ORON AMULAR

MICHAEL J HARVEY

malcolm down

PUBLISHING

Oron Amular is dedicated to Nana,
my first and greatest fan.
I hope that somehow, somewhere,
you get to read this.

ACKNOWLEDGEMENTS

The love and support of many people has helped to bring *Oron Amular* into being. I owe a great debt of gratitude to those whose belief and encouragement sustained me in both the writing and the hunt for publication. I wish to thank my parents, Ian and Lucie, for raising me in a home of love and faith, and for setting my feet on this path. I reserve special thanks for Kelly Jamieson, for being so vocal a fan, right from the start, and for your friendship since. Phil Dobbs, it wasn't quite your thing, but you always encouraged me along the way, and never stopping asking about it. Pat Eisner and Matt Taylor also deserve my appreciation, for being among the first to read it, and for much practical support and helpful input. Many other friends have encouraged me hugely, too many to name, but you know who you are and I really appreciate it. I'm also really grateful to the whole team at Malcolm Down Publishing for taking this chance with me and bringing *Oron Amular* to print. No one has done more to make this novel possible, than my beloved wife, Lucy, my *Soleithébar*. Thank you for letting me have all those hours; thank you for believing in me; thank you for walking this road with me as the best of companions. Most of all, though, I wish to thank God, from whom comes every good and perfect gift (James 1:17). You gave me this imagination, these ideas, and this talent, and I honour You with every word that I write.

CONTENTS

Map of
Astrom

Icy
Seas

Retorn
Ocean

Troizon
Ocean

Urunmar

Oron Cavardul

The Haunted Pass

Gulf of Urunumar

Tor Kenfer

Guard
Hills

Ciricen

Rohandur

Nalatot

Hendar

Onvich

Kalator

Beachbone Bay

Melatror

Poitole

River Goralar

Hamid

Kalimar

Oron Amular

Dorzand

Payeir

Black
Mts

Ithrill

Aranar

White Moor

White Hills

Silver City

Arkania Forest

Maristonia

Markros

Athra

East Fold

Silver Bay

Carthak Mts

Carthak

Mariston

Mariston Bay

Nimreil Bay

Swordhak Peninsula

Dagger's Cove

Marble Bay

Sapheil
Ocean

Lurallan

Rakhdun

Urundair

Southern Cape

© Michael J Harvey

Map of
**Oron
Amular**

© Michael J Harvey

✻

I

A Tournament

THIS was the day. Wasn't it? It must be. The thought kept him going as he climbed the hill during the night. He had been waiting for this day half his life. If his conviction were wrong, he wasn't sure he could carry on. He was at the summit in time to see the first hint of dawn colouring the sky behind the mountains in the east. He shivered as the wind blew away the last wisps of mist around him, leaving the view he had come for unimpeded. He was not disappointed. The tranquil violet of the slumbering world was blushed with peach as the sun peeped over the mountains. The light shifted imperceptibly through exquisite shades of rose and vermillion. As it did so, the landscape of tilled fields and little towns gradually took on definition. So too did the poplar-lined road, running east to west through it all. Settling down to wait, he watched the road.

The higher the sun rose, the more his eyes narrowed. Daylight imparted each contour of the land with a subtly unique tint of gold as it advanced westward, but the beauty of it was lost on him. His attention was fixed on the road. He would wait for the sign. He would wait all day if need be – but after that? He wasn't sure.

Fourscore years had given him patience, half of them spent in waiting. Yet an armist could not live on hopes and dreams forever. He was not yet past his prime, as some armists might view it, but he felt much older. Instead of the excitement and camaraderie which others of his age might have experienced, all he had ever known was sorrow, frustration and delay. He had spent forty years waiting upon a promise, clinging to a hope. His mane of red hair might look aflame in the waxing daylight, but the strength of that hope within was now scarce more than a flicker. He thought that today was the day. Or had he misread the sign? He had spent all his life in the mountains, had stood every night facing east. Hoping. Waiting. Willing. In his dreams, he had seen many times that towering flash of fire searing the mountain sky, so many times that when his waking eyes beheld it, he could not be sure that it had not been another dream after all.

If today was not the day, what would he do? He looked down at himself. The hose, tunic, coat and cloak which had once been such bright red and orange were now faded to dusty browns and yellows and a colour which looked depressingly like dried blood. His strong leather boots, studded with gripping nails, were starting to fall apart again. That's what came of constantly being on the move. Yet often he had nothing better to do than collect news of all kinds. He had no place to call his own; the only home he had ever known had been burned to the ground by bandits. So he simply wandered. Wandered from place to place and from town to town, seeking lodgings where he could or sleeping underneath the stars when no place could be found. Early on he had discovered that he could conjure and enchant like his father, and with the help of Prélan he had somehow managed to scratch a living. Some villages had shunned him as a vagabond, others had refused to let him stay after discovering what he could do, and even those few which paid for his entertainment soon grew weary of him and rarely had kind words to say. That had left him little choice but to mostly keep his own company. He had no one to call him friend. If he died here, casting himself from that high place, would anyone ever know?

Eyes squinting in the strengthening sunshine, he watched society begin to pulse in the world below him. Work parties tramped to the

fields and merchant caravans plied the roads. Their life was so alien
to him, bracketed as it was by the daily rhythms of purpose, and he
understood them little. Overlong locks of reddish hair kept falling
across his eyes, and time and again he brushed them away with his
hand. Then he saw it. One puff of dust among many, as of a swift
rider galloping along the highway, but there could be no mistaking
what happened next. His eyes widened when, out from the dust-
cloud, there bloomed a vision. It was the emblem of a foreign power.
Silver runes and a conical mountain, all on a sable field. Within
the mountain were successive roundels of different colours, whilst
flanking it on either side was a staff, fire pouring from their tips. This
banner mushroomed so large that it filled most of Roujeark's vision,
allowing him to see every detail. His eyes were drawn especially to
the device in the bottom corner of the vision: a six-pointed star with
strange words beneath it: *ce avar kalanor, genmos ey ce corpide*. His
father had taught him the elven characters, so he knew it said *the
brightest star, first and the last*, but he had no idea what it meant. Yet
there could be no mistaking it: this was the same emblem that had
appeared in all his visions. This was it. He closed his eyes, awash
with silent relief.

When he opened his eyes again, the vision had vanished as if it
had never been. All that was left was the fast-moving cloud of dust
that denoted the rider's rapid westward progress. Straightaway, his
mind tried to tell him that he had been seeing things, that he was so
weary from his night-climb that he had dozed and dreamt as he sat,
but his heart was pounding so hard that it seemed determined to
gainsay the doubts. No consternation anywhere in the land implied
that anyone else had seen the vision, but he trusted the insistence of
his heart. He got to his feet in growing excitement.

He turned his eyes back northward, towards the mountains.
Somewhere up there was the home he had been forced to leave

behind. A home he might never see again. With his waking eyes he saw a cottage burning, the mountain-faces above lit red by the glare. He heard breaking glass and vengeful voices. He felt again the thud of hoof-beats as the pony carried the boy into the unknown. He closed his eyes to shut out the memories, and slowly, with the unclenching of his fists, they died away behind his eyelids. Turning his back on the pain-filled past, he opened his eyes again and looked west to the white-walled city.

If the rider of the vision was heading for Mariston then so would he. He would go to the capital and find him. Would there be a message or set of instructions? A guide to take him back, perhaps? After so long, the old man owed him that much at least. Pushing those thoughts aside, he set off down the steep slope in an eager shuffle.

⅄

The rider wore no obvious mark or emblem. She was dressed in black with silver edgings and there seemed to be strange devices or runes on her cloak that only showed as the light directly caught them. She wore a silver helm with great purple plumes flowing back from it and her visor was down so that her face was hidden. Her belt was studded with gems and from it hung both an ornate scabbard and a satchel, which both bore the symbol of a great six-pointed star with burning torches about it, and flaming runes conveying some strange motto. She was going at a mighty speed, the flagstones of the road sparking as her horse's shoes struck them. The road wound around the feet of a great hill which overlooked the city, before leading down to Mariston itself. As she rounded the hill the rider cast the token into the air, watching over her shoulder as the vision sprang out of it to fill the sky. That was all she had been bidden to do. Here, in this exact spot. She hoped the recipient was watching, or her master would be displeased. But she had other business too, so she left the enchantment to work itself and kept spurring on towards the city.

She rode at breakneck pace up the road. Heedless of the people who leapt out of her way, she galloped all the way to the great outer walls of the armist capital. Others like her had ridden the length and breadth of Ciroken and Ebinnin to every major city in every realm. They had gone to Kalator and Rohandur in the north; to the Silver City of elven Ithrill; to the halls of all the major Clan-lords in Aranar; to Paeyeir, the ancient citadel of the elves in Kalimar; to Carthak, the deep and forgotten citadel of the dwarves; and even to the extreme south where dwelt roving sun-darkened tribes. It had fallen to her to come to the capital city of Maristonia and deliver not one but two messages.

With one already delivered, she focused now on the other. Pulling up in a cloud of dust, she patted her steaming horse and caught her breath. The fabled walls towered above her, impossibly high. She looked up, up, up, craning her neck to look at the top of the gatehouse. The sentries at its top were almost out of sight. Made of stone hewn from the Carthaki Mountains, the portcullis had been fashioned in impenetrable steel by the elven-smiths of old. Vast oaken gates glowered across a long drawbridge which ran over the lake-like moat. Cut from the biggest trees, they were covered in carvings and bound by steel bands. They were the outward symbol of Mariston's might and wealth. Not as fair as the jewel-encrusted citadels of Kalimar, thought the rider, but stronger certainly. The first armist chieftains had done their work well: this was an unbreakable obstacle, behind which a few could defy all the hordes of the world.

She could have joined the queue pressing through a door within the great gates, but she had no time for such formalities. Instead, she gazed at the first parapet where the lowest sentries looked out from just above the gates. Their comrades at the top of the wall were scarcely within shouting range. She fixed her eyes on one of the sentries, and waited for the silent scrutiny to take effect. Soon the armist soldier began to look distinctly uncomfortable, and, searching around for the cause, his eyes alighted on the strange rider below, standing apart from the rest.

'Who are you?' he called down. 'Why have you come to the gates of Curillian, Lord of Maristonia?' The rider sat quite still for a moment, then lifted the visor of her helm. From beneath it, her pale elven face looked up. The sentry gaped down, blinking in surprise. She reached down to her satchel and took from it a roll of parchment. It was rolled about a gilt wooden frame, sealed and hung with a silver tassel. Then she allowed her clear voice to ring up.

'I bear a message for the king. It is for your king's eyes alone; will he receive it?' The words, soft yet commanding, drifted up to the sentry, who looked uncertain, more at the rider's outlandish garb and accent than at her simple words. Ordinary people in the queue and other sentries had heard the foreign voice and turned to look. The first sentry had gone to fetch a superior, who promptly came down and out of the gates with a detachment of soldiers.

'I am Captain of the Watch; I will read your message and judge whether it is worthy of His Majesty's attention.' The elf messenger looked coldly down at him, and then shot a volley of foreign words at him.

'*Ai-va, Curillian Haretholin, Ar i ce del i ce alan, valoreé egin ce Ciryád i Amagaïd.*' The captain's face fell. 'Fool, do you speak the tongue this message is written in? Do not waste my master's time, set wings to your feet and find someone with the wit to understand me, and whom I can trust to deliver my message to the hands of the king.' Unhappily, the captain went about obliging this request, while the onlookers slowly lost interest as the rider waited, still as a stone. At length, a larger squad of soldiers arrived, this time with a more senior-looking officer at their head. Waving his armists back, he walked out to meet the rider. His importance was proclaimed by the long black cloak he wore over his mail-coat, and by the red-plumed helm of gold enclosing his face. He walked like he owned the gateway.

'Hail, visitor from afar.' He laid a hand across his breast by way of salute. 'I am Lancoir, Knight of the Order of Thainen and Captain of the Royal Guard. I have the ear of the king. I will convey your message. Since I hear you are in haste, surrender the scroll to me, and I will take it to my king.' The elf inclined her head and extended her hand with the scroll. Yet before she relinquished it, she spoke a warning.

'My master laid great emphasis on the fact that only the intended recipient should read what is contained herein. Know that if any hands but the sovereign's open this wallet, they shall burn and wither before their eyes.' Lancoir held the other's eyes steadily as she spoke, though they were both fair and fell. 'I have no need to wait for a reply, if the king finds the message acceptable, he will seek out my master.' In the blink of an eye, the strange rider had turned her horse away and galloped back the way she had come.

Lancoir watched the receding rider for a few moments, then considered the package in his hands. When he realised his armists were watching him, he sent them scurrying back to their duties with a bark. He himself hastened to his horse in the gatehouse's stable. With his escort he rode swiftly through the streets of Mariston, over the bridges, under the gates of all the walls (for there were five walls, each with its own moat, each circular, getting progressively smaller) and so came to the innermost area of the city. Here, on a small armist-made island, stood the magnificent palace of the kings of Maristonia, the Carimir. It was built of white stone and marble. Its many towers, domes, golden roofs and crystal spires gave it a skyline which defied description. In the heart of the palace, the king resided in the tallest tower, and thither now was the Captain of the Royal Guard bound, treading familiar corridors. He ran into no obstructions, for all knew him and knew his status; instead, each guard he passed snapped to attention and saluted.

On his way he passed many disconsolate folk going the other way. Their number increased steadily, so that when he reached the corridor leading to the Royal Audience Chamber they filled the passageway, grumbling and shuffling away from the doors. On either side of this broad corridor were apertures inhabited by the effigies of past kings and their families, and from these apertures scarcely noticed Royal Guardsmen kept careful watch. Despite his haste, his eyes missed nothing, making sure they were properly alert. Now at last he was checked. The Announcer put a hand on his chest to intercept him. Without even looking up, he told him, 'His Majesty is no longer receiving supplicants. Wait until tomorrow.' He had not noticed the dozen Royal Guardsmen, who were arrayed in two squads either side of the gilt doors, snap to attention, and it was only when Lancoir boomed in a voice of inimitable authority that he looked up from his parchment.

'Tell His Majesty that Lancoir is here.' The guardsmen smiled as the Announcer nearly fell backwards in fright, scattering his documents. He made several apologies as he scurried around picking up his papers, and in the meantime two of the guardsmen heaved the doors inward. Without waiting to be 'Announced', the Captain of the Royal Guard, the most celebrated soldier in the realm, strode into the vast chamber. Filled with unimaginable riches, the Royal Audience Chamber was designed to accommodate thousands. And to overawe those thousands. Every last inch of wall was covered in tapestries, portraits and artistic friezes. The ceiling dripped with gold and crystal, and even the floor, either side of a single, red carpet, was covered in carvings telling a thousand stories of the Harolin dynasty's greatness. All the light came from the far end of the hall, where great stained-glass windows filled the wall. The hall ended in a great projecting bay, where the red carpet ended and the royal dais lay. The chamber, and indeed the whole tower, had been designed to face east so that light could glorify the morning Audiences. Now the multi-hued radiance flooded in and bathed the dais in great rays, with the effect that the thrones upon it, and their occupants, could barely be seen. Thus, the King of Maristonia, whenever beheld up close by his subjects, existed in a world of dazzling glory.

Even Lancoir, who was not easily intimidated, never failed to be impressed by the effect contrived by the Harolins and their architects. And even he could not see the persons on the dais. He kept approaching, but long before his eyes could penetrate the glittering scene, he was hailed.

'Lancoir, I thought it might be you. Come in. Welcome.' It was the noble voice of Queen Carmen, though he could still not see her.

'Your Majesty?'

'I'm by the windows, Lancoir, come.' At last he saw her, standing by the window, looking out over the palace gardens. She was so bathed with light, and her dress so brilliantly white, that she was all but invisible from beyond the dais. Her husband, however, was nowhere to be seen. Beautiful and erect as a portrait, she turned and smiled at him. Seeing her face, Lancoir fell to one knee and waited for invitation.

'Rise, Sir Lancoir, son of Lorumon, rise. You are looking for His Majesty, no doubt? He grew weary of proceedings and expelled the supplicants, along with the entire court, and retired up yonder staircase.'

'I have with me an urgent message for his attention, Your Majesty.'

'You are free to seek him out, faithful Lancoir. I hope your missive offers some relief from his present boredom.' Polite and gracious to a fault, the queen showed no interest in further conversation.

'By your leave, Your Majesty.' Lancoir turned away and the queen turned back to the window. The staircase she had indicated was concealed behind a great hearth in the centre of the northern wall, and it was expressly reserved for royal use and those given special royal permission. Lancoir was one of perhaps half a dozen people not related to the king by blood who even knew of its existence. Climbing it, he knew he was entering the private warren of Maristonia's sovereign, which meant that King Curillian could be in any of dozens of locations. Not fully familiar with this tower-top labyrinth, Lancoir knew he could be searching for a long time if his master did not wish to be found. Not in the Library. Not in the Reading Room. Not in the Viewing Hole, with its 360-degree panoramas of the city and its many telescopes. Similarly he checked off the Games Room, the Chapel, countless hidden passages and even the Royal Bedchamber and Bathchamber. At a loss, he stopped in the Library and called aloud.

'Your Majesty, it is Lancoir. Where are you to be found?'

Footsteps, distant yet close by, a turning of levers and a small section of bookcase pivoted into the air. A most unkingly figure, with rolled sleeves and begrimed face, peeped out of the new aperture, and greeted him cheerfully.

'Lancoir, no less – this is a pleasant surprise. Well, you've uncovered another secret refuge of mine, so you might as well come in. Come along, come along. It's no good standing on ceremony, you have to get your hands dirty to use some of these passages.' With that he vanished back into the hole. Immaculate as his office required, yet not personally fastidious, Lancoir followed him in and found himself having to stoop in a rough-hewn tunnel. Before long, he was forced to crawl in order to keep going, while his quincentennial king scampered along somewhere ahead with the nimbleness of a chimney sweep. Eventually he dropped down into a most curious chamber, lit both by braziers and small windows. Its walls contained countless inset shelves containing all manner of paraphernalia, presumably relevant to the vast war-gaming table which dominated the pit-like bottom of the room. King Curillian was already back amongst his cavalry squadrons and battalions, hard at play.

'Antruphan says this particular passageway will be finished in a week, and then connected to the others a few weeks after that,' the king informed his new guest while charging a knight-figurine forwards.

'Truly, Your Majesty's Master-mason is the envy of the Architects Guild, to receive so many royal commissions.'

'My dear Lancoir, he is one of those rare armists who combines great skill with great discretion. When the others could say as much, I might consider them. Anyway, how many times have I told you, drop the formalities.'

'As you will, sire.'

'Better, but as to relevance and directness, nothing beats Curillian.'

'Yes...Curillian.' The king showed a curious attachment to his name, thought Lancoir. Here was an armist who possessed a dozen glittering titles, and yet who preferred his ordinary baptismal name. For his part, very few people ever called him Lancoir without using the knightly Sir before it. Most just called him Sir. He could have been called anything and he wouldn't have cared, so long as people respected him. Yet he kept his thoughts to himself whilst standing bolt upright and gazing fixedly above his king's head. Curillian took a seat and regarded him carefully. As ever, Lancoir felt sure his thoughts were being guessed with uncanny perspicacity.

'You know, Lancoir, an armist values a name much more when he has been deprived of it. Curillian I was in my youth – Amazing Whiteness – an odd name, but my parents must have had their reasons. That name I was forced to relinquish, and I wandered as the Exile, Nadihoan, before being baptised in battle as Ruthion, the Red Warrior. Long and hard I had to fight to be allowed to come home and be Curillian again. I prize that name above all others, because it represents everything that I lost, and everything that I regained.

'But you, Lancoir. Enduring Silver. Your loyalty and steadfastness are as true as silver, and as enduring as the purest silver that the elves say fell from the stars. Silver runs through your name and your reputation, just as it does for King Lancearon of Ithrill, the Silver Helm.'

'So I have been told,' said Lancoir, unconvinced. Curillian continued, unperturbed.

'Lancoir, hear me in this. Names, like salvation, are from Prélan Himself. And like salvation, which we must receive with faith, names must be grasped, taken to heart, and lived out.' He paused, still pondering his visitor. 'What do you think?'

'I think,' began Lancoir before hesitating, 'I think that you think too much about such things.' Curillian laughed.

'Well, that's true,' said he. 'I have plenty of time for thinking. Too much. But come, there are plenty with whom you could better discuss nomenclature in the University; why have you come?'

'I have a message to deliver, sire, a very strange message.' The king smiled as the old habit of deference crept back in unnoticed. 'It bears the mark of no lord or institution that I recognise. Wherever it has come from, it's beyond the bounds of my knowledge.' Curillian heard the unease in his captain's voice and his interest was piqued. 'Will you receive it here?' Curillian thought a moment.

'No, since you have disturbed my game, I will receive it in my Bedchamber…and let Carmen be present. Come.'

The king led the way back through the tunnel and through the labyrinth of apartments to his Bedchamber. The king's actual sleeping chamber was still further within, but this opulent outer chamber was where the most important of messengers were received. The king's ceremonial robes – gorgeous white patterned silk, edged with facings of crimson velvet – still hung where they had been discarded after the supplicants had been ejected. Preferring to stay in his tunnel-grimed shirt and trousers, Curillian settled himself in a seat and studied the message while Lancoir went to find the queen. The message was contained within a leather pouch, covered with runes and designs of the most outlandish sort. He was still scrutinising it when the queen entered with Lancoir in tow. Curillian was just about to jump up and greet his wife, but she moved swiftly to him, kissing his forehead and encouraging him to remain seated. Then she took another of the seats. Both then looked at Lancoir. Curillian tossed him the pouch.

'Do the honours old friend.' He raised an eyebrow when Lancoir, normally so efficient and unflappable, hesitated, looking worried.

'Sire, the message was expressly for your eyes only…on pain of… maiming.' Concerned and intrigued in equal measure, the king leaned forward and took the pouch back again. 'Well, if my enemies have hatched some plot, it's been a long time in coming…' Not without a little trepidation of his own, he untied the thongs knotting it shut. No sooner had the knot come undone than the message sprang out of the king's hand as if it had a life of its own. Lancoir stepped backwards, hand flying to his sword-hilt, and Carmen rose in alarm, but Curillian remained sitting, hunched forward in fascination. Suspended in mid-air of its own accord, the unfurled message looked just like an ordinary letter, but then it started glowing at the edges, as if being held too close to a candle. All of a sudden, it burst into a kaleidoscopic mirage of colours and forms. These filled the air for a fleeting second before suddenly contracting and coalescing like an explosion reversed. A small incandescent orb was all that remained, but slowly it grew, until a face could be discerned in its midst. On first glance the face seemed to belong to a tired old man, but then a mantle of snowy hair, like a garment of wisdom, and grey eyes full of memory and knowledge, became apparent. The face spoke, and its voice was invested with age-old authority.

Kulothiel, Keeper of Oron Amular, and Head of the League of Wizardry, to Curillian son of Mirkan son of Arimaya, King of Maristonia, greetings in Prélan's name. You must excuse the theatrics, but in this age of suspicion and doubt, I deemed it necessary to preface what is to follow with a small token of its authenticity. The world is changing, and my place in it is fast diminishing, but I find that my office has one duty yet to discharge for the benefit of the Free Peoples. Even as a third stormcloud gathers in the North, I invite you to a Tournament here in Oron Amular. Upon the first full moon of summer, many are invited to gather here. The prize for which you shall compete is an heirloom of Power Unimaginable. Other rewards you may also find. I trust I do not misjudge in appealing to your restless talents. Prélan's speed.

The mellifluous voice ceased and the whole vision faded. The room was recalled to normality from the stuff of dreams. As if a string had been cut, the letter dropped to the floor. Gingerly, Lancoir picked up the object. The leather packaging remained as it had looked before, but the page within was blank. He proffered it to his sovereign, who still sat hunched forward with the same expression of rapt fascination. Curillian did not appear to heed his captain, but instead muttered to himself.

'He speaks as if he knew me...' Recovering from the intensity of the spectacle, Queen Carmen spoke to her husband.

'All those times we heard his name, but never once did either of us meet him. Why does he address himself to you now?' Her eyes were sad but understanding when she watched the transformation in her beloved. The enchantment was replaced by boisterous excitement, as if it had been a crumbling sluice-gate washed away by a sudden spate. Curillian repeated the two words to himself three times, each time getting more voluble.

'Oron Amular...Oron Amular...ORON AMULAR...' With the last utterance he leapt to his feet, the light of adventure in his eyes. 'I am called...to Oron Amular? What a prospect Prélan sends me in His mercy to stave off senile dotage for a few more years. All these years I thought He'd forgotten me, but now, now at last a new game's afoot.'

'My darling,' his wife said soothingly, 'try not to get too carried away just yet. None now know how to find Oron Amular, and even if they did, it would be a long way away, and beyond many dangers.'

'Beyond many rivers and mountains, I've no doubt. Someone, I'm sure, can be found to lead me thither. Let me see now, how to get there, and who to take...' The king would have gone on apace with his plans had not the Captain of his Royal Guard interrupted.

'But Your Majesties...' They both turned to look at him. 'You speak as if this message is genuine, as if Oron Amular really exists...' Curillian smiled at him.

'Lancoir the Unpersuadable! Verily, even if a trickster took in every wise armist in the realm, still you would be unconvinced. Has it not brought you to where you are – so high in my service – along with your martial valour and unstained personal honour? Yet a cynical armist may become so cynical in filtering all the counterfeits aimed at a king that he may miss the real thing. Oron Amular does exist, though the world may have forgotten it. Carmen and I met several of the protégés of Kulothiel in Silverdom, and I fought alongside them in the Second War of Kurundar. Like most others, I do not understand High Magic, or Black Magic, but I've seen enough of both with my own eyes to be convinced that it does indeed exist beneath the sun. Is what we've just seen not proof of that? And yet we've heard nor seen nothing of it for hundreds of years…until now. My dear Lancoir, can't you see how exciting this is?'

'I can see how dangerous it is, sire,' Lancoir responded staunchly. 'The southern frontier is quiet, but far from stable. There is much to be done in your own realm. What if the barbarians should rise up again when you have gone to foreign parts?'

'General Otaken and the Constable of the South-fold can handle anything the Alanai can throw at them, just as their predecessors have done for generations uncounted. The southern front is as quiet as I have ever known it, and all else is quieter still. Can you *not* see? This is just what I have been waiting for.' Lancoir looked unhappy, but refrained from arguing further. Curillian turned to his queen. 'Beloved, will you excuse us?' Carmen nodded resignedly. Curillian sprang towards the door. 'Come, Lancoir,' he beckoned. 'We have many preparations to make.' Queen Carmen's voice checked him just as he reached the door.

'If you must go out, dear,' she said, 'at least put on a clean shirt and coat.' Curillian looked down at his grimy attire and smiled. To Lancoir's startled discomfort, he stripped his dirty shirt off right there and then. A forest of scars from old battles was plain to see, but the muscles were those of a much younger armist. He donned a new shirt, seized his white and gold brocade coat, bowed to his wife, and was gone.

He stormed along the corridor at a great pace, pulling on his coat and tidying his hair as he went. Lancoir, struggling to keep up, came up alongside. Never breaking stride around all the corners and down all the steps of his chambers, Curillian rattled off instructions to the Captain of his Guard.

'Lancoir, I want you to assemble a cohort of the Royal Guard. Which is the unit with that new commander?'

'Surumo?'

'Yes, he impressed me when we met.'

'Third Cohort, sire. Piron is his second-in-command.'

'Curillian, Lancoir, not sire. The Third? Yes, they'll do. Have them assembled and ready to ride in two days. They must have baggage and provisions for a month on the road. I want messages sent on ahead by the quickest errand-riders to summon the finest trackers and pathfinders of the Eastern Army. They will rendezvous with us at Arket two weeks from now. I myself am going to the Royal Library, where I will be investigating Oron Amular for the rest of the day. Have Arton, General Gannodin and My Lord High Chancellor ready to meet me in my State-room at sundown tonight…Oh, and make sure Téthan is there, too.'

'As you command, sire.'

Curillian stopped. They had now reached the public part of the palace and were standing at the top of the staircase which led down into the grand Entrance Hall. Here they parted ways, but Curillian remonstrated with his captain first.

'Lancoir?'

'Sire?'

'If you address me as 'sire' one more time, you won't accompany me to Oron Amular.' The king smiled when he saw the surprise register in Lancoir's face: clearly he had not presumed upon this honour.

'Yes...Curillian...' he said at length. Curillian clapped him on the shoulder.

'Good armist.'

⋏

'Are you telling me you really have no idea whatsoever?' Curillian demanded. The old scholar straightened up, creaking as he did so, and sneezed from all the dust covering the ancient tome in front of him. He looked apologetically at his king.

'My profound apologies, sire, but this is the oldest volume we have. Our records only go back so far. I'm afraid certain sections of the archives were rather badly neglected when...when Your Majesty was abroad for so long.' Curillian impatiently waved him past the awkward allusion and pressed him further. 'The section on Kalimar was among them. One or two of the older monasteries might have histories going back further, but even if they did...well...exact directions wouldn't often have been written down. The League was, by all accounts, very secretive about such things. I doubt whether even many of the works in Kalimar itself would shed more light on the matter. The League seems to have been defunct for almost five hundred years, and before that it had been getting increasingly more mysterious for centuries.'

Curillian sighed with frustration at the old scholar's lisping, wheezy ruminations. The Royal Library was located in the westernmost of the palace's three towers and took up several whole floors. Shunning the open way from his own apartments in the central tower in preference for the secret passages which he loved, Curillian had moved from the Writing Room of his Secretariat to the Royal Library without being seen by anyone. Now, after two hours of trawling through old parchments and manuscripts with old Comangen, he sat on a bench amid the stacks, irritated and grouchy. Old Comangen, practically blind and rheumatic, was the acknowledged expert amongst the royal archivists on Kalimar – the ancient elvish realm – and all things elvish. If anyone would know the whereabouts of Oron Amular, it would be him. But now, after enduring the slow unravelling of his long erudition, it appeared that even Comangen knew little more than his colleagues, some of whom had barely heard of the League of Wizardry. A thousand and a half years ago, or so it was said, the League had had its own resident ambassador at the court of the Maristonian king, but now the lore of Oron Amular in the armist realm had shrivelled to a sad level of ignorance. The thickness of dust covering all the elven manuscripts testified to the dwindling interest in that subject. Making one last effort, Curillian appealed to one of the newly dusted maps of Kalimar.

'Can you at least indicate a rough location?'

'Perhaps, sire,' mumbled Comangen, wiping his nose and leaning in close to the new resource. He hummed and muttered to himself for a while. 'Hmmm, yes, well, I think I could safely say it lies somewhere in this area.' Curillian inspected the chosen point on the map. Comangen's finger was tracing an infuriatingly wide circle in western Kalimar.

'But that's an area that covers most of the Black Mountains, and a lot of Dorzand and northern Kalimar with it! I could have an entire legion of trackers scouring such an area for months and still not find every mountain!' He put his fingers to his forehead in exasperation, trying to block out the sound of Comangen's breathing. 'Oh, it's hopeless,' he said after a while. Then, 'Or maybe I have a better idea...' He got up and made to leave, but before doing so, he rounded on the archivist. 'This archive's a disgrace, Comangen. When I'm back, I'll have words with the Head Librarian. You and he had better get it back into some sort of shape or I'll transfer you both to stable duty.'

Fortunately for the Head Librarian, he was not to be found when Curillian came back to the library's entrance. Returning by the secret passages to the Writing Room of his Secretariat, he summoned a clerk to him.

'Have a runner go to the Kalimari Embassy. If the ambassador is home, I want to see him in the Royal Audience Chamber an hour before dusk.'

⟁

The elf standing next to him was tall and saturnine. Together they stood watching the late afternoon through the windows of the Royal Audience Chamber. Shadows were fast growing in the east-facing room.

'I was delighted to find that Your Eminence could join me at such short notice,' Curillian told his guest. The ambassador of Kalimar never took his eyes from the window.

'Long has it been since I have been summoned so urgently. I am honoured by your eagerness, Your Majesty.' Curillian smiled inwardly. Despite the tedious official cordiality of diplomatic parlance, he knew as well as the ambassador that neither of them was happy at the hasty manner of this meeting. The representative of the oldest nation in the world did not take kindly to being summoned on a whim, and Curillian could practically smell the resentment rising off him like steam from a spent horse. Just as aloof as the Hendarian Ambassador, this misanthropic elf was even more reclusive.

'I've asked you here to have your help in finding Oron Amular.' Curillian cut straight to it, but the elf maintained his silent scrutiny of the view. Curillian studied him, guessing that the considered non-reaction was a likely indication that Kalimar knew all about Kulothiel's invitations. Eventually, unwavering examination induced the ambassador to turn and face him, looking down gravely at the armist king. 'Come,' said Curillian, 'you know the way, do you not?' The ghost of a smile hovered on the ambassador's lips.

'Your Majesty, it is with great regret that I cannot speak to you with candour on this matter.'

'Perhaps one of your kindred might be more forthcoming if I were to conduct enquiries in Alkala? Lovely part of the world, and I do so love to edge across the border every now and then...' The suggestion had barely left Curillian's lips when another evasion was proffered.

'I fear there is no one in Alkala, or anywhere along the Armist Road, who would be able to satisfactorily answer such an enquiry, much as they would like to assist Your Majesty.' Curillian sighed extravagantly.

'It seems that the obscurity of the Mountain of High Magic is not so much down to forgetfulness as to intentional design. Tell me, Eminence, what would happen if a large and inquisitive delegation were to cross the border with the peaceful intention of finding said mountain?' There was the ghost of another, entirely unamused smile.

'His Immortal Majesty, King Lithan, son of Avallonë, son of Avalar, would take a very dim view indeed of such an errand.' Curillian stepped away and began to pace a tight circle nearby. Soon he stopped and regarded the ambassador again.

'You will forgive me, Eminence, but I grow weary of these circuitous niceties. Talk plainly to me. Has Kulothiel dispatched invites to a tournament, or has he not?' Curillian read in the other's eyes exactly what he wanted to.

'Whether or not there is a tournament is for the invitee alone to know. Word has reached me, however, that I am not to extend any insight or assistance to anyone who might ask about Oron Amular.'

'No doubt similar instructions have reached your esteemed colleagues in Hamid, Rohandur and Kalator? Let us just suppose, for a moment, that Your Eminence knew about such a tournament as this – how would you expect the entrants to participate if they cannot even find the venue?'

'It is all part of the test.'

⋀

Five people were waiting for Curillian in his State-room. Smaller and more intimate than the Royal Audience Chamber, it was nevertheless just as grand. Being on the western side of the central tower of the palace, it basked now in the dying rays of the sun. Languid red-golden light sifted through the opulent chamber. The first to greet him was the small boy who came flying at him.

'Father!' Fondness suffused Curillian as his son Téthan ran up and hugged him. Picking up the little bundle of energy, he walked further into the room, nodding in acknowledgement to the others present as he did so. He set the boy down by his favourite chair and kissed the top of his head. Settling back into his seat, he turned his attention to those waiting upon him: a duke, a palace official and a soldier. Cardanor, Duke of Arton, was the seniormost noblearmist in the realm, not related to the king by blood, but whom Curillian thought of as a younger brother. Ophryior, the Lord High Chancellor, was Curillian's most important minister, responsible for both the Royal Treasury and Secretariat. Gorgeously apparelled in robes of state, he embodied the grandeur and majesty of the realm far more often than did his more casual sovereign. Gannodin, a grizzled old warrior, was the general in command of the Ist Legion, the prestigious elite unit of the Maristonian Army which formed part of the garrison of Mariston. And then there was Lancoir, faithful and vigilant as ever, standing quietly in a dark corner.

'Arton,' Curillian beckoned the young duke closer. 'In two days I will be leaving the capital on a discreet and private venture. I want you to head up things here while I'm gone. Are you up to it?'

'Of course, Curillian.' The king smiled.

'Good armist, I knew you would be. Ophryior here will help you in the running of things, won't you Ophryior?' The Lord High Chancellor bowed immaculately, his face a mask of uncompromising efficiency. Curillian turned to the general.

'Gannodin, can the Eastern Army spare a legion?' The general grunted in what could loosely be interpreted as an affirmative response. Curillian carried on seamlessly. 'Good, Horuistan's 15th should do – they're at Arket, yes? Prepare immediate open orders for them to conduct exercises in The Bowl, and prepare closed orders also, to let Horuistan know to expect me within two weeks.' Gannodin grunted again, but this time he followed it up with a short, barked question.

'You expecting trouble, sire?'

'It's not impossible. My guess is that this tournament may attract unwanted attention from those not invited, and I'd like some seasoned troops nearby, just in case.'

'And if anyone asks why a whole legion is exercising in the East-fold…?'

'Tell them we've heard rumours that the harracks are causing trouble.' Next it was Cardanor who leaned in with a question.

'Curillian, Lancoir has told us the basic details, but won't you tell us more? What is this tournament? Can you even find a way there?' Curillian reflected a moment, palms flat against each other.

'Whatever it is, Kulothiel must have good reason for breaking his centuries-long silence. The Hendarians tell us there's trouble in the north again, and it wouldn't surprise me if there's a connection. Some last throw of the League of Wizardry, who knows?'

'But can you find the Mountain?' the duke pressed him. 'I thought no one knew where it was.'

'Well, Comangen knows even less than the little I thought he did, and the maps are worse. The Kalimari ambassador was hardly forthcoming – my guess is Kulothiel's told the elves not to give anyone help that would be unfair. King Lithan wouldn't help, even if he wanted to, and I've got no intention of forcing his hand. He may even be competing himself. That leaves me with a couple of options, but you can let me and Lancoir worry about that.' The Captain of the Royal Guard pricked his ears to an extra level of alertness. 'Is my cohort making ready, Lancoir?'

'They are indeed…Curillian.' The king smiled, doubly satisfied.

'Good.' He pulled his son close. 'Now listen to me, Téthan, son, I'm going to be away for a short while.'

'Like when you were smashing the barbarians?' the boy piped up eagerly.

'Yes, just like then, only maybe not so long this time. I'm glad to see your history lessons are sticking.' Téthan had not even been born when Curillian had fought his latest campaign against the troublesome tribes on his southern border. 'But while I'm away, Uncle Arton here will look after you, and teach you lots of interesting things.'

'More interesting than old Gaeon?'

'Yes, even more interesting than your tutor. And,' he leaned in close, 'even more fun,' he promised in a conspiratorial whisper. Téthan beamed with pleasure. 'But remember,' Curillian warned his son, 'you must always obey your mother.' Téthan nodded. 'Now off you go with Uncle Arton, he'll take you back to your mother.' Duke and prince walked out by a side-door, both equally happy in each other's company.

Curillian stood up. 'Well, gentlemen, I think we're done. I bid you all a pleasant night.' His good wishes were returned elegantly by Ophryior, and rather less elegantly by Gannodin. After them Lancoir took his leave, and Curillian departed to be with his wife.

Carmen was already in bed, but not asleep. She sat up, waiting for him. She watched him as he slowly took off his clothes. With an effort, she kept her mind on other things.

'Did your meetings go as you hoped?'

'Well… yes and no,' he answered, casting aside the last garments. 'Everything has been set in order here with Arton and Ophryior, but the ambassador was less than helpful.' He settled in next to her under the bedclothes.

'How is Melnova?' One of the kingdom's greatest epic poets lay unread in the queen's hand; she had quite forgotten she was holding it.

'What? Oh, fine…fine.' Curillian leaned in and gave his wife a kiss on the cheek.

'She has quite a way with words, doesn't she?' he observed, then, changing subject abruptly. 'Téthan should get on well with Arton – they are a good influence on each other. Ophryior will hold the fort administratively, and the important matters can wait till I get...are you all right, sweetness? You seem preoccupied...' Curillian could tell she hadn't taken on board what he'd said, and yet she appeared unwilling to share what was on her mind. He shifted on to his side to attend to his bed-side lamp and stopped short, feeling the hands on his back. Her fingers traced the old scars, and he lay still, allowing her hands to move freely.

'Must you go?' The pent up question slipped out at last. Curillian gazed into the lamp's flame for a few moments before responding.

'Yes.' The pause was pregnant.

'But why? You've fought your battles, earned your stripes, lived your adventures. Isn't now the time to rest and enjoy the life we've worked so hard for?' He rolled back over, so as to face her.

'Carmen, I don't want to stop having adventures until I die. I was born to it, raised and confirmed in crisis, and ever after had my heart fixed on it, on the challenge, the excitement. Have you forgotten it, the headiness of the early days? It was like strong wine...'

'I remember. We came together in unusual circumstances, and our deeds against the Usurper are rightly glorious in the eyes of your people, but it was a long time ago. Things are different now. I find I no longer have the appetite for the breakneck life. Alas, I am not so evergreen as you, though much grace has been given me, sailor's daughter. I married the dashing prince, and now I want to grow old in contentment with the venerable king.' She snuggled up close to him, kissing his neck. 'Can you not be content with that?' Curillian smiled wryly.

'Venerable, am I? That makes me sound nearly six hundred.' She nuzzled him.

'You *are* over five hundred.'

He pulled away slightly. 'And yet I still feel two hundred. My hands and feet are restless, my mind is restless. I yearn for more...'

'You are *King*, lord of a wide realm and father of a free people. What more is there?'

'*Power Unimaginable.*' He breathed the response so lightly that she barely caught it. A look of concern came into her face.

'Do not let the old wizard tempt you. His day is over. You have no need of whatever relic or toy he cares to hold out.'

'And yet it remains for every armist to challenge the bounds of the ordinary, be he serf or sovereign. Do not ask me to deny my soul.' She saw the light in his eyes, the fire that burned from a depth she could not reach, and knew her words were in vain.

'I do not ask it. But your soul is not your own – it belongs to Prélan – and He has given you duties, to your wife, to your son, to your people.'

He fixed her with a challenging look. 'Carmen, if you do not want me to go, say so and have done.' She regarded him sadly.

'Curillian, most precious love, I do not begrudge you your freedom or wish to deny your dreams. Your heart will lead you where it will, as it always has. How many rulers and powers have sought to constrain your heart and failed? Yet I am here to counsel you, to share my heart with you, and my heart warns me. You will over-reach yourself in this.' The protest died on his lips and he listened gravely, knowing the time-honoured wisdom of his wife. 'You are not talking about a pleasure cruise along the Mastred, or a hunt in Tol Verenen, or even a campaign against the Alanai. You propose to seek out the hidden Mountain and compete in ancient halls of sorcery. You will meddle with the policies and devices of mage-lords when you don't even know where to find them? Beware, my love, lest you fail at too stern a test. I fear that you might spoil the honourable autumn of your life, even at the last. Stay.' *And yet I know, in spite of all my words, you will still go.*

Λ

In the quiet early summer morning, Curillian sought out his escort. Soft golden light filtered down on the gardens and smooth stone walls; birds sang sweetly, and many fair waters trickled in a peaceful music of their own. The world seemed good. And yet his heart was heavy from the conflict within. His feet traversing well-known and beloved paths, he made his way to the stable-yard of the palace garrison. Distinct from the much larger stables in the Royal Square outside the palace, this smaller abode was home to the steeds of the Royal Guards who lived in ceaseless vigil about their sovereign. A full *militar* – 600 warriors – were thus stationed in the Carimir, the Palace of Carinen, five cohorts of 120 each who were the personal bodyguard of the king, elite warriors all. Separate to this, two legions were garrisoned in the city itself, and one of these – Gannodin's Ist Legion, the seniormost unit of the Maristonian Army, occupied four barracks all around the perimeter of the Royal Zone, the moated island at the heart of the city. In the event of trouble, the legion's 12,000 troops could surround the palace in a matter of minutes and thwart any enemy.

When Curillian came to the stables, he found everything virtually ready. The armists of the Third Cohort were all there, either standing patiently by their horses, or hurrying to stow the last of their baggage. Curillian knew they would have been up since before dawn, meaning that their weapons were all honed and their scabbards oiled; their clothing and provisions for the journey were already packed in neat bundles before and behind their saddles; their farewells to loved ones had been made and their instructions for the first day given. Surumo, the commander of the cohort, strode over.

'Morning Commander,' Curillian greeted him. 'Everything ready?' The question was merely polite, and quite unnecessary.

Surumo had overseen the whole operation. As soon as he had been given orders from Lancoir two days before, he would have had his troops focused on this moment. Last minute training, procurement of special equipment, all had been seen to.

'Yes sir, all ready. The lads are just waiting for your word, sir.' The guards all about were looking at their king in full readiness; affection, pride and excitement in their eyes. Curillian took a moment to take in their fondness. It filled his heart with glowing satisfaction and eased his doubts. Lancoir walked up, leading two horses. His own, kitted out like those of the cohort, bore no distinction, but the king's horse, Theamace, was altogether a more noble beast. Bred from among the long-lived horses of Aranar, which were of elven pedigree, he had been a faithful companion of Curillian's through many years and adventures. His saddle and bridle were finer than the other mounts, but Curillian had given specific instructions that the grandest tackle should be omitted. Likewise, the guards had exchanged their gleaming plated armour for chainmail and the muted garb of rangers, both less conspicuous and more practical. This would be a testing venture, treading unknown paths in the wild, but even on the easier roads at the outset Curillian wanted his riding to be discreet. While they retained the two-handed swords of which they were so proud, they now also carried bows, quivers, throwing axes and hunting knives, which were less usual weapons for them.

Curillian's pride from surveying the fine soldiery around him had turned into an odd sense of foreboding, his mind focusing on peculiar small details. The rich carvings on the stable-doors, the hop-skip of a crow in the rafters, the lucky coin poking from behind the ear of a guardsman. As soon as he became aware of this, he shrugged it off by propelling himself into the saddle, prompting his escort to do likewise. As was his long-time habit, he personally checked his own baggage and weapons, even though Lancoir would have been minutely scrupulous in doing so beforehand. His left hand was immediately drawn to the hilt of his sword, quite helpless against the magnificent weapon's magnetism. Something in the touch of it electrified him. The smouldering embers of adventure in his heart ignited into sudden flame. In a burst of energy, he spurred Theamace out into the courtyard, where the lofty towers of the palace soared up above him. The Third Cohort surged into the morning light, the clatter of their hooves reverberating. Outside, two other cohorts were drawn up in formal dress, flanking the path to the palace entrance as an honour-guard. Many intrigued servants were watching furtively, but the only intended audience stood at a balcony in one of the towers above.

Queen Carmen looked on demurely, her calm demeanour quite concealing the inner turmoil from her companions. With her were ladies-in-waiting, Lord High Chancellor Ophryior, Duke Cardanor of Arton, several officers of the Royal Guards, and her little son, Téthan. This royal party watched as the king led his knights in dismounting and kneeling beside their horses.

Before joining his followers on their knees, Curillian unsheathed the Sword of Maristonia, *Falakinde*. Forged by elf-lord Torlas of Camelar for his grandfather Arimaya over fifteen hundred years ago, it was *the* weapon of the kings of Maristonia. Even more so than the great walls of Mariston, it was the symbol of their formidable strength and justice. Blessed with spells during the forging, the fear it engendered smote all the harder, and the gleam of its metal shone all the brighter. It was a blade of destiny, potent and compelling. Holding it aloft to glimmer in the rays of the sun, Curillian turned a slow circle, displaying it to all present. Only then did he kneel, holding it point down and gripping the crosspiece with both hands. He bowed his head. The prayer he uttered could not be heard above, only by his guards.

'Prélan, Lord of Heaven and Father of the Faithful, hear this prayer and be with us now. Bless this riding, and go forth with us to victory. Guide us and protect us on whichever paths we tread. Give us the strength to conduct ourselves with honour and justice, as befits Your warriors. Give us wisdom, that we might fight only the good fight. Grant that whatever success we find redound to the Glory of Your Name and the increase of Your Kingdom among us. In Your holy name, Amen.'

He should have got up then, but he did not, could not. His guards waited impatiently behind him. As soon as he had raised his eyes, he saw the emissary of Prélan, white-clad and glowing, come and stand before him. Angelic hands were clasped around his, still holding the sword. He heard the voice swirling around his head like an orchestrated storm of wind.

The Lord is with you, mighty warrior. Go in the strength that you have. Protect him, for he is needed at the Mountain. And whatever prize you win, be ready to relinquish.

Curillian choked and shook, overcome by the encounter. Lancoir was poised ready to spring like a cat to his assistance, but the king managed to get to his feet unaided. He looked unsteady at first, but strength grew with every step. When he raised the sword again, its brightness was redoubled as if it had sapped the morning light around it for its own brilliance. Raising their eyes, the awed guards saw the light of heaven in their king's eyes, a look which had inspired so many of his followers before, but which none of them had ever seen. Were the tales really true, then? Was he really the chosen warrior of Prélan? Was he really invincible? No enemy had ever withstood him, they had been told, and now they believed.

Curillian leapt again into the saddle, even more invigorated than before, and Theamace reared high, as if sensing and sharing his master's joy. Hilt first, he saluted his son. Sword sheathed, he blew a kiss to his wife. She in turn held out a hand of farewell and blessing, and Téthan waved enthusiastically.

In a flash of speed Curillian turned and led his cavalcade in a whirl from the palace. Riding down the paved slope and under the tower-flanked gatehouse, they emerged into the Royal Square. Normally a royal exit would have been in a measured pace and accompanied by much ceremony and attention, but now they cantered across the plaza and did not slow down until they had crossed the south-eastern bridge into the Third Zone. They trotted briskly, not wishing to arouse too much attention.

The Royal Zone was the innermost sanctum of the city, encircled by three others, the Third, the Second and the Outer, each one wider than the one before. Of the three great gates out of the city, Curillian had chosen to exit by the southern one, for it was the least busy, and to get to it one rode through the quietest segment of the city. To use the North Gate, or the East Gate, where the messenger had met Lancoir, would have been to meet half the city along the way and fight through enormous crowds of merchants and farmers, drovers and carters, soldiers and foreign visitors. Even so, as they went, many people heard the rumour of their passing and flocked to line the streets where they rode.

A

Most petitioners would have been duped by the king's evasive route, but not this one. His was a special petition, an urgent petition, and it had to be today. His task could not be delayed, nor his offer made again once the opportunity was missed. Unfamiliar though he was with the city, especially this part of it, some guiding force greater than the will of Curillian brought his feet to the right place. Hurrying at unaccustomed speed, he arrived in the nick of time, exploding out of the side street onto the main thoroughfare in a red blur. The king's horse had only just enough time to rear to a sudden halt without smearing him into the road. The onlookers gasped. The spectacle of the great horse rearing over him was terrifying, and he cowered back onto the road, thinking at any moment that he would be trampled to death. Yet no sooner had the initial terror of the lead horse diminished than a second horse advanced up. A grim rider, hugely tall and menacing on his big steed, rode down on him, sending him scampering back along the road. A sword was unsheathed, but as it swung round into an attacking position, a voice of command rang out.

'Leave him be, Lancoir.' The rider of the first horse was on foot now and level with the other rider, who stopped advancing, but still stood high in his stirrups, a hovering, bullish menace. The dismounted rider walked ahead of the horses and confronted the armist whom he had nearly crushed. The newcomer now saw that, unlike the other mounted armists, this armist's hood had fallen down in the near miss and a circlet of silver with a blue sapphire at its front was evident upon his head. He had not been led wrong: this was the royal riding.

'My friend,' said the king, 'whatever your haste, I hope it was worth nearly being killed for.' The younger armist could only just manage to speak in response, the shock still causing his heart to pound and his breath to come in frantic gasps.

'Lord King, I came to offer you my service.' At the mention of that title, a buzz went through the onlookers; they had noticed the jewel and circlet too, but now their suspicions were confirmed: the king was here. The king's captain, who had seemed intent on trampling him, spat his derision.

'You?! What service could a beggar like you offer us?' The

newcomer became keenly aware of his age-stained red and brown garments. He did indeed feel quite the beggar, but he was committed now; he might as well see it through. If the king was not amenable, then he had already done enough to merit the royal dungeons.

'I know where you are going. I'm going to the same place. I can help you.' Suspicion and wariness immediately came into the king's bemused face, but soon they were joined by a strange expression which the newcomer couldn't identify. They made a strange and vivid pair – the coroneted and mail-clad rider in rich green and black, and the dusty beggar in faded red – and Curillian suddenly became aware of the growing number of people watching, well within earshot. He strode resolutely towards his accoster; close enough so that only he could hear the next words.

'Where am I going?' The young armist now realised the need for discretion, despite having played the key role in its being thrown to the winds. He matched the king's low tone.

'Oron Amular, to the Mountain of High Magic. I can help you... I've been there.' Wonder and surprise showed in the king's face, but he mastered them within moments.

'Come then, and we shall see if your claim is true. Woe betide you, though, if you have spoken falsely.' He turned and beckoned to another senior-looking rider. 'Commander, a spare horse for this armist; he comes with us.' With startling speed, a horse with an empty saddle was brought up and the king remounted, ignoring the disapproving look of the knight beside him. In a trice, the whole cavalcade moved off again. They left behind them a bewildered crowd of city-dwellers rubbing their eyes and rummaging in their ears, wondering if they had really seen and heard what they thought they had.

The King's Cohort, though, was long gone. They slowed just enough for the lead riders to go on ahead and arrange clear passage at the South Gate. The guards at the gate opened wide the passage and cleared the crowds aside, so Curillian and his party of 123 were able to sweep through without so much as breaking pace. In a blur of green and brown they left the city behind and entered the townlands beyond. Now they spurred into a full gallop and were flying eastward. A tournament beckoned them.

＊

II

Reflections

THEY rode hard all day until dusk was falling about them, and then Curillian called a halt. Long shadows were falling across the plains of central Maristonia. They bivouacked in a small copse beside the road. The armists of the Royal Cohort busied themselves erecting tents, setting pickets and cooking an evening meal. The young armist tagging along was extremely glad of the halt. Unused to riding, he was chafed raw and his muscles were burning. He burned, too, from the shame of the jeers and smirks of the skilled riders about him all day as they watched his efforts to keep up the pace and remain in his saddle. Now that they had stopped, he was ignored by them whilst the hustle and bustle went on all around him. Feeling suddenly at a loss, he took himself off to a quiet corner away from the rest and sat down against a tree, trying to get comfortable. He had no desire to join the rough camaraderie of the guards, which was quite incomprehensible to him. Try as he might, though, he could not relax. He discovered the reason why when he caught the hostile glare of the captain, the rider who had nearly trampled him. The hard-faced armist was staring at him with undisguised hostility. He felt the force of the gaze like an over-hot fire too close for comfort. Closing his eyes, he did his best to ignore it. When he opened them again he saw that a guardsman had distracted the captain, allowing him some respite. This was going to be a long journey.

The soldiers gradually formed into small groups around dozens of small campfires. They talked and jested over bowls of steaming broth, and the trees rang with their voices. Roujeark watched on, stomach rumbling. He gave up waiting for food to be offered to him and took a biscuit from his pouch to nibble. He was not unused to meagre fare, having trodden many lonely paths far from inns or markets. It had been a long day though, and the stale morsel did nothing to sate his appetite. So he was grateful when a shadow loomed over him. It was one of the soldiers, a duty cook, and the armist wordlessly plonked a bowl of broth into his lap. He ate the meal, whose main virtue was that it was hot, and felt a grudging thankfulness. As he blew on a spoonful of scalding liquid he became aware of the king picking his way amongst the circles of troops, conversing and joking with them. He was surprised when the monarch kept going and came to stand over him. The king looked down, regarding him silently. He seemed to be scrutinising him for some answer.

'We should talk,' he said at last. Silence fell amongst the guards nearby, who listened in until an officer snapped at them to be about their business. As they dispersed, the king beckoned for his new acquaintance to follow him. Picking up a flaming brand from one of the fires, he led him off into the trees away from the main camp. The ever-vigilant captain made to follow them, but Curillian waved him away. He sat them down between two pine trunks, and thrust the brand into the earth beside them to illuminate their conversation. The night was warm and overhead nightjars flitted through the branches.

'You're not used to company, are you?' Curillian had studied the young armist's manner, full of wariness and unease, and wondered how aware the stranger was of it himself.

'I am not often in company, Your Majesty...' Curillian waved a hand.

'No, no need for titles...'

'...and certainly not company of this sort.' Curillian knew the guards of the cohort had given him a hard time, but he said nothing.

'And you don't ride, do you?' The other shook his head. The king fell silent then, leaving his companion unsure where the questions were leading.

'Of course,' the king said abruptly, 'none of my armists think you should be here.' His companion tensed, thinking he was about to be turned adrift. 'They don't understand why you've been brought', the king continued, 'and I would tell them, except I don't understand myself.' He paused. 'But since you are here, you may as well tell me your name.'

'Roujeark.'

'Roujeark,' the king repeated thoughtfully. 'What does it mean?'

'I don't know for sure. Someone once told me it meant 'Red Journey'. It is apt enough.'

'Red Journey,' repeated the king. 'That would be *Rutharth*.' Roujeark started at that pronunciation, which he had only heard once before. The king seemed not to notice. 'You must come from the mountains to pronounce it *Roujeark*. From near Arton?'

'The Upper Tribune Valley.'

'Ah,' smiled the king. 'Not too far off, then. Red I see you have in abundance from your garments...'

'Red was the only dye we had...'

'But why 'Journey'? Why did your father and mother name you so?' Curillian's perceptive eyes saw the sadness creep into the younger armist's face. It was even a sadness he could pinpoint – he had been there himself.

'I barely remember my mother. My first journey was forced upon me the night my father died.'

Again, the burning cottage and the desperate flight into the night blazed into his mind. Stronger than it had been for many years, the memories surged up. The last moments they had had together were spent frantically packing the pony's saddlebags. Roujeark had heard about the unfortunate death of the two children, swept away by the provoked river, a spell gone horribly wrong, but he had never thought it would come to this. The villagers wanted revenge, and his father had seemed resigned to it. But he had been determined that his son would escape and live his life. So he had spent the last minutes of his life in a frantic rush. Roujeark had seen the long line of torches advancing up the hillside to their home, peeking through the window, and he had got out only just in time. Tekka, their only pony, had barely carried him out of the yard when he wriggled off his back and looked back. Hiding behind an arm of rock, he could just see back down the winding path to the rear of his home.

The sounds were still alive in his mind. Angry shouts twisting in the wind…glass breaking…door crashing open…the grunts and shouts of a struggle. No anguished death-cry; only the heavy slump of a body to the floor. Then the rush of flames as the torches took hold in the furnishings, and the smashes as bottles and jars were thrown from the shelves.

The sounds were not just still alive: they throbbed in accompaniment to the inseparable images. Partners in his recurrent nightmare, together they were engraved in his heart. The dark interior of the mountain-cottage suddenly lit up with an orange glare…the shadows of many figures moving around inside…the confused shades of the struggle…the uprush of the flames, filling his wide-eyed gaze. Shock, and terror, but he hadn't been able to move. It had only been when the attackers had come to the back door, coming for him, that he remounted the pony and took flight. That black night, with all its chill wind, hadn't been able to cool the burning pain he took with him.

Feeling the hot tears streaming over his cheeks, he cuffed at them with red sleeves.

'Perhaps he foresaw it,' said he, almost to himself.

'Your pain is still near,' said the king, 'like a branding just administered. You have carried it with you all these years, with no one to tell, and it has multiplied in the carrying. Share your story with me – perhaps it will help? What happened that night?' Roujeark didn't know where to begin, and thought he couldn't bring himself to speak of it – it had been bottled up for so long – but after the first few tentative words it bubbled out like an unblocked spring.

'My father was Dubarnik...He was known in the valley as a magician...someone with power over the unseen. They supported him...us...because he was of use to them, and life seemed good. But then two children died when he made the river rise up. He was only trying to test a new device for harnessing the water's power, but it got out of control. He never told me the details, but I never thought he'd done anything wrong. Yet he blamed himself. He changed, and in the last few days he was silent and withdrawn, guilt-struck. The villagers blamed him too, and one night they came. They came with torches, fresh from the alehouse and eager for a blood-debt to be settled. My father became energised again only just in time to get me out of there, but no sooner had I left than they broke in. I never saw him fall, but I think I heard it. Then they set fire to our home, and ever since my father's ashes have lain among the ashes of our home. I have not been back.' Tears streamed out while he spoke, but so compassionate was the king's face that he did not feel abashed to weep before a stranger. By the time he had finished speaking they had dried up, leaving wet stains on his cheeks.

'And what was the journey?' the king asked.

'To Oron Amular.' The charged words lingered in the air and hung between them in the firelight, like sparks that would not go out. The king continued his questions.

'Why would an orphaned child from the Carthaki foothills seek out the Mountain of High Magic?' Across forty years, Roujeark heard his father's words again.

'You have a gift, young one, a special strain of the powers that run in our family. I may not be the mighty wizard I once hoped to be, but you have far more potential than I ever had. I have enough skill to recognise that, and I believe that, with the right tutelage, you could become great. You have great things in your future.'

'My father had some magic, and he saw it in me too. Although magic led to his death, he still hoped I could find training and become a real wizard.'

'And you came there? How did you know the way? No one knows the way, not even I, veteran of many adventures. Not many even among the elves know now, and they tell no one.'

'Prélan guided me. He led me by secret ways from the Aravell River.' Mistaking the king's pensive gaze for disbelief, he pressed his case. 'If you do not believe me, then why did you bring me this far?'

'I do believe you, Roujeark. I know what it is to be led by Prélan, and I have some skill in perceiving His hand on others. If nothing else, I can discern honesty in an armist, and I see it in you. But the real reason I brought you, if you want to know, is because I was told to. I was told to protect someone, *'for he is needed at the Mountain.'* I believe that someone is you.'

'Prélan spoke to you?' The relief on Roujeark's face was like rain on parched ground.

'Yes. Tell me how he spoke to you.'

Roujeark thought back into the happenings of that long-ago journey. 'I had just reached the land of Kalimar,' he began slowly. 'I hadn't been long in that land before an elf found me and warned me that I shouldn't be there, that it would go badly with me if I didn't leave. He frightened me. I somehow found the courage to go on, but not long after I was drawn into the woods away from the road. In a small dell I came across an old elf, or at least what I thought was an old elf...'

Λ

L ooking down into the dell, seeing all the broad, short trees, bushes and patches of fern, Roujeark felt that he had found a sanctuary for the night, but then he noticed the figure sitting hunched at the foot of a tree on the dell's far side, facing him. He gave a start, and would have turned back immediately towards the road, but the person smiled. He was like, and yet unlike, the elf who had accosted him. He was dressed in a cloak and hood of peculiar colour, a deep shade that seemed to shift between green and brown, and he clutched a staff in his hands between his drawn-up knees. His smile was warm.

'Don't mind me,' said he. 'This is my dell, but I'm happy to share it with you tonight.' Drawn by the warmth in the stranger's voice, Roujeark led Tekka cautiously down to the dell's bottom until they were only a few paces from the seated figure. Roujeark could not decide whether the person was elf or armist or something else entirely. He seemed old, but had an ageless handsomeness in his face and eyes as deep as the sea.

'I'm afraid,' he began timidly, surprising even himself that he was confiding in this stranger unbidden. 'I think that…that there are…'

'That there are elves after you?' the person finished for him, and smiled. 'Yes, I know, but do not fear, they will not find you while I am here.' Roujeark's knees buckled with relief, but a thread of worry tugged at him.

'Are you staying?' The person smiled again, apparently with a power to flood him with peace.

'I don't usually,' he said, 'but tonight my special vigil shall be here. Quiet now, unpack your things and settle down. You may sleep for the time being and have no fear.'

Roujeark did so, and slept for many hours with more rest than he had ever before experienced, but sometime in the middle of the night he awoke to the sound of hooves and the soft jingling of harness. He looked up over his blanket at the dell's lip and saw three riders standing there. He began to panic, but when he looked up at the cloaked figure still sitting beside him, he saw that his face was completely unconcerned, almost as if he was not aware of the horses. Roujeark felt calmer, but was still afraid, for the riders seemed to be looking straight at him. His fears vanished, though, when they turned and rode away, leaving him unmolested. He looked up again at his guardian, who was still serenely unperturbed.

'Please,' he began, 'how did those riders not see me?' His companion gazed in front of him, not looking down.

'The elves know this land almost as well as the land knows itself, and very little that goes on in it escapes their notice, but I am able to make things blind to them when there is need.' Roujeark thought for a moment.

'What need is there?' he asked. His companion seemed not to hear the question, but instead remarked,

'It is as well that you are awake, for now you must leave this place.'
Roujeark's face fell.

'So soon? Why?'

'There are things you need to see, someone you need to meet.'
Obediently, Roujeark rolled up his blankets and packed them away
again in Tekka's saddlebag. The old stranger got up and made to
leave, but Roujeark pressed him with one last question.

'Please, I must know. Why did you help me tonight?' The hooded
figure turned and looked at him. His words were as incisive and
knowing as his eyes.

'You are going somewhere, and it is important that you get there.
Therefore, it would have been a pity if the elves had been able to
carry you back to your own country. No, they must share their land
with you for a while. But come, the night passes, and there is much
left to do. That way lies your path.' Following his point, Roujeark saw
moonlight illuminating a path through the trees as they climbed the
slope outside of the dell. When he looked back, his helper was gone.
He followed the moonlit path further up the hillside. He had not
gone far when he came to a little tree-shaded hollow. A little stream
was issuing from a rocky surface and falling into a pool. And on the
surface of the pool was a single flame, broad and incandescent. He
marvelled, for no steam rose from the water, and no oil or fuel lay on
the surface to feed the flame. The heat issuing from it, however, was
unmistakeable. His curiosity overcame his incredulity and he took
faltering steps towards it. He came to the pool's edge and reached
out to touch the water, but a voice checked him. It was as terrifying
and benign as the flames whence it came.

'Roujeark! Roujeark!'

'I am here,' he heard himself say, though he had barely been aware
of the urge to speak.

'Do not touch the water, for this is a holy place.' Roujeark shrank back, but hearing the compassion in the deep voice, which stirred a recent memory into faint familiarity, he dared to speak.

'Please, Lord, who is it that speaks from the fire and the water? And how do you know my name?'

'I am Prélan, the God of your fathers, who was at the Beginning and who brought all things into being. I know the name your father gave to you, and I know the name I myself have for you. I know the cares of your heart, and its ambitions. You are seeking Oron Amular, but you do not know the way. Be reassured, child, for none ever come to this place and leave it still astray. Verily you are destined to go to the Mountain of High Magic, and I have drawn you here so that I might confirm you on your course and guide you.'

'I am glad, Lord, to meet you, and to receive your reassurance. I was glad also of he who watched over me this night when the elves came looking for me. But I am alone in a strange land, far from home, and without help or companions, and I am afraid.' The flame waxed larger and absorbed his vision.

'Look at this flame and know me, Roujeark. Now that we are met, you shall not lack for help or companionship again. I shall send more besides in the time to come. First, know me. Second, know that I created you and knew you before your conception; know that I love you and that I have plans for you. Plans to prosper you and to use you, for you shall grow strong. You shall confound the counsels of the wise and shake the towers of the mighty. Go forth knowing these things and take them in earnest of other things which shall be taught to you. Go back to the road with the first light of day, and there you shall meet a merchant's family. They are expecting you, and they will carry you as far as the Aravell Bridge. There we will meet again.'

⋀

'That was my first encounter with Prélan,' Roujeark concluded. Curillian sat entranced by the retelling.

'Your first?' the king asked, rousing himself from his absorption. 'What were the others?'

'I found the merchant's family, and they took me to the Aravell Bridge. There I was at a loss for what to do next, but when I took refuge under the bridge, hiding from more elves, I met Prélan again...'

⋀

The water's reflection flickered on the underside of the bridge. At first it was dim, but then the patterns grew in brightness and colour, though Roujeark could not tell where the light came from. As he watched, mesmerised, the patterns began to coalesce and produce a concerted shape. He was fascinated to see that it took on the vague but unmistakeable outline of a head. It was neither wholly elven nor armist in appearance, but it was seemingly generated by a power within the water. Then He spoke.

'Roujeark, welcome. Well done for trusting me, for you have come here, just as I asked.' Roujeark could think of no response, but had to cower slightly and cover his eyes, for the shape seemed to gather brightness as it spoke. The voice was soft, but in the confines under the bridge it seemed to boom and echo. 'Do not worry,' said Prélan, assuaging his unspoken fear, 'the elves will not overhear us. Indeed, they will again be blind to you as soon as you leave the cover of this bridge, where their eyes are most watchful.' Roujeark plucked up his courage and spoke, though still unable to look directly at the lights.

'Lord, is it still to Oron Amular that I go?'

'The Mountain waits for its last son. This is where you leave the road, and follow the Maker's paths on the last leg of your journey. The directions are written in the water: drink, and know.' Roujeark looked down, and was amazed to see foreign characters lingering amid the river's rippling current. Falling to his knees, he cupped his hands and drank deep. Instant revitalisation flushed down him, and a new confidence. 'See?' said the voice above him. 'My ways are now your ways. Follow them, and reach your destination. And remember, I will always be with you…' Straightaway, the symbols in the stream vanished and the lights dimmed. They seemed to drain into the current and rush away, like a spirit of the waters. Yet he could still feel the glow of some of it within his belly.

A

A look of rapture was on the king's face. A slight note of envy was in his voice when he spoke again.

'You are lucky to have heard Prélan speak in such a manner twice. I myself have only heard His voice audibly on one occasion, and I thought I was blessed indeed to have had just that. Yet ever after, throughout my life, I have heard His voice in other ways, and felt my feet guided by His paths. So you came to the Mountain?'

'Yes,' said Roujeark, 'but first I had a strange encounter…but it is late…'

'The moon has barely risen,' said the king. 'I will not be able to sleep until you have told me the end of your tale.'

'Very well. Climbing into the mountains, guided I know not how by Prélan, I came to a mysterious cave…'

⋀

Compelled from within, Roujeark entered into the cave, tugging a reluctant Tekka along with him. The cave inside was like a tunnel, comfortably high enough for him to walk un-stooped, and sufficiently broad for him and Tekka to walk abreast. After some time, the passage forked and went into two separate tunnels. At the end of both tunnels, there was a door, of standard size and shape, not unlike that of his old home. The final direction came from within him, like a voice issuing up his throat.

'There are two ways, and you must choose between them. One way will lead you to the answer, and the other will not. Trust not to your eyes, but rather listen to your heart, and follow it, even if the way seems uncomely.' He pondered the words and looked from one door to the other. As he got nearer, he saw that the door on the left was very well-made from varnished pine. It was bound with gold and a warm reddish glow issued from the cracks around it. The passage leading up to it was warmer and seemed much more inviting. The door on the right, however, was not so stately. The scarred and singed wood was falling apart and great holes were torn into it. It was hung with icicles, jagged and menacing, and the whole tunnel leading up to it was frosty and repellent.

He stood looking at the doors, turning from one to the other. The door on the left seemed so nice and warm and looked so comfortable. The heat issuing from it seemed to draw him closer so that he was several steps down the tunnel before he realised it. As he went, he expected the heat to increase, but instead the air about him grew colder. Soon he was shivering, and his breath was misting in front of him. His confidence peeled back like a curtain, and panic rose within him. His flesh broke out in goose-pimples and he shook violently, but still the door ahead looked so appealing that he strove to get to it. After another few painful steps, however, he began to notice that the door was not as well-made as it had first appeared. A veneer of finesse seemed to strip away, leaving a rotten, dejected layer underneath. He stepped quickly away, disappointed, and retraced his painful way back to the fork in the tunnel. Panting, and doubled up, he despaired to look at the two doors again: one harsh and cold, and the other whose magnetism he now knew was deceptive. He remembered what the voice had told him: trust not to your eyes, but rather to your heart. He breathed deep and decided to try the right-hand passage.

He steeled himself for another ordeal, and indeed, the first few steps in the right-hand passage was like trying to walk through a blizzard. Deadly cold clutched at him, but his heart was calm, completely against his better judgement. A few more steps and suddenly the fierce edge of the cold abated and the going became easier. Daring to look up, he noticed a change in this door also. The holes filled up, the singes disappeared and the wears of use and signs of neglect slowly faded. He traced his fingers against the passage wall, and what had at first been icy-burning to touch now became warm. The temperature in the passage was increasing rapidly, until, a few steps from the door, the walls were too hot to touch. Yet this time, instead of feeling more panicky as the temperature changed, he felt a warm sensation of peace spreading through him. His face flushed, and by the time he reached the door, he felt the homely heat that one might experience in the bath. On closer inspection, the door before him was the picture of finery, as if before he had viewed it through a distorting cobweb of filth, hiding the magnificence beneath. Hesitantly, he reached out and touched the doorknob. It stung his hand like a glowing coal. Yet as he held it, restraining his initial impulse to let go, he felt the heat reduce to a comfortable, reassuring heat. His other senses suddenly reported contentment too: his nose smelt fragrant, newly-cut wood, and his ears heard pleasant, yet indistinct sounds. Twisting the knob, he pushed the door ajar and went through.

Half expecting to be greeted by some impenetrable darkness, he found himself dazzled instead by some great light in front of him. As he stepped through fully and shut the door behind him, the light gradually subsided and he saw that he was in what looked like a garden. It was filled with the fragrance of flowers and trees and plants grew everywhere. The place was alive with colour so vivid that it hurt his eyes at first: orange, blue, yellow, red, green and turquoise. He heard the trickle of water and saw that a small but crystal clear stream was flowing over a succession of waterfalls. A very tall figure, all in white with hands clasped behind him, had his back to him. His garments were of the purest white, trimmed with gold, and upon his brown hair was a plain circlet of gold. When he turned, Roujeark beheld a face of astonishing handsomeness. It was dominated by golden-brown eyes which radiated warmth and power. As he approached, Roujeark found himself barely level with the other's waist, and forced to crane his neck to look up at him.

'Who are you?' was all he could ask, in a tone of wonder.

'I am a messenger from Prélan Arrion, The Lord Almighty. You may call me Ardir.' His voice was like rhythms of deep music, soft and noble. 'You have chosen well, son of Dubarnik, and to have come this far has proven your wisdom and worth.' Roujeark felt abashed, unsure what to say next.

'Truly, I am glad to be here, though I did not expect to find such loveliness at the end of such an unpromising route.'

Ardir smiled. 'Verily. Oft the more attractive way proves hardest, while the harder-seeming leads to unexpected rewards.'

'I don't know if it was all some kind of test for me, but it seemed that I had to shun the obvious path, and take the one which looked harder. I feel sure that only such wisdom as Prélan has given me enabled me to choose aright. By myself, I'm sure I would have gone astray. Ever since I first met Him at the pool He has been with me.' Ardir smiled at his words, the smile of one whose hopes have been fulfilled.

'You do well to pay homage to your Maker. Assuredly, I have watched Him guide you, and bestow upon you the right measures of humility and courage. Having passed through then, come, and see what I was bidden to show you.' He led Roujeark around the garden to a place where suddenly the ground came to an end. They were on a cliff, with clouds just above them. Looking down, they could see the land of Kalimar far below, spread out like a living map.

Roujeark had seen impressive vistas from mountaintops before, but this surpassed them all; he could even see parts of Maristonia, whence he had come. However, it was the Black Mountains which dominated his view, a dense thicket of jagged slopes and white-tipped peaks. He saw armies of trees on their slopes that eventually marched down into the great Ankil woods. He saw the other forests of Kalimar, mighty and humble alike, and glinting silver waterways threading their way through field and valley. Most captivating of all, he saw the sea for the very first time, where sunlight danced on its waves. Following them to the shore, he saw a great river plunge into a bay of golden sands and pure white cliffs. It truly was a beautiful land.

'Behold Kalimar,' declared Ardir, 'most beautiful of all lands. I rejoice in its beauty while I may, for soon I shall grieve for her.'

'Why do you say that?' inquired the armist, suddenly filled with curiosity and a foreboding of great sadness.

'Because, alas, the foremost fingertips of a great shadow are already groping at its edges; a great storm is brewing away north. If the storm itself can be withstood, the floods which come after may prove irresistible.' Up until then he had been gazing, like Roujeark, out at the magnificent landscape, but now he turned to look at him, and his face was very grave.

'This is the story which you are caught up in, and, as the Lord Prélan has decreed, your part will soon be made clear to you.' He took from his robes a piece of folded parchment and clasped it against the armist's smaller hand. 'Now it is right for me to give you this, to light the next steps.'

Opening it up, Roujeark eagerly anticipated a replica of the panorama beneath his feet, but no, it was...blank. He opened his mouth to speak, but Ardir spoke first. 'It is not as other maps, made to quench the beholder's curiosity all at once; yet nevertheless, it will guide you true, step by step.' Again, Roujeark made to speak, but Ardir held up a forestalling hand. 'More than that I cannot say. Trust in Prélan and he will not lead you astray.' And with that, he seemed to fade before him. Even as he looked, Ardir dematerialised and vanished into thin air. Roujeark blinked, and the world about him reverted to what it had been.

A

'You have spoken with Ardir?' Curillian was amazed, and Roujeark was not able to appreciate how difficult it was to amaze an armist like Curillian. 'Depending on your theological bent, some would account that a third meeting with Prélan...and... in person. Though whether he be Prélan incarnate, or one of His angels, I do not know. Your life has indeed been marked out in a special way, Roujeark, son of Dubarnik. But come, finish your tale.

Ardir's map guided you to the Mountain…?'

'It did. I set out hesitantly from there, all too aware that the map in my possession was blank. Walking in one direction, I found that the map remained blank, and so too for another direction, but when I tried a third, walking towards the setting sun, I saw that the map came alive. A dusting of colour blushed a tiny portion of it, showing the slopes across which I walked. The remainder of the crumpled page stayed resolutely blank, and if I wavered to one side or the other, it ceased to expand, but as long as I proceeded in the correct direction, it followed my feet.

'One day I was shown just how perfectly my path had been picked out for me. I finally breasted a long, steep escarpment, and what I saw from there took my breath away. Spread out before me were the Black Mountains, in all their formidable ranks. They are aptly named, composed of the darkest stone, like a sheet of obsidian crumpled and riven into a thousand peaks, folds and crevices. Almost the only colours among them were the crowns of snow mantling the tallest peaks, and the glint of sapphire waters in hidden recesses among their feet. They extended almost as far as I could see, but due south of me I could glimpse where steep valleys tugged them down into the plains of Kalimar. Surely, I thought, if I had come any other way, I would have had to find a path through that granite wilderness. Had Prélan brought me so far east with the merchant's family to circumvent those difficult passes, setting my feet on easier tracks instead?

'The sun, having cast a reddish tint over the dark mountains, had set behind a particularly high massif, but then, almost in a display for me, it peeked savagely out. The parting shot scorched the knotted landscape, but in one place, at the corner of my vision, it set it spectacularly ablaze. I turned to look, and gasped in awe. Was that a mountain with its entire top-half aflame? The vast ice-sheets and snowfields on one enormous mountain were rippling and shimmering with flames, captivating me. The great mountain stood apart from the rest, rearing like the neck of a proud horse far above the thin spur which connected it to the rest. Not only did it stand apart in location, but it soared twice as tall as any others which were in view. It dominated the skyline so effortlessly that I was amazed I had not seen it before. It reached up so high above the ridge in front of it that it looked like a vast tower enclosed by a garden fence. I blessed Prélan in my heart for arranging this perfectly clear evening in which the mountain could be seen in all its glory. My mind slowly caught up with my eyes. Could it be? Intuition built upon suspicion until my disbelief came crumbling down, and my knees with it. Oron Amular. This was what I had journeyed so far to see. Then the flames on the mountain's sides began to die down. Suddenly, the sun vanished and the great mountain was dowsed in darkness.

'So it was that I came to Oron Amular, and the sight of it alone made the whole journey worthwhile. Getting down to the mountain, however, was no easy task. The mountain seemed to grow no nearer, no matter how many ridges I scaled, or how many dales I traversed. Tugging Tekka along with me made the task much harder. I spent several days trying to get closer to it, and seemed to make only slight progress. Each evening I hoped for another sunset to kindle the snowy peak and recreate the vision of that first sighting, but each evening my hopes were denied by overcast skies. However, despite the cloud cover, the early summer air was hot and humid. Pausing at a shoulder of rock which offered a tantalising view of my destination, I wiped my brow clear of sweat and wondered how much further to go that night.

"Will I ever get there?" I said aloud to myself.

"Where is it you are going?"

"The Mountain, of course." I made the reply before realising that it was not I who had asked the question. I had been on the road for two months now, with only minimal contact with people, so I assumed that any voice I heard was either my own, or Prélan's within my head. Now, with a shock, I realised otherwise, and whirled around. It took a moment for me to spot him, but then I saw him, an old man sitting on a flat-topped rock, staff between his knees. The old man's dark purple robes blended in with the rock behind him, but his pale face and long wispy white hair stood out.

"Who, who are you? And what are you doing here?" I asked nervously. The old man seemed bemused.

"I live here. I am out for an evening stroll." He pointed a bony finger at me. "No, more to the point is, what you are doing here." He drew his hand back into the folds of his robes and settled himself for an answer. He seemed relaxed, but his eyes watched me ever so carefully. I shivered under the intense scrutiny, but I swallowed hard and decided to start from the beginning.

"I was sent here." The old man waited patiently for more elaboration. "Some time ago," I went on, "I lost both my father and my home on the same night." Was that the barest softening of the eyes, betraying some compassion? "Before he died, my father told me to seek out Oron Amular." I shrugged. "I know nothing of the place but the name." The old man leaned forward interestedly.

"Who was your father, I wonder, to have directed you thus?" Tears formed in my eyes as I brought my father to mind.

"He was a magician," was all I could say.

"A magician," the old man repeated thoughtfully. "Hmm, did he tell you anything about Oron Amular?"

"I had but the vaguest directions, knowing only that it lay in Kalimar, somewhere beyond the Delarom Pass, and I believe I am near its slopes now. Many weeks on the road, across fields and over hills, have brought me to this place."

"So, you come from beyond Delarom Pass? Then you are, as you appear to be, a son of Armanor?"

"I am an armist, yes."

"Maristonia is a long way from here. With such vague directions, how did you come to make it this far?"

"I had help," I said simply. "An elven family bore me through Kalimar in their wagon, and…" I paused, suddenly embarrassed by what I was about to say.

"And…?" the old man prompted me.

"And I think Prélan appeared to me several times, guiding me." The old man's eyes lit up, along with his whole face.

"Ahhh," he exhaled expressively. "One who comes in the name of Prélan is to be welcomed." He resumed his scrutiny of me, and after a few moments' thought, he pronounced, "I think your father sent you here because he wanted you trained; because he believed you had some talent with magic." I nodded, for that made sense.

"Whenever he worked magic and performed tricks, he always used to say I had greater powers than him. I didn't believe him."

"Did you not?" the old man mused. "And you do not know elvish? Not even enough to know that in elvish, Oron Amular means 'Mountain of High Magic'? No? Well, the training would be long indeed." He broke off, muttering to himself. "Many have heard of my Mountain…"

"It's your mountain?" I interrupted excitedly.

"Yes, it is *my* Mountain. Many have heard, but your father would appear to be among the few who guess that a fraternity of magic still lingers on here." Then he dropped his voice so low that I could barely hear him. "Perhaps it is you then…" He looked up and raised his voice to a more audible level again. He seemed to be in the grip of some strange emotion and had to clear his throat to regain his composure. "Tell me, what is your name?"

"Roujeark, sir. If it is your mountain, can you take me there?"

"And tell me, Roujeark," asked the old man, ignoring my question completely, "what does your name mean?"

"In the language of my land it means 'red journey', though I have never understood why." The old man chuckled, a sound strangely at odds with the sad kindness in his face.

"That is but an armist corruption of *Rutharth*, the Journey of Red. You are garbed in red, and your hair is red, but this is your first real journey. There are many reasons why the journeys ahead of you will be red, but that is not for you to know now." His voice deepened and his gaze took on a faraway look as he made this pronouncement. Then he seemed to remember my question. "And yes, I could take you to my Mountain, but it would do you little good, I am afraid. Soon it will be empty, and to go whither its inhabitants are bound would be far too perilous for an untrained youth such as yourself. Alas, weightier concerns have conspired to make this first journey of yours futile. But," he said, surveying his visitor with that unsettling intensity again, "it may be that there are things for you to do first, just as I myself have a grave task at hand. No, now is not your time."

My heart sank. The muggy evening turned suddenly chill, and a sudden weariness swamped me.

"But I've come so far, wasted so much time…" The old man raised his eyebrows.

"Is time something you are short of? Do others demand of you?"

"I have nowhere else to go," my voice was pleading now. The old man smiled sadly, but he was resolute.

"No, I can understand that this is a bitter blow for you, but now is not your time." Something in the old man's face cleared, as if a knotted problem had suddenly resolved itself. 'You will come here again," he declared with confidence, "but I see now that it will be in company. Very esteemed company, I think." He rose creakily to his feet, hauling himself upright with his staff. A strange red flash lit the sky by the mountain, and he looked impatiently towards the mountain, and then down again at me. His face softened, and he laid a tender hand on my red hair.

"Be blessed, *Rutharth*. You have done well to follow Prélan's promptings so far, see to it that you continue to do so. He has a place and a plan for you. And wait for my sign – then you will know that your time has come." He muttered some strange words over me, though whether it was a prayer or a benediction of some kind, I don't know. Then he pushed something into my hand. "When you come back, bring this with you as a token to any that might challenge you. Until then, son of Dubarnik, be blessed..." The hand lingered a moment, quivering as it imparted something that made my hair tingle, and then it was withdrawn. I closed my eyes in despair, and let tears course down my cheeks. When I opened them again, the old man was gone, with only the receding sounds of his footsteps remaining. The deepening night around me seemed to reflect my mood, but then suddenly I started, realising that I had not told the old man my father's name – how had he know it was Dubarnik? As I thought this, a surge of power, like a jolt of excitement, electrified every part of me.

'I slept that night at the place of my meeting with the old man, whose name I had not even learned. I felt very small in that landscape of giants, and very alone. I thought to delay my return journey at least until the light came, yet it was not the light of day which woke me, but a flickering of strange colours. Rising, I went to the overlook again, and in the darkness, I saw flashes of blue, green and red which illuminated the sides of the mountain. They were like the flash I had seen during my conversation with the old man the evening before. Eerie and comforting at the same time, they illuminated a small column issuing forth from some hidden door in the mountain. More flashes seemed to emanate from the column itself. As that column made its way north, like an army on its way to war, I prepared to make my own journey.'

Roujeark completed his tale at long last and looked up at Curillian, whose attention had never wavered.

'That is how I came to Oron Amular. I still do not know who that old man was, but I still have what he gave me…' He drew forth from his pocket a metal star, engraved with runes and decorations in intricate detail. Curillian gasped when he saw it.

'A Seal of the League of Wizardry. Do you realise this is probably the first time one of these has been seen outside of the Mountain since the Second War of Kurundar? Phew, even if I had doubted your tale up until now, this would confirm everything. The wizards each used to carry one of these, a token of authority and membership of the League of Wizardry, but now they must be among the rarest and most valuable trinkets in the world. Incredible! Why did you not show it to me before, when we first met in Mariston?'

'I had forgotten all about it,' said Roujeark truthfully. 'Telling my story for the first time reminded me.' Curillian ran his hands over the star.

'The old man you met was Kulothiel himself, I feel sure.'

'Kulothiel?'

'The Head of the League of Wizardry, and Keeper of the Mountain. He is a great power. An ancient man now, but he has long been the mightiest mage in Astrom. Yet the world has forgotten him, for he seemed to have forgotten the world. Verily, Roujeark, you are vindicated in seeking me out. I am indeed on my way to Oron Amular, summoned to a tournament there. But until I met you I had no clear idea, other than a couple of unpromising leads, about how to get there. Could you lead me there, by way of the Aravell?' Roujeark just nodded dumbly, slightly bewildered by the pace of the conversation and the strength of the king's sudden resolve. 'The elves won't like it, of course,' Curillian went on, 'but that's a problem for another day. So you will guide me, and I will protect you. Thus shall we serve each other, just as Prélan clearly intended.'

The king went quiet again, lost in thought. At first Roujeark thought the conversation was over, but something made him stay. Intrigue about this strange king, so gentle yet so formidable, so rough yet so deep, so simple yet so mysterious, was growing in him. Curillian, who had done most of the scrutinising so far, was surprised to find himself on the receiving end.

'What?' he asked gently. Roujeark seemed bashful.

'Oh, nothing. Well, it's just…you're not quite as I imagined the king would be.' Curillian smiled, having heard similar assessments many times.

'Really? And what do you imagine the king should be like?'

'I don't really know,' confessed Roujeark, embarrassed. 'But in the hills where I grew up, we have heard two things about the king. One says that his strength is legendary, that he is tall as an elf and brave as a hero. The legends of his deeds all speak of great feats and daring exploits.' Curillian smiled at this description of himself. He was at least six inches too short to be even a short elf. 'The other thing we have heard is that he is very aloof, very remote, too grand to be approached.' Again, Curillian smiled.

'That last part sounds more like my father Mirkan than myself. So you think I am not like these stories you have heard?'

'You are obviously a great warrior,' Roujeark said, struggling to find the right words, 'but your strength seems more down to earth than legend makes it. I mean, how many kings would take the time to sit down like this and talk to a simple peasant? You are more… well, accessible.'

'How many simple peasants would talk thus to a king?' rejoined Curillian. 'It seems we are neither of us as we ought to be.' The king lapsed into a long, deep silence. The brand crackled softly and in its light, Roujeark saw the far-away look in the king's eyes. It came as a surprise to him when, after a long time, the king spoke again. He was even more surprised when he heard the words which were spoken.

'I too was forced to make a long, hazardous journey when I was only young, and I too lost my father before I really knew him. An evil counsellor of my father, the erstwhile Lord Protector, caused me to be sent into exile and usurped the throne that should have been mine. Unlike many princes who have come to kingship through ease and privilege, I only attained it after long years of labour and testing. I wandered through Dorzand and Ciricen and Aranar, never knowing a true home. I was an outlaw, fending for myself and encountering many strange people and places. Later I came to Ithrill and there entered the service of the Silver Emperor, Lancearon. He gave me the name Ruthion.'

'Why Ruthion?' Roujeark interrupted without meaning to. Curillian seemed unperturbed – indeed, he even seemed to think the question significant.

'It means 'Red Warrior'. I wore red armour and apparently reminded the elves of one of their heroes from older days. Anyway, as Ruthion I kept safe the borders of the Silver Empire, fighting many enemies. When the Second War of Kurundar broke out, I fought in that conflict too, first in the emperor's cavalry, and later with my own army. After I recovered from a deadly wound, the time was deemed ripe for me to reclaim the throne of Maristonia, whose strength the empire so badly needed in that desperate war. I returned to Maristonia, and, with Prélan's help, I overthrew the tyrant Lord Protector and won back my throne. After leading the Maristonian Army to victory in the war, I came back home to live out my days in relative peace. Here I have been ever since – more or less – and here I am, just as you find me.' He didn't know why he had told this stranger all that, but he had felt able, for some reason, to open up.

'So,' responded Roujeark tentatively, 'Red Journey and Red Warrior?'

'Yes, it sounds like we'll make fine travelling companions, doesn't it? Prélan knows what He's doing, seemingly. A lesson I find myself having to learn time and again. But I marvel at you, Roujeark, to go seeking magic, the very thing which caused your father's death.'

'At the time magic was all I had…It still is. If I can learn to use it properly, and control it, then I might be able to make up for my father's death, mightn't I?'

'Perhaps. Yet I still say you are courageous. I remember, in my very earliest days, when my brother Aramist swam for the first time – he was carried off by a swift current and nearly died. His death came not long afterwards, from a sickness, but for all his remaining days he had been terrified of water. But you, you grapple with what nearly caused your death. Whether your gift of magic proves to be a blessing or a curse remains to be seen,' said Curillian. 'The more I think about you, the more I see a heavy doom lying on your shoulders. You have become entangled with the great affairs of the world. If you are to walk the path set before you, you will need to hold tight to Prélan.' As these words sunk in, Curillian stood up, plucking the brand from the ground. 'It is late, my new friend. Get some sleep. Let us see what tomorrow may bring.'

The last thing Roujeark saw, as he walked back to the already-slumbering camp, was the old king wandering amid the trees, taking counsel with himself in the torchlight.

※

III

Water and Fire

THEY broke camp early the next morning. With torturously stiff legs and back, Roujeark forced himself back into his saddle. They had not gone far along the road before they stopped. Standing up in his stirrups and gazing forward, Roujeark could just see the king deliberating with the senior officers at the head of the column.

'We'll leave the road here,' Curillian told Lancoir and Surumo, 'and make for Laston.' They looked at him in surprise.

'For Laston?' asked Lancoir. 'You mean to go the long way round?'

'I do,' Curillian confirmed.

'Markest would be better,' the knight ventured tersely.

'Only if you're willing to put up with prying eyes through the whole East-fold, which I am not. No, we shall avoid the main road through the pass and go via Welton.'

'The ferry at Laston will be a far quicker way to reach Welton,' put in Surumo. 'Much easier than negotiating all the traffic on Delarom Pass.'

'Just so,' confirmed Curillian. Lancoir's misgivings showed plainly on his face.

'I hope our footpad hasn't been suggesting any wild notions or strange paths,' said he. 'The armists don't trust him. They think he is a magician of unknown powers.' Curillian gestured for Surumo to get the column moving again, and then he laid his hand on Lancoir's arm as the first riders trotted past.

'Lancoir, Prélan has spoken to me. For better or worse, we will take Roujeark to Oron Amular, and he will be our guide. Do you accept this?' Lancoir returned his sovereign's steady gaze in silence for a while, and then nodded assent. 'Good armist,' said the king happily, slapping his captain's vambrace. 'It's just as well, really, since before meeting him our chances of finding the Mountain were slim.' Lancoir nodded in grudging acknowledgement.

'It's his idea to go via Phirmar?'

'It is no notion of his that I am following, Lancoir, but my own, so be at peace. Roujeark will guide us, but first I wish to talk to a friend in Welton. I may find out something useful. Going this way also has the added advantage of being more discreet – the whole country doesn't need to know I'm on the road. Plus, I'd rather not have news of my riding go ahead of me to reach the ears of any potential competitors. Leave them guessing for the time being. And as for the troops, they will just have to get used to Roujeark. Magician or not, he is no danger to them. Come.'

Having left the road, they made across country for a while before striking a new road. Not so large or well-maintained as the first, which was one of the main thoroughfares of the kingdom, it was nevertheless kinder to Roujeark's pain-wracked body than the rough uneven ground of the open country. This second road led them by mid-afternoon to the coast. During a noontime pause the king had sent errand riders ahead to make preparations, which meant that when the main company arrived they found the town in an uproar of excitement. A modest port of several hundred colourful stone houses, Laston's inhabitants made their living either from fishing or from trades connected to the great ferry which docked in their harbour. Many important visitors and delegations used the ferry – most notably the Duke of Welton – but the presence of the king was a rare and special occasion. Without the benefit of advance warning, the whole population had turned out of their brightly-painted houses or left their nets and lobster-cages at the waterfront and hurried to make the place ready for the royal visitor. Extra hands were assigned to make the ferry ready, and others cleared up the main street and then lined it with hurriedly cut flowers.

When the main company arrived outside the town's stockade and rode under its large, seashell-studded arch, most of the town's population was still lining the road. Making the most of this unexpected glimpse of their beloved king, they cheered him past with great enthusiasm. Similar enthusiasm was also directed at his escort, but unlike foot-slogging legionaries who might have availed themselves of the town's hospitality, these disciplined Royal Guards rode on through with professional smiles and cool reserve. Another shell-adorned arch, this time rearing out of a low stone wall, marked the entrance to the harbour area. Here the cohort dismounted and waited while the ferry was made ready. Their most strenuous task was to keep back the still-buzzing crowd who had followed them, hoping for another look at the king. Not a few of the younger guards regretted not being in their full, resplendent uniforms while talking to the town's pretty girls.

For Roujeark, it was a first close-up view of the sea. He had seen it from afar before, and smelled the salt-tanged sea breeze wafted up the River Ebinnon while in Mariston, but never had he been so close. While the cool wind was refreshing, the prospect of tossing about on waves after riding a horse filled him with consternation.

Unlike the guards about him, he was not able to enjoy the beautiful setting. Large mountains loomed away to the west, representing the uttermost end of the Carthaki Mountains, whose easternmost flanks fell sheer into Dagger's Cove, the great blade-shaped inlet which separated most of Maristonia from the East-fold and Swordhilt Peninsula beyond. The sun glinted off the sea and leisurely waves broke upon the shingly beaches adjoining the harbour-wall. The guards studiously avoided contact with him, as they had on the first day's ride, despite being more curious about the stranger after his late-night conference with the king, and so, as well as dreading the voyage to come, he felt despised and lonely. If it had not been for the kindly interest the king had shown in him, together with his reassuring references to Prélan, he would be perfectly miserable by now.

Curillian, Lancoir and Surumo were met at the quayside by the Harbour-master, a tough-looking seafarer who had hastily donned a jacket in an attempt to look more respectable. He bowed clumsily to the king, and then seemed rather taken aback when the sovereign shook his hand.

'My gratitude to you for getting the ferry ready at such short notice, Harbour-master.'

''Tis no trouble, Yore Majesty. As you know we always keep one o' the ferries free for military use. I've some hands aboard now re-arranging some o' the bulkheads to make room for yore horses. If Yore Majesty will be so good as to wait a little while, we'll 'ave her ready in a brace of shakes.'

'Good,' said Lancoir. 'How many can you take in one run?' The Harbour-master thought for a moment.

'Sixty with horses, or a hundred without.' The officers discussed this.

'We won't need the horses right away on the Phirmar side,' said Surumo. 'The Tonsor barges can take us on up to the Welton Road.' Curillian nodded his assent.

'Well Commander, choose twenty lucky victims to remain behind with the horses for the second crossing. Leave your second-in-command, Piron, to command them. They will join the main body at the barracks on Welton Hill while we conclude our business in the city. See that the whole cohort is ready to ride again on the fifth morning from now, 24 *Milariel.*'

'Very good, sir.' Surumo went off in search of his subordinate. Lancoir beckoned to the Harbour-master, who had been hovering nearby.

'Leave the horses till last – one hundred to go in the first crossing.'

'Aye aye,' said the Harbour-master, doffing his sun-bleached cap. Then he moved alongside the king surreptitiously. Dropping his voice, he told him, 'Are you sure you wouldn't like to wait for an escort? Well, it would seem only proper, Yore Majesty, and a-sides, there's been more than usual corsair-activity out beyond the peninsula…troubling merchantmen and the like, or so the patrols report.'

'I thank you for your concern, Harbour-master, but it will take too long to wait for a warship from Lecoin. They may be a damned nuisance, but no corsair has yet troubled the ferry, and if they do, we'll deal with any trouble.'

Curillian and Lancoir strolled onto the ferry, a great broad-bellied craft, and inspected it. It was a sparse, utilitarian vessel, its few concessions to comfort being aft cabins immediately below decks where high-ranking passengers could pass the crossing more easily. Hardly fit for a king at such short notice, but Curillian was not bothered. Above decks the ferry's masts were crammed with every yard of sail possible, for maximum speed. When the wind was contrary, as it was now, propulsion was by means of scores of oarsmen on the bottom deck. Half of them were unskilled local labourers for whom this was the best means of livelihood available; half of them were corsair prisoners put to work without pay and with considerably worse treatment. Of the three ferries in service at Laston, this was the largest, but the other two civilian craft were nowhere to be seen – presumably at sea or on the Phirmar side of the bay.

The king and his chief captain watched from the quarter-deck as the hundred chosen guards filed up the quay and across the gangplank. They quickly settled themselves on the main deck, preferring the sun-washed open air to the austere sickness-prone compartments below. Roujeark was awkwardly tagging along near the back of the line, clearly unsure as to whether he should be going as well. Piron, too, was unsure and held him back while he looked to the quarter-deck for guidance.

'What about him?' Lancoir asked of the king.

'He comes.' Lancoir waved his arm in a beckoning gesture, and Piron let the red-clad armist past.

The crossing began pleasantly enough. Although the going was slow, as the oarsmen bent their backs against the wind, the sun was out and the chance for resting was welcome. It was a fine early spring day, unseasonably warm. This was the closest a Royal Guard ever came to a holiday.

Roujeark sat apart, leaning on the ship's side and watching the waves twinkling in the sunshine. He saw patrolling fins, but was entirely ignorant of the size of the sea-creature under the surface to which they belonged.

'Sharks,' said a crewmember as he came nigh to slacken off a rope, though the name meant nothing to Roujeark. 'Our meals would be much the poorer without them.' Grinning, he left Roujeark to his solitude. He was on the starboard side, and was soon dozing in the warm sunshine. He did not know how long they had been sailing when an unusually large wave suddenly jolted him awake. Rubbing his eyes, he looked out over the azure water. His eyes reported a strange blur at the edge of sight, a sort of distortion on the eastern horizon. He blinked away the drowse, thinking he was still half-asleep. But no, there it was. Nothing distinct, just a blur like a heatwave. A stab of warning smote his heart, though he could see no reason why it had. Uneasy, he got to his feet and squinted into the distance. No one else showed any sign of concern – indeed, most were asleep on the deck – but he could not shake this sudden disquiet in his heart. Apprehensively, he approached the quarterdeck. The guard at the stairs was one of the few who were awake and alert. He barred the way resolutely.

'Please, I just need to speak to the king.'

'No one goes on the quarterdeck without invitation, least of all you.'

A

Curillian heard the exchange and strode to the top of the stairs. Predictably, young Roujeark was being obstructed by one of the guards.

'What's the matter, friend?' he called down. Roujeark took advantage of the guard's momentary relaxation to push past and climb a few steps.

'I...I think there's something out there,' he said, pointing out to sea. He fell silent after blurting out those words, suddenly at a loss. Then inspiration came to him. 'A ship on the horizon.' Another ruler would have dismissed him curtly, but Curillian wasted no time in calling the captain over, who in turn bellowed up to the crow's nest. The lookout shouted down that there was nothing to be seen. Many of the dozing passengers had been roused by the raised voices, but when nothing further seemed to happen, they resumed their repose.

'Perhaps you were mistaken, Roujeark?' the king suggested. 'The sea can play tricks on inexperienced eyes.' Roujeark was thankful for the gentle way with which he was being dismissed, and knew he should step back down and leave matters be. Yet the alarm in his heart, far from dissipating with the lookout's reassurance, redoubled in conviction.

'Please, Your Majesty, I really do think there is a ship out there.' Curillian studied him carefully. Then he turned again to the ferry's captain.

'Captain?'

'If my lookout says there's nothing, then there's nothing,' the Laston armist replied stoutly. Curillian looked from one to the other. He looked at Lancoir, and to Roujeark's surprise, the captain of guards did not look sceptical, but wary. The king walked to the side and looked out himself, gripping the gunnel with powerful forearms. After painfully long seconds of deliberation, he turned around.

'Lancoir, my sword.'

'What?' the ferry-captain exclaimed, momentarily forgetting himself.

'Surumo,' Curillian issued his second command. 'Wake the cohort; make sure weapons are to hand.'

'Did Yore Majesty mishear me?'

Curillian rounded on the ferry-captain, and Roujeark saw what happened to those who abused the king's easy-going nature.

'Do you presume to question my judgement, ferry-captain?' Roujeark saw just how intimidating the king could be when roused. Taller than most armists, his powerful frame loomed over the armist from Laston, and his eyes blazed. 'If, in half an hour, my instincts are proved wrong, then you can take me to task, but until then another insolent word will have you back mending nets in Laston so fast you won't be able to swallow the salt-water on your way.'

The ferry-captain, thoroughly cowed, turned away. Lancoir re-emerged with the Sword of Maristonia, and Curillian buckled it on. On the main deck, the whole cohort had been roused and was quickly armed and ready. The decisive posture of their king up on the quarterdeck was enough to let them know danger was at hand. Yet, for a long time, nothing happened. More and more passengers began lining the starboard side, straining for some sign of life out there. The ferry-captain was looking at Roujeark as if he were crazy, but with every minute that passed, the more that expression became smugness, as of one who is about to be proved right. Roujeark was just about to slink away and try and mitigate the humiliation when the lookout's voice rang out.

'Saaaaaiiil! Saaaiil ho!' Everyone strained their eyes, but although they could not yet see what the lookout could see, the tension on deck redoubled. Roujeark just caught a glimpse of the ferry-captain looking at him before springing into action. Gone was the smugness; all there had been in that split second was sheer incomprehension.

The moment passed.

'Helsman, bring her about,' the captain shouted. Curillian whirled around.

'Belay that order,' he commanded.

'Yore Majesty, there's still time to reach Laston…'

'We're not going to Laston,' the king said steadily. The crew looked nervous.

'But Yore…'

'You have your orders, captain.' Curillian rejoined Lancoir and Surumo at the gunwale. While the guardsmen streamed below decks to find weapons and armour, Roujeark went to the rail just beneath the quarterdeck, and overheard the king's conversation.

'How many on a corsair galleon?' Surumo asked.

'Two hundred at the most,' Lancoir answered tersely.

'They've got a bloody nerve,' said Surumo. 'I've never heard of corsairs molesting the ferry.'

'That's because they never have,' Curillian told him. 'They have indeed become bolder.'

'Of course, it might only be a big fisherman…Maybe we should have waited for an escort,' said Surumo doubtfully.

'No. We will get a message relayed to the fleet once we reach Welton. Right now, we have to make sure we survive and get there.'

'The corsairs will sink us from a distance with ballistas and catapults,' Lancoir said quietly to the king. 'What's your plan?'

'They won't sink us. We're no threat to them, and in their eyes we'll make a fine prize. No, they'll be greedy, and come in close. We will let them. Once they're up close, once they've grappled us, they'll find they have bitten off more than they can chew. A cohort of guards will be more than a match for a pirate mob, even if they're outnumbered.

Surumo, have a dozen archers stay above decks, enough to put up a token defence – they know the ferries aren't completely helpless. Have the rest waiting below decks or hidden out of sight. Hold them back until they come alongside. Then, on my command, spring the trap.' Surumo hurried off to arrange his troops. 'I wonder how on earth Roujeark knew that galleon was out there.'

'Wizardry,' murmured Lancoir.

A

In no time at all the clamour had receded and all was quiet and tense on the ferry. The oars kept up their motion, but they would never outrun an enemy with the wind at his back. Their scything through the water was the only sound to be heard except the preparations of the archers. Strings were attached, bows bent, and arrows laid out. Roujeark found himself next to them, unsure what else to do. Fear was clutching his stomach and rising like bile in his throat, but he did his best to look as calm and capable as the guardsmen. Looking out he could now see plainly with his eyes the vessel which some other sense had warned him of before. Even he knew it was too big to be a fishing boat. He watched it move slowly towards them, borne nearer with every wave, and tried to quell the panic gripping him. Interminable minutes dragged by. His nerves were frayed like string across sharp rocks, and he supposed that those of the guards around him were made of steel, for they showed no sign of panic, only grim professionalism. In truth they were out of their element – they were not marines or even sailors – but they had all faced battle many times, and knew how to approach it. Roujeark, on the other hand, couldn't bear the horrible waiting when nothing seemed to be done, when he was helpless, knowing every second brought death closer, and that there was nothing he could do about it. Now he could see the emblem stamped on the other ship's sails: a white skull on a black field.

'Corsairs,' muttered the guard next to him. Roujeark turned to glance at him. He was a big armist, with a handsome face and rangy limbs that easily flexed the big bow to full draw.

'Corsairs?' The question slipped out of his lips before he remembered that he didn't want to show his ignorance.

'Aye, corsairs – you know, scum of the waves? Pirates?' Roujeark nodded, but in truth the word was a hazy one for him. As a mountain-dweller living far inland, pirates had only lurked on the edge of the wildest stories he had heard in his youth. 'They come up from Lurallan in the far south and prey on helpless tubs like us. This lot are probably from Urundair.' Roujeark blinked, surprised but pleased that one of the guards was finally speaking to him.

'How do you know all this?' he asked. The big armist smiled.

'Corsairs plagued the coast of Carinen Peninsula where I grew up, curse them! There's a couple of us in the Royal Guards who hail from the coasts.' He grinned, and then extended a big, friendly hand. 'Andil,' he said. Roujeark shook the hand uncertainly.

'Roujeark.'

'You shoot, Roujeark?' he motioned to a spare bow lying beside him.

'A bit,' he said. It was barely true, but he wanted to appear competent next to this confident warrior. He took up the bow and struggled with the string, which seemed incredibly tight to him. Andil watched him struggle for a few moments and then offered some advice.

'Kneel side on, see? Pull the string tight to your ear, and point the arrow right at your target. Breathe easy and loose when you exhale.

Don't move the bow until the shaft is well away, otherwise it'll go wide.' And he demonstrated with his own bow. Roujeark flexed his bow a few times with a novice arm, but he was soon distracted by how awkward his spray-dampened robes were making the motion, and by how much closer the pirate ship had come. He thought he could even see figures hanging off the rigging, brandishing weapons and leering.

'Are we just going to wait until they're on top of us?'

'That's pretty much the thinking,' confirmed Andil. Roujeark gulped. He removed his outer robes to let him move easier, but fear made even that simple action clumsy and awkward.

'I'm sorry,' he found himself saying to Andil. 'I'm afraid I'm not much use.'

'You're doing better than the crew,' Andil reassured him. And it was true. The crew had been ordered to remain in view to make things look normal, and they shook visibly. Just then a strange snapping noise carried across the waves to them. It was followed by a long, trailing whoosh, and then, WHUMP! Something big smacked the water not far ahead of the ferry's prow. Roujeark cowered in terror. The strange succession of noises came again, and a second missile struck the water aft of the ferry, this time close enough to fling spray over them.

'What's happening?' The question came out with a shriek.

'Easy,' said Andil. 'They're firing stones from their catapult – they're only warning shots, meant to slow us down.' Orders were relayed from the king on the quarterdeck and the ferry's oars did indeed slow down. Orders also came for them to fire their bows. A pitiful volley of arrows spat across the sea between the two vessels.

'Count thirty seconds between each shot – it's only for show, see?' Andil told him. Just as well, thought Roujeark, for most of his feeble shots were just grazing the water harmlessly. All the time the pirate ship glided closer. Although she was actually the same size as the bulky ferry, her full rig of tattered sails made her seem dreadful and intimidating. Roujeark's panic kept threatening to resurface, but he fought it down each time by looking at Andil, or the king on the quarterdeck.

Now jeers and shouts could be heard across the shrinking gap. One voice, louder than the others, seemed to be ordering the ferry to stop, although Roujeark could not understand the language.

'Prepare to be boarded,' scoffed Andil, 'yeh, you can try.' Another order came and they dropped their bows and crammed against the ferry's side, hiding under the overhang of the gunwale. From there, Roujeark could glimpse the enemy ship looming up bigger and nearer through tiny holes in the wood. He could also see the king standing by the wheel. He and Lancoir stood unafraid, completely out in the open, seemingly heedless of the danger. Roujeark heard a massed creaking and many scornful voices as the pirate ship drew alongside. Slowly, Andil laid a long dagger in his hands, which Roujeark gripped like his life depended on it. He heard whirring noises, and winced as metal hooks suddenly latched onto the ferry, right above his head. His stomach lurched as the vessels came crashing together, lashed by many lines. When was the king going to do something? Was the adventure really over so soon?

⋏

One of the corsair leaders shouted down at Curillian. The king had had enough dealings with the Alanai to know their tongue, and even to discern the harsh, clipped tones of the dialect of Urundair.

'Surrender yer vessel, armist scum! Come quietly, and the Wave Brethren might be merciful.' Curillian spread his arms. The corsairs needed no further invitation, and started streaming across the makeshift gangplanks. Roujeark cowered into the overhang as many pairs of bare and booted feet crashed onto the deck in front of him. He tensed, and gripped Andil's dagger harder, knowing they would spot him any moment. The noise of whooping and screeching was horrendous. He lost sight of the king, but he heard his war-cry. Then bedlam broke loose.

'MAAAARISTONNNNN!' Had Roujeark been able to see, he would have seen how swift was the end of the first two corsairs. A group of them had approached the king, but hung back nervously. They could see his great sword and were wary of it and him. Then two of them came too close. Curillian drew the blade in the speed of a lightning-strike. Even quicker he swung it down, back up, and down again. Slash! Slash! The two corsairs fell at his feet, weapons clattering to the deck as their hands went to ripped throats. Their shipmates were appalled by the devastating speed, but before they had time to react, Lancoir struck moments after his king. Scarcely less lethal, he lunged forward and laid open the throat of another corsair. Then another terror confronted the boarders. From out of nowhere armists were appearing, streaming up on deck like swarms of ants. And not just any armists. Soldiers, warriors, armed to the teeth. The seemingly helpless ferry was now teeming with death.

Surumo had come charging up the companionway steps and burst into the open like a fiend, and at his back came roaring guard after guard. Roujeark watched as Andil and his fellow archers sprang from their hiding places and struck at the corsairs from the rear. Between them they caught their enemies in a vice of death. Deadly blows rained in from both sides. It was just as well they'd achieved surprise, though, for the guards were only able to emerge one or two at a time. Had the corsairs been expecting them, they could easily have bottled them up. As it was, the deck was soon alive with embroiled fighters. Roujeark saw the Royal Guards in action for the first time and watched the fearful efficiency with which they went about the business of killing. They employed compact, efficient motions and dealt out disciplined blows, always seeking the neck or groin. They moved with a fluidity and ease that was dreadful and hypnotic. Roujeark was petrified at the sight of blood-thirsty corsairs, dark-skinned and brandishing cruel weapons, but his fellow passengers did not seem fazed. The noise was deafening: a cacophony of shouts, grunts, screams and curses mixed with wooden thuds, meaty smacks, sharp cracks and the ringing of steel.

The young armist's spectating was rudely interrupted when a fearsome figure appeared in front of him and blocked out the view. He had been spotted. A corsair, black-skinned but swathed in tawdry orange garments and festooned with golden jewellery, leered in at him. The snarling face ducked under the wooden overhang and beringed hands reached out for him. He cried in panic and terror, and, not knowing what else to do, thrust his dagger out and swept it back and forth with wild swings. At first he didn't realise that he had made contact, and kept on lashing out like he was battering nettles out of his path. It was only when a spurt of blood sprayed all over him that he stopped. The corsair had slumped over his legs, face and arms lacerated. He could feel the man's punctured neck leaking blood all over his trousers. The eyes rotated in unfocused rolls and the last dying breaths came in horrible, frothing gargles. Roujeark gasped and recoiled in horror.

He could now see again: the carnage on deck went on unabated. He could see Andil, swordless now, but using his arms to throw his assailants in wrestling moves. Beside him, his comrades hewed great strokes with their two-handed swords. What the guards possessed in superior skill, their foes made up for in weight of numbers and sea-canniness, and the armist defenders were hard put to it. Not so on the quarterdeck. Above the main melee, a smaller battle had been in progress. Curillian and Lancoir swept the platform like angels of death. Curillian was accomplished in combat to a degree most corsairs never imagined possible. Many of them had been drawn to the rich-looking figures by the wheel, but the king and his captain put paid to their greed and had cut them to shreds before even Surumo was able to come to their aid. When Surumo reached the king's side, with half a dozen guards, he could only gaze at the ring of bodies in awe. When he looked back over the main deck, it was now plain that the corsairs were having the worst of it. The first wave of boarders had been well-nigh slaughtered by a well-armed and well-organised trap. Victory looked assured.

One corsair had other ideas. He too watched the butchery as one after another his shipmates fell on the ferry's deck, and he could see that no effort of fighting could retrieve this disaster. His own ship would be at risk next, and he wasn't about to lose her as well as his prize. He seized a boarding pike, wrapped the haft in an oily rag and kindled it in the galley stove. With his burning spear he swung across onto the bows of the ferry where few armists were. As quick as thought, he pitched the makeshift torch down the for'ard steps and into the lower decks. No one was around to notice it, and no one was there to extinguish the flames before they got out of hand. He completed his work by stabbing an unsuspecting member of the ferry's crew in the back before hurriedly making for his own vessel again.

Andil found himself in a lull of the fighting as he suddenly looked around and found a shortage of corsairs within grappling range. The last few boarders were being hacked to the deck elsewhere, but none remained near him. Rivulets of blood stained the deck at his feet.

Several of his friends lay among the pirate slain. This couldn't be it, he thought. He looked to the corsair vessel and saw many of its crew hanging back. His gaze was drawn to an agile figure dashing towards one of the gangplanks. He traced back where he had come from and saw the smoke billowing out of the companionway.

'FIRE!' he shouted. Not stopping to attend to that hazard himself, he sprinted towards the fleeing figure, looking to cut him off at an angle. With a leaping dive, he reached the corsair's running feet and pitched him to the ground. Immediately a boot crashed into his face to reward him for his trouble. In the split second's respite, the pirate made off again, swinging himself up onto the narrow bridge. Andil watched as he regained his own ship and set about hacking at the ropes lashing the vessels together. He saw the peril, and called to those around him. Curillian and others had also seen the danger and now a different kind of struggle began. The corsairs desperately tried to detach their vessel before their would-be prize became a floating inferno, and the armists shot with bows or flung daggers at the corsairs nearest them to interrupt their work.

While that struggle raged, Roujeark had been roused by Andil's initial shout. It had snapped him out of his stunned paralysis. He struggled free of the encumbering corpse and staggered unsteadily towards the nearest companionway. Stumbling down the steps, he entered the gloom below deck. It took a moment or two for his eyes to adjust to the reduced light, all the while inhaling smoke and coughing. Bodies coming the other way shoved past him and he realised that the rowers had abandoned their oars and were fleeing to the safety of the top deck. Above their clatter he dimly heard cries of panic. He grabbed one of the armists going past him.

'What's that noise – are there people still down there?'

'Only the oar-slaves.'

Roujeark looked at the armist uncomprehendingly. 'You mean you're leaving them down there to burn?'

'No better than they deserve.' The armist shook free of Roujeark's grip and carried on his way. The young armist realised he would get no help. Fighting against the torrent of fleeing rowers he ran along the deck, trying to find another companionway leading down. Already he was oppressed by the heat and choking in the smoke, and when he moved into the next compartment, he could actually see the flames. It had taken a grip in the bulkheads around it and was billowing out of control. The whole bow was ablaze and it must have already spread to the oar-deck.

At last he found the steps that would take him down. Fearing what he might find, he fearfully descended into the darkness. The heat nearly knocked him off his feet, and the overpowering stench of enclosed, exerted bodies made him gag. Through eyes made watery by the smoke, he glimpsed ahead and saw several of the for'ard-most oar-benches already wreathed in flame. He looked away in horror from the sight of blackened bodies, charred where they sat chained. He span around in a panic, not knowing what to do. As he did so pitiful cries called out to him from both sides, and he became aware of terrified oar-slaves all around him. These he could still save, but how to cut through their chains? Where were the keys? No chance to find them, so he scampered back up the steps in hunt of any implement he could use. Grabbing a hatchet from a guard's abandoned pack he swiftly returned and began hacking away at the wood around where the nearest slave's chains were secured. He made pitifully little progress, as if he were just clawing at it with his fingernails. The flames licked closer, their heat blasting him and the roiling smoke threatening to suffocate him. The wails of the oar-slaves grew ever more shrill and desperate. They would die down here, despite his efforts, and so would he if he did not leave soon.

The thought that he hadn't been able to save even one pumped furious strength into his hatchet blows. Finally, moved by some deep prompting, he abandoned the hatchet and strained his hands towards the chains. He didn't even know what he was trying to do, but his fingers tingled and grew hot, and the bolts holding the chains down began to quiver. And then...nothing. They moved no further. Just then a strong hand gripped his shoulder and thrust him aside.

He looked up and through the thick smoke he recognised the stern face of Lancoir, Captain of the Guard. In the light of the flames he looked like a mercenary of hell. Lancoir swung his own axe and in a few mighty strokes had released the chains of the entire bench. As he set to another bench, Roujeark helped the released rowers clamber free of the encumbering wooden fixings, and guided them to the companionway and safety. Meanwhile Lancoir had freed another bench, and another three slaves. Roujeark knew he couldn't last much longer. Their time was up. Lancoir didn't seem to think so, for he started to hack at another bench. Roujeark tried to intervene. He threw himself on the captain, trying to restrain the blows and pull him back. He was appalled by how much stronger the knight was, and he barely interrupted his flow. He choked hoarsely. Lancoir, too, in spite of his great strength, was nearly overcome. They would have both died down there had not a squall of flames suddenly blasted them, scorching their faces and hurling them backwards. Not even hearing the final screams of the doomed slaves, together they crawled up the companionway.

Staggering along the middle deck, they remembered nothing but retching, blinding smoke and withering heat. At one point they were nearly claimed by the inferno as burning planks gave way beneath their feet, but their forward momentum just carried them past the blistering hole. Spurred to greater speed by fear of similar near-misses, they shot up the final companionway and burst back into the open air like round-shots from a cannon. Then, for Roujeark, the world screeched to a halt. His own motion was checked by some invisible force as his senses demanded his complete attention with a hasty portrait. Sunshine, heat-hazy and smoke-strewn but dazzling after the darkness. Sails flapping, smouldering. Wounded moaning. War-cries. Screams. A spear aimed and drawn back. A spear flying through the air towards Lancoir. He was allowed to glimpse this portrait for a split second before the checking force was released and the full speed of life resumed. He arched his muscles and shifted his momentum to pitch to the side. With the weight of his momentum he pushed the captain aside. The spear grazed his left arm and he crashed on top of Lancoir with a burning sensation.

The Captain of the Royal Guards stared at him, stupefied. It took him a second or two to realise what had just happened. Gratitude of feeling might have been expressed elsewise by another, but Lancoir's intensity produced a countenance akin to hatred. Roujeark thought he would strike him, but then he realised that Lancoir's blood was up and anger at his would-be killer was coursing up like magma in a volcano. Even before this thought had finished forming in the young armist's mind, he noticed Lancoir's hand reaching for the spear. In an athlete's fluid sequence of motions the captain rolled Roujeark off him, grasped the missile in a throwing grip, propelled himself to his feet, sighted the spear's former owner, span round for extra velocity and launched the projectile into the air. Mesmerised, Roujeark watched it fly through the hazy sky, even saw it wobble in its course as if unnerved by the ferocity which had flung it. A lesser being would not have been able to throw so powerfully, nor so accurately, having just come near to death in a burning chamber. But Lancoir's throw found its mark. It not only found it, piercing the pirate's incredulous heart, it carried the body right off the crossbeam it had been perching on and overboard into the sea.

The urgency of the situation allowed for no more spectating. Released from the spell of the last few seconds' events, Roujeark took in what had happened while they had been below. The corsairs, having been scoured from the ferry, had put all their effort into cutting themselves away from what would soon be a floating furnace before it engulfed their own vessel too. Curillian and his followers, though, had succeeded in keeping intact some of the bridges between the two ships. Many of the guards' cohort had already fought their way across these avenues of escape and were now fighting on the pirate galleon's decks. Lancoir was already hurrying to join them. Andil directed those of his comrades who still had arrows left for their bows to shoot down the pirates lurking in the rigging above – where they couldn't be harmed any other way – and thus shelter the other guards from the missiles being rained down. Curillian was a firestorm all in himself, the enemy resistance blown away wherever he came.

The ferry itself was barely afloat. The entire for'ard portion of it was ablaze and tilting down as fire-burned holes let the sea in. A great cloud of steam and smoke engulfed both vessels. It mattered little that the fire would soon be extinguished by a greater force, for the vessel would sink all the same. The alarming tilt of the deck brought Roujeark's predicament home to him. Rivulets of blood were running down the planks. He darted towards one of the bridges. Slower than all his travelling companions, he reached it last of all and arrived on the corsair galleon with the battle nearly over. He jumped down in comparative safety, but he now knew of a greater danger. Whilst traversing the gang-plank bridge he had seen flames from the ferry catch amid the timbers of the galleon. Despite everyone's efforts, the two ships had been together too long. Now both were doomed.

'MY KING! MY KING!' Fear made his voice carry above the vast crackling and the multitudinous din of fighting. Curillian heard it even as he clove his latest adversary almost in two. He disengaged, allowing Surumo and Lancoir either side of him to finish the job, and turned his mind to the warning cry. Straightaway he saw the threat, without Roujeark having to elaborate. He knew the vessel was doomed.

'BOATS! LONGBOATS!' he cried to those near him, gesturing at the small rowboats lashed to the galleon's decks. Furiously the ropes were cut and the cumbersome objects manhandled to the vessel's sides. The pirate crew were now too few to contest the commandeering, and even as their last members were cut down by some of their enemies, others of the guards were casting the rowboats into the sea. The armists of Maristonia worked feverishly to jettison the life-saving craft before the insatiable flames claimed them. Then, in pairs and groups, they clambered down the outside of the galleon's bulging hull and into the new craft. Beside them the sinking ferry, with her stern reared into the air and shrouded by clouds of steam, made an awesome spectacle. More and more of the guards made it overboard before the galleon too began to list. Roujeark and Lancoir were among the last to leave. With no time for the luxury of clambering, they threw themselves overboard beside one of the rowboats.

The guards in the boats were already manoeuvring with oars to pull away from the sinking ships on either side. Other oars were waved like poles to fend off burning spars fallen from the galleon. Their comrades in the water were hastily pulled into the boats, lest they be dragged down by the weight of their mail-shirts. Lancoir and Roujeark were hauled on board, the latter by the king himself. Bruised, dazed, and still struggling to breathe after their ordeal in the smoky bowels of the ferry, they lay panting in their comrades' arms.

Only a few of the guards had fallen, but to an armist the survivors were battered and bloodied, sweat coursing channels through their fire-grimed faces. All they had with them were the clothes on their backs and the weapons in their hands.

'Roujeark.' The young armist was roused from his daze. Raising his head from the king's lap, he saw Lancoir sitting opposite, looking at him. It was the first word spoken between them since Lancoir had derided his offer of help in that Mariston street. Roujeark hadn't even known that Lancoir knew his name. 'You saved my life. Twice.' The words were few, but each one carried weight. Lancoir took a ring off his finger and leaned forward to press it in Roujeark's palm. It was just a simple silver band, the modest design traced on it nearly obscured by all the scratches. 'Where I come from, rings are given in token of a debt of honour. I give this to you. I will not forget until I have repaid.' Roujeark closed his hand around the ring, squeezing it, but unable to make any reply. Lancoir glanced at the king, and Curillian nodded approvingly. Then Curillian glanced in turn at each guard beside them. Humbled, they all made their gratitude known, whether it was a smile of acceptance or a comradely squeeze of the arm. Tears came to Roujeark's eyes, though whether they were from joy, relief or sheer weariness he couldn't tell. He fell back against the boat's timbers and closed his eyes as the oars pulled them out of the steam-haze and on into the long swells.

IV

The Watcher's Words

ROUJEARK awoke to find that it was nearly dark. He had dozed off in the boat and evening was in the sky. He was surprised by how cold he was. Half of the dozen guards around him were also resting or sleeping, and the other six were rowing stoically. In the front pair the king was setting a tremendous pace, rowing with great speed and endurance. Even Lancoir was struggling to match him. Truly was it spoken of Curillian that he was a great among armists, for in his veins ran the noblest blood in the land. So noble was it, some said, that it must be elvish and not armist at all. Roujeark watched him for a while, but could see no signs of him tiring. He looked about him, but the waves told him little about where they were. Behind him, the long-set sun had left a ragged red swathe across central Maristonia that was only just starting to fade. In that last ruddy light he could just make out the mountainous coast, and all that he could tell was that it seemed further away than it had before the corsair attack.

He looked at his hands and inspected them, recalling the strange impulse which had seized him below decks on the ferry. Had he been trying to work magic? Although his father had played all sorts of tricks and achieved strange effects, he himself had never even attempted magic. But the bolts had moved slightly, hadn't they? He was sure he remembered his fingers tingling, animated by a strange heat. Or was he misremembering? Had it just been the heat of the inferno? Or had his oxygen-starved brain played tricks on him? His fingers looked quite normal under his scrutiny, with nothing strange or unusual about them. He let them drop, his mind filled with new questions.

One of the resting guards manoeuvred his way forward and relieved Lancoir from his oar. As the captain came back, Roujeark ventured a question.

'How far from shore are we?' Lancoir shrugged and took a swig from one of the few canteens they had with them.

'Hard to say. The ferry can do the crossing in ten hours with the right wind, but who knows how long it takes to row?' Roujeark still felt nervous asking another question, despite Lancoir's earlier pledge.

'But do we even know where we're going?' He glanced up and saw that clouds rolling in from the ocean had covered most of the sky. There were precious few stars left to navigate by.

'Don't worry. The king has a better sense of direction than anyone I know.'

One of the nearby guards, who seemed familiar with this part of the country, added his own thoughts.

'We were well past the big headland east of Laston by the time we were attacked. With the currents coming in from the ocean, the only landfall we could make now is on the Phirmar coast. If we misjudge it, all we will have to do is row up the coast until we find the mouth of the Tonsor.'

'What about the tide?' put in another.

'True. if the tide's going out when we get near, it could make things more difficult,' conceded the first guard, 'but we're equal to it.'

The king did not seem to tire, but kept heaving his oar doughtily. When Roujeark caught glimpses of his face, he thought he could see peace there, and he was surprised. He saw his lips move in murmured prayers. Behind them five other boats were following their course. A strong wind from the south-east picked up on their right-hand side and the waves grew rougher, lifting them up and bringing them back down again. Thunder rumbled ominously in the distance, and drops of rain pattered into the boat. When the lightning started they could see that the coast was not too far ahead of them, but the rain grew heavier and chilled them. To take his mind off things, Roujeark took a turn at one of the oars, but his strokes were so clumsy that he was soon replaced and set to work with the other non-rowers bailing out the rainwater. Feeling the wind blast his soaked clothes, he suddenly regretted taking off his outer robe before the attack. With numb hands he kept bailing out water for what seemed like hours until Curillian paused in his rowing and looked round. Blowing rainwater from his face, he smiled grimly.

'Nearly there – see the coast up ahead? Those are the sandy beaches off Eithanunt; we are some way from the Tonsor. We have more work to do to reach it.'

So they kept going, following the coastline on their left. The stormy weather didn't make it any easier, and the tide was coming in, so they had to work even harder to keep from being washed onto the shore.

'Why don't we make for land?' Roujeark had to shout above the latest peal of thunder.

'Harder going on land,' shouted the guard next to him. 'We're miles from the nearest town, Eithanunt, and there's lots of fen and bog between us and Welton. We're making for the ferry-barges on the River Tonsor – they'll take us straight to the city and do all the hard work for us!' They passed a network of small river mouths, which his companion informed him was the Memitor Delta. After that they rounded a small headland. Beyond was marsh country, the outliers of a great system of deltas. Roujeark, on the starboard side, looking out to sea, thought he could see the outline of a large ship sailing away from them, barely visible in the night. When the lightning flashed again, he could see it for certain.

'What ship is that?' he asked. The others had seen it too, and the knowledgeable guard at his side answered him.

'One of the other ferries, going back to Laston. We're close.'

He spoke truly, for the next lightning strike illuminated a small river opening out amongst the fens on either side. They passed several such small waterways, but when they reached one which was wider than all the rest, they turned into it.

'Is that the Tonsor?' Roujeark asked of his neighbour, who seemed to know so much.

'Yes, one of the six great rivers of Phirmar, land of many streams. But the barges are some way upstream, where the banks are firmer.'

Lancoir's voice rose above the noise of the storm.

'The river flows against us, bend your backs. One last push.'

So it was that their little flotilla of six captured longboats entered the relative sanctuary of the Tonsor River, and battled upstream until it was nearly dawn. The sky was lightening overhead when at last, bedraggled and exhausted, they drew nigh a high wooden platform built on poles fixed into the riverbed. Armists stationed there jumped to their feet in surprise, some seizing spears, and others drawing bows. Lancoir, who was in the lead boat, stood up and hailed them.

'Ferry-armists, stand down! We are a company of armists in royal service. Lancoir, Captain of the Royal Guards, am I.'

That name was evidently well-known, and commanded immediate respect. They laid aside their weapons and hurried to help bring the boats level with the jetty. Ropes were thrown. All the while Curillian remained discreet and unidentified. One by one, the six long-boats drew alongside and their occupants disembarked. Lancoir found out which of the ferry-armists was in charge. He drew him aside.

'Your career is about to take a turn for the better. Curillian, your king, is here.' The king stepped forward, bright eyes shining from underneath the hood which hid his identity. Flabbergasted, the chief of the ferry-armists would have fallen to his knees had Lancoir not held him up. 'His Majesty has had a misfortune, and is in a hurry to reach Welton. What is your name? Arrange the passage quickly and word will be given for your promotion. Keep us waiting, and you'll be dredging the rivers for the rest of your life.' The ghost of a smile played around Lancoir's lips as he watched the alacrity with which his command was obeyed.

'Fear always gets them moving,' he remarked under his breath to the king.

'Most of the time. Love works better.' Lancoir looked at the king, expecting a rebuke, but instead saw a lesson. 'How many are we, Lancoir? Take a head-count.'

'Ninety-three, ourselves included,' Lancoir returned quickly. Curillian closed his eyes momentarily.

'Seven lost.' Just then, Surumo came up. Curillian grasped his shoulder. 'Glad to see you still with us, Commander.'

Surumo grinned wolfishly.

'Ah, wouldn't miss the next stage for anything. Your orders, sire?'

'Get the cohort to Welton as quick as may be. We will take stock there. Leave two guards behind to meet Piron and the horses when they arrive.'

Roujeark was seeing a different side to the guards. They were pale and weary, and grimmer than ever with their wounds. If only seven had perished, dozens more were wounded, and some badly so. He saw the toll that events had taken on them, and wondered what he himself looked like. How close he had come to death hadn't yet sunk in, but he was shaking with cold and fatigue. The rain was easing, but low clouds hanging over the delta and the eerie cry of seabirds made it a very uninviting place. He did not know what was supposed to happen next, but when he found himself shepherded along the platform with the others, he suddenly saw what lay behind the jetty.

The platform itself was high enough, and built sufficiently far downstream for the ferries to dock and then turn round where the river was wide enough for them to do so. Beyond the main platform were steps leading down to a lower platform lapped by the water. This soggy platform led right out into the river where a line of broad punts was drawn up. They all had strange mechanisms in their prows and chains linking them. Pilots were waiting in the sterns with long tillers in their hands. Slowly the weary cohort piled onto these new craft. Special attention, of course, was paid to the king's vessel, and Roujeark was disappointed to find himself separated from him. He raised a tired smile, though, when he saw he was in the same barge as Andil, the tall guardsman who had tried to teach him archery. His low spirits lifted when a hefty hand was clapped on his shoulder.

'Glad you made it through, Red-breeches. Not the nicest first sea-voyage for you, eh?'

'No indeed, but luckily I had stout company.' Andil snorted self-deprecatingly. The pilot of the punt overheard them and butted in.

So chirpy was he that it was plain that he was well fed and had spent the night comfortably, not rowing out on the open sea.

'So they was corsair longboats I saw you lot roll up in? Thought so. What happened? Marines normally stay dry when fighting pirates.'

'Barge pilots normally stay dry when going up the river, doesn't mean they always will,' Andil retorted testily. 'As long as you've got passengers aboard who can handle a tiller you'd best watch your mouth, ferry-armist.'

The pilot spread his arms exaggeratedly wide and pouted, aggrieved. Andil and Roujeark settled down on one of the benches. After a night cramped up in the longboat it was the last thing they wanted, but there was nothing for it.

'This damn sacking doesn't do much to ease the arse,' complained Andil. 'Maybe the king got a cushion. Blasted nuisance, those rogues. Still, one thing's for sure: they won't attack a ferry again for a long time. Word will get back to the other corsair captains that an entire galleon was lost in the Dagger.' He smiled grimly, still trying to get comfortable. From his seat, Roujeark investigated the craft they were sat in, trying to understand how it worked. The pilot standing behind them was grasping a tiller, not a means of propulsion.

'There are no oars, no sails,' he said. 'What are we going to do, paddle with our hands and feet?' Andil and one or two other of their fellow-passengers laughed.

'No,' chuckled Andil, pointing forward. 'See that contraption at the front of the king's barge?' Sure enough, a sturdy metal frame dominated the bow, supporting two chunky pulleys. Wet chains were looped through them, running off into the river. 'That thing is connected to a massive winch somewhere upstream. They have water buffalo heaving on them to draw the barges upstream. When more than one barge is required, like now, they're linked together by chains and get tugged along in convoy. All they do is hitch up some more buffalo to provide the extra muscle.' Barely had he spoken and the king's boat jerked away from the platform, some hidden signal having been given.

Roujeark let the small mysteries slide by him and tried to get comfortable. His tortured back, knotted gruesomely from the cramped night, gave him little respite, and the passage up the river was hardly smooth, but it was better than it could have been. His arm stung from where the spear had grazed him, but he was not seriously hurt. Strangers to these fens on foot might wander for weeks, lost in the shifting waterways, and would be lucky to emerge alive. Uncomfortable though it was, the ingenuity and industry of Maristonia had provided a solution. As they went, they passed many other craft going both ways, and dimly Roujeark began to guess at the importance of this river as a trade artery. When they passed areas of firmer land on the banks, they saw busy quays where sea-going vessels transferred their wares onto barges able to navigate the upper reaches of the river. Timber and amphorae of wine went upstream, and sacks of grain and vases of oil went downstream. At several points, their barges pulled into one of the jetties, and Roujeark realised that no one winch and chain system could span the whole river. Again and again they disembarked the old barges and boarded new ones, making what seemed to be painfully slow progress. Andil seemed unperturbed, though. The sun, having burned off the clouds, was beaming down hotly now, and he stretched out, lapping it up.

'One of the marvels of the East-fold – never been up the river so fast before.'

Eventually, after most of a day in transit, they came to a settlement with a bridge. It was a sort of trading depot, enjoying proximity to the only bridge over the river and The Waterside Road that ran over it. Between the river, which ran from top to bottom of the Phirmar, and the road, which linked the full breadth of that same province, this was one of the three key hubs of commerce in the region. Roujeark struggled to make sense of the chaos of boats clogging the river, or of the throngs of goods and merchants on the banks, but their barges were guided soundly to this last winching station. News of the arrival of important visitors had plainly gone ahead of them because every other river-user was careful to get out of their way. A special message seemed also to have gone on before them, for a group of horses and grooms in matching livery were waiting for them at precisely the point they disembarked. Roujeark wondered how this had been arranged, but then he glanced up at the white-stone tower dominating the depot's skyline, and saw colourful processions of flags rising and falling in signals he couldn't decipher.

One of the waiting grooms addressed the king as he reached the quayside.

'Your Majesty, word reached us of your coming, and of your desire for discretion. His Grace the Duke of Welton extends his compliments and begs you to make use of these horses for your advanced party. Lodgings are already being prepared for you in the ducal palace. If you'd like to follow me...'

In the commotion of the place, few paid much notice to the grim armed company pushing their way through to the road. The king, Lancoir, and a select detachment of guards mounted up on the horses. Roujeark thought he was about to be left behind again, but to his surprise he was beckoned forward to an empty saddle. His muscles protested as he heaved himself up into the saddle, but it was better than walking. Led by the head groom, they made their way to the road. There they were met by a mounted escort of knights also bearing the livery of the Duke of Welton, the king's cousin. Straightaway they took to the road, setting a brisk pace away from the river and towards the city.

They followed a small tributary stream as it ducked under wooded slopes and wound up a hill. The road was as well-maintained as any Roujeark had ever used, which was just as well. He was fed up with being uncomfortable, and wondered if this day were ever going to end. They splashed across the stream at a ford before rejoining the road. Now it led up a steep slope. Breasting a low rise, he finally saw their destination. Welton was a great city, dominating the hill on which it sat. The white stone of its elegant skyline shone faintly in the gathering dusk. Folk going to and from the city scattered to make way as the cavalcade thundered towards the city gates. They scarcely checked their pace when entering within, and then their guide led them through well-paved streets to the most graceful building of them all. The duke's palace was a gorgeous white-stone complex with colonnaded façades and airy courtyards. Its beauty was lost on Roujeark, who was sore in every part and nodding in his saddle. He had barely noticed Welton – the largest city, after Mariston, he had ever been in – as they had clattered through it. He didn't remember when he got separated from the king's party; all he could recall was being ushered into an opulent suite and falling asleep before the door was shut.

He must have only slept for a few hours when knocking awoke him. Through bleary eyes he was astonished to find the king himself at the door.

'Roujeark, my friend, I hope you're not too tired to visit the baths?' Roujeark didn't even know what he meant, but he followed all the same. Lancoir and several of the guards were also outside, and together they were led by a servant to a warmly lit building. Inside, the air was thick with aromatic steam. Sheepishly, Roujeark allowed a servant to take his robes, and the others did likewise. He felt suddenly puny next to the chiselled bodies around him. His eyes widened when they walked into a low dome-ceilinged room dominated by a large, steaming pool. Water was running in alcoves all round the outside and in smaller pools beside the main one, where eminent-looking armists were already bathing. Roujeark had heard of aristocratic bathhouses in the south, but he marvelled to see the reality. For him growing up, a bath had been a rare occurrence, and involved plunging into a cold mountain-stream; here, it was an art form. He soon discovered why it should be housed so ingeniously, for the water was deliciously, almost unbearably, hot, and as he sank into it, he began to feel his self-consciousness seeping away. Slowly his aches and pains went with it.

For a while their group sat in silence, but then a conversation started, discussing the venture so far. It turned out this was a rare treat for the guardsmen as well, and they were soon dismissed to another corner of the bath. Curillian smiled at Roujeark's obvious bliss.

'Nice, isn't it? I fear there won't be many places like this where we're going, so enjoy it while you can.'

'It was very kind of Your Majesty to invite me here, although I was surprised to find a saddle left empty for me.'

'Roujeark, nothing has changed since we spoke by firelight under the trees, you need not trouble with titles. You're as bad as dear Lancoir here. No, this is a place for relaxation. I thought you might enjoy it rather better than the tents of the cohort back at the bridge. But I can't go inviting all my armists into my cousin's baths, now can I?' Soon after he spoke, an important-looking armist came and stood by them at the pool's side. Much younger than Curillian, there was still a resemblance between the two.

'Cousin Illyir, how nice to see you.'

'Curillian, blessed am I by this visit. Come, shall we not enjoy the steam together and talk?' The two of them went off, leaving

Roujeark alone with Lancoir, who was reclining in an adjacent corner. He suddenly felt intensely conscious that he was bathing with an armist who only recently had exuded such hostility towards him. Lancoir was no longer hostile, but neither was he exactly warm. Still, Roujeark tried to glean a few answers from him.

'It is late – do you know if the king has any plans for tomorrow?'

'Plenty, but none that need get you early from your bed. Enjoy the duke's hospitality until the rest of the cohort join us.'

'I hope those we left in Laston have a safer crossing than we did.'

'They ought to. But it will be at least a day before Piron's lads join us.'

'Then what? Where do we go from here?' Lancoir gave him a funny look.

'You should know. You're the guide, after all.' Roujeark felt uncomfortable under his stare.

'I know the way from Kalimar, but to get to Kalimar I followed the Armist Road; I never came this way. This part of the country is wholly unfamiliar to me.'

'Well,' said Lancoir, apparently satisfied. 'His Majesty hinted at needing to find something out here in Welton before going on, but he hasn't told me what. Unless things take a very strange turn, we'll be riding north to the Broadsword Gap, which leads out into the open East-fold. Hopefully you'll know better than me after that…' That awkward question hung in the air until a servant-girl approached them.

'Captain Lancoir, what a pleasure to have you again,' she said coquettishly. 'Your usual?' Lancoir beamed a rare smile, and made to get out of the pool. Wrapping a towel around himself, he patted the girl playfully.

'Atellia, you and your skilled hands are the best thing about this soggy land.' Almost as an after-thought he looked down at the embarrassed Roujeark.

'Red, ever had a massage?'

⚔

Roujeark might have lost some sleep to the bathhouse visit, but the hot water and the ministrations of the masseuse had made it well worth it. Under skilled hands his knots and aches had disappeared, and now his skin shone with the oil. Exhausted, but at peace, he slid into sleep.

He was still sleeping soundly when the king rose with the dawn and set off alone into the city. Lancoir, who missed nothing, had tried to insist on going with him, but Curillian left him behind. The Captain of the Royal Guards could rest. A messenger was to be sent on ahead to Arket, and Surumo had orders to march the cohort up from the bridge depot to the barracks at the summit of Welton Hill, but nothing else needed to be done.

Curillian had deliberately dressed modestly so that he looked like an ordinary noble-armist and not like a king. He left the distinctive Sword of Maristonia behind and went with a humbler blade by his side. He liked being able to walk among his people unrecognised. It had been his practice at whiles to do so, and very rarely had any ordinary person known him for who he was. And he liked Welton, too: it was an ancient city, even more so than Mariston, and well-built. Its wide streets and beautiful buildings paid homage to the fact that elves had dwelt here long after they had forsaken the rest of Maristonia. The suburbs lower down the hill were more modern and armist-built, to accommodate a growing population, but the old citadel, here in the highest part of the city, retained the simple grandeur and curving masonry of sea-elf architecture. It was in this old part of the city that he wandered, passing the townhouses of great nobles, ancient churches and some of the city's public buildings: the library and amphitheatre. He stopped outside a lofty house. Walking up the path between peach trees, he knocked on the richly carved door. A servant admitted him, and, as expected, directed him to the top floor. It had been the same last time.

He knocked again at the door marking the end of the last flight of stairs. This time all he heard was a muffled voice within bidding him enter. It was a spacious, airy apartment, such as was beloved by rich merchants, but unlike the living quarters of well-off armists, this one was filled with extraordinary artefacts, manuscripts, decorations and hangings: the result of a lifetime's collecting. Warm sunlight and a breeze were flowing in from a wide balcony, and there he saw a lonely figure taking his ease. White-haired but fresh-skinned, the figure reclined on a couch which was positioned in the shade, but still able to look out over the city and the country beyond. Without a word Curillian occupied the empty couch next to him, and for a long time they both sat and contemplated in silence. Curillian took his time – you had to with Gerendayn. They looked out over a broad and fruitful land beneath blue skies. Sun-drenched orchards were in blossom and a sea of young corn was waving in the fields. Low hills lazed in the distance.

'The last time you came to see me,' Gerendayn began languidly, 'was when the harracks were making a nuisance of themselves. Mortals have seen nine and sixty summers since then. Dare I hope that something exciting has brought you to me now?'

Curillian looked over at the elf.

'Nothing excites you anymore, Watcher: you have lived too long and seen it all.' The tall elf smiled and stretched like a cat.

'I have been in this land since the elves first came here, many moons and suns before your people were even awake. I have watched the kings and merchants come and go. I have watched the armists take over. I have watched Welton grow old. The span of your life, deemed long by your kind who marvel at you, is like a beaker being drained next to a vat. I have...'

'I need to get to the Mountain,' Curillian interrupted him unapologetically. Gerendayn was shaken from his reminiscences and looked across at his guest, startled.

'Eh, what? What's that now? The mountain? *The* Mountain? Heh, you should be so lucky. Not even the elves remember where it is anymore. No one knows...'

'But you know,' Curillian interrupted again. Gerendayn threw out a careless arm.

'I know people who know...'

'People?'

'All right,' the elf confessed, '*a* person. A person who might not be too forthcoming at the moment.'

Immortals never are, thought Curillian. Obviously, he was wrong, years ago, to think he had aided elvendom enough to not have to play these knowledge games.

'What's your business at the Mountain, anyway?'

'Kulothiel is holding a tournament, as you well know. Just like you knew I'd be coming here, so you can drop the act. I've got a young fellow with me who says he been there, and whom Prélan wants to get back there, but he only knows a route through Lithan's backyard. How do I convince Lithan to let me pass? Sooner or later, one of you undying fogies is going to tell me something useful.' Gerendayn gasped in mock outrage.

'The cheek of youth! I was one of the obliging souls who elected to accept your long-sires as kings of this land, and this is all the thanks I get? Asking is cheating, O king. It is a tournament, after all.' Curillian smiled and helped himself to a date from the nearby bowl.

'What's the good of a tournament if no one can get there? Lithan's hardly going to let us stroll through and hunt around right under his nose. And even if I opted for stealth, accompanied by just a few, even *I* couldn't sneak past without him knowing,' Curillian explained.

'It's not any old tournament, you see. Quite a carrot the old Keeper's dangling, I hear. Who've you got with you, apart from this boy?'

'Lancoir, and a cohort of my guards,' Curillian answered.

'Only one Knight of Thainen? You are confident, aren't you? Where are the other eleven?'

'The usual. They're either with my ambassadors in foreign courts, or overseeing the frontiers. There was no time to collect them, and my realm is safer behind me with them guarding it. But if this is a game,' he went on, 'then the world is the board and all the things in it are pieces. You're one piece, and I just happened to get to you first. How do I get to the Mountain without offending His Immortal Majesty?' Gerendayn sniffed daintily and ate a date himself.

'So you need a way to keep Lithan happy? You may be in luck. There may be a service you could render him which would make it impossible for him to refuse you. This person I mentioned...'

'What person?' demanded Curillian. 'Do I know them?'

'I should say so. You saved each other's lives once or twice while gallivanting around in Lancearon's little empire. She might need you to again.' Curillian had long ago learnt not to take this elf's irreverence seriously, and so he took no offence at his labours being alluded to so lightly. Instead he thought about who he meant.

'*Carea.*' He breathed the name. Enchanting encounters from centuries ago flashed through his mind.

'Carea,' confirmed Gerendayn. And then, because he could not resist relating news, he spilled over into sudden loquacity. 'Yes, you remember her, don't you? The radiant daughter of Therendir, she who is one of the oldest, and one of the loveliest, creatures on this planet? The untouchable, shape-shifting princess of the forest, the spell-weaver and heart-breaker extraordinaire? Spurned the advances of just about every eligible wood-elf prince in the land, yet somehow found your tedious company compelling. Goodness knows what the two of you really got up to in those adventures, but I do hope all the tales are true.' He paused long enough to grin mischievously. 'But of course, they don't make songs about *those* parts, do they? Certainly not in the courtrooms of Maristonia. But if you went to the forest realm, now, well you'd hear some delightful yarns there...' Curillian jogged his digressing train of thought and steered him back on track.

'Where do I find her? You said she might not be too forthcoming at the moment?' Gerendayn sighed.

'There are some, armist king, who wouldn't thank me for getting her mixed up with you again. Last time she did that she fair near got herself killed, and you can thank Prélan that never happened, otherwise you'd have had every wood-elf bachelor from all the world's forests after your blood. Then again, she may be in worse trouble now. Her father, Prélan bless him, long ago gave up trying to predict what she'd do next, but he must be worrying his undying beard grey thinking about this latest fix. Always the rebellious child. To think that such single-minded stubbornness could reside within such serene fabulousness...'

'Trouble – what trouble is she in?'

Gerendayn looked remorseful for a moment, as if weighing

whether he'd said too much, but then his love of a listener won over again.

'Strewth, you don't want much do you? Find me the Mountain! Get me in Lithan's good books! Give me the name! Tell me the trouble! No one in the land knows what trouble she's in – one day she's a hawk, the next a deer, the next only the canniest wood-elf there ever was. Do you have any idea how hard it is to keep track of a girl like that through fen and fold, fell and forest?'

'Of course not,' said Curillian, 'but I reckon she tells you more than anyone else. You two have some way of communicating. Only not many suspect it other than me.'

'Well, if you will press me. Word from the wind is that she's fallen foul of the harracks.'

'Harracks?' said Curillian, amazed and alarmed. Gerendayn gave his most serious face.

'Yes, harracks. Nice symmetry, isn't it? It was those blighters brought you to me last time. Goodness only knows how she managed to get snared by the stone-huggers, but somehow she did, and now she's probably holed up somewhere in Faudunum. Get her out of there and Lithan will be in your debt. Never mind safe passage to your little tournament, half his kingdom wouldn't be too big a reward for you...'

Faudunum, thought Curillian. The city of the harracks. Hidden in the Black Mountains, it was a remote and mysterious hive of evil. He had been there before, and didn't relish the thought of returning. He stood up and ventured out into the sunshine, rubbing his arms. The mere thought of it had made him feel rather cold. Gerendayn had subsided into quietness again, tinged with sadness. His jollity had parted to reveal the anxiety beneath.

'Well,' announced Curillian, getting up. 'I suppose I'd better go and pay my respects to Dácariel, hadn't I?' He had nearly walked past Gerendayn when the old elf shot out a hand and seized his arm. When he looked down, he saw desperately worried eyes looking back up at him.

'You will rescue her, won't you Curillian?'

Curillian smiled reassuringly and detached himself gently. He patted the elf's shoulder. 'Don't worry, Watcher, I'll save your muse.'

V

By Way of the Broadsword

ROUJEARK gazed up forlornly at the map on the wall. Built out of tessellated stones of many colours, it depicted a portion of the world centred on the East-fold of Maristonia. It extended far enough west to show Mariston, and far enough east to show most of Kalimar. The teaching of his father meant he knew more or less what he was looking at. Yet when he tried to trace his journey to Oron Amular, he met with only confusion. He couldn't fit the pictures in his memory to the thick dark humps showing the mountains of Kalimar. He had been happy enough today, wandering about the palace and discovering some of its charms and wonders. The scholar in him had happily passed a few hours in the duke's archive, where dust filtered through the sunbeams. He had got his boots mended, and whilst waiting he had heard Lancoir and some of the others hard at work, sparring in the training yard. Some considerate soul had even laid out clean clothes for him. They fitted well enough, and they even matched his old colours, only not so faded. Yet now he had come to a disconsolate impasse. The king might have played down the difficulties of getting through Kalimar, but Roujeark still felt keenly a sense of responsibility for the path finding, and couldn't help but imagine what Lancoir and the guards would think if he came up empty-handed. They would think he was a fraud, wouldn't they?

'Are you all right? What is the matter?' A sweet voice spoke behind him, and he turned round to see a little armist-girl behind him. She wore the beautiful dress of a noble-born child, and spoke with the confidence of aristocracy.

'Well, no,' he crouched down to confide in her. 'You see, I don't know where I'm going.' In a gesture that took him aback completely, she reached out and touched his cheek.

'Don't worry. If Prélan wants you to be somewhere, he will show you the way.' He stared, amazed, into the soft brown eyes, thinking that instead of a young girl he was speaking with an angel. He was only persuaded that he was not when the girl's mother appeared at one of the arched entrances and called her daughter to her. She smiled kindly at the stranger, but took her daughter away in her arms. The child waved, and Roujeark, still stunned, waved back. He reverently touched fingers to his cheek, feeling as though Prélan Himself had touched him.

He was in much happier spirits at the meal that evening, but still shy amid so many lofty and well-born people. In another gesture of generosity, the king had obtained an invite for him to the duke's table, and now he ate well with the duke's household, albeit at one of the lower benches. Lancoir had spent the day like a caged tiger in the palace, unleashing some frustration by hacking at a stump in the palace's training ring – the sounds of which Roujeark had heard from the archive. The guards had been much happier to take their ease, chatting to the servant girls of the palace. No one knew where the king had been, but now he was back he was merrily enjoying the company of his family. Duke Illyir had responsibility for ruling the entire East-fold in the king's name, answerable only to his cousin.

He held forth merrily over his meat, but asked no questions about Curillian's quest. If he asked after every venture of his restless cousin, he would never stop asking.

The next day, Curillian summoned his companions to him and took his leave of the Duke of Welton. On horseback again, they left the citadel by a small postern-gate and crossed the head of the little valley, which ran down to meet the Tonsor where the bridge stood. Roujeark was pleased to find that they did not journey long, only up the slope behind the city to a small fort. Partially hidden by cypress and cedar trees, it looked down over Welton and the valley. It was manned by a small garrison, but inside the place was full, for the King's Cohort was there. They were greeted upon arrival not only by Surumo, but also by Piron, who had arrived the previous night. So the twenty left behind to mind the horses had re-joined their comrades. Save for the seven who had died at sea, they were all together again. Curillian went in search of Theamace, his horse, and left Lancoir to remind everyone that they were to depart the following morning.

The guards of the cohort spent the morning getting their gear ready. Extensive provisions had been laid on by Duke Illyir, along with some more unusual items. Curillian had requested spike-studded mountain boots, thick clothing, gloves and small picks. The cohort still did not know what their mission was, but as they packed the new equipment it became evident to them that mountain-climbing would be involved. What the mountaineering paraphernalia suggested, the long coils of rope for each guard confirmed. Questions were directed at Surumo and Lancoir, but neither let on anything, saying only that all would be revealed in due time. To divert the restless troops, Piron took them on a training run. Roujeark managed to escape that sentence, but he was soon enrolled by members of the fort's normal garrison to help them feed and groom the cohort's horses. Later they were taken for exercise too, to strengthen the limbs which had been cooped up aboard ship.

It was not until after the evening meal that Curillian called his followers together and addressed them. The guards were sitting around several fires in the courtyard, polishing off lamb and chicken and roasted vegetables from long spits. They licked their fingers as the king stood on the wall-steps. He was dressed in a white tunic, whose golden embroidery twinkled in the firelight.

'My Royal Guards,' he called, raising his voice above the sound of many conversations dying away. 'I trust you've enjoyed the trip so far? I can now reveal that we are bound for Kalimar.' He paused to let the round of surprised remarks run their course. 'You are my escort to a rather unusual gathering of many nations. More than that at this stage I will not say, but to satisfy the curious among you our next step will be northwards. You do not have long left amidst the comforts of the fat East-fold, so enjoy them while you can. Before long, we will be leaving our horses behind and climbing into the mountains. That is where our friend Roujeark comes in. He has a unique knowledge of our final destination, and so he will guide us. Although he is not one of you, I expect you all to treat him as if he were. Get some good rest. We leave at daybreak.'

Roujeark was conscious of many eyes on him when the king disappeared, going to hold conference with Lancoir and Surumo. The guards around him broke into excited chatter about the king's revelation, and many theories and suggestions were put forward as to their destination. None came close, though. Some of them plied Roujeark with extra food and more wine, but although he accepted the comradely gestures, he gave nothing away. When he went to sleep, he was aware of being the subject of many hushed conversations. He had aroused fascination before. In the uplands near his home many communities had debated, over many tankards of ale, the identity and purpose of the wandering conjuror who had visited them, but now he had the feeling of being involved in something big.

⋏

In the morning, their cavalcade left the fort just as dawn was colouring the sky. Watched by the garrison, their horses carefully picked their way down the steep slope at the back of the hill, which led down to the Tonsor again, and then splashed across the river using a ford. The washerwomen of a nearby village watched the large mounted company in astonishment, and so too did their husbands and brothers from the fields: such a warlike party was very rare so far from the road. Once across the river, they rode across gently sloping ground, skirting every now and then the tilled fields of settlements. In the distance to their left rose the hills which gave birth to rivers like the Tonsor. Roujeark had learned from the map in the duke's palace that high ridges like that ringed the Phirmar, completely fencing it in. Outside, to the north, lay the East-fold proper, where Roujeark had journeyed before. Beyond the southern fence, though, lay Swordhilt Peninsula, wild lands stalked by primitive tribes, which had never been subdued by Maristonia.

Scarcely a sign of life did they see all day: Curillian was deliberately leading a path which avoided the local villages. At the end of the day they crossed another river and made camp soon after by the banks of one of its tributaries. Roujeark sought out the king's company and attached himself to the royal campfire.

'What river is this?' he asked the king when he got a chance.

'The Wellain, the greatest river of the Phirmar. He's the older brother of Tonsor, and almost half as long again in his course. Follow its bank downstream and you'll come to Welham at the throbbing heart of the Phirmar: the second city and port of the region.'

Curious, Roujeark asked another question.

'And what is our next immediate destination?'

'Arket – we'll meet some friends there.'

Roujeark remembered Arket – a busy and prosperous market town that he'd passed through on his first journey to Oron Amular. Roujeark was still curious, but no more specific questions came to mind. He went to bed with a strange feeling of unease.

$$\Lambda$$

As they rode the next day, the uneasy feeling grew on him. Following the stream up its course, he noticed the land start to close in around them: they were leaving the flat plains and entering into a bottleneck between two of the ridges. Almost without realising it, Roujeark found that he had followed an advanced party out ahead of the rest. Apparently his subconscious desire to be close to the king had made him keep pace when the king and Theamace rode ahead with a dozen of his guards. Curillian, who knew the land better than any of them, acted as scout at the front with one other. The rest of them followed. They had to be careful riding now, for the land became difficult and broken. Lots of dips and hillocks rippled the landscape, and boulders of increasing size obstructed their path. Roujeark's feeling of unease redoubled, and he looked about for some cause of it. They had ridden into a defile now, a deep crease in the land which was filled with yellow gorse and great boulders fallen from the rock faces above. He scanned the stony walls on either side. The right-hand lip seemed to glow with a faint red colour. Roujeark blinked to make sure he wasn't seeing things, but when he reopened them the tinge was still there, even though no one else had seen or remarked on it. His skin prickled with a memory of its own, and he remembered his strange sensation right before the pirate ship had appeared in Dagger's Cove. Back then, he had discerned a warning, like a blur on the horizon, before anyone else was aware. Was it the same now? Was someone lurking beyond the rim above them?

Encouraged by the successful prediction he had made the last time, he called out to the king, his voice ringing in the ravine. The spear came crashing down like a lightning bolt. It stood quivering in the earth where it had fallen. It was quite unlike the spears Roujeark had seen among the soldiery of Maristonia: painted red, hung with golden tassel-threads, and coming to a broad, leaf-shaped point. It might have impaled the king between the shoulder-blades, but Roujeark's cry had brought him up fast in the blink of an eye. Ageless reflexes had brought his horse up fast and the spear flashed down in front of the beast's nose. The king's hidden armour remained untested. Theamace and all the other horses skittered in fright, ears twitching. What happened next, though, far exceeded Roujeark's faint suspicion.

Dark figures suddenly appeared all along the rim of the ravine, thirty, forty, fifty. Maybe the first spear had not been aimed to kill, and had been only a warning shot, after all, for a second, similarly directed weapon crashed to the ground behind the last horse of the scouting party. Hemmed in by spears and ravine-walls, the mounted armists were trapped. The ambushers had chosen their spot well: the rock-littered ground made it impossible for them to spur their horses and make a dash for it, even if they could have evaded more spears. Staring upwards, Roujeark could not tell whether the assailants were barbaric armists or savage men. They brandished decorated spears identical to those which had been thrown, and seemed everywhere to drip with red and gold. Short, ornate bows were also in evidence. They were eerily silent, making no move. The king sat fearlessly on his horse, gazing up. Slowly, resolutely, emphatically, he drew the Sword of Maristonia.

'TAKE COVER!' yelled Roujeark, somehow knowing what would happen next. Even before the shout had finished leaving his lips his legs were in action, kicking out of stirrups and propelling him sideways. The whole scouting party leaped from their steeds and crashed among the rocks beneath and beside them. Almost in the same instant a volley of weapons hailed down after them, spears and arrows. The king was the slowest to move, not because speed had suddenly failed him, but because he trusted his weapon. DRING. DRING. DRANG. The arrows aimed at him bounced back harmlessly off the Sword of Maristonia's broad blade. Curillian covered himself expertly, his hands knowing exactly where the weapon needed to be. His horse, however, had no such defence: Theamace reared high and screamed in agony as two arrows pierced his chest. Another arrow and a spear cut into him. Just before he fell, Curillian freed his legs and jumped clear. Theamace crashed in ruin and thrashed about as he lay amongst the rocks. Half of the other horses had died instantly, and two guards as well. The other guards, bruised and jarred, had made it to some sort of cover, but the remaining horses were left exposed. Some reared up where they were, and others tried to pick a hurried route of escape, but all were cut down mercilessly by the next volley.

'SAVAGES!' cried Piron, who had been with the party. 'BOWS!'

His troops knew exactly what to do, and as soon as the order was given, their bows were seized from their back-straps and brought to hand. Arrows followed quickly and then they began their answering fire. They sent half a dozen shafts buzzing upwards: a feeble reply, but at least a pair of savages were caught in the open. Their gaudy corpses tumbled noisily down into the ravine. Yet their comrades kept up such a successful covering-fire that the armist archers' next chances to fire were few and far between. The guards hid behind their boulders, unable to do anything other than keep out of the way and loose off the odd retaliatory shot. Curillian looked up at the cliff behind him: it was a good job their enemies were only on one side of the ravine's top, for if they had been on the other side as well there would have been no cover. They would all have been dead already. Chainmail might deflect indirect hits, but nothing else, and without their full plate armour their limbs, throats and heads were all unprotected.

Roujeark did his best to hide, but felt horribly conspicuous. The guards' green and grey garb might blend in amid the rocks and grass, but his red and brown certainly did not. He felt sure more arrows were coming his way than they were going anywhere else. They snapped and cracked on the rock in front of him, and he winced every time they came close. The sound of metal striking rock was like the deft touches of a master mason's chisel: CRACK, SNAP, CRACK. Flakes of broken rock flew through the air, grazing and blinding. Roujeark's nerves were being shredded. But anger boiled up inside him, too – anger at being attacked and anger at feeling helpless. Without thinking, his hands stretched up towards the attackers. His brow furrowed as he concentrated on he knew not what. His whole body shook. His hands shook too, but they also started to glow ominously. Mysterious thoughts and unintelligible words screeched across his mind, defying comprehension.

All of a sudden, his hand exploded into flame. But his hand did not catch alight. Instead, a small ball of fire sprang forth. It hurtled upwards and smote the ravine's side. A heartbeat later a second fireball leapt from his other hand. Unable to understand what was happening to him, let alone control it, Roujeark felt like a detached observer as more fireballs careered off into the sky, each growing larger and more furious. The first had not reached the savages – smashing the rock-face beneath them instead – but the last couple exploded on the rim. Shards of rock were thrown up in a deadly hail of splinters and garish robes caught fire. Several of the savages caught alight and danced along the rim, screeching in helpless pain. Somewhere in the distance, faint and remote, a horn blew, but Roujeark barely heard it. The momentum of the power coursing through him had thrown him off balance and now flaming missiles were exploding just in front of him. Somehow, he managed to wrench back control of himself, and he collapsed back behind the boulder, panting and smouldering.

Through the smoke and charred boulders he became aware of the guards gaping at him in astonishment, and not a little fear. He himself was too shaken to move, let alone tap into whatever resource had just welled up within in, and try and use it in a more controlled manner. Scenes from his childhood flashed before his eyes and he quite forgot the scene around him.

Curillian was no less amazed than his companions when the fireballs started leaving Roujeark, but he at least had seen such missiles before. They had been a stock-weapon of the warrior-wizards in the Second War of Kurundar, deadly and practically inextinguishable. Even now, as if fed by some otherworldly fuel, the flames licked around Roujeark's boulder, despite having precious little to burn. Such a display had not been seen for four hundred years, and yet here it was, unexpected, uncalled for, but more than welcome. When the fireworks ended there followed a brief respite in which the terrified ambushers tried to get hold of themselves. Taking courage from their numbers, they soon resumed their rain of arrows and spears. But it was not so dense this time. Before long Curillian noticed them thinning out. Were they running out of projectiles, or were they despairing of destroying their victims this way? Whatever the reason, Curillian's seasoned instincts told him that if the enemy did not retire, they would soon be coming down. He gripped his sword-handle, determined to make them pay. He saw that the sheer wall of the opposite cliff had been blasted away by some of the misdirected fireballs, and what was left was a gentler, if still steep, slope, leading down into the defile. Sure enough, the foreign raiders began to slide and scramble down the new slant, intent on pressing home their attack. They came on with scimitars and spears, howling and yammering.

Curillian, King of Maristonia, rose to meet them. Leaving his cover, sword-first, he closed with them. An arrow smote his breast but fell back, turned by his impenetrable armour. A spear was flung, but he ducked away from it almost contemptuously. The lead savage never had time to even deviate from his course before Curillian cut him down. Several others sought to take advantage of the momentary distraction and hack at the king, but when their blades came scything down, they met only thin air. He was no longer there. He had moved on, quicker than their minds, and was now beside them. With the speed of a striking snake, his sword sliced through the neck of one of them, came cleanly round, and ripped open the belly of the next. He booted that savage to the ground, where he lay writhing in his own entrails, and lashed his pommel-stone backwards into the jaw of the next savage who sprang toward him. Deftly Curillian righted the blade and split open the skull of the enemy who had crept up behind him. The savage whose jaw he had smashed was still trying to recover his balance when Curillian ran him through. Barely ten seconds had passed and five savages lay dead.

By this time, Piron and the other guards had barely broken cover. As they rushed into the fray in support of their king more horns sounded, closer this time. Not nearly so lethal as the king, but still deadly enough, the guards dropped their bows and went to work with their swords and daggers. Now they made their attackers pay for their cowardly ambush, slaying without quarter. But the enemy was resourceful. It took them less than a minute to start shying away from normal hand-to-hand combat and resort to other techniques instead. Swift and agile, they used the boulders like launching pads and flew through the air to jump down on their enemies from above. In this way several of the guards were brought down. Some of them never rose again, their throats cut as they lay dazed; others grappled their opponents on the ground, rolling and punching, heaving and battering with loose rocks.

Roujeark all the while hid trembling behind his boulder, clamping down on his smarting hands and biting his lip. Every now and then he twisted to glance out at the fight. He saw swords rise and fall; red-clad savages propel themselves through the air, figures wrestling desperately. He saw one guard cleave a savage completely in two with one mighty sweep of his two-handed sword. As the shorn halves fell away like butchers' shanks, the guard swung the sword free and raised it high for another blow. But as he did so, a two-footed kick caught him in the sternum and sent him crashing down. Unable to retrieve his sword in time, the savage who had felled him sawed his scimitar across his face and chest. Roujeark shrank away in horror. Terror suffused him and he was suddenly forced to confront death. Was this where their adventure ended? Even though the king was still fighting, unscathed, surely they would all die here. With his next panicking glance, he saw another two guards fall: one with a rock-blow to the face, the other's legs hacked from beneath him.

Concern for his companions wrenched Roujeark out of his shock and he began to focus again, striving in his mind for the magical formulae which had so recently clicked within him. Nothing came, only pricks of fear lancing through his concentration. But then he heard a mighty sound.

'MAAARISTONNNNNNN!'

An instant later a warrior came leaping through the air, sword brandished. Leaping off one of the boulders, just as the savages had done, Lancoir jumped into the battle with a blood-curdling war-cry. He was still in mid-air when a chorus of horns blared somewhere close by, filling the narrow space and shaking the loose rocks on the blasted wall. Each of Lancoir's outstretched boots connected with a savage, and he crashed to the ground, taking both of them with him. Lurching up, he attacked first one, then the other, and slew them both with fearsome strokes. Drawing breath, he yelled again.

'MARISTONNN!!'

The cry echoed in the ravine, and instantaneously answering cries came back as the main body of the guards came rushing into the fight. The savages, who had been exulting in the slaughter of their quarry, now looked up in dismay. They fled from the oncoming armists, and then remembered that the most dangerous armist of all was still behind them, unconquered. They saw the dozen bodies piled around the armist with the great sword, and their courage deserted them. They dashed for the steep slope which led back up to their ambush site. The guards were hard on their heels, and they would never have made it, struggling up the loose earth, had their comrades lingering above not thrown down ropes to rescue them. Seizing hold of them, or jumping over one another to clutch at them, they were hauled and dragged upwards. Surumo, now on the spot and organising his troops, targeted them with archers, and though they scored one or two hits, the majority escaped over the ravine's rim and out of sight. Scorning to ask for mercy, the few left on the ravine's floor were slain by the vengeful armists.

Roujeark emerged from hiding to peek over the top of his boulder, and looked out over a dreadful scene. Ten of the guards lay dead or horribly wounded. Piron, bleeding prodigiously, and one other were the only survivors from the advanced party. Curillian carried not even a scratch, but he wept as he walked amongst the gore. Roujeark watched lines of blood drip down more than one boulder. Tears poured from his own eyes as he counted the grey-green bodies amid the red-clad corpses.

The wounded were carried out of the defile and a camp was set up not far ahead on a low hill. A detail of guards was left behind to pile the enemy dead and burn them. Then they bore their fallen comrades, together with their weapons, in honour from the ravine. They were cleaned and tended and laid out on the grass of the hill. Roujeark learned that they would be borne to Arket for a proper burial, of the highest honours.

'We saw the explosions,' Lancoir told the king quietly as they stood over the slain. 'You hadn't ridden on that far...and yet just too far. Would that I could have arrived sooner.' Stolid as any, he shook like a leaf as he tried to contain the rage which blazed within him. Later, in a calmer mood, he would learn how Roujeark had fought them with the fireballs of wizards, and he was amazed. But for now, as he stood shaking, a single tear coursed through the layer of grime on his cheek.

Songs of death and mourning were sung by the guards over their fallen companions, and the wounds of the injured were tended to. Piron had been hacked deeply in his side. His right leg was gashed from knee to ankle, and three fingers were missing from his right hand, cut from where they grasped the rock as he fell. Andil had put an arrow through the eye of his mutilator, and it was Andil who now cleaned and bandaged his hurts. The only other survivor had a bandage wrapped around his head and a dozen other cruel cuts staunched, but no healing could come to the traumatised face and stupefied eyes. His mind had been skewed by the blow to his head, and his friends wept bitterly to see this proud warrior reduced to such a pitiable state. The rest of his life would be spent as a harrowed invalid in an army hospital.

Curillian turned to Lancoir, and his voice grated with anger.

'Take forty guards. Hunt those scum down. We will go no further until every last one of them is dead.'

Even Lancoir blanched from the king's anger, but he hurried to do his bidding. He hand-picked those he wanted to take with him. The chosen forty shed everything that would encumber them, taking only weapons and water-gourds. Lancoir tightened the vambraces on his arms and gave his detachment terse instructions. Swift and grim, they filed out of the camp on their vengeful mission.

The remainder of the cohort – sixty-three royal guards – stayed in the camp, resting. Over and over in his mind Roujeark tried to reconstruct what had happened to him in the defile, but all his efforts failed him. In the end he gave up trying and tried to rest his strangely weary mind. A lethargy came over him so that he dozed the afternoon away and didn't rise again until the sky was blood-red with a brooding sunset. The soldiers around him were quietly getting on with their various duties with a subdued air, but Roujeark saw the king standing at the edge of the camp, outlined against the ruddy sky. His back was to the camp, and he was looking out at the world, hands clasped behind him. He remained like that until night had fallen and an improvised evening meal was being doled out.

Roujeark was again feeling uneasy, restless. There had been no word or sound of the hunting party, and worries played around the fringes of his mind. Suddenly the king called a guard to him and gave some instructions. Whatever he said was not positive, for all were grim-faced as the orders were relayed and soldiers criss-crossed the camp. Roujeark saw that the sentry positions around the camp were being strengthened and expanded.

He got up and approached the king. No obvious worry showed in the king's face, but it was tight and grim-set.

'I was just about to suggest a stronger watch myself, but then I saw you were already doing it.' He felt impertinent, giving advice to so veteran a warrior, but the king gave him a solemn sideways look.

'Concerns have been in my mind, too. You seem to sense danger long before anyone else, Roujeark.'

'Maybe I have been lucky,' Roujeark suggested.

'There is no such thing as luck. Every small feeling, every tingle of the spine, is part of a Prélan-given instinct.' He paused. 'Is it for us that you fear, or the hunting party?'

'I'm not sure. Possibly for the hunting party,' Roujeark mused aloud, 'but then again, maybe for us.'

They fell into silence and studied the night together. The camp had grown quieter as a nervous mood settled in. Pans and dishes were left neglected as taut senses strained. The horses sensed their masters' anxiety, pacing and whickering nervously. The night itself seemed to grow quieter, eerily so. Soon all that could be heard was the gentle crackling of watch-fires and the occasional hoot of an owl somewhere in the blackness. Eager to help, but knowing of nothing that he could do, Roujeark just watched and listened. He was just about to retire, thinking his vigil was in vain, when the king stirred almost imperceptibly beside him. Roujeark watched his hand fall to the sword-hilt at his side, and felt his own tension screw up tighter. A few nerve-jangling moments passed and the king made no further sign, but then, very slowly, he bent his knees into a combat stance, and pulled the sword a few inches out of its scabbard.

Open-mouthed, Roujeark watched as the sword swept out and back in an elegant arc, its brilliant blade catching the firelight like a mirror. As it swung through the air with a whistling scythe, the darkness in front of them smudged and a dim figure came leaping through the air. A split second later the accompanying howl registered in Roujeark's ears. The sword and the figure met in mid-air, and the sword won. It clove right through the leaping head and brought the body behind it crashing to the earth. The tell-tale jewellery and bright red garments had been removed, but it was still undeniably one of the savages from before who now lay prone before them. Curillian, who had been unwilling to let the enemy know that he had spotted them, now yelled a war-cry to alert his comrades.

'MARISTON!'

Those who hadn't seen him prepare his deadly greeting, like Roujeark, certainly heard the cry, and weapons were brandished. All around the camp, figures suddenly came leaping out of the dark, howling their hatred. They had rubbed mud on their faces and hands and dirtied their bronze spear-blades and arrowheads, and had thus managed to creep up on the armist camp unawares. Only Curillian's long-honed instincts had detected them. The defenders were momentarily dazed; their night-vision was spoilt by gazing at firelight, and they were on the back foot straight away. The sentries were hard-pressed in desperate hand-to-hand fighting. Horses neighed and whinnied in fear as they heard the sounds of metal striking metal.

Roujeark looked around in rising panic. He saw the confused shadows of dozens of mini-battles raging in the firelight. There seemed to be hundreds of the enemy, scores of them drawn like moths to each watch-fire. The armists must have been outnumbered three or four to one. Unarmed, he had rushed within the rapidly formed defensive cordon, and now watched from inside like the injured. He watched the king fend off the enemies near him. He alone seemed unfazed by the darkness. He moved and fought with the fluidity of a warrior whose prowess derives from innate ability rather than drilled lessons. The Sword of Maristonia burned like a brand, catching and rejoicing in the firelight with every sweep and thrust. Roujeark thought he actually saw sparks fly as other weapons came into contact with it and were shorn away.

A cry behind him made him turn around and he saw one furtive attacker who had slipped through the defensive ring. He watched the line of his movement and saw that he was making for the wounded, who sat or lay huddled in the centre of the camp. With a speed that surprised even him, Roujeark rushed to where a guard's bow and quiver lay abandoned on the ground. With no more practice under his belt than a few pop-shots loosed at the pirates from the ferry, he notched an arrow and let fly. The attacking savage had closed to within a few feet of the wounded Piron when Roujeark's arrow plunged into his belly and threw him back. Piron shot him a grateful look.

Meanwhile the battle still raged, and Roujeark longed for something more that he could do. He couldn't shoot from inside the cordon, for fear of hitting the defenders by mistake. He took up a burning brand from one of the fires and held it aloft. Without command or focused thought, he felt the same onrush of intuitive knowledge that had come to him earlier. Raging formulas and flashing lights seared inside his head and his hands glowed again. This time it was so intense that it was painful, and he could only watch, stunned, as the flames of the brand shot upwards in a great jet of fire. Like a towering beacon the flames leapt into the sky, instantly illuminating the whole hillock. Where before only shadows and reflections could be seen, now garish firelight revealed the scene in harrowing clarity. It lasted only moments, though, for the pain in his mind grew and grew until it became unbearable. In agony he dropped the brand and slumped unconscious to the ground. The brand extinguished and lay smoking beside him.

Both defenders and attackers alike had been startled into abeyance by the sudden light, but when it faded, they fell upon each other again. They barely heard the war-cries in the distance coming rapidly nearer. Some of the less wounded who were near Piron rushed to help the fallen Roujeark, and so it was that they never saw the return of Lancoir. Along a huge segment of the fighting ring, the attackers were taken in the rear as the hunting party came to the succour of their comrades. Battle-fury glinted in Lancoir's eyes as he cut down a pair of savages, screaming aloud.

'MARISTONNN!!!'

With equal relish, his picked hunters slew the unsuspecting enemies and in an instant turned the tide of the battle. Having freed one side of the hillock, they rushed round to the other sides where their comrades were still beset. Only slowly did the savages become aware of the new threat, and many of them were cut down where they stood by avenging swords materialising out of the night. As realisation gradually dawned that their night-attack had failed, they started to slip away. Soon the few survivors were in headlong retreat into the night. One or two of the guardsmen tried their luck shooting into the night, but they were rewarded with only a handful of hits.

Blood-spattered but beaming, Curillian and Lancoir met on the battlefield and embraced, still holding their swords.

'Two timely appearances in one day, Captain of the Guard – anyone would think you did it by intention!' Lancoir flashed a rare, wolfish smile.

'The day hasn't come yet when my king is attacked and I don't get a say.' He proffered his blood-rinsed sword in evidence.

Together they strode to the centre of the camp and the sight of Roujeark lying prone, surrounded by worried guards, immediately drew their concern. Their fears abated when he was roused just as they came up. He looked pale and exhausted. He moaned, and when he rubbed his head, they saw that his hands were scorched and his robes singed. Curillian squatted beside him and laid a hand on his shoulder.

'Roujeark, my friend, what is wrong?'

At first, the wide eyes didn't seem to register the sight of him, but then they focused and a look of alertness crept back into the face.

'My king, forgive me for failing you...blinding light, scorching heat...' Curillian shook his head in amazement at the wholly unnecessary apology.

A faint voice spoke up nearby.

'He seized a brand from the fire, as if to see the battle better. But then he transformed it into a pillar of blazing light. I thought all hell was about to break loose, but then he shrieked in agony and fell down like a stone.' It was Piron, telling of what he'd seen.

Lancoir nodded and came to squat on the other side of Roujeark. Like the king, he laid a reassuring hand on his quivering shoulders.

'We'd hunted fruitlessly for hours before we came upon a small group of them, guarding all their booty and bright red cloaks. It wasn't much of a fight, but we realised the main body was out on a hunt of its own. We were part-way back when we saw the pillar of fire. Then we came at a sprint. Prélan only knows how many more of us would have died had we not seen that sign. You didn't fail, Roujeark. You did well.'

VI

Whispers from the Wood

ROUJEARK was in such a daze that he didn't even realise it when they reached Arket. Between throbbing pain, weariness and bewilderment at his experiences, he only just had the energy to remain in his saddle on the ride. He had been oblivious when they emerged from the higher ground on either side and left the Phirmar behind. He hadn't noticed the openness of the new country or the long, gentle slope leading down into that vast, shallow depression known as 'The Bowl'. Dominating the East-fold, The Bowl boasted some of the best arable land in the realm. Skirting its rim was the Armist Road, which ran between Mariston and Kalimar, and this they now joined, riding eastward. Even though Roujeark had trodden that road once before on his previous journey, he didn't register that he was now retracing his steps. Now that they had left the empty, half-wild lands behind and returned to civilisation, they passed through many market towns lying on the road, and shared the road with many people travelling between the towns. Roujeark took in none of it.

Arket was larger than most of the other settlements on the road, being, after Markest and Aldia, the largest town in the East-fold. With its encircling wall – a relic of old troubles – it was more of a city than a town, but the wall was not in good repair, and the gates had been enlarged to allow for better trade access. Its gates were not even closed at night. Threats did still exist in this part of the realm – bandits and harracks in the wilderness to the north, savages beyond the hills to the south – but Arket was so well protected by the legion stationed nearby that its walls were merely decorative. The 15th Legion, commanded by General Horuistan, one of five legions making up the Eastern Army of Maristonia, was garrisoned in permanent camps strung between the great road and the rugged highlands to the south. Well-maintained pickets, forts and watchtowers kept the commerce of the East-fold secure. General Horuistan was usually so busy patrolling these facilities that he rarely came to Arket, and kept no permanent residence there, but having received the message from the capital, he made sure he was in the city in time to meet his king.

The burgesses and guild-masters that ran the city were much perturbed to find a meeting taking place between the king and a general, both rare visitors to the city, in their Guildhall. Curillian reassured the anxious businessmen and sent them away. Lancoir watched silently from the edge of the room as the king gave the general his orders. Curillian did not share many of the details, but told Horuistan to carry on holding exercises and maintain a state of readiness until informed otherwise. The meeting was short and sharp, and the general soon left to return to his command headquarters. Curillian and Lancoir together walked through the city towards the home of one of the city's dignitaries, whose hospitality they had imposed upon.

'He was surly,' remarked Lancoir, who had never met Horuistan before.

'Yes,' agreed Curillian. 'Horuistan is one of a breed of capable but over-comfortable generals who keep our peace-time army ticking over. I believe he feels aggrieved at having been passed over for promotion to Constable of the East-fold. He may be the oldest and longest-serving officer in the Eastern Army, but I am not in the habit of rewarding the unremarkable. He will serve his purpose, though, and with luck, won't be needed at all.'

'That fussy, mouse-like fellow didn't seem too pleased to see us either.' Curillian smiled at the description.

'The President of the Municipal Council, you mean? He's cooperative enough, but I'm sure he'd very much like us to clear off as soon as possible. He needn't worry; we won't disrupt his careful routines for very long.'

They arrived at their destination. The armist who'd found himself playing host was the Master of the Grain-guild, one of the most important officials in the area.

'A delight to have you here, Your Majesty,' he kept saying over their roast beef and wine. 'And, of course, what a privilege to entertain one of the valiant Knights of Thainen,' he added on several occasions. 'An honour to make your acquaintance, Sir Lancoir.' The portly armist, who seemed to have a somewhat story-book notion of soldiering, far from being put out at the sudden obligation, seemed rather taken with his guests. 'We don't get many visits from heroes like yourself out this way. Even His Majesty is a rare guest. Though, if I may say so, Your Majesty as often appears out of the blue mid-way through some adventure, as he does on official state visits, with his court in attendance.'

Lucky for you, Curillian thought as he sipped his wine. I expect you wouldn't want to waste too much of this best Redmar vintage on my courtiers. To entertain my full royal court would strain even the resources of someone as wealthy as yourself. But Curillian did not voice these thoughts. He was quite used to mildly impertinent remarks about the eccentricities of his kingship. Instead, he responded politely.

'I'm sorry to have given you so little notice, but it is very kind of you to put us up. It is so much nicer to keep up with important subjects than to hide away in one of my villas, or in an abbey.'

The dinner and the conversation ran its staid course until a steward came in with a message for the Master. The otherwise impeccable armist seemed in a state of some distress.

'Your Eminence, a crowd of ruffians has arrived at the door, and demands an audience with His Majesty.'

Lancoir hastily rose and pulled off his napkin. 'By your leave, sire, I will deal with this. Your Eminence,' he nodded curtly to the Master and left the room.

Some of the anxiety of the steward seemed to have transferred to the host. With a worried expression on his fleshy features, he leaned towards Curillian.

'We're not expecting any trouble I hope, are we, Your Majesty? I'm sure Sir Lancoir has the matter in hand, but might I enquire who these people are?'

Curillian smiled disarmingly. 'It's quite all right. I have contracted the services of some specialists for a particular task. It is nothing to cause you any alarm.'

'Ah, I see. And will they, er, be staying the night?'

'They will be making their own arrangements, and will be no bother at all to you.' The anxiety left the Master's face. 'In fact, we will all be gone by morning, so as not to indispose you any more than necessary.'

Quite recovered to his normal dignified self, the Master concealed his relief rapidly.

'So soon? I am sad to learn that I cannot enjoy any more of Your Majesty's company. I shall by the envy of the Council just to have had this encounter. Still, I must say that I'm glad to have your reassurance that everything is in order. You see, as long as the right grain gets on the right waggons, as long as the right amount of bread gets baked and the urbanites are kept are happy, I may be said to have done my duty. I really don't go in for anything else, and must confess to having no experience whatsoever of more, er, exciting matters. It is just marvellous to have had an opportunity to assist Your Majesty.'

⁂

The 'ruffians' were waiting for the king in the stables of the Guildmaster's mansion. There were ten of them. Ruggedly dressed in hooded cloaks and sturdy well-worn boots, they were sufficiently unkempt and sported enough unusual weaponry to alarm any comfortable city-dweller. Surreptitious yet confident, they exuded an intensity that only the inexperienced could mistake for unscrupulousness or hostility. However, only the most trained of eyes would be able to spot the marks of insignia about their persons. These marks were all that remained of their uniforms. Crested rings, tattoos, subtle devices woven into their dark clothing, each marked them as belonging to one or other of the Eastern Army's five legions. Scouts, trackers, pathfinders, hunters, they were highly specialised legionaries whose attire and equipment was tailored to their role.

'Gentlemen, glad you could make it,' Curillian welcomed them. He greeted several of them by name, having worked with them on previous enterprises. Lancoir had brought them round to the most inconspicuous part of the mansion, away from prying eyes. 'I'm sure friend Lancoir here has briefed you on the basics already.' They nodded confirmation. 'Now we've got representatives here of all five legions, yes?'

'That's right, sire, two of us from each,' said one. 'The rest are waiting outside the walls. We didn't want to attract too much attention.'

'Good. I need to know how many of you have been to Kalimar, and I'm especially interested in those who've been through the Black

Mountains. I want those armists to meet me at the royal hunting lodge, half a day's ride downslope of Hearthel. I will be there in a day's time, so see that they get there before me. Messages have already been sent to arrange for provisions to be made ready there. Now I realise I've asked for quite a specialised group, but there's work for the rest of you. Lancoir?' The Captain of the Guard stepped forward and handed sealed scrolls to a representative from each legion. 'Three cohorts to scour Broadsword Ridge and the lower Saneth to identify the routes of heathen incursions. They will then co-operate with the 17th at Welham to flush out any threats. The remainder should keep themselves in readiness in the vicinity of the 15th's barracks – General Horuistan may have need of you. He is aware of your availability, and will deploy you as and when needed.'

'Questions?' barked Lancoir. As was to be expected from such capable armists, there were none. Curillian cocked a quizzical eyebrow when one of the trackers, a seasoned old campaigner, cleared his throat.

'Not a question, sire, just a comment. A pleasure to be of service to you again. It's been too long since we had a proper job to do.'

Roujeark slept through all of the meetings and planning. All he knew in the morning was that he was being turfed out of bed before it was light and ushered through a hasty sequence of breakfast, toilet and packing. Before he was properly awake, he was in the saddle again. Seemingly only a score of guards were currently with him – he didn't even know where he'd spent the night – but soon their group was joined by others emerging out of the shadows. If he hadn't been riding alongside Andil he would have felt thoroughly disorientated. Gradually the King's Cohort coalesced and by the time they reached the city's eastern gate, with only the merest suggestion of predawn light in the sky ahead of them, they were all together again. They left Arket before even the early-rising market traders and stallholders were about, and townsfolk who thought they'd been disturbed by the massed hooves of a mounted company assumed they'd had a bad dream.

With unusual speed, they thundered along the road as if straining against a pressing deadline. Wretchedly uncomfortable, Roujeark rode in their midst. Fresh air whistling past his face and the beauty of dawn unfolding in the open sky had brought him more fully awake. To his surprise he found that his burnt hands had been salved and bandaged whilst he slept, so that he was just about able to control his reins, but they were still raw and painful. They must have covered a good many miles at their breakneck pace, for the normally busy road was still virtually deserted, when, without warning, they changed direction and turned off the road, plunging into the open country to the north. Once off the road they slowed down, as if some danger had now passed, or possibly also because the lightly wooded land through which they now rode was less easy going than the neatly paved highway. Roujeark, who had originally thought himself the expert guide, was fast abandoning the notion as he found that travelling with the King's Cohort was simply a matter of trying to keep up while trying to guess the king's mind. Thankfully they had now slowed down enough for him to fire a couple of questions at Andil. Their brief conversation was punctuated by numerous ducks, swerves and jolts and the scream of disturbed birds as they cantered downhill through scrubby heathland.

'What was all the rush this morning – the sun's only rising now – and why have we left the road? Isn't that the quickest way to Kalimar?'

'Orders,' Andil replied tersely. To Roujeark's immense gratitude, he went on to elaborate. 'It seems the king is keen to be as inconspicuous as possible. He normally travels by main roads with an entourage of thousands; this is different.'

'Why are we not all here?' asked Roujeark, whose rough headcount kept coming short.

'Some of us are still not here – they went south off the road as a diversion.'

'Why?'

'Don't ask me the ins and outs of it. But basically no one knows we're here now – we left the road before people were abroad to notice us. My guess is we're headed for one of the king's private lodges, somewhere nice and discreet. Another day or two and we'll be in Kalimar.'

⋏

Andil's guess turned out to be quite a good one. The sun was approaching its zenith when they came to a hunting hall. Far off the beaten track, it lay in a clearing in a large wood. Roujeark was alarmed to see mounted armists waiting for them outside the hall, but evidently the king was unperturbed. The reeve who maintained the royal property was clearly expecting to see them, for no sooner had they been spotted than vast amounts of provisions were arranged on the patio outside the hall. The king disappointed Roujeark's hope of having a quick word by immediately vanishing inside the hall with the resident servants, so the young armist found himself enrolled in helping to transfer the victuals to the horses of the cohort. Loaves of bread, bags of flour, flitches of salted and cured meats, packets of nuts and dried fruit, wedges of cheese and linen-wrapped cakes and biscuits, gourds of wine, skins of water, flagons of cider, there was enough here to sustain an army. Bewildered, Roujeark wondered what the onlooking horses thought of this soon-to-be doubling of their loads. While he helped, a gang of the horsemen who had been waiting for them here accosted him.

'Look here, lads, I didn't know the king's cohorts rode with mascots these days.'

'Cor, will you look at this fellow? Not conspicuous at all is he? I don't mind these other fellers, they'll blend in at a pinch, but this one's asking for trouble.'

'Stick out like a sore thumb he will, spot him a league off.'

'He'll get himself shot right enough.'

'Shot?' said Roujeark, alarmed. 'By whom?'

'Elves?' suggested one of them helpfully. The voice was behind him, and Roujeark turned to face him, the other armist fierce but smiling happily. 'Savages? Harracks? Bandits?' he went on cheerfully.

Roujeark turned again when the original speaker gripped his shoulder. Shocked, he found the armist was almost nose-to-nose with him, all aggression and hostility.

'Who knows?' he said, his deep voice grating. 'Maybe they'll all have a go. Seriously though, is this some kind of joke?' Roujeark winced under the heat of his enmity and recoiled from the stale cider on his breath.

'Soldier!' A stern voice made the pugnacious armist step away. Roujeark noticed, with surprise, that it was Piron who was intervening. The armist who had accosted Roujeark clearly held a rank of his own, but he did not pick a fight with the officer. Reducing his animosity to a restrained malevolence, he listened respectfully to the guards' officer.

'You'd do well not to make an enemy of the king's friend. After watching him incinerate more than a few savages, I'd be doubly careful. Now, get your people in order.'

'Incinerate, is it?' the armist muttered. 'Interesting.' Eyeing Roujeark curiously, he moved on, and one of those with him gave Roujeark a playful shove as he passed. Piron bit on an apple as they moved away.

'They're trackers, expert pathfinders. Some of the most skilful, and least courteous, members of the army.' Roujeark surveyed Piron and saw that his wounds had been dressed neatly, just like his own.

'I'm surprised to see you're still with us, Piron, I thought you had been too badly wounded. Surprised, but glad.' Piron shook his hand, acknowledging the kindness. 'Ordinarily I would have been, but I wasn't being left behind, was I? Nearly killed me again, but just had to show them I could keep pace. I'll be fine, provided I'm not attacked within the next few days. I believe it will be worth sticking around.'

'What do you mean?' said Roujeark.

'Well, between Lancoir's presence, the sudden emergence of a wizard in our midst, and the fact that we've been attacked twice already inside our own borders, I'd say we're in for one hell of an outing.'

'Oh, I'm not a real wizard,' said Roujeark, embarrassed and intrigued in equal measure. Piron gave him a comical look of feigned apprehension.

'By Prélan, if you're not, then I'd hate to meet a real one.' He continued to eat his apple while doing just enough to seem like he was supervising the activity about them.

'What is this place?' asked Roujeark.

'A hunting lodge of the king's. He has hundreds of them across the realm, probably doesn't visit any of them more than a couple of times a century. Curillian's not even much of a hunter, by comparison to some. He prefers to hunt enemies, not game. Guardsman Andil here will know more.' Andil strode up, happy to join the conversation.

'Don't know the place personally, but judging by the state of readiness here I'd say orders for this lot were lodged some time ago – how else could a country reeve get so much tuck assembled in time? Must have called in all the tax owing to the king in kind from the local landowners. The king's chosen a good spot, ideal as a base for operations, but nice and discreet.' Roujeark could see that Andil thought a lot more about what went on than the average member of the riding. Piron added another surmise of his own.

'We'll only be waiting until the chaps in the diversion rejoin the main party. Then we'll be off again. Any idea how the king plans to sneak into Kalimar?'

'I don't think even Lancoir knows that,' said Andil. 'No, that knowledge is for the king only, and perhaps also for our guide?'

⋀

Roujeark, however, didn't know. Having left the road, he had totally lost his bearings. He kept close to Piron and Andil as they left the following morning, riding further into The Bowl and angling slightly towards the rising sun. Roujeark didn't mind revealing his ignorance to his two friendly companions, and he gleaned everything he could from them.

'We're steering a very deliberate course,' said Andil. 'We've given a wide berth to all the busy farmland over there to the right. The town of Irlaton's probably not more than a couple of leagues upslope.' Their puzzlement grew as they rode. Presently they came to a river with a strange, greenish hue.

'That can only be one of the waters that issues from the forest,' declared Andil. Piron paled slightly.

'Surely we're not going through Tol Ankil? No armist I ever heard of has been through there and returned to tell of it.'

'Maybe the king has,' said Andil.

They followed the course of the river upstream for a time, and as they did so the banks became increasingly wooded. Up ahead, the trees appeared to get much denser. Clouds had been gathering overhead, and now a light drizzle was falling. Then they noticed Lancoir come riding back down the line. He reined in alongside them, and Surumo, sensing instructions were afoot, spurred up to meet them.

'The king sends word,' Lancoir told them, 'that there'll be a brief delay soon. Surumo, there's a confluence not far ahead. Halt the armists there. From there only a small group of us will ride forwards. Roujeark, you're wanted in the king's company.'

Roujeark shrugged and left his companions, riding up to the head of the line with Lancoir. They came to the expected confluence and then the guards, who now numbered 91, were left behind. Those who rode on with Lancoir, Roujeark and the king were the ten trackers who had joined them at the hunting lodge. Ignoring the surly glances of his newest companions, Roujeark was far more concerned about the trees ahead. Nervousness was mounting inside him, and his skin seemed to tingle as if reacting to something in the air. It was quite unlike anything he had ever experienced in Maristonia before; only his meetings with Prélan came close.

The clouds were low and the rain heavier now, giving the whole country a mysterious, uninviting feel. Roujeark started in his saddle when they suddenly rode within sight of a thick wall of trees. They had reached the forest. He had never imagined it would be so great. Even though the clouds were so low as to be almost fog-like, he got the impression that before him was a vast tract of unguessable woodland. When he had ridden into Kalimar before he had only heard rumours of the great forest near the border – it had always been just beyond the edge of sight from the road – but now the forbidding nature of it struck him. This was not a place where mortals strayed lightly. He sensed an anxiety similar to his own in his companions. Only Curillian took it in his stride, but even he was warier than normal.

Out of nowhere, an arrow sped and buried itself in the turf before the king's horse. Green-flighted and almost invisible against the backdrop, it seemed to vanish into the ground. However, the message it bore was all too clear. Horses and riders alike jolted in alarm. Even the trackers seemed taken aback. Wherever the arrow had come from, their sharply honed skills hadn't detected a nearby threat. Ahead of them the line of trees, half-hidden by the film of heavy rain, seemed to brood like a garrison enduring a siege. Unperturbed but grim-faced, the king freed his feet from his new horse's stirrups and dismounted. He entrusted the reins to Lancoir.

'I go alone from here. Do nothing until I return.' His tone brooked no argument. So Lancoir took the reins and, fidgeting in his saddle, watched anxiously as his sovereign strode ahead into the rain. There were keen eyes among them, but even from their sight he had disappeared by the time he reached the treeline, apparently without suffering harm. The trackers were grim and silent, seemingly quieted by the forest's oppressive presence. Lancoir too said nothing, straining his eyes for sign of the king. After a while, however, he sensed the futility of his vigil and relaxed a little. Roujeark edged closer, and, no louder than he dared, spoke to the Captain of the Guard.

'You care for the king a great deal, don't you?' Lancoir seemed to bridle, as if sensing an insult, but then his features softened slightly.

'He's like a father to me.' Roujeark sensed the weight of unspoken history behind those words. Fingering the ring which Lancoir had given him, he wondered if it gave him the right to pursue this conversation further. He decided to try.

'Curillian is more paternal than I thought a king could be. I would give much to have a father figure like that. My own father was taken from me when I was a small boy.' The words were true, though he hadn't planned them. Although he had walked the world for many years and learnt much of its ways, Roujeark still felt young and vulnerable, somehow conscious of an incomplete upbringing. Lancoir did not speak for so long that Roujeark thought he would not respond, that he would not be interested, but eventually he asked gruffly,

'What happened to your father?'

'He was slain by the folk we lived near. He tried to help them, but they did not appreciate the practice of magic.' Lancoir narrowed his eyes at the mention of the word, but his expression became more interested.

'My father was murdered too,' he said at length, confiding almost reluctantly. Roujeark had to coax more out, for nothing else came freely.

'What happened to him?'

Slowly, stiffly, Lancoir conveyed his story. Had the trackers been any closer, he probably would have stifled it, but they had spread out, trying to keep busy while not actually doing anything. Rain dripped from the knight's hood as he spoke.

'He was a Knight of Thainen, just like I am now. Sir Lorumon of Markest. He was one of the greatest warriors in the land, but unlike most of the Order, he came from humble roots. He served the king well, but well-born armists around him, craven and weak, were jealous of his status, his fame. Driven by the devil, they brought false charges and evidence against him. The king took no action, but the conspirators took the law into their own hands. Ambushing my father on the road, they executed him and left his body to rot. We never recovered it. The king paid them in their own coin and executed all the known conspirators, and denied them burial honours, but I am convinced that some of them still live. There is nothing I can do to bring justice down on them, but justice will find them sooner or later. As for me, I always keep a blade by me when I sleep. They didn't want my father to be a knight. Nor me. Nor my son, Lancaro. He will be a knight after me, when he comes of age. But every day that I am a knight, and a good knight, I pour burning coals on their heads. They will never stop me being who I am meant to be.' He paused and gave Roujeark a direct look from beneath his hood. 'Never let anyone stop you from being who you were meant to be.'

A

Curillian walked across the wet grass, feeling the eyes on him the whole way. His boots pressed deeply into the turf with every step. The great sword was by his side, but he spread his arms wide in token of peace. Soon, he knew, he would be hidden from the sight of his companions. He hoped he would not have to leave them in the dark for too long. The trees grew nearer and nearer. He passed under their eaves. The boughs and foliage were so dense that the precipitation slackened almost instantly to a pattering trickle. Above the earthy scent of damp loam, the odour of strange plants wafted into his nostrils. Droplets of rain ran down his neck. All he could hear was birdsong in the trees. When a greeting didn't come, he called aloud to the trees.

'We've been through this before. You can show yourself.' His voice echoed under the thick canopy. Long after the last echoes had died away, the whisper came, like an utterance of the trees themselves.

'And every time you come, you fail to appreciate how fortunate you are to tread here at all.'

Curillian responded in kind.

'And if you didn't want me here, I wouldn't have been allowed to come.'

Silence. Only the sounds of the forest and the rain. He shivered and felt his skin twitching. Was that the flapping of a bird's wings? He had been expecting it, but the grey form which suddenly appeared beside him still made him start. Tall and slim as a young tree, cloaked in invisible grey, the wood-elf turned his head and only then was his pale face visible beneath the damp hood. Unreadable brown eyes transfixed him. Of all elves that he had ever had dealings with, the wood-elves, Firnai, were the most secretive, the most alien.

'So, Falakai king, you are here. The fear of the wood keeps all mortals away, but not so the doughty son of Mirkan, protégé of Lancearon, scion of ancient chieftains. Your troop did well to halt where the arrow checked them, else they would all have died without a trace ever reaching mortal lands. We knew of your coming, and of your number.'

'Our riding was secret and known to few. Are we expected? We took great care...' The brown eyes were implacable, as was the face, which hadn't moved at all, save the lips.

'Not careful enough. Your folk, who look only to the ground, may not have marked your passing, but we who also inhabit the skies were well aware of your movement. Did you hope to creep across the border undetected? Even the Avatar in their stone houses would have been aware of you. We are aware of all, even the passing of your red companion, forty years ago in the mortal reckoning. Even as now, it was early springtime when he vanished into Avamar. No, Curillian, son of Mirkan, son of Arimaya, we knew of your coming.'

Curillian looked at him, allowing a slight smile to play on his lips. *You don't know why I'm here, though, do you?* He scrutinised the face next to his, and realised he knew it, though it had taken two minutes for the recollection to come back to him. Sin-Solar, or was it his twin brother, Sin-Tolor? The great yew bow hidden by his side was the mighty emblem of both, and their sister too, inescapable marksmen and guardians of the forest all. Did the princes often stand sentry in these latter days, or had other word reached them?

'Gerendayn,' he said, searching for a reaction. There was none whatsoever. 'Has Gerendayn sent word from Welton? I know he has the capability. You probably know the conversation I had with him word for word. Whatever else you may or may not know, you at least know I'm here to see her. Take me to the queen.'

'Come, she is near.'

The elven prince had not been exaggerating. Curillian had followed the fleeting grey figure only a few hundred yards through the trees before they came to a great fallen oak, a giant of the forest. The prince led him to the foot of the slanting trunk and gestured him up it. Pacing up the broad wooden slope, Curillian reached a point where lightning had cloven the trunk in two. He stood near the edge of one of the spars and wondered what was meant to happen next. He started when the blackbird came and hovered in front of him. It looked strangely at him for a few moments, and then it changed before his eyes. He had seen wood-elves shapeshift before, but never so close up. The surprise of it nearly knocked him off the trunk. Where before there had been a beautiful bird, now a beautiful elf-woman stood before him, dark-haired, dark-eyed, graceful with ageless elegance. The eternally young body was only visible for a heartbeat before what had moments ago been feathers were drawn about it in a dark cloak, swathing her like a robe. His mind shot back to another elf-woman, to another glimpse, in another life. Then he forced himself to focus. He knew this face, too. Eyes like dark opals, but as penetrating as arrowheads, gazed out at him from pale, angular features that were hawk-like in their beauty. The top of the black cloak was drawn up in a tall collar which framed her imperious visage. He stepped back and bowed low.

Here was Dácariel, Queen of Tol Ankil, daughter of woodland kings. So alike was she to her aunt, Carea, that Curillian thought it was she, and had to fight against being transported back to long ago days. He blushed, knowing she read his thoughts.

'Welcome, Curillian, King of Maristonia,' she said. Her voice was tough as oak roots, and yet as free and as light as wind through the trees. In wood-elven song, all the textures of the forest were given vocal form.

'Lady of the Forest, hail Dácariel, daughter of Carion.'

'Twice met are we,' said she, still maintaining an aloof regality, and then suddenly smiling like a tree in blossom. 'Far too seldom for those who have been neighbours down the long centuries.'

'I am honoured by your friendship, Lady, but I am just a sapling in the grove next to your ancient evergreen. How small a chapter in your life have been the four hundred years of our acquaintance?'

'And yet we have been comrades-in-arms in that time, an honour you have bestowed upon many of my kin. Great is that bond…nearly as great as love.' She gave him a direct look, and he lost himself in

those eyes. And she was the younger, and less potent of the two...
'You have come for her, have you not?'

A

All the horses reared and Roujeark nearly fell from his saddle. Lancoir's sword came singing to his hand, but the cloaked figure that had suddenly materialised before them made no move of attack. Without so much as looking up or showing his face, he spoke, beckoning them.

'Come. My queen bids you join your king as her guest. You and all your company.'

The King's Cohort was brought up to the forest eaves and there they were met by Curillian, damp, but unharmed.

'Lancoir,' he said happily, 'pass the word. Leave the horses and baggage here, they will be brought after. We have been offered alternative transportation.' He saw the look in his captain's eye and added, 'Have no fear. We are welcome guests. Let there be no doubting heart, we are here as a necessary part of our quest. Come, enter under the eaves where few mortals have been and gone in peace.'

Presently a group of wood-elves materialised beside them and took charge of their mounts. If Lancoir and the officers were surprised, the trackers and ordinary guards were practically goggle-eyed – most of them had genuinely believed elves to be myths of a legendary past. Now here they were, taking their reins and gesturing kindly to them. Once shorn of all their baggage, they were led off on foot into the trees by one of the elves. As they went, Roujeark looked back over his shoulder to where the horses were disappearing in the opposite direction. He started, thinking that he had seen one of the elves leading them suddenly change into a horse herself. It had been but a brief, leaf-obscured glimpse, and a heartbeat later the whole herd had vanished with hardly a hoof-beat to be heard. He turned back, certain his eyes were playing tricks on him, and followed his comrades through the dripping trees.

After a while they began to descend into a wooded valley, which led them to a swift river. Rafts were waiting down by the riverbank, and they were ferried across the fast-moving water by tall cloaked elves wielding long poles in skilful strokes. No sooner had they disembarked than they were led up a damp slope, back down the other side and to the banks of a sister river. More craft were waiting beside this bank, but this time they were more like a cross between log-boats and coracles. They piled into these boats, surprised to find that there were enough to accommodate them all, and took up the leaf-shaped paddles. Curillian looked in surprise at Sin-Solar, their guide.

'What, are we going to paddle the eighty leagues to Firnon against the Sachill?'

'No,' said the saturnine elf. 'Since you are our guests, Sachill herself will bear us. Tell your followers to put aside the paddles.' The guide then got into the lead boat and from the prow leaned down to the river. Dipping a paddle into the current, its blade pointing upriver, he whispered a few flowing words over it. The river seemed almost to shudder in response. Then he adopted a trance-like posture in the prow, from which he did not emerge for a long time. The guards in each boat were treated to an eerie sensation when, as soon as they were all aboard, the boats started to inch out into the current as if of their own volition. At first the current started to tug it downstream, but then it held fast, as if kept in place by a restraining hand. Astonished and fearful, the guards gripped the boats' sides and eyed the water suspiciously. Then, one by one, the boats started to move off upstream, against the current.

'What is happening?' Roujeark asked the king, whispering lest he offend the sentinel elf, who shared their boat along with Lancoir and four others. Curillian smiled.

'As one who is gifted in magic, you should be telling me that. It is the spirits of the water. According to the wood-elves, every waterway, from the smallest stream to the mightiest river, has its own spirits, and they are friendly to the elves. The elves are very careful to keep running waters pure and unpolluted. Some say the spirits are the living tears of Prélan; others that they were handmaidens among his angels who were sent to Astrom to steward the waters; which it is, the elves do not tell the armists. A river like the Sachill might have hundreds of spirits, or possibly one great one. See?' He pointed. 'They glint in the water.'

Roujeark looked over the boat's edge into the river, and there he saw, to his amazement, flashes in the water. They looked like the glinting of fishes' scales, only they all pulled in one direction, not deviating from side to side. Captivated, he watched them ripple and wriggle. He trailed a hand over the edge, wanting to touch the water, but as his bandaged fingertips came close, they started to feel heat and resistance. Hastily he withdrew. He contented himself with watching the gradually changing scenery on the banks. Slowly the trees changed from the oaks, horse chestnuts and sycamores common in the East-fold to less typical species. Elms, birches and beeches started to predominate. They were normal at first, but then they started to diversify into strange shapes and varieties Roujeark had never seen before. Willows lined the bank the whole way along, but the further they went, the larger and more luxuriant they became. Were they throwing out their limbs further across the river, or was the river shrinking? A confluence came and went, and then suddenly the valley became steeper. Gradually upward they travelled, but no slackening did they notice in their pace. As they climbed into the higher recesses of the valley the trees started to change again, as the deciduous lowland species gave way to higher-dwelling conifers, cypresses and firs.

Above them the rain stopped, and as evening drew on the sky cleared to reveal the early stars. Some while later they were travelling by starlight, which danced and flashed upon their ethereal conveyances. Quite at odds with the fresh evening air, a strange drowsiness started to come over Roujeark, and seemingly over his companions too. Occasionally Roujeark thought he saw lights shining faintly in the distance in the trees, but with sleep creeping over him, his tired eyes couldn't be sure. Then he thought he heard soft singing in the trees, and it lulled him to sleep.

So smooth was their going that nothing disturbed his nodding until he was thoroughly asleep. He only came awake when a hand shook him by the shoulder. He opened his eyes to see the king looking at him.

'Wake up, we're here.' Roujeark rubbed his eyes.

'We're where?'

'Our destination. Welcome to eighty leagues deeper into Tol Ankil than you'll ever likely come again.' As Roujeark unsteadily exited the craft on to a finely manicured landing-bank, he tried to get his sleepy mind around the king's statement.

'Eighty leagues? How long have I been sleeping?'

'Not long, but your snores scared the magical fish away,' a guard said helpfully.

'We were travelling for less than a day,' said Curillian, starting to follow after the guide, who had not said a single word throughout the voyage.

'No wonder news travels fast in the forest,' Roujeark overheard Lancoir say. 'I wish we'd known about this last time.' Roujeark wondered what last time was.

'You don't know the half of it,' the king told his captain.

⋀

They had come to a sheltered bay created by a wide sweep of the river, which was much narrower here. The boats were stowed in subtle niches cut into the bank, and then they were led up a steep slope. Before them rose a steep hill, about whose waist the river ran. And around them were the most marvellous trees Roujeark had ever seen, broad-boled and impossibly tall. The trees were widely spaced, and in between them wood-elves were living out their daily lives. Some were washing clothes, some were weaving baskets or fashioning strange garments; others sat about in groups, talking or playing instruments of wood and wind. They seemed barely to notice the company of armists suddenly come into their world – they just carried on as normal. Roujeark gaped at them, never having seen anything like it. In a community of armists you might see one or two fair people, and every so often a real beauty; here, every elf was fair to behold, and many of them had a beauty that was rich and striking. No signs were there here of the dirt, disease and disorder which marred the existences he had known. It was not until they saw elves entering and exiting out of doorways set into tree-trunks that they understood that their dwellings were in the trees themselves. Looking up, they saw windows, platforms, treetop walkways and stairways.

Like many of the guards, Piron was wandering about as if in a daze. The very ground on which they walked seemed to whisper and laugh, and in the air above, vast colonies of all kinds of birds seemed to thrive. The trees themselves seemed alive, quivering and vigilant. The movement of their limbs and boughs was like a music in the forest, accompanied by the lyres, harps and pipes of the wood-elves. The atmosphere was peaceful, but it was close and seemed inexplicably stuffy, like a cosy, fire-warmed living-room. The air was filled with fragrance, sweet but so heady that it seemed to catch in their throats.

'Why have we come here?' Piron asked, his voice strangely muffled.

'To help, and be helped,' Curillian told him succinctly. Loosening the cloak at his neck, Curillian followed Sin-Solar up the slope, treading a path only faintly discernible from the grass on either side. As they passed through the wood-elf dwellings, Roujeark had the odd feeling that the elves didn't even know they were here, that it was actually some kind of waking vision of the past. He hurried to fall into step beside the king.

'How long has it been since our kind came here?'

'Guess.'

'A thousand years?'

'No. Never.' Roujeark looked at him in amazement. 'The Firnai have dwelt here unchanged for nine thousand years, since the early days of the First Chapter, millennia before our species even awoke... And in all that time, no foreigner has ever come here. Until now...'

Roujeark's mind span. In treading here with mortal feet, they were creating history. He drank in the sights, sounds and smells of this virginal encounter, but then a slightly unsettling thought announced itself to his brain. If the wood-elves' isolation was so rigid, what had happened to make them break the habit of eternity?

As they went on up the path, they left behind the wood-elf dwellings like armist suburbs. Up ahead of them loomed a hedge, a living wall. From beyond it rose up towering trees of mountainous height, a city-like cluster of green and brown columns. No guards or sentinels could be seen, but watchful eyes tracked them as they approached. Two enormous intertwined holly-trees formed a gateway by breaking the hedge and arching over the path. Once within the hedge, they seemed to enter into another world, another era. As they stepped over the threshold, everything seemed to slow down. The closeness and drowsiness of the atmosphere redoubled, but at the same time their senses heightened to report stimuli they had never before been conscious of. They had to crane their necks to look up at the trees, whose mighty summits joined together in a living vault. In the branches above them flitted birds of marvellous colours that none of them had ever seen before. Under this enormous canopy everything on the ground was thrown into shade, illuminated only by some startling radiance deeper within, while above them a thousand lamps lit the sky. Cast in shadows, the great trunks of the trees made it seem like they were trespassing in some primordial temple of titans. Many arm-spans wide and as high as towers, the armists were utterly dwarfed and cowed by these forest-giants.

Sin-Solar, seeming to glide over the grass, led them into the centre of the city, where stood a ring of the greatest trees yet. Twenty metres wide at the base and over a hundred high, it seemed impossible that they could have sprung from the same earth which elsewhere nurtured normal trees. And yet not just huge were they, but graceful and artistic also. Vast, arched limbs of trunks were flung out and enchanting patterns were drawn in living wood. Carven thrones, stalwart towers, leaping arches, mysterious recesses, spiralled boles and gossamer curtains; every conceivable type of feature was represented here in this natural architecture. It was as if all the trees they had ever seen were just essays in some fantastic art which was here mastered in a pinnacle of sculpted finesse.

At the summit of the hill, a flat crown was occupied by a great fountain, the source of whose copious waters could not be guessed. Every one of its many tiers and springs were lit by crystal lamps, so the water flashed and scattered liquid radiance far and wide.

Around the fountain the colossal trees grew in a large circle. In between each pair of trees gurgled a rivulet sprung from the fountain. Discrete pathways led from the fountain to ornate doors at the foot of each tree. Suddenly, at Sin-Solar's gesture, they were made aware of a deputation emerging from the tree at the northern edge of the circle. The cohort crowded past the fountain and watched, awestruck, as the king went to meet the elves and bowed to them. Unlike the folk outside the hedge who had been dressed in modest green and brown, these three elves were clad in silver-grey, like the smooth bark of a venerable old beech. In the luminescence of the fountain they seemed to shimmer like apparitions. Many of the cohort could not endure the sight for long, and others backed away from the fountain, fearing what effect splashes of its waters might have on them. To allay their fears, Curillian came back to them.

'My friends, welcome to Firnon, the city of the forest. This is as far as you can come. You have already come further than any mortals before you, and from here I must go alone with one or two others. Have no fear, the Lady Dácariel, queen of this forest, has made her realm welcome to you. See, here is a servant of hers, who will guide you to quarters which have been prepared for you. There, in a little while, we shall meet again. Lancoir, Roujeark, come. Surumo,' he summoned the commander as he went past. 'We are guests here, see that my armists conduct themselves with due decorum.' Surumo nodded and led the dazed cohort in following the elf-servant off down the hill. Then Curillian, Lancoir and Roujeark were left alone.

They approached the northern tree's doorway, where Sin-Solar and the two other elves stood waiting. Roujeark felt tiny standing under the tall figures, whose chests were level with his face. When he looked up into their faces, though, he saw solemn kindness and welcoming smiles. The elves turned and led them through the doorway.

Roujeark marvelled at the carving in the tree's interior, but he was not able to do so for long, as their guides led them right through the trunk and out on to a broad, balustraded walkway emerging from the opposite side of the trunk. Lit by lamps and small gems set into the handrail, the walkway instantly left the ground and led them up into the night, hugging the trunk all the way. Round and round the trunk the walkway led. Here and there it branched off to houses in the branches, or back into the trunk itself, but they continued upwards until the ground below was lost in a sylvan shadow. After a while, they realised that they had climbed so high that they were above the canopy of the forest. Enchanted, they paused on a north-facing platform and looked out over the living carpet of green. For miles and miles the trees stretched, but straight in front of them they gave way to dark slopes, and, in the distance, snow-capped peaks glimmering in the starlight.

Already giddily high, they had further to go. Their guides went on ascending tirelessly until they had led them to a wide hall perched amidst the uppermost branches. Woven screens and rich tapestries enclosed it and gave it shelter from the breeze, but they were so in keeping with the woodland colours that it seemed like a natural feature, the crown of the great tree. Little did they see, though, other than the majestic figure seated upon a raised dais. Here was the Lady of the Enchanted Forest. Many tales depicted her as a fell sorceress with her mysterious forest filled with strange servants, so the armists had heard tell of her, but the fables told in Maristonia fell far short of the reality. Beautiful and bewitching, she was dangerous and benevolent in equal measure, a mistress of many cunning arts beyond the reach of others. The elves knew her simply as Dácariel.

She sat upon a great carved throne whose arms were life-sized embodiments of stags, so lifelike that Roujeark thought they would spring at him at any moment. The dais was covered with rich green cloth and where it ended, the interwoven branches which made up the tree were interspersed with fabulous carvings depicting stags and centaurs and fawns. The whole place had a dryad charm, but there was nothing rustic about the queen herself. Dressed in a sleek robe the colour of forest berries, she wore warlike vambraces and a plumed helmet of steel. She grasped a great spear and against her throne a circular shield rested, bearing the image of a stag. No crown or adornments fit for a lady of great rank, only the martial accoutrements of a warrior queen. Ruling the largest settlement of Firnai outside of their ancestral home in the heart of Kalimar, she maintained her realm against its enemies with strength.

No less warlike were two figures standing on raised platforms around the edges of the chamber. Dressed in hunter's clothes, they held enormous yew bows which measured from throat to toe. So still were they when they entered that Roujeark thought that they were statues. He knew better when Sin-Solar, garbed and armed in similar fashion, went to take up his place on the third remaining platform. Surely these were his close kin?

It therefore fell to the other elves who had climbed the tree with them to usher them forwards.

Curillian, ar i ce Falakai, ey anionarteh maray. Curillian, king of the armists, and his companions.

The words seemed to have been spoken aloud, but they resounded in Roujeark's head like a thought. He recognised the word Curillian, but none of the others. Lancoir was no less dumbfounded than he in this surreal setting, but the king approached the dais and knelt before it. The queen arose from her throne and came towards him, speaking rich words which seemed to take wing and echo in their ears.

Graceaa Ruthion! Rol castothir lanim hánen nomille ilyadir eres marua des ton hánen. Welcome Ruthion! It makes my heart glad to have you here in my home.

Curillian kissed her outstretched hand and then rose. She stepped down from the dais, towering above him, as he made his introductions.

'This, My Lady, is Lancoir, High Captain of my Royal Guards, and Knight of the Order of Thainen.' Dácariel bowed low and spread her arms wide in acknowledgement. When she spoke, suddenly they could both hear the words properly and understand them.

'Of course, who could forget such a valiant ally of battles bygone? Welcome, Lancoir. May your strong swordarm here find rest for a time.'

'And this,' said Curillian, gesturing to the second of his companions, who hung back shyly, 'is my new friend, Roujeark.' Dácariel glided towards him, intrigued and smiling.

'Come, King of Mariston, you can do better than that.' She reached out and held Roujeark's face in a lingering caress. Her skin was warm, and her penetrating gaze made him feel like he had drunk heady wine. 'Why not say…wizard-to-be…pupil of Kulothiel…your guide to the Mountain?' Roujeark gaped at her, astonished. 'Oh, yes,' she said tenderly. 'We have heard much about you, young one; more, probably, than you have heard yourself.'

She paused, contemplating him. *So, you're the one*, he heard inside his head. His ears reported differently. 'So this is the mysterious armist wayfarer who crossed the border into Kalimar forty suns ago and then simply vanished, eluding even the best efforts of the Avatar patrols? One of such high destiny is always welcome in my court.'

She removed her hand and moved away.

'Now that we know who you are, it is only right that you should know us. Dácariel of the House of Firnar am I, queen of the woodland realm of Tol Ankil. These are my children, the guardians of my northern marches, my western marches, and my southern marches: Sin-Serin, Sin-Tolor, and Sin-Solar.' One by one they nodded their heads, but so alike were they that they could not be told apart, except one, whose face had a more feminine cast. 'They have come from their vigils in the far-flung eaves of the wood to greet you. Yet you may also find interest in the news that they bear.'

'What news, Lady?' Curillian asked.

'See for yourselves...' And suddenly a living vision was cast before their eyes, a recent memory brought to life, filling the tree-top chamber.

It was a dark evening at the edge of the forest. An armed company of men were venturing into the forest, treading warily. There was a score of them, and although they tried to be stealthy their noise spread far and wide. It was evident from their hesitant steps that they did not know where they were going, but even so they went a fair way through the trees before halting. They paused and produced axes, preparing to make a camp. The axes were only just laid against the smaller branches of the nearby trees when the arrows fell. It could not be seen where they came from, but there could be no mistaking their great number, nor the terrible accuracy with which they were fired. In the space of a few seconds, the intruders were all struck down by green-flighted arrows. Fear and shock had only just registered in the first faces as their companions fell before to a man they all lay dead, arrows protruding from eyes and necks. For a few moments all was silent, and then shadowy figures entered the scene. The vision zoomed in to show the newcomers picking among the dead bodies, investigating the fallen and retrieving their weapons. The same design was on all their hauberks, surcoats and shields: a double-headed grey falcon against a quartered green and black field.

'These are men of the Falcon Clan,' burst out Lancoir. 'They are erstwhile allies of ours.' He was shocked and angry. Curillian's face was neutral. The vision faded before them, leaving the throne-room as it had been before.

'And yet they dared to trespass in the forest, a place sacrosanct for our kindred ever since we first came here. By intruding thus, on earth forbidden to mortal feet, they invited their own deaths.' Roujeark thought it was Sin-Tolor who spoke in answer, though in truth he could not be sure. Lancoir likewise did not know which of the queen's children to face, but regardless he confronted them dauntlessly.

'So why not kill us also?' Sin-Solar stepped down from his pedestal and came close.

'You are here by special and unprecedented invite. Your king solicited permission first before bringing armed retainers within our realm. Had he not, my archers would have slain you all just like the Aranese. If they were trying to find a path to Oron Amular, they were woefully off-course, and my brother has paid them for their folly.'

'If others try, they will fare alike.' The succinct promise was uttered by Sin-Serin, the third of the queen's children, her voice barely discernible from her brothers'. Then the voice of Dácariel herself spoke again.

'All the champions and heroes of the world are abroad, responding to the call of Kulothiel. These men of the Falcon are not alone: the Hawk, the Charger, the Lion, the Unicorn, the Pegasus; all the Clans have sent contingents, and many others also. The Jeantar himself is with them. The King of Hendar rides with a strong mounted company in this direction and many of his vassals are also on the move. Courageous Ciriciens, intrepid Ithrillians, gallant Hendarians, even a dauntless warlord from the south, all are on their way. All have been seen. However they try to approach the Mountain, it will not be permitted for them to come through Tol Ankil. You alone, Curillian, friend of old, have been granted passage. For you alone have another purpose here, besides finding the Mountain.'

'What other purpose?' Roujeark piped up, his voice sounding horribly shrill and boyish in his own ears. Almost immediately he wished he hadn't spoken. All the elven eyes turned to him, before Dácariel fixed her gaze on Curillian again.

'Have you not yet told your companions, Curillian? Then let them see…' Another vision materialised in the centre of the room, so vivid and lifelike that it seemed like a world within a world.

A hooded figure was picking her way up a rough, mountainous path. It was a slender elf-woman, all alone. The wind clutched at her cloak and sent it streaming. Even from behind was evident the striking likeness of this person to Queen Dácariel. No clue was given as to where she was going, only that her path through the stones and grass was leading her up into the mountains. Up ahead, all was dauntingly black and bleak.

None of the armist viewers were unmoved by her seeming frailty and vulnerability. Curillian's jaw trembled as he watched.

'That is enough,' he said. 'You need show no more. It is true, then? Carea is in Faudunum, in the hands of the harracks?' The vision faded at his request and the face of the queen became visible again. It was drawn and pained.

'What you have been told, you have been told aright. It is so.' Having struggled to stay silent thus far, finally Lancoir could contain himself no longer.

'What is so? Who is Carea?' Roujeark looked at him side by side with the king and saw the yawning gulf of knowledge between them. Lancoir, many hundreds of years the junior, had not had the benefit of the king's royal education and wide-ranging experience. He looked pitifully out of his depth. Even the king's customary cool suddenly seemed less assured. But Curillian did not answer. Instead, Dácariel herself answered the knight's question.

'Carea is one the oldest elves still residing on these mortal shores. She is the daughter of an ancient wood-elf king, and possessor of some of the noblest blood in existence…and she is my mother's sister. What you have just seen is the last we ourselves saw of her, walking in the direction of Faudunum, the harrack stronghold in the midst of their mountainous realm of Stonad. We doubt not that she is now their captive.' She spoke patiently, but the pain was evident in her words. Lancoir was unsympathetic though.

'And what is she to us?' he hissed sidelong to Curillian. The three elf children bridled at the disrespect, but a three-fold glance from their mother calmed them. From a mass of unspoken words, Curillian answered him tersely and calmly.

'She can help us. She alone of all those who know the location of Oron Amular might be willing to help us.'

'But what about him?' Lancoir demanded in Roujeark's direction.

'You forget yourself, Lancoir, son of Lorumon,' Dácariel said firmly. 'You are here as a guest; no one here is answerable to you. But restrain your anger for when it is needed, and perhaps you will have your questions answered.'

Curillian went first. 'Roujeark knows *a* way to Oron Amular, but it is a way we cannot use without High King Lithan's consent. Roujeark did not know that when he offered us his help – he slipped past unbeknown to anyone one – nor did I know what way he had taken when I brought him along. If we tried to rediscover his route, even two or three of us, let alone a hundred, we would be accosted by the elves of Kalimar, disarmed and escorted back to Maristonia before ever we came within thirty leagues of it.'

'Then why did you bring...' Lancoir interrupted. Curillian held up his hand and spoke over him.

'He *does* know a way, we just can't use it yet. I hope to still make use of it, but we must perform this task to be allowed to go that way. We must persuade King Lithan to permit us passage. Don't you see, dear Lancoir, that we have no other choice? If we attempt the western passes of the Black Mountains, we could wander for months without ever finding another way – the Tournament would be long finished, won by someone else, even if we lived to rue it. But to go the way that Roujeark knows, uninvited, to defy the High King, is to court disaster. Yet if we rescue one of his most beloved subjects, a kinself no less, then he would be in our debt. He would permit us to retrace Roujeark's route. And, regardless, Roujeark needs to get back to the Mountain. Whatever the problems with the route, still I would have brought him. Prélan wished it so. He spoke to me on the day we left Mariston. He wishes Roujeark to come again to Oron Amular.'

As Curillian subsided, Roujeark remembered the king speaking similar words to him by firelight in the woods. He felt again the warm glow of reassurance that he had felt then, hearing confirmation from someone else of Prélan's calling on his life.

Sin-Serin spoke for the elves.

'As for us, we do not know the way to Oron Amular any more than you do. It is not common knowledge, even among the Firnai.

But in rescuing Carea, you would be putting all Elvendom, not just the High King, in your debt. Every service has its price. If you want passage, you must first rescue her.'

Lancoir was not yet placated.

'So that's it? The quest must be set aside for a mad rescue plan? Why haven't you rescued her, if she's as dear to you as you say? Has no one here remembered?' he demanded, raising his voice. 'We fought the harracks before, and the victory was as hard-won as it will prove unmatchable. Few can contend with the harracks in their own terrain. Even we who beat them never ventured deep into their domain, nor came within sight of Faudunum. If anyone has a chance there, surely it is the wood-elves and not us armists at all?'

Sin-Serin answered his question.

'Our power is in the forest; it is not in the mountains. We have learned, through bitter experience, that we are as vulnerable in the uplands as the harracks are under the trees. One of us may go with you as a guide, but that is all. The task is yours.' Lancoir was as discomfited as Roujeark had yet seen him. The knight appealed to his king.

'To challenge the harracks in Stonad, in their own back yard, is to needlessly risk the lives of the whole cohort. Better that we should go home and forget this whole business than die ignominiously in the mountains.'

'There is nothing to stop you returning to Mariston,' Dácariel told him. 'But if return you do, you will have fallen at Kulothiel's first hurdle, and others will contest the great prize without you.'

Curillian shook his head, refusing to contemplate the thought. For better or worse now, he was committed to this quest. Roujeark had listened with mingled excitement and fear in his belly, electrified at the thought that Prélan actually wanted him at Oron Amular, yet mind reeling with the thought of his current uselessness in the expedition. Scarcely thinking about what he was saying, he spoke up.

'I'm not sure what I can do, as a guide...or anything else...but whatever I can do, I am at your disposal, Lord King.' Curillian nodded and smiled faintly. He turned to look at his captain.

'I am invited to Oron Amular, and to Oron Amular I will go. I am resolved on this, and I can see no other way to ensure getting there on time and alive. Our quest depends on this. Besides, there is nothing ignominious about trying to save someone in need. I would go even if the quest were not at stake.' He looked up at the queen solemnly. 'I will go.'

Lancoir's face struggled to contain his misgivings, and Roujeark sensed the intensity burning in him. His eyes smouldered and his voice was thick with barely controlled wrath when he spoke.

'Then I, too, will go.'

VII

Rock and Snow

ONCE Back at the bottom of the great tree, Curillian took Lancoir and Roujeark aside before they rejoined their companions and spoke to them. The journey back down the wooden walkway had been fraught with tension and unspoken disagreement.

'I know you are not in favour of this mission, Lancoir, but I will undertake it nonetheless. I ask no armist to come with me, and no pressed armist – you least of all – will I suffer in my company. Whoever comes, we must be few. We cannot carry war into the mountains with any hope. We will neither overmaster the harracks nor lay waste their cold citadel. Rather, it is as shadows and thieves we must go. With stealth we will penetrate their stronghold and steal the captive back. Therefore, there is no risk of the casualties you fear. But make your decision swiftly: either stay here with the main cohort, or come with my volunteers.'

Curillian went straight to bed then, letting no task come between him and sleep. Lancoir instead went and reviewed his kit. Roujeark went with him, seeing him as the more likely source of answers. They joined the rest of the King's Cohort in the lodge that had been made available to them. It was a wooden structure built into a bank of earth, so discrete that you hardly noticed it until you were right outside. A carved wooden doorway gave onto a wide hallway running back into the earth. The hall was filled with a long wooden table at which the Royal Guards reclined in shirtsleeves. In their king's absence all had evidently been washed and well-fed, judging by the aromatic steam filling the air and the well-scraped bowls littering the table. Arms and armour had been piled to one side, and some of the guard had already taken to their beds in curtained niches cut into the walls. Overhead, the ceiling was a mass of tree-roots which had somehow been twined into wonderful patterns.

The happy banter died away almost immediately as Lancoir stomped in. Fists clenched, he took in the scene with a scowl and the armists' jests died on their lips. They knew the Captain of the Guard well enough to know when he was angry. Lancoir looked as if he might speak, and the armists braced themselves, but then he stalked off down the hall. Gradually the conversations resumed once he was past, and Roujeark felt the atmosphere recover as he followed the angry captain. Lancoir went right to the far end and sought out his own gear. Roujeark watched as the captain's anger seeped out in kit slammed down, weapons slotted resoundingly into scabbards and knots tied unnecessarily tight, the rope positively whistling and cracking in his hands. Some of the guards nearby were already asleep, but one or two were wakened and made nervous by their captain's ire.

'What are harracks?' Roujeark ventured to ask at last. Lancoir continued sorting his gear, but eventually answered.

'Harracks...' he snapped, but too loud, startling several others. He fixed each with a furious glare that made them turn away and mentally block up their ears. 'Harracks,' he repeated more softly, but hardly with less venom, 'are squat little bastards who live in the mountains that spawned them. They're so at home in stone that they're practically made of the stuff. Some say they're born of the stone itself. They're tougher than dwarves, slow-moving but ridiculously hard to kill. They blunt blades and smash shields. It's like trying to fight the mountains themselves. You've probably never heard of them, because the only time they've ventured down into the lowlands they've exposed weaknesses and been beaten, but get them in the mountains, around plenty of rock, and they thrive on it like elves in trees. That's why we've never taken them on at home, nor tried to flush them out, and that's why we shouldn't be trying now.' He thumped his backpack in frustration. Roujeark could tell that eavesdropping was still going on by the way some of the prone guards nearby jumped slightly in their feigned sleep.

Lancoir gripped his bag like he was going to rip the leather apart with his bare hands, but then slowly he relaxed.

'I just don't understand why he's doing it,' he said quietly, almost to himself. He was quiet for a moment. His next words were dropped so low that Roujeark had to lean in to pick them out. 'I've seen him impulsive before, we all know his quick-fire instincts on what's right, but never have I seen him risk so much for so little reason.'

Roujeark tried to mollify his wound-up companion. 'You heard the queen, Lancoir; all the great men of the world are on the move, converging for this tournament. Do you really want to miss out on that, or not even find out what's at stake?'

The captain was silent for a long time, eyes boring holes into his pack.

'No,' he conceded, muttering at the ground. 'We should be there.' Then suddenly he reached out and seized Roujeark's tunic and growled like a bear. 'But mark my words, Roujeark, nothing this big happens without trouble. The greater the prize, the greater the price.'

Ⴑ haken, Roujeark sat on his bed watching as Lancoir rooted out some volunteers. All thought of sleep was soon forgotten.

'Right, you deceitful dogs, I know you've been listening in. I know you're not asleep, so hear me now. Next bit of the mission's for a few only: I want a dozen volunteers to accompany myself and the king up into the mountains. Rescue mission. You know what's up there, so declare yourselves quick.' Roujeark felt dread creep up on him as he watched these courageous warriors daunted by this prospect. What's up there, he wondered, that they're so afraid of? Should I be more afraid? Piron and Surumo cast their bedding aside and stood up, but Lancoir instantly snarled them down.

'Not you Piron, you're not fit. Nor you, Surumo, someone's got to keep this rabble in order till we get back.'

The rest of the guards found it far harder to find their feet. Slowly, two stood up. A few moments passed and then another two stood also, and finally two more. Eventually twelve were standing. None could conceal their fear, but none were willing to back down now. Roujeark was both encouraged and dismayed to see his friend Andil among the standers.

'Andil, Aleinus, Haroth,' Lancoir called their names. 'Cyron, Edrist, Norscinde, Utarion, Antaya, Findor, Manrion. Good armists.' He paced up and down before them.

He surveyed the others, letting his gaze settle on two who were not Royal Guards. They were from the ragtag group that joined them at the royal hunting lodge. They wore different garb and had been sitting apart in a small group, yet nevertheless two of them now stood with the others.

'State your names.' Lancoir barked.

'Caréysin, sir,' said the one who was tall and slight.

'Lionenn,' said the other, not bothering to add 'sir'. He was shorter by far, but sturdier and thickly muscled. With a thick beard and mysterious marks upon his face, he was a fearsome sight to behold. Roujeark noticed a great battleaxe resting just beside him. He looked a match even for Sir Lancoir. The captain was sizing them both up.

'Lionenn, Konenaire are you?'

'Aye.'

'Been in the mountains before?'

'Once or twice.'

'Good. Keep your axe sharp.'

'Ah always do.'

Lancoir turned on the other figure. 'And you? Do you have the profession to match your name?'

'Yes sir, never missed yet.'

'Good, don't start now.'

Lancoir moved away, and Surumo spoke. 'I'll await the king's orders for the rest of the cohort.'

Lancoir nodded.

'What of the other trackers?' Surumo asked, jerking his head in the direction of a surly group further up the hall.

'We'll think of a use for them,' said Lancoir, scowling at the group. 'They know their stuff in the mountains, and more of us may yet need to cross them. Await your orders. Stay alert.' He turned back to his kit, then suddenly whirled around and barked a name. 'Aleinus,' he singled out the armist who had been the first to stand. 'Aleinus, why are you going?'

The guard in question, who looked quite young, forced a smile of bravado.

'Captain, if the king is going to fall, how glorious will be the deaths of those who fall beside Curillian, greatest of the Harolins?' Lancoir growled acceptance of that.

'Glory in death is what we all seek,' said Haroth, morbidly.

Lancoir smiled grimly.

'As so you should. But make no mistake about it: you may not know what the game is yet, but Curillian won't fall before it's all played out. The only question is how many of us will die along the way.'

Curillian allowed them a day's rest. The following day, he woke before the dawn and walked through the mists. He didn't know who his volunteers were yet, but he knew they would be ready when he was. He had one last conversation to have before he left, so he followed the shadow through the misty trees. Leaving the leafy citadel behind he pursued the blackbird ahead of him, certain that it meant him to follow her. The bird left him some way behind, and he lost sight of it in the mists. Hurrying forward, he came to the mossy shore of one of the many lakes which dotted this northern part of the forest. There, standing on a great boulder in the shallows, the black-cloaked Dácariel stood, motionless. He joined her, walking through the water until he reached a small boulder beside the one she was standing on. She spoke practically at first.

'The easiest part of your journey is over.'

Easy? thought Curillian. I've had a ship burnt out from under me, been ambushed twice in my own realm, and many of my armists already lie dead. What does difficult look like? He voiced none of these thoughts, knowing she guessed them all too nearly.

'This seizure of Carea is not an isolated act,' she went on. 'The harracks have been very active of late, and my folk have seen them consorting with the goblins. They have given the snow-elves much trouble and even raided some of the high valleys of Kalimar itself. Together they are a great threat, and they may even attempt an invasion of the lowlands. My heart forebodes about the timing of their unrest, so close to the tournament...If you have forces nearby, it would be well to deploy them closer to the mountains, and have them closer at hand in the event of need...'

'I will do so, Lady. Those in my cohort not coming on the mission will redeploy to the foothills north of your realm, ready in case of trouble. They shall not impose on you any longer than necessary. By your leave, I have prepared orders for other units to march and join them. Indulge me and spare a guide to lead two of my messengers by the swiftest routes to the southern border – that way, word will reach my nearest legion as fast as possible. If you are in need, the Eastern Army of Maristonia will be on hand to assist you. Consider it a token of my gratitude for your hospitality.'

'It shall be done.' They fell silent for a while, and the mists enveloped them. When Dácariel spoke again, it was no longer about strategy.

'You're going to a lot of trouble, Curillian, to rescue her...' The queen left the thought hanging, neither wholly statement nor question.

'Lady, you know that I would go to her aid even if nothing else were at stake.' His voice was solemn, even though it was muffled by the mist. She turned imperceptibly towards him.

'They say that no armist and wood-elf have ever been joined in love. Yet I doubt that anyone has ever come closer than you and she.' Curillian was suddenly aware of her making intense eye-contact.

'Some thought the rumours grotesque. For myself, it only showed just how special you were, that you were able to move such a one as she in her soul. We all knew you were special, Curillian, right from when you were born. The Silver Emperor, the High King, myself, we all knew. And yet, it may be that your great deed in the judgement of history was to reclaim the throne of your forefathers after being exiled for so long; or that your greatest deeds came and went in the wars long ago. Think you that you can surpass the glory of your youth? So, I ask myself, what do you seek at this tournament? Power Unimaginable? You have already wielded great power, O King of Mariston. Glory has its limits. What makes you think that this great thing is not reserved for another?'

'There is only way to find out, Lady. I go to compete not merely for the prize, but to discover, if it may be, what Prélan's will is in all of this. My heart forebodes that this is merely the start of great and terrible things. I go also to strive for the best of myself. It has ever been so. I challenge the greatest, defy the deadliest, and strive to emulate the best and noblest. The quest for excellence has defined me.'

'No, Curillian, it has not defined you. There is no doubt that you will leave a mark on history of surpassing excellence and nobility, but those things do not define you. They are merely the symptoms of true greatness. You are, and always have been, defined by your love of Prélan, by the closeness of your relationship with Him. Verily, Prélan blesses abundantly those who walk with Him. What could you ever have achieved without His guiding, enabling Spirit? You may go and compete, O mortal king, but you must be ready, if, in this case, the will of Prélan differs from the desire of your heart. I do not ask much of you – just do as you always have done, walk with Him. You will not fall from greatness unless you fall from Him.'

He said nothing. Staring out over the water he contemplated her words. He did not look at her when he felt her long hand caress his cheek. The hand withdrew. He heard the flutter of wings and knew that she had changed and left him.

⚔

Lancoir, Roujeark and the twelve volunteers were ready. They stood outside the lodge with their gear, and to it their wood-elf hosts had added many valuable supplies.

'Nourishing food, and warm cloaks, to help keep you alive in the mountains,' one of the elves had said. The rest of the cohort had been reunited with their horses and expected to be going again soon, but word had got round about a chosen few being taken on a special mission, and now they were disconcerted. Through the mists Roujeark could make out their worried faces. With the king still gone, none of them knew what to do next, but they did not have to wait long. Curillian came back to them, solemn and quiet. He spoke first to the officers, Surumo and Piron, calling them forward.

'My friends, with great patience you have been kept in the dark till now and asked no questions. But no longer. Up to this point, all I've told you is that we are bound for an unusual gathering in Kalimar. I can now tell you: we are bound for Oron Amular, the Mountain of High Magic.' He gave a few moments for the words to sink in and the amazement to lodge in their faces. 'Yes, Kulothiel, Keeper of the Mountain and Head of the League of Wizardry, is hosting a tournament to which all the princes and champions of Astrom have been invited. Between us, we will contest momentous prizes. Roujeark, our new friend, is bound thither, and he will be my guide. But to persuade the elven High King to grant us passage, there is a task I must perform first. That is why I venture into Stonad, the land of the harracks, now. It is a rite of passage. When I return, successful, then the main quest can resume.'

'However, I do not ask you to sit here idle in a foreign place. New counsel has reached me, warning me of dangers close by and far off. The two swiftest riders, with wood-elf guides, must make haste to the southern border of the forest whence we entered and speed messages to General Horuistan of the 15th. He is to march the entire legion north and encamp between the north-western reaches of Tol Ankil and the River Amretu. You will attach the cohort to his force and be under his command, unless new orders reach you from me. Be alert, for you may well be called for before all this is over. While the messengers travel, the rest of you may take a few days' respite, but after that you must rendezvous with the legion. On no account should any of you return into the forest, and the main legion not at all. Is that understood?'

'I have my orders, sire,' said Surumo in acknowledgement. 'For my part, I am content. I have no desire to intrude into old legends. But our swords will be sharp and ready if you need us.' They both saluted, but Piron could not hide the longing in his face.

'I would go with you, sire,' he said plaintively. Curillian clasped a hand to his shoulder, then his neck.

'I know, Piron. But you're not yet fully fit, and you need to be for this mission. Gather your strength now, for there is plenty ahead of you, great deeds and danger alike.'

Roujeark watched the king brief his two officers, watched him answer their questions, and watched him bid farewell to his cohort of guards, who were desperately sorry to be parted from him. Not many were eager to march into harrack territory, but they had come to an alien place, and were uneasy about lingering here without their king. But such was Curillian's authority that they accepted his strange decision.

Then Roujeark noticed Queen Dácariel materialising as if out of the mist itself. Swathed in her tall black cloak, and accompanied by one of her formidable offspring, she watched the farewells before gliding to Curillian's side. She spoke soft words to him that only he could hear. He looked at the queen's companion and nodded.

'Lancoir, we are ready?'

The captain gave the barest inclination of his head, his face set grim.

'Good, then let us lose no time. Sin-Serin here will accompany us, and be our guide, as her brother was before. We march to the northern border of the forest, and thence into Stonad in the mountains beyond.' The armists all bowed their heads and each in turn received the elf-queen's blessing. Then she spoke words over them together.

'...*Tûh Prélan ábécos érese livon ey allédos rol amaluph*...May Prélan smile upon your mission and grant it success.'

⋀

Sin-Serin led them along a faded and ancient path through the trees. When dawn came, it drove away the gloom and revealed a fresh and glistening forest. Droplets of water left over from soft rain in the night dripped all around. They caught the sunlight as they did so and flashed, making the leaves look as if they were made of gold. The springy grass swayed in a light breeze and vestigial shreds of mist flitted amongst the trees.

The way was long on foot, and the ground was steadily rising, but Sin-Serin marched them at a stern pace and in four days they had reached the edge of the forest. They took their leave of the sentinels at the border and found that their feet were on an ancient and faded track. As they exited from under the eaves of the forest, they saw it march uphill, away north alongside the River Pharaphir, the parent river of the Sachill.

'Ought we follow the river?' Curillian asked of Sin-Serin. 'It will surely be watched.'

The elf nodded sagely. 'There is nothing for it. It is too easy to get lost in the mountains using any other path.'

So they climbed, nervous and watchful. At first the gradient was gentle, and the river lay open beside them under the sun, glinting in the warm light. It was not as hot as Roujeark was expecting out in the open air, but he did not realise how high they had already climbed – almost the same elevation as his home in the Tribune Valley, where the fierce heat of Maristonian summers softened into alpine warmth. He enjoyed the sun but, looking up, he saw that the foothills above them were beset by glowering clouds. He shivered looking at them. Gone were the days when the uplands had positive associations for him, happy childhood memories buried beneath a layer of pain.

On the first day, their path wound in zigzags up green slopes made damp by a hundred tiny rivulets racing to join the great river below. Roujeark was a little out of practice, but he was enjoying the hike. It was obvious, though, that the guards around him, less used to trekking in the uplands, were not so happy. On the second day, the grass gradually thinned out and lost its glossy green as browner hues started to take over. Where before they had marched through miniature forests of fern, now they trudged past clumps of heather, mossy hummocks and grass-crowned stones. Down below, the unobtrusive valley sides started to close in above the river and it shrank as it flowed past steepening slopes and overhanging banks. Behind them, the forest which had seemed so vast now looked small and far off. Looking down, Roujeark felt like he stood on the ankle of a giant whose legs the trees were forbidden to touch, such was the abrupt change between forest and hillside. Again he looked up, and the crags above him flitted in and out of dark clouds like furtive titans. With increasing regularity, the sun disappeared behind clouds and swathes of shadow fell on the valley sides. The low clouds started to envelop them in an uncertain welcome. Time and again they paused to look back, but the receding forest was now only intermittently visible, peeking sometimes from behind curtains of wandering vapour.

Sin-Serin permitted them only rare and short breaks. Each time Roujeark paused, flushed with the effort of climbing, he soon became chilled and found himself piling on more clothing. Before long they were walking exclusively in clouds, condemned to dank, muted conditions. The temperature dropped alarmingly as a cold wind blew down from the mountains. It was a good thing that the king's foresight had made them well-prepared for an environment such as this. Warm layers were donned and over the top they had sheepskin coats and waxed cloaks to resist the moisture in the air.

'I'm rarely pleased to see clouds,' Roujeark overheard the king saying to Lancoir, 'but these are more than welcome – they'll hide us from unfriendly eyes.'

'For the moment...' came the guarded response.

They passed sidestreams braided with stones and caught occasional glimpses of the rocky staircases by which they had fallen into the main valley. They crossed more and more stretches of scree and loose rocks, which lay in their path like gnarled blankets casually draped across the hillsides. Ankles were turned and knees and shins were scraped. By the end of the second day, the landscape changed again. The tight valley suddenly opened up into a great U-shaped trough, flat-bottomed but walled with towering slopes fearsomely sheer.

The path, such as it was, led them past a spitting waterfall, which fell, as if from nowhere, out of an unguessed shelf above. Soon it was not just splashing falls which assaulted them with water: the damp mists in the air turned into driving rain and soaked them through. They made a sodden camp in the shelter of a low overhang of rock and conjured as good a meal as they could. The night was passed fireless and cheerless.

The morning, though, was splendid. Gone were the rains and the low clouds, and now revealed to their sight was a stunning theatre of rock. Roujeark had seen such places before, in the Carthaki Mountains. The more pious mountain-dwellers said that Prélan had scooped out the broad channels to display His majesty; the less pious were of the belief that they had been dug by giants to ease their travels. The wide valley looked like the empty hull of a rock-ship, and it stretched off into the mountains as far as they could see. Shimmering waterfalls cascaded down its flanks, gracing the sombre, rounded peaks above. Up at the rims of the valley, though, clouds lurked like distant spectators.

'Long ago,' Roujeark heard the king's voice beside him, 'when it pleased Prélan to keep the world colder, vast floods of ice gouged out these mountainous valleys like frozen warships, their broad prows snapping off all the rock that lay in their paths. In those times the world was changed, and what was once jagged became smooth.'

Roujeark listened with interest, hearing lore that was scarce heard by any outside the privileged class which could afford to attend Maristonia's universities.

'See the Pharaphir there, making its lonely way through the flat bottom of the valley? The river's all that remains of a monolith of ice – what the scholars call a glacier – which once would have soared so high as to fill this basin, right up to the rims.' Roujeark looked up at the cloudy rims, scarcely able to believe that all beneath had once been locked in ice.

'Somewhere up ahead,' the king told him as they trudged along together, 'way up in the mountains, where snow lies year-round, the Pharaphir probably still springs from a shrunken glacier, though I confess I've never seen it.'

'I've heard the tales of such places,' enthused Roujeark. 'Of high valleys where plains of ice groan like living things. And snow-folk dwell there, or so the story-tellers say...'

'Snow-folk?' Curillian laughed. 'I think they're a fairytale even to the elves.'

They would have continued to wander, marvelling, through that mighty open-air cavern, but Sin-Serin took them close to the cliff-like sides and had them hugging the steep slopes as they walked.

'This is the harracks' porch,' she said. 'Our knowledge stretches no further, but we know this is the beginning of their domain. We must take great care.'

From then on, they grew to dread every stone-fall and constantly craned their necks up, fearfully expecting hidden foes to reveal themselves in ambush. Rounding a bend in the valley, they saw that the valley did not stretch on unimpeded for ever, as it had at first seemed, but was filled with a great narrow ridge, tall and sharp as a ship's prow. Shard-like, and obsidian-dark, it virtually cut the great rounded trough into two smaller valleys. Two branches of the Paraphir opened out, rushing either side of the ridge.

A bitingly cold wind rushed down from the mountains to greet them, and they felt the temperature plummet. With the wind came fresh clouds and new rain, icy cold this time. Their discomfiture soon turned to concern as the rain started to harden into snow. They trudged onwards, sometimes leaning acutely to keep making progress against the wind. The vicious precipitation stung their faces and any other patch of flesh left exposed. None of their voices had been raised above murmurs for days now, but Curillian had to shout into Sin-Serin's ear just to be heard.

'Which side of this ridge ought we to go?' The wood-elf seemed unsure. She, too, shouted to make her response audible.

'I do not know – it is likely that any path up this valley will take us to the stone city.'

The king made his decision for her.

'We go left.'

Roujeark grew more and more miserable – the snow showed little sign of letting up, and if anything the air seemed to grow colder, making his throat and nostrils smart. His feet were well-shod, but even so he began to feel them grow damp. Curillian led them now, since Sin-Serin had come to the limit of her knowledge. Desperate to gain some shelter from the terrible wind, the king led them to the western side of the left-hand valley. There they were sheltered from the worst onslaught, and found a narrow path cutting up the rock-face. Barely broad enough to walk on, it seemed to have been purposefully created, but so many rocks, fallen from the heights above, littered the way that it was hard to be sure.

They forged up for as long as their strength held out, and then they were forced to stop. They made the most of a little overhang to shelter from the snow and minimise the risk of being struck by falling stones. They swept out the worst of the encroaching snow and laid out blankets. Their wet cloaks they took off and fastened to the overhang as crude windbreaks, replacing them with spare dry cloaks. Roujeark huddled down, shivering, and found himself between two different conversations. To his left, the king and the elf debated in low tones.

'This is a fierce storm for early *Pleuviel*, anyone would think we had set off in winter. The snow is already shin-deep on the track ahead, it must have been snowing here for some time', the king surmised.

'Snowstorms can strike at any time in the mountains. It may shelter us from the harracks', Sin-Serin replied. 'But it will be perilous as we climb higher. You may find that the weather is a worse enemy to you and your comrades than any stone-foot.'

On his right, several of the guards were grumbling, teeth chattering, as they huddled together and tried to keep warm.

'Coming up here was a fine idea, wasn't it? Hope our bloomin' guide knows where she's taking us.'

'Look at her there in her tunic and thin cloak, hardly affected by the cold. Maybe she doesn't feel it?'

'Or maybe she's too proud to show weakness in front of us...'

'She's magic, just like that elf-lady back in the forest. It'll be her magic keepin' her warm.'

'Well why doesn't she bloody well share the goods?'

As if to take herself away from their envious looks, Sin-Serin disappeared off into the snow, and Curillian ducked under the overhang to join them.

'Whatever magic she has, she isn't using it right now.' Apparently he had overheard, or guessed, their conversation. 'Elven powers are less potent up here in the mountains, just as the harracks are weaker when out of their element; any attempt to use unnatural abilities here would send an unmistakeable signal to watchers.'

Roujeark looked up at those words, but the idea vanished just as soon as it had appeared – he was too cold to think about any magic.

'Right now,' the king went on, 'she is simply scouting ahead. If she appears to be less susceptible to the cold than us, it is simply because of the natural grace bestowed on elven constitutions. It was the same with men once, long ago, before they turned away from Prélan and forfeited many of His blessings. Now, though, try to get some sleep, we'll move off before dawn.'

True to the king's word, Lancoir roused them all while it was still dark. The barest glimpse around their improvised curtains told them it was still snowing, and that it had accumulated deeply on the narrow path outside. They awoke deeply stiff and unspeakably cold. It took a lot of stamping and flexing before Roujeark could even feel his fingers and toes. They moved off carefully, practically wading through the snow, knowing that even a slight miscalculation could send them sliding down the sheer slope to their right. Sin-Serin was back with them, but if she had gleaned any particular insights on her reconnaissance, she did not share it with them.

Roujeark was no longer merely miserable, just deeply worried. A child of the mountains, he had never known exposure like this. His experiences of snow had been limited to brief forays, and during the heavy stuff he and his father had kept snug inside next to the fire. He was not sure how much longer he could last in conditions like these. Full springtime might be burgeoning down on the plains below, but up here in the mountains winter could re-exert itself whenever its capricious mood took it. Up ahead, he heard one of the guards complaining to Lancoir.

'Why don't we go back? We'll die in this snow without shelter or fire...' Lancoir, though, was unmoved.

'We will not go back. We will make use of this snow for as long as we can. Endure it or be left behind.' Whatever discomfort he himself was feeling, Lancoir, tougher than all of them, was ruthless in dragging the others along with him.

And so they plunged on, braving the snow as best they could. Several times they heard ominous rumblings above them and were soon after showered with snow falling down from the cliff. On one such occasion, Aleinus, the first volunteer, was nearly knocked off the path and into thin air, prevented only by the steady hand of Lancoir, who reached out and caught him.

After an interminable stretch of time, their path seemed to bring them above the level of the trough-valley's rim, for the ice-sheened rock wall on their left gave out. Shaking with cold, Roujeark was dimly aware of gentler slopes stretching away into a blurry distance. All was white here, covered in snow deeper than any they had yet come across. An ill-judged step brought the snow up to his waist, and he had to be tugged out by two of the guards. He could no longer feel the deadly burn in his limbs, and an eerie numbness started to settle over his body like a suffocating blanket. He lost all awareness of where the others were in relation to himself. He barely heard the latest rumble, although it was louder than the ones before. A deep thrumming built up in his ears, soon accompanied by waves of crunching, coming rapidly nearer. Too late he looked left and his vision was filled with a powdery juggernaut. His feet were swept out from under him, his mouth and nose filled with snow and he instantly lost sight of his companions. Terrified and panicking, he was carried along, now submerged in the snow, now just gasping clear. He was turned over and over and around until finally he came to a halt, thoroughly disorientated. By great luck, in his final position he was only covered by a thin film of snow. Scrabbling frantically at it he broke through and glimpsed the muffled grey of the world above. Fleeting relief was soon swamped by a lethargic blackness which stole over him. In the last few seconds before losing consciousness, he heard soft feet crunching near him, and then, as his eyelids slammed shut, a pale shadow reaching down to him.

※

VIII

In the Company of Legends

ROUJEARK Came to and did not know whether he was still in this world or in the next. Wherever he was, he was resting, and the space around him was warm. A pale blue light was about him. Feeling was coming back into his limbs and they burned like fire. His head swam. Gingerly exploring his environment with his fingers, he felt thick furs under him, soft and warm. Looking up, he could see nothing except a blue haze. Gradually though the details filtered through, and he felt sure his eyes were telling him that they could see a ceiling of ice – neatly shaped into blocks – but ice nonetheless. The incongruity of it baffled him. Where was he? He had no memory of coming here; he must have been brought. He turned his head one way, and saw a figure lying beside him. One of the guards, pale and unmoving. Caréysin, he thought. Yes, his bow lay beside him, unbroken. He turned his head the other way. On the other side of him was another figure, another guard, Lionenn, clasping his great axe.

It wasn't until he mustered the strength to sit up that he began to make sense of it all. He was in an enclosed space, barely a dozen feet wide. A low domed ceiling ran overhead. Whiter light peeped through cracks in the blocks to pierce the pervading bluish hue, and through a small aperture like a vent. Both the walls and the ceiling were made of ice. The only way of exit was a narrow tunnel opening out of the wall. Despite the cold light, it was oddly snug. Inside were his companions. Or most of them. Arrayed with their feet inward to form a snug circle, they were packed into the ice-chamber as tight as sardines in a pan. All were out cold, showing no signs of life, except two who were sitting up like him. Lancoir and Curillian both had their knees drawn up to their chests, and both looked drawn and pensive. Roujeark started to share their sobriety as his curiosity about his surroundings gave way to concern about his companions. Two of the guards and Sin-Serin were missing, even after he had recounted twice. He did not know them all by name yet, but three were definitely missing.

The king and the captain did not seem about to be forthcoming, so Roujeark resumed his inspection of their accommodation. Each armist had ample furs both under and over him, wrapping them in a cocoon of warmth, and the collective generation of body heat made for a very comfortable atmosphere. As the warmth and life flowed back into him, he became impatient.

'What is this place?' What he had thought was just a whisper seemed devastatingly loud in that confined place, and his own words rang in his ears. No one answered him. Perhaps even the all-knowing Curillian was as mystified as he. Then there came a scuffling from the tunnel, and all eyes turned that way apprehensively. It continued, growing louder, until an odd conveyance emerged from the tunnel's mouth. A long sled glided into the small space between two of the sleeping figures. Bulky-looking contents were well-wrapped in skin covers and ropes. Once it had nosed fully into the chamber, the person who had been pushing it entered in after it. Roujeark watched a lanky white fur-clad figure unfold itself and stand upright, pushing back its heavy hood as it did so. Underneath was a tall face, delicate yet gaunt, and covered with thick hair the colour of liquid silver. Yet Roujeark saw nothing but the eyes. Two piercing eyes of a blue so pure and deep they couldn't possibly be real. Twin pools of icy sapphire they were, beautiful, and utterly transfixing. They regarded each of the figures in turn, and if any expression could be read in them, it was neither hostility nor love, but curiosity. Curillian gaped back, with as much unabashed amazement as the other two.

'I thought you were a legend...' he breathed, barely loud enough for Roujeark to catch the words. Unoffended and uncomprehending, yet apparently satisfied by her silent survey, the newcomer bent over her sled, deftly threw back the wrappings and produced, as if from nowhere, bowls and spoons made of horn. Roujeark marvelled as he watched a pot uncovered. Its cunning fastening was removed, and steam sprang forth. All of a sudden, the small space was filled with a wonderful aroma. Roujeark's stomach growled volubly, but just as he had plucked up the courage to address the strange host, the newcomer left as suddenly as she had arrived, darting back into the tunnel with the litheness of a mountain-cat.

Roujeark and Lancoir looked at each other for a moment, and then they both lunged for the food, only Curillian maintaining his dignity. They scarce had time to admire the cunning of the pot's placement and portability, so absorbed were they by the food. It turned out to be a broth, full of strips of meat and fragrant with rock-herbs. The meat was of some lean mountain-creature, tough and stringy. It would have been considered uncouth at a genteel lowland banquet, but here, after near-death in the snow, it was satisfying beyond measure. Those guards who had not been roused by the heavenly aroma were soon awakened and given horn bowls full of the nourishing broth. They did not speak, and before they were finished eating, the stranger came back. This time she came with Sin-Serin in tow, the wood-elf looking quite at ease and none the worse for wear.

With ever so slightly more friendliness in her startling eyes than before, their mysterious host surveyed them once again and then spoke a few words in a soft, melodious language. It was as soft and furtive as snow, quite unlike the tongue spoken among the wood-elves, yet lovely in its own way. Sin-Serin interpreted for them, though even she did not seem wholly fluent.

'Aiiyosha of the Cuherai declares that you are welcome, and bids you follow her to her house.'

They were given no chance to respond, for even as the words finished leaving Sin-Serin's lips the mysterious Aiiyosha vanished again, diving into the tunnel. The wood-elf wordlessly ushered them to follow, and so, one by one, they entered the tunnel. Only when he tried to bend down did Roujeark realise just how stiff and weak he was. And there was small comfort to be had in the tunnel, which was cold and alarmingly narrow. The ice was painfully cold under hand, so he pulled down the sleeves of his coat to cover his palms. They had no idea where they were going, but from up ahead, the scuffling of their more agile host came echoing back to them. It was just as well, for they came to a junction in the tunnel, where two ways branched off at right angles to each other, and only the sound coming from ahead told them which to take.

The journey was not actually that far – it just seemed to drag on because their awkward limbs made heavy weather of it – and eventually they came to an opening. They stood upright in another warm blue chamber, but this one was larger than the one they had left. Furs and patchwork quilts hung from the icy walls, and deep recesses lined the far wall. More thick furs were spread lavishly on a raised circular area in the chamber's centre. There sat Aiiyosha, with two others beside her. All were cross-legged and dressed alike, and all regarded the king's party with the same intelligent ice-blue eyes. They were gestured to come and sit with the trio of fur-clad figures. As he settled himself stiffly down, Roujeark could scarcely see any differences between the three hosts, except two were female and one male. Aiiyosha, in the centre, spoke again, and Sin-Serin translated the same welcome as before.

'Aiiyosha of the Cuherai bids you all welcome, children of the southern mountains.'

Curillian bowed low, and then, once seated, introduced himself and his companions.

'Curillian, son of Mirkan, king of Maristonia am I, and these armists with me are members of my royal guard...'

Aiiyosha spoke again and watched Curillian as the translation was made.

'Here among the Cuherai we do not count ancestors or titles, for we are few, and we are simple.' More words were spoken, and Sin-Serin dropped the first person. 'She says she is the daughter of Cuherl, which makes her a princess among the snow-elves. She and her family are the only ones of their folk living in this part of the mountains, although others are elsewhere.'

Now Curillian had something to go on. Like everyone not of that race, he had believed the Cuherai, the snow-elves, were a myth, a unique people long since vanished from the world, if they had ever walked it, but the name of Cuherl was familiar, for the great lineages of the three elf-kindreds of Kalimar were still part of a Harolin prince's education. Cuherl was the great-grandson of Marintor, king of the sea-elves, and therefore his daughter Aiiyosha was in the equivalent generation of her kindred as Sin-Serin was in hers, separated from the head of the kindred by four generations. The wood-elf addressed their host directly in her own tongue.

'Let me say again, Aiiyosha, how honoured I am to come into your home. Alas, too seldom do the children of the wood and of the snow meet, but I am delighted to make your acquaintance.' Aiiyosha nodded in acknowledgement, and then spoke in Curillian's direction again.

'She says that two of your party were lost in the avalanche. They were buried too deeply by the snow, beyond reach. She says she is sorry.'

Curillian could see the sympathy and sorrow in his host's face and was amazed at how tangibly the feelings were etched there. Eons of dwelling in this rarified world of ice and snow had clearly done nothing to stem the expression of emotions.

After an appropriate pause, more words came. 'She wants to know why you have left your realm and come to hers,' Sin-Serin told Curillian.

Curillian told the brief tale of their mission in the mountains, how they had come from Tol Ankil with Dácariel's blessing to rescue Carea, whom they believed was being held captive by the harracks of Faudunum. At the mention of those last two names, the sympathy went out of Aiiyosha's face, and those of her companions, and all three made hostile growling noises.

'So, they're not any fonder of the stone-foots than we are...' muttered Lancoir to Roujeark, earning a brief, mercurial glance from Aiiyosha. The snow-elf chieftain regarded Curillian for a long time, and then spoke through Sin-Serin again.

'She says you are a friend of hers if you are not a friend of the harracks, but she hopes you will not bring about trouble for her people. The Cuherai avoid the harracks and the harracks avoid them, but a confrontation in the cold city might spell danger for her family. She wants to know what you plan to do.'

'Tell her we are very grateful for her succour, without which we would all be dead, and that the last thing we want is to repay her with distress. Yet we cannot leave our mission unfulfilled. I simply intend to rescue the princess, getting in and out as quickly as possible. I do not intend to confront the harracks or fight them any more than is necessary. She has done much for us, and we are in her debt, but can she help us further, in Prélan's name?'

Curillian held the snow-elf chieftain's eye as his plea was conveyed, and waited quietly as she weighed it up. The three snow-elves turned slightly towards one another and conversed in tones so soft that the armists would have been unaware of it had everything else not been so quiet. After a long discussion they turned back to their guests, and Aiiyosha spoke her answer.

'She says she will give you food and supplies to keep you on your way; what is more, she says she will lead you back to the path to Faudunum, for we are far out of the way here, and much higher up. Yet neither she nor any of her folk will go with you to the city or raise arms to help you.'

After the main message was delivered Aiiyosha spoke a final sentence, softer than the rest. Sin-Serin hesitated before passing it on. 'She says that if any of her people come to harm, you will none of you leave the mountains alive, though you may escape Faudunum.'

⚐

The armists returned to their own chamber, but Sin-Serin remained behind, closeted with her distant kin. They mourned their comrades who had fallen, praying for their souls and drinking a toast of the snow-elf cordial in their honour. Manrion and Haroth were their names, brave warriors now buried deep in the ice, far from home.

In spite of their weariness, Curillian pressed them to haste, adamant that they should leave soon, and that time was running short. So, they made sure they were ready to leave as soon as Sin-Serin returned. More snow-elves, who might have been Aiiyosha's sons and daughters, came and brought them packs of food and skins of a sweet and refreshing cordial. They also gave them fur garments which were much warmer than the clothes they had brought with them. The armists tried to convey their gratitude, but the snow-elves merely smiled and took their leave without speaking. Some time after they left, Sin-Serin returned, and Curillian was eager for further information from her.

'I have learnt much from Aiiyosha and her folk. It seems we took a wrong turn back in the valley,' the elf told him. 'We should have gone to the right of that great ridge, not left. But going right would have led us to the harracks' first outpost. Coming this way, though it has brought us trouble, perhaps spared us trouble of a worse sort. The Cuherai were aware of us before ever the snow fell. They kept a close eye on us, and so were at hand when the avalanche came. Those of us who could be saved were hauled from the snow and borne miles uphill to the abode of the Cuherai, where we now rest. Since today is already far gone, we will leave with first light on the morrow, and the Cuherai will guide us. We are far above the valley of Rumuron, a rocky brother of Pharaphir, but they will lead us back to that valley, only further along. They say we should not be worried, for the snow is not so bad across the river. Apparently, there is a rope-bridge above Rumuron's rapids. Once across that stream, and the dry gorge beyond, we will be in sight of a harrack fort and the track to Faudunum, and thus be able to guide ourselves.'

⟁

In the morning, they reluctantly left their shelter. This time taking the other route at the fork in the tunnel, they crawled up a slope and emerged out into the open. Roujeark gasped as a blast of chill wind hit him. The air was thin and cold, and he felt light-headed. Then his eyes took in the view, and he was amazed. From this glistening snowfield, a wide panorama of the mountains could be seen. Mountain peaks, hard and black and draped with ice, rose behind them, and before them the ground fell away into the valleys far below. They all stood and stared, awed by the majesty of the view. None of them had realised how high up they had come.

'Where there is snow, there the harrack treads not,' Aiiyosha told them through Sin-Solar. Then she produced strange shoes for them to wear. Wide and circular, they were made of light wooden frames criss-crossed by strings of animal tendon. They strapped them to their hob-nailed boots and suddenly found that they could walk on the snow without sinking. Now they could look at the snowfield differently – it was no longer a wearisome barrier to be crossed only with great difficulty. Thus-equipped, they made good progress downhill, led by the snow-elf chieftain, who was towing a heavily laden sled. At one point she stopped and called Sin-Serin and Curillian to her. Pointing away to the north-east, she uttered a single word.

'Faudunum.'

Curillian traced her finger down to the valley, which just showed as a slit in the ground. Then, he followed the valley along as far as it could be discerned. Although he could not see the city, he now knew roughly where it lay. For the meantime, though, they carried on downhill, barely pausing and hardly speaking all day. Only at the end of the first day did the snow start to thin out. Now it was no longer a deep field, but a thin blanket. Aiiyosha led them into a secret shelter, which had been completely invisible to them until she revealed it. It seemed to be some sort of frequently used outpost of the snow-elves, for inside were bedding, sleeping compartments, and best of all, stores of food. They ate heartily, then rested gratefully in that place, nursing aches in a whole different set of muscles after the long downhill march.

When they left in the morning, the entrance to the shelter vanished to sight as soon as Aiiyosha concealed it again. Though they took great precautions, Roujeark thought, the snow-elves really didn't need to worry about anyone finding their shelters. Halfway through that second day, still descending steeply, they came to the edge of the snowline, where the ground beneath starting patching through. Aiiyosha halted abruptly.

'She will go no further,' Sin-Serin told them. 'But fear not, she has told me the rest of the way.'

Now they saw what the sled was carrying. The snow-elf chieftain unloaded it of packs of food, one for each of them. They gratefully stowed them in their own packs and gave her thanks. Curillian bowed low and thanked her again. Aiiyosha seemed somewhat bemused by their manners, but she did not drag out the farewell. She placed her hands on Sin-Serin and Curillian in turn, and uttered over each a blessing in her own tongue. Then she was gone. At first, they watched her amazingly nimble progress back up the mountain, but very soon they lost her amid the snowy contours.

'Well,' said Lancoir, 'I doubt if we'll see her again.'

'Maybe not,' answered Sin-Serin, 'but she'll see us. They have eyes capable of following us wherever we go in these mountains. Do not take her threat lightly.' Then the wood-elf turned to Curillian and spoke softly to him as they surveyed the terrain below them.

'After you left on that first night, Aiiyosha told me a strange thing. She said that one of her kin has gone missing. Apparently, he vanished in the vicinity of Faudunum.'

Curillian looked up at her. 'What? Why would one of their kind stray so near the stronghold of their enemies?'

'It is strange indeed.'

'Well,' said Curillian, 'maybe we'll end up rescuing two captives, not one.'

'Perhaps,' the elf agreed. 'Or we may end up repaying our host in a different way.'

Curillian did not stop to ponder Sin-Serin's riddle, but struck off downhill, eager to be going. He was conscious of time ticking away – they only had until the first moon of summer to reach Oron Amular, and he still had no idea how long yet was the road thither.

After a few more hours of tramping they came back to the rim of the valley and found that it plummeted down no less sharply here than further down where they had left it. Its side was like a cliff dropping away beneath their feet. Looking out across it, they saw the same high ridge rising out of the valley floor, sheer and precipitous. They watched eagles launch themselves from eyries nestled in its impossibly steep sides to patrol the skies. Behind the knife-edge ridge the opposite rim could just be seen, with rugged slopes rising beyond. There would have been no way across but for the bridge. It was a rickety structure of ancient wood and rope, swaying and creaking in the breeze. None of the guards looked keen to use it.

Curillian and several others advanced up to it. Lancoir tested the first plank doubtfully with his foot and jerked the rope hand-rail. They all watched the whole bridge shudder and jump about like a skittish colt, and nerves fluttered in their bellies. For Roujeark, though, there was a deeper dread. Apprehension flooded him, making all his senses tingle and the hairs on the nape of his neck stand on end. He scanned both sides of the gorge with deep misgivings.

'Clearly this was not put here for our convenience,' said Curillian.

'This bridge can only have been put here by the harracks,' mused Sin-Serin, 'for the Cuherai would need it not.'

'And yet they cannot use it often,' observed the king. 'See what bad repair it is in. If they do not like to come near the edge of the snow-elves' territory, then perhaps there is hope that we may cross in peace.'

Sin-Serin gave answer enough by remaining silent, doubt etched in her normally unreadable face. Lancoir voiced his own thoughts.

'Consider, my king, were we to cross, this would be our only retreat from trouble. I like not the thought of such a bottleneck at my back.' He gave the bridge another speculative shove to emphasise his point. Curillian nodded, acknowledging the fact. He looked to Sin-Serin, who seemed absorbed in private concentration.

'Can you...change?' the king whispered to his elven guide. Disquiet furrowed the elf's smooth forehead.

'Would that I could,' she whispered softly. 'A hostile will pervades the valley and I find my senses diminished in this strange environment. The chances of successfully completing even a simple *morph* are slim, and even if I could, it would merely serve to announce our presence.' Roujeark had not heard the elf's words, but he, too, sensed animosity in the air, even if he couldn't say what caused it. Having weighed up what both Sin-Serin and Lancoir had said, Roujeark now saw the king turning last to him. In spite of his fear, he could not help but feel a stab of pride at being consulted along with such veterans.

'Roujeark,' Curillian said to him. 'You have been more attuned to danger than any of us on this journey – what do your instincts tell you?'

'It scarcely needs to be said that we are in danger, Lord, but I cannot tell from what quarter it will first assail us. All I know is that I feel sure our peril will increase with every step taken from now on.' Curillian went quiet, taking counsel last of all with himself. They watched him staring out across the chasm. He gripped the sides of the bridge with both arms, as if trying to gauge its reliability through touch alone. Finally, he swung around to look at them again.

'We will cross.'

Roujeark's heart jumped in alarm – he had felt sure the king would veer away and find another route. But no, he actually meant to attempt it. Curillian saw his doubt, and the same doubt in the others, and addressed it.

'Our quest lies on the other side of this gorge.' He pointed across the gulf. 'And I mean to fulfil it. And since I see no other way, we will tread this bridge.'

Even Lancoir's devotion faltered in that place.

'I implore you...Curillian...do not...'

'I will not turn back,' the king said sharply. His eyes glared out, challenging the fear in them. When he saw them hesitating still, he spoke again. 'I will cross, alone if needs be.' With that he set foot to the first plank and trusted his weight to it. With hardly a falter he took another step, and another. It took barely a heartbeat longer for the magnetism of his will to drag them after. Lancoir started after him, and then the other guards. Trembling, Roujeark joined them, and last of all came Sin-Serin, as calmly as if she had meant to bring up the rear all along. One split-second glance down at his feet, and the gaping emptiness beneath, convinced Roujeark not to look down again. Feeling sick and faint, he kept his eyes firmly on the guard in front of him. Gripping the sides fiercely with both arms tensed, he felt every vibration and wobble made by the others. The whole bridge seemed to lurch and bounce up and down like a living thing as they inched forward. His feet felt for the planks almost with a sense of their own. The planks were not as evenly spaced as he might have wished, and without the collaboration of his eyes he more than once stumbled into a gap or lost his footing. Each time his heart thundered and his head swam. There were stunning vistas to both sides, but they were completely lost on him. He would have closed his eyes altogether, but the gusting of the wind made him feel like he would be blown into oblivion if he did not keep them open.

When he felt they were roughly halfway across, he started to feel a bit more composed. But then he realised the guard in front of him had stopped. Obliged to stop himself, he felt the vibration of footfalls fading away until it was just the natural movement of the bridge he could feel. Why had they stopped? Another glance down, into the deepest recesses below, brought all his panic to the surface again. Looking sharply up again, he repositioned himself marginally to be able to look up ahead, leaning as far out as he dared. They were situated in the greatest extent of the bridge's sag, and from that precarious position they had to look up quite a way to see the top.

Someone was standing at the far end of the bridge. Short and stocky, a dark figure stood framed between the posts and the sky behind.

Roujeark looked round as quickly as his nauseated state would allow him, and all was clear behind them. They could still retreat. But the king advanced instead, treading up the steepening gradient with bold determination. Then he stopped again, and Roujeark saw why. More figures could now be seen, and still more, until they clustered around the bridge's exit in a forbidding obstacle.

'Back!'

Lancoir's shout, buffeted by the wind, barely reached him, but when Roujeark and the others looked behind again another figure, exactly the same as those in front, suddenly materialised to bar the entrance to the bridge. Both sides were sealed. They were trapped. Roujeark and those near him took several steps back, thinking one was better odds than many, but even as they did so more figures appeared as if from nowhere to reinforce the one. Through waves of nausea Roujeark tried to reach the mysterious power within him, but it wouldn't come. What before had emblazoned itself boldly if illegibly in his mind now fled before the groping fingers of his mind like shreds of smoke in a gale. He stretched out his hands, but nothing would come, and the instant loss of security made him seize the rope again quicker than thought. The newcomers made no sound, but they remained eerily and immovably in place. Above the wind's blasts, only the murmurs of fear of those near him could be heard. The elite soldiery of Maristonia had hitherto seemed fearless, but now they quailed. It was the only realisation at that point which could have disconcerted Roujeark further.

A tremor running through the wood and through the rope announced the intrusion of heavy feet onto the bridge. Still none of them knew what to do, and icy fear coursed through Roujeark's veins. He heard the scrape of swords being drawn, more in desperation than out of any realistic thought of success. Slowly, unstoppably, the grim figures thumped further onto the bridge from both sides. Roujeark steeled himself for the end. An arrow sprang from Sin-Serin's bow in front of him as the only defiance from the little party, but though it found its mark unerringly in the lead figure, it had no effect, and the figures kept coming. Resignedly, the elf put her bow away and drew her long daggers. Just then Roujeark felt an almighty tremor run through the bridge, more violent than anything yet. His hand leapt involuntarily away from the rope-side as if burned, and the whole bridge lurched. The structure beneath swayed drunkenly, as if being rocked by some new force, and when he turned around again to the front, he saw why. Curillian had hurried forward, as close to the advancing foes as he dared, and taken to the rope-side with his sword. Roujeark put his hand back to the rope only to feel the tension it in vanish like a whiplash. He staggered, somehow managing to keep his footing. One side of the bridge was cut. Now it sloped dangerously to one side.

'HOLD ON!'

The king's bellowed warning came back to them even as his first stroke landed on the other side. The keen metal shore straight through the top rope in one cut. Roujeark felt his bowels weaken and his legs give way as the loosened integrity of the bridge communicated itself through his feet and fingertips. Their accosters, having seen the danger and hurried to thwart it, were nearly on Curillian now, but with one last swing he severed the bridge. One moment the fading support of the bridge gave the illusion of safety beneath Roujeark, the next it fell away beneath him in an awful whoosh. The speed of his survival instincts, swifter by far than any reflex or intention, was all that saved him as he clutched unthinkingly at the disappearing rope strands. Another moment and the drag of gravity would have wrenched it beyond his grasp and left him to plunge freely into space. Having seized the rope with one hand, he swung himself round and grasped a plank with the other, holding them both tight with desperate strength. Hanging on for dear life, he was hurtled through empty space like a slingshot. The gut-wrenching heave that accompanied it felt like some capricious force was trying to inwardly rearrange his bodily organs. Now, facing inward, he could see the cliff-wall speeding towards them like the end of existence. He barely heard his own shrill scream, subtle as an extra keen edge to the wind.

He screwed his eyes tight shut and clenched his whole body ahead of the dreadful impact. Nothing could have prepared him for the bone-crunching, breath-depriving, thought-swamping, reality-shattering force of it. His feeble grip was loosened in an instant and he was falling, rock and wood and rope flashing upward past his terrified eyes in a kaleidoscope of incomprehensible motion. He tried to snatch at the bridge as it tore past, but his fingers could find no purchase. No sooner did they touch wood than it was wrenched away again. Almost imperceptibly his rate of fall decelerated, just enough for him to achieve a fleeting finger-hold. Once, twice, he managed to check his downward progress before losing his grip and falling again. Utterly unaware of those falling above and below him, his world shrunk to just a narrow shaft of consciousness intent upon somehow living through this. At last his fingers caught again, and oblivious to the wrenching pain shooting from the nails through to his shoulders, he felt himself shudder to a stop. He had no idea of how far he had fallen or had left to fall; he just felt his battered body hanging by the frayed strand of his own strength.

He held on just long enough for the *what now?* thought to occur to him, and then he failed himself. He could hold on no longer. He lost his grip. Eyes struggling to focus dimly reported a length of rope flitting by as the last hope, but even as his hands successfully reached it the dangling length blistered through his palms, taking the skin with it. Then he was falling unchecked again. Something hard yet flexible struck his back and the back of his head and turned him round in his fall. Sharp bristles scratched his face and hands as he fell through the branches of a tree, crashing from one to the other before finally rolling semi-conscious onto an unforgiving stone slope. Rolling over and over, bludgeoned by the merciless passage, he tumbled down the foot of the cliff where its sheer wall relented into the valley with a steep curve.

Somehow he was still conscious when he came to a halt, but only hazy vision came to him through a throbbing head. All he could see was the collection of stones nearest him, partially veiled by a cloud of dust from disturbed rocks. Blood poured from his lips, knuckles and elbows, his robes were tattered as if savaged by a pack of wild-cats and every square inch of body screamed with agony. He tried to move but could not. He lay unmoving for a little while before sounds started to register. Dimly he heard gruff voices yammering urgently, and footsteps crunching the loose stones near him. Suddenly he was hauled upright by some monstrous strength and he found himself looking at a fearsome squat-faced figure, like a grotesque statue come to life. Others were nearby, and they fell upon the fallen armists like vultures. There was nothing he could do to resist, but just then, he felt himself falling again as the harrack that had picked him up crumpled to the ground. Lancoir had tackled him like a charging bull, and now scrabbled in the dust with him. How the Captain of the Guard had emerged from the fall with any kind of ability to fight was beyond Roujeark. But now, ferocious as a banshee, Lancoir gained the upper hand and used his heavy boots to crush the brawny figure into the ground. Rising with a whirl he took up a huge stone and smashed it into the face of another harrack. Out of the corner of his eye, Roujeark saw Sin-Serin fighting also, leaping like a gazelle and slashing with daggers, and one or two others, but then he had to concentrate on evading the stamping boot of another harrack. Rolling in the dust with excruciating pain, he tried to get away from the fighting, losing sight of the embattled Lancoir. He heard scuffling feet, blows connecting with sickening crunches, and the thud of falling bodies. When firm hands grasped his shoulders, he feared the worst, but it was Lancoir again, heaving him to his feet and propelling him upward and away.

Making the most of some miraculous opening, they fled the scene. Staggering round an outthrust spine of the cliff, they hobbled into some dead ground. Behind them, the sounds of fighting grew dimmer. A solitary harrack followed them, brandishing a mattock, and Lancoir had just the presence of mind to trip him, casting Roujeark off to one side as he did so. Brutally, he leapt upon his fallen foe and grappled with him. He tried to throttle his enemy, but the harrack's neck was as thick as an ox's haunch, and even more unyielding. The harrack picked up a rock and smashed it into Lancoir's face, knocking him out flat. The knight lay sprawled, unmoving. Slowly, creaking like an old cart, the stocky figure rose and turned his attention to Roujeark. Still woozy, Roujeark felt a surge of fear and panic, but then new adrenaline pumped into him and took over. He flung a stone at the harrack, and in the momentary pause he leaned down and grasped Lancoir's sword, which still lay in its scabbard. Tugging it free just as the harrack was on him, he swung it clumsily and scored it across the thick leather jerkin. It made no more impression than a thin cut, and it did not deter the harrack from coming again. Roujeark was too slow with his swing this time, and a thickly muscled arm punched into his forearm. Yelping with pain, he lost his balance and dropped the sword. Another meaty blow connected with his sternum and he crashed onto his back.

Struggling for breath, and tasting blood in his mouth, Roujeark felt helpless as the horrid figure retrieved his fallen mattock and came to loom over him. The harrack leaned down and seized his robe with a gravelly fist, pulling him up. Up close, Roujeark was appalled by the sight, and the smell. The skin, if you could call it that, was cracked and leathery, and so thin and drawn that it looked like too little skin had been stretched over a skull much too big. The eyes were brutish, but not stupid, and set in an expressionless face that might have been daubed on stone for all the life there was in it.

Even as he took in these ghastly details, his smarting fingers were scrabbling desperately for the fallen sword. His fingers locked on it just as the mattock was drawn back for a killing smash. Roujeark swung the sword up, pommel first, and caught the harrack a ringing blow on the cheek. There was a resounding crack. The sparsely lashed eyes blinked curiously, and Roujeark hit him again. Capitalising on the precious advantage, Roujeark shoved up with all his might and helped the stunned harrack topple backwards. Groaning and struggling to get up again, Roujeark leapt upon him and smashed the big pommel-stone down again and again, like a frenzied stone-carver. He kept smiting until the unfamiliar weapon clattered free from his numb grip.

He looked down, appalled at the lifeless mess he had made. Sickened, he pushed himself away. Just then he heard Lancoir stirring. Somehow finding his feet, the ragged knight stumbled forward.

'I...must...help...others...' he mumbled. Summoning his final strength, Roujeark lurched over and grasped his retreating ankle. It was just enough to pitch Lancoir onto his hands and knees. Roujeark crawled up and tried to pin him down. But neither of them had any strength left. So there they lay, battered, broken, barely alive, and not knowing what had become of their companions.

IX

Faudunum

COLD. The floor beneath him was so cold. He could hear nothing, see nothing, smell nothing; the only sense he had was touch, the rigid embrace of the ground. Had he been lying there so long that it had seeped deep into his bones, settling in with a deadly ache? There was no mattress, nor even any straw, just unforgiving stone. And it was dark. Impenetrably dark. Curillian tried to lift his head, only to be rewarded with waves of groggy pain that threatened to engulf him in oblivion again. His reward for the effort was to discover than he could in fact see nothing, not even the merest suggestion of light. He tried to stave off unconsciousness, but the freezing cold weight of it was irresistible. Slumping back down, he sank back into dark dreams.

Weightless, unsupported, he saw the gorge again and again. Poised in mid-air, he was condemned to a constant re-evaluation of his decision to cut the bridge. Sometimes he was gazing almost peacefully at the serene peaks away in the distance, sometimes he was looking straight down into the ravine. Sometimes he saw his enemies falling, sometimes his friends. The remorseless dream seemed determined to play before him every possible way in which the scene might have played out. Sometimes he caught hold of the rope before it vanished, sometimes he didn't. Once he saw the sword reach out, almost of its own accord, and wedge itself into the wooden planks just before they fell away, but most times it remained frozen at the end of its fateful last swing. Then he would be falling, always falling...

The impact never came. But when he awoke again on the cold floor, he felt its aftermath. The pain wracked his body, and he did not even know where to begin inspecting his hurts. At least he was more alert this time – or had his previous waking been just another path in his dreams? It seemed familiar, though: unremitting dark and freezing cold. His head throbbed with an awful ache, but at least he felt his thoughts coming clearly to him. Now as well as feeling the cold stone, he was able to discern a dreadful smell, if not its source. He might not be able to see even the walls of his cell, but he knew for sure that cell it was. He knew he was in Faudunum. Nowhere else south of the Haunted Pass could be so cold or so unwelcoming. But he had no idea how he had come here, much less an answer for any of the other questions that queued up in his mind.

He tried again to get up, but his body wouldn't obey. He was still flat on his back when a metal scrape sawed across the silence. The sound startled him, and he looked over to where the sound had come from. A red bar of light emerged, feeble but bright enough to hurt his eyes after all that time in complete darkness. A torch was held up to a small aperture of some kind, and in its flickering, he glimpsed a pale face looking into the cell. He saw the curiosity in the gaze. He saw a part of the wall, and the outline of a huge door. Then the torch withdrew hastily, and the metal plate grated shut again. All the faint outlines he had seen at once melted back into the blackness.

Curillian was unable to measure the passing hours, but some time later he was able to haul himself into a sitting position, numbed muscles cramping with the sudden effort. Gradually he managed to stand up and, once standing, he patted himself all over to discover what state he was in. Though bereft of the warm outer cloak the snow-elves had given him, he was dressed in all the same clothes. A chain pendant from Carmen still hung about his neck. His other effects were gone, though. His pack had been taken, together with all his provisions. Feeling round his belt, he found his dagger gone, and, worst of all, his great blade. The Sword of Maristonia was in the hands of harracks! Wretched as he was, the thought burned in him like acid in his stomach.

With nothing else to do, he investigated his cell also. He stumbled blindly in search of the nearest wall. Locating it with an outstretched hand, he paced around the cell. He found only two features to break the otherwise square perimeter. His nose warned him by the smell before he came to the small, sloped orifice in one corner. There could be no doubt of its purpose: a latrine had been provided, not so much for his convenience as to spare the guards the need to clean his cell. Nauseated, he lurched to the other wall and found the sloping indent which was the second feature. He thought this was where the light had come from, and, sure enough, as his fingers groped out, they touched something even colder than the stone. Metal. It was the plate sealing the spyhole, but he could not move it, nor find any handle or lever.

He jumped back when it moved from the other side. Again, the sudden light of the torch was dazzling, and he held up a hand to block it out. When he removed his fingers, he saw the same face looking in at him. Its eyes looked surprised to see him so close by. They were not the eyes of a harrack. They were elven, set in a pale smooth face. Immediately Curillian thought of what Sin-Serin had told him, about one of Aiiyosha's folk who had gone missing near Faudunum. Was this he? The voice too, when it spoke, was elven.

'So, you are up. I have been eager to speak with you.'

'Who is it that wishes to speak with me?' Curillian was shocked by how hoarse his voice was – he scarcely recognised the sound of himself.

'One who knows who you are, so do not waste your time in denying it.'

'And who am I?'

'The King of Maristonia, Curillian the Mighty. A catch of singular value…'

'That's an ambitious guess. The harracks…?'

'The harracks also know who you are. They might not be the most perspicacious of creatures, but they never forget a sword like yours, one that has done them so much damage in the past. Do you deny it?'

'I do not deny it. And yet I thought I'd done enough damage to the barbarians for them to have no hesitation in killing me. Why have they not done so?'

'I convinced them not to.'

'Why? They must know they'd never be able to ransom me. Or do they simply delay to prepare a slow death for me?'

'You're probably right about the ransom, though it would be interesting to watch them try. The loss in prestige to your house alone would be incalculable. And yes, given half a chance, they would take great delight in subjecting you to the tortures of the deep. But I have persuaded them otherwise…for now…and I had another reason for so doing.'

'What reason?'

'I believe you possess information which would be very useful to me.'

Curillian shot forward, pressing his face close to the open grate. The person on the other side stepped hastily back, casting torchlight over the rough passage outside. He was swathed in warm furs, but the stature of the snow-elves was unmistakeable, very similar to Aiiyosha.

'And who are you that guesses?' Curillian demanded. 'An elf, certainly, and most likely a snow-elf. But whoever you are, I will not converse through a hole!'

'King of armists, it may be the hole or nothing. Perhaps I was too quick to rouse you and should have left you a little while longer for the cell to cool your ardour. At least be willing to eat and drink what is passed through the hole.' Curillian brought his hands up and objects were placed in them. 'I will return soon,' the elf said. '… when, I hope, you will be more amenable.'

The grate snapped shut, but in the last second of light Curillian saw what had been given to him. He was amazed to see a flask and a hunk of bread from his pack. Amazed, he slumped down against the wall and tore hungrily at the food and slurped the water down. All too soon it was gone, and then he was left alone with his thoughts in the darkness.

With great caution, Roujeark and Lancoir made their way back to the scene of the fallen bridge. They peered from behind a concealing rock for a long time before feeling sure that no harracks were about. Then, apprehensively, they emerged from hiding. Nursing their bruised and aching limbs, they crept down the rocky slope and out into the flat open space of the gorge's bottom. The scene was carnage. Broken lengths of the bridge lay draped over stones like so much firewood. Roujeark looked up and was astonished to see how high the ravine's sides looked from below. There, waving gently like bones in a drafty tomb, were the broken ends of the bridge, hanging from either cliff face. Looking down again, the humps they had seen proved to be just what they had feared: bodies, half-buried in dust and fragmented rock. Ignoring the fallen harracks, they hurriedly identified those which were armists: five of them. Lancoir pulled them free one by one and turned them over to see their faces.

'Cyron…Edrist…Norscinde…Caréysin…Andil.' He called out their names mournfully and wept over them.

The last three were still breathing faintly, and Roujeark was relieved to see his friend Andil among them. He and Caréysin seemed more or less unharmed, just stunned, but Cyron and Edrist were unmoving. Norscinde was conscious, but when his dim eyes looked up, Lancoir was only able to see the life draining from him. The knight clasped the dying armist's hand until it went limp.

Roujeark sat helplessly by, wracked by grief but too exhausted for tears. The three guardsmen had seemingly been killed by the fall, their backs and necks broken like twigs. All they could do for them was to straighten out their crooked limbs and pile cairns of stones over them. Caréysin and Andil they revived as best they could, though both were injured. As they were doing so, the sound of rocks being disturbed startled them. Lancoir dropped the stone in his hand and reached for his sword, and Roujeark prepared a rock for throwing. There, trudging across the stony watercourse, was Lionenn, the Konenaire. So covered in dust and rocky debris was he that he looked like a corpse risen from some mountain tomb. Limping with a wound in one leg, he came up to them and rested upon the great harrack mattock he bore.

'Lionenn? Where have you come from?' Lancoir said in gruff welcome. The grizzled armist was no less gruff in reply.

'Killing harracks. Lost my bloody axe. Catching the last one took me away yonder.' He gestured stiffly up the valley. 'Bastard smashed my leg with this club, but I smashed his head. Bastard.' He spat out dust and blood but weighed the mattock approvingly. Lancoir smiled grimly and thumped his arm.

'Good armist. We should have brought a few more Konenaires,' he said. No sooner had he finished speaking than a new sound came from across the river. A figure was stumbling down towards them from the scree slope at the far side of the gorge. It was not a harrack. It was an armist.

'Aleinus!?' Lancoir said in amazement. The guard in question fell to his knees, sobbing uncontrollably and clasping his hands in front of him as if in prayer. They helped him up and he joined them in burying their comrades. When asked how he survived, he told his story in the fragments that came to him.

'I was at the front, near the king. When he cut through the bridge, I flung myself forward to try and catch him, but his momentum took him sideways and instead of reaching him I just managed to grab the other half of the bridge as it fell away. That meant I ended up on the other side of the gorge, away from the rest of you. When the harracks fell around me I just managed to hold on, having gained a good grip. I just hung there, not able to do anything. Eventually I could hold on no longer, and I fell. I expected the impact to kill me, but instead I must have been knocked out. When I woke up again, the ground beneath me was somehow softer than rock. It took me a while to realise that I'd landed on a pile of dead harracks. They're hard enough, though, jolting pains were shooting up my back. Even now, every movement is agony. I waited, in the shadow of the cliff, hoping against hope. When I saw you...I can't tell you...' He broke down again, tears coursing through the dust caked on his face. Roujeark laid a comforting hand on his shoulder.

'So you're alive, and we're alive,' said Lancoir slowly. 'That makes five, but where are the rest?' Together they searched the floor of the gorge desperately. Through waves of pain, they were overjoyed to uncover two more bodies half-hidden by the stones. They could scarcely believe it when they found that both bodies belonged to live armists. Utarion and Antaya were just coming around from deep concussions. They were even more battered than the rest of them, but somehow, they had survived the fall in one piece. They kept searching in growing desperation. They turned up fallen packs, but no more bodies did they find.

'There's no sign of the king,' Roujeark said, voicing the thought troubling all of them.

'I wish someone saw everything, someone who could tell us what the hell happened.' Lancoir spoke into his hands as they massaged his weary face.

'I don't remember much. I was dazed, and everything happened so quickly. I remember harracks attacking us, and I think I saw Sin-Serin alive and fighting, but it was only a glimpse,' Roujeark recollected with difficulty.

Aleinus was little help. 'Everything had happened by the time I came to. The gorge was empty when I regained my senses. Nothing happened until you two came back...'

'I can barely say more,' said Lancoir, looking at Roujeark. 'How I got up at all I'll never know, but when I saw you being attacked, I was up before I knew what I was doing.' He rubbed his wounded shoulder as he recalled tackling the harrack which had picked Roujeark up. Roujeark slotted this memory into his own and fingered the ring Lancoir had given him. He looked at it, covered in dust, but unbroken. the debt was repaid, if nothing else. Suddenly he became aware that Lancoir was berating himself.

'I should have stayed. My first thought was to get you to safety, out of harm's way. I thought that once I'd done that I could return in good conscience. But I never made it back...'

Roujeark tried to comfort him.

'You had no strength left, and there was nothing you could have done anyway...' Lancoir swatted his hand aside, and rose, suddenly furious.

'But I left the king! I shoulder never have left the king.' He shouted the words and they echoed off the gorge walls. Wincing, he lowered his voice. 'I abandoned him, and now he's either dead or captive. I shall offer my life in penance, if only I can find him again.'

His shout reminded them that they were all in terrible danger out there in the open. Roujeark was just about to usher them back into cover when they heard a moaning. Fearing attack again, they prepared to defend themselves, but all that happened was more moaning. It seemed to come from the trees. They staggered back up into the trees, following the noise, and found a body dangling from the lower branches of a fir tree. Incoherent with pain, it was another live armist. It was Findor, the last of their ill-fated company. As gently as they could, they lowered him down, and then took stock of things. Hidden for the moment by the trees, they allowed themselves a rest. They took on water and food salvaged from the shattered packs.

Lancoir, Roujeark, Andil, Caréysin, Aleinus and Lionenn were all battered and bruised, but they could move unaided. Antaya was able to get up with some assistance, Findor lay groaning in pain, but Utarion was unable to move. Apparently only his eyes and lips were still active. They laid him on his back, devastated by his pitiful condition. His fingers scrabbled by his side, and, following his gaze, Lancoir placed his sword in his hand. The inert guard grasped it weakly, and then murmured to his captain. Lancoir held his other hand tightly, watching as he slowly expired. There were no more tears to come from the exhausted captain, but the pain disfigured his face as he complied with his comrade's last request. His passing did not take long, and at the end there was peace in his face. They covered him with stones like the others. Then Antaya, who prized his faith, and honoured that of his fallen comrades, spoke words of prayer and farewell over the sad little cairns.

It was a pathetic, dishevelled little company that left the cover of the trees and struck out across the gorge. They went at a slow, limping pace, the best they could manage with their collective injuries. Its shell-shocked members proceeded with little clear idea of where they were going, and with even less hope, but Lancoir led them forward with his slowly recovering strength. Wearily, painfully, they inched along the far wall of the gorge, feeling as small as ants, and following it blindly in the hope that it led somewhere. They came to a deep fold in the cliff-face and the sound of stones being disturbed made them all freeze with fear. Fumbling for weapons, they looked up a steep slope, seeing nothing at first. Then, with extraordinary slowness, a statue-like figure became outlined against the rocky backdrop. The figure was kneeling, bowstring pulled back taut. Gradually Sin-Serin became recognisable, as if she had temporarily been part of the cliff itself and now came back to life.

'*Falakai*,' she breathed softly to herself in relief. Marvelling at her camouflage, their fears dissipated. The tension eased with her bowstring, and then, incongruously, she smiled down at them.

'Well met, friends. I'm glad to see you still alive. But come, our mission is not over; far from it, it is now harder than ever. If you think surviving this far was hard, think not of what lies before you. Let us beseech Prélan that he spares you also through what comes next. Come. Follow me...'

When his visitor came again, Curillian thought he now had some idea of how to play things. He seated himself with his back to the far wall, facing the aperture. When the faint red light came through and illuminated him, it revealed a very composed figure.

'Well, king of armists, I hope you will make my visit more worthwhile this time. I doubt I shall be able to come alone many more times...' Curillian stretched out the silence before answering levelly.

'I may know something which would be valuable to you...' His benign interrogator waited expectantly. 'But why should I tell it to you...?'

'To spare yourself worse treatment,' came back the hasty response, obviously prepared. Curillian scoffed.

'You must do better than that, snow-elf. Don't take me for a fool. The harracks will kill me one way or another. You must give me a reason to loosen my tongue...' This time his questioner took longer to respond.

'I...may be able to help you,' he said hesitantly. 'But I cannot tell you how without knowing what it is you offer.'

Looking up from where he sat, Curillian could not see the snow-elf; he was just talking to the red slit in the opposite wall. He smiled to himself.

'Why don't I tell you how you could help me?' he said, long practice infusing his voice with more confidence than he felt. His questioner paused, unsure of this proposal. 'You can take me to the elf-woman held captive here.'

'Impossible!' the voice on the other side of the wall hissed quickly. 'I cannot just go guiding you round the dungeons...'

Curillian smiled inwardly again. So, she is here. He waited, sensing the indecision behind the snow-elf's refusal.

'She is held in a deep cell, far from here. It would be extremely difficult to access, and even harder to do so undetected. You would have to know something very valuable for so much trouble...'

'I'm sure you would like to know why I am really in these mountains,' Curillian offered. 'I'm even more sure that the harracks would. What's more, I think you knowing such a thing would give you great credit with your friends...'

Curillian wished he could see the other's face as he spoke, gauge the reaction, but even talking to a wall he could sense the temptation and uncertainty. He held his breath. There was silence for a long while, but then the metal panel was scraped shut and footsteps retreated down the passage outside.

Curillian got up and paced around. He needed to keep his mind active and focused, lest madness start to creep in. Whoever this elf was, there was a reason why he and not the harracks were attending to him. An elf would not reside easily in a place such as Faudunum, so he must have some use, or render some service to the harracks. Curillian felt sure, though, that he was a duplicitous character, trying to play both sides. The very fact that he was contemplating assisting a prisoner showed that he was willing to damage the harracks' cause. Or at least, so it seemed. He had admitted that Carea was here, and even if he didn't know who she was, he must know how valuable a prisoner she was from how secure cell she was kept in. His outright refusal to go near her had changed very quickly to a willingness to bargain. Whatever his agenda was, whatever it was he wanted, he wanted it badly. But how badly? Curillian felt sure he would come back, but he hoped it wouldn't be too long. He must play this just right, for this snow-elf might be his best chancing of escaping. The thought of being trapped in the darkness of Faudunum for the rest of his days didn't bear thinking about. Already even just losing the pathetic red light from the viewing hole had made his heart sink. He must get out, and soon…

⅄

Now with Sin-Serin leading them, the battered little company of nine continued on its way. After a long trek, they rounded the sharp end of the great ridge which filled the wider valley. Beyond it, the far side of the valley rose up as a long steep wall. Welcoming the thick mists that had come over, they trudged up that steep valley-side. After a wearisome climb, they emerged out of the mists which filled the valley and found themselves on a rough, barren plateau. It proved to be quite narrow though, for they soon came to its far side. There they were brought up short by another obstacle, and another breath-taking spectacle.

It seemed that they were on the roof of the world, looking down upon it. Again, the ground fell away before them in sudden precipitous cliffs and plunged to unguessable depths. To either side they heard the trickle of little streams falling into the abyss, only to be blown away in fine spray. Across from them, many miles away, they saw another area of high ground, which seemed to be the same height upon which they now stood, only curved round like a horseshoe. All the vast gap in between was filled with mist, as if it were a cauldron containing mysterious vapours. Yet out of that great emptiness rose a peak, its sides as sheer as the cliffs at their feet but flat enough at the summit to accommodate a forbidding fortress. Squat, crude and grey, the fort sat foursquare on that improbable pinnacle, seeming almost to float above the sea of mist. They were left in no doubt as to its ownership. Even from this distance they could see sentries as squat and hard as the fastness itself: harracks. Nor were they just perched in the building, like would-be eagles in a hand-built eyrie: they also manned what looked to be the only approach to the high place. A ludicrously steep staircase, hewn out of the living rock, climbed up to the fortress. The steps were broken every now and then by a level of flat rock where sentries skulked. Leaning over as far as they dared, they saw a knife-thin bridge of living rock emerge from under the cliff on which they stood and stretch across the yawning mists to the fortified crag.

All this they saw with mixed dread and wonderment.

'Cor, would you look at that place?' exclaimed Antaya. 'Can you imagine having to attack it?'

None of them wanted to, and with one mind they pushed the thought aside. Instead, their attentions fixated on where to go next. The steep staircase vanished into the mist after a few of the level places, giving no clues as to what lurked below; nor could they see any way down from their present position. They crouched down in congress to consider things.

'We were indeed fortunate not to come this way originally,' declared Sin-Serin. 'Aiiyosha told us that this is where the right-hand turn in the lower valley would have led us.'

'So somewhere down there is a gap which would lead us back to where we started,' Roujeark observed.

'A straighter road,' agreed Lancoir. 'But it would have brought us right to their door-step.'

'The question is where to go now,' Roujeark told them.

'Can we bypass this fort?' Caréysin asked.

'Perhaps,' said Sin-Serin. 'My guess is that there is a path which leads from this outpost to the main stronghold of Faudunum. Somehow we must get down to that path, but without being seen. Let us hope we have not been descried already upon this height.' Roujeark shivered with that thought, drawing his cloak tight about his aching shoulders. Lancoir was already up and ready to move.

'Come; let us find what way we can. One thing is certain: however we get to Faudunum, the longer we take, the less chance we have of finding the king alive when we get there...'

The metal scraped again, breaking the silence, and the red light appeared again. Curillian had been expecting the third visit, but all the same, he was relieved when it came. The aching still throbbed all over his body, but he forced himself to concentrate.

'Does my visitor have a name?' he called out.

'Perethor,' the voice came back. *Perethor*, Curillian echoed thoughtfully to himself. *And who is Perethor?*

'And what is a snow-elf doing in Faudunum?' was what he asked out loud.

'I will ask the questions,' Perethor snapped. 'What are you doing in Stonad?' Curillian broke in, keeping him off balance.

'I know who you are,' he declared, taking his questioner aback. 'You are of the clan of Aiiyosha, whose hospitality we have just enjoyed. She told us that one of her kinsmen went missing, near to Faudunum...that kinsman is you, isn't it Perethor?' He got no answer, but he knew he was right. He spoke his thoughts aloud. 'I thought we might be able to rescue you, but maybe you don't want to return to your kin?'

A nerve was struck.

'I would do anything to live among my people again.' Perethor's voice was sharp and bitter. 'Do not judge me or make guesses about me, armist; what would you know of exile?'

A rush of memories swept up from hidden places to engulf Curillian. *All too much.* His jaw clenched, but he stayed calm, and the moment passed.

'Actually, my friend, I know as much about exile as anyone alive. I know what it is to be deprived of hearth and home and honour.' He got up and walked to the red slit. He wanted to see Perethor's face for this. The snow-elf did not like having him closer, but he stood his ground. He seemed to be in the grip of some strong emotion. 'Were you driven,' Curillian asked gently, 'or did you run?'

Perethor grimaced. 'What does it matter now? I came here, and here was I snared. You have been a captive here for two days, armist king, but I have been a captive for many circuits of the sun.' Compassion rose in Curillian.

'I will help you if you help me.' Perethor looked at him sharply.

'Do you really know something that would buy us both our freedom?'

'Yes,' said Curillian. 'I believe I do. But how can I trust you?'

'That is a chance you must take. If you have not guessed it already, both our lives are at stake. The harrack has no more love for the traitor than for the trespasser. Come, what is this knowledge you possess?' Curillian hesitated, weighing up the rightness of what he was about to say.

'Would I be right in thinking that the harracks are desperate to strike a blow at their lowland enemies?' Perethor nodded, waiting. 'What if I were to tell you that they might soon have an opportunity to strike at many enemies?' His conscience pricked him even as he said the words, but he felt he had no choice. Perethor's eyes widened with interest.

'Truly? Where?' Curillian smiled thinly.

'I will say no more until you release me. Get me out of here, and we shall talk again.' It was Perethor's turn to hesitate. He stood there, transfixed with indecision. Curillian watched many emotions go across his face. He willed him to a positive decision; his heart rose within him when he seemed to reach inside his robes for a set of keys, and then his hopes were dashed as he reached out a hand and slammed the viewing hole plate shut. The metal clanged in front of Curillian's nose and he heard shoes slapping hurriedly against the stone floor, beating a hasty retreat. He struck the walls with his fists and cursed aloud to the darkness in his frustration. He had been so close…

A

Roujeark didn't know how they managed it, but eventually they found a way down. Not before several of them had nearly fallen to their deaths, not before countless slips and twisted ankles, not before hours of bone-chilled toil, but eventually they found a way. They clambered down a slope so steep that Roujeark would have sworn beforehand that it could not be scaled. Without the ropes in their packs, and close co-operation between them, they never would have made it. Every minute spent clinging to that wind-buffeted rock-face, scrabbling for handholds and places to rest his feet, felt like an hour. More than once, he nearly slipped into misty oblivion, and the others fared little better.

Their luck had nearly given out when they had drawn near the level of the bridge that connected the cliff with the outcrop. A sudden noise, as of deep horns blowing, came from within the fort and startled them so that they nearly lost their grips. All of them came to a halt and clung to the cliff as best they could. Those that were able to watched as the fort's great doors were flung open, and out of them issued a column of harracks. Perhaps forty in number, they came tramping out of the fort with heavy booted feet. All were armoured with chainmail and leather and pointed iron caps, and all bore sturdy shields and thick, short spears. Over everything, they were swathed in thick black bear-skins, in which they very quickly seemed to meld into the night as soon as they had left behind the glare of the watch-torches. Yet they gave no sign that they had seen the armists, but followed the bridge to the cliff-face, where they picked up a steep path descending down into the valley. The doors of the fort were slammed behind them, and noisily they marched away, chanting war songs in deep throaty voices.

The company waited until the harrack patrol was gone and then resumed their descent. With bruised and bleeding fingers barely able to relax from their clenched gripping positions, they eventually managed to get down. Roujeark would have liked to rest, but Lancoir drove them on mercilessly. Until he could get back to his king, he was like an armist possessed. Riding their luck, they hurried across a broken valley floor and splashed over a narrow stream. The heights above from which they had descended were lost to view.

'This must be the upper reaches of Pharaphir,' said Sin-Serin. 'Prélan be praised that her waters are cleansed from harrack filth ere they reach the forest. Come, let us be swift and gain the cover of those trees ahead. Danger is all around.'

Half-running, half-stumbling, nearly blind with weariness, they followed her suggestion and came to the trees. It was a narrow stand of fir trees. The cover offered was thin, but it was better than nothing. They paused briefly, and then went on. Creeping now, they cautiously approached the far side of the stand. From the far trees, they could see a rough-beaten road running alongside.

'That road must link the fortress we passed with Faudunum,' Lancoir guessed. 'At least we now know the way.'

Roujeark seized his arm fearfully. 'But how will we escape their notice, being so close?' Lancoir smiled grimly at him, the smile known only to veterans of a hundred campaigns.

'We must hope they are looking the other way!'

They carried on, full of fear, expecting discovery any moment. Their pace of march was the best compromise they could manage between a desire for speed on the one hand, and the need to be as quiet as possible on the other. They might have gone quicker, but their tortured bodies slowed them down with grating pain. All of them were fortunate to be mobile at all. Several times Sin-Serin, leading again, had them down flat on their bellies when she suspected some danger. Caréysin kept an arrow ready on the string while all the rest of them watched Sin-Serin's shadowy outline in the gloom. She would have them wait, faces pressed to the pine-needle-covered ground, for interminable ages before she judged that the danger had passed. None of the rest of them could guess what made her fearful, but on the last occasion, they were still lying flat when they heard the faint thrum of heavy feet. Not daring to move a muscle, hardly daring to breathe, they waited in agonising tension as the booted feet came nearer. Glancing up, Roujeark just made out a patrol of ten or so harracks stomping down the road. They were dressed and armoured like the other patrol, but now they were close enough for him to see that above their huge boots were strange greaves and gaiters of fur. He felt certain they would turn aside and find them, but their stride never faltered. They kept going; back down the valley in the direction of the fortress.

Gradually they eased up and got going again, but it was not long before Sin-Serin had them down on one knee again. Roujeark's heart started to thud again, but this time their elven guide gestured through the trees. She pointed out a hill up ahead, rising out of the valley. Manoeuvring into a better position, Roujeark could see what she was pointing out. The bleak hill was crowned with a fell citadel. Low, crumpled and gnarled, the city ran around the brow of the hill like an iron circlet. It looked more like a grave-ring than a habitation of the living. The path beside them ran up to it, flanked all the way by trees. Red torches flickering above the gates were the only evidence of colour in all that mass of grey. They could see their destination, but could they get to it...?

Curillian knelt in prayer. Ignoring the discomfort of his posture, he poured out his heart to Prélan.

O merciful Father, do not abandon me here in this darkness! How long will You let me languish here? The days merge into one and are as night to me. My hope falters within me. Yet I remember You, the God of my youth. Ever were You faithful to me, and always You preserved my life against my enemies. Arise now in strength, and deliver me from my foes. Fill this tired and aching body with new strength, and give me what it takes to reclaim my freedom. Grant that I might bring Carea out with me, and continue on my quest...

The words melted into the darkness and fled before him. No answer came, only that familiar inward peace. Lying down and closing his eyes, sleep took him again, one darkness replacing another.

The scraping of the key in the lock startled him awake. He opened his eyes, not that it made any difference. He had lost track of time, so he did not know whether hours or days had passed since he had scared Perethor off, but now something was definitely going on outside. It was not the viewing-hole – this scuffling was coming from the door. Ignoring the ropes of pain in his back and the howls of complaints from his knees and elbows, he eased up into a crouch, tense and ready for action. He heard, rather than saw, the door open. In a few quick strides, he was across the cell. Cannoning into the barely open door, he threw his weight against it and heaved it ajar, letting the red light from the corridor spill into the cell. In doing so, he knocked over Perethor, who was just unbending from the keyhole. With the catlike reflexes of an elf, Perethor was up again, darting to block Curillian's escape. Curillian had intended to take only a split second to take stock of his new surroundings, but the torchlight was dazzling after so long in the darkness and his eyes smarted. Gradually he got the measure of the corridor, which was low and narrow. Perethor could not stand fully upright, but had to stoop. He realised there was only one exit, and the elf was now between him and it, tensed ready for trouble.

'Don't even think about running, armist king. You won't get anywhere if you break faith with me. All I have to do is shout and harrack guards will be upon you.' Curillian stared levelly at him.

'It'd already be too late for you if you did. How did I get out of my cell, they'll want to know.' Perethor had no answer; he knew he was right. Curillian made it doubly clear for him. 'No, you stand complicit now, and you won't get me back in that cell without one of us dying. We need each other.' The elf relaxed almost imperceptibly.

'Well then, I have released you. Now tell me what you know.' Curillian shook his head.

'Take me to the elf-woman first.'

'That wasn't our agreement.'

'It is now. You take me to her, or you'll get nothing from me.' Perethor looked desperate. He wavered, and Curillian rushed at him. The elf was quick, but Curillian was quicker, and in a flash he had his accomplice pinned against the wall. 'Take me to her, Perethor. You need me now more than I need you. I can take your keys and find her on my own, but you need what I know, or they'll show you no mercy.'

He was bluffing – he doubted he would find Carea at all, let alone in time before he was caught – but he infused his voice with all the aggression and confidence he could muster to keep Perethor from realising it.

'I've never seen her...' Perethor prevaricated.

'But you know where her cell is. Take me there.' Still the elf dithered, his courage deserting him. Curillian thrust his face close. Desperation gave his voice a ruthless edge. 'I've never killed an elf before, but believe me, with these bare hands I'll tear your head off if you don't do as I say.' Perethor resisted a moment longer, and then buckled.

'All right, all right,' he whimpered. 'But for pity's sake we must be quick.'

He wriggled out of Curillian's grasp and shuffled, wincing, to the door at the end of the corridor. He placed another key in the lock, turned it with impeccable care, and then looked over his shoulder at Curillian.

'Make any noise more than a patter, and we're dead.'

With oily speed, he inched open the door and vanished through it. Curillian made haste to follow. Evidently knowing the way very well, Perethor scurried down the eerily-lit passageways like a rabbit, but as stealthily as a cat. It was all Curillian could do to keep up. Only briefly were they exposed in the inhabited parts, and after that, they were flying down dim corridors of stone to another clutch of dungeons. Deeper and deeper they went, and the way became tighter and narrower as they went. Eventually, panting and alive with nervous energy, Perethor came to a halt in a low tunnel. He paused at a corner, and peered round.

'Good, there is no guard here,' he whispered in relief.

'Is there normally?'

'No, we are so deep now that none are needed. There is no way out of here except back the way we came. We were fortunate, though, not to run into any guards on the higher levels...' That thought seemed to trouble him, but he pushed it away and slipped round the corner, whisking Curillian with him. In this last section, the tunnel got so low that they had to stoop almost double. At its end was a portal, small but sturdy, and fastened with many locks. It looked almost airtight. Perethor turned to Curillian again.

'Well, here we are, just as you asked. Now make good your end of the bargain.' Curillian shook his head.

'Not yet, I need to see her, make sure she's alive.' Perethor looked aggrieved, and, very suddenly, like he was on the brink of breaking down completely. Curillian reasoned with him. 'If I tell you now, what's to stop you dashing off and leaving me here? The information would save your skin, but I'd be doomed.' He saw the fear and rising terror in the elf's eyes. With a will, he hardened his heart and kept his resolve. He gripped Perethor's arm, and looked him deep in the eye. 'I will not abandon you, friend Perethor. One way or another, I will get you out of this city. Now, open this up.'

Trembling, Perethor opened the locks one by one, and then turned a small wheel in the portal's centre. Each turn of the wheel relaxed the pent-up tension of the barrier further until, at last, it swung open with a gasp of released air. Cold, clammy air wafted into Curillian's nose. His heart thudded with foreboding, and a sudden hesitation seized him. Perethor was even more unwilling. He cringed away from the mysterious opening, as if mortally afraid of it.

'I will not go in,' he murmured. Curillian overcame his hesitation and crammed himself through the opening. It was barely big enough for him. As he squeezed through, he heard Perethor muttering balefully to himself.

'Hurry, hurry, make haste, make haste...'

The opening was actually just one end of a small extension of the tunnel. He fought down the panic of being so enclosed under the earth. Had he only swapped one cell for another? Eventually he scrabbled through, landing on what appeared to be a high shelf. All about him was dark. Not so dark as his former cell – he could just make out the shape of the chamber he was in – but dark enough. The shelf he was on seemed to go all the way around an empty space, hugging the walls near the ceiling. Below, the air fell away into a deep, dank pit. The shelf almost seemed to be a platform for looking down at what was below. He swallowed in horror, to think that a living person should be kept here in the bowels of Faudunum. There was something sinister about that thought that made his own cell seem bearable by comparison. If a prison were to be specially devised for the incarceration of a dangerous shape-shifter, it would be difficult to surpass this place. At first, though, he thought no one was there. He could see nothing, hear nothing, and smell nothing but damp rock. Had Perethor tricked him, and brought him to the wrong place? He lay still, straining, all too aware of time slipping by and his heart thumping furiously in his chest. At last, he called out.

'Carea?'

He sensed the barest change in the atmosphere, as if the name had hit home somewhere. Straining his eyes, he thought he saw the tiniest movement and a scrape of something light against a dark backdrop. He thought he was seeing things, but then, with painstaking slowness, a piteous figure uncurled itself and stood up on shaky legs. Thin, frail, covered in filth and grime, the identity was nevertheless unmistakeable. The confinement had not subdued the tall elegance yet, nor had the darkness managed to wholly dim the immortal beauty. Just as he and the others had feared, Carea was here. He had never quite fully believed it until now. He shuddered to see the awful reality of her predicament. Had he not come, here she would have remained, her immortality no longer a virtue but a condemnation to eternal bondage. No death would have intervened to cut short her suffering. Choked to tears by these thoughts, it took Curillian several moments to counter them with the realisation that he was here now, and could do something about it. Pushing aside his revulsion, and the nagging thought of how she had come to be here in the first place, he called to her again.

'Carea...' The pale figure stepped unsteadily towards him, looking up with shocked eyes. Her voice came up to him, distant and wondering.

'That voice…I know that voice. My heart remembers those tones. Out of darkness I am transported to rolling green fields where the horses ran strong, to a time of unlikely fellowship, and courageous common cause…' She paused as tears and sorrow overtook her. Her sobs cut through the damp air like whiplashes. Through the grief, she spoke again, welcome words welling up from improbable hope. '…Oh my Ruthion, is it really you…? Are you really here?'

To hear her voice plead so piteously cut him to the heart, laying bare the emotions that had been covered by centuries of forgetting.

'It is. I am here.' He felt more tears coming to his own eyes, and emotion catching in his voice. 'Carea, I've come for you. You're leaving this vile place…now.' He held out his hands, stretching downwards.

'*Prélan étyr lauthaeyes, miel Maren ilyades gevron ídavalir Maray gaälésus hán.*'

She reached up with her arms. She could not reach. Curillian slithered forward, stretching as far as he could. Fleetingly their fingers touched, but they could not grasp the other's hands. Swallowing hard, Curillian swung his legs round and launched himself down into the pit, all his pain forgotten. As soon as he was down, he knelt by her, then reached up for her hands. She understood what he was doing, and placed her feet on his shoulders. She weighed nothing. Trusting the balance of an elf, Curillian heaved upwards, lifting her into the air. He felt her let go of his hands and reach upwards for the shelf.

'I cannot reach…' she cried. A rage took him then. He would not be defeated; he would not let them remain here in this pit. Summoning strength that for all but the most extreme of needs lay well out of reach, he seized her calves, crouched down, and with a pain-filled roar of defiance, he launched her upwards. He felt the miniscule weight leave him. He heard her scrabble against the rock, heard her exertion as she rolled up onto the shelf. Now for him. She could not reach down to him anymore than he had been able to reach down for her, so he rushed to the far side of the pit. He hurled himself back, sprinting across the floor, and leapt up onto the wall. Needing no handholds, his feet ran up the vertical face like steps. His momentum carried him up to her waiting arms, and then she took over before he fell back down. Long imprisonment could not totally atrophy the ancient strength of the noblest race that ever walked beneath the sun, and she lifted him upwards until he could seize the shelf for himself. He hauled himself up, and then lay panting, the extra strength deserting him as quickly as it had risen up.

The urgency of the situation jabbed him like an elbow in the ribs. He forced himself to first sit up, and then crouch. She too crouched, and for a moment, they beheld each other's eyes. What she was thinking, Curillian did not know, but he was gauging her strength. What lay before was surely more difficult and dangerous than what had already passed. She looked so weak, so pale and drawn, that he doubted she could manage shape-shifting or any other magic. He hoped she could run, but he would carry her if he must. He took her hand and yanked her to her feet.

'Come, we must be gone.' He paused at the open portal to whisper through. 'Perethor, we're coming out.'

There was no answer.

When Curillian had crawled back through, he found the elf gone. 'Curse him!' he hissed savagely. 'The coward has deserted us.'

'Who?' Carea asked as Curillian turned to help her through also.

'Perethor, a snow-elf – it was he who led me down here.'

'I do not know him. Only harracks...'

'Come, we cannot worry about him now. If he's fled, he'll be dead soon, and so will we if we don't get out of here. Can you run?'

'My legs will carry me if they must.'

'They must.'

He whisked her away and then they were flying, hand-in-hand, blindly back up the low corridors of Faudunum. Without Perethor he did not know the way, but he retraced their steps as best he could remember. The faithless snow-elf was nowhere to be seen. At any moment he expected the hue and cry to go up. Stealth was still possible, but if the alarm should sound, he knew all they could do was make a run for it. He needed to recover his sword also, but if that were not possible, then Carea was by far the more precious of the two. He would get her out if he could, and then come back for the sword. The tournament could wait; he would not leave the Sword of Maristonia in the hands of heathens.

They saw no one, and with every corner turned, their fears redoubled. Cold sweat ran in chilling drops down his spine. At last, they seemed to come to the upper levels. Curillian fought to control his breathing as Carea collapsed against him. Her weakened legs gave way beneath her. He would have to support her from now on.

He led her out into a grey corridor where receding daylight told him that evening had fallen. They passed the nightmarish shapes of harrack carvings that leered at them in the half-light. With Curillian half-supporting, half-carrying the princess, they staggered along the corridor, their feet slapping against the stones. They passed the misshapen apertures of a miserable cloister, but no sign of life did they see in the hard courtyard beyond. Curillian's suspicions began to grow. He was about to lead her out towards the open sky, thinking that way offered their best hope, when his way was blocked by falling stone crashing down in front of his toes. He leapt back and tangled with Carea, the pair of them falling in a heap. The building itself remained standing, but stone barriers, moved by some cunning of the harrack masons, fell down over the cloister apertures. He blinked through the dust – he had never seen anything like it. Were the harracks able to manipulate stone like a potter would clay? He picked them up, and stumbled in another direction, the only one which had been left open to them. Up some stairs they limped, and then, again, when they tried to turn in a promising direction, they were brought up short by stone angrily reforming into a barricade. Were they being watched, their way barred only when they came to a favourable route? He felt like a mouse trapped in a changing labyrinth, but he struggled on.

They made their way heavily along another tunnel, hoping for another glimpse of open air. If they could only find a way to the battlements, find a postern gate, or something… As they were hobbling along, the floor itself turned against them. The lifeless flagstone lurched up beneath them like a catapult, tipping them off balance. At the same time, a treacherous hole appeared in the wall, which moments before had been solid stone. They were pitched down a long slope and deposited out into another corridor. The burning pain of all Curillian's hurts returned, but he had to pick himself and Carea up again. Another corridor, another turn, another sudden dead end.

Hopelessly disorientated, they saw ruddy light ahead and stumbled up a wide staircase. Suddenly they emerged out into an open space. It was what he had hoped for – a glimpse of the city's outer battlements, and a clear way to reach them – but his hope cheated him. The vast courtyard they had entered was not empty. Through thin nighttime mists, he saw Perethor, and with him were a hundred harracks. Their torches blazed all around, garishly illuminating grim stones and mocking faces alike. The way of escape was blocked by a hundred mattocks and maces, while above them, more harracks stood ready with crossbows and slingshots to shoot them down.

The wretched snow-elf looked terrified, and well he might, for next to him stood an enormous harrack, greater than any of the others. He was shorter than the elf, but almost three times thicker. He wore a chieftain's helm and bronze glittered among his furs and leathers. Across the shoulders of his chainmail were draped the claws of a bear. He leaned nonchalantly on an immense war-hammer, smug satisfaction etched deep in the stiff fissures of his granite face. Perethor's small voice came shrilly over to them.

'I'm sorry, Curillian.' Was he apologising for betraying them, or for failing them?

It was the harrack chieftain who spoke next, barking with laughter and then grinding out a coarse take on the common speech. It came out like the grating of a portcullis against a gatehouse's stone floor.

'Harrharrharr. So armist king, you pay visit to the city? But, leave so soon?' The harrack was barely capable of inflecting different intonation, but something like sarcasm was conveyed. 'I see you find one my treasures, the elf-witch. But, in haste you not find another...' He beckoned a crony forward, and the Sword of Maristonia sparkled in the torchlight. Almost as tall as the harrack who bore it dutifully forward, it glimmered like a jewel in a coal-heap. Curillian started, rage rising in him.

'That sword is mine, and was my father's, and his father's before him,' he shouted, full of wrath. 'You will give me back my own.'

He reached instinctively to his side to grasp his sword and then remembered that he had none. The harrack's guttural voice came again. The other harracks joined in too, filling the courtyard with a horrible grating noise. Then they stamped their feet in delight.

Curillian felt the ground throb between his own feet. Behind him, he felt Carea stir. She crouched down, arms flung forward, and started to incant, but her words were cut off. From out of the ground came stone bonds with vicious speed. Bands of stone, as malleable as any metal, snapped around her ankles; others shot up to seize her wrists, holding them fast, and another encased her head from behind, clamping down over her mouth. Curillian stood aghast, seeing the wild fear in her eyes. She was held fast, unable to do or say anything. The demonstration of harrack power over elven magic was brutal and overwhelming. Curillian turned his anger on the harrack chieftain.

'Is this how you defeat your enemies? You fear to face them so you encase them in stone? Cowards! Fight me!' He strode forward, eyes blazing his challenge. The lack of response made him shout all the louder. 'Give me a sword, and fight me!'

Still throatily chuckling, the chieftain nodded and beckoned another minion forward. He tossed a sword nonchalantly to Curillian. It clanged dully as it hit the ground and scraped towards him. It was notched all over and as battered as a squire's training post. All the same, Curillian picked it up. He would rather fight with a butcher's cleaver, but it would have to do. Hefting it in his hand, he looked up at the sky, where a few stars peeked through the mists.

Father, I've never needed You more than now. Time and again I've faced death, when all hope was gone, and always You delivered me. Let me win through, let these heathens who curse Your name be delivered into my hands. Give me the strength I need, I have such need of it…

Fortified, he looked down again, sweeping his eyes round the assembled harracks. He sought out one set of eyes after another.

'Who will fight me? Send your best against me!' He looked challengingly at the chieftain. 'If I throw down your champion, you will let us go, myself and the two elves. If I fall, you may take their lives too…'

To his astonishment, the chieftain shrugged, and then nodded.

'As you say, grass-eater. You win, you go free. You lose, you all die. NOW,' he raised his harsh voice. 'SEE MY CHAMPION.'

As if at some hidden signal, the whole place started to shake. The courtyard trembled as if it was in the grip of an earthquake, and masonry flaked away from the surrounding walls. Harracks scattered as something came bursting out of the ground. What Curillian had thought was just a squat statue now turned out to be the head of something much larger. A stone-helmed head rushed upwards, followed by battlemented shoulders and a granite torso. Up and up it rose, straightening legs like mighty arch-posts. The diabolical figure loomed out of a cloud of dust, leaving a mess of rubble and gaping earth. It was ten feet tall, a stone gladiator brought to life. Baleful red eyes looked out in a mockery of true life.

Curillian steadied himself after having been shaken by the thing's emergence. Here was an old legend become reality in front of his eyes. In the Great Wars, seven thousand years and more ago, the elves had fought all the manifold demons of hell's host. If the tales were true, one breed was made of stone but given a monstrous semblance of life in movement and malice, and they had proved unstoppable juggernauts in battle. Carea, had she been able to speak, might have told him more, for it was her kin who had courageously fought against such demons. Not in his worst nightmare did Curillian ever think that he would have to face one. Yet it seemed that one had slept here, beneath the cold floors of Faudunum. Long ago, it must have sought refuge here from the vengeful victors of that ancient conflict. Now it had awoken, rising to meet his challenge.

The demon did not wait long to press its attack, and came stomping towards him like a moving tower. No weapon did it wield or need but its club-like hands, and it came on seeking to trample him like a charging bull. Curillian did the last thing it expected and charged towards it, closing the gap between them even faster. Eyes wide, he slid under the giant arm which came scything round, and as he passed he struck at the demon's thigh with his sword. His momentum took him well past the charging demon, sliding across the flag-stones. He glanced down at his sword. It was snapped off at the hilt. *So much for my weapon.* He flung it away, knowing he had to reach the Sword of Maristonia somehow. He had never taken it to stone before, but if any blade could harm this monstrosity, then it was the great sword of his forefathers. Forged from a fallen star-shard, blended with unbreakable Zimmerill, the metal of heroes, it was the mightiest weapon ever created. He needed it now.

Slow to realise what its enemy had done, and even slower in lumbering to a halt and turning round, the demon came back for another charge. Curillian saw that his sword was still with the chieftain, who had withdrawn to watch the fight from the safety of a stone platform set in the corner of the courtyard, like a royal viewing box at a tourney. No time to get to it now, he fled before the demon's next onrush, struggling to keep his feet as the earth lurched under the force of the pistoning footfalls. Sprinting for all he was worth, Curillian reached a set of wall-steps and thundered up them. The stone-demon caught up with him and brought a trunk-like arm down, shattering the steps just behind Curillian's heels. *Speed,* thought Curillian, *speed is the key. I must out-manoeuvre him.* He tried to think how the elf-heroes of the ancient days had felled their enemies, or what tactics the fabled Demon-slayers of the dwarves employed, but the thoughts fled before his mind in the panic of staying alive.

Quicker than its lumbering frame would suggest, the demon crashed down its other arm, this time just in front of Curillian, bringing him up sharp. The top of the stairs disintegrated into demolished stone, and he had to fling himself up to reach the parapet. All his pain was drowned in a wave of adrenaline, and he swung himself nimbly up. Suddenly he found himself looking out over the battlements, but only into the next courtyard. He had hoped they were near the outer walls, whence they could escape, but no, they were right in the centre of the fossilised honeycomb of Faudunum. He picked up a dislodged stone, as large as he could manage, and flung it at the unearthly face. It smashed into the stone helmet, and momentarily gave the demon pause, but it did no more damage than a rock-fall to the mountain. The stone-demon returned a stone of his own, one the same size as Curillian. Curillian threw himself flat and gasped as it screeched an inch above his head and crashed into the crenellations. Looking across, Curillian saw a six-foot stretch of battlement blasted clean away.

He catapulted himself to his feet and started to run. He sprinted around the top of the courtyard, following the ramparts, which exploded behind him into smithereens as the stone-demon flailed wildly. No sooner did the demon start to find his range than Curillian quit the wall and hurled himself back down to the courtyard. Crashing into an awkward roll, he came up running like a madman and ducked through the archway that loomed up before him. The harracks were laughing again, enjoying their grim sport. They didn't care where their quarry went, for their pet demon would catch it; nor how much of their city was wrecked in the chase, for it could be rebuilt in no time. Curillian dashed down the corridor he found himself in, hearing it boom and echo with the sound of what was following him. Charging through a hail of falling dust and stone, he hurtled back into the courtyard by another arch, choking and barely able to see. The stone-demon, too big for the corridor, stopped striking the roof and made to give chase in the open again.

Curillian found another set of wall-steps and took to the battlements again. He raced around, making towards the corner where the harracks were watching from their platform. Between him and them, a great bulwark protruded, breaking the run of the rampart with outthrust stone. He saw a long chain hanging down from it and hoped it would reach far enough. Before he could get to it, though, a furious fist struck the stone beneath his feet, trying to pummel right through it. He staggered against the battlements as the rock crumbled under him. Scrambling up again, he ran, hopping and jumping from one embrasure to another. He saw the latest swing of a mighty arm coming, and he leapt right over it, launching himself in a desperate lunge for the chain. He was fully horizontal and just about to plunge down when he caught it, and then he was hurtling through the air on it. He swung, screaming, right around the corner of the bulwark, and just as he sensed the arc come to its limit, he let go and thrust his body forward. Then he was flying through mid-air, borne by the momentum of the swing. He crashed down amongst the harracks feet first with the force of a battering ram. He flattened several of them, and lay stunned and winded.

They were shocked at his sudden appearance in their midst, and were slow to react. Perethor stared at him in abject amazement. In those precious moments, he forced his mutinous body to respond and regained his feet. Shoving violently, he caused further consternation by heaving the harracks nearest to him against their fellows. Picking up a fallen mattock, he lashed out, using the harracks' own weapon against them. He did not intend to fight for long; he just needed to win through to his sword. He focused on the harrack bearing it and battered his way through to him. Evading the swipe of the outraged chieftain, he bulled into the harrack holding his sword and pitched them both from the platform down into the courtyard below. He landed on top of the harrack, breaking his fall at the other's expense. Taking up his sword, he hacked open the harrack's throat and left him spluttering in the dust. Ignoring the tumult above him on the platform, he turned to face the stone-demon.

His opponent had not been idle. With a wrench, it had pulled the chain free from the wall, pulling down half of the tower with it. He was upon Curillian scarce two heartbeats after he had dispatched the harrack. Curillian flung himself backwards in a half-roll, half-somersault to avoid the vast foot that came stomping down to squash him. Coming back up with a war-shout, he attacked the foot while it stood planted. He watched the Sword of Maristonia score along the stone, sparks flying. It did no harm, but it did not break either. It felt good to have it back in his hands, stronger yet lighter than the crude length of iron he'd held before. With it, he felt he had a fighting chance. He struck again, putting all his dwindling strength into the blow. His arms jarred as it connected with the back of the demon's knee, but still it did not bite deep enough. As he withdrew the unbroken blade, its gleam dulled by stone-dust, the demon swung at him as an armist might at an annoying wasp that has just stung him. He was too slow to react, and as he leapt away, the stone fist caught him a glancing blow. He clattered to the floor, head swimming. He just saw the foot coming, and managed to fling himself out of its path in a desperate roll. The demon then tried to pick him up, and Curillian paid it for its folly by shearing off one of its fingers with a flash of his sword. This time the demon reacted, lurching upwards and roaring in pain. *That got him*, Curillian thought.

Taking advantage of the demon's pause, he dashed to where the chain lay torn from its fixings, and took it up. Quick as he could, he flung it round the demon's nearer foot. He was just about to run it around to the other foot when the demon reached down and with surprising dexterity seized the chain. Heaving on it, he sent Curillian flying. Skidding across the ground in a blaze of agony, Curillian forced himself to his feet again as quickly as he could. When the demon let go of the chain, he kept hold of it, dragging it with him on an impulse. He fled the courtyard again, this time by another exit. Larger than the others, it seemed to be a main thoroughfare, which meant the demon was able to follow him. Carrying the chain over one shoulder, and brandishing his sword in the other hand, he darted into a narrow doorway and hurried up the spiralling stairway within, chain clanking behind him. He heard the whump and thump of the demon striking at stone outside, trying to find where he had gone. Curillian came out on a flat rooftop, and had long enough before the demon spotted him to take his bearings. The flat roof he was on now was joined to another across the street by a narrow bridge, and that rooftop opposite led back to the battlements of the main courtyard.

Dangerously unbalanced by his burdens, he shuffled across the bridge and on to the other rooftop. Now the demon had spotted him and, seeing that it could not reach him from the street below, had found another way up. It battered a whole wall down and used its ruins as a staircase. Meanwhile, Curillian used his bought time well and hurried to where the rooftop backed onto the battlements. He picked a spot between two squat towers and looked out over. To his dismay, there was no rampart beneath him here, only a straight drop of thirty feet down into the courtyard. Hearing the awful noise of his pursuer, he turned and saw the demon scrambling up his makeshift steps. Thinking quickly, he saw iron hooks protruding from the walls of the towers. Hurriedly, he dropped his sword and fastened one end of the chain to one of them. The demon had gained the rooftop now and was rumbling towards him, intent on putting an end to this chase. Curillian felt an odd calm descend on him. He stood, obvious and unafraid in the gap. In his hands, he gripped the length of chain fiercely. Like an avalanche of stone in the mountains, the demon bore down on him, desperate to catch and kill. Either it did not know the courtyard lay so near, or it did not give thought to it. It charged right up to where Curillian waited, and at the last possible second, Curillian dashed to one side, carrying the chain with him.

'MARISTON!' he yelled, fear giving his feet wings. In the blink of an eye, he was gone, and hurled himself against the opposite tower. With all his might, he stretched the chain taut and leaned all his weight against it. The stone-demon had no time to react and clattered into the chain. Its vast weight and momentum carried it forward until it tripped and fell headlong into the courtyard. The whole city shook and dust rose in plumes as the great gladiator crashed down in ruin.

In the eerie silence that followed, Curillian retrieved his precious sword. He cast down the chain and lowered himself wearily down into the maelstrom of stone and dust. Picking his way forward, he walked past the stone helmet, which lay quite still. From their high platform, the harracks were looking down, appalled. Curillian staggered out into full view of them, and looked up. For a long moment there was silence, except for the sound of small bits of stone pattering down. Curillian heard the stirring behind him even as he saw the expression on the harrack chieftain's face change from one of shocked horror to smug triumph. He turned to face his enemy, knowing he had no strength to fight again. The stone-demon was trying to rise, prying itself up from the indent it had made in the floor of the courtyard.

Then, something else happened. Snaking tendrils of vegetation suddenly appeared, emerging out of cracks in the ground. Vines and tree-roots, thin at first, but then waxing thicker, crawled all over the demon, festooning it like overgrown ruins. The weight of them tugged it back down to the floor. More and more came, and tighter they tugged on the scarred stone. Curillian turned his head, and through clouds of dust, saw Carea, still bound fast but with one hand free. The fall of the demon must have broken one of her bonds. With her one hand, she wove the spell, controlling the vegetation. Slowly the roots exerted intense pressure, and Curillian saw them bunching like muscles. He watched as all the age-long grip of trees condensed down into the fury of a few seconds. A deep groaning sound arose and grew louder and louder until suddenly an almighty crack rent the air. A dozen other cracks followed and then all was still. Slithering away as quickly as they had come, the vines and tree-roots vanished, leaving the stone-demon splintered into a dozen different pieces.

Turning back to Carea, he watched her other bonds fall away, as if they had been held in place by the life of the stone-demon. She was weak, though, and with the spell now done, she collapsed back to the floor, spent. Curillian went to her and cradled her in his arms. He feared the awesome output had killed her already frail life-force. She smiled wanly up at him. Weariness overcame him as he knelt there with her. He heard the tramping of boots as the harracks stomped down from their platform and surrounded them in a wide circle. Crossbows were shouldered and aimed at the pathetic pair of figures in the courtyard's centre. Looking from Carea to the poised harracks, Curillian blinked away tears. His end had come. Grasping his sword to him, and still hugging Carea tight, he turned his mind to Prélan. His prayer muffled the sound of the crossbow bolts being loosed, but when they burst into flame in mid-air, his mind snapped back to reality. The war cry seemed to come from all sides at once.

'MARISTON!'

X

Into the Black

AGAINST All hope, they made it to the foot of the walls without being spotted. Evening was fast falling into night. Skirting round the outer ramparts, they had come to the back of the eerie fortress and crouched now in the shelter of a few sparse pine trees. The armists paused, trying to get their breath back, but Sin-Serin looked fearful and anxious to press on. Did she sense something the rest of them did not? The obstacle of the wall daunted them all, for there seemed to be no way up it. They had ropes with them, but no grapnel-hooks to latch onto the battlements. They had taken great pains to avoid the guarded main gate, but now they had come to an insurmountable barrier. No postern gates or sally ports were there, just sheer stone. Sin-Serin looked around, surveying the terrain immediately around them.

'Cut down one of the trees,' she commanded. They looked at her as if she were mad, but Roujeark saw that even saying the words pained the wood-elf.

'What are you thinking, elf?' Lancoir challenged her. 'We've got no time to play at lumber-jacks!'

'I will get us in, but I need a tree.'

Roujeark looked up and saw that the trees, although poor stunted specimens, were nearly as tall as the wall. Did Sin-Serin think she could make a ramp by leaning one of the trees against the wall? Lancoir looked as if he were about to object again, but then he gave the nod to the other armists. Aleinus, Antaya and Findor took out their axes. Lancoir and Roujeark joined them and together they hacked at the nearest pine. Fearful of the chopping noises giving them away, they bent to the work with feverish haste. With a crack and a drawn-out groan, the tree surrendered its uprightness and toppled over. Roujeark was dismayed by the noise it made, and even more so to see it fall short of the wall – maybe it wouldn't reach after all? But Sin-Serin was not perturbed. Under her direction, she had them strip away all the smaller branches, leaving just the long, thin trunk.

'Now pick it up,' the elf ordered. The armists hesitated again, but they complied when they saw the determined confidence in her face. Heaving, the five armists lifted the fallen trunk and held it waist-high. Sin-Serin looped one coil of rope over her shoulder and took up the front of the trunk. She looked up at the wall, sizing it up.

'Back up,' she hissed, and they shuffled awkwardly backwards. Speaking softly, the elf gave them last instructions over her shoulder. 'When I give the word, run for all you're worth toward the wall. When you can't run any further, keep holding the trunk and push it upwards. I'll do the rest.' The armists exchanged bewildered looks with each other, none of them understanding. They weren't given time for further reflection.

'Now!' hissed Sin-Serin.

They started forward and soon broke into a lumbering trot. They built up all the speed they could thus encumbered and charged towards the wall. When Sin-Serin reached the foot of the wall, she flung her legs upward, planting them on the wall. Keeping a hold of the trunk, she walked quickly upwards. Aleinus was the next to reach the wall, and he came up short. Staggering under the weight, he nevertheless managed to angle the trunk upwards, levering Sin-

Serin higher. One by one they all came to a halt and then switched their efforts to lifting the trunk. Intuitive understanding came to them as they watched Sin-Serin propelled higher, and they strained upwards. Lancoir was at the back with the heaviest section of the trunk, and he thrust upward with the force of two armists. Hand over hand they passed the trunk upward, ignoring splinters, and the higher it went the more they struggled to keep it steady. Had Sin-Serin not been guiding it from the top, it would have fallen. Eventually they ran out of trunk and gave one last heave. Sin-Serin was nearly at the top. Their last upward shove unbalanced them and they lost control of the trunk. With no support beneath it anymore, the trunk swayed to one side as if in a re-enactment of its original felling moments before. Sin-Serin, though, was equal to the challenge, and even as the trunk lurched sideways, she let go of it and stretched upward for handholds. Another few inches and she would have been out of reach of tiny skirting-shelf of rock just below the battlements. The trunk crashed down sideways, deflecting off the wall and rolling down the slope.

Sin-Serin was left hanging by her fingertips, agonisingly short of the battlements. Had it all been for nothing? Roujeark thought. But no, as they watched, craning their necks upwards, she shifted her grip and turned herself so she was no longer facing the wall but outwards. They had no idea how she managed to maintain her grip in that position, but she did so, fingers straining. Momentarily she looked as helpless as a criminal chained to a wall, but then she rocked her legs outwards. Again and again, she swung her legs, building momentum, and then, just as she lost her grip, she surged upwards in an acrobatic summersault. Defying gravity, she let go of the wall and soared heels over head in a backward arc. Their hearts were in their mouths as they watched her, but she landed on the embrasure between two flanks of parapet with all the poise and finesse of a professional tumbler. Not wasting a second, she sprang lightly down out of sight. She disappeared for such a long time that they began to grow disconcerted, but then they heard a muffled thump. Moments later, she reappeared and cast the rope down to them. She had made its end fast to the battlement so they would be able to climb up. One by one, they shinned up the rope, thankful that they had had an easier time of it than their guide.

'That was a neat trick,' Lancoir told her grudgingly as he dropped over onto the rampart's walkway. Roujeark was astonished to see unshed tears shining in the elf's eyes as she answered.

'The pine may only have been a poor stunted creature, living in shadow, but it gave its life for us.' Lancoir nodded, acknowledging the sentiment for no more than a split second. Then he was up.

'Time is short, we must go.' They passed the slumped figure of the harrack sentry that Sin-Serin had dispatched, but they did not see any others.

'Where are they all?'

'Something is happening in this city,' Sin-Serin responded, as if she could sense it through the stones. 'A distraction is benefitting us, and there's only one cause I can think of.'

'The king,' said Lancoir grimly. He redoubled their pace. Suddenly their progress round the outer rampart was brought up short by a great tremor, which ran all through the city and shook the stone beneath their feet. Sin-Serin spoke urgently to them, fear in her normally serene eyes.

'A great evil is stirring, we must hurry.'

'How do we know where to find the king?' asked Caréysin.

'Follow the noise,' the elf told him, rushing past. True enough, there followed an ominous series of sounds, thumps and crashes, all of it portending destruction. Roujeark even saw a cloud of dust rising in the night air ahead of them, out of the heart of the city, and he wondered fearfully what was going on.

They saw other harracks as they went but none of them paid any heed, or even showed any sign that they had seen the intruders at all. The armist party had kept to the rooftops and upper ways, but down below, at street level, harracks were hurrying towards the centre of the city in their scores. Unmistakably, something had them so concerned that they were heedless of all else. Roujeark could understand their preoccupation: the tumult sounded as if the city was being torn apart. What was going on? Up ahead, torchlight peeped garishly out from a great open space, the only light in the whole cold citadel. It was partially obscured by clouds of dust, but it gave them something to aim for.

After an infuriating series of wrong turns, they finally found a way to reach the torchlight. A crooked stair brought them up a squat tower, which overlooked a great courtyard. Through the roiling dust, they saw first a ring of harracks with crossbows, and then a forlorn pair of figures huddling together in the middle. Heaps of stones and fallen masonry lay everywhere, and Sin-Serin, normally so taciturn, gasped when she saw the broken stones still resembling the outline of an enormous stone figure.

The armists crouched helplessly, even Lancoir unsure of what to do, but Roujeark's mind was suddenly sharp and incisive. Even before he had taken in all the details of the scene below, he knew that the king was the figure in the middle of the harracks, and he knew also that their crossbows were about to fire. Feeling a throb of power bursting to life within him, he stretched out his arms, and the wildfire surged down them. The crossbow bolts were loosed with ragged, mechanical coughs. Simultaneously his fingertips ignited into flame, and, quicker than thought, that flame spread to the bolts in mid-air. No trail of fire connected his glowing hands with the bolts – this time he had managed to ignite the flames where he wanted them. The bolts never reached their targets – so hot did the flames burn that they were consumed in an instant and fell in showers of ash to the courtyard floor.

Lancoir was shaken out of his uncertainty by the spectacle of Roujeark's power. It was the turn of him and his guards now. He bellowed a war cry that was soon taken up and repeated by his companions.

'MARISTON!'

With ropes tied to the tower's battlements, Lancoir and the six guardsmen flung themselves over the edge and abseiled rapidly down into the courtyard. Caréysin fired a quick succession of arrows at the harracks and then followed the others. Once they hit the floor, they charged towards their beleaguered king. The suddenness of their appearance gave them the edge of a few crucial seconds. The bewildered harrack crossbowmen had barely recovered from the shock of their vaporised bolts when the armists were on them. Swords crashed down onto the crossbows, splintering them, but the harracks themselves were harder to destroy. The heaviest blows managed to bite into them, but anything less than a full-blooded chop seemed to jump back, thwarted. It did not take them long to begin fighting back, nor for more harracks to lumber into the fray, brandishing their mattocks. There followed a desperate skirmish in the courtyard, garishly illuminated by the flames.

Lancoir made straight for the king. The moment the crossbow bolts had burst into flame Curillian had leapt to his feet, brandishing his great sword in defence of the elf slumped beside him. Lancoir knew better than to underestimate his king, but all the same, he looked bone-weary, just about ready to collapse. He dared not think what he had already been through. So, he rushed to his side and stood back to back with him. Several harracks drew near, menacing brutes in the firelight.

'Lancoir,' Curillian called over his shoulder. 'We must get out of here. We'll be surrounded soon.' Lancoir glanced back at his king.

'We'll have to fight our way out. Can you manage it?' The king's look was savage.

'I'll die before this sword leaves my hands again.' As if to prove his point, he lashed out and hewed a harrack's head clean from his shoulders. The Sword of Maristonia had no trouble cleaving the thick, leathery skin that was turning other blades.

The armists were hard-pressed to defend themselves when the harracks came up in force. Killing them was hard enough, but until the killing blow was dealt, they seemed to feel no pain at all. All the remaining Royal Guards were thrown back and staring death in the face when Lionenn came to their rescue. Wielding his stolen mattock, he came charging through the harracks like a maddened bull. Sweeping his weapon left and right, he bludgeoned several harracks and stamped them into the ground. His victory was brief, though, for a heavy mattock blow from behind knocked him down, club clattering on the courtyard floor. The harracks pressed in close again and the armists were hemmed in with their king and captain. Sin-Serin was nowhere to be seen, although visibility in the courtyard was poor.

Lancoir was just readying himself for a hopeless last stand when the harrack in front of him burst into flames. His thick furs caught fire like a pitch-soaked torch. Then the same thing happened to another, and then another. Just then, Roujeark came striding through the ruddy dust-clouds like an avenging angel. Utterly different from how they had seen him before, he looked like an armist possessed. He was now wielding his fire with full confidence, and at his coming, a whole ring of the harracks had been ignited. Panic-stricken, they dropped their weapons and went into a mad, whirling dance. They rent the air with unearthly shrieks and caused mayhem among those of their own kind who were not yet on fire.

'NOW,' shouted Lancoir, 'RUN FOR IT!'

Curillian paused only long enough to sling Carea across his shoulder, and then they were all moving. The harracks had fled before them, and Roujeark and Findor followed as a rear-guard. They stumbled blindly forward, tripping over fallen masonry, and then met Sin-Serin coming back through the dust. She beckoned them forward, seemingly knowing the way. She led them to a small archway where a pathetic figure was huddled. Curillian saw that it was Perethor, cringing and sobbing.

'He comes with us,' he told Lancoir. No sooner had he said the words than an enormous figure leapt down at them from above. Curillian and Lancoir were knocked flat in opposite directions, but Curillian was the first up, sword ready. It was the harrack chieftain, whom he had not seen since he had won back his sword. A mad angry light was in the chieftain's eyes, and he came at his erstwhile prisoner with a mace studded with metal barbs. Curillian backed away from the savage onset, evading the massive swings of the mace. Then he stepped smartly to one side and cut down, cleaving the chieftain's mace-hand off at the wrist. Weaponless, the enormous harrack still tried to rush him, seeking to crush him against the wall with his sheer weight, but again Curillian gave way before him. He bought himself enough space and then crouched low. Putting all his strength into a great sideways swing, he cut the harrack's legs out from under him. The chieftain went down heavily, screaming like a wounded boar. Curillian glanced at the hateful face, twisted in a paroxysm of pain and rage, only for a moment before ending his enemy's life with a sword-tip through his neck.

The fight had only lasted thirty seconds, but it had given the other harracks a chance to regroup. Curillian pointed his sword at Perethor, and said again, 'He comes with us.'

'Yes,' agreed Sin-Serin, 'my kinsman here will show us the way out.' The wood-elf looked at Carea, eyes full of concern, as her unconscious kinself lay slumped over the king's broad shoulder. But when she returned her attention to Perethor, the snow-elf hurriedly pulled himself together and led them through the arch-way. He nearly died a moment later when a harrack swung a mattock at him from round a corner, but the brutal blow missed by a hair's breadth and struck the wall, sending shards of stonework flying. Lancoir slew him with a mighty thrust and, pushing him aside, cleared the path. More harracks had returned to harry them from the rear, but Findor kept them at bay until Roujeark put the fear of fire into them again. Then they were on the move, fleeing through the cold passageways of Faudunum, dodging the slingshots and crossbow bolts loosed at them. Along chill tunnels and through cheerless streets they ran, all weariness forgotten in their desperation to escape. Perethor led them unerringly through many twists and turns, though barely a landmark did they pass. Several times they were accosted, but Lancoir seemed invincible as he cut down all who stood in his path.

Perethor led them round one last corner and suddenly they came to a downward slope that led to the outer walls thirty yards away. But he stopped abruptly, brought up short by what unexpectedly lay before him. The harracks had opened up a gutter in the street and filled it with an oily substance. No sooner had the escapers emerged round the corner than they set torches to the oil and instantaneously, a wall of fire scorched before them. Roujeark was not the only one who had fire at his disposal, it seemed. Through the searing heat, they could glimpse a gatehouse on the other side, their way of escape now beyond reach.

Perethor did not tarry long, leading them instead down another street. Running round a few more corners, he led them into an open space that was dominated by a hillock of rock. In the rock-face an arch was set, beyond which all was dark. Perethor plunged through the arch and into the blackness beyond. The armists hesitated only for a moment before following. Inside, all was pitch black until Perethor struck up a torch. Its fiery light revealed a well-hewn tunnel that sloped down before them, twisting away into the bowels of the city. Down the slope they ran, following its spiralling course deeper and deeper. Over the sound of their feet, they could hear the pursuit close behind, following them down underground. Where was this strange elf leading them?

At the bottom of the slope, they came to a smaller opening, a narrow gallery running into the rock at a slight downward angle and supported by wooden posts. A warm wind wafted up to them out of the depths. At the entrance to the shaft was a bulky dram made of cast iron. The huge dirty conveyance had four under-sized wheels, which rested on crude iron tracks on the shaft's floor. When Perethor told them to get in, the armist guards looked at him as if he were crazy, but he insisted.

'There's only one other way out of this mine, and its way down there,' he pointed down the shaft. 'It's either back up the tunnel to where the harracks are hunting for us, or further down, and it'll be faster by dram.'

Curillian led by example. He laid Carea in the dram and climbed in after her. Hurriedly the rest piled in, squeezing themselves into the narrow space. Perethor jumped in last, and as he did so, he released a huge iron lever beside them. With a grating sound, the dram seemed to come alive, and started to inch down the slope. The armists were alarmed to be moving, but Perethor was quite calm, and stayed holding another lever like a helmsman at a ship's tiller.

Their nerves grew as the dram quickly picked up speed, rolling on its tracks down into the darkness. Lancoir crouched at the front, holding the torch aloft as their only light and staring wide-eyed down the tunnel as it sped by quicker and quicker. Suddenly a gust of warm wind extinguished the torch and they were plunged into darkness. Screams were stifled, but panic-stricken terror surged up within all of them as the wobbling dram hurtled down into the darkness. They were sloshed around like slops in a bucket as the dram rounded corners, and their stomachs leapt into their mouths when they plunged down sudden drops. Above the whistling of the wind, Perethor's voice came to them out of the darkness.

'Stay calm, we'll slow down soon. We're coming to the habitable parts. There's light there.' True enough, they entered onto a long slow incline and they decelerated gradually until they were just rolling at walking pace. The darkness lifted somewhat as a ruddy light waxed stronger ahead and above them. Perethor insisted they all lie flat and be silent, so it was only by peeping over the edge that Lancoir saw their destination. They rolled slowly into what looked like a docking station, wooden boardwalks built on either side of the tracks, which now reached their terminus. Wall-braziers flickered, and in their light he could see a pair of harracks guarding the station. They seemed surprised by the unannounced arrival, and got slowly to their feet to inspect. As they approached, Lancoir gestured to his companions, and swords were readied. The two harracks leaned over the dram to look in from opposite sides, and the reward of their curiosity was a blade in the gullet. Their blood poured down, drenching the huddled fugitives, but they never had a chance to make a sound above a fleshy gurgling.

Disgusted, Roujeark couldn't get out of the dram fast enough. They all scrambled out, but Perethor went ahead, stealing quietly up the boardwalk to check their situation. While he was gone, the rest waited around anxiously, straining their ears for sounds of pursuit. Was there another dram to bring harracks after them? What lay ahead? Carea was barely conscious, leaning against Curillian, but they heard her say one intelligible word.

'Cloaks…their cloaks…' With a vague arm gesture, she pointed at the dead harracks. Lancoir quickly took her meaning.

'A disguise. Quick, take their cloaks, their helmets too.' He and Curillian fastened the thick bearskin cloaks over the top of their own clothes, wrinkling their noses at the smell, and placed the ugly iron caps on their heads. More apparel of the same sort was hanging from hooks beside the boardwalk, as if the station were meant to have more guards but was under-manned. Very soon, all of them were transformed into passable harracks. By that time, Perethor had returned from his reconnaissance.

'The coast is clear…for now. Come, we must be quick.'

When the boardwalk ended, the tunnel broadened and the ceiling opened out above them into a cavern. The light of wall-torches grew stronger and side passages started to appear. They soon saw that what they had taken for a mine was really an underground settlement, and quite an extensive one at that. They realised that there was more of Faudunum below ground than there was above. The chinking of hammers was all around, and the grinding of wheels and the echoing of distant feet and voices. They drew their stolen cloaks about them, and looking around they spotted harracks here and there. Some gave them suspicious looks, but none accosted them, and they hurried on. There were workshops and forges, sleeping areas, halls full of tables, benches, and kitchens, which smelt of red meat and strong ale.

Just as more attention was starting to be paid to them, they left the open caverns behind and passed into another tunnel. They were astonished to find a team of mules harnessed to a big waggon, full of barrels and boxes. It seemed to be some sort of supply vehicle. The mules were grazing from troughs of hay built into the walls, seemingly unattended. Fearing discovery at any minute, Perethor ushered them up into the waggon. As hurriedly as they could, they stowed themselves uncomfortably amid the cargo, while Perethor and Lancoir took up seats on the driver's bench. Just as a couple of harracks appeared in the tunnel behind them, they cracked the whips and rumbled off. The waggon's rickety wooden wheels bounced and trundled over snags and divots on the tunnel floor. The creaking of the waggon and the clip-clop of the mules' hooves seemed loud in their ears, but no trouble came.

After a while, though, they rounded a bend and saw a crossroad ahead. Wooden barricades and sentries guarded the underground junction. Involuntarily they pulled on the reins and slowed down, pulling their hoods down over their heads. They were spotted, and there was nowhere they could go except back up the tunnel. Lancoir hoped they could somehow bluff their way through. Was Perethor known down here and able to come and go? One of the sentries stepped into their path and the mules stopped of their own accord. The guard barked a word. Lancoir looked sidelong out of his hood at Perethor, but the elf beside him gave no sign. The order was repeated, more fiercely, but still Lancoir did not answer, but just sat hunched on the bench. He could feel the tension among his comrades in the bed of the waggon behind him. Impatient and suspicious now, the guard walked right alongside Lancoir and looked up at him, hefting a spear. Slowly, almost delicately, the harrack used his spear-point to push Lancoir's hood back. For a lingering second there was a startled silence, and something like bewilderment showed in the guard's face. Lancoir smiled at him, and booted him full in the mouth. Stunned, the guard fell back, and as he did so, Lancoir seized his spear. Beside him, Perethor cracked on the reins, geeing the mules on. Lurching forward, they burst through the wooden barricade, accompanied by the angry shouts of the other guards. Lancoir righted the spear and hurled it at one of the harracks as they careered past, pinning him against the wall of the tunnel.

Suddenly they were clear of the crossroads, plunging down the tunnel on the opposite side. The passageways behind them were alive with hoarse shouting now, a din that echoed menacingly down the confined space to them. They thundered on at breakneck pace. In one place, they passed a more open stretch where harracks crossbowmen stalked on a gallery above them. Bolts were loosed, but in a few seconds they had passed safely back into an enclosed tunnel. One quarrel had pierced a barrel of ale, and as they went, it spewed a frothy trail behind them. Aleinus cupped his hands together and slurped down a handful, breaking out into something between a grin and a grimace.

'Bleugh, it's not good stuff, but if I'm going to die, I'd rather have a drink in me!' Little did he or the others realise, though, that another bolt had hobbled one of the mules, and already they were slowing. Lancoir cracked the reins, but then they slewed and struck a protruding rock. It snapped off the back-left wheel, and the whole waggon lurched down to one side. The pierced barrel of ale teetered off and smashed on the floor, its frothing contents washing down the tunnel. They could go no further in the waggon, so they extricated themselves from the wreck, and prepared to go on by foot. But just then, they heard voices, and saw torchlight flickering up out of a side-tunnel. Lancoir looked down and saw a detachment of harrack soldiers storming up some stairs towards them. He knew swords wouldn't last long, so he called for the only missile to hand.

'Antaya, Andil, roll me one of those barrels.'

The two guards retrieved one of the casks, and rolled it along to their captain. In a show of tremendous strength, Lancoir lifted it up on high, just as a crowd of harracks emerged round a bend of the stairs into plain view. Lancoir hurled the barrel at them. It smashed into them and the wood burst asunder. Wood and ale exploded outwards in a foaming explosion, and the lead harracks were knocked back down the stairs, taking those behind with them. With the raucous din of their dismay ringing in their ears, the company carried on their way, hurrying as quickly as their tired limbs would allow. Perethor's call was a welcome relief when his words sank in.

'Not far to the gate now, keep going!'

They did, following the crooked tunnel ever downwards. Before long, they could see a brighter light ahead than the occasional wall-sconces. It came from a large space at the tunnel's bottom, where it expired in a great underground porch. Large pillars hewn into the hillside marked a smooth section of the rock-face. Two harracks were manning the gate, and they were ready for them, having heard them coming. Lancoir hacked down one, but the other nearly accounted for Curillian. Encumbered by Carea, Curillian just managed to avoid an axe-swing before Andil came to his aid and chopped off the harrack's arm, axe and all. In a few moments both gate-guards lay dead, but then the fugitives were brought up short. The gate appeared to be no gate at all, just a wall of stone where a gate should have been. It seemed the harracks didn't use wood for anything if they could use stone.

'How do we get out?' cried Aleinus, angry and frustrated. Wordlessly Perethor darted into an enclosed space to one side of the gate. Moments later, they heard a grinding noise as some hidden mechanism kicked into life. Before their eyes, the whole wall started inching upwards like a solid-stone portcullis. Throwing himself flat, Aleinus shouted that this was indeed the way out; he could see the world outside, but it was twenty feet away with solid stone hanging over the exit. To make matters worse, the gate was infuriatingly slow, only creeping upwards.

'Better get it to hurry up,' called Findor, who had gone back to the tunnel mouth to watch. 'They're coming!'

Sure enough, they could all hear the rumbling of many booted feet bearing down on them. Sin-Serin dropped flat as soon as there was enough space, and rolled herself through the aperture. Lancoir watched her do it, and shouted for the others to do likewise.

'Follow the bloody elf!' he roared, pushing Aleinus flat again and practically kicking him through the opening. He beckoned for Roujeark to do likewise. Curillian had rolled Carea under, where Sin-Serin took her up, and then followed himself. The gate was now waist-high. Antaya helped the groggy Lionenn down and then ducked through himself.

Just then, the harrack pursuers appeared. Dozens of them came pounding out of the tunnel like a rock-fall, and with barely a check in pace, they charged at the gate. Lancoir and Findor stood as a rear-guard, ready to do battle. Lancoir's blood was up, and he booted the first harrack back before cutting into him with a sideways swing of his sword. Findor accounted for another, before Lancoir blazed at him to get gone. Perethor reappeared a moment later, dragged from the guardroom by some harracks. In the confusion, he managed to snatch himself away and dive for the growing aperture. Lancoir cut down the harrack who lunged after him, flattening him with a vicious downward chop of his sword. Then he himself dove for the gap, rolling into the space and out into the world beyond. He was up and running in the blink of an eye, but Perethor stumbled and fell. The harracks, who came pouring out of the gate in pursuit, were on him in a moment, but Lancoir changed direction hastily and bulled into them. Hacking all about him, he bought enough time for Perethor to get away before wrenching himself free and retreating himself.

The terrain outside the gate was a rough downward slope, set well down the hill from the citadel on the summit. Not far ahead of them, though, the isolated Hill of Faudunum ran into the steep slopes of the valley beyond, which led back up into the mountains. A narrow, dipping saddle of land joined the hill to the mountain slopes beyond, and the whole area was covered with small, stalwart fir trees. The escapers fled down to the saddle, thinking to take refuge in the trees, but the harracks followed them, bent on revenge. Sin-Serin, still carrying Carea, led them on up the far slope, but they did not have the strength to go far.

Roujeark's energy was giving out, drained by the power that had burst out of him. Was it the fire within him subsiding, or was the air suddenly getting colder? They were running into a fine mist that seemed to be thickening with every step. Finally, they could go no further. As one, they turned to face their attackers, resolved on a final stand. The harracks themselves were toiling on the slope, squat figures on short legs, but when they saw their enemy at bay, they put on an extra spurt. The armists brandished their swords, and Sin-Serin and Caréysin bent their bows, as two-score harracks charged closer. But even as the escapers looked on-coming death in the face, strange war cries suddenly rent the cold night air. Wild ululating voices filled the misty air like fell beasts issuing forth. Then, the air around them became alive with angry objects whizzing by. Buzzing past their ears like maddened wasps, the missiles came from behind them and smacked into the oncoming harracks. Roujeark looked behind him, but in the mist, he could only see vague shadowy forms darting here and there. More missiles came, missing them, but striking down the harracks. With unerring accuracy, they struck the harracks in their eyes, felling them instantly with horrible squishing noises. The harracks thumped to the ground in droves.

Roujeark looked back again, and this time saw ghostly white figures running down-slope, swinging slingshots and screeching strange war cries. It was the Cuherai, the snow-elves, come to their rescue. They came through the trees like frozen banshees, and the missiles they hurled were lethal little pellets of ice. Little more than irritating when they struck armour or thick clothing, they were deadly against vulnerable parts. The snow-elves knew to go for the eyes of their tough-skinned enemies, and their accuracy was appalling.

Half the harracks were dead already. The snow-elves surged past the fugitives' defensive line and on down the slope. As they went, the very breath of their mouths seemed to freeze the air around them so that the world became like the inside of a winter cloud. The tendrils of freezing vapour dampened sound and visibility. As though from a great distance, they heard muffled groans and gasps as the remaining harracks either turned and fled back to their gate or were frozen solid were they stood.

Just as soon as the snow-elves came, they departed again. While their out-runners were dealing with the harracks, others came and hurried the escapers away. There were not many of them, but they seemed to be everywhere at once. Swiftly they retreated back up the slope, urging their friends up with them. When the exhausted armists could go no further, they collapsed. Silent sledges were brought up, and the fugitives were placed on them. In a trice they were on the move again, vanishing uphill at breath-taking speed. They did not stop for a long time, not until Faudunum was left far behind, and by that time the night air had cleared. They were in the Black Mountains again. Most of the guards lay asleep, and Carea and Curillian, side by side, seemed overcome with weariness. Even

Lancoir had submitted himself to the necessity of riding on a sledge, and now sat nodding, countless wounds left untended.

Roujeark, although bone-tired, found himself prickled by a strange wakefulness. He saw now that the sledges' sinewy hide ropes had been whisked upwards by packs of white wolves, slim but exceedingly fleet of foot. Now they sat around in a pack, panting and steaming. While the beasts were resting, the snow-elf leader came up, Aiiyosha herself. She made straight for where Perethor stood apprehensively among the armists. Several snow-elves stood nearby, like guards. The chieftain stalked right up to Perethor, stopping inches from his face. No words were spoken, but her fierce gaze made the rescued elf quail. Upon some hidden understanding, Perethor cringed and began to whimper pitifully, even as both arms seized him. Startled, Roujeark stumbled after as Perethor was dragged away into the night. The rest of the armists were oblivious as he was led away to the edge of a precipice. Fearing what was about to happen, Roujeark tried to intervene, but a snow-elf shoved him away. He came on again, but this time he was brought up short by the ice-blade suddenly held under his chin. All he could do was watch as Perethor was forced to his knees. Standing behind him, grasping him by the hair, Aiiyosha produced an ice-blade, pale and wickedly sharp. Looking up to heaven, as if in sacrificial ceremony, she uttered baleful words and drew the dagger redly across her victim's throat. While Perethor's life-blood was still gushing forth, he was picked up and hurled bodily into the depths.

✳

XI

Potent Persuasion

'HE Was a wanted elf,' Curillian told Roujeark. They were sitting together on a mossy stone. The shock of what he had witnessed still trembled in Roujeark. 'I thought he had just gone missing near Faudunum,' the king continued, 'but truth is that Perethor was an exile. He entered into it willingly, to escape the penalty for his crime.'

'What crime?' Roujeark asked.

'He raped a kinself. Fleeing to Faudunum was his only way of escape. It was a desperate measure, for there is little love between snow and stone. There he became a traitor, buying his life with secrets harmful to his kin. Wretched soul that he was, he soon yearned to return to his kin; yet he had no means of escape, nor any certainty that he would be received back with forgiveness. Maybe he hoped to expiate his sin by rescuing the princess, but he dared not attempt it until I came along. In the end, he helped, and I couldn't have done it without him, but he burned his bridges with the harracks. The traitor betrayed his masters, but he must have known he was going back to his death. Now I have lived to see the ruthlessness of Cuherai justice.'

The king fell silent, contemplating the right and wrong of it. In the end, he laid the matter aside, and, rising, he went to say farewell to his host. All his company was ready, refreshed and waiting for him. For a week, they had been succoured by their rescuers, strengthened by their broths and kept warm by their curious shelters. Now they were ready to set forth, and Curillian thanked Aiiyosha for all her kindness. The enigmatic snow-elf smiled and uttered over her guest a blessing after the fashion of her own kind. Carea and Sin-Serin said their own farewell, the wood speaking to the snow, kindred yet alien.

The snow-elves vanished almost before their very eyes, leaving them alone in the wilderness. Thick clouds were about them, obscuring the vistas on either side. Curillian took counsel with Sin-Serin and Carea, who had spent long hours in silent companionship with each other.

'Where are we to go next? Back to the forest?' he asked them. The princess was much stronger now, thanks to her time with the snow-elves, but her ordeal still lay heavily on her shoulders. She was frail and hunched, grey of face and withdrawn. Not a word had she spoken since their escape until now.

'No,' she said. 'Not to the forest. Your path lies ahead of you and not back. Sin-Serin, take us along the mountains' feet to Eldaphir's spring.'

'To Eldaphir I will go,' agreed Sin-Serin. 'It is the longer road home, but the fairer, and the safer.'

So their journey began again. Leaving that cold high place, they struck northward, leaving the perilous vale of Stonad behind them. Sin-Serin led them, and for a time their going was slow as they kept to the pace of Carea. She was silent, completely withdrawn into herself, and though she stumbled often and tired quickly, she kept going. Curillian watched her with worried eyes, but gradually he saw the colour coming back into her cheeks, if not the shadow lifting from her soul. Their going was slow also because of the terrain, which was difficult and tangled. Through deep ravines and over rock-strewn moors they trudged, winding ever northward through the tangled foothills. Every once in a while the persistent clouds would lift to reveal tantalising glimpses of glistening peaks above them, but to their right, the lower slopes seemed trapped under an impenetrable blanket of grey.

⅄

One night Curillian felt himself wakened by a strange sensation, like the caress of a passing mist. Looking up, he saw the outline of Carea stooped over him. It was still night, and he feared that something was wrong. But she put a finger to her lips, and bade him follow her. As he stumbled through the darkness, Curillian noticed that the stars were visible for the first time in many a night, and his breath misted in front of him. Unerringly Carea led him out of their little camp and into the darkness. She made for a pinnacle of rock rearing out from the dark hillside and started to climb. Up and up they went, the rock slope becoming steeper and steeper until they were climbing almost vertically. Her energy has certainly returned, thought Curillian. She was not satisfied until they had climbed right to the top, and inched along a narrow finger of rock, which overhung the hillside beneath. She sat them down, facing east, and Curillian saw the first hint of dawn tinging the horizon. Nothing obstructed his view to the east: all of Kalimar lay before them, shrouded in sleepy mists.

Giving no word of explanation, Carea just sat beside him in silence. There was no wind, all was still. Together they watched the world come slowly alive. Time as slow as the unfolding of the world passed as the light blue ribbon waxed larger, reaching into the sky until it was a broad swathe. Behind it came the vermillion band of nascent sunlight, creeping above the rim of the world and flushing into a thousand shades as it did so. Behind its fiery out-runners, the brilliance of the sun's onset lit up the sky, and suddenly the land below them began to be revealed. Curillian gave an involuntary gasp as the first slither of the sun's disc peeped above the horizon. Shy at first, then bolder and brighter, the sun rose until the whole elven kingdom was awash with golden splendour.

'I feel re-born,' Carea told him. He turned to look at her, and saw her face suffused with life. 'I have waited for just such a morning as this, a sign that all will be well. I have been lost in dark dreams...'

Curillian felt himself drawn in by her words and lost in the dream world they conjured about him. The great elven minstrels and storytellers could bring waking visions to life before their audience's eyes with the power of their words, and scarcely less potent was Carea's voice in that hour. Soon he ceased to hear them at all, but seemed to know them in his own mind. Vividly she retold the story of her capture, of how she had come to rescue a friend who had become ensnared in Faudunum, only to become caught herself.

Many allies strove with her to uncover the plots of the mountain-dwellers, but this one had probed too deeply, and needed rescue. Dread of the harracks and their rock-magic had not held Carea back, for she was of the royal line of Firnar, and great in power. Truly, had her mind not been focused on rescuing the captive, her power could have overthrown the city of the harracks, but the trap had been well laid. Keeping her within sight, the harracks had taken the captive ahead of her, leading her deeper and deeper into the earth. Wrathful, Carea's radiance in that dark place had been like a star fallen into a mine, but too little did she heed her surroundings. She took on the form of a sparrow to penetrate in through the narrow opening of the prison and, once within, was too late in changing back to prevent the slaying of the captive. Only then did she mark the form of the prison, an impervious square of delved rock with but one opening. That opening was now shut behind her, airtight and sealed with many locks. They had lured her into a tomb beyond the reach of any.

All of her magic could not avail her in that place, shut off in a lightless void. Bereft of the sunlight, wind, and wood that she thrived upon, she slowly faded in that place. As her vitality ebbed away, she came to understand all too well the efficacy of rock-magic in its own environment. Before her powers failed altogether she had perceived the presence of the stone-demon, and how through it the harracks could control the very rock itself, fault and vein. Wasting away, she lost all track of time, oppressed by the darkness and in peril of losing even her sanity. This was how Curillian had found her: weak, shrunken, beyond all hope. The red warrior from her past had reappeared and borne her back into the light. Only it wasn't really light at first, for the darkness clung to her even after she came into the open air again. She remembered the onset of great danger and trying to summon her powers against it, only to be constrained. Then there was a blank that she remembered not at all, and even after the stone-demon's fall, there was deep vagueness in her mind about their escape.

In fact, she recalled little until the snow-elves started to minister to her. With their arts, she was brought back to herself, and a little strength was imbued into her gaunt frame. Retrieved from the brink of forgetfulness, her spirit resumed its rightful place and the rest of her being soon followed. Yet not until now, with the rising of the sun on a clear morning, had the last of the darkness been washed away.

'Now I feel strong again; now many pathways lie open to me.' She looked at him and the vision of her tale receded. He saw her smile, brilliant in the sunlight, and his heart was warmed.

'I wanted to ask...how it was that you came to be trapped.'

'And now you know. You've come to my rescue before, Ruthion, but never again, my heart tells me. The former days are gone, and time hurries on to a new age. I cherish this time alone, for we shall never have it again. Very soon our paths shall sunder, we who were once comrades-in-arms for Prélan. Who knows wither He will lead you and I in the end? But now? Now it is my turn to come to your rescue, for your quest threatens to fail before it has begun. Follow the river below you until you come to the Eldarell Water-Meadows. There you shall have the audience that you need. See? I go ahead of you...'

Before his eyes, she changed. Casting off her raiment, she exchanged her skin for feathers and her arms for wings. With one last look, she unfolded her falcon's wings and launched herself from that promontory. With a keening cry, she soared over the wide valley below and was lost in the golden haze of the sun. The tug on Curillian's heart was so strong that he nearly leapt after her, but he gripped the edge of the rock and held himself tight. For a long time he watched after her, pangs of loss welling up inside him. In the confusion of his heart, he did not know what he had lost. A comrade? A friend? A lover? His memories cheated him so that he could not look back and clearly recall their encounters; all was lost in a blissful haze. He tried to leave the giddiness of those emotions behind on the high rock place, but in his climb down, he was heavy of heart. Yet when he reached the bottom of the outcrop, he perceived a door opening up before him, and an avenue closed and hidden behind him.

A

'Where is the princess?' Roujeark asked as Curillian returned to the camp. The rest were up now, assembling a breakfast round the cooking-fire, but they all stopped to look at him as he drew near. Each one marked something strange about the king, though to each of them it seemed different.

'She has gone ahead,' Curillian answered, 'to prepare the way.' Lancoir gave him a strange look, but no more was said. As they broke the camp, Curillian enquired of Sin-Serin.

'We are near to our goal now?'

'Verily,' affirmed the elf, 'the Spring of Eldaphir is near.'

'Good,' said Curillian. Then, turning to his armist companions, he told them, 'Our toiling in the foothills is at an end; soon we shall descend into the Vale of Nimrell.'

They spent one last night in the high country, exposed and cold. They built up a fire and, out of deference to Sin-Serin, went to the toil of scouring far and wide for wood that was dead. The wood-elf left them to their own devices, slipping off into the night. So the six armists were left alone.

'Come,' said Curillian. 'We only have the cordial of the snow-elves, but let us toast our fallen comrades.' They all stood. Curillian pronounced the roll call of honour. 'Haroth, and Manrion, who were lost in the avalanche.'

'They did their duty,' Lancoir intoned. 'Prélan keep their warrior's souls.' They drank.

'Cyron, Edrist, Norscinde and Utarion, slain by the bridge's collapse.'

'They did their duty; Prélan keep their warrior's souls.' This time they all chorused the words with their captain. They drank again, and, in unison, they tipped the last measure of their cups into the fire. It rushed up in sudden blue-white fury, and then settled back down, hissing and moaning.

'So there *was* something good in it after all,' said Aleinus wryly. Having satisfied honour, they sat down again around the fire. Curillian gazed into the flames awhile.

'Would that I could have brought them back home for a proper funeral.'

'Sire, they died happy,' said Findor. 'There's not an armist under arms in the land who wouldn't want to die in your service. They none of them had wives or children left behind. Their souls have gone to the right place, so what do the bodies matter?'

'And Haroth always sought a glorious death,' added Andil, who had been his friend. Lancoir, who had not spoken yet, now gave his verdict.

'His glory shall be that he died in courage, for he went where others dare not.' None seemed to care to add to the captain's words, and there was silence for a time. Then Curillian spoke again, lighter of heart.

'Ah, but you all fought well, my loyal guards. It is no small thing for you to have come through unscathed.' They all nursed cuts and bruises, but grinned nonetheless. 'The deeds of those on this expedition will be sung with praise in the palace and the academy, but great indeed shall be your renown if you live through what is yet to come. The armists who infiltrated Faudunum and came out alive, who went on to compete in the Great Tournament at Oron Amular? Centuries shall come and go and still such prestige shall remain undimmed. And what about you, friend Roujeark? Very glad I am that you were with us. You grow mightier with each passing fight.' Roujeark blushed and looked at his hands. They had not been scorched this time, though the flames had burned hotter, and been sustained longer.

'When I first met you,' Lancoir said, 'I despised you for a peasant weakling. Yet soon you will prove harder to kill than I.' Roujeark looked up at the Captain of the Guard and shivered. Such a compliment was not lightly given. He pulled his cloak tighter about him.

'Then let the other contestants beware,' exclaimed Caréysin. 'For Knights of Thainen are hard enough to kill.'

'It is not the other contestants you need worry about,' said Curillian. 'The Keeper of the Mountain will likely prove a sterner test than they. Prélan only knows how long Kulothiel has been preparing the tournament ground. We shall be competing in a mountain-kingdom that was already ancient when our race first awoke. We shall enter into halls where the deadliest weapons known to history were made and the most subtle minds trained. Every artifice and device contrived by the elven mages throughout the depths of time shall be deployed between us and the prize. Elves and men and armists shall compete, but the Mountain itself will be our foe.' There was silence again, as each armist contemplated the king's words in the flames.

'What of the harracks?' Antaya asked at length. 'Will they be there to compete?'

'No, I do not think so,' the king answered. 'They have longed to discover the Mountain and conquer it too long to be given an invitation. You have seen your last of them, I hope.'

'I've crossed blades with them,' pressed Antaya, 'and yet I still do not have it clear in my mind what they are. Do they have souls, or are they beasts?'

'No one knows for sure,' answered the king. 'When we first encountered them, they were already at odds with our people, so all we have learned of them we have discerned from afar as enemies. Beasts? I think not – they are too skilled in craft for that.'

'Some of their architecture was very impressive,' Roujeark offered.

'Indeed,' agreed the king. 'As shapers of stone and delvers of mines they have few equals, which lends credence to the theories that they are degenerate dwarves, sundered from the kin of Carthak long ago and fallen into evil, like the Black Dwarves of the Goragath Mountains. They are even more secretive than the dwarves, adept at concealment and camouflage, but they have shown no evidence of the dwarves' nobler arts: runes and literature, and the fashioning of gems and marvellous works of skill. We may never know who or what they are. I count them enemies as long as they menace my realm, but I will never hunt them without cause as things not worthy of life.'

One by one, the armists fell asleep around the fire, until only Roujeark was awake. His mind struggled as the implications of what he had done amongst the harracks sank in. He had taken life, and taken it with ease. He sensed tremendous power within himself, and it frightened him. He almost longed for the doubts that had once wracked him, for at least he did not need to guard others from them. *Who am I? What will I become?*

'You are learning to control it,' a deep voice spoke from across the fire. Roujeark looked up, startled. So long had he been gazing at the fire that it took his eyes some time to adjust and discern Curillian beyond, not slumbering as he had thought. The king's voice was thick with the authority of discernment.

'When my father said I had the same gift as he, I thought I might be able to move small objects, or create fleeting lights. I never saw my father do what I have now done.'

'Your father did not face danger as you have, nor fight alongside comrades whose plight would move him to greater things than he had known before. I do not know if magical ability is hereditary, but I do know that it is a gift of Prélan, bestowed by His Spirit where He wills it to be. He has bestowed it on you. And for a reason.'

'Am I to be a killer then?'

Curillian hesitated. 'Everyone feels remorse after their first killing. The barbarians who crossed you back in the Phirmar probably died, but this time it is certain. Moreover, back then what came from your fingertips was wild and undirected; now it is becoming harnessed and deadly.' Curillian saw the young armist was unconvinced, full of confusion. 'Roujeark, the first person I killed was, like yours, out of necessity.'

A distant look came into the king's eyes as he recalled that far off day.

'Do not torment yourself over death in battle,' he went on. 'For everyone present has embraced it as a possibility. The harracks would feel no guilt in slaying you, for even now they would be melting the skin off your bones had you not denied them. You killed only to defend your friends. If Prélan has called us to nothing else, He has called us to love, and, if necessary, to give our lives for those we love. Listen to me: I have been given many gifts in my life, and all of them to a purpose. It will be the same with you.'

'What purpose?'

'Roujeark, the wizards are gone. Their mighty deeds belong to the pages of history now. Kulothiel may well be the only one left. And now another has arisen? Why would Prélan call forth such a one unless for an errand of surpassing greatness?'

Curillian stood up, stretched, and walked around the fire. He looked down at the seated Roujeark. 'My young friend, all I can say is what is plain to my eyes. I have not lived so long by being blind to what is before them. Yet it may well be that you will not get your answers until you get to Oron Amular, so you must be patient. My task is simply to get you there.' He squeezed his young companion's shoulder. 'Now, let me see if I can find our elf...' With that, he strode off into the night.

The elf had not gone far, for she was still with them in the morning. If she had scouted through the night, she had found what she sought for. That very day they left the mountain glens behind and descended into an eastward-plunging valley. The top of the valley was marked by a window of rock, through which trickled a gurgle of water. *Eldaphir's Spring*. Unmistakeably the trickle grew into a stony stream, carving its way downhill. All they did was follow. It dropped steeply down, taking them to warmth and fecundity. Sin-Serin laughed with sheer joy and ran dancing on ahead, to the bemusement of her travelling companions. This was the first time they had seen their grim guide like this, joyful and carefree. It gladdened their own hearts to behold it.

'My friends,' interpreted Curillian. 'Though you may not be transported to such delight as our guide, do you not feel it in your feet? We tread now on immortal grass, for we are come to Kalimar. It would go ill for us if we came here uninvited, but do not fear, we have one to vouch for us. Ah, truly, it is only now that my weariness falls from me...'

They lost sight of Sin-Serin and walked on for a time without her through fields of fragrant early wildflowers. Full springtime was burgeoning around them. Birds and butterflies, brighter than they had ever seen, darted and sang all about them. They were passing a forest on the far bank when their guide called to them. Looking across, they saw her sitting at leisure on the green bank under branches that overhung the stream. Her foot rested carelessly on the prow of a long slim rowboat.

'Friends, worry no longer about your aching feet, for we have been given alternative means of transport. Our coming was known, and folk were waiting with this boat, here, where Eldaphir first becomes deep enough to bear one.'

The armists looked around, but they could see no one. Roujeark thought he could hear laughter off among the trees, but it might have been only the wind. Still, the boat looked sturdy enough, and larger than expected, for when Sin-Serin brought it across to them, nimble as an otter, they found it had plenty of room for all ten of them and what remained of their packs. So they continued on their way by water, now paddling, now drifting with the current through lands as lovely as a dream. The air was warm and still. Summer was not far off. They relaxed under sunny skies and watched the peaceful banks slide by with their willows and alders. When Roujeark dangled his arm over the side, his fingers grazed the waters of the shallow stream and felt them almost warm to the touch.

The stream grew wider and deeper, meandering through places where the trees grew densely on either bank. For a time they seemed to be gliding through an enchanting tunnel where the leaves above and the waters below joined in a hundred wondrous shades of green.

'Where are we bound?' Roujeark asked. Curillian looked back over his shoulder to answer as he helped paddle.

'To the Eldarell Water-Meadows.' The name meant nothing to any of them, and indeed, Curillian himself had never been there. He leaned forward to Sin-Serin, who paddled from the prow.

'How far off are we?'

'Soon we shall come to where Eldaphir joins Nimrell, her cousin. Then we shall be but half a day's journey as the river will take us.'

'What waits for us there?' Lionenn called from the stern of the boat, his voice uneasy.

'You will see,' Curillian answered.

Just as the wood-elf had said, they came to the confluence where the small Eldaphir joined the larger Nimrell River. Curillian knew enough Kalimari geography to know that the Nimrell was one of the great waterways of Kalimar. Here they were, still well above where the valley's main habitations started, and the river had hundreds of miles to go before emptying into her namesake bay, whose waters also lapped a tiny part of Maristonia's eastern coast. Yet the Nimrell was already a great river. She was sprung from a hundred streams, which tumbled down from snowfields in the mountains. As they swung into the main channel, they could look back and see those mountains clearly for the first time. The mighty peaks, glistening in the distance, were beautiful to behold, and Roujeark wondered whether they were as tall as the Carthaki Mountains whose shadow he had grown up in. Yet for all the youthful vigour of the mountain waters, the Nimrell here entered into a sluggish stretch, spreading out in wide meanders as the valley floor swiftly broadened out. They passed many small lakes beside the banks, and saw wide watery floodplains extending on either side. Herons stalked, swallows wheeled and warblers burbled amid the reeds.

They paused to make camp for the night, and resumed on their way in the morning. Sin-Serin had them up and going very early, while mists still clung to the river. Flotillas of giant swans were their only companions. Sin-Serin surely chose this hour knowingly, for the place they came to seemed achingly lovely at this hour. The river gave out into broad meadows where multiple channels wended their way lazily. Clumps of reeds grew up, and little tree-clad hillocks poked up out of the waters. The mists slowly burned off as soft sunlight dappled the peaceful world. The only noise was that of the birds all around them. Fish seemed abundant and waterfowl fluttered about, ducks, geese and waders in great numbers. Again, the armists never saw a sign, but Sin-Serin told them, 'The Avatar are all around us.'

The name made Roujeark nervous, for it reminded him of the fierce riders who had tried to expel him from the land when he first came to Kalimar. A higher power had turned their eyes away on that occasion, but this time Roujeark did not know what to expect. Sin-Serin too seemed slightly less at ease, for while the Avatar were elves also, they were a kindred distinct from the Firnai wood-elves.

'The Avatar,' began Curillian, answering unvoiced questions, 'are a high and excellent people, but they are perilous and jealous of their realm. Leave the talking to myself and Sin-Serin.' A strange air of nervous expectancy settled over them, and even the quacking and honking of the birds seemed to subside.

'Behold,' said Sin-Serin, suddenly and softly. 'Your rendezvous approaches.' They all looked out into the hazy light, but could see nothing but huge dragonflies skimming above the water. Several moments passed before the sharp-eyed Caréysin called out and nudged his companions.

'Look, there, coming through the mists.'

They followed his pointing arm, and there, sure enough, coming through the mists, was a large waterborne conveyance. It was a vast raft, serenely guided through the water meadows by silent, golden-haired puntsmen. The details only slowly became apparent, but it was obvious that this was no common vessel. As comely and well-built as it was large, it was fit for a king. Devices of a six-pointed star were held aloft on shields and banners by silent sentinels, still as statues. The raft shimmered with the reflected light of precious metals and stones as it glided towards them. Many persons were on the raft: four puntsmen, one at each corner, and stern warriors watching out. A group of people stood near the middle, but the spellbound armists had eyes only for the spectacular figure seated on a throne at the very centre. This person was taller seated than any of those standing around him and, though he wore no crown, his bearing and countenance was regal.

Curillian was taken aback to see Lithan, High King of the elves, drawing near. He was not sure whom he had expected, but it had certainly not been the ruler of Kalimar. Here was a being who had been alive for over two and a half thousand years, and who was yet considered young among his kindred. Descended directly from the Elder King, Avatar himself, six generations distant, Lithan was the last scion of the House of Avatar to remain in Kalimar. In all his adventures, Curillian had never come within sight of him. He had met his older cousin, Lancearon, when he was still the Silver Emperor, but as awe-inspiring as Lancearon was, he was a very worldly elf, monarch after a pattern recognisable to mortal eyes. Lithan was very different. He was set apart, ethereal and aloof, and the grace of the elder line of Avatar's dynasty was in his face.

Even more so than Curillian, the other armists were spellbound as their boat nudged alongside the great raft and they were beckoned aboard. None of the other elves batted an eyelid as they assembled clumsily before the throne, and High King Lithan sat still as a carven statue. It was a voice coming from behind the throne that welcomed them, and it was a voice they knew.

'Welcome, and twice-met, warriors from afar.'

Carea stepped into view. While her voice had been recognisable, the rest of her was completely changed. The elf-lady they had parted with only days before had been a pale, dark-cloaked waif, tired and weak; but now there stood before them a tall, radiant queen. And they were dazzled. Health and vitality, such as a mortal could never hope to possess, shone in her face, and the beauty that had before been shrouded now smote them like the noonday sun. With familiar courtesy, she introduced them to the High King.

'Armists of Maristonia, behold His Grace the High King of Kalimar, Lithan, son of Avalar, chieftain of the Avatar and overlord of all elves.' The armists went to one knee before him. 'Lord King, see here your neighbour and brother-king, Curillian of Maristonia, of the House of Carinen. By his side stand Lancoir, Captain of the Royal Guards of Mariston, and his valiant comrades-in-arms, Aleinus, Antaya, Findor, Andil, Caréysin and Lionenn. With them stands Roujeark, the last pupil-elect of Kulothiel.'

As she spoke the words of introduction, it was as if a spell had been lifted from Lithan, for his grave regal countenance broke and he leaned forward with a welcoming smile upon his lips. He rose from his throne and stood by Curillian as he returned to his feet. If the armists had thought he was tall while he was still seated, they now saw that he was fully eight feet tall. He towered over Curillian. The armist king was the tallest of his companions, but still he only came level with Lithan's breast. The elven king laid hands upon his shoulders.

'How is it, valiant Curillian, that it is only now that we meet? For all the mighty deeds of your ancestors, yours surely is the greatest renown. Verily, our realms have drifted apart with time, but I bear you no less love than your forebears.'

'Majesty, the honour is mine,' Curillian responded, his words sounding awkward in his own ears after Lithan's lordly tones. 'Glad I am to have met you, O High King, but I have never presumed upon an invitation.'

Lithan moved on from Curillian, but while he acknowledged all the others, and embraced Sin-Serin as a cherished kinself, he did not pass over Roujeark as the young armist had expected. Roujeark was startled and abashed when the elven High King crouched in front of him so that their eyes were more or less level.

'My young friend, you are certainly not the least welcome here. Twice now have you come to my kingdom, but only now do I bid you welcome. My riders thought nothing of it when you vanished forty suns ago, but clearly, Prélan was at work in our land that night. I am not so privy to the counsels of the League as were my fathers, but I still know that your coming was foretold.' He straightened up to tower over them again.

'Curillian, son of Mirkan, you come to me via a strange path. Do I not guess rightly that you are bound for Oron Amular?'

'I am, Your Grace.'

'Evidently you chose not to ride the straight road, which would have brought you to my home, but instead emerge from the mountains bearing gifts unlooked for. Prélan, it seems, has ordained it so. Had you come to Paeyeir, even with an escort, you would have been welcome, for Kulothiel requested that I hinder not the invited who came peacefully, but I could have done no more; it was for each contestant to find the road to the Mountain without aid. Come, elf-friend, ask your boon.'

Curillian looked to Carea, who smiled, and then up to the elven king.

'Your Grace, I request passage to Oron Amular, and ask your leave to pass freely through your domain.' Lithan looked down on him with kingly pleasure.

'It is granted full willing, Curillian of Mariston. You are a noble and excellent armist, descended from a house of elf-friends, and held in high esteem by my cousin, Lancearon; for these reasons alone, you have claim upon me. But now, you come with even more potent persuasion, for you have rescued Carea, daughter of Therendir, she who is even more senior in her house than I am in mine. She was lost, and feared dead, but you have brought her forth out of the cold shadows. All of Kalimar, and the House of Firnar in especial, is indebted to you, heroic descendent of a blesséd house.'

'You are kinder than I deserve, O High King,' said Curillian, bowing low. Lithan proved to be kinder still, for he invited them to eat with him upon his raft. Surrounded by the beauty of the water meadows, they broke their fast upon warm loaves, divinely soft and fragrant. The fruits they ate were so flavourful that they could scarce believe they were the same as those that they knew in their own country, and the hibiscus flowers steeped in clear elven cordial was so refreshing that they quite forgot the toils they had come through. After they had eaten, more of the same foods were bestowed on them in generous packets to take with them for the road. As they retired replete from the table, Lithan declared a further kindness to them.

'It is my wish to bless you with the loan of horses, and furthermore, I consent to escort you to the start of your path. The young wizard, I believe,' he said, turning to Roujeark, 'knows the lost way to Oron Amular which starts in the Aravell Valley.' Roujeark nodded nervously. 'If he can remember his steps, then you will come to Kulothiel's hidden gates. Should the Keeper think I have helped you too well, he will indulge his liege-lord, for my thankfulness for the deliverance of Carea outweighs my willingness to abide by his wishes.'

Sin-Serin and Carea took their leave of the armists then, for their time had come to return to Tol Ankil, where Dácariel waited for them. Carea made her thanks to each of her rescuers, kissing them farewell. Sin-Serin laid her forehead against Curillian's, and they too exchanged farewells.

'My thanks to you, Sin-Serin, daughter of the forest. You have been a good guide to us.' Last of all, Curillian went to one knee before Carea, and kissed her hand tenderly. She smiled on him.

'Farewell, and Prélan bless you, Ruthion-Curillian, comrade and friend. If ever we meet again, it shall not be for long, and the tides of providence will bear us apart. Yet my friendship to you shall endure beyond the confines of this world. In the meantime, I shall repay the last of my debt to you by preparing the help you will need.' With those words, she was gone, and none of those that looked on knew what a painful parting they had just witnessed.

Lithan gave orders for the raft to clear the water meadows and make landfall on the eastern bank, where horses were waiting. None of the armists saw where the two wood-elves went, though when he turned back, Roujeark saw two waterbucks leaping gracefully through the watery tracks. He blinked, not sure if he had seen aright, but all he saw when he re-opened his eyes were two wild horses on the distant western bank, running strongly south.

XII
Retracing Red Steps

HORSES Were waiting on the banks beyond the water meadows, the same horses which had borne Lithan and his entourage in haste from Paeyeir, the Kalimari capital. Spare mounts had been purposefully brought, and these were now given over to the armists, their stirrups already shortened ready for them. With little delay, they rode away, following the eastern bank of the Nimrell downstream. Coming to one of the great river's tributaries, they rode upstream until they found a ford. Once across, they left the river valley behind and rode across rolling green hills. In two days' gentle riding, they came to the crest of a steep ridge and, looking down, beheld the Aravell valley. This valley neighboured the Nimrell, and it marked the very heartland of Kalimar. Across the river rose a mighty hill, surrounded by a spherical forest, and upon whose summit sat a fair city. Thus, they became the first mortals for many years to behold Avarianmar, the demesne of the High King of the elves, and Paeyeir, his ancient ancestral abode. Pale and graceful as a thicket of frosted saplings, its many towers, gables and domes glimmered in the westering sunshine, and its banners danced in the breeze.

The armists sat in their saddles and gaped at the sight; even Curillian had never seen this. However, Roujeark had, if not from this vantage point. His eye was drawn to the road, which crossed the river, ran through the forest and climbed up the hill to the city, the very same road whose western reaches he had walked before. The

Armist Road, whose one end was used by armists, and whose other served the elves, was the oldest highway in Astrom. Then he turned his eye to the great stone bridge by which the road crossed the Aravell. He was taken back to the day when, after being smuggled through the immortal lands, he was set down at that bridge to continue his quest for Oron Amular. Now, forty years later, he was on the same quest again. Would he enter the Mountain this time? Or would he be turned away a second time?

Following Lithan's lead, they left the ridge-top behind, and followed a small stream down into the valley. Keeping parallel to the great road, they intersected the river a few furlongs upstream from the bridge. As Lithan rode up to his armist guests on his great white horse, they knew the time had come for parting. As one, the armists looked longingly to the place where the road plunged into the immortal forest, wishing they could follow it up to the mythical capital, of which so many tales and legends told. Instead, the High King gestured upstream, to where the Aravell hugged the forest as it climbed slowly up into the highlands.

'My adventurous friends, the time has come for us to part. Our time together has been brief, but full of pleasure. I go back now to my halls, but your way leads up into the mountains. It is time for your guide to come to the fore and play his part. With Prélan's blessing, I leave you in his capable hands.'

They bade the elven king farewell with fitting words, and surrendered their borrowed mounts to the grooms who had ridden with them. They watched as king, grooms and knights, the whole royal entourage, rode down and across the bridge. In a flurry of hooves and streaming pennons, they vanished into the forest as if it were a portal that took them to another time and place. They were left alone, elf-less for the first time since coming to Tol Ankil. As they had left Mariston, so now they would go on, a company of armists.

Curillian was just about to address Roujeark when the young armist hurried off, running in the direction of the bridge. Fearing lest he might outstep the bounds of their welcome, the king called after him, but he was gone.

'Shall we fetch him back, Curillian?' Lancoir asked. The king watched the receding red figure, red cloak flying.

'No, he is called.'

A

Roujeark ran as close as he dared to the bridge, mindful of the sentries who stood there, and then he scrambled down into the reeds on the bank and crept the rest of the way into the shadow of the great stone arch. He had come here once before to meet Prélan, and by Prélan's grace, he had been left unmolested. He trusted to that protection again now, and settled himself down between the water and the stone. Everything seemed different. Last time it had been night; now it was daytime. Last time strange characters in the river had lit the underside of the bridge with luminous instructions; now the water was dark and still. Last time he had heard Prélan's voice speak to him; now all was quiet.

He tried to concentrate his mind to hear Prélan, but his thoughts were in turmoil. A frustration grew in him that made him squirm and fidget where he sat. Finally, despairing of hearing anything as he gazed into the river, he looked around. As he did so, a memory came to him of words spoken long ago...

Now, it is right for me to give you this, to light the next steps...

They were the words of Ardir, the angelic being from whose hand he had received the living map that showed the way to Oron Amular. Why didn't I think of that before, he wondered? Suddenly excited, he reached into his innermost pocket and drew forth the map. It was his most treasured possession, even though he didn't look at it very often. He lovingly unwrapped the leather bindings, and opened up the parchment within. His heart sank immediately. That's why I didn't think of it: it's blank. It had been like that when he first received it, and it only began to reveal itself when his feet found the right path. As he went, it had confirmed his route by remaining blank when he was astray, and only filling in when he was on the right track.

He remembered the time when he had come within sight of Oron Amular. The whole map had been revealed, a stunning tapestry of colour so richly textured that it was as if the land itself had been captured inside it. The path he had trodden showed, in a stippled red line. A red line for a red wanderer. *Rutharth*, Red Journey, indeed. He had put it away when he had retraced his steps back to Maristonia, for it showed not that land. Somewhere along the line, as it lay unread against his skin, it had reverted to its original state, blankness reclaiming the paper like desert sands engulfing an oasis. The first time he had discovered the loss the blow had smote his heart, for he had counted on using it to find the way back some day.

It is not as other maps, made to quench the beholder's curiosity all at once; yet nevertheless, it will guide you true, step by step.

Ardir's other words winged into his mind as he sat wracked by doubt. The revelation that followed struck him like a stone on the forehead. Would it happen the same way again? Would the map come alive again if he found the right path?

Trust in Prélan and He will not lead you astray...

Roujeark realised he had all he needed after all. His memories of the journey first time around were only vague, but he felt sure that they would become clearer when he came back to each place in turn, especially if the map helped him again. Pushing himself up on his haunches, he clasped the map tight against his chest.

Prélan, guide my steps, he prayed. *Help me retrace my steps. Take me to the Mountain. Let me enter in this time, and ascend, that I might meet with You again.*

His companions were restless and impatient by the time he rejoined them.

'Right,' he told them. 'Follow me.'

⋀

Packs hoisted and boot-laces drawn tight, they trekked up the river bank. For a time, while the forest hugged the bank, they felt like they were being watched. Yet soon they reached a fork in the river. The forest arched away northward, following the right-hand channel; whilst the left-hand way curved away to the left into quiet green country. Roujeark remembered taking the left-hand way here before. That had been before he had received the map, which came to him when he gained the hills higher up, but he saw now that the map backed up his memory. In its bottom-right corner, it flushed suddenly and showed the confluence in the river. Yet while the right-hand river was immediately lost over its edge, the left-hand way was illuminated as it crept diagonally up across the parchment. Delighted, he made haste to follow.

⋏

For days they wound their way up the river valley through a quiet and empty land. They passed through woods and splashed over fords across side-streams, but always they followed the main river. One day they scaled a steep bluff beside the river and found that they had reached a similar vantage point to the ridgetop where, in the High King's company, they had looked out over Paeyeir and Avarianmar. Now at the same height, they could see the royal elven city again, rising on its hill clear of the surrounding forest, only this time they viewed it from the west, as opposed to the south. They also saw, much closer to them, that the other river was very nearby, only separated from them by a narrow ridge of intervening land. The two waterways flowed south through the land together, staying close as brothers unwilling to be parted. They came down from the same highlands, which, turning north-west, they could now clearly descry. Somewhere up ahead, the green grass and shady copses of lowland Kalimar gave way to more rugged heaths and moorland and beyond them, on the horizon, rose craggy hills and plateaus. The view, long forgotten in Roujeark's memory, now came back to mind as fresh and familiar as if it had never gone away.

Knowing he had to reach those uplands, Roujeark kept following the river. Curillian, Lancoir and the guards followed him without question. Now that they had left the watchful forest behind they felt more at ease, alone and untroubled. They took delight in each new flower and butterfly they saw, but kept going, up and up. They made cheerful fires by night, and sang songs and told stories by day to pass the long hours of trudging. Curillian had a great store of wonderful tales to share, great events that he himself had lived through or participated in. His companions drank up every word, though in the telling of those long-ago deeds he seemed as old to them as the land around them. Roujeark ignored one side-stream after another, sticking to the main channel, but then he came to a confluence where he could not tell which branch was the main river and which the tributary. His memory failed him here, so he struck out left with a guess. He had not gone far, however, before it became clear that he had left the map behind at the junction. They were walking in a blank section. Abruptly he turned around and, somewhat to his companions' alarm, led them back to the junction. He tried again, following the right-hand channel, and this time the map went with him, revealing a narrow strip along the valley.

Every night he took the map out and contemplated it, though he was careful never to let his companions see it. For a reason he knew not why, he wished to keep it to himself. The next day, walking through terrain that was noticeably hillier, the hairs on his neck began to prickle. The country, which for so long had seemed devoid of life, no longer felt quite so empty. Several sensations in his body were trying to tell him that he was coming to a significant place. Casting his mind back, he thought the hidden city he had discovered last time was nearby. He had discovered it quite by accident, and never found out its name or history, but the memory of it stood out clear amid mists of vagueness on either side.

He was out ahead of his companions when he stopped dead in his tracks. Barring the way ahead of him, standing as still as a statue, was an elf warrior. Resplendent in the armour and weaponry of an Avatar prince, he looked like he had stepped right out of the pages of history. His head was bowed and both hands were at rest on an upturned great-sword in front of him. Behind him, the riverbanks reared up in canyon walls through which the water tumbled frothily. As Roujeark gaped at him, the warrior raised his head and transfixed him with a terrifying glare, though he could see little through the gaps in the ornate helmet. Lifting one gauntleted hand, he pointed westward, away from the river and up the bank to one side. So intimidated was Roujeark that he let out a little cry and turned to his companions, who came hurrying up behind him. They asked what had startled him, but when he looked back upstream, the forbidding figure had vanished. Where he had stood, his sword alone remained, thrust point-ward into the turf. The guards fingered their weapons nervously. Fascinated, Curillian started towards the abandoned weapon.

'I think we should leave the river now,' Roujeark said nervously. Curillian went on a step or two and then came to a stop, hand resting on the hilt of his own sword. Then he retreated.

'Our way is barred,' he whispered to Roujeark. 'Let us find another route.'

Together they climbed away from the riverbank, up onto the shoulders of the canyon, which heralded the start of the hills. To Roujeark's relief, the map approved of their deviation from the river, divulging details of a narrow corridor through this mysterious land. They picked a way up the slope among moss-covered boulders and straggling trees. As they climbed, the churning thunder of the river down below receded, and they came into beech-woods perched above the canyon. Caution dictated a route on through the trees, but curiosity tugged Roujeark towards the canyon rim. He wandered off in that direction, but a sight in the trees brought him up short. His breath caught in his throat. A well-camouflaged figure perched on a branch in a tree forty yards from him. The menacing hooded figure held up a gloved hand, palm outward in a gesture of rejection. Then he drew his bow and crouched poised, ready to release. Roujeark caught a glimpse of baleful eyes from under the rim of the hood that chilled his heart. Stumbling backward, he returned to his original course.

His companions had seen nothing, and they followed his abortive detour away from, and then back to, their original course. They might have asked questions, but strange noises sounded in the trees, and they felt none too safe. They hurried on. A little further on, a break in the land lay across their path where a tributary of the river had carved a fern-filled side canyon. Roujeark led them down into the moist green cleft in search of a place to cross to the other side. His companions were strung out on the steep slope above him when he strayed too near the main river below. A dripping figure emerged out of the river. Clad in scaly blue and white, he was virtually invisible amongst the foam and boulders of some rapids. Crouching in a martial stance, he brandished a trident drawn back on a taut arm. The other hand was held out rigidly towards him in the same palm-outward gesture of denial. Roujeark stumbled back in fright and lost his footing. Again, the guards saw nothing, but the vigilant Curillian was quickly at his side.

'What is it?' he hissed. The guardian of the river had disappeared, but Roujeark was pale with fright.

'Nothing,' he told the king, and hurried to get up and move on. Going on from there, his heart barely stopped pounding all day. None of these apparitions had been there before, nor did he remember the canyon. He could not remember when or why he had left the river first time round, but he surmised sketchily that he must have followed a course off to the side. They spent an uneasy night under the trees, keeping their weapons close.

⋀

The next day a strange prompting roused him early. He left the guards still sleeping and crept off into the dawn half-light. Soon he was aware of Curillian coming with him. They looked at each other strangely.

'You feel it too?' the king asked him, but Roujeark did not know what to say. Together they followed their feet to an out-jutting promontory. Feeling increasingly nervous as they approached an overhang, they got down first to hands and knees, and then flat on their bellies. Crawling, they came to the edge and peered out over. A hidden world lay beneath them, now exposed. Elemental forces from a forgotten age had carved a vast amphitheatre in the hillside, and now it was filled with a marvellous city, like a jewel in a hollow. Out of morning mists, tall houses and needle-thin towers rose like icicles. Elegant arches supported domes and spires, from which issued soft and beautiful lights, like undying lamps. They glimpsed unkempt gardens and channelled waters flowing under graceful bridges. All of it bespoke the finest architecture of the Avatar, the High Elves, the finest builders ever to labour above the earth. Fascinating suburbs delved into the sheer sides of the amphitheatre and some dwellings even clung to the very rock faces. A river emerged out of a rocky tunnel on one side, wound its way through the city, and then departed southward by another tunnel. The whole place was sealed off on all sides, invisible except from above.

And it was deserted.

Not a single soul was in sight. No traders sold their wares in the market squares, no horses' hooves clattered down the paved streets, and no gardeners tended the neglected and overgrown lawns. Not even wild animals haunted this place. Forgotten by the outside world, the city seemed to have forgotten itself. If the three apparitions had been guarding this city, it was a dead place they watched over. Nature was trying to reclaim the place with groping roots and spreading briers, but the buildings themselves had a timeless quality, as if their makers had intended them to stand until the end of days, even though they themselves should depart.

'This is Aramar,' whispered Curillian beside him. As the first fingers of dawn touched the tallest turrets with rosy hues, there was a look of rapture in his face. The name flittered at the back of Roujeark's mind, as if trying to elicit a long-forgotten memory, but Curillian evidently knew more.

'Roujeark, do you realise? We've come to a place where our kind has never been before – we're looking at a fabled city which no armist eyes have ever beheld. And yet, the beginnings of our history are bound up with this place, for from this ancient citadel of the elves came the host which first settled Maristonia, centuries before my forefathers first awoke. Aramar. City of Arvaya, Avar, and Arvarion. City of many kings. Birthplace and home to many generations of Avatar's elder line, and a place that once rivalled Paeyeir as the capital of Kalimar. The folk here used to be called the deep-elves, the Irynthai. It was one of the fairest cities of the elves, and one of the most industrious too, for many fine things were invented or discovered here.

'Kurundar lusted after it so much that, although he lacked the strength to invade Kalimar properly in the Second War, he sent a special taskforce to sack it. Whilst I fought in the west, we heard tales that the fabled city of Aramar had been besieged. It remained so until the ending of the war, at the dawn of the Fourth Chapter. Avallonë, King of Kalimar at the time, and father of Lithan, whom you have met, died defending his gates, but he preserved the home of his fathers. Much damage was said to have been done, and most of its folk departed to the Inner Isles, despairing of the war-torn homes they had lost, but some stayed, and rebuilt it in the image of its former glory. They rebuilt it, and then they too left, for as you see, the city lies deserted. Now it is naught but a memorial to the ancient greatness of the Avatar.'

Roujeark, who had known none of this, listened with rapt attention. Curillian had more to tell.

'It was the most secretive part of Kalimar, save Oron Amular itself. Foreign ambassadors and embassies might come to Paeyeir, down in the lowlands, but none were ever permitted to come to this place – it was kept sacred. And so, we are the first mortals to ever see it, what some have deemed to be a lost treasure. Some even doubted that it had ever existed, save in song and legend only. I never doubted, but I listened to the stories like everyone else. One particular legend told of three guardians who were left behind by the departing population to guard it.'

Roujeark stirred, and looked at Curillian keenly.

'An Avatar, a Firnar, and a Marintor, brothers-in-arms representing all three kindreds,' the king went on. 'It is said that they watch over the approaches to this city with sword, bow and trident, and suffer none to pass. Theirs was a solemn and eternal duty: to preserve the inviolate mystery and serenity of Aramar, city of elven dreams. That tale I did not believe, until now. I think you saw these three watchers, Roujeark, even though none of the rest of us glimpsed them.'

'But why have we been allowed to come here, and look out over the city?' Roujeark asked, puzzled and nervous. He kept expecting the three to appear again, each in their own element.

'Who knows? Seeing is not trespassing, perhaps. We would never have been allowed to come to the city itself and set our feet upon it. There may come a day when men or armists try to venture here, seeking treasure and ancient lore, but even if the three guardians let them pass, it will be a perilous undertaking. The Irynthai were the most cunning of all elves, well able to booby-trap the city they had kept secret for so long. Yet we have the leave of the High King himself to come this way; you are beckoned by Prélan and drawn by a powerful doom. Notice how all of our companions slumber strangely on past daybreak? Their eyes have been closed, but ours are permitted to see. Roujeark, it sets my heart beating faster. If Aramar may be glimpsed, then who knows? Maybe even Oron Amular will give up her secrets...'

A

When they returned to their companions, they found them slumbering still, held in the grip of a strange drowsiness. When they were shaken awake, they seemed strangely vacant and unobservant of what was around them. Even Lancoir was lethargic. Roujeark and Curillian hurried them away from that secret place, and it was not until late afternoon, when they had left it far behind, that they became their usual selves again.

All that day and the next, they climbed up and up, coming across hillsides ever more barren and windswept. The trees were now almost exclusively evergreen, and they clung to the slopes in serried ranks. Roujeark searched for the cave that had been the setting for his third encounter with Prélan all those years ago, but it eluded him. He felt sure it would be nearby if he stuck to the correct path, for that had been the way he had come before, but he couldn't find it. Maybe he had taken a detour the first time that he didn't remember, or perhaps the fir-trees had colonised the cave-mouth in the years in between and hidden it. Or maybe the cave had been a secret portal to Prélan's own country, which, having served its purpose, had now been swallowed up by the earth and closed forever?

He did at least find the lake he had visited before, which they reached after much toiling and scrambling. He remembered the steep escarpment that rose behind it, and the flatter ground west of it, which he had been grateful to traverse instead. They had come far enough into the hills now that the lowlands were hidden, but they knew that the waters stored up here fed one of the great rivers of Kalimar, for out of the lake tumbled myriad little streams which gradually convened to form the Aravell.

They trod the wooded shores of the lake until they ended and then followed the buttress of higher ground above them. Low clouds and persistent rain dogged their steps for the next few days, and Roujeark feared going astray in the poor visibility, but he kept the high ground on his right like a guiding fence, and every time he checked the map, it reassured him that he was on course.

One morning they finally left the clinging clouds behind and, breasting a low crest which jutted above the plateau, they were given a spectacular view west and south. To left and right the northern and southern flanks of the plateau tumbled away gradually into the lowlands, but ahead of them lay the Black Mountains in all their glory. Stern dark masses of rock reared upwards like the shoulders of the world. Above they rose into jagged spires and fluted pyramids, and below the bitter cliffs and craggy flanks plunged away into dank labyrinthine networks of ravines and sunless clefts. Only the glistening snow covering the greatest peaks softened the forbidding prospect, like the flowing white hair that makes a grave elder seem somehow more benevolent. The sunlight glinted off that snow, and glittered among the ice-clad valleys where rivers birthed.

They had had a limited view of this range before, from the south, when they were in Aiiyosha's company, but now the view was untrammelled on any side, and it was as if the whole world lay spread out before them. Yet the mountains themselves were still many miles distant. Between themselves and those far-off peaks was a great flat-topped ridge, many miles broad, which jabbed out from the massif like a blunted blade. Following its long miles with their eyes, they tried to descry their path, but all they could see was a trackless wilderness of rock where no green thing grew. Roujeark strained his eyes westward, hoping for some glimpse of the Mountain, for he knew it stood apart from the others. But either he was looking in the wrong place, or the enormous peak was still too far distant to see, hidden behind nearer peaks. Disappointed, he returned to his job of path-finding.

Down they went, leaving the height behind and going back down to the plateau. That night they had their first glimpse of the moon for many days, and Curillian paused to take his bearings from it.

'The new moon rises,' he said. 'The last one of spring. The next full moon will be the first of summer, and the date set for the Tournament. That means we have only two weeks to reach the Mountain if we are to get there on time. How far away are we, Roujeark?'

But Roujeark did not know. He thought they were getting close now, but he could not even begin to put a guess in days on it. He was totally dependent on his enigmatic map, and the others were totally dependent on him. Curillian and his warrior escort learned a new appreciation for Roujeark in that place, knowing they would have become hopelessly lost without him. The great ridge was not as flat as it had looked from above, but instead was crumpled in folded ranks of troughs and outcrops. Prehistoric torments had riven and rent it with elemental forces, and numerous crevices scored deeply across their path.

So their going was tough, and their progress frustratingly slow. Even with the aid of his map, Roujeark still went wrong several times, and many days were lost in difficult detours and temper-fraying retraced steps. When they were sure of their direction they could still only go slowly, for the way was fraught with dangerous places where one of them could have plummeted into mysterious depths, never to be heard of again.

Roujeark consoled himself with the thought that the Mountain must be close now, for his first proper view of it had come whilst lost in terrain like this. He wondered how long it would be before they finally saw it. Wearily they hoped for a glimpse every day, just enough to reward their bone-jarring labours and spur them on with fresh impetus. But every day, they found their view cut off by looming outcrops of rock, or curtained off by thick clouds. In the meantime, they just kept trudging on, trying to ignore the growing number of blisters that made their steps increasingly painful. Their hardwearing mountain boots and cold-weather clothing was tested to the limits in that rugged wilderness, but they proved their worth, keeping them warm and much drier than they would otherwise have been.

Day by day, they forged on, encouraging each other by turns whenever one of them stumbled or tempers frayed. Still, at whiles Andil or Antaya would sing a few verses to keep their spirits up, and Aleinus told ridiculous jokes to keep them smiling. By night, they built fires whenever they came across wood, even if it was the gnarled limbs of wizened old pines crammed into some crevice. Taking sentry duty by turns, the rest of them reclined about the fire, getting as comfortable as they could in that desolate place. They kept close together and huddled under thick cloaks and blankets to keep out the mountain chill. Roujeark would discretely study his map or gaze at the stars. Curillian caressed Carmen's pendant and thought wistfully of home. He kept his wife and son ever in his prayers, and wondered from afar how Téthan was getting on. *He's been growing so fast these days. What a prince he would become one day.* His companions kept their own private thoughts or talked with each other, but Lancoir was ever restless, always whetting a blade on a rock or strolling about on patrol.

At the end of one long, soul-numbing day, they came to a rock-face that barred their way like a great ruined staircase. Vowing to find shelter as soon as possible on its far side, they drove themselves up the broken ledges and steps in half-light as evening fell. Leading as ever he did, Roujeark was the first to reach the top, and he came up short. Grasping the lip of the topmost step, he hauled himself up and found what he had been yearning for. Perfectly framed between two upward-jutting fingers of rock, like a window with no top, was a clear view to the north-west. The great Mountain, standing clear of the slopes beside her, dominated the view. Impossibly tall, snow-clad and starkly beautiful, the mightiest peak in Astrom was unmistakable. Oron Amular. Immeasurably loftier and incomparably fairer, it made the other bastions of the Black Mountains look like misshapen lumps. Standing upon a vast, leaf-shaped plinth of rock, the central tower rose in a diamond formation to knife-edge parapets and sheer faces. Amidst the lesser peaks, rising high above the mighty crown, the uttermost pinnacle soared to its tapered summit. The roof of Astrom was as slender and as unbreakable as a spearhead. Defying the sky and wrapped around by gale-blown snow, it looked down majestically over all.

Roujeark just stood and stared, perched precariously where he was. Cramming themselves into any nook available, his companions came and did likewise. Each one gasped as the view greeted their weary eyes. Curillian perched precariously on a rock, utterly transfixed by the sight.

'More beautiful than I dreamed…' he murmured to himself. Here it was, the object of all their toil. A new fire was kindled in each of their flagging hearts. Finally they could see, if not yet reach, their destination.

'Behold, my friends,' declared Roujeark. 'There lies Oron Amular.'

XIII

An Ancient Landscape

DAYS Were running short, so they hurried along. They had been buoyed by their first view of the Mountain, but even now that it was periodically visible, it proved exceedingly slow and difficult to approach. Curillian had been counting the days off as notches on his mountain-staff, but now the skies above cleared at night and he took his reckoning from the moon again.

'We must make haste,' he urged them repeatedly. 'The moon is waxing to its full, here on the threshold of summer. The Tournament will begin soon. We must not miss the start and gift a lead to our rivals.'

Roujeark was happy to oblige, but a strange experience gave him pause one day. They were now more or less constantly in view of the Mountain, and today they were following a crude path that wound around sharp rocky bends as the crooked hills slowly descended towards the lowlands again. Suddenly he paused, the hairs on the back of his neck bristling. What was familiar about this place? The others were kept waiting behind him as he cast about in his mind. It was not until he approached the strange, flat-topped rock in a dark recess that he realised what this place was. Running his hands over the smooth rock, he remembered an old wizard sitting there. This was where he had met Kulothiel, though he had not known him at the time. In this very spot, he thought he had reached his journey's end, but in this very spot, he had been turned back. Forty years had passed between that day and this. Tears welled in his eyes as he realised that the long detour was finally over. At last, he would step closer to the Mountain. This time he would go on and reach it.

Oron Amular stood apart from the rest of the mountains, sat upon a bastion thrust out from the northern face of the range. Despite being so tall, it was exceedingly difficult to catch sight of because the mountainous approaches to south, east and west were so broken, rarely affording a clear view. Indeed, the tallest ridges to the south of the great peak were also the nearest to it, so for a long time they blocked the view of anyone coming from the east, as Roujeark and his companions were. Only from the north was there a clear view of Oron Amular, a direction well-guarded by the most secretive part of the elven realm and by the wooded fastnesses of Therenmar, the wood-elf domain.

The Mountain stood at the head of a great twin valley, where the rivers Varell and Amulir began their journeys. At first the two rivers were separated only by a long crooked ridge, but leagues and leagues downstream they separated, one skirting round the western fringe of Therenmar, and the other plunging straight through it, before they both emptied into the Troizon Ocean on Kalimar's northern coast. The Amulir was *the* river of the Mountain, issuing from right under its feet. That provenance, together with its long slow passage of the mysterious Therenmar, gave it a perilous reputation, hence its name: the Magic Water. Between Therenmar and Oron Amular, the twin valleys were practically empty of folk, the first habitations being many miles downstream. Jealously guarded of old by the League of Wizardry, even the elves had long learnt to give Oron Amular a wide berth. Therefore, the Mountain presided over a silent and untamed country.

All this they could see clearly now, but each passing day brought the prospect into sharper focus. From further off, the Mountain had seemed completely isolated and cut off from all other features, but the nearer they got, the more they realised that was simply because its sheer size dwarfed what lay about its feet. Far from being flat, the terrain about the Mountain was full of tangled forests, sharp hills and deep cloven vales, making even the northern approaches difficult. Yet all around the Mountain, immediately about its steeply-sloping feet, was a looping trough like a ditch around a fort. Tucked between mountainous slopes, it was the Mountain's own little garden.

Passing around the precipitous southern spur of the Mountain, they made their final descent into the trough, reaching its flat grassy floor in the middle of the day. They were now right underneath the Mountain, utterly dwarfed by its looming bulk. They craned their necks upwards in awe to see its lofty turrets and ice-clad flanks glittering in the sun. It was Antaya who found words to express what they were all feeling.

'This is a place Prélan paid special attention to in His work of creation. There can't be a more wondrous place in all the world, or more fearsome.'

Having arrived at last, none of them had any clear idea what to do next. They scanned the vast mountainsides, more formidable than any hand-built bastion, but no entrance or sign of life could they see.

'Well,' said Curillian, leaning on his staff, 'our great journey is at an end. We made it. But what comes next, I fear, will prove much harder.' That thought hung in the air between them before Andil asked the obvious question.

'What way in did you use when you came here before, Roujeark?'

'I fear I never actually came this far,' Roujeark answered him. 'I only came within sight of the Mountain before I was turned back.

There must be a door somewhere, but I don't know where it is.' The armists with him looked disconsolate at this revelation, but they held their peace. For want of a better plan, they followed the trough northward to see what they could find.

'It would take us days and days to walk around the whole Mountain,' said Curillian. 'I hope we get a clue before it comes to that.'

The trough was only a quarter of a mile wide, and the slopes that hemmed it in on either side were dizzyingly steep. They all felt uneasy, being trapped in such a narrow place and confronted with such formidable works of nature. The afternoon passed as they walked and they were soon cast in shade, whilst the sunlight swiftly retreated up the side of Oron Amular like a golden curtain being drawn up. When dusk fell, they settled down in a camp. As Aleinus and Caréysin prepared a meal, the stars gradually came out overhead. Being lower in altitude than they had been for some time, the guards settled down to enjoy the balmy night, but they didn't rest easy. They felt something was strange in the air here, a foreboding presence. They looked around anxiously, fearing that in every wisp of mist they might see a ghost stalking the ancient landscape.

If Curillian felt the same, he hid it well. Swathed in his cloak, he kept a patient watch, waiting for the moon to rise over the Mountain. He had waited half the night, refusing all attempts to relieve him, before the moon finally appeared over a sharp spur of ice and rock. Excitedly, he shook Roujeark awake to inspect it with him.

'Three days off full, I'd say,' judged Roujeark.

'Close enough,' agreed Curillian. 'We're early. For so long I worried we'd be late, having to come so far, but Prélan has blessed our journey.' He fell silent, regarding the luminous orb. 'I don't know what Kulothiel has planned,' mused the king, 'but whatever it is, my guess is that it will start on the day of the full moon itself, and probably at nightfall. We'd best be ready, but there's nothing we can do now except watch and wait.'

⟁

Which is exactly what they did. After a night under the stars, the morning dawned chill and misty. They did not venture far while the visibility remained poor, but remained in camp. As with the moon during the night, so the sun took a long time to appear over the mountainside, but when it did, the mist burned swiftly away and the deep cleft was warmed. Then they continued their explorations, following many twists and bends in the trough. Everywhere they went, though, the heavy, watchful atmosphere followed them. Not a soul did they see all day, and they were beginning to wonder whether there was a Tournament at all; or, if there was, whether anyone else would come. They were about to make another camp as evening fell when Lancoir, who was taking his turn as scout, called back to his companions.

'A light,' he informed them tersely when they came running up. 'Away there in the distance.' As they watched, the light came again, flickering like sparks being struck. Suddenly the flame caught in a fire of some sort, but it was immediately screened so that all they could make out was a faint glow.

'A campfire,' said Caréysin, who had the sharpest eyes among them.

'It would seem we're not alone in this valley after all,' said Curillian.

'Are they friends or foes, do you think?' asked Findor.

'Unless they are sentinels appointed by the Keeper, they can only be here to compete,' answered Curillian. 'I do not think Kulothiel will have invited any who might be thought of as enemies, only rivals. Come, let us go and find out who they are.'

They advanced cautiously, taking care not to be seen until they were as close as possible. Caréysin's judgement of a campfire proved correct as they drew near, but whomever it belonged to was wary, for they had taken precautions to shield it as much as possible. Night was now thick about them. Coming closer, they saw that it was a fair-sized camp: not a large gathering, but home to a larger party than their own. The owners of the fire had made their camp upon a grassy knoll rising out of the trough's bottom. Looking up from below and a little distance off, the armists inspected it as best they could. Many figures could be seen milling about, but all of them had cloaks and hoods concealing any tell-tale signs.

'It doesn't look to be a welcoming party to me,' observed Aleinus.

'There seem to be a dozen and a half or so of them, Sire,' murmured Antaya, 'but I see no banners or devices by which we might know them.'

'Sensible to stay anonymous while in a strange land,' muttered Lancoir softly.

'They are men,' declared Curillian. 'That's clear enough. But of what nation? Too discrete to be Hendarian, and too large a company to be Ciricien, I'd say. If they're from Aranar, then I may well know them. I mean to find out.'

Tiring of skulking and peering from a distance, the king straightened up and walked forward. Either the sentries were dozing, or they were looking the other way, but Curillian got quite close before they spotted him and then suddenly the whole camp was astir. A pair of figures advanced, swords drawn, but Curillian stood his ground.

'Who goes there?' shouted one, in the Common Speech. 'Declare yourself!'

Curillian strode forward another two paces and then halted on the edge of the firelight. From the challenger's voice alone, he knew that they were men of Aranar, and he chose not to speak, waiting for them to realise who he was. Unnerved by his silence, the sentries edged forward, trying to see his face.

'Who are…' the second question was cut off when a torch was brought closer and Curillian's face came fully into view.

'King Curillian,' said the other, in a wondering voice. There were two men facing him. The one who had first challenged him was tall and clad as a man-at-arms. He had not recognised Curillian, though the signs were there to see: bright hauberk of mail under a tunic embroidered with the Harolin arms, regal cloak, the great Sword of Maristonia. The other was short and stocky, better dressed, in knightly attire, and he needed no signs to recognise the armist before him. He bowed respectfully, in Aranese fashion. Curillian knew him. He was looking at Sir Hardos, Clan Knight of the Pegasus Clan, a comrade and ally of times gone by. And if Hardos was here, then his master, the Pegasus Lord, would also be present. Sure enough, a large, dark figure loomed towards them from the fire, accompanied by several others.

'Hardos, who is it?' The deep booming voice of Southilar, Jeantar of Aranar, was unmistakeable.

'An old friend, lord, sprung from the shadows.'

'Is that so? Well, let us see who our nocturnal visitor is.' As he was speaking, Southilar came into the torchlight. He was a great bear of a man, tall and broad as a gatehouse and muscled like a champion wrestler. He stood six inches taller than Curillian, and much broader. His close-cropped hair was black, though his small, neat beard was salted with grey. His dark suspicious eyes took a moment to take Curillian in.

'An old friend indeed,' said he, with barely a hint of emotion. 'No wizard's phantom this.' Then his forbidding exterior broke into a broad grin and he enveloped Curillian in a crushing bear hug, effusing as he did so.

'Curillian the Renowned, no less! And there I was thinking it was a bandit or a prowler of the night. Have you come all the way from Mariston? Great stallions! It makes me feel young again to be near you, you old campaigner!' Eventually he released Curillian and stepped back again.

'Gentlemen,' he said loudly to the men standing by, 'I give you Curillian Harolin, son of Mirkan, fabled King of Maristonia. Curillian, you may not know these milksops, for they were still slurping at their mothers' teats when last we went to war together. Here you have the baggage that no Pegasus Jeantar can do without – Clan Knights of the other clans: Lindal of the Unicorn, Deàreg of the Falcon, Acil of the Hawk and Romanthony of the Eagle.'

Next to Southilar, who was in rough garments that made him look like a travelling blacksmith, the Clan Knights were richly dressed in brocades and velvet, their weapons glittering with gems and their mail studded with ornate roundels. He did not know any of them, but he could tell their clans from the heraldic insignia each one sported proudly, and he recognised their names, for he made it his business to know about his neighbours, however new or distant. Each one bowed in turn, correct but cold in their courtesy.

'You're not alone, surely, O King of Armists?' boomed Southilar.

'No,' replied Curillian, breaking his silence at last. 'I too have companions with me.' He half-turned, and just at that moment the other armists came up into the torchlight. Lancoir and Southilar knew each other already and grasped forearms like old soldiers, but other introductions had to be made. Southilar and his knights greeted the Royal Guards of Mariston with cool aloofness, knowing the wide gulf that existed between them, for they were the nobility of their land. Southilar smiled wolfishly and boasted.

'So, you have only one Knight of Thainen, and I have no fewer than six Clan Knights – perhaps we will be a match for you this time?'

Curillian smiled easily, unfazed, while Lancoir glared challengingly at the Aranese knights, like a wolf weighing up its prey. Southilar went on volubly. 'You the noble king, me the up-jumped horse-master, and I have a larger party than you? Seldom did your ancestors, the great kings of old, go about with so little retinue. But ever was it your wont, old friend, to keep few companions and cloak yourself in mystery. Curillian, the Adventurer-king.'

If any scorn was intended in the Jeantar's jesting, the armist king chose to ignore it. 'This may be the greatest adventure of all, Southilar,' he said, 'and one where quality may count for more than quantity.' One by one, Curillian introduced his companions. Last of all, he came to Roujeark.

'Lastly, I present Roujeark, son of Dubarnik, my guide, who is known at this Mountain.' Southilar had dismissed him with a glance, but then, realising what Curillian had said, he did a double take and looked at Roujeark with amazement.

'Get away! Do you mean to tell me, Curillian, that you've got an actual wizard in your ranks?'

'I am no wizard,' spoke up Roujeark. 'But I've come here to be trained.'

'Not a wizard yet,' warned Lancoir, 'but one in the making.' Southilar laughed a deep rumble like the rolling of barrels on wooden floors.

'Careful then, my lads,' he said to his knights. 'Don't annoy the novice. I've got a wishes-he-was wizard around here somewhere. Caiasan. Not the real thing of course, blasted nuisance of a scribbler, but useful from time to time, if truth be told. Come,' he beckoned the armists. 'Come and share a flagon of ale around the fire.'

The armists followed their burly host through a makeshift camp of tents, baggage and picketed horses. They were nearing the central fire, which was well screened with tents, when a tall, dark figure stepped into Southilar's path. The shadowy figure was even taller than the Jeantar, and slim as a sword-blade next to his muscled bulk. He spoke with an elegant voice, much more cultured than the other men of Aranar.

'My lord, if it please you, I would meet the armist king.' Southilar hesitated and looked annoyed, but then stepped aside to let him through.

'Curillian, it would seem that Sir Theonar wants to make your acquaintance.' Roujeark felt a chill of foreboding as he stared up at the tall, mysterious figure, whose face was hidden by a deep hood. After a moment or two, in which he seemed to be studying the king, the tall knight went to one knee in a fluid motion and swept back his hood.

'Lord King,' he said, 'it is my deepest honour to meet you. Long have I prayed that Prélan would bring our paths together.'

The mellifluous words seemed to weave a spell before their eyes. Even Curillian, who stood barely taller than the kneeling man, seemed affected by it, regarding the knight with wonder. Wonder, too, was in Roujeark's eyes, for never had he beheld a man or armist so beautiful. He was clean-shaven, smooth-skinned and possessed of striking eyes, but it was the way that his face seemed to *shine* that really smote the beholder.

'Sir Theonar, is it?' asked Curillian, emerging swiftly from the spell. The knight nodded. 'How is it that we have not met before; you seem older than you appear?'

'Lord King, I have only had the honour of serving my lord of Pegasus for a little while.'

Southilar butted in to say more. 'If you call twenty years a little while. He's been by my side all the time I've been Jeantar, sometimes a help, sometimes a hindrance. He, Hardos, and the others helped me as I wrested the sceptre back from the other clans. 'Twas many years ere I first triumphed at Hamid that we met. My predecessor, Celkenoré, snatched him from the Unicorn Clan, which was little to their liking.'

Theonar, who had been on one knee all the while, now got up, saying as he did so, 'It is not unheard of for a common knight to transfer between clans,' he said humbly.

'Though, from what I've seen,' remarked Curillian, clearly curious, 'it is only for a rare talent that a Clan Lord will risk the controversy.'

'You are generous to suggest thus, Lord King, but I claim no such ability for myself. Lord Celkenoré saw some use in me, brought me to Hamid, and made me a Pegasus, for which I am grateful.'

'Had you always been a Unicorn prior to that?' asked Curillian. Again, Southilar interrupted.

'The horned-horse was always vague about where they found him, and neither I nor anyone I knew had seen him long on the tourney circuit.'

'The tale of my former years is, I fear, a dull one.' Roujeark watched the man's eyes flicker as he said those words, and knew them for a lie.

'Humph,' snorted Southilar. 'Wherever he came from, he came a faster swordsman and a finer horseman than he had any right to be. It's come in useful at times, I'll not deny,' he said grudgingly, 'and now he's a Clan Knight. It's a good job he doesn't yet compete in all the events, else I'd have my hands full, or more so than they are already...'

One of the other Clan Knights distracted Southilar then, and they retired to the fire together.

'Sounds like you're a good man to have around at an event like this,' said Curillian after they'd gone, looking up at the tall knight. 'We'll need to watch our step. Outside we're all friends, but inside we'll be competing against each other.' Theonar smiled deprecatingly.

'The Tournament may not be as clear-cut as that,' he said. 'My heart tells me that not all will compete alike.'

'You will compete for *the* prize, though, surely?' blurted out Roujeark. '*Power Unimaginable*?' Theonar turned to gaze at him, and held him with his eyes for an unnervingly long time.

'To each his own prize, friend. That which I seek is elsewhere.' A faraway look came into his eyes as he finally released Roujeark, and he left his last remarks unexplained. Turning back to Curillian, he said courteously, 'I hope you and I can find some time together, Lord King, before Kulothiel beckons us inside.' He nodded briefly in the direction of the looming mountain. 'There is much and more that I would know of you.'

'Then let us make a start around the fire,' said Curillian, striding in that direction. 'Have you any wine?'

Lancoir approached the king's elbow, but Curillian, taking his meaning straightaway, waved him down and made him wait. Soon they all settled down around the merry blaze, together with all those knights and men-at-arms who were not standing sentry. Apart from

Curillian and Lancoir, who sat with Theonar, the armists sat together and the Aranese for the most part left them be, but one figure came to stand over them. Roujeark looked up to see a languid man with unruly hair who was chewing roasted meat from a spit with one hand and clasping a jug of wine in the other. If his scruffy bookish clothes had not been matched by a short byrnie and dagger-belt, Roujeark might have taken him for a clerk. The smooth-cheeked newcomer stood regarding them for a few moments, swaying slightly as he did so, and then plonked himself down beside them, just before he fell over.

'So you're armists, are you?' he asked to no one in particular, although he was facing Roujeark more than the others. The direct question was good-natured, if a little slurred.

'We are,' said Antaya, annoyance grating in his tone.

'Splendid.' The man took a swig from his jug. He happened to have seated himself between Roujeark and Lionenn, and he did his best to ignore the hostility that was radiating off Lionenn like a second campfire. The Konenaire's expression left no doubt that he did not suffer fools gladly, but the genial man was undeterred. 'Never met an armist before. Seems they're just as tough, but less ugly than rumour makes them.' He smiled winningly around at all of them. Finding a mixed reception of smiles and frowns, he settled on Roujeark. 'Here, you look like my kind of chap; I'll talk to you, if you don't mind?'

Bemused by his new companion, Roujeark could only smile and nod his assent.

'Half a moment,' announced the man. 'Hold this.' He gave Roujeark custody of his jug while he finished the last chunk of meat on his skewer, which he then cast into the fire. Wiping grease on his sleeve, he took the jug back and swilled the morsel down.

'Friend, have you had any beef or wine? Come, there should still be some to go round, and for your companions too, to silence their bellies and loosen their tongues. That's the thing, for all the discomforts of the field, at least when you're on the road with the Falcon and the Hawk you're well-provisioned.' He went to collect some food, hailing Sir Deàreg and Sir Acil as he did so, who both glanced up from their conversations to nod coolly in acknowledgement. He returned laden with more spits and clutching some cups, which he duly handed round to the armists, spilling much wine and grease in the process.

'I say, lads,' he said, surveying them seriously, 'I've brought the tuck, and the wine too. Don't s'pose you brought the women? I hear armist women are much better looking than the chaps, but just as tough, eh?' He raised his jug and toasted all of armist womanhood, seemingly. 'None to be found? Just my luck, privations of the camp and all that. No flipping fillies, ah well.'

'Our women would be too much of a handful for you, friend,' Andil told him.

'Caiasan's the name, old scout, schooling's the game. And don't worry, the more of a handful the better I say. So,' he raised his voice to proclaim, 'here's to women who are too much for us.'

Aleinus alone cheered his toast, and then promptly declared the wine to be excellent stuff.

'Proper Redmar stuff, this,' Caiasan told him. 'Some of these philistines insist on swigging beer, but just 'cos you're in the field doesn't mean you have to let standards slip, right?' Shortly after this statement, Aleinus got talking to a man-at-arms on his other side, drawing Andil and Caréysin with him. Findor and Antaya, repelled by Caiasan's conversation, fell to speaking amongst themselves, and Lionenn just sat glowering.

'Cor, he doesn't say much, does he?' Caiasan said, nodding toward the Konenaire. 'Looks like it's just us then, old lad,' he told Roujeark winningly. 'Probably for the best.' All of a sudden, he became more serious. 'Seems to me that you stand out amongst your lot no less than I do amongst mine; do we pursue similar professions?'

'I am not yet a scholar,' said Roujeark, 'but I hope to be one soon.' He let his gaze wander unwittingly to the great bulk of the Mountain, shimmering in the starlight.

'Here?' Caiasan paused mid-bite, half-choking, to ask the question in surprise. Then he let out a long soft whistle of admiration when Roujeark nodded.

'Strewth, this place is a bit beyond the likes of me. I've devoted a great part of my adult life to finding out about Oron Amular and other antiquities, but I never knew they were still admitting novices.'

'I fear I know nothing about the Mountain that would satisfy your curiosity. With his dying breath, my father sent me here forty years ago, but I was turned away with a promise that I would be able to return one day. Now, maybe, that day draws near.' Caiasan watched the far-off look smouldering in the armist's eyes. He saw too how his hands seemed to glow briefly with an inner fire when the Mountain was mentioned, even though the armist himself didn't seem to notice.

'Blimey, this is real life for you, isn't it? I mean, you're here for a real reason, not this silly Tournament?' Roujeark looked at him, surprised.

'You think it's silly to compete for *Power Unimaginable*?'

'Too bloomin' right,' Caiasan affirmed, with another swig of wine. Wiping his mouth with the back of his hand, he leaned conspiratorially close. 'Listen, friend, with some of the chaps as are here I don't think the likes of me will get much of a look in. No, they'll fight this one out between themselves, and whatever other champions turn up. And they're welcome to it. It may be that all my studies haven't turned up much, or then again, maybe they have, but I reckon whoever wins will find they've bitten off more than they can chew. Settle for scraps, I will. I mean, it's Oron Amular. You must have an idea. Think what secrets and lost knowledge lie within that Mountain. Even a fleeting peek at some of them would make my reputation. Blasted nuisance of a scribbler indeed,' he snorted indignantly, evidently well acquainted with Southilar's opinion of him. 'I'd like to put pay to remarks like that, and mayhap get one over on my peers. No more "yes, Caiasan, well done Caiasan, but now go and muck out the stables", and no more "back to your fairy-tales and fancies Caiasan, leave the real business to us". If I get out of here, I intend to be much more of a somebody when I get me back to Hamid.'

The more he drank, the more Caiasan seemed happy to chatter on about himself. And Roujeark, glad to have the attention deflected away from himself, was content to let him.

'Truth is, friend Roujeark, I'm little more than the jester on this little outing. The high 'n' mighty Jeantar's pet. You'd think they treat me better, seeing as how I got 'em here, not to mention cleaning up their cuts and scrapes along the way. Unappreciated, that's my trouble.' He sniffed loudly, and wiped a sleeve across his nose.

'You guided your party here?' Roujeark asked, thinking he was not quite as unique as he thought. Slowly, the rambling truth came out, meandering ever more so as the wine claimed the scribe's wits.

'Yes...well, mostly. Knew vaguely where the Mountain might be, but got a little stuck after the High Falls. Good job that chieftain from, whaddya call it, Ilk, 'at's it, turned up. Never seen such a strange chap, but he set us right for a while...then we ran into that older blighter, claimed 'e was from old Ithilia, flipping fibber. Anyhow, he led us a right merry dance through most of eastern Dorzand before one day he just vanished in the fog.' By now, Caiasan was practically lying in Roujeark's lap, having started off slouching against him. Still cradling his wine jug, and talking more to himself than to the armist, he carried on, fending off sleep and discoursing blearily on.

'Oh, how we struggled in that accursed waste of rock and bog. Day after day, never getting anywhere. Food running short.' He interrupted himself with a loud belch. 'We would have been in a real tight spot had we not been spotted by the elf border-guards. Least, think tha's what t'were. They took pity on us, remembering kindly some good turn or other that our ancestors did 'em back in the Second War. 'Gainst the rules they packed us down some steep valley, and then, flip, we were in Kalimar...avoided the towns and cities...crossed the rivers quiet-like...eventually wound up here. Fine service I rendered.' Another belch, this one less volcanic. 'And how was I rewarded? With...with...' he raised his jug feebly for another sip, but it never made it to his lips, as he finally fell asleep.

A

Curillian smiled when he saw the Aranese scribe slumped in sleep against Roujeark. The young wizard was trapped and couldn't get up, but he seemed close to sleep himself. Half the camp was drifting back to their tents by now, and the sentries were being changed. Judging this as good a moment as any, Curillian had Findor and the others pitch their own shelters in the Aranese camp, and then he slipped off with Lancoir. They made their way to a smaller knoll some way from the larger one, and stood talking, out of earshot of the camp.

'A jolly evening,' Lancoir said mirthlessly. He looked bored and restless.

'You mean you weren't riveted by the endless tales of prowess with which we were regaled?' Lancoir scowled for answer. 'Yes, brave and reliable they may be, but the men of Aranar can be more than a little brash. Count yourself lucky if you can ever get them to talk about more than horses, tourneys and ale.' In truth, Curillian had found the evening just as tedious as Lancoir, having been ignored by Southilar for most of the time and left to converse with small-minded Pegasus knights.

'That Sir Theonar seemed a bit different,' remarked Lancoir.

'Yes, but he wasn't there for long. I didn't see when he slipped off.'

'He retired quietly when Southilar started on his third tankard. Just melted into the night.' Curillian smiled.

'A pity,' said the king. 'His conversation would probably have been more engaging than what I ended up getting. I didn't get much of the Jeantar's time. Truth be told, he seemed far more interested in the company of the Hawk and the Falcon.'

'I noticed that too. Strange bedfellows.'

Curillian smiled. 'Not much gets past you eh, Lancoir?'

'Except me, just now,' said a new voice.

Curillian and Lancoir both whirled around, swords in hand instantaneously. For a moment, they could see nothing, but they could hear the heavy breathing. Then the darkness of night thickened into a deeper shade. Slowly, an old, unsteady figure shuffled out of the darkness, leaning heavily on a curious staff. Lancoir stepped in front of his king, brandishing his sword in a defensive stance.

'Aye, but I've marked you now. Who are you?'

Curillian laid a soothing hand on Lancoir's arm. 'Not so loud, Lancoir, maybe our visitor doesn't want to alert the whole camp.' Slowly he felt the tension in the knight's arm relax, and then he straightened into a more relaxed posture.

'Might we know who you are, sir, and why you sneak up on us in the dark?' The figure kept shuffling forward, nearer to them, and he seemed to be making an odd sound, like an old man chuckling softly to himself.

'An old man has little other option for approaching folk in the night when he has no light. As for who I am, my name would not do you much good I'm afraid – it is very difficult to pronounce.'

'Still, a name would be a comfort,' said Curillian. 'An honest name, however difficult to pronounce, would make the wise man feel better about his unbidden night-time guest.' Again, the chuckling sound came, but still the old man had not raised his head enough for them to see under his hood.

'Fairly said, but you are an armist, not a man. Even more fair is for the stranger to declare himself first, for I am more at home here than you, I think. I was curious to see who would be first. But an old man has to be wise too, you see, in times when folk lie, cheat and steal to come to the Mountain that was lost.'

Curillian bridled. 'We did not lie, cheat or steal to come hither. Ours is a noble motive, and honest have been our steps.'

'*Indeed*, is that so?' said the stranger. 'Then you are singularly set apart from many who draw nigh. Invites they may have to the Tournament in yonder mountain, but that does not mean that their conduct in the approach will go unmarked. Pride, greed, envy, lust – do these sound to you like traits that will be rewarded?'

'Sir,' countered Curillian, 'you seem to know a lot about what passes in the hearts of contestants who are not even here yet. How may that be?'

'Do you not know that those who walk in this land have many ways of knowing things? Secrets stay less easily buried in these vales. Come, I bid you, can you declare that you come here for reasons other than those I have named?' The voice was undoubtedly that of an old man, but it had grown in power since the first soft words.

'I come to see what else my life may yet hold in store,' declared Curillian. 'I live and compete in the name of Prélan, the living God.' The old man raised his head a fraction at these words, enough for them to see a jut of chin, and the glimmer of eyes hidden deep in the hood's recesses.

'And what would be the hallmarks of a contestant thus conducted?' The question and queer glance together chilled Curillian's heart, though he could not think why, for he spoke in good faith. The virtues rattled off his tongue almost before he was aware of them.

'Courage, steadfastness, humility, temperance, mercy, clemency.'

The old man nodded along as the words came. Then he swept back his hood. For a split second, he loomed large, eyes blazing, and then he seemed to vanish in a gust of wind. Curillian and Lancoir turned away, shielding their faces with their arms as the chill draught flowed over them. But the single word uttered could not be warded off, and Curillian heard it within his head and without, penetrative and lingering.

Remember...

A

332

Roujeark sat alone on the edge of the camp. Having finally extricated himself from the slumbering Caiasan, he had settled down to gaze at the Mountain, dark beneath, and luminescent above. The more he gazed, the more he seemed to lose himself in the otherworldly sight. The air seemed to grow warmer and a strange breeze wafted up. Then suddenly he heard hot words within his head.

'Are you ready to begin? Is this truly the path you wish for yourself? Will you be ready to leave them all?'

XIV

The Contestants Convene

The next morning dawned upon a somewhat dishevelled camp, one which slowly came to life as the last sentries and duty cooks were joined by knights and men-at-arms waking tender-headed. On stools around the breakfast fire, Curillian and the armists found themselves joined by Sir Theonar. As they ate their bowls of porridge, talk inevitably fell to the Tournament.

'Still not much sign of anything happening on the Mountain,' remarked Aleinus. 'How long will we just sit here?'

'Last night the moon was still two days off the full,' said Roujeark. 'That means it isn't due to start until tomorrow night.'

'Fear not, Aleinus,' said Curillian. 'I shouldn't expect much to happen before more competitors are here. We are the only ones at present, but my guess is that others will arrive today.'

As they talked, others came and joined them, including an unshaven Caiasan, looking much the worse for wear. The conversation widened, and as it did so, Curillian and Theonar began talking between themselves.

Lancoir was too disciplined a soldier to remain idle for long, so as soon as he'd devoured his porridge he abandoned his bowl and walked the circuit of their camp. Their situation was not as defensible as he would have liked, but the position atop the knoll was better than anything else in prospect. He finished his circuit on the west brow of the knoll and joined one of the Aranese sentries, a Pegasus man-at-arms whose stomach was growling.

'Go get some food,' Lancoir told the man. 'I'll keep watch.' He looked out west in the dim morning light created by the Mountain's shadow. The sentry had not gotten far before Lancoir recalled him. 'No, wait!' Despite owing no obedience to this armist, the man-at-arms scurried back, curious as to what had alerted his new companion. For a long time Lancoir didn't say anything else, but stood straining his eyes against the half-light. Before them was the widest stretch of the trough they had yet come across, where there was quite a gap between the mountainside and the opposite slopes. In that wide space the mists were already mostly lifted, but beyond, where a great spur of the Mountain reached out almost to within touching distance of the cloven trough's far side, fog still lay heavy in the narrow place.

'There,' said Lancoir, now more confident of his sighting. 'Yes, there. See, figures moving through the mist.' The sentry strained his eyes thither as well, but by the time he had even located them, Lancoir had counted their number. 'Seven. Men on foot.' He turned to the sentry. 'Go give word to His Majesty the King, tell him there are new arrivals. Ask him to join me here.'

Others heard these words, and so a small crowd had gathered by the time Curillian came up with the armists and Theonar in tow. Lancoir pointed out the distant movement to his king.

'There, sire, men moving in the mist. Seven of them. I think they may be men of Ciricen.'

'Yes, they come from Ciricen,' pronounced Theonar. 'See how dull and sombre their apparel is, all grey mail, dark fur and hardened leather? They move with the accustomed caution of their race, and come well-armed. They each bear a skux, the axe-like weapon that only the Lordai wear, as well as more besides...'

Curillian smiled, marvelling. 'You are far-sighted, friend; I cannot see any of that.'

'Believe him, lord king,' piped up one of the Pegasus men. 'Sir Theonar has the best eyes I know.'

Gradually the newcomers came on, and slowly the distinctive characteristics of their garb and gear that had been apparent long before to Theonar became visible to the others. Around the same time, the small company halted, seemingly now aware that their approach was being watched. After a short while they came on again, their caution redoubled. In the time they took to draw near, Curillian was able to answer some questions posed to him by those around him.

'Who are the Lordai, Curillian?' asked Roujeark. 'Are they the same as the men of Ciricen?' To Roujeark, growing up in one of Maristonia's high valleys, Ciricen was just the name of a distant land, its people little more than a vague rumour beyond the edge of firm knowledge.

'No, Roujeark, Ciriciens and Lordai are not necessarily the same, for although the Lordai are a clan only found in Ciricen, not every man of Ciricen is reckoned to be a Lordul. The distinction is centuries old, coming from a time when the character of the men of Ciricen began to greatly diverge, between those who remained noble on the one hand and those who fell into darkness on the other. The Lordai were those who retained their dignity, named for their first chieftain. They opposed the Sordai, who forsook the lore and traditions of their forebears and conspired with the Northmen for their own profit. Ever after Ciricen was a realm divided, doomed to endure long ages of evil and chaos that culminated in the Second

War of Kurundar, when I was young. After bitter struggle, the Lordai emerged victorious to reclaim the throne of Ciricen, but they had become a grim folk, iron-hard and dour.' All were listening with great fascination, for such lore was not commonly known, in Aranar or in Maristonia. Findor asked another question.

'Sire, that is ancient history and long ago. What do you know of these men and their purposes today?'

'Thónarion sits on the throne in Rohandur today, Findor, as you should know well. He is beset by war and sedition, both of which arose again to trouble Ciricen in the time of his father, Liotor, but a little while after the royal authority had been restored. Bleak is his outlook, with the return of the Sordai and the rebuilding of Haracost. So much, at least, my Royal Guards should know,' said Curillian, with gentle reproof. 'As for what their purposes are, that is harder to say.'

'If I may speak, lord king,' said Sir Theonar respectfully, 'I am surprised that men of Ciricen have come hither at all. They are too much occupied with their own troubles, or so I deemed. But since some have indeed come, perhaps one of the Lordai has it in mind to win a weapon of great power. Now that the fell city of Haracost has been rebuilt, his kin are in desperate need of some such aid if they are to prevail again over their ancient enemies.'

No one knew how Theonar came by such knowledge, which was hardly common, even amongst the great lords of Aranar, but few of his countrymen at hand seemed surprised. Curillian was surprised, and marked it, but he was also in agreement. While they had been speaking, the men had drawn near. One of their number, a huge man, stepped forth and held his weapon aloft, haft-first in gesture of peace. It was a curious weapon, somewhere between a short halberd and a throwing axe, single-bladed but surmounted by a vicious-looking spike. This, and many other strange things about the Ciriciens, could be discerned as they came closer, but nothing that looked rich or princely.

Responding to the big man's gesture, Curillian went partway down the knoll's slope to meet them with Lancoir at his side. Since Southilar was nowhere to be seen, Sir Theonar went to represent Aranar, and with him went Lindal, the supercilious Unicorn Clan-knight. The whole Ciricien party came forward, but five of them hung back slightly. The big man who had waved the skux led the way, another close behind him.

'Hail, men of Ciricen,' spoke Curillian loudly. 'Unless you mean to start the Tournament prematurely, then come in peace and be welcome in this place of waiting.' The big man, with scarred face and hard eyes, looked Curillian up and down, but gave no answer. Instead, his companion stepped forward. He was a smaller man, but stern and well-built all the same.

'I am not a man of lore, but even one from far Centaur knows that only Curillian of Mariston could speak thus. Did ever an armist live so long and yet look so young? And if I guessed not from your bearing, I know the Sword of Maristonia by your side truly enough, of which we have heard, but not seen, in my country.'

Curillian bowed stiffly. 'Is it the earl of Centaur that I speak to, Culdon, of formidable repute?'

The man slammed a fist into his armoured chest by way of salute. 'I am he, and here with me is Garthan, my master-at-arms, and five others of my household. But I see men of Aranar beside you, King Curillian, and not armists only. Do we look to compete against you together, or severally?' Theonar gave answer for his people.

'My lord of Centaur, you find the two here together by happy chance, not conspired design. Oft have armists and the men of

Aranar stood side by side as allies in war, so do not be surprised to find evidence of friendship between them. Yet you need not worry, both now welcome you, and both will compete against you in their own right if you mean to enter the Tournament.'

Earl Culdon came forward then, and scarce could he have looked less like an earl in the eyes of Roujeark. In his small experience, the great lords of Maristonia were far grander in their appearance than this grim, simply clad warrior. But he was relieved to see the newcomer accepted in friendship by the king and Sir Theonar. Coming closer, he heard the other members of the Ciricien company named.

'Anrhus, my scout...and these here are warriors of my household: Rufin, Narheyn, Rhyard and Kaspain.' Each looked as severe and doughty as the last. All were armoured in leather and mail beneath their cloaks and furs, and armed to the teeth with swords, daggers, hunting spears and skuxs. The first three, who were all dark-haired, bore three faded chevrons on hardened-leather surcoats, while blond Kaspain, the last-named and youngest-looking, had only one. Roujeark missed some of what was said, but one thing he heard was very interesting, although it made him nervous.

'We are not the only ones who will arrive to disturb you today,' Culdon told Curillian. 'We have travelled far now in company with the Hendarian host, though at the last we tired of their slow pace and came on ahead. I think they were happy to let us do the scouting.'

The men of Ciricen set to making a small bivouac for themselves a little apart from the existing encampment. As they did so, Lancoir seized Curillian's elbow and hissed urgently in his ear.

'A host of Hendarians? We are too few if they decide to make trouble...'

'I don't think you need worry, Lancoir. How large a host can they have sent on such a road? If King Idunar is too old to give thought to this Tournament, then doubtless one of his brothers will have sent a champion with a suitable escort, but I do not think they will be many. Besides, competitors will need more than numbers to win this Tournament. If these Hendarians think they can bully through with sheer weight of men, then they have sorely misjudged Kulothiel's mind. Still, let us be on our guard.'

A

They did not have to wait long before the next arrivals turned up. They heard them long before they saw them, because a fanfare of trumpets smote the air and set the quiet air of the mountain vale to ringing. The noise was enough to bring Southilar forth from his tent at last. Drying a newly washed face with a towel, he strode grumbling to join them.

'What cur is winding trumpets at this hour?' he demanded gruffly. 'Are we beset by an army?'

'Behold, my lord,' said Curillian. 'Hendar has arrived.'

'Trust the Hendarians to make such a racket, always showing off...' grumbled Hardos, who stood beside his master.

The sun had now risen high enough to glance off the helms and spear-points of the cavalcade that was emerging from the last of the mist. Issuing out of the narrow place, the mounted party fanned out into a broad line of horses. They seemed to be mostly clad in metal, because when they came clearly into view, they caught the sun like mirrors and dazzled from afar. Shielding their eyes, the waiting leaders watched their onset.

'Only twenty,' breathed Theonar. 'But there was something strange about that fanfare…' His voice trailed off.

'It seems we need not have worried,' murmured Curillian to Lancoir. 'The Hendarians come with as much pomp as ever, but not so many in number as we might have expected.'

Roujeark was struck by the contrast between these men and those who had arrived before. The Hendarians were mounted, and came on arrogantly and full of confidence, where the Lordai had been on foot and so discrete as to be almost secretive. And after the nondescript drabness of Earl Culdon's party, the Hendarians were gorgeous in bright and ostentatious colours. Wealth and distinction were much in evidence as they drew nearer. After a while, the mounted group halted, and suddenly great banners were unfurled. As they caught the breeze, the brief relaxation of the waiting onlookers twitched rapidly into new anxiety, and murmurs of wonder rippled through them. Roujeark wondered why this flag had agitated them all so. He saw a great shield divided into five parts, each bearing its own token. Over all was set a crown and crossed spears, and stars twinkled in the scarlet field. Precious thread and sewn jewels made the whole device sparkle and glitter in the sun.

'The royal banner of Hendar,' said Curillian aloud. 'Has King Idunar come in person?' Southilar was incredulous.

'What? The old miser himself? Must have finally gotten sick of those squabbling brothers of his…'

'My lords,' said Sir Theonar, demurring. 'King Idunar has been wracked by illness for some time now, and hasn't been able to ride for months. This cannot be he.' Southilar ignored him, but Curillian looked troubled. By now, the Hendarian riding had started moving forwards again, coming swiftly closer.

'If this is not Idunar,' declared Curillian, 'then it can only be one other. The dukes of Malator and Nalator do not ride under the royal emblem, they would bear their own ducal arms. This can only be the Crown Prince, Adhanor.' New murmurs greeted this identification, as men wondered what it might mean.

'Lord king,' said Theonar quietly, 'the Crown Prince has his own token. If he rides with the king's banner, surely it means that the old king is dead and a new star rises in Hendar?' These words, spoken softly enough, were caught by enough ears to cause widespread amazement and shock. The king of Hendar, dead!

'But why would the prince be here if he has a kingdom to secure?' asked Sir Romanthony. 'This would be a dangerous time to go questing.'

'The allure of Oron Amular is stronger than we thought,' remarked Curillian. 'But certainly, strange tidings are afoot.'

Soon it was beyond all doubt. Five riders broke away from the main party, and, cantering forwards, they reined in their horses at the foot of the knoll. One bore the great banner, and he that led them bore a golden circlet on his elaborate helm. No old man could ride thus. The five riders waited at the foot of the knoll, as if expecting the onlookers to come down, but eventually they tired of waiting and dismounted. All five came up, led by the crowned man who now took off his helm to reveal a shock of fair hair. The knight who struggled on foot with the great flag remained behind armour and visor, but the other riders also removed their helms. One was old and grizzled, but the other two were as young and handsome as the leader.

His face full of wonder, the leader halted and surveyed the faces above him. The older man, all in plate armour, stepped forward and announced his master in an uncompromising bark.

'Behold His Most Serene Highness, Adhanor, King of Hendar, Master of the Five Cities and Guardian of the North.' So, thought Curillian, it's true. The old king was dead, and yet his son and heir was here, hundreds of leagues away. That's inconvenient timing, for the invite to arrive just as the kingdom changes hands. This Adhanor was young, barely into full adulthood. Curillian had never met him, but already he began to guess at his character. An impulsive youth, and daring, but reckless and irresponsible.

'Strangers,' the older man barked again. 'Declare yourselves.' Only now did the leaders on the brow of the knoll come down, and none of them really looked the part. Curillian and Lancoir were road-worn and travel-stained, and Southilar was not even fully dressed yet. Only the Clan Knights Romanthony of the Eagle, Lindal of the Unicorn and Hardos and Theonar of the Pegasus bore any insignia of rank and realm. Curillian was foremost in courtesy and greeting.

'Hail Adhanor, King of Hendar, and well met. I did not know your late father the king as well as I would have liked, but I am glad to meet you so early in your reign.' Adhanor looked searchingly at Curillian, as if trying to place him, and then seemed to arrive at an answer.

'Curillian? Curillian of Mariston?'

The armist nodded.

'It is you!' Adhanor gave a perfunctory bow. 'Lord King, the honour of this meeting is mine. Earl Culdon I know already, for he and his men were good enough to accompany us on the road for some time. And these,' he said, looking at the men beside Curillian, 'are surely my neighbours of Aranar, knights and princes of the horse.' He spoke with an easy gallantry, but there was conceit in his eyes, and in the eyes of his companions who looked on. 'Southilar I know, at least, the noble Jeantar, but who are these others?' Southilar grunted noncommittally, so Sir Theonar introduced himself, Hardos, Romanthony and Lindal.

'Well met, sirs,' declared Adhanor. 'And let me introduce my companions.' He gestured first to the big man in full plate armour who had announced him. 'Onandur, Count of Oloyir, Captain of my Bodyguards and makeshift royal herald. Xavion, Count of Koros, who has grown up at my side, and my particular friend, Reubun, Duke of Lalator.' The two elegant young men stood apart, aloof, and surveyed the ragged welcome committee with cool eyes.

'Your Grace,' said Curillian, 'it is a great grief to us to hear of the passing of King Idunar. On behalf of all Maristonia, I offer you my condolences. I hope that his passing was in peace?'

'An illness took him,' Adhanor said carelessly, 'but his time was ripe.'

That's true enough, thought Curillian, for 220 years old was well-advanced even for a king of Hendar in these days, but there's more to this than the boy lets on. Rather than continue the conversation there in the open, Curillian disengaged and Adhanor returned to his horse. The rest of the Hendarian cavalcade came up, and soon their tents were sprouting like velvet mushrooms on the ground before the knoll. Curillian sought out Adhanor while his great royal pavilion was being erected around him. The young king was standing while a squire unfastened his bulky outer armour. Duke Reubun and Count Xavion were there also, seated discretely off to one side.

'Ah, my lord Curillian, good of you to come and visit me. This is Athrick, my squire. Athrick, meet the king of the armists.'

The stout teenager looked up bashfully, but could not muster a greeting. He hurriedly finished his task and withdrew from the pavilion.

'A good lad,' Adhanor told Curillian, 'but shy.' He sat back in a camp chair and sipped from a goblet of wine that Athrick had poured earlier. Curillian declined a goblet of his own, looking around the richly decorated interior. He had something similar himself, but he rarely used it, for when on the road he either stayed in one of his estates, or with a noble host or a religious house. On ventures such as this, though, he preferred the simple trappings of an army officer. To regain his attention, Adhanor began speaking.

'So, it looks like we've got quite an international crowd already. Men of three different nations, and armists. Do you think many more will come?'

'I believe so, Your Grace. It is my understanding that invitations went out to the leaders and lords of every nation and race. We will probably see elves and even dwarves before long.'

'Dwarves?' Adhanor seemed astounded, and shared a smile with his noble attendants. 'Well, that *will* make it interesting.'

'And more men may yet come...' added Curillian.

'There will be no others from Ciricen,' announced Count Xavion from the half-shadows in the pavilion's eaves. 'Friend Culdon told us as much. He nearly didn't come himself.'

'Well,' said Curillian, 'our friends the Lordai have many concerns at the moment, some more pressing than this Tournament. Will there be any more of your own folk, Your Grace?' Curillian was not genuinely worried, but behind the casual enquiry was a faint suspicion that Hendar might be seeking to turn the situation to its own advantage. Once more, it was not Adhanor who answered, but one of his companions, Duke Reubun this time.

'No others shall come from the kingdom of Hendar,' he declared loftily. 'I have seen to it that no lord or knight rode forth without leave. All those in this riding were carefully vetted. As you can imagine, my lord, the kingdom is much astir because of recent events. Each nobleman, from the great dukes to the lowliest knight, is busy making ready for the new reign.' Curillian instinctively disliked the pompous young aristocrat, who reclined so languidly, cup of wine in hand, and he marvelled at the casual hypocrisy in the words.

'And yet, you, my lords,' he addressed the young noblemen, 'are here?' Adhanor made a deprecatory noise, sipping again from his wine.

'My uncles are taking care of everything. My crowning is not due until the end of summer, and nothing else required my immediate attention. But this, on the other hand,' he gestured vaguely out of the pavilion entrance-flap. 'How could I pass this up? You've had your fair share of adventures, my lord, or so I was taught. Surely you understand? And why else would you be here...?'

'That is true enough,' conceded Curillian. 'Though it is probably not as romantic as your tutors may have made it out to be. I too was young when my father was taken from me, but unlike yourself, I did not have the good fortune to come straight into my own. Long years and dangerous roads I walked before ascending the throne, and those trials prepared me well for it, teaching me to value it properly.' Reubun seemed to sniff dismissively, but Curillian ignored him.

'Come, my lord,' said Adhanor, 'I hope you aren't here to lecture me? Or is it that you're afraid of a little more competition?' The young king smiled disarmingly, but his challenge was unmistakeable. Just at that moment, two other men entered the pavilion, as different as chalk and cheese. One was a small, wry-faced man, immaculate in scholarly robes, whose faint smile showed that he had heard the last exchange. The other, bulky and red-faced, stood uncomfortably by the entrance in ill-fitting royal livery. The neat little man introduced himself and the other.

'Lord King, allow me to introduce myself. I am Equerrin, Physician to His Grace, and most pleased to make your acquaintance. That sweating oaf by the door is Rothger, a sheriff of the realm, and our pathfinder.' Curillian looked at Rothger.

'You guided the king's party all the way here?' The sheriff looked uncomfortable being addressed, but his eyes were shrewd enough. They darted around, and then settled on the floor as he mumbled an answer.

'Me lord? I found paths for His Grace and their lordships as best I could, but 'twas the bishop who did it really.' Curillian nodded, and cocked an eyebrow at Adhanor, who, in turn, gestured for the physician to elaborate.

'What Rothger means is that Bishop Nurvo, an esteemed member of our expedition, has a rare knowledge of this Mountain that he was only too happy to put at the disposal of his new sovereign.'

Curillian took this information in, and then turned his attention back to Adhanor.

'You are fortunate to have such a person in your following.' Then he changed tack, curious. 'The Lords Malator and Nalator are well, I trust?' Rumoril, Duke of Malator, and Dencaril, Duke of Nalator, were the greatest magnates in Hendar, and brothers to the late King Idunar. They had dominated his reign, and Curillian wondered what sort of dynamic would reveal itself between the old tyrants and the young successor.

'They are well,' Adhanor replied. 'It is a great relief knowing I have two such experienced men of government to rely on while I am here.' He scrutinised Curillian curiously for a while, as if pondering some great question, and an uncomfortable silence grew. Curillian paused a few heartbeats and then took his leave.

'Your Grace, I am glad to see you settled. Now, if you will excuse me.' He had reached the flap and was halfway out when Adhanor called after him, voicing the question which had obviously been needling him.

'And you, my lord, how did you find your way here?' Curillian paused and then looked back over his shoulder.

'I, too, have a guide.'

Ducking out of the tent, he had only gone a few strides in the waxing morning light when he bumped into a dark-robed figure. The figure made respectful apologies and made to move on straightaway, but Curillian checked him. The man looking at him had oil-slicked hair above strong aquiline features and glimmering black eyes.

'You are the bishop who guided King Adhanor?' Curillian guessed. The man smiled modestly, but his eyes gave nothing away.

'Your Majesty is well informed. I am Nurvo, Bishop of Losantum, a lowly priest in the service of the Hendarian church.' Curillian's skin prickled and he remained alert and firm.

'Yet you know of Oron Amular?' Again, the modest smile.

'Some of my, ah, rather…unique studies have led me here, yes. If Your Majesty will excuse me, I must attend to my services…' Without a backward glance, he moved suavely on.

Curillian watched him go, and only then did he notice the other priest who shadowed the bishop, black-clad and surreptitious. After a while, a third man went by as well, another nobleman, older and pale, but whose concentration was wearily fixed on the two priests. Curillian was puzzled by the atmosphere and the peculiar body language, and he mulled over the morning's conversations on his way back to his own tent. With several parties now joined together, the camp had swelled to a small temporary village, but the different nations had separated themselves out now into distinct quarters. Lancoir waited by the armist tents.

'Lancoir,' the king said, 'strange things are going on amongst the Hendarians. It may be nothing, but see what you can find out.'

A

The day wore on and Curillian found some more time to talk to Sir Theonar, sitting together on the brow of the knoll facing Oron Amular. The tall knight told him many tales of his life, but all vague and unassuming. Presently they were interrupted as Adhanor came up, all brash confidence and bullish charm.

'So, when will the wizard make his move?' he called. Roujeark, who had also joined them and sat nearby, started, afraid, but then he realised that the Hendarian king had no idea who he was, and had been referring to Kulothiel. Adhanor was dressed for action. He rubbed his hands together eagerly as he surveyed the Mountain, as if expecting its hidden gates to be flung wide at any moment. He was soon distracted, though, by sounds coming down the valley. His head turned to look in that direction, and soon all eyes were turned thither also. Curillian and Theonar came to stand by the Hendarian king. A lot of noise announced the arrival of many people into the valley. Not long had passed before it became clear that several different parties were arriving at once.

Aided by Theonar's sharp sight, Curillian did his best to tell them apart. A doughty contingent of dwarves came marching into the broader part of the valley, throwing up much dust beneath their heavy boots. Iron-shod, mailed and armoured, they were a grim folk who looked ready for trouble. Behind them, and to the side, rode a large ragged group, free-riders of Aranar by the look of them.

Male and female, hardened soldiers of fortune all. Hardly needing a closer look, Curillian had rarely seen such a surly and disreputable band. Unless the watchers' eyes were mistaken, there seemed to be more distinguished persons dotted amongst them, tall enough to be elves, but way-worn. Curillian could not guess what had brought together such a combination, nor where this band ended and the next began, for dozens of lordless mortals were now milling about in the confusion of the valley. Most astonishing of all, there came a crew of Alanai, barbarian men out of the south. Curillian wouldn't have believed it had anyone other than Theonar announced them. It was to them in particular that his attention was turned as the assorted newcomers gradually came closer to the camps.

'They are olive-skinned and proud of face,' Theonar told Curillian.

'That makes them sound like men of Raduthon,' Curillian guessed from the description. 'For the tribes and city-dwellers further south are darker of skin, some as dark as charcoal and ebony. Do they have curved sabres and flowing robes?'

'Yes,' said the Aranese knight. 'Their heads are covered with gem-set turbans, and scarves cover their faces up to their noses. They wear sandals and carry short bows and wicker quivers. And if my eyes do not deceive me, I believe there are both men and women in this crew, equally fierce of face and equally well-armed.'

'This is astonishing,' said Curillian. 'I know the invitations went far and wide, but I am amazed that they went as far as Lurallan. Truly, Kulothiel means this to be a varied gathering.'

'I do not know what surprises me more,' agreed Theonar. 'That they were invited at all, or that they managed to get here. Kulothiel's influence with the elves of Kalimar must still run deeper than I guessed for them to suffer such as these to pass.'

'They're savages,' spat Adhanor contemptuously. He knew the Alanai far less well than did Curillian, whose constant concern was to guard his southern frontier against them, but his prejudice was none the less keen for his ignorance. 'However they came, they will yield to better men in this tourney.'

A

Now, with such a blend of different races and nations present, the leaders of each group went among their followers to make pre-emptive preparations. Suspicions ran high, with many fearing and guarding against ambush. Not a few old grudges and grievances were now thrust uncomfortably close together, making for a tense atmosphere. Curillian took counsel with Lancoir and Roujeark.

'This will require great care. With so much fuel, the slightest spark could cause a conflagration. I mean to bring the various leaders together and secure a truce until the Tournament starts. Lancoir, go to the dwarf company and assure them that they are welcome and not under threat. Bid their chieftain come to our gathering, so that his kind may be represented.'

Curillian sent Antaya with a similar embassy to the Alanai. As messages went also to the other contingents, Curillian took stock with Roujeark.

'9 *Alanciel*. Last day before the full moon. It will begin tomorrow night.'

'Everyone's here now, do you think?' asked the wizard.

'It may well be, Roujeark.'

Just then, though, Curillian noticed three discrete riders passing up the valley from the other direction, whence the armists themselves had come. Tall, elegant, beautifully garbed and riding magnificent horses, they were unmistakably elves of Kalimar, and yet each as different to each other as the sea is from the plain, and the plain from the forest.

'Three kindreds, three representatives,' breathed Curillian. 'An Avatar princess and lords from the coast and from the forest.' The three riders kept well apart, and went unnoticed by most of those present, but Curillian watched as a slight scuffle broke out and three others broke away from the rudimentary camp of the free-riders to join them. His guess that elves had been among the free-riders was proved correct, but the reason for it still eluded him. Now, watching them ride across the valley, it became clear to his eyes that they were Ithrillian elves, dressed more sombrely than their Kalimari kin, and yet also distinct in other ways less easy to describe. The six took counsel briefly together on horseback, and then withdrew silently.

𝕬

The gathering of the leaders was a surreal experience, like nothing Curillian had ever seen before. He had travelled far and wide, and fought beside folk of most free nations, but never had he seen so many brought together in one place and time. He looked round the bizarre circle, marvelling at the wide array of faces, garments, accoutrements, stances, and weapons. There was Southilar, Jeantar of Aranar, still dressed like a blacksmith but lordly in stature; Culdon, the dour earl of Centaur in Ciricen, grim as a guard of graves; Adhanor, King of Hendar, boisterous yet regal; Hoth, a stout dwarf-lord out of long-forgotten Carthak, proud and wary; Parthir, the Alanai captain whose dark eyes glowered above a half-hidden face, and who was flanked by two female members of his crew, faces half-hidden like his own but regarding all about them with a fierce glance; and a long-faced Aranese knight errant who named himself Sir Losathen the Luckless. Last of all there was himself, armist king of Maristonia. Curillian doubted such an assembly of lords and kings had been seen since the Great Alliance overthrew Kurundar in the First War. And yet this was just a flavour of the mix of free-folk milling about around them, where walked bishops and knights, scribes and healers, mercenaries and rogues. Quite a cast.

'My lords,' he addressed them. 'We are all here with the same purpose, and by the same invitation. Let us compete long and hard for this prize that has been set before us, but let us save our energies for the Tournament itself. There should be no enmity among us here, lest this ancient valley be filled with needless blood. Some of you I know, and some I have had dealings with in the past, but I have no quarrel with any of you.' He fixed his eyes especially here on Parthir and his attendants, the Alanai representatives, who had been so reluctant to come. Whatever lay in the past between their two peoples, there was no need for any of it here. 'We have but one more day to wait, I deem, before the Tournament begins. None of us should suffer harm before we hear the wizard speak. So, my lords, help me keep a truce until we are inside the Mountain. Let old scores be forgotten until we are inside. Help me, by each of you restraining his own folk. We shall soon all have the chance to test ourselves. When the time comes, may the greatest of us prevail, but until that time, let peace reign among us.'

After a brief clamour and argument, they all assented with varying levels of enthusiasm. Gradually, and not without some muttering and jostling, they dispersed to preach this accord to their followers. Only as the council was breaking up did Curillian notice a latecomer who had not been present at first. He recognised the tall elf, despite the new scars on his face and the rents in his armour.

'You ask more than you know, Curillian,' he said, eyes smouldering.

'Elrinde! Are you Lancearon's representative here? It's so good to see you after all these years.' This Ithrillian lord had been right-hand elf to Lancearon for many lifetimes longer than Curillian could remember. Whether as king of Ithrill, or Silver Emperor, Lancearon had relied heavily on the many talents of Elrinde, both as a warrior and a politician. Now it seemed Elrinde was resuming the role of ambassador that he had played on several previous occasions. Curillian had fought under Elrinde's command, and alongside him, for many years during the Second War of Kurundar. As a young armist, living in exile and not yet come to the height of his powers, Curillian had been trained and encouraged by the noble elven lord. He had learnt so much. Through many battles and skirmishes, he had never seen Elrinde suffer so much as a scratch, nor lose his ready smile, but the elf that stood before him now was battered and bruised. Suppressed anger radiated from him.

'I will observe your truce, Curillian, because you ask it. But there are some in this gathering who will die very quickly after they have entered the Mountain.' Curillian shivered – Elrinde did not issue idle threats – but he was mystified. He thought Elrinde must have been one of the elves who had come with the free-riders of Aranar, but who had left them immediately upon arriving at the camp to join the other elves.

'Elrinde, what has happened? You look like you've fought every step of the way here.'

'What you say is not far from the truth. I am Lancearon's ambassador here, an observer more than a contestant. The mysterious tournament seemed like a good opportunity not only to learn what Kulothiel is up to, but also to make contact with our Kalimari kindred. So Astacar, Linvion and I were sent. Yet we had not gotten far beyond the borders of the old empire when we were ambushed. It was a gang of Aranese outlaws. Thieves, rogues and murderers. They are led by a captain named Raspald, whom his followers name Kin-slayer.'

'How many were they?' Curillian struggled to imagine how mere bandits had discomfited the famous Elrinde, Lancearon's 'holy sword'. This was an elf who had single-handedly cloven his way through orc armies, a swordsman with no equal in all of Astrom.

'Fifteen.' Anger flickered in Elrinde's face at the admission. Anger and embarrassment. Curillian was speechless. Each of Lancearon's chosen three would normally be worth a hundred others in a fight: deadly, skilled, and lightning-fast.

'How did it happen?'

'I had only slain a couple of the scum before one of them got behind Linvion and took her hostage. She is clever, but more of a diplomat than a soldier. To purchase her life, Astacar and myself had to yield and surrender our weapons. Somehow, they had heard of this Tournament. I was forced to guide them here, in return for which they let Linvion live. They deliberately waylaid us when chance brought into their path just what they needed. They didn't let down their guard the whole way here, until they were distracted by that circus out there. Seizing our chance, we took back our weapons and left them. They have no idea how little they will profit from their cunning. Fools! Oron Amular is holy ground. Even if they had not injured the subjects of Lancearon, they would forfeit their lives for daring to tread here. Each one will die. Raspald Kin-slayer, Benek Thunder-Eye, Sampa the Smooth, Vampana the witch-healer, Sceant, Lucask Lightfoot. They have all been marked.'

Curillian recoiled from the force of Elrinde's words, and only then did he notice the other elf standing by. Clad in various hues of blue, grey-eyed and sombre, he was a sea-elf, older than Elrinde, but no less noble. He smiled graciously at Curillian, showing none of the thirst for vengeance harboured by his companion.

'King Curillian, I am Nimarion, Lord of Marinia and representative of the Marintors. I came with here with two others, representatives of Avatar and Firnar.' That made him a very senior figure in the sea-elf realm, scarce a rank or two junior to Marintor himself, the sea-elf king. 'Your reputation is well-merited, for it has been borne out by your conduct here. I see and hear that you have established a truce between all these volatile guests, for which I am grateful, on behalf of all my kindred. It would not do for blood to be spilled before the Tournament has started, but it would have gone particularly ill for those at fault. The Mountain is not as blind as many here might suppose. Kulothiel knows you are here. He is ready for you, and he will summon you soon. Fare thee well, king of the armists.' In one suave motion, Nimarion turned to go, but Curillian checked him.

'Please, lord, before you go. Do you know what this is all about? What is Kulothiel up to?' Nimarion lowered his sad, benevolent eyes to Curillian's, and spoke soothingly.

'The Keeper is his own master. His full devices and true purposes are known to none, not even the wise in Paeyeir. We shall see…but you, Curillian, have as good a chance as anyone here of finding out the truth when all is finished. But survive the many snares before you, or Mariston will never know why her king died.'

A

The elves were gone in a rustle of robes and soft feet. Curillian's heart was heavy, grieving at the thought that his old friendship with Elrinde was forgotten. So many friendships won and lost over the years. For the first time he felt old. Old and tired.

The night passed, and the long-awaited day dawned. Curillian awoke refreshed and revitalized, the lethargy of the previous night fading like a thought. Not all seemed to share his energy. Some were excited, itching for the off, some were scared, and all were nervous. The day was hot and the air humid. A stifling atmosphere lay over the various camps, where elf, man, dwarf and armist kept studied distance between each other. Frugal meals were eaten half-heartedly, and private thoughts were nursed in a thousand internal conversations.

The armists broke open their packs and dressed for action. Their travelling clothes were stowed and exchanged for battle-wear, leather and mail. Routine took over as kit was checked and weapons sharpened. Curillian called them all together as the light was fading.

'My friends, the time is nearly upon us. This is what we've come all the way from Mariston for. There will be danger inside, and great fear. As such, I do not command any of you to enter; but I welcome the company of each one of you who comes willingly. Lancoir, Antaya, Findor, Aleinus, Andil, Lionenn, Caréysin and Roujeark, there are none I'd rather have beside me. Many challenges and tests both stern and strange lie before us, so let us be prepared. Remember, our brains will be needed just as much as our muscles. Do not assume anything in there is safe, so touch cautiously and tread lightly. Look around you. Some here are allies, friends, grudging admirers, and plenty too are enemies from of old. Once we get inside, we're on our own, and we'll need to stick together. Antaya, say a prayer for us.'

The devout guard led them in earnest prayer. On behalf of all of them, he besought Prélan for protection and guidance, wisdom and strength…and success. When he finished, their eyes met, and they all clasped wrists. They were ready.

And they waited.

The whole valley waited. Fuller than it had been for centuries, all eyes were turned towards the Mountain, elves, men, dwarves and armists alike. As darkness fell, no one so much as thought of food or sleep. Warriors fidgeted and fiddled with weapons, and lords stalked back and forth. The darkness deepened, and still nothing happened.

Roujeark, though, felt something that no one else did. He sensed the onset of something in the dark. Eerie winds picked up and rushed tauntingly among them, but behind the unsettling sound, he felt the air prickle. His fingertips tingled, as if responding to some unseen force. The air thickened so much it took his very breath. The Mountain seemed to intensify its magnetism, tugging him towards it. He raised his eyes, and watched the full moon rise above the icy ridges and escarpments. Curillian saw it too, and held his breath. Roujeark's stomach lurched and all around him cringed, as if some invisible irritant stung their ears. From deep within the Mountain, a vast pressure rose up and up until it burst from the summit like a volcano. An eruption of light and sound shook the still night air, illuminating the valley floor like daylight. In the sudden glare, the icy flanks of the Mountain glimmered fell and terrible.

Even as the first eruption subsided, a second explosion of lights went off much lower down the mountainside, kindling an archway of fire above a narrow shelf. All eyes strained up towards that sight, wondering what it heralded. Slowly the fires subsided and went out. They saw that the shelf where the lights had been could be reached by a steep but viable slope up over the Mountain's toes.

In ones and twos, small groups, and wary companies, they were drawn towards it, all under the same spell. If some had thoughts of turning back, none now found it possible. Even those who quailed inwardly realised that their feet were summoned. Fears heightened and bowels clenched, but all kept going forward. They quite forgot each other, heedless of the friends, foes, and soon-to-be-rivals that advanced all around them. The contestants scaled the lowest paths of the Mountain like ants, slowly converging on that shelf where the beacon had burned.

Gradually the path beneath their feet became smoother and broader until it led them up onto the shelf and beneath a tall, smooth cliff-face. As they arrived, they saw a dark outline in the lower portion of the cliff, a great rectangle of glowing runes. The lights and fires had gone out, but the runes still gleamed in the night. They framed a great dark door, but faintly visible in the darkness. The first men to arrive approached it nervously, but soon came up short. The way was shut.

As the armists came up behind, they could hear the mixture of fear, disappointment and consternation rippling through the crowd of questers in front of them.

'It's locked,' some cried.

'There's no way in,' others wailed, their voices stinging the cold night air.

Gradually a passage opened up before them and Curillian and his company found themselves drawn forwards to the front. When they got there, they could see what had been hidden before. The door was indeed shut. It loomed over their heads, dwarfing all of them. It was featureless except for a circular impression halfway between the doorposts. Roujeark's eye was drawn there immediately and he could hear his heart thudding within him. Almost without thinking, his hand went to the star-seal beneath his clothes. His fingers seemed to get a shock as they brushed its cold metal. Roujeark jumped as he felt Curillian's hand laid on his arm. He found the king looking at him, almost as if he had had the same thought. They alone knew that the young armist bore the seal, but now he slowly drew it out.

As he stepped forward, the others around him became aware of him and dropped back. A buzz and a murmur arose as they regarded him, wondering what he was going to do. Roujeark could feel their eyes on his back as he took another step forward, cradling the star-seal uncertainly in his hands. He looked around for the elves, feeling sure that they would know what to do, or even that this was something for them to do. But no sooner had he located their bright eyes in the crowd than they melted into the darkness, ceding to him.

He looked back at the crowd of faces, men stern and women proud, dwarves in their fearsome helms and his own armist companions. He quailed under their expectation, and looked to Curillian for reassurance. The king just nodded. Behind him loomed Sir Theonar, who gestured forwards with his hand. Swallowing hard, Roujeark turned back to the door and approached it with trembling steps. Visions of his former days rushed through his mind, all insisting that his whole life had led him here, to this moment.

The closer he got, the more detail he saw in the circular feature. It was a raised area standing proud of the dark doors, and a circle of glowing light ran around it like a residual fire from the explosion of lights. Inside the circle was a carved surface full of runes. He could not read them, but the star-shaped impression in their midst was unmistakeable. Raising the star-seal, he found that it was the exact same shape. With a trembling hand, he lifted it and slotted it into the indent. It sank neatly into place and did…nothing.

Nothing happened. Roujeark's heart continued thudding but he could almost hear the collectively-held breath behind his back. A few more agonising seconds past, and then the seal began to glow. A word was illuminated amongst the runes. It flashed bright and the seal dropped out of its fitting with a loud, startling hiss. Roujeark stepped back in fear, and the entire crowd behind him went back several paces also, cringing away as if expecting to be struck down. Hesitantly Roujeark leaned down to retrieve the fallen seal, and as he did so, he felt rather than saw the doors swing inwards. They did so soundlessly, and so dark was it inside that only the disappearance of the glowing circle and its fitting persuaded him that the doors really had opened. A waft of suppressed air issued forth and the night air seemed to crackle and fizz, suddenly alive.

The whole host of questers was suddenly under some strange compulsion. The spell allowed for no hesitation, no second thoughts. They entered inside as if drawn by some great pressure within. Elves of Kalimar and Ithrill, dwarves of Carthak, mortals of Hendar, Ciricen, Aranar and Lurallan, they all plunged into the blackness. Roujeark resisted the tug long enough on the threshold to turn his eyes upward and behold the forbidding bulk of the Mountain soaring steep overhead. The moon-washed heights of ice and rock, framed against the pale stars, was the last thing he saw before darkness engulfed him.

※

XV

Oron Amular

INSIDE The Mountain the darkness was complete. For the first few steps they had been aided by the faint moonlight outside, long enough to see that they were in a tunnel, but very soon they must have turned a corner, for even that small light was lost, plunging them into utter blackness. Roujeark's eyes strained uselessly against the darkness, but he couldn't even see his hand in front of his face. He could hear, though. Hear the sounds of others blundering blindly up ahead, of feet scuffling and armour clinking, of curses muttered under various breaths and the nervous calls of one to another. Yet even those sounds seemed to fade after a while, as if the various parties were being separated and devoured by the terrible darkness, one by one.

Roujeark reached out his hand to feel for the tunnel wall, but it was further away than he thought. Straining for it, he nearly fell over before coming to rest against it. To his surprise, the rock wasn't rough, but smooth to touch. Feeling with fingers and feet, he found that both the wall and the floor were smooth as polished gems and flat as paving slabs. No blemishes or snags could he find. But he had only gone a few doubtful steps when he bumped into something. It was one of his companions. Clutching the arm, Roujeark felt the armist quivering.

'Who is that?' he whispered, hearing his words vanish in the swallowing darkness.

'Aleinus,' came the barely audible reply. In fact, they were all there, stopped dead in the middle of the tunnel. Groping darkness was before them and behind them, above them and below them. The very air was thick with potency, harsh to taste and seeming to tingle on the tongue and fingertips. In the face of this invisible barrier the lion-hearted armists faltered, unnerved and uncertain. Here, normal boldness was of no avail. Even Curillian was at a loss. When Roujeark discovered the king by touch, he found him still and tense, staring into the impenetrable darkness. Long moments passed in silence, with only the sound of shallow breathing hanging in the air. Slowly, Roujeark stepped forward. The air seemed to be full of whispering spirits, murmuring long-forgotten secrets and creeds. He was terrified, but the feel of this place, heavy, forbidding, mysterious, was slightly less daunting for him than for his companions. He felt some sort of affinity with it.

He stepped forward into the watchful air, having to drag himself against unseen resistance. Even with so little a step he had moved out of sight of his companions, but after a heartbeat or two the king moved up behind him. Curillian was completely out of his comfort zone, but his courage was conquering his fear. Lancoir defaulted to sticking as close to his king as possible, and each armist followed suit, all afraid of being left behind in the gloom. Roujeark had them link hands and stretch out so they could fill the tunnel, touching it on either side. Yet it was wider than any of them had imagined, a vast corridor fit for princes. The wide space quite belied the sluggish movement of the airs and cheated noises, which seemed not to behave as normal. But stretched out, and hands joined, they felt slightly more at ease, and proceeded cautiously forward.

Reluctantly, the blanket darkness gave way before them. Now and again they felt the tickle of some wind filtering down from an unseen vent above their heads, and occasionally they caught muffled sounds from ahead. With a veritable army ahead of them, they might have expected to hear more, but the sounds just weren't carrying. Nerves tautened like harp-strings and hairs stood on end as each member of the company began imagining what end had already befallen their competitors. Their powers of reason and deduction seemed to have been left behind outside, like their courage, so they found themselves at the mercy of their senses, quite convinced by the distortions that were being reported to them by eyes, ears and noses. The cool night from outside had been replaced by a stuffy heat, such that beads of sweat started to form on their brows and hands, and they twitched and crackled as if toyed with by delinquent sparks in the air.

They followed the tunnel, feeling it bend and twist in slow, deliberate curves. The darkness seemed to lessen an iota, or so their hopeful eyes claimed, but still nothing definite could they see. Their feet were more certain in reporting a gradient and, following that long smooth slope, they came to a place where the tunnel walls gave out on either side. The air suddenly felt very different. Still queer and laden with intent, it now scurried about and carried sound more easily. They began to hear other groups about them. Suddenly sounds seemed to be all round them, boots scuffing and scabbards banging, leather creaking and mail clinking, heavy breathing and sniffing. The place was teeming with life. Voices began to call to each other, some in fear and some in suspicion. Then an almighty clatter split the air as two metal objects collided. The armists drew close and stuck together in a tight group, but even so, they bumped and jostled with unseen neighbours.

Roujeark felt the tension ratcheting up inside him as he groped blindly in the intolerable darkness. He felt enclosed and exposed at the same time. With every passing second he feared a collision, or a sly knife sliding out of the jet black air. Panic was building up within him, ready to burst out in a shrill scream, when all of a sudden a silver flame burst into life. Poof! Up above them, it seemed to hover in mid-air. Then another joined it, and another. Poof! Poof! Poof! In the blinking of a suddenly seeing eye, there was a ring of silver fires up above them. In their velveteen light, the inhabitants of the hall might have seen one another, except they were all straining their eyes upward. Glimpses they caught of ancient grandeur, carvings, friezes and sculpted vaulting, all dancing in a firelit ceiling high above. The fires seemed to burn out of sconces set on some sort of raised gallery.

Just as the contestants were adjusting to take in this vague information, a blinding light filled the roof like sheet lightning. A moment later there came a multi-layered boom like rolling fireworks, then cascades of iridescent sparks were falling among them. Those who had the presence of mind raised their shields to ward off the hazard, but still many eyes were dazzled and not a few burns caused. Yet the sparks had not been without purpose, for their passing had ignited wall-torches all around the place, and now there was enough light to see by. Not enough as could be wished, but enough to fit everything else together. The contestants were now able to take one another in, resuming their uneasy acquaintance after what seemed like an eternity. Together they found themselves in a vast and glamorous cavern, like the anteroom of a strange old palace. It was a perfect circle, flat and smooth and painted in a colour that one moment seemed terracotta and then mahogany the next. There were portraits and engravings everywhere, depicting strange scenes of wizards and magic.

Above these murals, which were uncannily lifelike, there swept a lip of bronze, crowning and encircling the walls. Beyond that lip there seemed to be a circular walkway, lost out of sight. The only thing marking the head of the chamber was a little indent in the bronze lip, where a small balcony jutted out. So awed by their surroundings were they that it was some time before the contestants noticed the figure standing there, still as stone. The murmuring amongst the company died down as one by one the contestants became aware of the statue-like person above them. Their eyes were drawn irresistibly towards him, and then were locked, unable to look away. The figure was clad in a dark green robe. His long hair was white, and silver was the wispy beard that fell to beneath the rim of the wall. He looked old beyond reckoning, but he stood erect, unbent by whatever years lay upon him. His gaunt face was proud and grim, a study in fascination, yet unknowable. Long clever hands rested on the bronze lip in front of him, and a curious staff leaned beside him. Beneath his unwavering gaze, each and every person in the chamber felt like a child, tiny and inordinately young. After what felt like an eternity, the words came.

'Hail, contestants from afar, the Keeper of the Mountain welcomes you to the Tournament of Oron Amular.'

The words seemed to emanate out of the rock itself, impregnated by the slow march of all the years this chamber had witnessed. They didn't even see his lips move. Quiet but booming, unguessable but certain, each person heard the words as if from within his own head.

'They who were summoned here by invite are welcome, and their retinues with them, but woe to him or her that cometh here unbidden. Guest and intruder alike, both have passed within the doors, and they are now shut. They shall not reopen until the Tournament has run its course. The signal moon waxes in the night sky above, and she shall have passed away ere this business is done.

'Eight doors there are...' Immediately as he said this, eight portions of the spherical wall, in which no join or crack had before been evident, swung noiselessly inward. '...Eight doors, eight routes beyond, and eight leaders to tread the way. Each way leads into the

Tournament, and though the aspect of each may vary, each will lead inexorably to the same destination. Which of you can know what you will find upon the way? But verily, at the end awaits the prize which you all seek…Power Unimaginable…'

The last two words echoed and reverberated around the chamber, rumbling on and on, and as they did so the silver fires went out as suddenly as they had been ignited. The wall-torches too were extinguished, and the timeless speaker vanished. The only light that was left was a faint glow around each of the eight newly-revealed doorways. As if by some hidden signal, the eight parties gravitated towards their own entrance. The elves of Ithrill went to one, the elves of Kalimar to another; the dwarves of Carthak had their own, as too did the armists of Maristonia; one each was set apart for the men of Hendar, of Ciricen, of Aranar, and of Lurallan. None of them saw the additional opening prepared for the interlopers, they who had seen no invite and followed no flag. None saw them go, but the screams that marked their expulsion from the chamber, like the hunting cries of vampire-demons, transfixed with horror those that heard them.

That terror was only deepened by the menace of the doorways, the eerie light around them and the complete lack of light in the blackness beyond. What lay without? Would they step into a void and tumble into oblivion, or would other horrors be waiting? Some tried to get out of the chamber, back the way they had come, but to their consternation they could find no trace of the broad sloping passage that had brought them hither. While the others were gripped by panic, Roujeark took it upon himself to lead. He stepped under the glowing arch and then into the blackness beyond. His companions were hesitant to follow him into so dark a place, so a sudden idea came to him. He conjured a small flame in the palm of his hand. Turning, he raised it to his companions, shedding a little light on their fearful faces. It looked for all the world like he was holding a small oil lamp. In its small light, they could all see that what lay beyond was just a tunnel, a tunnel like any other. Now revealed, its terror diminished somewhat.

Roujeark could not keep the flame in his palm indefinitely, but just as it was starting to waver, bringing all the guards' fears back, he came across a long disused torch in a wall brazier. Once the torch was alight and burning brightly, the young conjuror handed it to Findor, who looked glad to receive it. Now they could proceed faster, but trepidation still made them slower than they could have been. Roujeark could sense the growing air of hostility. He guessed that obstacles and hurdles awaited them. For a long time they followed a descending slope which wound and wound round many bends and twists. As they went the air grew noticeably warmer.

After what seemed like an age of walking, they came to a small cavern. Much smaller than the main cavern where Kulothiel had met them, but still a curving open space with a low ceiling. Running around the opposite side of the cavern was a series of doors. They all came to a stop, uncertain what to do next. There were six doors, but no clues as to which way to go. Fear rose and magnified the decision: what if they chose wrongly? A poor choice here could be disastrous, sending them plummeting down into an abyss or into a lair of monsters. The torchlight danced about as Findor trembled noticeably. Steeling themselves, Lancoir and the guards tried each door, and found that every one opened. No locks to narrow their choice.

Roujeark looked closely at each door, going slowly from one to the next and feeling his hands over them. All were alike, heavy seasoned oak with brass bindings and locks. Yet on one the varnish of long-vanished days was peeling, the brass was tarnished and the wood was slightly discoloured. There was even a different smell from behind it, even though all that could be seen through any of them within the reach of the torch was a dank passageway. A memory fluttered in Roujeark's mind and a warning came to his heart. In the long past journey when he had met Ardir in the mountain tunnel, he had learnt then that the most attractive-looking option was the wrong one. The way which had looked worse in fact turned out to be right. Like a caged bird suddenly set free, this memory whirred around inside his head and then was gone, and he was left looking at the odd door out, the door that seemed older and in worse repair. Its contrast with the others was not as strong as it had been on that far-off day, but he felt sure the same lesson still applied. He motioned to the others.

'I think it's this way,' he told them. Curillian looked doubtful.

'What makes you say that?' was his question. Roujeark frowned pensively.

'I cannot be sure, but it reminds me of something I encountered long ago. I feel in my heart that Prélan is leading us through here.' Lancoir looked even more dubious than the king, but he had no better suggestion to make. Curillian looked appealingly around the room, as if they had missed something.

'There is nothing else to guide us. So, let Prélan lead us aright.'

The old door was opened. One by one, they plunged through.

XVI
The Gauntlet

THE Tunnel they entered was much lower and narrower than the one before. Nor was it smooth and well made, but jagged and scarred, full of dents, undulations and imperfections. They ducked and eased past the fingers of rock that blocked their path, making their way slowly onwards. Curillian was up at the front of their file with Roujeark. Suddenly he put an arm out to check Roujeark. He looked forward with suspicious eyes and sniffed the air. Roujeark looked at him questioningly but then saw what he was looking at. A thin, almost invisible silver strand, like a spider's thread, was stretched across the tunnel. Another one like it was at shin height. The torch was brought up, and in its light they could inspect it more closely. Curillian touched it very gently and gave it the slightest twang. They felt, rather than saw, the shower of rock flakes patter onto their heads. Looking up into the still-falling trickle of powdered rock, they eyed the ceiling nervously. They both swallowed hard as they caught one another's gaze.

'Haste yes, Roujeark, but not too much,' whispered Curillian. 'We need to be ultra-cautious.' With exaggerated care, they all ducked under the taut strand, stepping over the lower one in the same motion, and moved on up the corridor. Lancoir was the last armist past, and as he went, the tunnel shook. Their hearts leapt to their mouths, but Lancoir hadn't touched it. Taut as a crouching cat, Lancoir slowly eased himself up and straightened. Then they heard the booming report from somewhere else in the mountain. It sounded far away, but all too near.

'Sounds like someone wasn't as careful as us,' breathed Caréysin.

Recovering their composure, they carried on. There were many more twists and turns and uncomfortably narrow sections to negotiate before the tunnel finally dumped them out in a small sandy chamber.

⋀

Their relief at being out of the tight confines of the tunnel was short-lived when they realised that they were in a chamber with no exits.

'Well so much for this way,' exclaimed Aleinus. 'Roujeark, you've brought us to a dead end!' Roujeark didn't answer, but Antaya started back into the tunnel on his own volition. He paused to lean against the tunnel wall and peer back up into the gloom. The portion of wall he was leaning on gave way and sank back into the mountain. An ominous rumbling sound built in volume and tremor. Antaya threw himself backwards only just in time, regaining the safety of the sandy bay just as the roof of the tunnel collapsed. A gust of air whooshed over them, carrying a cloud of rock dust. Choking and temporarily blinded, they all staggered back. When the dust settled, it was all too plain that the only exit was blocked. There was now no going back.

The guards slumped against the wall in despair, but Andil and Lionenn started to investigate the walls. Lancoir, who had taken the torch from Findor, planted it in the ground, and by its light he too joined the exploration. Though they ran their fingers over every face and into every crevice, and though they pored through every nook and cranny, nothing could they find. The mood darkened, and Roujeark felt glaringly conscious of his responsibility for their predicament. *I was sure this was the right way*, he murmured to himself. Aleinus began chucking rock shards at the rockface opposite him.

'There's no way out,' he moaned, 'we'll die down here.' He carried on flinging bits of rock. 'Not much food, barely any water, and the torch won't last long...'

'Shut up, Aleinus,' Lancoir snapped. He had heard something strange and, having silenced his subordinate, he strained his ears. He motioned for another rock to be thrown. Sulkily, Aleinus obliged. The rock smashed into smithereens barely a foot from Lancoir's face, which was flattened against the wall, but the captain didn't care. A faint smile played upon his lips, and he pushed himself away. Slowly, deliberately, he brought his foot down in a powerful kick against the wall.

'Lancoir, what are you doing?' the king asked. 'That's not going to help.' Lancoir took no notice but kicked again.

'It's hollow,' was all he would say. Again and again he kicked, and part of the rock face broke off and fell away. Lionenn caught on quick and used his battle-axe to smash in more of the brittle wall. Others lent their boots to the task and soon large gaps were appearing. Lancoir backed off, and then charged shoulder-first against the wall. It smashed under the impact and fell in pieces around the upended captain. They had to dig Lancoir out of a pile of rock, but he had done his work well. A false façade of rock had disintegrated under his assault and what it had been concealing was now revealed. Behind it was a curious feature. Running up the real rockface behind was a series of tiny little ledges. Upwards they climbed, like an awkward staircase to the ceiling. And there, in the ceiling, was a dark hole. Lancoir rested his foot on the lowest step, bruised but triumphant. It held his weight. Having come this far, he retained the initiative. Placing both feet on the lowest step, he stretched up to the next step, hands scrabbling at the rockface to help himself up. The gaps between the steps were large and daunting, but progress was possible.

One by one, step by step, they climbed up the wall, leaving the mess of rubble and the apparent dead end behind. Curillian stayed behind with the torch to light his companions' way, but when his turn came, he couldn't climb with the torch ablaze, so he reluctantly extinguished it and tucked it into his sword belt. Roujeark now conjured another light, which was not easy as he balanced precariously on a narrow step. They had all come to a halt because Lancoir had stopped. He called down to say that the hole didn't open onto a passage or tunnel but went upwards in a vertical cavity. Leaving the steps behind, he wedged himself into the narrow space, back to one wall and legs stretched out in front, bracing against the rock.

'Follow me, do as I do,' he grunted. Then he vanished into the hole. Guided by Roujeark's wavering light, they ascended with aching slowness and stomach-lurching uncertainty. The cavity became a vent, a hollow vein in the heart of the mountain that seemed to go on forever. Lancoir gritted his teeth and continued to shuffle, inching his way up. At long last he came to a place where a gap opened out on one side. A breath of air confirmed that he had come to another passage.

⋀

Roujeark's flame was too far below to cast more than the barest glimmer of light here, but Lancoir didn't need sight to know what lay all around him. He could *hear* it. Hear *them*. Sibilant hisses caressed the darkness in every direction. Slithering bodies slunk past each other and rustled through something dry. Lancoir had encountered snakes during his tours of duty to the southern frontiers of Maristonia, and he did not relish the memory. Hastily he dropped back down. He hissed down to the next person below him, which was Findor.

'Snakes!' He heard the guard gulp before relaying the message downwards. After a while another chain-message came back up. Findor reported Curillian's words.

'What's the lie of the land? Can we get past?'

'I can't see a thing,' Lancoir retorted. 'I need light.' He waited, his muscles burning with the effort of holding him in place, every moment expecting a sinuous body to drop down on him. Beads of sweat ran down his forehead. A musty odour of decay filled his nostrils. After what seemed like an eternity, he saw the light from below grow brighter, and then Findor was passing him the relit torch. Steeling himself, Lancoir inched back up. Hissing angrily, the snakes backed away from the flames, but in their light the Captain of the Guard could see now that there were hundreds of them. Twisting fearfully around, he saw that the whole floor around him was a roiling sea of reptilian flesh, writhing around each other like some sort of demonic rope. The light of the torch came back at him from a thousand beaded eyes. Wanting nothing more than to get away, he forced himself to hold firm and summoned the presence of mind to properly assess the immediate vicinity. He was in a sort of bowl-shaped hollow, perhaps thirty feet in diameter. The gentle slopes led up to a wide rim at the foot of the walls, and from that rim was a crooked ramp that led up to a dark door near the ceiling. The entire bowl was full of snakes and worms.

He slunk back down again, fighting hard to control his breathing. His heart pounded as he strained to think clearly. The way back was blocked; this was the only way. But how to get past? Even if he could rise out of the vent without being struck, he could hardly hope to reach the rim or the ramp without being bitten. All it would take was one bite to fill him with venom and end his quest in frothing, seizing agony. He glanced up again fearfully. Something above him had caught his eye. The torchlight was reflecting off something metal. A large circular candelabrum hung down from the ceiling, dangling from a rusty iron chain. It was long disused and looked ready to fall at any moment.

'Pssst,' he hissed to get Findor's attention. 'Get some stones passed up.'

'Stones?'

'Stones. Pebbles. Rocks. Something to throw. Hurry.'

Fortunately, the collapse of the tunnel and the false façade below had provided plenty of suitable ammunition. Lancoir grabbed what came up and stockpiled it in his sleeves. When he had enough, he raised himself to throwing height. One by one, he hurled the bits of rock at the point in the ceiling where the iron chain was fixed. He hoped he could dislodge whatever was holding it in place. His first few efforts clanged off the candelabrum and rained back down on the snakes below. They raised their heads in anger and started to seethe. Lancoir's fears rose to fever pitch but he kept throwing. He managed to hit the chain itself and set it jangling, and the ceiling around the fixing, provoking a shower of rock chunks. The snakes nearest him were leaning towards him, cold fury emanating from them. The corners of his vision were filled with shimmering scales and glinting fangs. He paused throwing to swish his torch about, forcing them to back off. He knew his time was running out. There was no shortage of ammunition, but he had only seconds before he was struck at. His fall would likely doom those below him, and any that survived would still have to face the venomous obstacle. He took a particularly large rock and hefted it. Using all his daring, he spent precious seconds sighting it, and then threw it with as loud a yell as he could summon.

'PRÉLAN!!!' In the confined space the shout seemed deafeningly loud, and it seemed to echo out of the aperture above and spread throughout the mountain. Other contestants heard it and trembled; Kulothiel heard it far above and smiled; the snakes blanched before it. Lancoir's hearing was so taken up with the booming report of his own shout that he scarcely heard the rumble from the ceiling. His rock had hit home, thudding into the loose fixing with ample force. In a flurry of rock and dust, the chain came loose and crashed down into the chamber below. Scores of snakes were crushed beneath it and blinding dust spread throughout the whole space.

'NOW, MOVE!' Lancoir yelled back down the vent. Using the torch, he swept the rim clear of snakes and vaulted himself upwards onto the sloping ground of the bowl. He had no time to think or fear, he only knew instinctively that the fallen metal was his bridge. With terror-fuelled speed he crashed over the candelabrum, snakes hissing and snapping about his ankles. When he reached the rim, he did not stop but powered up the ramp, not caring what lay ahead. Through the throbbing adrenalin haze of his head, he heard his companions following in his wake.

Curillian came last, sprinting behind the flowing robes of Roujeark with the speed of an armist possessed. He brandished his sword like the railing of a sinking ship, drawing strength from its hilt as he charged up the ramp. Vaguely he heard cries up ahead, but he kept going. As he approached the dark door, he thought that once they were clear of the snake den they would pause and take stock, but no such time was given him.

A

Passing through the door he found himself in utter darkness – the torch ahead had vanished. The last cry he heard more distinctly, a yelp of dismay from Roujeark, whom he couldn't see. His foot reached out and found nothing to rest on. It plunged down, hit something slippery and then flew out from under him. The rest of his body followed, his own momentum thrusting him forward, out of control. He thumped down onto rock slick with water. In darkness that his eyes could not penetrate, he was carried along in a sort of rocky gutter. Moments later he passed under a torrent of water falling from somewhere overhead, gaspingly cold. All of a sudden, the water beneath him was not a trickle but a powerful cascade that swept him away, bearing him into the darkness ahead.

Soaked through and chilled to the bone, he hurtled down a very steep, sloping tunnel. If he had been on a purpose-built waterslide he couldn't have gone much quicker, but no slide in the world was so treacherous. Every few seconds he came to another sharp bend and was hurled round, smacking painfully into the rock walls, only to be righted again and resume his plunging descent. He was whipped back and forth viciously, bruising all parts of his body, but he could do nothing to protect himself. He was completely out of control. Above the sound of the water and his own shouts he could hear the echoing cries of his comrades below, each of whom was having a ride as rough as he.

Roujeark slammed into something hard. In a split second his hands reached out and managed to grab a chunk of rock. The torrent tugged powerfully at him, threatening to carry him away again, but he clung on grimly. He felt movement beside him and realised that he had collided with someone else. He tried shouting to the person, who could only be one of the Royal Guards, but above the roar of the water it was useless. He thought he heard another body go shooting past in the stream, but he could not be sure. Roujeark felt the armist moving, and he feared he was about to be swept away, but it was not so. By chance, the line of their descent had taken them near the tunnel edge where they had thumped into a spine of rock. The spine marked the entrance of another opening, where the tunnel seemed to fork. His companion was not losing his grip, but rather clambering up out of the torrent. He felt boots slide past his fingers, and a few moments later a hand was reached down to him. Glad to let go of the slippery rock, Roujeark clasped the hand. Between it and his own scrabbling feet, he managed to haul himself up. The second hand reached under his armpit and pulled him up.

Next thing he knew he was sitting up in a damp aperture with the underground river gushing past beside him. He took a few moments to rid his ears of water and shake himself off. Blowing water out of his mouth, he looked across to see who his helper was. The armist had to lean close to be seen in the gloom. It was Antaya. He had not been immediately ahead of him in the headlong dash across the snake pit, so Aleinus must have been carried away by the stream while Antaya managed to cling on. Then, more by touch than by sight, he found the protruding knob of rock that had been their salvation. Carried close enough to grab it, they had managed to escape the strongest pull of the current. Without someone else, though, Roujeark felt sure he wouldn't have been able to hold on.

The side-tunnel they were in wasn't exactly dry, with damp walls and puddles underfoot, but at least it didn't have the churning cascade of the main vent. He and Antaya looked at each other.

'Well, we managed to get out,' said the guard.

'Yes, but now we're separated from the others,' Roujeark commented. Antaya looked rueful.

'Should we go back down and try and follow them?' They both leaned over, peering down. They could see nothing but the white froth of the water.

'We don't know what's down there,' said Roujeark, his voice echoing. Somehow, neither of them could summon the courage to lower themselves back into that cold torrent. Reluctantly, they agreed to go on together. Knowing Antaya was an armist of faith, Roujeark encouraged them to stop and pray before going on.

'Guide us, Prélan,' they prayed in the blind blackness. 'Lead us through, and back to the others.'

A

They had to stoop to follow the tunnel, which ran gently down and round several bends. The ground underfoot became gradually drier and the rushing, gurgling sounds of the water died away into the background. They were deep underground, in a capillary of the Mountain, one of thousands for all they knew. They didn't know where they were and certainly had no idea where they were going. After a while, the slope started to level off and then became entirely flat. They followed a faint glow that appeared ahead of them and, rounding a corner, came into a long, narrow hall. A series of wall sconces held waiting torches. It took quite some time, cold and wet as he still was, but eventually Roujeark managed to light one, and once one was lit it was easy to set the rest ablaze. They were suspicious of this sudden provision, but too thankful for the heat and warmth to be deterred. Sitting down to rest, they regarded the hall in the light of the torches.

It was a curious space, natural-looking and yet contrived at the same time. A series of rib-like protrusions stuck out from either wall, demarcating sections between them of roughly equal length that ran down the length of the hall. At each set of ribs, grooves could be seen in floor, walls and ceiling. The bays in between were rough-walled, and each held a torch on alternating sides. It was curious arrangement, like a framework which had once held a succession of long-vanished doors. It seemed they were at the threshold of some kind of portal, with perhaps a significant part of the Mountain beyond. Cautiously they moved forward. The quiet seemed so complete that they could hear the beating of one another's hearts.

Then Antaya unwittingly trod on a weak stone. Only too late did he see that it was slightly raised, and a different colour to the floor around it. An ominous series of grating, creaking noises came from all around them. For a few moments they stood frozen in terror, watching as slabs of rock a foot thick began lowering from the grooves in the ceiling. The grooves were actually gaps through which partitions were now descending, ready to slot into the matching grooves below. At first Roujeark went back, but then realised that would only lead back to the river. He recovered from his panic and followed Antaya, who had instinctively gone the other way. The first partition they passed easily enough, still high overhead, and the second, but by the time Roujeark reached the third one he had to stoop to get under it. Groaning with the strain of suspense, the next few slabs kept lowering. The end of the hall, on the other side of them, suddenly seemed very far away.

They broke into a run, dashing headlong through the hall. Antaya was faster, leaving Roujeark behind and grabbing a torch, but they both had to crouch to get under the fourth partition. Antaya threw himself into a roll to get under the fifth and last one, but when Roujeark got close it was barely two feet off the ground. He dropped to his belly and squirmed frantically through. He pulled his sopping wet cloak through after him, only for the rock slab to come down on it, pinning it fast. With a sound like a sigh of satisfaction the slabs all came to rest in their allotted places, sunk deep in their grooves and unmovable. Breathing hard, Roujeark got to his feet and tore his cloak free, leaving a strip of it trapped behind. In a fit of anger, he tore the rest of the cloak free and tossed it to the ground. It would only continue to encumber him. At least they had a torch, which Antaya had managed to keep alight. When he was able to compose himself again, he said to his companion, 'This Mountain has tricks and traps everywhere, we must be wary with every step.'

⅄

The next section seemed easier though, as if the beguiling Mountain was feigning innocence. They followed a flat sandy path that seemed featureless as it led through bare tunnels. At length they came to a room, plain and empty. Once again, there appeared to be no way out.

'Is nothing simple in here?' complained Antaya. Roujeark, though, was beginning to get used to nothing being as it seemed.

'Come, friend, let us search the floor and walls.' Scrabbling around in the sand by the light of the torch, they covered the whole floor until Antaya found something in the far corner.

'Hey, Roujeark, come and look at this.' The other armist hurried over, and together they inspected what Antaya had found. Parting the sand, he had uncovered a small board type object, roughly a square foot in size.

'It looks like a puzzle of sorts,' exclaimed Roujeark, 'but one made entirely of rocks.' He played around with the loose rocks. 'See how these rocks move around. Together they seem to form a picture of some kind, but they're all muddled, so I can't see what it is.' The board had sixteen rocks on it, all fixed to iron sliders so that they could be moved around both horizontally and vertically. They were painted with parts of an overall picture so that when they were rightly aligned, they would depict a scene or portrait of some sort. 'Here, help me move them around. Let's see what it shows.'

Together they experimented with the pieces, which proved to be rusty and unwilling to move, but slowly they explored the different alignments. Gradually they found the right configuration for the pieces, and an elusive illustration began to be revealed. After a few more minutes of fiddling, they gazed down at what they had discovered. It was an ancient motif: a mighty elven prince in glamorous armour, brandishing a twohanded sword overhead. Only a few seconds had passed when, with a sudden snapping sound, the marvellous picture disintegrated and vanished in a puff of dust and tiny stone particles. They both winced, fearing another collapsing ceiling, but nothing happened, so they looked on with amazement as the scattering dust revealed a stone slab with a protruding button of stone. They looked at each other hesitantly. With no better option at hand, Roujeark pushed the button with great apprehension. A long groan filled the room, and then a resounding clang made them both jump. Looking over, they saw a small square hole in the previously unbroken floor.

They scuttled over to see a metal trapdoor hanging down from two ancient, squealing hinges. The hole was big enough for them to fit through, but the vertical tunnel it led to was another matter. It looked perilous, and there was no knowing what lurked inside or where it led to. Yet their fears were trumped again by the knowledge that there was nowhere else to go. Gingerly they lowered themselves down, one by one, dropping again into darkness.

Curillian shot out of the tube like an arrow from a bow. The jet of water that came with him carried him over a large expanse of water. After a few soaring seconds, he plunged down into the water. When he surfaced, spluttering, he saw that he was in yet another cavern, bigger than all the rest. A low, sinister light illuminated the cavern, emanating from a string of wall-torches that looked like they had been prepared for visitors. Lurking half in shadows were forbidding cliffs, moss-covered walls that rose up sheer all around him. He splashed around, turning in the water to see what the rest of the cavern held, and saw to his surprise a large galley riding high in the water. It was an ancient bireme, a type of ship that hadn't ploughed the main for millennia. It was thirty metres long and had a single mast where the ripped and tattered remains of a sail could still be seen, clinging like bedraggled garments to the rotting wood.

He saw that he was not the first to arrive. Between him and ship were many of his companions, swimming in the direction of the vessel. Lancoir was already aboard, waving. Curillian could see no obvious exit to the cavern so, in the absence of any better options, he swam to the ship.

The bireme had two decks, one below for the rowers and one above, the latter just a pair of fighting platforms running the length of the hull. Arrayed in two columns either side of a central aisle, the rowers' benches ran the entire length of the ship, save for a closed off section in the bow and another raised platform at the back for the steering oar.

The seven armists explored the ship. Andil, who had grown up on the coast, ran his fingers over every surface and grew more suspicious with everything he touched. Everything was brand new, scrubbed and polished. There was barely a drop of bilge-water down among the ballast stones. The smell of pitch was still fresh, and the leather of the slaver's whip might have newly come from the tanner's bench.

'This ship has never sailed in anger, if it has sailed at all,' he told the others. Lancoir was completely in agreement.

'Then I'd like to know what it's doing in the middle of a subterranean lake,' he growled suspiciously.

'And how did it even get down here?' wondered Aleinus aloud. Curillian walked the length of one of the fighting platforms and rested his hands on the polished rail.

'It can only have been set here for a purpose,' he mused.

'A trap of the wizard's...' muttered Lancoir, coming to stand beside him. He continued to mutter inaudible words, his hands gripping the rail reflexively.

'What are you thinking?' Curillian asked him.

'This lake, this ship, I don't like them. I don't like any of it, the whole mountain,' Lancoir grumbled.

'I was just thinking about those rocks over there,' said Curillian. 'It's the only part of the cavern wall that's not solid rock – there might even be a way out there somewhere.' For a while they studied the rocks and nothing could be heard except dripping from all around the cavern.

'Well, we'd better go and investigate,' said Lancoir, but even as he voiced the thought Andil spoke at the same time.

'What?' said the king. 'What is it?'

'I'm not sure, sire, but I thought I heard something.' Suddenly they were all on edge, straining every sense.

'Bubbles!' shouted Lionenn, who was standing at the stempost. Curillian and Lancoir practically catapulted themselves down the ship to stand with him. Together they peered down into the lake. Suddenly it was not so placid. Over a growing area tiny bubbles were breaking on the surface, creating a frothy lacework of foam. Before long the surface was boiling and the deck beneath them quivered. An ominous whooshing noise rose up from the depths and then the lake positively exploded. A monstrous head appeared and reared up like a primordial leviathan, showering the ship in water. After its initial breach it sank down a bit, and a hefty wave smote the ship. As the spray subsided, they found themselves facing an enormous octopus-like creature. Its head was half as large as the ship itself, huge and hideous, scaly contours lining its face. The mouth was a bristling mess of teeth and foul-smelling gunk. Hideous as it was, they had all too little time to study it, for suddenly the air was alive with snakelike tentacles, more numerous than the mind could count. Lined with pulsating suckers and swung with battering-ram force, they attacked the ship in a whirlwind of ferocious flesh.

Recovering from the shock of the beast's arrival, they tugged their weapons free, only to be knocked willy-nilly by the forest of tentacles. Curillian rolled away from a tentacle that seemed to pursue him and retrieved his sword. As the tentacle latched onto an oar, he swung mightily and cut the limb in half. The creature gave a huge bellowing scream that pierced above the thrashing of the lake, but another tentacle replaced the severed one almost instantaneously. Caréysin had managed to fit an arrow to the string of his bow, but time in the water had ruined the fibre and caused the arrow to flop uselessly when he tried to loose it. Lancoir found himself surrounded by the arms, but he was freed by Curillian and Aleinus, who slashed them away furiously.

Hopelessly beset, the seven of them hacked away for all they were worth, but for every tentacle they hewed another took its place. One tentacle caught Aleinus square in the chest and flung him against the ship's side, where he slumped down amid fractured timbers. The others darted and dived to avoid a similar fate, but a bireme's deck was a treacherous place to try and evade pursuit, especially as waves created by the monster's movement kept up a violent rocking motion. Lionenn struggled to keep his balance and managed to get in one good blow before he lost his balance, bashing a tentacle with his mace. Curillian was backed against the forward cabin, slashing all the way, but he ran out of room to retreat. Whilst fighting off half a dozen tentacles in front of him, another one snaked low and wrapped around his ankle. The king was yanked off balance and hauled into the air. Full of dismay, the others watched helplessly as their leader was swung upside down like a ragdoll. But Curillian wasn't finished yet. Lurching to right himself in mid-air, he arched upwards and hacked relentlessly at the tentacle holding him, screaming like a madman. It squeezed him tighter, and he feared it might break his shin, but he kept attacking it until the great sword finally found purchase and bit deep. Another blow severed the limb and suddenly Curillian was falling. He slammed painfully onto the ship's side, the wind driven completely from his lungs. The sword fell from his grasp into the ship and he clung on for dear life. It was surely death to go into the water with that thing.

Lancoir hurled a knife at an encroaching tentacle and smiled grimly when it withdrew. Then, quite unexpectedly, something other than octopus flesh caught his eye. From out of the cavern's high ceiling a square chunk of rock came plunging. Big as a table, it struck the squid full on its head with an almighty squelching smack. Barely a moment later there came a deep groan from within the lake and the whole surface seemed to lurch. As the dazed creature slid below the wild surface, the waters took on an altogether different character. They were whipped into a whirling circle, with some great force from below sucking them down. Like the draining of some colossal basin, the lake began to recede, taking the creature with it. The ship bucked wildly, caught in the grip of the whirling current. Lancoir lost his footing. Out of the corner of his eye he saw two figures plunge from the ceiling into the lake, one red and one in grey and green. Then he saw the king in dire need. Still clinging to the rail, he was being tugged from below. The ship was tilted downward by the weight of the octopus grasping it in an attempt to not be washed away. Also alert to the danger, Findor and Aleinus seized the king's arms and held on tight. Fighting the centrifugal force of the ship's motion, Lancoir staggered across to them. He saw the Sword of Maristonia still lying discarded and scooped it up. Never before had he brandished the fabulous blade, but no time for wonder now. Leaning over the side, he struck at the tentacles holding the king. Sharper than a razor, the sword cut through the grotesque flesh. One, two, and gone! The pressure vanished and they all ended up in a heap inside the ship.

Fighting waves of nausea, they clambered back up to the rail. Looking over, they saw the lake circling down in a spiral towards some hidden aperture. The waters roared and crashed as they were whipped against wood and stone, sending up huge spouts of foam and spray. Suddenly they were shaken from their vantage by a tremendous force. They crashed into the hull as the ship grounded against rocks beneath the surface. Planks were rent and torn as fingers of rock smashed through the keel as if it were a rotten log. For a moment the ship swayed crazily as the waves continued to batter against it, and then it came to rest.

Roujeark felt powerful coils encircle him, crushing his legs in a vicelike grip. One moment he had been falling through the air, having lost his grip in the shaft, the next he had plummeted into a maelstrom of water. He was underwater and could see nothing but boiling chaos, but the tug on his lower half was remorseless. He flailed his arms in search for something to help, and his fingers brushed rock. Somehow his hands managed to get a hold and, for a split second, he was convinced he was about to be torn in half. A heartbeat later he heard a dull whump and the pressure on his legs eased. Kicking desperately, he shook free of his assailant. As soon as his legs were released, he swung them up and away from trouble. The next thing he knew, was water breaking over him and lowering around his shoulders. At last he breathed, gasping deeply and hoarsely.

Beneath him he saw the last remnants of the lake slosh and disappear through a series of long channels set in the cavern's floor. Dead or dying, the hulking mass of a great monster lay half-in, half-out of the giant sluice, a disgusting mass of bunched and slimy flesh. Higher up, stuck fast on the rocks, lay the ship it had tried and failed to destroy. Then, as if in answer to some hidden signal, a gust of wind blew and the torches went out, their fitful luminance extinguished in an instant.

Eerie darkness fell, but in the last moment of the light he had seen Antaya above him on the rocks. He had survived the ordeal too. Wincing with pain, Roujeark hauled himself up level with him. His whole body was ablaze with pain. Then oblivion took them both.

⁂

It was a shout that roused them.

'Roujeark! Antaya! Are you there?' It was Andil's voice. Slowly they roused themselves, still unable to see a thing. Following the sound of each other's voices, they somehow found their way to each other, slipping and stumbling across the slime-covered rocks. They touched in the darkness, counting to make sure they were all present. Close to Roujeark's ear, the king's voice was full of relief.

'How did you manage it, Roujeark?'

'Manage what?'

'The rock that struck the squid. Did you drop it?' Roujeark thought back.

'There was a room with no exits, but we solved a puzzle that opened a trapdoor. We climbed down into a dark shaft and lost our grip almost immediately, and the next thing we knew we were falling. A small circle of light rushed up to us and then we plummeted down into this cavern.'

'A great rock came down first.' It was Lancoir's voice this time. 'When we first arrived, there were no shafts in the ceiling, so you must have opened one. Somehow, you dislodged that rock. It smashed the monster square on its head. But for that, it would have killed us all.'

'You saved us, Roujeark.' The king's voice again. 'You too, Antaya, albeit inadvertently.'

'You never know what will happen in this place,' said Antaya wonderingly. 'Whatever you touch does something. Everything in here wants to kill you. Still, I'm not keen to repeat that drop, my stomach's still lodged somewhere in my gullet.'

'What do we do now?' Caréysin's voice came out of the darkness.

'Before the squid came, I thought I saw a gap in the cavern wall somewhere,' Curillian said. 'But now the lights have gone out, right on the Keeper's cue. If we could see, we might be able to find that gap and see if it really is a way out.'

Roujeark pulled himself together. 'I may be able to start a light – do you have any wood?'

Findor chuckled for answer. 'There's plenty in the ship, damn thing was nearly smashed to pieces.'

'Well, then go get some,' snapped Lancoir. Findor slunk off unhappily into the pitch black. He had not been gone long when the sound of an explosion filled the cavern. At first they cowered, thinking that the roof was collapsing on them, but when no stones fell on them they realised it was not so. The deep boom had been far off, so too the sounds of crumbling ruins that followed it. It struck fear in their hearts, but nothing like the next sound. Blood-chilling screams, neither near nor far away, a chorus of many voices raised in terror then suddenly cut off.

When Findor finally rejoined the others, he was as shaken as they were. Yet as he slid back down to them, he dropped an armful of wooden splints at their feet. Roujeark took one up and held it in his hands. Forcing himself to concentrate, he tried to reconnect with what he had done before. Long moments passed and nothing happened. Aleinus started to speak, but the king shushed him immediately. Only their breathing could be heard in the darkness as they waited for their friend to conjure something. Slowly, almost imperceptibly at first, a faint redness appeared, like a trick of the mind. Hesitant at first, then waxing stronger, the glow spread and lit up Roujeark's face in the darkness. None of them who beheld that sight ever forgot it: the wizard-to-be, surrounded by blackness, staring enraptured at the flame springing from his hand.

A second later the moment had passed, for Roujeark had transferred the flame to a wooden spar where it caught and grew stronger. Slowly the terror of the noises in the dark receded. They touched other bits of wood to the torch and created a series of brands. Roujeark looked normal again, and a glowing radius of light brought a part of the cavern's back into view: slick rocks and steep walls and a glimpse of gore below.

'Roujeark, my friend,' announced Curillian, 'you're a marvel.' He helped him to his feet and only then, in the flickering torchlight, did Roujeark see the angry red sucker marks that covered both his and the king's legs. Bracing themselves for another effort, they struck off into the gloom, seeking the way out. With much slipping on the treacherous rocks and cursing in the shadowy light, they made their way above the water line and up to the cavern walls. A brief exploration discovered that the rocks led on up the cliff, ascending like a broken staircase. Soon the ship and the sluice were lost to the blackness behind, but in front of them their torches took them up over a crest and into an alcove beyond. The space they found themselves in rapidly narrowed to a rough tunnel, which led away from the cavern. They paused at the entrance, uncertain. But Roujeark stepped past them, going in boldly.

'Prélan is with us,' he told them. One by one, they followed him in, wondering what they would find next.

⋏

The tunnel was harmless at first, containing nothing more intimidating than a steep slope. The damp floor gradually dried out and then became quite sandy. After a time, they came out into a large room, again conveniently lit with torches.

'Kulothiel leads us to one death trap after another,' muttered Curillian. This latest space was no vast cavern like before, but a smaller, foursquare room carved out of the mountain. Just like the neatly-hewn walls, the room's contents also bore the marks of careful design. The floor was made up of dozens of large, buff-coloured tiles, each with an elven rune painted on. The only opening was in the far wall, but it was covered by a lowered portcullis.

'So, what's the game this time?' asked Caréysin. 'Spell a word?'

'How am I supposed to spell anything?' objected Aleinus. 'I can't even read elvish.'

'I can,' said Curillian, 'but the letters are in no particular order – they don't spell anything.' They stood for a moment, stumped.

'What's that on the far wall?' Andil pointed. 'It looks like faded writing.' They all looked. Sure enough, there were characters on the wall, two words, one each side of the portcullis, but faint and worn by the passage of time.

'It's elvish also,' said Curillian, 'but I can't quite see.'

He stepped closer, squinting. He still couldn't see properly and stepped forward again. This time his foot sank as the paving slab he had stepped on depressed. His whole body tensed, wondering what he had done. Sweat beaded on all their brows and eyes flitted fearfully around. Behind them a second portcullis appeared from nowhere and rattled down over the tunnel mouth from which they had come. They were trapped again. Then the floor beneath them started to quiver and there came a groan of tortured rock from above them. For a few seconds the room became still again, and they all stood riveted to the spot, looking fixedly either at the ceiling or the floor. Then the tremors and the creaking noises returned. This time, to their horror, they saw dozens of tiny iron points piercing the ceiling above. Grating and rending, they slowly pushed through, lowering down like huge fangs. Suddenly the ceiling collapsed under the pressure and rained down in a cascade of dust and rock. But it had only been a false ceiling, a framework hiding the true ceiling, which now came into view. This one was solid, and studded with long, vicious spikes. And it was lowering.

In the same moment that the false ceiling fell apart, Curillian had a blinding flash of inspiration.

'ORON AMULAR!' He shouted back to the others behind him. 'The name of the Mountain! The TILES!'

They didn't understand what he meant, but they soon did when he sprinted to one of the tiles and began jumping up and down on it. This tile bore the elvish 'O' rune, and under the king's onslaught it smashed into smithereens. Beneath it was empty space and the king lost one foot into a hole. The others looked at him in shock, but he waved urgently and shouted at them.

'The other letters – QUICK!' In blind panic, they each ran to a different tile and beat at them, stamping with their boots. Lancoir broke through his first and was almost impaled on the spike waiting underneath.

'NO!' yelled Curillian. 'In order, spell the name!' When they didn't know which ones to go for, he pointed them out frantically. 'R...O...N...' Hurriedly they smashed each tile in turn, opening up a patchwork of cavities below the floor. Lionenn proved more proficient than the rest of them, his mace and brute strength making short work of the tiles. All the while, the ceiling lurched lower. Curillian kept shouting his directions. 'A…M…U…' The tiles were smashed in order, but it seemed to take forever – the descending spikes were barely above their heads now, and in their panic they destroyed some of the wrong tiles, revealing more spikes. With hazards above and below, and gaps all over the floor, they were herded into a smaller and smaller space.

'L…A…' Now the spikes had fallen below standing height, and they were all bent double, preparing to be pinned to the floor and crushed. With their necks bent sideways, they desperately hunted around for the last few letters. Findor and Aleinus gave up and clung to two of the spikes, bracing themselves for the end, but the others kept their presence of mind. The 'L' and the 'A' both disappeared, but by now they were all wedging themselves into the spaces between spikes, doing anything they could to prolong the end. Some were clinging to the descending spikes like monkeys, being carried remorselessly down. There was no room for movement now; the space was so constricted. It fell to Roujeark to attack the last letter, the second 'R'. He struck out with the only thing he had to hand – the torch – and he soon extinguished it in the attempt. Being plunged into darkness once more brought forth screams of terror, the seasoned guards reduced to whimpering wrecks. They were all pressed against the floor now and Roujeark had barely any room to strike. The pressure built on their bodies as the last barrier of air was squeezed away. Pinned flat, it felt like an enormous foot was being forced down on their faces. Roujeark kept hammering with puny little blows, but still to no effect. The cries of terror now turned to groans of pain from compressed lungs. Finally, Roujeark felt the tile break. It gave way under his feebly beating hand. Another second passed, and another, and the pressure above them kept building. Then the grating sound of the mechanism stopped. It was as if a rusty key had stopped turning in a giant lock. Roujeark gritted his teeth and shut his eyes, waiting for the end, but the ceiling remained where it was.

They were still alive, but with no escape. They were held fast in an immovable vice. It was totally dark. They could barely move, much less see the way out. They all heard the portcullis being raised, but they couldn't get to it. Roujeark explored the hole made by the final tile and he found no spike. With just enough room to wriggle sideways, he dropped his legs into the hole. Pivoting awkwardly, he manoeuvred his body down into the cavity. It proved deeper than the others, which gave breathing space at least. He sat wheezing and gasping on the floor, gratefully gulping the dry dusty air. When he had recovered himself, he found that there was more space than he'd thought. He couldn't see anything in the pitch darkness, but he was able to explore, and he found what seemed to be a tiny tunnel leading off. Returning to the hole, he poked his head up and called to the others, though his voice came out in a croak. Antaya and Curillian were nearest him, and they managed to extricate themselves, worming past spikes above and below. For the others it was not so easy, and they had a very unpleasant time squeezing themselves through tiny gaps. Lancoir, the furthest away, had to be dragged from his spot, where he had been stuck fast.

Eventually, sore, bruised and traumatised, they all found themselves in the tunnel. With oppressive blackness all around, they crawled blindly on hands and knees. Roujeark had neither torch nor the state of mind to relight it. But the tunnel wasn't long, and it opened up into a long trench that seemed to occupy the whole length of the far wall. Dragging themselves upright onto shaking legs, they found the doorway by feel. Ducking the downward-pointing barbs of the raised portcullis, they passed through and left the torture chamber behind.

In the tunnel that followed, they did not go far. Still in darkness, they slumped down with their backs to the wall and tried to pull themselves together. Their hearts were only just starting to slow down from a wild galloping beat.

'I'll never be able to use an apple press again,' said Aleinus. His voice was serious, genuinely remorseful, but it sounded so absurd in the situation that the others laughed. The incongruous sound of their mirth helped to ease the tension and bring them back to normal. They regained their feet and carried on following the tunnel.

⋏

The tunnel grew steadily warmer until it became positively stifling. They sweated in the darkness until a faint red glow broke through. The glow grew brighter and more distinct until the rock walls were clearly outlined in red, like the throat of a dragon. They began to hear strange noises, hissing, bubbling and frothing. Turning a corner, the light became much brighter and a wall of heat hit them like a blow. It was like opening an oven door. Reluctantly pressing on, they came to the tunnel's mouth, which opened out onto another cavern. The heat was fantastic, and they all soon saw why. The path they were on dropped suddenly into a cauldron of fire. They all crowded together, looking down on a gully of lava which lay between two twisted slopes like a molten spearpoint. The path snaked down one slope, clinging precariously to its side.

'First a lake monster and now this!' said Findor wearily.

'There's a whole world in here,' exclaimed Antaya, with awe in his voice.

'Verily,' said Curillian, 'we have come to the very bowels of the mountain. We are so far beneath the earth that we have reached the fires of the abyss. Come, we must follow the path to its end; let us see where it leads.'

With every step they took the temperature increased, and the fierceness of the air was exacerbated by tongues of molten liquid that every now and then would bubble up and spatter through the air. Each one of the armists was pouring with sweat, and as the beads dripped off them onto the floor they sizzled and evaporated in seconds. Noxious fumes made them lightheaded and unsteady on their feet, which made the going hazardous when they reached the level of the lava. Only the slight raise of the path separated them from molten lake. They picked their way with care through a furnace-like defile, round a spur and then out into a wider space. Passing under a cracked and blackened arch, they found themselves in a square chamber of colossal proportions. A giant staircase of hewn rock twisted down from each of the ceiling's four corners, and in the middle where they met was an island-like platform in the middle of a molten lake. Each staircase appeared to lead to an exit, but they were so broken and treacherous that ascending them would be no easy task.

Warily they edged along the perilously narrow path towards the central platform, hoping to avoid the hissing jets of lava and steam that spat occasionally. Caréysin, who had scouted ahead, reached the platform first and suddenly shouted back in alarm. The rest of them hurried to meet him. The platform was not as stable as they would have liked; it dipped and wobbled alarmingly. But it was not the platform that had caused Caréysin to cry out. Looking down, they discovered what had startled him. Dead bodies lay on the platform, half a dozen of them. They wore the motley leather jerkins and tunics of Aranese free-riders.

'These were not men of Southilar's company,' Curillian said, looking down. 'Six men of Aranar. They got here before us, but they will go no further.'

'They must have been overcome by the heat, or caught in a jet of lava,' said Roujeark.

'No,' said Lancoir, 'they weren't killed by heat or lava. They were slain. Look.' Even as he was speaking, Roujeark looked closer and saw the death-wounds. Blades had cut deep into their necks and bodies, and lacerated limbs lay ragged and askew. The six of them had fallen in a small circle that had been fighting on every side, overcome by a hidden enemy. Curillian rolled one over. Horror was stamped on the dead face.

'They died in terror and pain,' the king said. 'Who knows what they came through, only to die here.'

'Which of the other contestants killed them?' Findor wondered aloud.

'It could have been any of them,' said Roujeark.

'Or none,' the king countered. 'There are enemies in this mountain that did not enter with us.'

'Well, whoever it was,' said Findor, kicking a fallen blade into the lava lake, 'they aren't here now.'

⚔

No sooner had he spoken than they heard the sound of voices. They all jumped, standing up from their examination of the scene and brandishing weapons. Other than the chilling screams, it was the first people they had heard since leaving the first chamber. Following the noise, they saw what looked to be a path identical to their own leading into the chamber from a different direction. The voices, which before had been distorted by fear and crooked passageways, gradually became more distinct.

Out of the passageway stepped an armoured figure, complete with helm and shield. He did not see the armists but stood gaping at the cavern into which he had entered. He had a Pegasus on his shield and on his hauberk. This was a man of Aranar, but not one of the free-riders like those who lay dead at their feet; this man was in Southilar's entourage. After a moment, he turned back and called to others in the passageway behind him.

'Fiery hell, no wonder it's been getting hotter. There's a bloody lake of fire out here.' Others stepped out of the passageway to join him, all uttering violent exclamations of surprise and consternation. Like the first man, all were armoured. The men of Aranar had come fully dressed for war. Among them was the unmistakably tall figure of Southilar, and Theonar, who was taller still.

'They must be absolutely cooking in that armour,' muttered Aleinus. The armists still wore the light mail and travelling clothes in which they had journeyed. Curillian stepped forward and called across the fire.

'Well met again, friends. Welcome to the furnace of Kulothiel.' They looked up in surprise, not expecting anyone else to be in the cavern already. Weapons were raised ready for defence, but Southilar also stepped forward. Raising his voice above the menace of the lava, he called back.

'Still alive, Curillian? You ought to have died several times already, if you've faced anything like what we have. But then you always were lucky.'

The men of Aranar looked uncertain how to reach the armists, but then they spotted the pathway that led out to the central platform.

Warily they came across and joined the armists. The first man had been Hardos, one of Southilar's Clan Knights, and he nodded curtly at Curillian and his party. Southilar, sweating like a blacksmith, was more voluble.

'God's teats, Curillian! But what the bloody hell have we let ourselves in for?' He threw down shield and sword and peeled off gloves that were practically steaming. Many of his followers followed suit, only too glad to be free of their burdens. The armists squatted down to rest too, and Caréysin took the opportunity to fit his bow with a new string, which had been in a pouch at his belt.

Curillian had to blow sweat out of his eyes to see the Jeantar properly. 'I tell you,' the big man complained, 'so far we've nearly been crushed, pulverised, ripped to bits, drowned and eaten. And that was just in the first half an hour.'

'You look like you have fared little better,' observed Theonar, joining them, 'but I'm glad to find you yet living, lord king.' Curillian acknowledged his words gratefully.

'And I you, Sir Theonar. And you other knights and lords of Aranar.' In all Southilar had 14 men with him, a couple short of the total he'd had in camp outside the Mountain. Even Caiasan, the irreverent scribe, had made it, looking even more dishevelled than before.

'Strewth,' he exclaimed, 'what a place! Best watch your step here, lads.' He himself tottered and took a swig from a flask at his side.

'This is an evil place,' insisted Sir Lindal, the Unicorn Clan Knight, but before he could expand further, Southilar spoke again.

'I've lost two men getting here,' he told Curillian. 'A man-at-arms ground into mincemeat under a falling rock, and Sir Acil of the Hawk emerged out of the waterslide dead as an anvil. He sank in the lake before we could get to him.'

Off to one side, Caiasan whispered loudly to Roujeark, whom he had sought out. Even above the nostril-singing smell of brimstone, the armist could smell the liquor on his breath.

'He arsed to the left, he arsed to the right, but he don't arse no more.' If anyone else heard, they ignored him.

'How many have you lost?' Southilar asked.

'None,' said Curillian, 'though we too have been beset by many perils.' Southilar looked aggrieved that the armists had sustained no losses, but he said nothing, merely grunted. Sir Romanthony of the Eagle spoke instead.

'What fools we are to have ventured into this wizard's funhouse. Tournament? I'd sooner be back at the Hamid Tournament, or Stable or Rikemord. Men die there, but at least they have a fighting chance. We'll all die in here without ever seeing the prize he spoke of.'

'If it ever existed,' chipped in another. Curillian was unmoved.

'Still, prize or no prize, we must find a way out, and we'll do better together than apart.'

'There's sense,' muttered Southilar grudgingly.

'Have you seen anyone else?' Curillian pressed him. The big horse-lord shook his head.

'Seen? No. Heard? All too much.'

'Screams?' Roujeark asked. 'Explosions?' The Jeantar looked strangely at him, but nodded.

'What's that noise?' Theonar said, breaking into their conversation. He had remained aloof so far, alert and watchful.

⋀

As soon as he spoke, men and armists alike were on the alert. At first they heard nothing, but then came strange sounds. Harsh, gravelly sounds, like a burrowing through rock. Southilar and Curillian stood back to back, tightening their grips on their blades. They saw nothing, but the odd rumblings continued.

'Whatever this new devilry is, I'm ready for it,' declared Southilar through gritted teeth. Curillian said nothing, but despite the dampness of his skin the hairs on his nape were standing up. Apprehension rippled down through his spine. Then Theonar spoke again in cool warning.

'Look, the walls!' All eyes snapped like clockwork to the wall he was pointing to and took in the horrified sight of grotesque figures emerging out of the rock. Clawed fingers outstretched, cadaverous forms seemed to be ripping their way out of the solid rock. They were skeletons apart from a few layers of thin skin stretching pale over their bones. They carried hammer-headed blades and crooked cutlasses. Seemingly oblivious to the lava, they waded towards the platform with alarming speed.

Even Curillian, a seasoned campaigner, had never seen anything like this. His stomach churned and his limbs quivered. Lancoir did nothing except raise his eyebrows and adopt a defensive stance, but Roujeark could only gape, eyes wide in frightened amazement. Caréysin got off two arrows, each of which plucked its target down into the lava. Then the other skeleton warriors leapt up out of the lava, striving to reach the platform, and they were upon the armists and men before most of them had had a chance to react. Horror slowed their reactions and many were late in bringing up their weapons. The undead corpses leapt upon them and they grappled in a life and death struggle. Those defenders used their weapons to brutal effect, cutting through gruesome skin, cracking fire-blackened bones and severing heads. Curillian's sweeping cut knocked one straight back into the fire where its bones splashed with a vicious hiss. Lancoir, Southilar and Theonar likewise threw back their assailants, but then they all watched with horror as the slain corpses re-emerged. Bones reconnected and scarce skin stretched taut again. Weapons came to hand, and they leapt once more to the attack. Again they hewed them down, but with the same result.

Elsewhere on the heaving platform the struggle raged, blades scything and bodies wrestling. Yells of fear pierced above the clash of steel and the roar of lava jets, only to bounce back off the walls and reverberate around the battlefield. So unsteady did the platform become that one man-at-arms lost his balance and tottered into the lava. Unlike the skeletons, he did not survive, but vaporised moments after his horrific shriek was extinguished. The noise of his passing shocked man and armist all around, and the pause cost two more Aranese dearly. Disregarding weapons, a pair of undead clambered up on their backs and tugged them backwards. Overborne, they too fell into the fire and perished with screams of blinding agony.

Their comrades fought on, but every split limb reformed and every severed head snapped back into place. Not only were their hard-swung blows having no effect, they struggled to keep their feet as the platform bucked and swayed. Then matters took a turn for the worse, as more skeletons emerged from the opposite wall, and still more followed from the other two walls. They closed upon the platform from every direction and looked set to overwhelm the gallant band trapped there. Embattled on every side, Curillian clove another skeleton in two and roared his war cry above the din. His arms were so quick, his thrusts so rapid, that he outmatched even the ability of the attackers to recover from wounds. Side by side with Lancoir, they fought recklessly, keeping a corner of the platform clear.

Nearby, Southilar was surrounded by the skeletons, standing head and shoulders taller than them, whirling in his greatsword in one hand and using his other hand to punch at his assailants. But then they jumped up on his shoulders and grabbed at his legs and he started to lose his balance, swaying dangerously near the edge. He was about to fall when Curillian threw himself at him, kicking one of the skeletons away from his legs and using his own weight to haul him backwards. He and Southilar struggled free of one another and got back to their feet. Curillian kicked another corpse flying and hacked his sword into another, while Southilar caught two by their throats. Lifting them bodily, he threw them into another pair, sending all four toppling from the platform.

Roujeark felt less than useless in the fight and it was all he could do to bob and weave clear of the whirling blades and punching fists. He knew his fire would have no effect on these attackers – even if he'd had the presence of mind to summon it – since the lava had not harmed them. Little skilled with blades, he did not try to attack the skeletons but devoted all his attention to staying alive. Then, in the midst of the melee, he noticed something around the neck of one of the skeletons. A weirdly green medallion, glowing with some fell power. Might it control them? Acting on his half-formed guess, he tried to get close to the bearer. He ducked a wildly swinging blade and ricocheted off Lionenn, who was bludgeoning his attackers. He stumbled over a pile of bones on the floor and tried reaching for the medallion. He nearly reached it when a hilt struck the back of his head, leaving him stunned on the floor.

Through waves of throbbing pain he glanced up, fixating on the bearer of the amulet. Armists, men and undead spun round him in a madcap dance, but he ignored them all. Dagger in hand, he finally closed with his enemy. For a split second he locked eyes with its baleful, unthinking gaze, and then his eyes darted away to warn of the rusty blade swinging at him. Somehow, he managed to parry with his dagger, and in the moment before his foe recovered, he lunged forward and snatched at the medallion. He ripped it free from around the undead neck, even as his legs were knocked out from under him. Staring at the glowing green orb, he felt himself being hypnotised. But he wrenched his eyes away, upended his dagger, and brought it down hilt-first with all his might. He wasn't even aware of the owner's sword swinging down, aimed for his unprotected neck. In the second before it struck, his pommel smashed into the medallion, shattering its fragile glass and spilling green ooze everywhere. In the same moment the sword above his neck disintegrated into ashes. So too did its owner. All across the platform, the skeletons crumbled. Where a heartbeat before had been indestructible enemies, now there were only piles of dust.

Breathing hard and still dizzy, Roujeark rose to his knees and looked dazedly around. The fight was over. The rocking platform was slowly subsiding to stillness. He saw each of his companions in turn, singed, bloodied and harrowed. Most of them seemed not to realise what had happened, but were simply glad to collapse to the ground, exhausted but alive. Only Theonar looked at him strangely. The tall man came over and stooped to inspect both the strange viscous fluid on the ground and the silver chain still gripped in the armist's hand.

'So, they were controlled by a spell locked in an amulet.' A strange look came across his face as he said the words, deep and far-off. 'How strange that Kulothiel should use that trick.'

'What do you mean?' said Roujeark in a frightened voice. The look vanished from Theonar's face as he turned his eyes on Roujeark.

'You found and destroyed the enemy's source of power. You saved us all from certain death. My thanks to you, friend of the king.'

Curillian came over to hear the words. Though he was as shaken as the rest, he found it in him to speak lightly.

'Roujeark to the rescue again?' He clapped him on the shoulder, making him wince. 'You'd better leave us to save ourselves every now and then, or what will we do when you're not around?' Curillian in his turn felt a heavy arm on his shoulder as Southilar drew alongside.

'And you have my thanks, Curillian, I would have been toast back there but for you. I'm indebted to you once again.' Curillian stepped clear of the big man, patting his armour.

'Don't talk nonsense, Southilar. I've done it before and I'll do it again, there is no need for repayment. I have no doubt that you will do as much for me someday.'

'Curillian, my lord,' Lancoir cut in. 'Let us leave. They may attack again.'

Caiasan staggered over. Somehow he had survived the fracas, bruised and bloodied though he was.

'How the blazes do we leave?' he demanded. Lancoir said nothing but stared grimly at him. 'Yes, I know you're the strong silent type, but stop glaring at me and answer the flipping question. You see those staircases, do you not see a problem with them?' Caiasan pointed up as he upbraided the captain of the guard.

The company all looked up to try and follow his logic. Three of the four staircases joined one of the corners of the platform they stood on, but they all had gaping holes in them higher up. The fourth one was more intact, but it didn't even reach the platform. Most of Caiasan's companions among the men of Aranar seemed genuinely surprised to find that he had a point. 'There's whacking great holes in all of them, meaning we can't climb them, all except that one.' They looked at the one he indicated. The scribe had spoken truly; it alone was more or less intact, free of the gaping holes which rendered the others completely unusable. But it was far from safe itself, twisted and crumbling, riddled with holes and, worst of all, broken away where it should have met the platform.

'But we can't reach that one either,' said Andil. 'It doesn't reach the platform – it must be twenty, thirty feet above us where it ends.'

Caiasan clapped his hands, exclaiming. 'Exactly! Bonus point to that blighter. We can't reach it, a...' Theonar grasped the overwrought scribe's shoulder and squeezed, silencing him.

'Caiasan, be quiet. Listen for a moment. You're going to get us out of here.'

'I am?'

'Yes. You're going up there.' He pointed at the broken end of the staircase above them. 'To let a rope down for us.'

'But h...' Theonar squeezed again to turn Caiasan's next protest into another gasp.

'We're going to help you.' He turned to the others. 'Right, I need the five biggest men.' Bemused, Southilar came forward, along with Sir Romanthony. The others looked at each other, measuring themselves. 'Come on,' urged Theonar. Eventually two men-at-arms and Rane, one of the Pegasus knights, joined the other two. 'Kneel down next to each other,' Theonar instructed them. They looked at him as if he were crazy. 'Well, go on,' he said firmly.

'Do as he says,' ordered Southilar, as he got down on his knees. The others followed.

'No, not like that,' said Theonar. 'Prostrate, right down, with your noses to the floor.' The men of Aranar complied with bad grace, assuming the position with much muttering. As they were getting into position, Theonar looked round at the rest. 'I need others to stand at the other corners of the platform and balance it out. Roujeark, find me a rope and be ready with Caiasan. Now, another four.' Four more knights and men-at-arms came forward, and Theonar arranged them on top of the original five, each one straddling two of the broad backs below.

'A living pyramid,' observed Curillian. He glanced up at the gap, gauging the distance. 'Hope you've got a long reach, Sir Theonar.' Then he volunteered himself, Lancoir and Lionenn as the row of three. The men beneath groaned and grumbled as the extra weight was applied. In the meantime, Roujeark was fashioning his rope. They had no actual rope, so he, Caiasan and Sir Lindal were lashing together belts and shoulder straps. Antaya and Findor climbed up as the penultimate row, and as they did so, the platform swayed alarmingly underneath them.

'Hurry up!' growled Southilar from the bottom row. Quite apart from the lava which was uncomfortably close, he found that the platform was hot to the touch. The growing pyramid wobbled as the men on the bottom row fidgeted to try and protect their fingers and relieve their knees. When the two armists were in place, Theonar beckoned to Caiasan.

'Got a good grip on that rope? Good. Now be ready to follow me up. The rest of you, do what you can to balance the platform.' Caiasan gulped visibly as he waited, while the others spread out to keep as even a weight as possible on the platform. Already the weight of the pyramid, placed directly below the targeted staircase, was dipping the platform dangerously close to the lava line.

Sure-footed as a mountain goat, Theonar sprang up the pyramid to the top. Only now did they see quite how tall he was – almost seven feet in height – and he went a long way to bridging the remainder of the gap. He called down to Caiasan, letting him know he was ready. Roujeark feared that it wouldn't be enough. He didn't think the scribe could reach the lowest step, even perched on Theonar's shoulders. Caiasan clambered up with considerably less elegance than Theonar, kicking several comrades as he struggled upwards and nearly pulled the whole shaky edifice down. At last he reached Theonar, who crouched down ready. With breathtaking poise and balance, he lifted the shrieking scribe upward. The whole pyramid quivered with the motion and the noises of discomfort from lower down rose to a whole new pitch. Caiasan strained upwards, but he was still out of reach.

'I can't reach,' he yelped.

'Stand on my shoulders,' said Theonar.

'What? No chance.'

'Do it, or we'll all burn!'

'Can't hold much longer!' came a grunted shout from below.

Somehow Caiasan managed to place his feet on Theonar's shoulders instead of his thighs, where the knight gripped them firmly. Crying for dear life, he straightened up uncertainly and reached again. Still the step was an arm's length too high. The watchers below held their breath.

'Should we add another layer?' asked Sir Deàreg.

'No, the pyramid would be too heavy, and tip us all into the fire,' said Roujeark.

'But he can't reach!' said a man-at-arms, panic rising in his voice.

'Get it done!' growled Hardos from the second row. 'We're about to collapse.'

Roujeark saw every braced arm shaking with the effort and knew he had to act. If they didn't accomplish this, they were trapped forever in this furnace. Shutting out the noise around him, he concentrated all his mind on the swaying figure of Caiasan. Nothing but fire had ever come to him before, but now he envisioned a wholly different power. Nothing happened, but he kept his focus. The pyramid was at breaking point when Theonar crouched down again. Keeping tight hold of the scribe's ankles, he shot upward, this time heaving his burden into the air. With nothing left to hold onto, Caiasan found himself flying through the air, screaming one long continuous exhalation of terror. He had reached the end of his trajectory, about to fall back, with his outstretched fingers barely inches from the step, when something took hold of him. An invisible force lifted him the last few inches, even as Theonar got ready to try and catch him. With feverish intensity, his fingertips gripped the elusive step, knowing his dangling life was on the line.

At the same moment he took hold, the pyramid collapsed. Men's arms finally gave out, and they fell in a heap. It was many confused seconds before they managed to extricate themselves, several of them coming close to falling in the lava. But when they forgot their own privations and looked up, Caiasan was still dangling.

'He made it!' exclaimed one,

'But he can't get up!' said another.

'Come on, Caiasan,' they all yelled. 'You can do it.'

'HEAVE!' bellowed Southilar, as if he might lift the dangling man by the power of his voice alone. No one noticed Roujeark, standing like a zombie, his outstretched arms rigid as he poured his attention into what he was doing. When Caiasan's leg came up and wrapped around the step, they thought it was by his own efforts. Now with enough purchase, and with raw ability lent from his survival instinct, Caiasan managed to wriggle onto the step. He collapsed on his back, panting fit to burst. At the same moment Roujeark slumped down, even as the others cheered about him. Only Theonar noticed him. The tall knight came over to check on him, full of concern.

'You're one of them, aren't you?' he said. 'One of the wizards?' Roujeark nodded silently, quite exhausted.

'I'm not sure I want to be, if this is what it takes.' Theonar pulled him up and gazed at him with his intense blue-eyed stare. 'Whatever your heart says now, Prélan has destined you to be a saviour of others. Because you are here, this isn't the end for us. But for you, this is only the beginning.' Another cheer interrupted them, and they turned around to see that Caiasan had recovered enough to let down the belt-rope.

'Here we go,' Curillian said, coming to join them. 'On to the next challenge.'

One by one the party pulled themselves up on the rope. As each man or armist reached the lowest step, the one before moved upwards, and so the party inched up the twisting staircase. It was a nerve-wracking experience, being so high up on so perilous a path with neither rail nor bannister to keep them from falling into the fire. It might once have been even and regular, but the staircase now was rough and unsteady, full of holes and crumbling in places. They picked their way carefully, scrambling more than walking. In places they had to leap across gaping holes with their hearts in their mouths. But each time they got past such an obstacle, and looked over at the other staircases, which had much larger gaps, they were silently thankful. If anything, it got hotter as they ascended, but they kept their eyes on the dark hole where the staircase disappeared into the ceiling.

Lancoir let the others go first. He brought up the rear with the belt-rope coiled round his shoulders. He kept one eye on the treacherous path and one on his king, who was immediately in front. Above them the other members of the party vanished one by one into the ceiling, leaving the furnace behind. Just as Lancoir came to the hole and was about to do likewise, he stopped, obeying a sudden instinct. He turned round and looked back down into the fiery chamber, cuffing the sweat from his eyes. For a moment all he could hear was the seething of the lava, but then he heard distant voices echoing from one of the approach tunnels. He paused long enough to see the first figure emerge out into the open. By the fur garments he knew him to be a man of Ciricen, one of Earl Culdon's following.

'Prélan save you,' he muttered. Then he was gone.

⟁

He found the others bottled up in a narrow tunnel that wound upwards in tight spirals. After a while of following this, he heard a frustrated cry and soon after came to a halt, as the men in front had stopped. Gradually the word filtered back that they were stuck on the wrong side of a locked door. At least it was slightly cooler in here. The armists waited patiently while the men of Aranar argued uproariously, until Southilar's voice subdued the others. They heard him pushing through to the front, then a few moments of strained silence. Next came a slow, rhythmic banging. Southilar was trying to kick the door down. Even his great weight and strength couldn't budge it, and he heard him bang it with his fists in frustration.

'Give me room!' Lionenn's voice growled in the dark. Repeated hammer blows crashed in the darkness as mace and door met. Evidently the mace prevailed, for shortly afterwards there were cheers of success and they were able to move again. But the cheers soon faded, and the armists followed the men out into an open space in awed silence.

They were in a tall smooth-sided atrium. In front of them was the longest staircase any of them had ever seen, stretching upwards out of sight. As different from the one they had just climbed as could be imagined, its smooth masonry was flawlessly straight and level. All the way up it was flanked by frescoes of ancient scenes and lines of sentinel statues. From somewhere up above there issued a wan bluish light, the faintest shards of which just touched the place where they stood. The door by which they had broken in was one of three, but the other two, towering up to left and right, were quite different. Tall, tapering and richly ornate, they gave onto twin passageways altogether more wholesome than the ways had followed up to this point.

'It seems we came by the hard way,' Southilar observed gruffly.

'Verily,' said Curillian, 'but that was surely intended. Unless I'm mistaken, we are come now to the habitable parts of the Mountain.'

'Yes,' agreed Theonar. 'I think our experience from now on will be quite different to what we've just had.'

'So we've crawled through the sewers and fought through the bowels of the place?' Hardos complained, his voice sharp with resentment.

'Maybe,' Curillian allowed, 'but from what I've heard, I wouldn't necessarily call them sewers. Legend has it that Oron Amular had vast caverns for the training of its acolytes, places designed to be difficult and uncomfortable. If that is so, then what we've come through are the same challenges once used to test warrior-wizards.'

'All very interesting,' said Sir Deàreg, 'but I for one am glad to have got the hard part over. I'm looking forward to an easier stretch.' The Aranese made to start moving forward, but Roujeark's voice halted them.

'Don't count on that, sir knight. The higher we go now, the more potent the magic will become around us. This is the very birthplace of magic, is it not?' He caught Theonar's eye, but the tall knight gave nothing away in his face. 'Everything we see here could be dangerous. Hard part over? I doubt that very much. Nay, the closer we come to the prize, the more Kulothiel will test us.'

His words cast a dread over the lords, knights and men-at-arms of Aranar, and when they walked forward now there was significantly less confidence in their steps. Curillian encouraged his armists.

'Come, friends, what Roujeark says is probably truer than he knows, but we've come this far together, and we'll go on together.' His party followed the men and Curillian himself was striding towards the lowest steps when he noticed Sir Theonar hanging back to catch him. The tall man came close and whispered in his ear before hastening up to rejoin his companions.

'Before your Konenaire broke the door down, we heard sounds out here. It was empty when we came out, but I am convinced that someone was here just before us. Watch your step, my lord king.'

Curillian let him go on ahead and hung back until his comrades were well above him. Then he turned, making no noise, to watch the atrium. Several long moments elapsed, then a shadow moved. Out of the left hand passageway, a tall figure materialised. From the other side came two others, elves all. Elrinde of Ithrill nodded in wordless greeting. Curillian returned the gesture, holding his eye for a while. When neither he, Astacar nor Linvion moved, Curillian turned and continued on his way.

The staircase proved to be even longer than it had appeared from the bottom. The whole way up they passed scenes of history and legend painted on the walls, though in the gloom they couldn't guess at their subjects. At regular intervals the steps were interrupted by wide platforms, each with a brace of tall marble lampstands, their lights long since extinguished. As they climbed, the ghostly luminescence from above grew gradually brighter. They were almost drenched in it when at long last they reached the top. The stairs gave onto a vast room, cathedral-like in its proportions and layout. Rows of enormous carved pillars supported a vaulted ceiling whose painted details could not clearly be seen.

Right in front of them was a metallic gateway, gleaming silver-blue in the light of whatever lay beyond. Two great statues flanked the opening at its centre, intricately sculpted into the likenesses of ancient mage-lords. Their outstretched staves barred the way, and though no barrier was in evidence, all beyond them was obscured as if by thick glass. They all walked up to the forbidding obstacle, mesmerised and chilled at the same time by the eerie light. Lancoir was foremost now, and he strode towards the crossed staves. After gazing up for a moment at the ancient engraved faces, he reached out and touched the staves. A blinding moment of pain and the next thing he knew he was picking himself up from the top of the stairs, having been hurled back fully thirty paces. His companions, who had been knocked willy-nilly by his backward flight, were just getting to their feet again, marvelling at the flash they had seen and the glowing blue forcefield that had momentarily been revealed.

'I...don't think we should touch them,' Caiasan said, overlate.

'Now he tells me...' Lancoir muttered. Dusting himself off, he returned to the statues, this time to inspect them, in company with Curillian, Roujeark, Theonar and Southilar.

'Who are they?' asked the Jeantar, looking up in awe, his face bathed in the spectral glow.

'I know not,' said Roujeark. 'Some long-past champions of the League, I would guess, defending their realm even in death. But these are not pieces of art. Did I not say everything here could be dangerous?'

Aleinus, standing behind them, overheard and muttered aloud, 'Great, down there everything we pressed triggered some booby-trap; up here, anything we touch is likely to give us a shock. I like this place more and more.' Caiasan shrugged expansively in sympathy, but everyone else ignored him. Back in the leaders' discussion, Sir Theonar made his contribution.

'It matters not who they are. All we need to do is find a way to get past them.'

'Any suggestions?' growled Southilar. Theonar had none to make, and nor did any of them. After a while they tired of their inspection and sat down to think.

'Kulothiel isn't giving up this last stage so lightly is he?' said Caréysin with a rueful smile. Curillian nodded agreement and sat back, propped up against a pillar. He felt wearier than he had in years.

For some while they sat about, racking their brains for a solution, but none came. Then Roujeark felt a strange sensation surge through him and, when he looked again, there was no one about him. Gone was the pale blue glow, replaced by the blaze of a hundred lamps. Then he heard footsteps coming up the stairs, which now looked resplendent in golden light. A wizard strode energetically up and passed him by. He took no notice at all of Roujeark. The wizard went straight up to the statues, which stood staves crossed as before. Roujeark followed, full of curiosity. Head bowed reverently, the wizard uttered a strange word, so softly that Roujeark couldn't catch it. However, there could be no mistaking the effect of that mysterious word. The staves separated and snapped into an upright position. The rest of the statues hadn't moved, but now the way was clear.

Roujeark saw the opportunity and hurriedly made to follow. He passed through the barrier hard on the wizard's heels, moments before the staves came back down. With a faint hum the forcefield came back into operation.

A cry of amazement from his companions tugged him back to reality, and he shook his head with a start. The blue light was back, shining softly all around him. He looked for his comrades, and there they were, on the wrong side of the magical portal. They had leapt up in astonishment when they saw him scurry through, and now were looking at him in amazement, their faces somewhat distorted by the intervening barrier. One of the Aranese knights chucked a ration-biscuit at the barrier to test it, and sure enough the object was hurled back, spraying across the dusty floor in a thousand pieces.

'Roujeark!' The voice was Curillian's, though it was muffled by the forcefield. 'How did you do that? You walked straight through. The staves came up, let you through, and then slammed back into place. What did you do?' Roujeark was no less bewildered than the king.

'I don't know sire. I had a kind of vision, and I watched a wizard approach this very spot. He spoke a password to open the gate, but I couldn't hear what it was. I was up before I knew it, following him, and no sooner was I through than the vision faded. Now here I am.'

'Amazing,' exclaimed Caiasan, pushing forward. 'It's like the Mountain recognises you as one of its own. You truly are a wizard!' There was awe in his voice.

Sir Hardos was less impressed. 'But that still doesn't help us! Unless he's going to finish the Tournament by himself, how do we get through as well?' There followed a loud, futile argument with lots of wild suggestions thrown around, but somehow Theonar's soft suggestion cut through it and silenced them all.

'Search the statues. There may be a clue.' He stepped away and let them search, but through the forcefield Roujeark caught a strange look in his face, a glimpse of withheld brilliance.

The search was conducted gingerly, the examiners fully expecting to get zapped at any moment, but it seemed that the defensive power was only in the space between the staves, not on the rest of the statues. Ornate though the statues were, no words were written upon them.

'There's nothing here,' Andil said dejectedly.

'Wait…wait a minute,' contradicted his fellow-guard Findor, 'there's something inscribed on this ring here…only I can't read it.'

'Let me see.' Curillian pushed in. What Antaya had found was tucked away on the finger of the right-hand statue, the hand not holding the staff. A word was set on a stone ring, on the side facing away from the staircase. Craning his neck, Curillian peered at the elvish script.

'*Nahtiere.*' He breathed the word to himself. He extricated himself. 'It's no word of elvish that I recognise, but here goes.' He turned back to face the barrier and bowed his head. '*Nahtiere.*' He did not look up but heard the swish and eerie whisper as the two staves slid smoothly up and shuddered to a halt by the wizards' sides. Awed gazes were replaced by hasty steps as everyone began moving forwards. Curillian led them through, while Sir Theonar stood under the barrier to keep it open until all had passed. And so they stepped over the threshold, into the very heart of the mountain.

⅄

Now, with nothing in the way, they could at last see the source of the light. In the middle of the pillared hall was a strange edifice, shaped in the likeness of the Mountain itself. The inexplicable glow emanated from a plinth at its top, filling the hall with unearthly light and scattering the shadows into recesses between the pillars. With dread and awe they slowly approached, but only a few dared go close. Curillian, Theonar and Roujeark. They were deaf to the imprecations of Southilar, urging them to remain.

The sculpture was star-shaped, like the mountain it evoked, with four out-flung spurs. Between those spurs were four sets of steps ascending to the high platform. Reverently, the three questers climbed them and met at the top. The structure was fashioned of a material like nothing any of them had ever encountered, obsidian-dark, smooth as marble, cold as the stars. In the steps and on inlaid panels to either side were runes of power, glowing with their own unquenchable fire. On the platform was a font, a carved pedestal of perfect white stone. Like everything else in the vicinity, it was bathed in the blue light. A shallow pool in the font held crystal clear water, fresh as mountain dew. And in the pool was a marvellous gem, though so incandescent that they could not tell what it was. Brighter than all the stars of the sky gathered together in one place, it was beautiful and terrible. They could not look directly at it, but it seemed to be curved in a graceful oval, as large as the egg of some giant bird.

'It is the Tear of Mírianna.' Curillian and Roujeark stood entranced, robbed of the power of speech, and they were barely aware of Theonar speaking. Had they known it, his voice was strangely changed, grown in power and dignity. 'No less than the greatest treasure ever wrought by elven hand. If wrought it was; some say it was one of the few heirlooms Avatar brought with him to Astrom from the stars. Undimmed by all the years, the League may have passed into the night, but the Tear still shines. If all else is conquered, can any evil ever draw nigh so heavenly a radiance? Let the shadowy heart of the Fire-demon himself be illumined if ever he gazes hither, and let no mortal eyes ever forget the sight.'

'Avatar.' Curillian mindlessly echoed the name, gripped with unthinking awe. Somewhere in the back of his mind, Curillian remembered what Theonar was talking about, but it was beyond him to articulate it. Avatar was the High King of all elves, the eldest member of that ancient race. Legend had it that he and his spouse, Mírianna the Star-Queen, had crashed to Astrom in a fallen star, sent along with two others from *Eluvatar*, the Holy-Star and dwelling place of Prélan. The other two stars contained the kings and queens of the sea-elf and wood-elf kindreds, just as Avatar and Mírianna ruled over the high-elves. Legend it might have been for all that any mortal knew, but Curillian had spoken with ancient elven lords like Lancearon who swore to it as a Prélan-given truth.

'The High King discovered Oron Amular and its Pool of High Magic,' Theonar went on. 'He founded the League of Wizardry here before he departed these shores, creating an institution which for seven thousand years has protected and enlightened the Free Peoples. This tear he bequeathed to the Mountain in honour of Mírianna, a light to grace the threshold. And verily these are his parting words, engraved in a circle around the rim of the pool.' As his companions stood still transfixed, the tall knight circled the pool, reciting the ancient script as he traced the words with his finger.

Though I leave these shores,
This legacy of light I leave forever
To shine by the grace of Prélan in
The heart of His hallowed Mountain.

Here let the Tear of Mirianna dwell,
A token of hope to all who behold,
And a promise of deliverance
To all who believe that He shall come again.

Just as they both marked but could never remember afterwards the change in his voice, so Curillian and Roujeark both saw but couldn't grasp the look in his face. Theonar stood rapt in the holy light, his face displaying wonder and intimacy mingled. Adoration and long-harboured pain swirled through his eyes, quivered in his lips and rippled in his skin. Or so it seemed to Roujeark. Then the moment passed, and he turned away.

'Be released. Let us go.' Suddenly the armists were loosed from the spell. Dazed, they followed Theonar back down the steps. On their way back to the others, both chased after elusive thoughts that flittered ahead of their groping minds, refusing to be tied down or retained. Whose voice did we just hear? How does he know such things?

Their comrades waited for them with fearful expectancy in their faces, wary of what dreadful magic might have rubbed off on the explorers.

'Curillian? Is all well?' Lancoir asked, but his question was overtaken by others.

'What is it? What did you see?'

'Whence comes the light?'

'Is the Tournament over? Have we won?'

Curillian looked at them, blinking. He still felt foggy-headed and disorientated by the dazzling light. The glistening Tear still seemed to fill his vision.

'It is a tear,' he said slowly. 'Left here by Avatar. His bequest to the Mountain.'

Caiasan burst forth in excited response, sounding more cogent than any had heard him for a long time. 'Avatar? The same Avatar who founded the League of Wizardry? Who was the first forefather of King Lithan of Kalimar?' Curillian could only nod. 'The same Avatar who slew the Fire-demon and singlehandedly vanquished his great armies? The noblest and greatest being who ever was or shall be?' The young scribe was suddenly showing off his knowledge, reminding his countrymen why they had put up with him all these weeks. Curillian and Roujeark could say nothing in response, so Theonar spoke instead, in gentle correction.

'Verily, that is he. Avatar. High King of the elves, first and eldest. But he did not slay the great demon, only defeated, banished him; a feat which nearly cost him his life. Next to him Lithan is but a child, he who outshines all others that remain today. Avatar was the greatest and fairest of all the elves, for in him was found the sum of elven greatness: strength, beauty, power, wisdom, kindness and grace.' Southilar could contain his curiosity no longer.

'Sir Theonar!' he barked. 'How do you know such things? You speak of this long-dead elf as if you knew him personally!'

Theonar shook his head sadly. 'Not dead, only gone. And no, I did not know him, though I would that I had.' Raising his head, he looked his lord in the eye. 'It is my fate to know what others know not, and to have seen what others cannot conceive.' All were now looking at the two tall men, locked in confrontation.

'No, that's not good enough,' snapped Southilar, spitting his words in sudden anger and pointed a gloved fist at his subordinate. 'Enough evasion; no more of your oh-so-humble dissembling and wordsmithery. You'll tell me, your lord, exactly who you are and where you come from, right now.' The contention between the two men, which before had been concealed like glowing embers under ash, now burst forth in flame, plain for all to see. On the one hand, Southilar's bristling anger and brusque demands; on the other, Theonar, standing in quiet defiance.

'You would be wise, Lord of the Pegasus,' Theonar said, still not raising his voice, 'not to insist here and now. Whatever you guess, however much you fear, you must lay aside your demands of me. Greater things are at stake. My identity and my past are for me alone to know. You need me, not so much to win this Tournament, but to help get us out of this Mountain alive. With your questions unanswered you will have my help, or not at all.' The two men's eyes bored holes in each other, waging a silent war of wills.

Curillian intervened. 'Come, Southilar, Theonar, we need you both. Lay aside your quarrel for the time being. There will be plenty of time for you to resolve it later. For now, there's a tournament to win, and a wizard's lair to escape.' The tension prevailed a moment longer and then Theonar turned away, striding off down the hall.

'Come then,' he called over his shoulder. 'Let's get this done. The guardsman's question I can answer. No, it is not over, we have not won. This is merely the start of the next stage.'

XVII
The Wizard's Lair

THEONAR Strode off down the hall, leaving the monument and its light behind. The rest of them followed him, plunging into what seemed to be utter darkness. They had no more torches, and no more means of conjuring light, so they braced themselves for a dark journey. But as the radiance fell further and further behind, they came to realise that the halls in which they walked were otherwise lit. The great wall-braziers were out of reach and without fuel, but from mysterious apertures high overhead filtered the soft radiance of starlight, as if from window slits in the mountainside. In that celestial light they saw that though their path wound much round corners and up and down stairs, the grand ecclesiastical feel all about them remained strong. Rarely were they without pillars and statues on either side, and never once was the high ceiling anything but ornate, filled with the adornment of many years' abiding.

What did change was the feel of the air. They all marked it to one degree or another. The air seemed thicker, somehow charged. It seemed to tickle their nostrils and eyelids, and ever and anon they would feel strange sparks about their person. To their ears came faint voices in tongues unguessable, whispering of enduring secrets and deep knowledge. An acrid taste was on their tongues. Bittersweet, like the aftermath of perfumed gunpowder, the odours of long-cast spells filled their noses and infused their imaginations with peculiar thoughts and strange imaginings. They all walked in a daze, suffused with sensations they had never felt before, at once wondrous and unsettling.

Now there was a carpet beneath their feet, a long, unflinchingly straight carpet of a shifting midnight blue that never seemed the same colour twice. To match the carpet, the bare walls were hung with gigantic tapestries that went on as far as the eye could see – huge, fantastically coloured needlework that must have been centuries in the making. In the imperfect light they could not discern them clearly, but they portrayed scenes of myth and history. They were in an immense corridor of tapestried history. The skilful threads showed wars waging, nations rising and falling, people toiling, monuments lifting and tragedies unfolding. Elves and men were shown, armists, dwarves, orcs and trolls. Kings and wizards were depicted, serfs and merchants, diplomats and warriors, traders and priests. Good and evil intertwined, joys and sorrows.

'It cannot be,' gasped Antaya. They all looked and saw what he saw. The very end of the tapestry showed their own exploits in the Tournament so far. The slaying of the great beast and the wreck of the bireme, the travails of the men of Aranar; the tapestry was alive, growing still further. Its newest threads wove themselves before their very eyes with no hand visible, and they saw other parties of men and dwarves struggling elsewhere in the Mountain. There was the Hendarian bishop, puzzling over a riddle in the rock while his king waited impatiently; there were the sun-darkened men of the south, treading warily down a rodent-infested tunnel; and there were the dwarves, toiling to clear a blocked doorway. Their deeds were being recorded even as they performed them.

'Surely Kulothiel is up there somewhere,' wondered Roujeark aloud, 'sitting with a pen and dictating this magic.'

They rewalked the corridor with necks craned upwards in awe. Each was astounded to find his own life recorded, and they became strung out as every man and armist stopped to gaze at his own story. A strangled sob rent the air, but they were all too sunk in their own little worlds to heed each other. The wondrous hall suddenly became a place of nightmare where painful memories from the past rose up to assail those who thought they had left them behind. Roujeark was full of suppressed anger when he saw the many wasted years of waiting in the threads, but his anger turned to tears of anguish when he traced them back to the night of his father's death. Through blurred vision he saw the fallen Dubarnik, and his wrathful killers standing over him. When he managed to wrench himself away, he almost stumbled into Lancoir, who stood still as stone, gazing up at the tapestry. He had found his own portion, and now he was rooted to the spot, emotion seizing his face and making his body quiver. Roujeark stood by him and looked upon the valiant knight unjustly slain by envious rivals. He shuddered, remembering the tale of woe Lancoir had told him under the eaves of Tol Ankil; he never thought he would live to see it retold with his own eyes.

Curillian walked further than any of them to find the beginning of his tale. When, much later, Lancoir and Roujeark reached him, they found him transfixed. They had seen his great deeds as king; the warrior armist crowned at the peak of his powers; his legendary deeds in the Second War of Kurundar made real; his service to Lancearon and the strange paths of his youthful exile. Yet, in the end, his story also began, just as theirs, with the loss of a father. They stood in solidarity with him for a while, sharing his pain. When at last they moved on, unspeaking, they all felt a much closer connection with the armists beside them.

Curillian's life, long as it was, came and went, yet it was still but a breath in the great tale of years. Using the intermittent light, Curillian interpreted the scenes for them.

'Look,' said he, 'see Lancearon's campaigns and the rise of the Silver Empire...the days of the Great Union...the First War of Kurundar, and the final battle at the feet of Oron Cavardul.' And so they walked back in history, back to where the knowledgeable king's lore faded and his identifications became guesswork. They passed back beyond the Great Betrayal and the dawn of men into the days of the Second Chapter, further back than any mortal could peer with certainty. The scenes became the stuff of distant legends, of ancient plagues and mythical wars. They walked on, overwhelmed by the weight of years, stepping into primeval chapters of the world when the elves were young and first walked on Astrom.

Finally, when it seemed like they had been walking for years, they reached the beginning. That tall, impossibly beautiful pair of elves, must surely be Avatar and Mírianna, rising out of a fallen star to become the first living souls to inhabit the world. Then they saw something that none of them could understand. Serene, majestic, unfathomable, it stood at the very beginning, hovering over the waters, though whether it was a person, a storm cloud, a star shining, or something else altogether, they could not tell.

'It is Prélan,' Curillian said at last, his voice thick with awe.

'How do you know?' whispered Roujeark, equally awestruck. Curillian pointed.

'He is at the beginning, but He has been there all along, all through the tale of life...' Roujeark looked and saw that the upper edges of the divine depiction swept into the topmost reaches of the tapestry. What he had taken for a decorative border was in fact the unsleeping presence of Prélan. Roujeark fell to his knees, unable to move for the moment. He wept uncontrollably. They all wept, without knowing why. When at last the tears subsided, Roujeark spoke.

'If nothing else awaits me here, I would have come just for this.'

Curillian rose, and then raised him up too. 'The Almighty Father is not just in the tapestry, Roujeark. He's all around. He's in here.' He tapped Roujeark's chest. 'He has always been with you, and always will be.'

Roujeark stared at his king, marvelling at how attuned to Prélan he was, how much he knew, how deeply he believed. The king reached out both arms and clasped both Roujeark and Lancoir by the neck. They linked arms with him and with each other. In a triangle, they summoned fresh strength.

'We have glimpsed the glory of the One and Only and have not perished,' Curillian declared. 'We will go on. Let us finish this.'

Having now come to the end of the tapestry, they noticed for the first time that Sir Theonar was still ahead of them. It seemed he had not stopped, nor been affected as they had been. He stood, leaning against a great doorway, which stood at the end of the hallway. All this time they had been wandering down the same great corridor. The doorway was immense, covered with gilt inlay a foot wide and set with glowing red runes that none could read. Yet whatever they said, the great gates stood open, and so they passed through. They found themselves in another corridor, full of closed doors. They were about to press on when they saw one door that was open, on the left-hand side of the passage.

Walking through it, they stumbled upon another marvel. From a viewing platform they gazed down on a huge, living map that filled the chamber. There was Astrom, with all its mountain ranges, rivers, valleys, forests and plains. There too were the great nations, full of cities and roads and all the handiwork of mortals and elves. And what was more, they could actually walk down and tread the fields and coasts. It was in there that the others caught up with them, having finally broken free of their own private reveries in the hall of history. The men of Aranar found their own lands where horses foaled and clans vied; the armists explored the long coastlines and mountainous backbone of Maristonia. Curillian paced across to Kalimar, tracing out their journey with giant steps. He came to stand by Oron Amular, so obvious now he knew where to find it. It stood up tall amid the Black Mountains like a spire of pearl out of crumpled rock.

'What did they use it for?' called Sir Lindal from his Unicorn lands.

'If not merely to marvel at,' answered Curillian, 'a map like this could be of great use in planning out campaigns and considering policies.' He was thinking of his own strategic maps, which until now he had thought large and unrivalled. 'All this time the wizards bestrode our world, and we knew it not,' he muttered to himself.

Reluctantly they left the map chamber and continued on down the passage. It reminded Lancoir of the imposing corridor that led to the royal throne room in the palace at Mariston, with its alcoves and high ceiling, but this place was altogether more unnerving. A cold draft came down to meet them from somewhere up ahead, and they perceived another great doorway. Passing through it, they had their breath taken away again.

They were in another colossal chamber, through which the path ran straight like a highway. About the road were strange shapes, like waves in the rock. There were four of them, each issuing from a gateway above and each running down to meet the main road with tributary paths. The lowest was also the broadest, as if designed to accommodate many wizards marching abreast, and each successive one was narrower and descended from a higher starting point.

'It's the strangest group of paths I've ever seen,' exclaimed Roujeark. Curillian moved past him, clasping his shoulder.

'Indeed, but can you imagine it when they were in use. These roadways full of warrior-wizards and mage-lords marching to war against the enemies of the League,' he paused, overtaken with awe at the picture he had painted. 'What a sight that must have been.'

A

The main path squeezed through a narrow section between the raised areas on either side, shepherding the party into a short tunnel. When it opened out again, they saw rock walls smooth as masonry running towards the cavern's end, which curved like the rim of a goblet. A great closed gateway awaited them there, but between them and it the walls of the cavern narrowed again to form a bottleneck. Standing guard either side of that bottleneck were two titanic figures. Immense figures of stone, they stood with their backs and shoulders braced against the curved ceiling of the cavern, as if they were holding it up. Unarmed and unadorned, they gazed down on the trespassers who approached their feet. The men of Aranar quailed under the baleful stare of the guardians, and hung back. Even Curillian's followers were unnerved, so that he was alone when he drew level with the giants. He came up only to their shins.

They watched as the king stopped, laying hand to his sword hilt as if warned of peril by some extra sense. Curillian drew his great blade and held it down by his side. Then he moved off again. He passed over a delicate red line on the floor, and straightaway there was an ominous grating sound. Far above, stone eyelids snapped open and the previously immobile arms flexed and started to move. The men of Aranar fell over themselves trying to get away, Roujeark cowered back, and even Lancoir stood aghast, but not Curillian. He was already moving, sword up and ready to fight. He sped past the feet of the giants and into the open space before the doorway. He took up a defensive stance, sword brandished, but the giants were only just lowering their arms. With slow stiffness they reached down, as if to grasp at the intruder, but then their fingers detached and dropped to the floor.

Only they were not fingers at all, for they took on a new shape as soon as they hit the ground. What rose up were small warriors, faceless and terrible. They wore no clothing or armour but seemed to have jet black skin of some malleable metal. There were ten of them, five from each right hand, and all were differently armed, sporting everything from nets and tridents to cutlasses and flails. As one they faced Curillian, standing between him and the door. He had just long enough to stare into their unseen eyes before they leapt into action. To the terrified onlookers it seemed as though Curillian must be overwhelmed by that first onslaught, but somehow he slewed his way through them, hewing left and right as he passed them. The metallic warriors veered away from his blade and jumped through the air, fluid as molten metal and agile as tumblers.

'CURILLIAN!' Lancoir bellowed, running to join the fight. For a few heartbeats the rest of them could only watch, mesmerised by the sight of the two armist warriors doing battle, all alone and beset by faceless foes. Then the other armists plunged into the fray, and some of the men of Aranar would have gone too, had Southilar not held them back. He thought all had obeyed his craven order, but Theonar went forward regardless.

'Sir Theonar! Get back here!' Southilar shouted after him, but he was ignored. Yet Theonar went not to the fight, but to the right hand of the two guardians, who, having deployed their fighting denizens, had straightened up to resume their vigil. Using any crack or hold he could find, he shinned up the great leg like a squirrel. His countrymen were agape, not sure which spectacle to watch: the whirling fight or the dauntless climb. Curillian and his comrades were hard-pressed, unable to land a proper blow on enemies who moved like greased smoke. Only the king's fabulous blade found its mark, and though it came away unscathed, it had done no damage. The other blades did not fare so well, being chipped or turned by the devious metal their foes were made of. Roujeark aimed a blast of fire at one of them, but his victim just soaked up the fire, almost revelling in it, before hurling it backward with redoubled fury. He dove out of the way, robes singed and face scorched, and then had to get up and flee as his adversary pursued him.

Lionenn was swinging his mace with might and main but couldn't seem to land a blow. Instead he himself took a pummelling, but each time he somehow managed to get to his feet again. Caréysin's arrows had no effect whatsoever, even those that hit their marks, and his firing was put to a stop when a black metal figure hurled him bodily against the wall. Andil was bleeding from a dozen cuts and retreated out of the fight. Findor took a sword-thrust in his arm and cried out, but Lancoir came to his rescue by bulling over the warrior who had wounded him. Then Lancoir himself went down, cracked round the back of the head by the haft of a trident. Antaya found himself without a sword and Aleinus was backed into a corner; it was looking bleak for the armists, and only Curillian fought on unimpaired.

Death was staring the Royal Guards in the face when suddenly Theonar leapt down from on high. Landing in their midst, cat-like, he took off at a run and nimbly somersaulted over the enemy. He ran for the closed doorway, and the ten warriors suddenly stopped in the middle of their attacks. It was as if they were alerted to some hidden peril. Forgetting the armists, they chased after Theonar with terrible speed. Theonar reached the doorway and slotted home a giant key. The ten were almost on him, weapons outstretched, when he turned the key with an almighty clunk. Some giant mechanism had been set in motion, and hidden wheels turned. The ten warriors stopped dead in their tracks, then turned and scuttled back to their parent statues. They clambered up the stone guardians like dark monkeys in the forests of the south. When they reached the right hands, they seemed to fuse back into the stonework, and lo, they were fingers again. In eerie silence, there was no hint that they had ever been anything but inanimate.

The sounds of their retreat echoed round the chamber and slowly died away. The men of Aranar looked on speechless, unable to believe what they had witnessed. But when they looked away from the stone statues, they saw Theonar standing by doors which were swinging open. His countrymen came towards him fearfully, half-expecting the grim warriors to leap down again when they passed the red line, and wary of Theonar himself, who seemed to have become virtually superhuman all of a sudden. Theonar stood aside respectfully to let the Jeantar past. Southilar eyed him darkly, more suspicious than grateful, but Caiasan blurted out, 'How...how did you do that?' His voice was laced with amazement. The tall knight shrugged modestly.

'I saw the key hanging from the right-hand statue. I guessed, rightly as it turns out, that it would open the door.'

'But the way you climbed...' Caiasan persisted, as his companions filed past behind him. Theonar turned him by the shoulder and prodded him onwards.

'Caiasan, my friend, when a man is pressed, he can do things he would normally think impossible. Necessity is a great means of redefining your limits.'

Back in the cavern, Curillian was tending to his armists. Andil had light wounds, not serious, but both Caréysin and Lionenn were battered and shaken. Roujeark, Aleinus and Antaya were unhurt, and Lancoir was just groggy from his head-blow, yet Findor was in a bad way. Covered in blood, he was helped to sit upright by his friends. A sword had torn a huge gash in his arm. Nerveless, it now hung uselessly by his side. Roujeark tore a strip of red-brown linen from his robe, which Curillian then tied above the wound to stem the bleeding. Findor looked pale and shaken, and they had to haul him to his feet and support him as he walked.

'It's a miracle we didn't suffer greater loss,' said Antaya as they paced slowly.

'Indeed,' agreed the king. 'If Theonar hadn't acted when he did, then we would all be dead.' Roujeark swallowed hard as that realisation hit him. The Aranese knight was waiting for them inside the elaborately fashioned doorway.

'That was a mighty climb, sir knight, and a daring leap. My armists and I are beholden to you.' Theonar bowed low, graciously accepting the thanks.

'Come,' said Lancoir. 'Let's see where the horse-lords have got to.' He led the way and the others followed him. Curillian motioned Theonar on ahead.

'Go on ahead, friend Theonar, we will only be going slowly with Findor here. Feel free to leave us behind and join your comrades.' Theonar shook his head in declination.

'No, lord king, by your leave I'd like to stay and walk by your side. I can no longer abide the company of the Jeantar.' Curillian nodded his consent.

'Sire,' said Andil, plainly concerned, 'we cannot let the men of Aranar get too far ahead. What if Southilar should reach the finish line before us? We've come so far, I couldn't bear to lose now.'

'We can go only as fast as our slowest armist,' replied the king. 'But fear not, Antaya, it's not over yet. Let Southilar try and fail. Then it will be my turn.'

They were on a broad, well-made staircase that led up from the door. Wall torches burned, as if in welcome, and illuminated their way. When the stairs levelled off, they walked down a passageway filled with doors and side passageways. They smelled the musty aroma of dormitories, classrooms, armouries, refectories and storehouses long disused. They caught glimpses of the ordinary day-to-day life of wizards, but they had no time to stop and explore.

They could hear the sounds of Southilar's party up ahead, and they were content to not hurry until those sounds took on a different note. Suddenly they heard alarm, and they picked up their pace. They hastened up some more stairs, and along more passageways. They heard swords being wielded, but when they came upon the men of Aranar, they saw no enemies. Southilar's party stood on the far side of a great fissure, across which stretched a flimsy-looking bridge. The sword strokes they had heard were not aimed at any foe, but against the bridge itself. They caught Sir Hardos, Southilar's right hand man, in mid-swing as he hacked at the bridge. He looked up, red-faced, and seemed momentarily ashamed of what he was doing. The armists and Theonar came up short, appalled by what they saw, but Southilar did not relent; in fact, he added two more men-at-arms to help Hardos in his work. Together they hewed at the bridge and succeeded in breaking it asunder. Shorn off from its shorings, it groaned and toppled into the chasm. Above the rending and the clattering of its fall, Southilar hailed them.

'Thank you for all your help so far Curillian, but I go on alone from here. This is a tournament after all, and I'll not share my glory with you.' With that he turned, and he and his party hurried away.

The armists and Theonar stood aghast on the wrong side of the chasm. The treacherous Aranese soon disappeared into the gloom, while below them nothing could be seen of the bridge they had destroyed. Peering over the edge, they could see no bottom, for the light of the wall-torches was soon swallowed up in the black emptiness.

'Treacherous scum!' exclaimed Theonar, with surprising vehemence. He faced his companions. 'This, my friends, is why I no longer wish to serve that man. What a coward – he is so afraid of losing to you, lord king, in a straight contest, that he has stooped to this perfidy.' The tall knight turned his anger upon himself. 'I heard him speak of you as unbeatable so many times – I should have seen this coming.'

Curillian, taken aback by the revelation, patted the knight's shoulder. 'Don't berate yourself, my friend, this betrayal was not your doing.' Theonar balled his fists, staring after his vanished master.

'I will make amends for this,' he promised. 'Curillian, I will challenge that man for the clan lordship and depose him if it's the last thing I do. I should have done it long ago; now it's well overdue. Then, when I rule in Jaglalir, I shall make good Southilar's actions and clear the stain of this betrayal.' Curillian looked out over the chasm with him.

'My friend, I wish you success, but let there be no debt between us.' Theonar looked down at him with fierce earnestness.

'Lord king, be it debt or unprompted kindness on my part, you will need my help soon. This Mountain Tournament is just the beginning. Greater tests lie ahead. And if ever I become Jeantar, the better shall I be able to help you.' Curillian clasped his hand and shoulder.

'Let it be so. Sir Theonar of the Pegasus, you shall ever have the friendship of Maristonia, and whatever challenges lie in the future, let us face them together. But first, let's find a way to get across this gap. There's a tournament to be won, and Southilar must be stopped.'

While the two of them had been talking, Lancoir and the others had formulated a plan. The captain ducked out of the belt-rope still coiled over his shoulders and dropped it on the ground.

'Apparently no one stopped to get their belts back,' he said tersely, with a savage grin.

'So let us use them,' said Roujeark. 'We must be able to get across somehow with these. Look, the posts of the bridge are still there – can we loop the end of the rope across one of them somehow?' Antaya took the rope and hefted it doubtfully in his hands. Andil, who had a much better throwing arm, took the responsibility instead. Sighting the post, he cast the rope out over the chasm. He missed his mark the first time, but second time around he succeeded in looping the end belt around the bridge-post. He gave a firm tug, and it held. He then gripped the rope's other end hard, preparing to swing himself across.

'Wait!' barked Lancoir. Taking the rope from Andil, he tugged again, much harder this time. The bridge-post cracked, snapped and fell into the chasm. Grim-faced, Lancoir hauled the rope back in, wooden spar and all. He dumped it back in Andil's hands. 'You're welcome,' he grunted. Andil just stared dumbly down at it as he held it in shaking hands.

'To think I nearly trusted my weight to that,' he whispered to Aleinus beside him.

'Now what are we going to do?' demanded Aleinus pleadingly. Lancoir cuffed him over the back of the head.

'Shut up and let me think, that's what,' he growled.

'Let me try something,' Roujeark volunteered. He took the rope and had his companions tie it underneath his armpits. He looked at Curillian, smiling bravely. 'Swing me across,' he said simply. Curillian hid his surprise.

'Are you sure, Roujeark? It's not enough just to get across – you also have to swing the next armist over by yourself.' Roujeark nodded resolutely.

'I have newfound strength I never knew I had.' Curillian considered for a moment, then nodded assent. He took up the end of the rope as Roujeark steeled himself and sat on the edge of the abyss.

'Let me,' said Theonar. 'I'm stronger.' Not many could have said that to the King of Maristonia, still less been willing to actually say it, but Curillian acquiesced. Theonar took up the rope in strong hands and paid out plenty of slack into the darkness.

'Whenever you're ready, master wizard,' he said. Roujeark nodded, gulped, and slid himself off into thin air. With a stifled yelp he dropped suddenly for a few feet and came up hard as Theonar caught him. Gasping, he took a few moments to come to terms with dangling above the unguessed depths, and then he turned and kicked off the wall, launching himself further out. Theonar followed him with the rope, paying out extra length as was needed. Gradually Roujeark gathered momentum until he was swinging wildly from one side to the other. Fearfully, Roujeark let go of the rope, which he had been clutching for dear life, and reached for the rift's far lip. There was still a bracket of wood where the bridge-post had once been fixed to the rock, and he aimed for that. Coming close, he snapped his hands on thin air before swaying back out of reach. The next time, he seized it and held fast to it against the backward tug of the rope, which was almost at its full reach. He let out a shrill yell of triumph, his heart pounding in his own ears. Gathering his wits and his strength, he found tiny toeholds with his boots and started to climb up. The rope was stretched taut when he wriggled up onto the level ground, and he lay precariously on the very edge, lest he pull it out of Theonar's reach on the far side. Slowly, his breathing calmed.

His companions cheered his effort then prepared to follow. There wasn't enough rope left on their side to tie around themselves, so Aleinus, the lightest of them, just had to cling onto it for dear life. When he propelled himself off the edge, his weight nearly pulled Roujeark down into the void, but he just about managed to steady himself. Aleinus' weight carried him across the blackness to ricochet off the wall on Roujeark's side. Bracing himself, Roujeark strained against the weight and waited until Aleinus' momentum expired and left him dangling. Then, concentrating mind and body, he hauled upwards. At first the effort was too much, and he slipped forward himself, but digging his boots into the broken bases of the posts, he stopped himself and strained again. Hand over hand he hauled, and then suddenly the weight lessened, as if new strength suddenly flooded into his system. White-faced, Aleinus came above the rim and latched himself onto the side. With relief, Roujeark felt the strain disappear and he switched his effort into helping Aleinus up and over. The two of them lay panting side by side for some time before they could muster the energy to think of their stranded comrades.

Roujeark now untied himself, and holding one end jointly with the guardsman, they flung the rope back to Theonar's waiting hands. The knight seized it and jumped out into the chasm without a second thought. With two of them now hauling, the job of bringing him up was much easier, and when he was beside them it became even easier still. Antaya came next, followed by Lancoir, Caréysin and Lionenn. Curillian stayed behind to help Findor, whose left arm hung useless by his side. Praying to Prélan for extra strength, the king took his wounded comrade under his arm, gripping him tight about the waist. With his other hand he grasped the rope and launched them out across. Many willing hands brought them safely over, but even so Curillian's arm was burning by the time he let Findor go.

And there they all were, safely across the chasm. They gave themselves a few moments to recover, then went on again. They met further obstacles as they went, other gaps and holes in the tunnel with dreadful drops beneath, but none so wide that they couldn't leap across, albeit with their hearts in their mouths. Other times they had to inch along narrow ledges, not wide enough even for the length of their boots. Slowly but surely, with hearts thudding, they traversed the hazards. They had only just negotiated the longest of these when a cracking sound split the still air of the tunnel. Curillian looked down at the floor beneath his feet, which was already starting to crumble into the gap.

'RUN!' he shouted. They all took off with the speed of terror, yelling at the tops of their voices as the floor gave way behind them. The gap was widening as it swallowed the tunnel floor, snapping at their heels even as they sprinted. Most of them succeeded in reaching a point of safety where the ground held firm, but Lancoir was hindmost and in real trouble. Curillian saw the gap catching up with him and hung back at the edge of the solid ground to help him. The captain of the guard was only too aware of his peril, and he put on a burst of speed…but it wasn't enough. With a great yell he threw himself into a despairing dive as the ground gave way beneath him, and at the very same moment Curillian lunged back towards him. Lancoir tumbled into the blackness, an uncharacteristic look of fear etched into his face, but their outstretched hands met. For a split second they fell together before they came up hard. Theonar's long arms had caught Curillian's feet. The tall knight had been dragged well over the rim himself, but his legs in turn were held fast by Lionenn.

'Hurry,' called Roujeark. 'I don't trust this ground.' The king's grip was unshakeable, and slowly the fear left Lancoir's eyes as they were hauled up together. Muscles bulging on his tattooed arms, Lionenn barely needed help from the others to lift his comrades out. Wearily they were hauled onto the firm ground and lay there, panting. Sweat poured down their faces. Slowly they dusted themselves down and waited for the ringing of their own cries of fear to recede from their ears. Willing hands helped them away from the edge and then, stumbling, the whole party put as much ground between themselves and the gaping chasm as they could.

⋀

'We should get out of this tunnel before it gives way again,' said Roujeark fearfully.

'Do you hear that?' said Theonar, checking them. Faint but unmistakeable, there came the sounds of combat from somewhere up ahead.

'It sounds like Southilar's reward has been to run headlong into trouble,' remarked Curillian. 'Let's see what's become of him.'

Soon they could see a fringe of ruddy light which marked where the tunnel came to an end. The clash of swords and cries of pain came louder now, but when they came to the doorway, they found it led only into a narrow space. Almost immediately they were brought up short by a smooth curving face of rock rising high above them. To left and right were narrow pathways squeezed between this obstacle and the cavern walls on the other side. There was only room for one to walk abreast. A few more clashes of steel, some thudding noises, and then the din ceased. After that, all they could hear was some faint whimpering. Curillian held them back from rushing.

'We do not know what lies ahead,' he whispered. 'Just be ready.'

They all brought up weapons and cautiously trod forwards. They branched left and right in two groups: Curillian, Lancoir, Caréysin and Findor to the left; Theonar, Roujeark, Andil, Lionenn, Antaya and Aleinus to the right. Slowly they followed the curving rock wall round until it started to lower. When they had reached the end, and it had come down nearly to their own height, Curillian paused and peeked round the end. Glancing across the cavern, he saw Theonar looking out from the opposite side. They were behind a great amphitheatre, whose immaculately carved tiers of seats swept back and above to the top of the wall that faced the tunnel mouth. Yet they both ignored the amphitheatre, for their eyes went immediately to the armoured figure standing at the edge of its central platform. It appeared to be only the statue of a mighty warrior, wrought from black iron, helmeted head gazing down at the floor as it rested upon a great two-handed sword.

Commanding the platform from which a speaker could address the whole amphitheatre, the warrior stood unmoving, except for a wisp of unseen wind which stirred the red plume atop his helm. He barred the way to a great doorway in the cavern wall behind him, which could only be reached by a narrow bridge connected to the platform. Between door and platform was a gulf of nothingness.

Curillian stepped out of cover, moving out onto the platform. Only as he did so did he notice the men of Aranar, lying about as if flung asunder by some great force. They all looked much the worse for wear. Some had scored mail or dented swords, others had helms knocked askew and the wind driven from them. Yet no sign was there of what had caused their discomfiture. It was as if a band of enemies had descended, smashed them about and then vanished. Only Southilar yet stood, occupying one of the lower tiers. Sword drawn, he glared at the warrior. His face was suffused with a mixture of anger and shame. Only slowly did he become aware of the armists' presence as Curillian's followers filed out behind their king and Sir Theonar. The Jeantar tried defiantly to meet the armist king's gaze, but he soon broke down and looked away.

'What happened here?' asked Roujeark, going to where Caiasan the scribe lay crumpled against the stone, quite subdued.

'We tried to get across,' he managed to whisper through bruised lips, 'but he denied us. We none of us could get past him.'

As he was speaking, barely heard by anyone other than Roujeark, Curillian had been slowly approaching the immobile warrior. He still showed no signs of life. Blade in hand, Curillian stepped closer still. Suddenly the helmeted head snapped up as if some mechanism had just kicked into action. Through a thin slit in the visor, his dark eyes glared out. They were like no eyes Curillian had ever seen before, and he had faced many kinds of enemy. Yet where the eyes were dark and hostile, the voice was fair and courteous, despite being given a metallic edge by the helm.

'Hail noble competitor, my master's congratulations on passing the challenges and reaching this place. Victory is within your grasp, if only you can overcome the final test.'

'Beware Curillian,' croaked Caiasan's voice in warning. 'He spoke even thus to us, before attacking us.' Curillian tightened his grip on his sword but stared levelly at the guardian.

'And what, pray, is the final test?' he asked, even though he knew the answer.

'You must defeat me,' the warrior declared. With those words, he brought up his greatsword and adopted a defensive stance. Lancoir and Theonar came up, weapons ready, but Curillian waved them back.

'No, my friends. Leave this to me.' Looking back at the knight, he spoke to him, 'Come, stranger, you don't want to fight me. I've reached the end of this accursed Tournament. There is no need to fight.'

'Nevertheless,' said the knight, 'there are times in life when one must fight. Now is just such a time.'

'Look,' snapped Curillian, 'I've been nearly drowned, crushed, incinerated and slaughtered, and I'm angry. I'm in a mood to speak to Kulothiel and claim my prize.'

'Don't be a fool, lord king, who but my master bade me hold this bridge against all comers? The Tournament is not over and remains unwon while I stand here undefeated. You've slain great beasts, unlocked many doors and survived all the wizard's snares, but conquer me or it's all for nothing, and you can go back to Maristonia with your tail between your legs.'

Swift as a striking snake, the knight brought his greatsword down in a great arc upon the armist king's head. All those looking on thought he would be cut down where he stood, but at the last moment he brought the Sword of Maristonia up to parry. There was an explosion of light and sparks as the two great blades met, each a match for the other. The two combatants recoiled from the force of the encounter, and then began to circle one another slowly. Curillian tested his opponent with some probing feints, looking for an opening, but the knight was equal to it, agile and watchful. Then suddenly the knight struck again, darting forward in a quick thrust which Curillian had to turn aside. A third and a fourth time their blades clashed, and still neither managed to gain an advantage. Roujeark was struck by how similarly they moved.

Lancoir looked on anxiously. Curillian was the finest warrior he knew, stronger and faster than any, but he was not at his best. He was tired and moving slowly. The Tournament had taken its toll. Curillian still moved well, with the customary footwork of a lifelong swordsman, but there was none of the dazzlingly swift ferocity with which his king normally destroyed his enemies. Suddenly, as if to disprove Lancoir's silent doubts, Curillian leapt into action, abandoning his watchful stance and throwing himself into an attack. He feinted left and struck right. Peeling away in the blink of an eye, he ducked under his foe's elbow and made to cut at his back, but the knight had turned. The manoeuvre would have been the end of any ordinary warrior, but the knight anticipated the move. He blocked the killing blow and threw the armist back. Curillian came again in a blur of blows, but each one was warded off. Back and forth they fenced, blades working so swiftly that the onlookers could barely follow them. It was a mesmerising display of swordsmanship, but at the end of it Curillian was no closer to winning.

At last the fighters separated again, stepping back and regarding one another.

'You cannot defeat me, armist,' declared the knight, 'for I am the equal of any swordsman.'

Curillian refused to be drawn. He just glared at his foe, breathing hard. The knight swayed slightly but was unhurt and watchful. In much less time than this, the knights of Aranar had been beaten down one after another, and the watching armists knew with a chill certainty that if Curillian could not prevail, then none of them would. Roujeark knew that as well as any of them. He considered wading in and trying to use his magic, but some intuition forestalled him. Magic would not win this contest. No, this was Curillian's moment, and he would have to win with his sword or with his bare hands.

Curillian stared wearily at the knight, summoning up the energy to try again. He could not remember a challenge like this. How long had it been since he'd met his equal? Not since the darkest days of the Second War, when Kurundar's fell champions had yet walked the earth. He was unnerved by how easily the knight was anticipating his moves, almost as if he knew what he was thinking. Pushing the thought aside, he launched himself forward. Running at the knight, he jumped high to one side of him and swung down a killing blow with all his might. Yet the knight danced back knowingly, and all Curillian's momentum went to waste. Caught off balance when he landed, the knight's counterstroke came fast. Curillian was only just able to fend it off, but the force of it sent him sprawling.

'Get up, armist king,' the knight said. 'We're not done yet.'

Now Lancoir was really worried. To see Curillian worsted was so rare he could not remember the last time. Going into every battle alongside the great king, he had had the utmost confidence in his survival and victory - but now? He felt a sharp twinge of doubt ripple up his spine like a shiver. With a knot in his stomach, he knew he would have to fight next if Curillian failed, and how could he hope to succeed where his king failed? He might intervene and save his master from death, but they would be defeated, now, at the bitter end. To come so far and fail in the end was unbearable.

Curillian picked himself up, ignoring the screams of his weary muscles. He dug deep into his vast reserves of stamina and attacked again. But whether by hacking and bludgeoning or by trickery and guile, he could not find a way through. After every attempt, the forbidding guardian of the bridge still barred the way. Was he even weary? He showed no sign of it. *Damn it*, thought Curillian, *I will not be beaten*. He struck with hellfire fury and drove his opponent back under a rain of blows. The two warriors were locked in a struggle that was much more than just a swordfight, but a mental clashing of wills. Curillian felt as if he had transcended to a new plane of reality, where every aspect of his being was bound up in the fight. Finally, he succeeded in getting a thrust behind the knight's guard, but there was no force in the blow. He only managed to slice the wrist, cutting just deep enough to get through the armour. But even as he did so, he felt a sharp pain in his own wrist. Crying out in shock and fear, he looked disbelievingly at his hand. It was cut and bleeding, even where he had hit his enemy. Reeling away, holding his wounded hand, Curillian felt an unfamiliar panic rising. *Prélan help me*. Out of the corner of his eye, he saw Lancoir dashing in to attack the knight, all anger and passion. There was a brief flurry of swords, but then the knight's elbow smashed into Lancoir's face and sent him lurching away.

Prélan help me, Curillian thought again, praying this time. *How do I beat him? He fights like...like me...* Sudden suspicion flooded into his mind and gave birth to a flash of insight. Wiping a hand across his bleeding mouth, he smiled grimly at his opponent.

'You'd beat anyone who came here, wouldn't you?' he called to him. The knight stared back impassively. 'You bleed, I bleed, eh? Man, woman, armist, elf, dwarf – you'd defeat them all. How can anyone defeat themselves? Bravo to the victor, who in winning slays himself. I don't know whether you be a living being or a phantom of wizardry, but Kulothiel has surpassed himself in this last challenge, hasn't he? Maybe this Tournament is unwinnable? Well, you may be my equal, but no one is the equal of Prélan, the lord of battle, and *He* is my strength.'

One last time he ran at the knight, legs pumping in reckless speed. The knight took up a stance ready to deflect him, but at the last moment Curillian flung his sword up in the air. The spectators gaped open-mouthed in awed surprise. The knight was distracted by the unexpected abandonment of the sword and Curillian seized his split-second opportunity with both hands. He cannoned into his enemy, knocking him flying. With a crash they landed together near the bridge. The force of the impact and the unforgiving armour nearly did for Curillian, but he somehow kept his focus. On his back, the knight's heavy plate armour put him at a serious disadvantage, whereas Curillian's cunning mail fitted him like a second skin while losing nothing in strength. Awkwardly the knight tried to strike with his sword, but Curillian wrenched it from his hand. Then he seized the black helm and tugged it free.

The shock of what he saw nearly stopped him from following through with his desperate plan. The face staring back at him was familiar from many palace mirrors and the reflection of his own sword. The craft of Kulothiel had made his last challenge the very embodiment of whomsoever should approach. Curillian steeled himself, knowing it was a trick of magic. His face a rictus of determination, he reached inside the protective mesh coif and wrapped his fingers around the exposed neck. Swordless and encumbered by his armour, the guardian knight could only move his arms and legs in feeble blows, which Curillian easily subdued. He kept squeezing, applying more and more pressure until his hands were white. The knight suddenly croaked in submission. He raised a gauntleted fist in surrender.

'Enough,' he gasped, barely audibly. Curillian relaxed his death-grip slightly. 'I yield,' said the knight. 'Advance, victor, and claim your prize. The way is clear, and the door is open.' Curillian glanced up, and the door beyond the bridge which had been closed now stood ajar, inviting yet repellent. Swiftly the bloodlust drained from him as relief and weariness swamped him in equal measure. All of a sudden, the black armour under him became very hot. He scrambled back and off as the whole body, armour and all, melted into a puddle of steaming liquid. Then a sudden gust of wind blasted through the chamber. It knocked them all from their feet and blew the liquid away into the void like dust and ashes. Curillian slumped onto the floor. He had done it. He had won the Tournament. But he felt not even remotely triumphant.

❊

XVIII
Power Unimaginable

CURILLIAN Retrieved his sword and used it to help him back to his feet. Leaning on it, he stumped back to his companions, who were waiting, wide-eyed, at the foot of the amphitheatre. Lancoir came to him, nursing a bruised face, and soon all the armists had crowded around.

'No, my friends,' he said, 'all is well, I'm just tired.' They backed away again to give him some room. 'It's over, but never have I been so tested.'

'Curillian, you're hurt, we must tend you,' insisted Theonar, full of concern, but the king waved him away.

'He's right,' Lancoir said flatly.

'No Lancoir, it's nothing.' The captain of the guard swallowed hard and acquiesced. 'Now I must finish the Tournament at last,' Curillian went on. 'Only one can go.' He looked over the bridge to the forbidding door. 'I shall go and claim the prize on behalf of you all, and in the name of Maristonia. Stay here and see to it that no one follows me.' Then, walking slowly but stiffly, he left them and moved towards the bridge. As he went, he passed Southilar, who stood agape, amazement and jealousy vying in his face. Curillian glanced contemptuously at him and went on by.

Cautiously he stepped onto the bridge, trying hard not to look down. Feeling faint and dizzy was not the best time to attempt such a perilous crossing, but he took his time and passed over safely. Cold airs eddied about him, chilling him, and a hostile presence seemed to issue out of the door to confront him. Curillian hesitated, looking up at the door. It was more intricately carved than any he had yet passed through, but the details were lost on him, for his head was spinning. He bowed his head, spoke a quiet, fervent prayer, and then plunged in. His nervous companions watched as he was engulfed in the shadow and lost.

The tunnel was much like those he had already passed through. He found to his relief that there were no overt dangers, but there was a latent menace in the air. Sweet saccharine odours hovered in the air, redolent of bygone spells, and the air itself felt abrasive, as if it prickled against the presence of a stranger. It was a peculiar and unnerving sensation that Curillian would never forget.

Like the passage with the bridge that Southilar had treacherously thrown down, there were many side-tunnels and openings to both left and right. He was overtaken by visions of dusty old scholars bent over ancient volumes and expectant faces reflected in the surface of sinister liquids. Though the passage and its side chambers were cold and empty, he felt that some other will was showing him glimpses of what they had been used for in days long past: workshops, classrooms, infirmaries and apothecaries. The tunnel ended abruptly at a broad balcony which overlooked a vast octagonal cavern. In the darkness Curillian could not discern much, but he held onto the rail of the balcony for fear of falling. Breathing hard, he was unsure what to do next, but then suddenly a great gust of air blew through the cavern. With its passing, a hundred torches were lit as if by magic, and suddenly the great chamber was revealed in all its glory.

Each of the eight walls were cut into a honeycomb of rock shelves. The shelves were full of manuscripts and scrolls, thousands upon thousands of them; tomes and volumes of all kinds, the collected knowledge of the League of Wizardry accumulated over long millennia. On the floor of the cavern were long tables set with chairs for study, but Curillian could see no means of getting to the higher books, no steps or ladders. Curillian's own library was impressive enough, but nothing compared to this. Every secret in the world might have been captured on parchment in this chamber, but no one was there to read them anymore. All was covered with a thick layer of dust, untouched for decades. He found himself suddenly filled with a fierce desire for erudition, to listen to the words of ancient masters and to be considered a loremaster himself. The names of every mountain, the number of feathers in an eagle's wing, the deepest teachings of Prélan – what could he not learn in this place?

With the light of the torches, Curillian could now see that spiralled stairwells led down from the balcony to the library's floor. He descended and traipsed across the floor, full of wonder. Gnawed with helpless curiosity, he forgot his business for a while and inspected the books. He could not make head nor tail of the runes on the cracked leather bindings, which were obscured by dust and spiders' webs. Yet when he reached out to touch one of the spines his hand leapt back as if burned, and another vision blazed into his mind, vicious as an angry bird of prey. He saw the scenes of a terrible and nameless battle in a frozen wasteland, of dying wizards and the air alive with bolts of fire and coils of mystical power. He heard infernal blasts, horrendous screeches and cries of pain so dreadful that he had to cower to the ground, covering his ears and shutting his eyes. The vision passed, and he straightened up to see an empty library again.

The silence was oppressive after the sudden sharp sounds of a faraway tragedy, and sadness hung in the air like a pall, impregnating the very fibres of the rock. His mind struggled to comprehend what terrible secrets he was being exposed to, but it seemed that a cataclysmic doom had befallen the League of Wizardry, reducing the once teeming mountain to an empty husk. With some extra sense he felt their pain and sorrow, even though he did not know the facts. He quickened his pace to get away from the oppression of it and exited the library by an archway in the far wall. He came into a triangular atrium with three passageways leading off from the three points. Drawn by what power he knew not, he entered into the passageway straight ahead of him, which led up wide, cold steps. As the library had been, so this staircase was dark and menacing. All that could be seen at first were endless rows of glowing runes, one at both sides of each step, ascending into blackness. Another pulse of magical energy throbbed through it. Curillian was thrown onto his back by the passing of what felt like a moving wall. Looking up from his fall, he saw that countless wall-sconces had been kindled to life so that the way up was now illuminated. This time a voice spoke audibly to accompany the striking change in his surroundings. Kulothiel was speaking to him from somewhere far above.

'Welcome Curillian, victor of the Tournament. Long have I waited to meet you. Ascend to my chamber, and we shall speak.'

Aching and weary, Curillian picked himself up and climbed the stairs. The sconces were filled with uniquely beautiful flames like dancing fountains of liquid gold, but the air was still hostile and coarse, in seeming contradiction to the sorcerer's welcome. He came to yet another cavern, smaller than the library yet still cavernous in its own right. This one was already lit by great wall-braziers whose light was conveyed to the furthest corners by a series of burnished mirrors. On a raised dais stood a vast table lined with dozens of ornate, gilded chairs. Curillian approached and saw that each one was a masterpiece of craftsmanship, the carving and embroidery far surpassing anything that mortal skill could produce, but the plush upholstery was moth-eaten and sunken, the gilt woodwork chipped and peeling. He ran his fingers over them, and through the deep covering of dust on the table top. From the centre of the great table issued a glowing light, as of blue flames kept perpetually alight. They emanated from an enamel hollow, about which was a golden band inset with runes he could not read. Kulothiel's voice spoke again, providing the wording.

"'*May Prélan grant us the wisdom to use His gift for the good of His people and for the glory of His name.*" The very words we lived by...'

Yet of Kulothiel himself there was no sign, so Curillian surmised that he must go on, penetrating further into the highest and most lordly parts of the mountain abode. His footsteps took him to a great archway crowned with a glowing halo of sapphires, in which was set a portal like no other. Spiralling ribs of glistening metal swirled from every edge to meet in the middle at an enormous blue diamond. It blazed with its own inner light, resembling the eternal flame on the table in colour and heat. Curillian could see no handle or knob, but when he brought his fingers close to the diamond it suddenly retracted and disappeared. As it did so, the spirals of metal unlocked and separated, gliding away from each other with the smoothness of oiled hinges. Without a sound they vanished into hidden recesses, allowing him to step through. No sooner had he done so than the same mechanism kicked into reverse. The spirals hissed shut, clasping around the diamond and locking the door securely behind the intruder.

Trapped, he found himself in a narrow circular space which was bathed in warm blue light. There was no way out other than the eerie portal behind him, but when he tried to open it again it would not budge. Fighting down panic, he looked around for some means of escape, but there was nothing. He was on a perfectly circular panel of flooring and above him was a gaping chimney of nothingness.

Suddenly the floor moved and he found himself shot upwards into empty space. Quite disorientated and full of terror, he lost his footing and sat in an ungainly heap as the disc whisked him upwards through the bluish shaft. Just as suddenly as it had started, the disc came to a silken stop at a platform which opened out from the top of the shaft. Giddy and feeling sick, Curillian staggered off the disc and onto what he hoped was less treacherous ground.

As he recovered, he saw one final staircase leading up into what seemed to be the very roof of Oron Amular. Stabbing through his waves of nausea was an overwhelming sense of power. The atmosphere swamped him like a blanket. It throbbed through his ears, dazzled his eyes and baffled his brain. It was a most extraordinary sensation that left him feeling like a spirit gliding through a pool of floating particles. His head swam, but instead of fighting the alien feelings, he allowed himself to be pulled upwards by the magnetism of what awaited at the top of the stairs.

Ever after he could remember very little of his time in that place, his memories being of an incredible variety of sensations, only blurry like a smudged collage. He ascended the stairs in a sort of daze. What he saw from the top took his breath away.

There, in all its eternal glory, lay the Pool of High Magic. He had never seen it before, but what else could it be? Of all the secret waters in the deep places of the world, there was surely none like this. All the legends spoke of it, a great pool at the very pinnacle of the Mountain, an energy source and the beating heart of the world's magic. And here it was, spread before his mortal feet. The pool dominated this topmost cavern, tranquil as a millpond and glowing with an ethereal light. Looking up, he saw that the gnarled ceiling and walls, which no hammer or chisel had ever touched, were bathed in the bluish radiance like some primordial grotto. He could well believe that only just above his head was the uttermost crown of Oron Amular. He shivered slightly. Although it was cold, it was nowhere near as cold as it should have been. Vitality seemed to exude from the pool as if power were constantly evaporating from an inexhaustible source and it warmed the otherwise frosty air, though it also made it heady and beguiling.

Entranced, he tottered towards the shore of the pool, treading close to where the limpid water lapped gently at a glistening slope of rock. Intensely curious, he leaned forward and peered into the depths, wondering how deep it was or where it all came from. He was amazed to see currents and eddies contorting the great body of water, as if its own power kept it constantly writhing in motion, and yet the surface was completely still, like a lid of crystal over a tempestuous receptacle.

'Do not fall in,' said a voice, just as he was beginning to lean dangerously far. It seemed both near and far away, quiet yet gaining strength in a long series of echoes. 'Only the staves of the wizards were ever dipped into the pool. Twice only in all its history have unfortunate souls fallen in: one never came out, his life-force consumed by the pool; the other was fished out almost immediately. Nevertheless, he emerged scarred but with superhuman strength, and much woe befell us before he was subdued.' Curillian jerked away from the pool and looked around for the source of the voice. For a while he could see nothing, but as he trod carefully around the edge of the pool and as his eyes adjusted to the strange light, he glimpsed a raised area beyond the pool's far edge. A brilliant object was shining there, like a sun veiled by gossamer clouds. He made his way slowly towards it, feeling very small and insignificant. He had never felt so completely immersed in the presence of Prélan, and it awed him to his core.

It seemed to take him forever to reach the other side of the pool. Not only was it bigger than it had first seemed, but there was also a ring of mysterious menhirs surrounding the pool like guardians. There were twelve of them, fashioned out of some smooth tapering stone, each set with a glistening rune. They radiated power no less than the water and he took care to give them a wide berth. Yet eventually he came to the foot of a svelte staircase, which led up to a dais nestled into the corner of the cavern. On the dais was a sculpture of an eagle, whose outspread wings bore a great shining orb. Far more luminous than the Tear of Mírianna in the lower cavern, it was impossible to look directly at. All the rest of the cavern slumbered in the pale gleam of the pool, but this area was lit up like moonlight enhanced a hundredfold. So dazzled was he by the orb that he could not see the further parts of the dais. Thus, it was only when Kulothiel stood up from his chair and moved in front of the great orb that Curillian could see him.

The king of the armists gasped. The figure standing before him was bent and aged, haggard and horribly scarred. The king's mind flashed back to the figure he had seen in the entrance chamber of the Mountain, when Kulothiel had revealed himself to the contestants, and the person before him could scarce have been more different. The proud and dignified mage-lord of unguessable power bore no resemblance to this shrunken apparition. He was equally unlike the mysterious stranger who had accosted him and Lancoir outside the Mountain, and different again from the benevolent old visage which had accompanied the invite to the Tournament. Kulothiel, it seemed, had many faces – but which was his true form?

The old man hobbled down the steps and came to stand before Curillian. He was so bent, and so utterly dependent on the staff he grasped, that it was impossible to tell what his real height had once been, but now his face was level with the king's shoulder. Reeling from shock and distaste, Curillian looked awkwardly down at him.

'Pity and contempt are in your eyes, O Curillian.' All power and authority was stripped from the voice. Up close, and without guise, it was thin, cracked and wheezy. 'Would you prefer it if I looked thus?' As he spoke, he changed before the king's eyes into the wise old grandfather from the invite. 'Or like this?' He changed again, becoming the tall, stern wizard-lord from the entrance chamber. Both forms faded, leaving the pitiable bent old man again. 'I am not as you expected, am I, king of the armists?' Curillian could find no response, but Kulothiel didn't need one. 'I am Kulothiel, and this is how I truly am now. Yes, Kulothiel, Head of the League of Wizardry and Keeper of the Mountain.' He trailed off into something like laughter which turned into a coughing fit. 'Alas, Curillian, we can none of us retain our vigour indefinitely. I yet possess the power to mask my decay, but all mortals must expire sooner or later, even I. But would you be so good as to climb the steps? Stand by me, I need to sit...'

With that he turned and climbed the steps with torturous difficulty. Following him beyond the immediate glare of the orb's brilliance, Curillian watched as he lowered himself slowly into an ornate carven chair with worn velvet upholstery. Beyond him was a dark window that seemed to have been cut into the very side of the Mountain. It looked out onto a black night, but he could imagine what a spectacular view it must command out over Kalimar. And for the first time since entering the Mountain, he could guess at the time of day – between dusk and dawn. How long had they been inside?

'Two whole days now,' announced Kulothiel, answering his unuttered question. 'That is what you were wondering, is it not? How long you've been here? Yes, the moon is already setting on the second night since you entered, and little do you guess it, but in that time you have climbed right up from the feet of the Mountain to its summit. Were you not dazzled by the orb, you would see the valleys and plains of Kalimar stretching away eastward. There is another window on the opposite side of the chamber which looks west.'

'How can I have climbed so high in just two days?' asked Curillian incredulously. 'It has taken me longer than that to scale peaks in the Carthaki Mountains, which are surely much smaller than this Mountain, and even on them I felt lightheaded from the altitude – why not here?'

'Little do you guess, O King, of the ways of this Mountain. Your own adrenaline in the heat of the Tournament brought you further and higher than you may have deemed, but you had only climbed a little more than half way up before you reached my levitator.' Curillian thought of the disc which had shot him up that impossibly high chimney to deposit him at the threshold of this topmost chamber. 'That brought you up more than ten thousand feet in just a few moments. Did you think it was just weariness that made you feel woozy when you stepped off? Believe me, but for the power of the pool you would collapse in minutes from the thinness of the air at this height, and even if you survived that, the cold would claim you shortly afterwards. You are on the roof of Astrom, Curillian, a place where life and death are separated only by Prélan's grace.'

A rush of tiredness swamped the king and he nearly fell. He steadied himself on the chair, but still his mind swam. This was a place of extremes that his mind could not even begin to comprehend.

'Do not feel ashamed, O King, for this is a place that has overawed many a first-time visitor. Many wizards came here only once in their whole career, and every one was affected just as you are now. Indeed, few of us ever dwelt here for long, for the very force of life in this atmosphere merely quickens the passing of normal existence.

Nowadays I only rarely come here, but it was meet that you should come here, the winner of the Tournament.'

'Why?' asked Curillian. 'What does it mean, to have won?' Kulothiel looked at him long and hard, as if weighing his ability to cope with what he had to say. If the rest of the Keeper's face was half in the grave, the eyes remained spirited and piercing. At last he spoke again, gesturing as he did so at the pool with a weary arm.

'Curillian, what you see here is the source of all good magic in the world. It is the place where Prélan's fingertip rests permanently on Astrom and the highest measure of His provision to us. You are breathing more rarefied air than is anywhere else in the world to be found. Alas, it is not as unique and singular as we all would have hoped. In the land of Urunmar there lies another such pool, high-crowned amidst ice and fire. Whether once it was it was as pure and holy as this pool we can never know, but it became a dread place, a channel of evil into the world. Just as this pool was the source of the wizards' power, so the other pool gave strength to the great enemy of the world.'

'Kurundar,' breathed Curillian.

'Verily, Kurundar. My nemesis. My opposite. My brother.' So, there was truth in the legend that the evil sorcerer was Kulothiel's twin. In a split second's vivid realisation, Curillian saw that the world's fate had, in large part, been governed by two men, both workers of magic, both deriving unnatural long-life from these pools, but where one was good the other was evil. Between them lay a contested world that had been fought over and menaced for three thousand years.

'Curillian,' Kulothiel went on, 'your spies and diplomats have sent back rumours that the north is troubled once more. I can tell you now that not only are they right, but that the situation is far worse than they suspect. Dark powers are on the move once again, some new and some old. For a third time, Kurundar will try and subjugate the world you know. Hendar, bulwark of the north, will soon be beset, and the Free Peoples are all threatened. Yet, just as the Pool of Dark Magic in Urunmar is the source of your great peril, so in this Pool of High Magic lies your salvation. That is why I have brought you here. So that you may understand your peril, but also so that you may know where your help comes from.'

Curillian reeled under the force of Kulothiel's words and tried to regain his footing in the conversation.

'But we thought that magic had already passed from the world, that we had entered a new age. I thought Kurundar perished in his defeat in the last war, that Roujeark was the only wizard left, if even he is...'

Kulothiel's tone became scathing. 'Perished? Did you see his slain body or witness his soul brought before Prélan for judgement? No... Kurundar escaped. Again. Twice now the Free Peoples have tried and failed to destroy him, and for their failure they must endure a third war. He has returned, and new devilry has been added to his power of old. As for Roujeark, he is certainly not the last wizard, for several others, curse them, survive in Kurundar's service. Nay, myself aside, Roujeark is the last *Godly* wizard, and I am not long for this world. That is why he was summoned to this Mountain, why you had to bring him here, do you not understand?'

Curillian remembered the voice of Prélan speaking to him in the courtyard of his palace back in Mariston, telling him to protect an unknown person and take him to Oron Amular. He had rightly guessed that Roujeark was that person, but little had he known just how important he was.

'So why am I here, and not he?' he asked at length, still trying to gather his wits.

'You are here, Curillian, son of Mirkan, because you won the Tournament. You are the answer to my prayers, the champion I have been seeking.' He paused, deliberating. 'Have you heard of The Oracle?' That name was just a legend to Curillian, a story from out of the mists of time telling how Prélan spoke in a special way to the Keeper of the Mountain. Whether it truly existed or not he could not say, still less what form it took. 'The Oracle is a mouthpiece of Prélan in this world. Forty years ago, its embodied form rose out of the pool and revealed to me that doom was near, for myself, for the League, and for the world. I passed on to my few remaining mages what it foretold about the coming of Roujeark, the last wizard, but I did not tell them what I believed had been spoken to me alone. I was told that the tools of doom had been found, that an unlooked-for ally would bring them forth. All I needed was the hands to wield them, and so Prélan decreed that I should hold a tournament to discover the chosen people. *This* is that tournament, and *you* are its winner. A great prize I have for you, but a great mission also.'

Curillian swore he could feel every single part of him alive at that moment, alert and tingling. His neck hairs stood on end, his hands quivered, his heart thumped and his mind raced. The weariness and the fog in his head were passing, and a fearful excitement was igniting in his veins. With his mind clearer, he asked another question.

'Is the prize for me alone? I did not win this Tournament alone and could not claim as much. Roujeark, Theonar, Lancoir, there are many others down there who contributed just as much as I.'

'My dear Curillian, how much I regret that we have not met until now. What an alliance we would have made in the days of our vigour. Truly, it is a sign of your fitness to be standing here that you display such humility. Other champions would have grasped the prize for themselves with no regard for others, and that is why the Tournament was arranged as it was, to bring forth a victor not only of the greatest strength but also of the soundest virtue. You are the champion given me by Prélan, and I give thanks for that. A prize awaits you, but not the only prize. Rewards await many of those you have named, and more besides, and just as there is more than one prize so there is more than one mission. The great task that lies ahead is too big for any one pair of shoulders, and so many have been assembled, and a few have been chosen. But it falls to you, O King, to see the overall picture, to have the full revelation. You will have the responsibility to guide and sustain all the winners in their various roles in a great undertaking.

'Kurundar threatens the whole world, and he is mightier than any nation alone. So, all the Free Peoples must unite against him. New weapons must be wielded; and new quests must be fulfilled to bring about his final destruction. Your forebear King Firwan fought in the Great Alliance that overthrew Kurundar in the First War, and in your youth the Silver Empire staved off his second onslaught; now a new coalition is needed to fight a Third War. Hendar, Aranar, Ciricen, Ithrill, and especially Maristonia, are all needed, or all of them will fall one by one.'

Curillian swallowed hard, the prospect of another war making him feel suddenly old. The moment of elation had passed; dread was creeping over him like a living thing. The last war had been so terrible – how could there be another? So many long years of toil and tears. The broad fields of Hendar had been tilled with blood, Ciricen had been engulfed in flames, Aranar was laid waste and the enemy had even shaken the ancient towers of Kalimar. The land of Maristonia might have been spared, but its sons, late come to the slaughter, were cut down in their tens of thousands. A hundred old memories of strife and loss passed through his mind, chilling his bones and oppressing his mind. Slowly he became aware of Kulothiel speaking again.

'Would you know of your competitors? Soon you will meet them again, but come now and see how they fared.' The old mage-lord gestured to the orb. Shielding his eyes at first, Curillian watched it grow dim enough to look at, and then he saw that pictures were moving through it like a conjured vision, one scene rapidly succeeding the last. Some of it seemed oddly familiar. There were the men of Hendar, the splendour of their armour dulled by soot and dust, their faces grimed and weary. They had fallen from a collapsing bridge and passed through a waterfall into a subterranean tunnel where terrible beasts lurked. Some of them died there before the rest struggled through tight holes into an icy compartment. There they had shivered and frozen nearly solid before the bishop, Nurvo, had solved the puzzle which unlocked the exit. Other riddles he had had to solve to save their lives from deadly perils. Killer bats had assailed them, and clouds of noisome darkness had choked them; flames had scorched them, and a long hall of nothingness had afflicted them with madness, from which they barely escaped in time. Now, led by Adhanor, the soiled, battered survivors were climbing the steps towards the wizard-guarded forcefield before the Tear of Mírianna.

Earl Culdon and his fur-clad Ciriciens had scaled a mighty wall that seemed to go on forever, before losing several of their number to a hail of great ice chunks. They had been hunted by giant serpents in a horrible maze and become trapped in a spinning cylinder where they had been hurtled round and round, half to death. Dark assassins had stalked their steps and giant pulverising levers had nearly pummelled them as they issued across a high and windswept bridge of crumbling masonry. They were now climbing by a different route up to the habitable parts.

The men of Aranar had braved many dangers and overcome many problems before meeting the armists in the firepit where the skeletons had attacked. The rest of their journey he knew first-hand, but now he saw the grisly fate that overtook the villainous free-riders who had been led to the Mountain under duress by Elrinde and the elves of Ithrill. Raspald Kin-slayer, their leader, had been stabbed by Elrinde on a high precipice and cast into an abyss at the roots of the Mountain. Benek Thunder-Eye had lost his other eye and been condemned to wander lost, blind and alone in the bowels of the Mountain. Sampa the Smooth, Vampana, Sceant and Lucask Lightfoot, all had been slain in dreadful ways as Elrinde, Astacar and Linvion took advantage of the Tournament's imaginative opportunities – almost as if they knew of Kulothiel's secret traps and could spring them on others. Yet other free-riders of Aranar, knights errant and soldiers of fortune, had survived the wrath of the elves and somehow stayed alive through all of the Tournament's nightmarish dangers. In ones, twos and small groups they now groped towards the same destination as the men of Hendar and Ciricen.

Curillian kept watching and saw the dark-skinned Alanai swimming across a great subterranean lake before being washed over a tall waterfall and subjected to boiling rapids full of rocks. They had fashioned a raft and braved extremes of heat and cold, as well as the attacks of crocodiles and sightless cave monsters. Some had perished as the raft melted in waters turned acidic, but the rest had gotten away to walk down wearisomely long tunnels infested with rats. They, too, drew near.

The dwarves had walked through beguiling lights and sorcerous visions to do battle with fire-breathing salamanders. Withstanding the flames, they had toiled on only to be crushed beneath fallen rocks. A remnant had burrowed clear and laboured mightily to clear a blocked tunnel. Using long-honed skills and every last ounce of resolve, they had made a way for themselves, coming up to the Tear by yet another path.

'Even as you struggled up your own road,' Kulothiel commented, 'the others trod paths of their own, for this Tournament had many ways. The challenges were different, but the danger was the same. As you can see, you came further and faster than any of them, through a mixture of luck, skill and bravery. And a little pinch of the bloody-minded refusal to be defeated that has been the leaven in your ancestors' bread. That helped.'

Then, the visions sped up, and Curillian watched the different groups converge in the habitable parts, so fast that it happened in a few heartbeats. Exhausted and bloodied, they slumped down to rest. For the moment they were too weary to wonder what would happen next. He watched the rest of his own party join the other groups near the Map Chamber. Together they discovered tables of food and pitchers of wine in an anteroom. Curillian glanced at Kulothiel – evidently the Keeper had made provision for famished contestants whose own food had long since been consumed or lost. Suddenly his own stomach growled long and deep, as if stirred by the sight of food, and his own long-ignored hunger flared up. Looking again at his companion, Kulothiel did not meet his eye, but with a gentle gesture of his hand he pushed a laden plate towards the king.

Curillian fell eagerly upon the food, quite forgetful of his own dignity and his exalted surroundings. For a while the two of them watched the scene in silence. As they did so Curillian continued to eat, refusing nothing that was on offer. Within the orb, his friends and rivals alike were also refreshed, and some among them took advantage of the lull to bind up injured limbs and staunch bleeding wounds. As some of them ate and some of them rested, others returned to the long hall where the tapestries of history were hung.

Curillian was vividly reminded of the newest section, still being added to, and his question came back to him.

'The tapestry of history…how…we saw some of these things… though they had only just have happened. How can that be…?'

'Verily, the story of Astrom is kept and recorded in Oron Amular,' Kulothiel answered.

'But we watched it growing before our eyes, as if it were alive,' Curillian persisted. 'Roujeark thought that there must be a magical pen somewhere, and that you were up here, dictating it all.' Kulothiel smiled.

'Yes, yes, the pen in the Keeper's Chamber writes in real time. No hand directs it but the hand of Prélan alone, for it is His story that it records. With it, magical threads are woven upon bare rock, continuing the story of this world that began in the dawn of time, starting with my original predecessor: Avatar, Eldest of all. No, the tapestries are no work of mine, though I study them often and learn much thereby. For things nearer at hand, I have other means of gathering news. I have eyes, O King, in every nook and hollow of this Mountain, and what they see is conveyed to this orb, another of the Keeper's heirlooms. Very useful, and with it I have followed each of you in your progress. I felt sure you would overcome the lake monster, but the spiked ceiling was nearly the end of you. But for Roujeark you would all have perished in the lava, where several unfortunate rogues of Aranese blood met their demise. And in the upper chambers you had some rather timely help, but we'll not speak of that. Here you are.'

While the old wizard was still speaking, Curillian glanced back at the orb in time to see elves ascend to the higher levels with much less trouble than the others. This was not Elrinde and his two Ithrillian companions, but the deputation from Kalimar, representing each of the three kindreds. Tall sombre elves all, from the city, the sea and the forest. He watched them ascend right to the Council Chamber with its eternal flame and hold counsel with Kulothiel. Looking back at the wizard, he glimpsed a faint look of irritation quickly smothered in the other's face.

'My neighbours, O King, the ambassadors of Paeyeir, Marindel and Therenmar. They are below us even now. They came not to compete, but to consult with me. Whether that which they heard was to their liking, who knows? Yet I think you will not have much help from King Lithan in the war that is coming, except perhaps once.'

Curillian watched as Kulothiel raised himself painfully from his throne.

'Walk with me, King of Mariston,' the wizard commanded. Curillian went slowly back alongside the pool, gently assisting his enigmatic host.

'Where are we going?'

'Unless you wish to stay here until the magic quite overcomes you, then we must finish our talk elsewhere. Come, I know just the place.'

In what seemed like an eternity they plodded back to the steps which had brought Curillian up to the pool. Just before they descended, he turned and look back, regret tugging on his heart. Never again would he behold such otherworldly beauty. Kulothiel plucked impatiently at his mailed sleeve.

'Come, Curillian, there is still greater beauty in the life that follows death. Do not linger overlong.'

With that he guided him back onto the strange platform in its blue-lit shaft, what Kulothiel called his Levitator. Kulothiel tottered on after Curillian and twisted a ringed finger in a curious looking panel that the king had not noticed before. Nothing happened. Curillian looked expectantly at the mage, who had closed his eyes as if sleeping where he stood. Suddenly he opened them again, smiled mischievously, and an instant later they were whisked off. They flew through the air with such velocity that Curillian's stomach rose right into his throat. His senses were scrambled, but he felt sure that they weren't going straight down the whole time, instead shifting directions through unseen passages of various orientations.

His suspicions were confirmed when they at last came to a halt and a hidden door rose, allowing them out into a chamber which was not the one Curillian had left. Somehow they had come to the map chamber, that great cavern filled with its wonderful living map. They had stumbled across it after walking down the corridor of tapestried history and before fighting past the giant guardians of the gatehouse chamber. Now Curillian beheld it again, awed anew. He had not noticed before the hidden portal through which they had stepped, so captivated had he been by the marvel at his feet. Kulothiel lingered on a platform above, letting the armist king go down alone. Curillian was lost in reverie when suddenly the lamps in the chamber were doused, leaving just one part of the map illuminated – a singularly lofty peak in Kalimar. Kulothiel spoke in a professorial voice which seemed to swirl around him.

'We are here, Oron Amular. And this is your home.' The Mountain went dark and another part of the map was lit up, showing distant Mariston. 'Maristonia, just one of the free realms. Here are the others: Aranar, Ithrill, Hendar and Ciricen.' As he spoke, each country in turn was lit up, then all together. 'The lands of the Free Peoples… all menaced by the north, by Urunmar.' The south of Astrom was cast in shadow whilst Urunmar took the limelight, only now the map seemed to come truly alive, as the sounds of gathering war thrummed in his ears and vivid, lifelike characters moved across the map. 'Kurundar has gathered yet another army. Orcs and trolls bred in the mountains of the north and their northern allies on the coasts of Urunmar. But this time, Kurundar has meddled with arts and powers darker still. He has opened a portal to the underworld and recruited the mercenaries of hell. The great Fire-demon is still trapped down there, where Avatar cast him, but lesser demons have escaped and come to swell Kurundar's strength; foes such as have never been seen since the Great Wars of ancient Kalimar, immortal and terrible.' As the vivid pictures crawled across the landscape, massing for an attack on the south, demonic faces reared up out of the map as if to attack the armist king.

'I do not know how much Kurundar controls them, but I suspect the Great Enemy is now using him as a puppet to prepare the way for him. One thing is certain. They are allied against us, both bent on our complete and utter destruction. Kurundar has come close to that goal twice before, but now he believes he finally has the power to achieve it. Verily, even now his forces are mustering, ready to invade south.' In the map, an innumerable host was accumulating in the narrow base of Urunmar, where that land of mountainous winter was joined to Astrom like an ugly head to a body. In between lay the neck-like isthmus of the Haunted Pass – the time-honoured corridor of invasion – a bleak rocky strip of land long made dreadful by the passage and abiding of evil. Through its centre, like a rotten gullet, ran a crooked canyon, so twisted and filth-ridden that none but the emissaries of evil would use it. Through this haunted highway the soldiery of Kurundar was poised to pour.

Now Urunmar faded again, and the light moved south to the northern part of Hendar, whose broad flanks tapered towards the neck of the isthmus. The Guard Hills of that border-country were festooned with fortresses which were now illuminated in turn by Kulothiel's unseen touch.

'Curillian, whether in a year, two years, or ten, Kurundar's demon-led hordes will come south, and the Guard Hill forts will be overrun.' Swathes of flame swamped the fair rolling uplands of Hendar. 'So too, Ciricen. This time you don't have the mighty legions of the Silver Empire to slow their advance – you will hardly have time to react before Nalator, bastion of the north, is besieged.' Nalator was one of the five dukedoms that made up Hendar, and the city of the same name was the greatest fortified city in the north, a place to rival Mariston. Kulothiel continued to demonstrate the likely narrative of the coming war in visual form as he spoke, with coloured lines, warlike figurines and moving colours.

'Lancearon will march from Ithrill with what strength he has left, and you must come north with all the strength Maristonia can offer.'

'Just Lancearon and myself?' Curillian asked.

'No, the Hendarians will be in the midst of the fight, as ever, and you must persuade the clans of Aranar to leave off their bickering and ride north also. Other help you may have, some unlooked-for, but do not count on Ciricen or Kalimar, for they will be unable or unwilling to give it. You must get to Nalator as soon after the outbreak of war as you can. If Nalator falls, all will be lost. Kurundar will seek to drive a wedge between you, coming from the southeast, and Lancearon, coming from the southwest. If you cannot unite, you will be overwhelmed piecemeal. Only Nalator has the strength to hold out long enough for your forces to come together. Nalator will draw the enemy like flies to a corpse, for there will be something there that they seek.'

'What do they seek?'

'This.' Kulothiel's voice gained still more in power and fervour. All the lights dimmed now except one, which illuminated Kulothiel.

He was standing at a stone font which Curillian had not noticed before, and something he could not see was in his hands.

'Power Unimaginable.'

Curillian strained his eyes forward, but he could not see in the gloom what Kulothiel held.

'Patience, Curillian, you will see in due time. Here, in my hands, lie the prizes of the Tournament. The three greatest are for you, one for each of you.' Curillian thought he had misheard.

'What three? I'm the only one here.' Even as his voice echoed around the dark chamber, his skin prickled to tell him it was not so. Slowly, from the shadows at the edge of the chamber, two figures stepped. Roujeark looked quite shaken, as if recovering from a shock. Theonar loomed over him like a well-groomed tree, serenity in his handsome face. Curillian gaped at them. He had left them in the amphitheatre chamber, far away, and yet here they were.

'How did you get here?' he asked. Theonar answered for them both.

'The Keeper summoned us here. While you were gone, he provided a road hidden from the others.'

'While I was gone? How long was I up there?' He looked for an answer in Kulothiel's face, but the old wizard was inscrutable. Suddenly though, his questions did not seem so important, as his eyes and mind were drawn back to the items held in the stone font. A deep solemnity was in the air as Kulothiel beckoned them all forwards.

'King Curillian, Sir Theonar, Roujeark, son of Dubarnik,' the Keeper addressed them. 'You have each contributed to your success here in my Tournament. Sir Theonar, you kept your comrades from Aranar alive until they joined the armists, you organised the escape from the lake of lava, you uncovered the password which opened the way into the Chamber of the Tear, you unlocked the gates guarded by the stone giants, and you helped get the stranded Maristonians across the chasm where your lord abandoned you.

'Roujeark, despite being the youngest and least experienced fighter here, you showed courage at every turn and displayed great resourcefulness under pressure. You outpaced the collapsing ceiling, you solved the rock-puzzle which doomed the great squid, you destroyed the undead attackers, you got behind the forcefield barrier, and you risked your life in going to Curillian's aid against the ten jet warriors.

'Curillian, you thought of the escape route when the spikes nearly crushed your party from above and below, you confronted the jet warriors alone when everyone else was rooted with fear; you led your small party with courage, you guided them through the treacherous course, and you overcame your very self in combat with the final guardian. You reached the finish line before all others and won the Tournament.

'You three have proved yourselves above all the others, and thus showed yourselves to be Prélan's anointed. I was told how I would know you, and now I see you revealed. Prélan calls you to save His people.' He paused. An eternity of silence seemed to press in on them. At last the Keeper spoke again. 'To each of you a task is given, and to each of you a tool is given. Behold your prizes.' With that he lifted his arms and a great light filled the chamber. When its radiance receded, they saw that he was holding a glowing object.

'Sir Theonar.' Kulothiel beckoned the tall Aranese knight forward first. 'To you is assigned the Amulet of Avatar.' Curillian gasped – had he heard aright? From over Theonar's outstretched arm he could see a golden device, shaped like a half-star and hanging from an ornate chain. The links were all tiny gilt oblongs with concave ends through which ran a shimmering wire. Ancient power seemed to ripple across the magnificent artefact and seep out of it into the air around them.

'This is the great treasure and weapon of Avatar, the Elder-King. As well you know, with it he cast down the Fire-demon in the Great Wars and spellbound him in the underworld, deferring doom for another day. When he retired to the Triumblen Isles, he bequeathed it to his son, Avarone, with the charge of watching over it, lest the Fire-demon stir again. Each elder son of the House of Avatar, the glorious princes and kings of Kalimar, has borne this amulet in turn, until Avalar was slain for it. Lithan's grandfather fell far from home and the amulet was broken in two pieces, both lost to the knowledge of the League for long ages.

'This half was recovered but recently from the hoard of the last dragon and came into my possession. I entrust it to you. Not only must you guard it, but you must also find the other half and take it to safety. On their own, each piece can do nothing but entrance the beholder; together they become the greatest power source the world has ever known. In it is all of Avatar's strength and power of old, all the virtue he derived from Prélan as His eldest child. That same power which threw down the Fire-demon and incarcerated him could also be used to set him free. As long as it is in the world, it is a menace to the Free Peoples. So, you must take it away, from under the very nose of the enemy, and deliver it to Avatar. The Elder-King now dwells on an enchanted isle removed from mortal sight, but the bearer of his amulet will be able to reach him. Yet only with this one half can you find the lost half, and so you must bear it into the greatest danger before you can redeem it.'

Theonar took hold of the amulet and drew it to his breast. He clasped it against his breast and hung his head in silent prayer. Then he looped it over his neck and hid it beneath his tunic and armour. He stepped down and to one side. Next, Kulothiel looked to Roujeark.

'Roujeark, wanderer from afar, you have been called from your humble home to do a deed beyond the power of anyone else. With the noble blood of long-lost ancestors in your veins, you must rise up and fulfil the great gift given to your family. Your father had but the dying embers of magic in his soul, but you have it a hundredfold, more so than any of your forebears. You will be the last wizard after me, and so you have been brought here to be trained. Prélan has called you forth because a great task awaits that is beyond my strength. The Pool of Dark Magic must be destroyed forever, never again to blight the unhappy world. While Sir Theonar undertakes his labour, the throbbing heart of Kurundar's stronghold must be laid bare and emptied, or else the rescue and removal of the amulet will count for nothing. With this Star-shard you will accomplish this deed.' He held forth a glittering rock in his hand and Roujeark stepped forward to take it. Although no larger than an arrowhead, it shone like a heavenly jewel, for its light and wondrous pattern was like no earthly rock. 'Take this shard to Oron Cavardul, cast it into the Pool of Dark Magic, and all its foul waters will be drained. The shard came from Prélan, and to Him it will return once it has removed a great evil from the world.'

Roujeark gazed down at the great jewel in awe, his face bathed in its light. Curillian was no less stunned. He felt the ground had been shaken beneath his feet as he heard his friends assigned such staggering quests. Kulothiel seemed to be a merchant of dreams, a trader in the impossible, and Curillian's already reeling mind blanched as it tried to contemplate what undertaking he himself would be called to. Half-expectant, half-afraid, he looked at Kulothiel, awaiting his turn.

'Curillian,' said the old wizard, 'no less a mission is set before you than the defence of the world. Your prizes are here, but you must wait a while longer for them. Others must be dealt with first.' Curillian's heart lurched, wondering what was coming next. He held the wizard's weary eye, looking full in his haggard face, and then had to turn away as a blinding flash of light seared in front of him.

XIX
Reluctant Pupils

WHEN He was able to open his eyes again, shielding them with his arm, he saw that Kulothiel had been transformed into the stern mage-lord once more, standing erect and grave of face. Before he had time to wonder why, he heard noises from behind him. Many people had come into the chamber. Turning, he saw contestants of every race approaching the map-floor. Man, elf and dwarf, they all looked stunned, bearing the same expression Roujeark had shown a few moments before. Where they had come from, none could say, but here they were, all the surviving contestants.

There were the battered and bloodied figures he had seen in Kulothiel's orb: Elrinde and his elven comrades and King Adhanor at the head of his Hendarians. There were his armist comrades: Andil, Caréysin, Lionenn, Findor, Antaya and Aleinus. With them came Southilar and his party, and beside them were the grim-faced Ciriciens. Steel-clad dwarves stalked into the chamber, and there also were the swarthy southerners and many a free-rider from Aranar. All were assembled again, as they had been at the start, just reduced in number. They all looked exhausted, but they were not too weary to greet each other with hostility and suspicion. Where had these others come from? Why did they look so much better off, when they themselves had gone through hell? Wild questions broke out and angry accusations were made. Yet few of them had actually encountered each other during the Tournament, so their rancour was overtaken by curiosity. They turned their eyes and their anger on the statuesque figure of Kulothiel on the raised platform.

'There he is, the wizard!'

'He's responsible for all this, it's on his head!'

'Come down, conjuror, and explain yourself!'

All the while Kulothiel had been waiting patiently, but now he stirred and lifted up his arms, staff held aloft.

'HEAR ME!' he cried, and every ear was seized, willing or no. A peel of thunder smote the chamber, silencing all the words which sprang to various lips, and bolts of light crackled over the wizard's head.

'Hear me!' Kulothiel cried again, though less insistently now that he had their attention. 'Elves, dwarves, armists and mortals, kings and knights and warriors, brave contestants all. Forget the trials behind you, lay aside your petty quarrels and hearken to me. The Tournament is over, and you, the survivors, have been summoned here for a purpose.' All were captivated by the sight of a mage-lord in his majesty, wielding magic before their waking eyes. Every doubting heart was convinced and every angry thought was forgotten. Wonder overcame all else. Kulothiel went on.

'Look about you, my lords.' At his bidding, they turned to look at each other. During the wizard's outburst, each company had subconsciously arrayed themselves in that part of the map which represented their home, and now they stood in their relative positions. 'All the great nations and principalities of the free world are here assembled. Never before has a company of such mixed creed and colour been convened, not even in the days of the Great Alliance. Those not here are of small significance in the coming struggle. Look at each other, you who are neighbours, who have been allies and adversaries by turns down the long centuries. Look at each other now and see friends, for so you are. You have a common bond of civilisation, a mutual belief in freedom, a shared revilement of true evil. Think no more of past grievances, but consider how much you share in common reverence.'

The various groups and parties studied each other reluctantly, weighing up the wizard's words with dubious expressions. At Curillian's bidding they had kept their peace in the camp outside the Mountain, and now the wizard seemed to be asking the same of them. They had been expecting to fight each other once inside, but they had barely crossed paths, and now they found they were too weary to cause trouble. Their leaders exchanged glances, but it was Earl Culdon of Ciricen who spoke out.

'All right wizard, we're listening. Speak your piece.' Kulothiel turned a stern face on him, but his eyes were glittering with amusement at the impudence.

'Then listen well, man of Ciricen, and all you others. Events in the world outside hurry on to great deeds, so let us conclude our business here with no delay. Friends, prizes I have for you, and words of counsel. Accept the one only if you are willing to receive the other.' He waited, holding the eye of each chieftain in turn, until they had all nodded their assent.

'In the Tournament just finished, many here have displayed extraordinary skill and courage. In token of this, I have many prizes to award. They are as varied as the acts of valour which earned them and each suited to the recipient's future needs. Step forward first, Anthab the Undubbed.'

It was a name none of them had expected, and indeed, which few of them even knew. The man who stepped forward was big and scarred, with livid branding marks on both cheeks. He was dressed in Aranese fashion, though he was ragged and wayworn.

Theonar, who stood by Roujeark, leaned down discreetly and murmured in his ear, 'An Undubbed is a knight stripped of rank and position for some great crime. They are lawless outcasts, shunned and despised.'

Kulothiel told them more. 'Anthab, you came here a hunted man, a soldier of fortune. You came here with nothing to lose, seeking redemption from the shame you bear. Instead of the death which you several times cheated, you live, and shall be exonerated for the gallantry you have shown, for the lives you have saved. Let your dishonour be cast off; take this ring as a symbol of your pardon.' Grateful and abashed, the big man lumbered forward and took the proffered ring. Churlishly, Southilar growled from out of the company.

'Such a one will never find employ in my Clan.' Kulothiel eyed the Jeantar coldly, but addressed the prize-winner.

'No longer are you a mercenary, but a man with a mission, and perhaps you will find some other lord with a readier heart.' Kulothiel did not explain what his mission was, so Anthab turned and walked away, confused but appreciative. Kulothiel moved on speedily.

'Next I call your compatriot, Jeannor, he who is called Hoofbeam. The speed you have shown throughout this Tournament is truly remarkable, fleetness of foot and of mind. Such a one will be of great service as a messenger when desperate haste is needed. In token of this, take these shoes for your horse, Rowardo. Never again will he need to be reshod, and never again will he tire. He shall run quicker than ever, outflying even the arrows of the enemy. Take them, and ride to good fortune.' Jeannor, a rough-clad but baby-faced man, stepped forward eagerly and received his prize. He did not share the limelight for long though, since Kulothiel swiftly called the next recipient forward.

'Lord Hoth, step forward.' All eyes turned to the leader of the dwarves, who trudged into the limelight. He was a burly figure, made even larger by the suit of heavy armour that he wore as if it were a thin cloak. The steel was scorched and fire-blackened, his face smeared with soot and his plaited beard singed, but he still stood proudly, using his great double-headed battle-axe like a walking stick. 'You represent Carthak, the realm of the dwarves, do you not?' Kulothiel asked him.

'Aye,' the dwarf affirmed. 'Hoth, son of Hoth, of the house of Kharad, I am. My lord, Arthond IV, King of Carthak, has bidden me be present and know what passes.' Roujeark stared in fascination. Like every other child of the Carthaki Mountains, he had heard the tales of the fabulous underground city for which the range was named. Yet neither he nor most armists had ever seen a live dwarf, for they surfaced seldom nowadays. Great indeed must the dwarf-king's curiosity have been for him to send a champion to this Tournament.

'And to get here,' Kulothiel told him, 'you passed through fire which would have destroyed any other competitor. Great is the hardihood of the sons of Carthak, and great is the skill of their smiths. But ahead of you lies fire hotter than any you have known. If you are to emerge unscathed, then you must suitably attired. My gift to you is new armour.' The wizard lifted up a suit of sleek metal, tailored to encase the whole body. It shimmered in the light, its close-woven links gleaming. Hoth took the prize and hefted it doubtfully. It looked ludicrously flimsy next to the heavy plates he already wore, but Kulothiel explained. 'Its mail is of star-steel, as light as feathers and as hard as dragonhide. The mail is woven onto a flameproof lining which turns heat and foils flame. In it, you will never burn.

See, here are hose, gloves and a masked helmet to match. Take an old man's advice…don't wait too long to put it on.'

Hoth took the armour back to his place, where his companions gathered round to examine it with interest. As they conversed in low, gruff whispers, Kulothiel called another forward to the font.

'Culdon, Earl of Centaur, it seems you too are in need of armour. You've come through many scrapes with as many wounds. If I don't equip you properly, you will never survive the skirmishes ahead of you. You will fight in tight places and rarely in the open. For you too I have prepared armour, star-steel mail which will cheat the darts of evil and the assassin's dagger. But be alert, and always on your guard.' Culdon muttered thanks, and looked ready to speak further, but Kulothiel ignored him.

'Next, I summon Adhanor, King of Hendar.' The young sovereign stepped forward, armour dented but pride redoubled. 'No weapon have I for you, but a limitless supply of what you need.' A look of disappointment passed over the handsome face when all that Kulothiel poured into his outstretched palm was a single gold coin. 'Lord King, if the coffers of the treasury which you have inherited are less full than you would like, then fear not. This is a coin that when spent departs not. It is given so that you shall have no lack, for you are to be the treasury of a great endeavour. If Hendar's full strength is to be nurtured, then armies must be recruited and strong places made fast. But beware, young monarch: if you are tempted to spend this coin on unworthy things, you will find that it does not stretch so far.' Bemused, Adhanor returned to his compatriots, clasping the coin close.

Southilar, hoping to catch the wizard's eye, was again disappointed when a most unusual name was uttered next.

'Where is Parthir?' Kulothiel asked. From the shadows at the cavern's far side, a dark figure stirred. From the southernmost extremity of Astrom, he strode into the light. If he was surprised to be called upon, then the others were more so. As he walked past them warily, they eyed him coldly and murmured disapprovingly.

'Savage...'

'Pirate scum...'

'No good can come from Lurallan...'

'A barbarian like this has no place here...'

Yet Roujeark noticed how the man held firm and kept on despite the abuse on either side. There was a nobility in his olivine features, a hawk-like hauteur. He was indeed dressed like a pirate and armed for brigandage, but Roujeark sensed a cultivation to him that softened his buccaneering apparel. Kulothiel, too, took no notice of the comments of the more northerly nations, but beckoned the Alanai chieftain to the font. From the gift-giving font, he produced a most curious item. A garnet-studded shoulder-belt, hung with half a dozen bulging skins.

'Parthir of Raduthon, I have a prize here fitting for a seaman such as yourself, an apt reward for the deft touch you have shown on the waters barring your way in this Mountain. Keep these skins well, for in them is a substance like no other. Simultaneously a propellant and a caulking agent, this matter will give a sheen to your vessel that even the spirits of the ocean will covet. Caulk your ship with this and no craft upon the waves will be able to vie with you. Yet like Jeannor on land, this gift is given for the good of others, so that the beleaguered may have reinforcements sped to them.' Raduthon bowed his head reverently and accepted the strange gift. As he stepped away, a voice of dissent was raised from among the crowd.

'Armour for the Ciriciens and pardons for the felons of Aranar I can accept, but are we to stand by and watch a marauding corsair rewarded?' It was Xavion, companion of Adhanor who spoke. Outrage and indignation were in his face, and several others voiced agreement. The corsairs of Lurallan, though mainly the ancestral enemies of Maristonia, were loathed by all. 'What has this sea-scum done to warrant such a gift?'

'More than you,' Elrinde the elf answered Xavion mildly, but with an edge of scorn in his voice. Xavion choked on his rage but could find no words. Although he was a man unused to swallowing his pride, the elven warlord's reputation and the look in his eye dissuaded the young Hendarian noble from pursuing the matter further. Ignoring the ongoing consternation, Curillian broke ranks and walked through the men of Aranar towards the font. He confronted Parthir.

'I have more cause to hate this man than any of you,' he announced loudly to the gathered contestants. 'The desert tribes and corsairs of Lurallan have done great injury to my realm and people down the centuries.' Parthir looked like he expected a fight, one he knew he would lose, but nevertheless he braced himself and stood defiant before the armist king. Yet Curillian moved no hand to his sword hilt. Still talking to the hall, half over his shoulder, he went on.

'And yet Raduthon is a nobler city-state than some in the south. Urundair and Caulrir are hives of villainy and frequented by all manner of wave-scum; Cavard is a half-starved desert outpost; Arthon and Mouraxar are inhabited by snake-charmers and devil-worshippers. By comparison the Raduthites are cultured men, a race of merchant-warriors. They are more like to us armists in taste and temperament than any of the others.' Curillian looked Parthir straight in the eye. He held out his hand. 'And I would welcome them into the fold of the Free Peoples, since there are greater enemies at hand.' The last he said loud enough for all to hear, but then he spoke softly just to Parthir.

'You can either cut off my sword-hand or make a better friend than you deserve. Choose.' Parthir looked at him a long moment, trying to discern a trick. Finding none, he clasped Curillian's paler hand. Wordlessly they walked back from the font together, and in the sudden silence everyone heard Caiasan's stage-whisper.

'Bloody hell. Armists and barbarians making friends. *Now* I know something strange is afoot.'

When Curillian and Parthir reached the men of Aranar, Southilar planted himself squarely in their way, arms folded. The Jeantar towered over both of them. He said no word, but disgust was stamped across his frowning face.

'Get out of the way, Southilar,' Curillian told him. Southilar stayed where he was, the truculence deepening on his face.

Curillian dropped his hand to his sword hilt. 'I won't ask again.'

Slowly, reluctantly, Southilar moved to one side. The unlikely friends resumed their places, and the silence was replaced by a ripple of murmurs that spread throughout the cavern. A new figure stood forward to raise his voice above them. It was Nurvo, the mysterious Hendarian bishop. He was rather less well-polished than before the Tournament, but he still had an air of confidence and charm. He appeared to relish the chance to speak directly to Kulothiel.

'Well, my Lord Keeper, we're all friends together it seems. Have you other prizes to give?'

Roujeark felt sure the suave prelate wouldn't have minded one himself, or, better yet, the chance to rummage around the old wizards' workshops for a few days, but the Mage-lord answered his question at face value.

'I have indeed. Lord Elrinde of Ithrill.' The elf looked up sharply, and Roujeark could not tell whether he seemed surprised by the call or not. 'A message I have for your master, Lancearon. Will you hear it?' The Hendarians stiffened at the mention of their erstwhile conqueror, but held their tongues. For his part, Elrinde looked half-eager, half-hesitant, a sudden dilemma breaking through his cool façade. At length he nodded, then he and his two compatriots left the chamber. How they knew where to go, Roujeark knew not, but they left behind them an atmosphere of awkward curiosity.

'There are four more prizes,' Kulothiel announced, 'all of them weapons, and all reserved for the valiant armists who reached the finish line before all others.' His eyes rested on the Maristonian contingent, and slowly all their neighbours turned to look at them, faces full of mingled jealously and admiration. 'Step forward, Lionenn the Konenaire; step forward, Caréysin the Archer; step forward, Lancoir of Thainen's Order; step forward Curillian, king of the armists.' Curillian led his small band forward, clear of the throng. Roujeark remained behind with Findor, Andil, Antaya and Aleinus. No one else would know that he too had been given a prize, nor Theonar, he felt quite sure. He watched as his comrades all took a knee, and as Kulothiel called them by name.

'Lionenn, the mace is the symbol of your ancient order, and with them your predecessors have fought since before even I walked the world. Do me the honour of laying aside your own mace, and taking this new one instead.' The wizard held forth a mighty mace, a great iron-bound club with vicious metal spikes all down its length. 'You will not find a better, for the blow struck with this mace has power to lay low trolls and demons. It is a demonbane. It has been dipped in my pool, so that you will strike with the power of ten armists.'

'Caréysin, your unerring accuracy with the bow is no small part of why your company managed to win through. Such skill deserves deadlier arrows with which to shoot, for the targets you will one day aim at shall not be stopped by mere steel. Thus, I have prepared for you star-steel arrows: their shafts are unbreakable and their tips will punch through any armour. They too are a demonbane, but I have only twelve to give, so use them wisely.'

'Lancoir the Stalwart, it is my pleasure to honour and arm a Knight of Thainen. For you I have prepared this demonbane dagger. It is of a kind with the mace and the arrowheads, forged of star-steel, and imbued with the power of the pool. Alone among all the arms of Astrom, these weapons can slay demons. Alike in fashion, they are to be used in concert, for the greater good. Let the bearer of this dagger never depart from his king, lest evil befall.' As Lancoir returned to his place, Kulothiel addressed them all.

'Armists, bear these weapons to good fortune, and may the blessings of Prélan Almighty go with you.' Dismissed, the armist prize-winners took their trophies back to the Maristonian part of the map.

Curillian alone was left. He had remained kneeling, head bowed, during the whole ceremony. Now Kulothiel called him last of all. Every eye was on him, as was a light, which fell suddenly around him, whilst all else was plunged into shadow.

'Last of all I summon Curillian, son of Mirkan, King of Maristonia, bravest of the brave. You are the winner of the Tournament. To you falls a double prize, and a great responsibility. Receive these mighty heirlooms, long set aside in waiting for this hour. Firstly, a demonbane dagger, the twin of Lancoir's, to be your weapon when evil presses close. And secondly, this amulet is a Soul-Shield. The wearer shall confound the mightiest servants of the enemy and bring new heart to those who flag. Let its virtue be ever about your neck, to put hope in your heart and fire in your belly.' Kulothiel spoke commandingly out of the darkness, addressing the assembled lords.

'My lords...' The wizard stepped into the spotlight so that all could see him hold Curillian's arm aloft. '...Behold your victor.' Curillian had always been respected, even feared, but in that moment, he was held in awe by his peers. They gaped at him, for the amulet flashed at his breast and he seemed to have grown suddenly taller. No one missed the significance of the display. Here was the wizard's champion, a warrior anointed for battle. But Kulothiel was not done. His final words he spoke in a ringing voice that roused them all to unprecedented fervour and unity.

'The Tournament is over, the prizes have been given. Power Unimaginable is now bestowed in your hands, but hear now the true purpose for which you have been assembled. Kurundar has arisen again in the north, his strength of old fully regrown and his hatred redoubled. What your forefathers faced has returned to plague your days, only now the sorcerer is in league with the demons of the underworld and fell abominations are in their train. One day soon, a storm such as you have never known will break upon you out of the north. All your collective strength will be needed to weather it, and only complete unity of resolve will spell survival. So I say to you, men, elves, armists and dwarves, put aside your enmity with one another, and take up arms as allies.

'Curillian will be your leader, the standard-bearer of this great endeavour. He is Prélan's chosen champion; to him has been revealed the means by which not just survival but victory will be achieved. Therefore, put your trust in him. Pledge yourselves to follow where he leads.

'Free Peoples! Unite, or fall. Stand together, or die. With you is the light of civilisation and all the heavenly heritage that Prélan has bestowed. Do not suffer it to be extinguished. I have fought all my life to keep the darkness at bay, but my strength is all but spent, so I bequeath the struggle to you. Prélan grant you the victory that has eluded me. Leave this Mountain, but forget not my words. Go forth now, your way out will be shorter than your way in. Farewell.'

A blinding light flashed, the walls shook. Roujeark heard the Keeper's voice speaking on in his head.

Roujeark, you will be my final apprentice. When all the others have left the Mountain, you must remain.

When the blinding flash subsided, the room was plunged into darkness. The wizard was gone. None of them saw where he went, nor indeed could they see each other, so sudden was the blackness. The stunned silence lasted only a moment, then it was shattered by shocked consternation. Scores of voices rose in alarm and protest, splitting the pitch darkness, but so flabbergasted were they at first that no sense could be made of them. For a while all was noise and anger. Each party turned in suspicion on their unseen neighbours and soon scuffling broke out, just as it had in the entrance chamber at the beginning of the Tournament.

Roujeark was just as shaken as any of them, but he was concerned more with the voice he had heard in his head than with the darkness. Suddenly his elbow was seized by a strong hand.

'Roujeark, fire.' No trace of panic was there in the king's voice, just a cool certainty of what to do. Roujeark tried to focus his mind, and heard the king speak to Lancoir also.

Above the din, Lancoir's stentorian voice rose like thunder.

'HOLD! HOLD FAST! NOBODY MOVE!'

His parade-ground lungs had the desired effect, bludgeoning all the others into obedience. In the silent eerie blackness that followed, a sudden flame flickered into life. Piercing the darkness, it moved swiftly into the centre of the map. It grew stronger, illuminating Roujeark and those around him. The fire sprang from his hand and hovered there. Spellbound, the jostling men and dwarves gathered round. Bewildered faces were drawn like moths. Curillian and Lancoir moved into the light and stood either side of Roujeark, the other armists behind them.

'So the Tournament ends as it began, in darkness and confusion,' Earl Culdon commented drily. His battle-hardened face flickered in the flamelight.

'A cursed waste of time it's been,' blurted out Reubun, one of Adhanor's attendant noblemen. Xavion, next to him, spoke in agreement.

'True. We've come all this way and for what? A few pretty lights and some trinkets.'

Caiasan the Aranese scribe stuck out his nose pugnaciously. 'Trinkets? Didn't you hear what they could do? They're powerful gifts. And we-mmpf...' he was cut off suddenly as Sir Hardos clamped a big hand over his mouth.

Southilar rumbled discontentedly in place of his scribe. 'Some of us have completely wasted our time. What's in it for those of us who got nothing?'

'Survival,' Lancoir answered him tersely.

'Survival?' Southilar scoffed. 'From what? The wizard's half-crazed, doesn't even know what century it is. Kurundar's dead and gone, there's naught but a frozen rabble left in Urunmar. Our Hendarian friends are quite capable of dealing with them.'

'Is that what you think, my lord Jeantar?' Bishop Nurvo spoke up for the Hendarians. 'Perhaps it has been some time since last you visited the haunted frontier, but evil is truly stirring there. You would do well not to ignore it.'

Hoth the dwarf elbowed his way into the firelight.

'The Keeper has done enough to convince me,' he growled. 'Magic is not forgotten in the halls of Carthak, even though the halls of Carthak may have been forgotten by all of you. In the past some of our own fought with the League of Wizardry, and what little we heard from them told us that we could trust Kulothiel.' He turned to Curillian. 'King Curillian, I will go back to my lord and report what I have seen and heard. I will urge him to ally himself to you. If I can convince him, you will have the axes of Carthak at your side when the time comes.' Curillian nodded in acknowledgement, but others had yet to say their piece.

'Nobly spoken, dwarf,' sneered Earl Onandur of Hendar, 'but how will we know when the time comes? For all we know, it could be years yet. The wizard spouted mighty fine rhetoric, but we can't plan an alliance nor a strategy of defence on this basis of this alone.'

Curillian stepped forward then, and seized the acrimonious debate by the scruff of the neck.

'My friends, there will be a time to speak of details. For now, it is enough that we have all been brought together. I do not believe that we have been deceived, nor brought together only to amuse the whims of a dying wizard. The League of Wizardry was ever a friend to the Free Peoples, bringing succour, counsel and military aid in times of trouble. Its last Head has spoken words of clear warning to us, and our children will condemn us if we fail to heed it. We're in a strange place, and have seen strange things, but let us nevertheless weigh carefully what we have heard. If any of us are to secure a future for the people we represent, then let us heed the words of Kulothiel, for I believe that he speaks with the authority of Prélan himself.' Several in the shadows around him murmured assent, but just as many faces were unconvinced. Curillian turned slowly, holding every eye in turn.

'There will be a role for all of us,' he told them.

'Easy for you to say,' spat Southilar. 'The wizard named you leader. Well, I won't follow your orders, nor will any of my people.' No sooner had he finished speaking than someone contradicted him.

'I will.' The voice spoke from the shadows, and both Southilar and Curillian knew it.

'Theonar, you'll do as I tell you and not forget your place,' Southilar told him. 'So long as I am Jeantar, I will have the final say for Aranar on all this madness.' Theonar paused, the silence suddenly thick again, before answering.

'You will not remain Jeantar for long.' Southilar's knights had to restrain him from finding the other man and lashing out at him, and commotion reigned again. Curillian spoke once more, raising his voice above the din.

'Aranar needs a Jeantar who'll look beyond Hamid to the good of us all.'

Southilar rounded on him. 'Did you not hear me, Curillian? I'll not follow you.'

Curillian stood his ground, keeping his voice level. 'If you can't follow then you've got no business leading.' The Jeantar looked as if he had been slapped. White-faced, he was unable to respond. Curillian again appealed to them.

'I'm not looking to rule any of you, nor is that what Kulothiel had in mind. But just let any man here say that I won't give my heart and soul for the free world. Let that man speak now, and back up his words with his sword.' No one spoke. 'No, I don't seek command. But whatever needs to be done, I'll do it. Whatever comes, I and my Maristonians will be in the thick of it. When Kurundar strikes,

I'll fight alongside any one of you, and I pledge my sword to that now.' He drew the Sword of Maristonia and held it up by the blade, turning in a slow circle and showing it to all of them. None of them failed to be impressed by the legendary weapon. Ever since the time of Arimaya, Curillian's grandfather, it had been a mighty force for good in the world, and never more so than in the hands of Curillian. Sheathing it again, he said, 'No one need commit to anything now. I propose we assemble for a proper council in one year's time. Will you all agree to that?' The lords around him all nodded or muttered agreement. Southilar alone demurred, insisting that he would have no part of it.

'A sound proposal,' said Earl Culdon, speaking over the Jeantar's sullen whisper. 'Decisions will be easier made in the light of day than in this wizardly gloom. Nothing more need be said. Come, let us eat what little food we have left and then depart.' Weary as they were, everyone was only too glad to agree.

'But how do we get out?' asked Parthir. 'We have only this one small torch, and there's much danger out there.' Only then did he appear to notice that the flame was coming from Roujeark's living palm, and he did a double take.

Theonar spoke again, drawing their attention to a single illuminated doorway.

'See, Kulothiel has provided a route. Remember, he said the way out would be shorter than the way in. Follow the light.'

Slowly they started to depart, minds chewing on all that they had heard. Adhanor of Hendar came close to Curillian. In the flamelight, the young king looked at the elder statesman with a worried expression.

'Do you really believe Kurundar will attack again?'

'Yes,' said Curillian, 'I do.' Swallowing his anxiety, Adhanor nodded, and then moved on. Bishop Nurvo went with him, but not before he gave Roujeark a lingering look of unsettling interest.

Roujeark, Curillian and Theonar were the last to leave. The tall Aranese knight held them back and spoke quietly but forcefully in the small light.

'We three are keepers of a secret trust. Only we know of the missions that Kulothiel gave to Roujeark and I. Do not forget.' He held out his hand, and in it was the gleaming piece of amulet. The others held forth their own tokens too. The firelight rippling across the otherworldly objects was enough to send shivers down the spine. 'Curillian, you must forge an alliance out of that unlikely material; I must find Avatar's amulet and return it to him; Roujeark must take away Kurundar's power. Amulet, Soul-shield and Star-shard: all must succeed, or all will fail.' Theonar folded his other hand over the artefacts, clasping both their hands with his. 'Prélan give us strength,' he said feelingly.

'Prélan be with us,' Roujeark offered.

'And Prélan guide us,' Curillian rounded off the tripartite prayer. Then he looked at Roujeark with a weary smile. 'So, you will remain here?' Roujeark nodded, reluctant now that the hour had come. 'Come down to the gates with us at least,' Curillian said. 'Say a proper farewell?' Roujeark was glad to accept, even though he could already feel the Mountain calling. The king looked from the wizard to the knight. 'Friends, we part for now, but let us come together again, when the time comes. Whatever help we can give each other, let there be no hesitation. We'll do this together.' They looked at each other and in silent understanding pledged faith. Then Theonar broke away and strode from the chamber. The armists followed him, joining their compatriots who waited outside. The great hall outside was dimly lit, and the footfalls of the others were receding along it. Smiling wearily, they took their first steps on the road home.

XX

The Uninvited

ONE By one Roujeark counted off the landmarks they had seen on their way in. Along the Hall of Tapestried History, past the wash of blue light about the Tear of Mírianna, beyond the twin statues of the guardian wizards – whose staves parted willingly enough from this side – and down the long staircase. When they at length reached its bottom, they found themselves in the atrium with the three doors. Ahead of them, like a blemish on the ornate wall, was the small iron-bound door through which they had forced an escape from the tunnel above the lava lake. To the left and right were two others which were four times the size and infinitely more decorative. Roujeark wasn't sure he would know which way to take, but when they came to it, they found the right-hand portal illuminated for them. The Keeper's directions prevailed.

Roujeark didn't even know if he should go through at all. Kulothiel had beckoned him to remain. Wasn't the whole point for him to get here and stay, not leave like everyone else? As everyone else trudged through the magnificent archway, he hung back, uncertain. Curillian noticed his reticence and paused by him.

'The Mountain is calling, isn't it?' Roujeark nodded wordlessly. Curillian squeezed his shoulder. 'Come down to the main gate with us at least?' the king suggested. Roujeark gratefully accepted the idea. It deferred the painful prospect of parting. Most of him couldn't wait to study and learn at the feet of Kulothiel, but a part of him dreaded losing the friends he had so lately won. So, they descended together, at the rear of the weary exodus.

They were now in a part of the Mountain they hadn't been in before. These were more civilised parts, the pathways by which honoured guests would enter, rather than the sewers and dungeons through which they had crawled. The décor was grand and imposing, but not so intricate or otherworldly as the upper chambers from which they had just descended. They passed along wide echoing corridors and through many-pillared halls which were lit as if for their convenience. They went carelessly, the different races conversing amiably enough as they went along together, and their voices echoed in the shadowy ceiling.

As they passed from one smaller chamber into a larger, Roujeark stopped, feeling a check in his spirit. This was not the reluctance to part from his friends he had felt before, but a tremor of remembrance. He shivered, feeling the inexplicable wariness he had felt on previous occasions. The other armists did not notice but walked on ahead of him. All the while he stood rooted to the spot, fingertips twitching. In his mind's eye, he saw himself in a great library somewhere inside the Mountain. A gust of chill air rushed over him, and the whole chamber around him seemed to bend and flex. Then a book fell from its place. He watched it fall in slow motion, wondering what it was. He felt the thud of it hitting the floor like a blow on his back. It landed spine-up, but he had to come closer to see its title. *The Wars Against the Harracks*. He straightened upright in a flash, feeling suddenly hot and sick despite the cool air. Unbidden into his mind came a succession of images from his horrific time in Faudunum, and he felt hot pulses running down his arms.

'Harracks,' he whispered to himself. Both visions faded, and he found himself back in the lower chamber. His comrades were some way ahead now, their footsteps echoing in the distance. 'Harracks,' he said again, louder, but still no one heard him. All of a sudden his feet were moving, alarm rising in him, and he said it a third time, panic amplifying his voice to a shrill cry.

This time the others heard him, for the echoes winged around the larger pillared hall. Running now, he caught up with them to find men, dwarves and armists all staring at him, confused and irritated. Even Curillian looked bemused.

'What did you say?' he asked. All was suddenly quiet, the clinking of mail and the squeaking of leather fading away to dead silence. Roujeark swallowed hard, much more afraid of his intuition than the others' annoyance.

'Harracks,' he repeated, somehow unable to say more. They all saw that his face was pale and beaded in sweat, and their expressions changed to ones of concern.

'What did he say?' Onandur asked, puzzled. Evidently the name meant nothing to him.

'Harracks,' Culdon said, adding nothing to the big man's understanding, but the grimness in his voice and the gripping of his sword hilt spoke volumes.

'Roujeark,' Curillian pressed him gently, 'what are you saying?'

'Harracks. Here. In this Mountain,' he managed to say, at last able to add more words. 'There are enemies out there.' Alarmed, many of them turned to look fearfully around at the partially lit hall, whose further parts were filled with great shadows.

'Are you sure?' Curillian asked. Roujeark nodded.

'Ah, what does he know?' demanded Sir Hardos. 'He's as crazed as the old man, or so exhausted he's delirious.'

'He's been right before,' Findor protested stoutly.

'What are harracks?' demanded Earl Onandur, adding to the fraught atmosphere. Suddenly many voices were speaking, and Curillian for once looked indecisive. Maybe it was weariness, maybe it was some other factor clouding his mind, but he just stared at Roujeark, not heeding the hubbub around him. It was Lancoir who acted. Seizing Roujeark's hands, he inspected the palms. To his horror, he saw a fierce red glow welling up in each like an evil boil. That was enough to convince him.

'Quiet,' shouted the Captain of the Guard. 'QUIET!' His ferocious tone cut across them all like a whiplash, and silence settled once more. Only this time, it was not quite silence. Small pitter-patter sounds came from the hall's shadows around them, like the falling of little stones. The silence thickened, pressing close like an unseasonal garment. More noises followed. Quiet, far-off, strange, but definitely there. It was as if a horde of insects were crawling about in the dark corners, like the shards of a nightmare pricking the edge of consciousness. Hands fell to weapons and feet shuffled nervously about.

A sharp whizzing cut through the thick air and sped towards them like a berserk hornet. An arrow ricocheted off a dwarf's shield, and behind it, somewhere in the darkness, came an evil snicker. The dwarf turned, indignant, but the assailant could not be seen. Theonar's sword came into his hands as more arrows came spitting and zipping towards them. The air was suddenly alive with them, vicious little black-barbed darts. Theonar deflected several of them with his sword, and many struck armour or clattered on the paving stones beneath them, but one found its mark. An Aranaese man-at-arms cried out, clutching his throat. An arrow seemed to grow out of his neck, and he slumped to the ground, gargling and bleeding copiously. Curillian seemed to come out of his trance and stooped by the fallen man. He inspected the weapon and came to a speedy conclusion.

'Never mind harracks, these are goblin arrows,' he cried. Even more than the arrows themselves, his words sparked panic. All around him the warriors leapt into action, unslinging shields and whipping out swords. The group fanned out, unsure what to do, but desperately peering into the gloom for sight of the enemy. Another man fell dead, this time one of Parthir's crew. The arrows weren't coming in a deadly rain, but well-directed pot-shots and accompanied now by blood-chilling howls. Curillian felt sure that this was but the vanguard of a great enemy presence. Every now and then they caught glimpses of little figures darting between columns or climbing up pillars like demonic monkeys. How many were out there Curillian couldn't guess, but then he heard the drumbeat. BOOM!

It was deep, so deep that it sounded like the heartbeat of some giant at the Mountain's core. Sinister and compelling, it brought fear into all their hearts. BOOM. Another drumbeat reverberated the floor under their feet. Not all of them there had ever seen a goblin, much less fought one, but Curillian had, and he knew that war-drums were not in their repertoire. But harracks used drums. Monstrous great things that could shake mountains. He had heard drums like this before, borne by harrack war-bands and used as weapons in themselves.

BOOM.

'Back!' he shouted. 'Back to the smaller cavern!' Suddenly he was thinking clearly again, and he knew that an enemy as agile as the goblins could quickly outflank and surround their little company. They must get back to a narrower place, somewhere they could hold.

'BACK!' Lancoir repeated Curillian's command, lifting it above the din of panic and drumbeats. BOOM. BOOM.

Men and dwarves were only too glad to follow his order, and as one they hurried back to the great chamber's entrance, pursued by mocking laughter. Between this chamber and the next was a short, broad corridor, and into this constricted space they piled.

'Is this some kind of sick joke by the wizard?' demanded Culdon.

'Curse him!' shouted Southilar. 'He's lured us here to our deaths. We are betrayed. Look at us – all the leaders of the Free Peoples caught together in one sorcerous trap.' Curillian didn't believe the Jeantar's wild assertion, but if that had been Kulothiel's plan, he could hardly have done a better job. They were trapped. Between them and freedom was an unseen enemy, and behind was only a haunt of wizards. BOOM. BOOM. The drumbeats were getting louder and nearer.

'But why would he do that?' wailed Caiasan.

'Someone had better find him,' suggested the bishop, who was armed with a wicked dagger, priest though he was. 'Now more than ever we could use his help.'

'This is not his fight,' said Theonar, though no one took any notice.

Curillian looked at the warriors around him. They had different weapons and equipment and different experience of fighting. His eyes lighted on the dwarves.

'Hoth!' he called. Men parted to reveal the dwarf squeezing into his new gift of armour. Angry eyes looked out from the leathery face. 'Hoth, I need your dwarves to form a shield-wall across the entrance,' Curillian told him. 'Your shields and armour will block the corridor better than any of us.' Hoth just nodded grimly and hefted his enormous battle-axe. 'The rest of you,' Curillian ordered, 'form ranks behind the dwarves. We hold this place.'

The shield-wall locked together, the dwarves' great iron-bound limewood shields clacking as they formed an overlapping barricade. Hoth's fighters were well-versed in this kind of warfare – underground clashes in tight spaces where victory went to the strongest arms and the most disciplined formations. BOOM. BOOM. BOOM. The throbbing drumbeats came more insistently, their pounding noise filling the subterranean world. In between each beat they could hear the lesser drumming of many heavy feet. The enemy was coming for them.

'What is happening?' Curillian looked around to see Elrinde and the other two Ithrillians coming up from behind. Wherever they had been, they were here now, and Curillian couldn't have wished for a better ally.

'Harracks,' Curillian explained abruptly, 'and goblins. It's an ambush.' Elrinde nodded. It was not fear in his face, but some other emotion that he had to quickly suppress as he took in the news.

'I thought as much. The racket they make is like the Black Dwarves of the Goragath Mountains. I hope they don't fight like those bastards.'

'Come and find out.'

The pounding of feet was coming much closer now. Goblin cries rent the air and as they gathered around the radius of the opening, they started to concentrate their fire. Most of the missiles snapped harmlessly against the dwarves' shield-wall, but some went over their heads. One Ciricien warrior didn't duck quick enough and took an arrow in his upper arm. Soon they were all crouching behind the shield-wall, and Lancoir and Onandur between them marshalled them all into place as second, third and fourth ranks. Suddenly the arrows stopped and a furious rolling wave of drumbeats burst over them like an orchestral climax of thunder.

BOOM. BOOM. BOOM. BOOM!

'BRACE YOURSELVES!' Hoth bellowed above the din.

'BRACE!' echoed Lancoir. None of them save the dwarves saw the enemy coming, but the booted feet came at a run and the bass war-cries rang loud. Then a wave of enemies hit them like a storm surge, and the impact shuddered through all the ranks to the very back. The dwarves were smashed back a few paces, and the men and armists behind were powerless to stop the backward momentum. The sound of shields smashing shields was like a rockfall in the mountains, and maces and hammers beat loud upon wood and metal. Then the dwarves pushed back. Grunting and cursing, they heaved at their enemies, and won back one of the lost yards. Axes forgotten, they used short stabbing swords to jab between the gaps in the shields, and the harracks did likewise. For harracks they were. Allied again to their old partners in crime, they had somehow come to Oron Amular with the goblins. Late, and uninvited, yet they seemed determined to have the last word. But where the short, sinewy goblins were good skirmishers and archers, it fell to the sturdier harracks to hammer home the main assault.

Hoth's dwarves gritted their teeth and put all their weight into resisting, but they were being driven slowly back. Between the shields they could see tight-skinned savage faces that were parodies of their own. All leathery skin, squint eyes and wild bushy beards. Mouths full of rotten tooth stumps spat and cursed, growled and roared. No one knew how many of them there were, but the weight of their shield-wall kept growing. Like an unstoppable juggernaut, it ploughed forwards. Their blades were forgotten; they seemed intent only on pushing their enemy out of the bottleneck.

Curillian and Lancoir knew the danger, but they could do nothing. Side by side in the second rank, squeezed up against the dwarves by the row behind, all they could do was push and heave in vain. A dwarf craned his neck back to look at them, red-faced and full of strain, his veins nearly bursting out of his head. Their world had shrunk to a claustrophobic oblong of noise and sweat, grunting and heaving.

Theonar, though, was at the back with Roujeark, Bishop Nurvo and Caiasan, the lightest of the company. The tall knight seized the young armist's elbow and hissed in his ear.

'They can't last long now. When we break, be quick and follow me.' The vague notion had formed in Roujeark's mind that as soon as he had clear sight of the enemy he would let fly with his bolts of flame, as he had done in Faudunum, but Theonar sounded like he had a plan. He hoped so, because the situation looked bleak. They numbered a little more than a hundred, by his best guess, but the harracks seemed to outnumber them many times over by themselves; with the goblins, they were a great horde. Their numbers mattered for little in the corridor, but as soon as they were out in the open again, they would be horribly vulnerable. Unless they could find another place of defence, they could be encircled or cut down by a rain of arrows.

BOOM. BOOM. BOOM. The drums in the larger cave beyond still throbbed, like a deep and insistent headache. Every drumbeat seemed to instil fresh encouragement in the harracks, and they heaved anew with each new beat. Roujeark and his immediate companions were forced out of the corridor now and into the dimly lit cavern behind, and still the men in front of them were being forced backwards. Roujeark searched around for some feature that might serve as a refuge, but there was nothing, nor could he hear himself think above the awful noise of the drums and the war-cries and the thunder of hammers. He noticed Theonar studying what looked like a small groove in the floor. It ran the width of the cavern. The knight then looked up, scanning around the cavern's walls. Whatever he saw, he looked more hopeful than Roujeark felt. His hands were hot with pent-up power and he shook uncontrollably, but in his mind, he was fending off the despair that threatened to swamp him. Refuge or no, unless they could overcome this enemy there was no getting out. No future, no hope for the Free Peoples.

'Ready?' Theonar asked. Parthir's crew in turn had been pushed out of the tunnel, and instead they took up positions on either side, fitting arrows to their short bows and hefting throwing knives. Elrinde and his two companions dropped back also, long slender elven swords at the ready. Back and back went Curillian's shield-wall and the harracks, scenting victory, gave an almighty push that sent men, dwarves and armists staggering.

'Now!' cried Theonar, and off he sped into the gloom. Roujeark half-turned to follow him but tarried a heartbeat to see what happened. One minute there was a shoving mass of bodies, the next a human explosion as warriors were thrust willy-nilly from the confines of the corridor. All order vanished, and everybody found himself alone and with no clear idea of what to do except flee. Roujeark broke into a run, following where Theonar had gone.

'Back!'

'Retreat!' The desperate orders were hardly necessary, nor even audible, for the scattered contestants were already in headlong flight, and the deep victory chants of the harracks drowned out all else. They came pouring into the second cavern like an avalanche of bodies and jeered at the routed enemy. Yet for all their impressive pushing power, they were not fleet of foot, and so their foes were out of reach for the moment. The harracks parted ranks to allow the goblins through, and they came like an evil tide through sluice-gates, all slimy skin and dull iron. With horrible speed they flooded the cavern, shooting off arrows with nimble fingers even as they ran. Several arrows found their mark in their fleeing targets, and the archers danced and screeched in exultation.

Curillian ran through the pandemonium, his armists by his side. He had no more idea of what to do than any of them, all he knew was to get to somewhere more defensible. They were fleeing blindly back the way they had come, urgently seeking somewhere to use to their advantage. They came to some stairs at the far end of the second cavern and surged up them. A doorway was in front of them, but Curillian couldn't remember what was through it. Instead, he turned about to see what was happening. What he saw made his heart sink. The cavern was in absolute chaos. His friends and allies were scattered all over the place, some fleeing, some turning to fight. They were being shot at from every angle and yelling mobs of goblins were closing fast to commence their butchery. A dozen or more men already lay dead with arrows protruding from them. Hoth's dwarves were hindmost, weighed down by their armour, and looking like being engulfed. Behind him, Lancoir was ushering some through the doorway, while anyone with a bow and arrows he deployed as a flimsy rearguard. Their shafts were like spitting into a hurricane.

Then suddenly the king's eyes and mind were filled with a wall of fire. The floor seemed to erupt in flames that seared all the way to the ceiling, filling the cavern with lurid light and appalling heat. A line of goblins was caught in the inferno and incinerated. The roaring of the flames and the hideous screams of those caught in them raised the cacophony of noise to a crescendo of horror. Curillian's first thought was of Roujeark, but he was nowhere to be seen. The flames receded as quickly as they had burst forth, dying into the thin trench whence they had come. Curillian vaguely remembered passing over a little gutter in the floor, but he had thought nothing of it. For a split second he hoped that the flames would remain as an impassable barricade, but that hope was cheated. It had won them precious moments though, and once the initial shock passed the dwarves were able to make good their escape, jogging towards the steps. Just ahead of them came the heavily armoured Hendarians, the last of the contestants.

Not quite last.

A

Roujeark had placed his hand where Theonar indicated, a small panel in the cavern wall. It had not been visible before, but Theonar had smashed the coloured glass that had covered it with his sword hilt. Pressing his hand against the panel, Roujeark felt a tremendous power throb up his arm like someone was pulling it off. Theonar waited not a second longer but pulled him away and they were running again. Seconds later a whooshing sound went up behind them and a wave of heat threw them on their faces. From his hands and knees, Roujeark looked back in awe at the wall of fire. He had done that. Horror filled his tear-blurred vision as he glimpsed flaming figures running around and heard the awful shrieks of the dying.

Theonar tugged him upright again and ushered him to another spot. Already the enemy were overcoming their terror and coming on again, passing over the trench that had proved so deadly to the front-runners. Again, Theonar smashed the glass, and shouted, 'Here!' Roujeark put his hand to the spot and felt the same heat and twinge of pain. This time, a deafening series of clangs announced the falling of many trapdoors. A chequered pattern of holes appeared in the floor. Some goblins who had been standing on them fell instantly to an unseen fate, and many more followed them who couldn't dodge or stop in time. Scores of them vanished, their forlorn cries drowned out by the alarm of the survivors. The goblins' forward momentum was brought up short, but again they weren't stopped for long. Madder than ever, and howling for blood, they rushed forward once more, harracks lumbering up behind.

Roujeark had time to steal a quick glance to where Curillian was conducting the escape of their friends before Theonar hauled him away. Together they ran to a corner of the cavern. Theonar turned and yelled to attract the attention of the goblins. A large band of them broke away from their headlong dash towards the steps and came charging at them. Arrows whistled and clattered all around them.

'Find the next panel, Roujeark,' the knight called urgently. Roujeark searched the rock walls, and behind a brazier he found a protruding stone that seemed a little loose. Pushing it, he felt it give and retreat into a hidden recess. Then there came a rumbling noise and a whole section of the wall swung inwards. Not a moment too soon, he and Theonar ducked inside. In total darkness, they hid to one side as fifty or more goblins came hurtling in after them, screaming and hollering.

Once the goblins were inside, the section of wall swung back to its original place, sealing them inside. The noise of them was an assault on Roujeark's ears, but in all the bedlam he and Theonar remained undiscovered. The awful noise only subsided when a dazzling light materialised in the centre of the dark chamber. Roujeark watched in amazement as the light dimmed somewhat to reveal Kulothiel standing there, a Mage-Lord in all his glory. The goblins surrounding him cowered away in fear. Their dark green hides, grimy leather garments and patchy iron armour were thrown into sharp relief by the light. For the first time, Roujeark got a good glimpse of them. They were short, slight and sinewy, mis-begotten creatures of filth and malice. They did not have even the traces of civilisation that the harracks could claim, only those instruments of evil that they had found a use for: sharp-barbed arrows, wicked knives, whips and light javelins. They were the skirmishers of Kurundar, his light infantry, bred for ambush and harassment.

One seemed to be a leader of some sort. He stood taller and more upright than the others. Gold was at his neck and wrists, and his armour was more complete, though still roughly made and primitive. Roujeark could not see his face, for it was turned towards Kulothiel. They stood locked in silent struggle, each seeming to know the other. The Mage-Lord looked at him with cold fury.

'This far you shall come,' he told the goblin chieftain, 'and no further.' The goblin barked in defiance and raised his scimitar, but Kulothiel was quicker. Incanting fell words of power, he raised both arms, fingers splayed, then quickly drew both hands into his body as fists. Instantly the goblins looked stunned. They held their hands to their ears in seeming agony, as if assaulted by sounds that neither Roujeark nor Theonar could hear. The wretched creatures danced, cringed and writhed in distress, but Kulothiel was implacable. He kept his fists clenched and maintained his measured words of command. No longer afraid of being overheard, Theonar backed away.

'Turn away now, Roujeark.' He drew the young armist away, leading him up a hidden flight of stairs. Behind them the goblins' screams reached fever-pitch and then cut out suddenly as each and every one of them was crushed like an egg. Theonar led Roujeark up and away before pausing at a blank wall. Just then they heard someone behind them, and they turned to see a solitary surviving goblin. Roujeark gaped as it dashed up the stairs, seemingly oblivious to their presence. Both hands were still clamped over its ears, as if trying to keep out some awful noise, but the only noise they could hear was its own screaming, a dreadful keening cry, like a pain-maddened hawk. It closed the distance between them in a few prancing bounds and bulled into Roujeark. The armist was caught off-balance and knocked to the floor, where he fumbled desperately for his dagger. But the goblin had a weapon of its own and removed a hand from one ear to brandish a javelin that had been strapped to its back. Still screeching in pain, it prepared to strike, seemingly more enraged by the hindrance to its escape than by out-and-out enmity. Roujeark saw the javelin point come glinting towards him, aimed straight for his throat, but then there was a swoosh in the dark and it stopped. The goblin's severed head toppled onto him, and he twisted away in loathing. Glancing up, he saw Theonar sheath his long blade. Roujeark expected him to extend a helping hand, but the knight was looking down at him with something akin to annoyance.

'Roujeark, what are you doing?' he said, half-puzzled, half-angry. 'You're better than that.'

Embarrassed and angry, Roujeark booted the headless corpse back down the steps and struggled upright, rubbing an elbow that he had fallen awkwardly on. He looked reproachfully at Theonar, but the knight seemed not to notice. Instead, he clasped Roujeark by the back of the neck and pulled his face close.

'You're not some mongrel man-at-arms who has to scrap in the gutter or scrabble for a blade. You have faster and better weapons than any of us; use them! There are hardened warriors out there who will one day quake at your coming. You're worth a hundred others in this fight. Next time, don't hesitate.'

Theonar released him and turned back to the dead end at the top of the steps. Another hidden button opened a door, and out they sprang into the tunnel passage where only moments before the last of their friends had passed by.

They found them in yet another cavern, by far the smallest of the three. Men, elves, armists and dwarves were all arrayed there, fleeing no longer but determined to make a final stand. Their leaders, Curillian, Southilar, Adhanor, Culdon, Elrinde, Hoth and Parthir, stood out in front, grim and resolved. Roujeark made a hasty count. Ninety-two were there, stretching nearly from one end of the cavern to the other. Sixty men of various nations, twenty dwarves, nine armists and three elves. A pitifully small force, but well-armed and counting in their number warriors of great renown.

Curillian looked relieved to see the two of them and beckoned them into the ranks near him.

'Prélan be praised you're still alive! Was that you back there? Well, we need more of it. This fight's not done yet.'

'It's just getting started,' said Lancoir. He was flexing his muscular forearms and tightening the cords that held his vambraces in place. He nodded at Roujeark, and the wizard smiled wryly at the wordless compliment. Lancoir wasn't the only one getting ready. As the harrack war-drums thudded in the nearby caverns, the whole company readied themselves for battle. The armists were dressed alike, leather-padded mail-shirts under their travelling clothes, with hardened leather plates over key areas like forearms and chests. The flaming sword emblem of Maristonia was etched into the leather and embroidered on the cloaks, which were now cast aside. Their bows and arrows were laid out in readiness on the floor in front of them, and their two-handed swords were strapped across their shoulders, ready to be drawn at a moment's notice.

Next to them, the men of Ciricen on one side were also in mail but with the added protection of thick fur cloaks. Brandishing their formidable skuxes, which were half-axe and half-halberd, they waited silently for the next round. On the other side, standing uneasily next to their armist neighbours, was Parthir's ragged crew with their curved sabres and long pikes. Beyond the pale Ciriciens, in the centre of their line, were the Hendarians in plate armour and Hoth's dwarves more heavily armoured still. They held great battle-axes and mattocks at the ready, eager for another chance to get at their ancient foes. The men of Aranar sported the badges of their respective clans. Swords were in their hands and small shields were unslung from their backs. On the far-right were the three Ithrillian elves, but they followed Elrinde as he came to take counsel with Curillian. He twirled his elegant sword as he came, almost absent-mindedly, and his casual swordcraft earned him many admiring glances. They had been allowed a short time of respite as the enemy gathered for a fresh assault, so the leaders came together.

'You know these scum best, Curillian,' said Culdon. 'What's the quickest way to kill them?'

'There is no quick way,' Curillian told him. 'They are tough and thick-skinned. Their armour is not as good as some of ours here, but the leather and fur they wear is enough to stop all but the strongest thrusts...'

Hoth interrupted him. 'They're nought but clumsy savages. They try to fight like us, only they're weaker and less good-looking. Leave it to us, watch how we do it.' Curillian smiled.

'But for those of you who find yourself facing a harrack and there isn't a dwarf to hand, listen to Lancoir. Captain...' Curillian gave Lancoir centre stage, and the stalwart armist raised his deep voice so all could hear.

'Slashing's no good, it's like hacking at a rock. They'll carry a thousand scratches and keep coming. Thrust and stab. Hard. Put all your strength into your blow. Make it count. They're slow, but they won't give you many chances. Keep moving, don't stop. Wait till they've committed themselves to a swing of their hammer, then step inside for the killing blow before they can recover.'

'And get close to the goblins.' Elrinde added his wisdom to the battlefield tutorial. 'Don't give them room to shoot. Keep your eyes on them, because they're quick and their knives will find the weak spots in your armour. An...' Whatever else he might have said was drowned out by more furious drumming. BOOM. BOOM. BOOM. Curillian saw the nervousness in their faces and stepped out in front of them all.

'Do not be afraid. Prélan is with us. We fight as one, and we fight with His strength.' The sound of many feet in the tunnels outside rose to a thundering din and Curillian had to shout to make himself heard. 'I say again, do not fear. There will be a tomorrow, our stories do not end here. If you could see the living tapestry in the halls of this Mountain, telling the story of time, you would see that there are other battles to fight, other struggles. It does not end here. We do not end here.'

Then the harracks were spilling into the cavern, stamping and snarling out of the corridors that led in. Behind crudely painted shields, they fanned out into the chamber. Gone was the mad rush of their first assault; this time they came with measured caution. More and more kept coming, filling the far side of the chamber until barely fifty yards separated them from their enemies.

For the first time, the contestants got a good look at them, for some had never encountered harracks before. To the Hendarians they looked like something out of their folktales, which told of Black Dwarves who haunted the Goragath Mountains in centuries past. They had the same primitive clothing, the same brutal weapons, the same eerie appearance of rational beings long fallen from grace. The Hawk and Falcon knights saw old enemies who lurked at the edges of their frontiers and whose mountain fastnesses they had never been able to eradicate. The Ciriciens saw barbarians who seemed to resemble the wild hill-men of Dorzand, the windswept plateau south of their realm in which they had fought for time out of mind. The dwarves of Carthak saw beings who had once been like them, but who had never achieved the heights of their underground civilisation, and who had already begun their descent into ignorant savagery when Carthak was still rising to new levels of power and skill. Elrinde looked with disgust at this stunted and unlovely race, and bitterly he regretted the far bygone day when his ancestors had first awoken them.

Roujeark saw the same implacable lifeforms he had encountered in the cold city of Faudunum. With faces like stone and animal eyes, they looked and were armed like maniac blacksmiths. He tried to stop his legs from shaking as fear crawled all over him like a plague of insects. The cavern seemed hot and he felt sick. More than once his hand strayed to his dagger, and more than once he checked himself. Instead he looked down into his palms, which were glowing angrily and throbbing with pent-up energy. Clenching and unclenching his fists, he resolved to give a good account of himself. He repeated as many of Theonar's words to himself as he could remember, but he doubted that he could live up to them. Whatever he had within him, he would throw into the fight, for himself and for his friends. He did not want to die here, before he had even begun his apprenticeship. Not after coming so far and waiting so long. No, he would use his untrained abilities in every way he could to make sure that he could live out his destiny.

Remembering how Curillian would pray before every action, he turned his mind to Prélan and his eyes to the cavern's roof. *Help me*, he pleaded. *Be with us. We need you. We need you badly. If you don't come through for us, this is the end. Help me to control my fears.*

Help me to control whatever power I have. Give me strength. Looking down again, he saw Curillian's head bowed and lips moving. He too was praying, as were many of them. Not all there were devout: some just stared balefully at the enemy, steeling themselves.

A sudden noise made Roujeark jump. It was a great war-shout and a clatter of arms. The dwarves had advanced into no man's land between the two armies and taken up a strange formation. Their deep voices boomed out in a ritual challenge, chanting words of hatred and power. Accompanying the words, they made a war-music of stamping feet, gesticulating arms and axe-heads clashed against armour. Far from random noise, the sounds they made were rhythmic, beautiful even, in a haunting sort of way. Their eyes were locked on the harracks as they put on their defiant display. The harracks started a chant of their own, and their front rank broke out into a thumping war-dance, similar but completely different.

Curillian at least had seen this before, or had heard of it in the tales from when his ancestors had fought the dwarves in the Second Chapter. He knew what was coming, so he raised his sword, turned, and yelled an encouragement to his followers. The other leaders did likewise, and the whole line shifted forward a pace, tense and alert. The dwarves bellowed out the last of their challenge, and the harracks finally lost patience. With an almighty shout, they came forward at a slow, lumbering run. There was no order to them, just a rage-fuelled charging mob. But the dwarves were ready for them. Before they met, they changed swiftly into a new formation. They pressed close together and presented their shields outward and above their heads. In the blink of an eye, they had become an armoured mass and the harracks crashed against it like a wave against a cliff. The din was ear-splitting as battle was joined. The harracks wrapped around the dwarf formation and beat at it with their hammers and clubs. They seemed to make no impression, but every few seconds a gap would appear in the shields and a short stabbing sword would flash out, hacking into the nearest assailant. Roujeark saw several harracks fall like this before he lost sight of the dwarves altogether.

But he didn't watch for long. He charged forward right behind Curillian and Lancoir. Beside them the whole line was moving, dashing up in support of the dwarves. Before any of his comrades could strike a blow, Roujeark let loose with a fireball from each hand. He didn't think, he just did it. A far cry from the raw and misdirected missiles he had discovered in the ambush at Broadsword Ridge, these fireballs were bigger and much more concentrated in power. They scorched into the harracks and exploded, filling with cavern with garish light. Harracks were blasted from their feet and a ragged hole opened in their ranks. Yet he didn't have time to fire again, because Curillian and Lancoir were into the gap like foxes after chickens. They laid about them with their swords in terrible blows. Moments later, the Royal Guards joined the action, and in a brief glimpse Roujeark saw the dreadful power of the demonbane mace given to Lionenn. The stocky warrior swung it against the nearest harrack, whose shield crumpled as if struck by a thunderbolt. That harrack was thrown backwards and the force of the blow took half a dozen others with him.

Then Roujeark himself was engulfed by the fight and he forgot all else. His world shrank to a few square feet of cavern floor, which he shared with Antaya and a trio of howling harracks. He had but a split second with which to duck the swinging hammer right in front of him. He evaded it so successfully that he found himself flat on the floor and his eyes had to adjust to the unusual angle as the battle lurched above him. The harrack passed over him only to have its head cloven by Antaya's two-handed sword. For a second Antaya looked exposed, but Findor appeared beside him and drove back the enemies menacing him. Roujeark's feet were trampled on and he launched a fireball at the offender, who disappeared upwards and backwards in a gout of smoke and sparks. Two of the dead harrack's comrades looked down and in their inexpressive faces Roujeark was certain he could see shock and fear. He didn't give them a chance to recover but blasted them as well. He rolled aside as a hammer came crashing down from the side, and he was scrambling upright as it smashed a chunk out of the floor. He kicked the hammer out of the harrack's grasp before he could retrieve it and then blasted him backwards. Yet the harracks pressed thickly about him, those behind quickly taking the place of the slain. He had to twist and drop to one knee to avoid the next blow, and from his kneeling position he swept his arm round in an arc of inspiration. A sheet of flame scythed round and ignited one harrack after another until all those near him were aflame.

He was suffused with exhilaration at the revelation of what he could do, but it was swamped in seconds by the realisation that he was confronted with flaming harracks who could not escape because of the press of the battle from behind. He backed away in alarm, lest his own fire engulf him too, but the harracks followed, mad with pain and seemingly determined to have revenge before the flames killed them. Out of the corner of his eye, he was vaguely aware that a new presence was ploughing in where Antaya and Findor had been before. The harrack to his right was flung aside as Lionenn's mace smashed into him. Roujeark winced at the tremendous violence as the guardsman waded into the melee. Again and again, Lionenn swung his mace, imbued with the magical power of Kulothiel's pool, until he had cleared a space in front of them. The harracks who had been there were either mangled on the floor or cast aside in a wide radius of carnage. Roujeark breathed a sigh of relief and leaned on his saviour's shoulder as he caught his breath.

ᴀ

All the along the line, the Free Peoples had crashed into the harracks and joined the battle. Ciriciens, Hendarians, Alanai, Aranese and Ithrillians, they were all soon embroiled in a desperate fight and hard-pressed. None of them could see any of the others except their immediate neighbours, their world full of noise and flailing weapons, and none of the leaders could gauge how the battle was going. If any of them had been able to get up high and look down, they would have seen the cavern filled with an ungovernable mass of embattled warriors. No order or formation was there, just a deadly fight at close quarters. In the confined space, few of them had room to swing and strike a proper blow, so they resorted to punching, grappling, shoving and stabbing with short, powerful blows.

The dwarf formation still held firm, but it was completely encircled now, and their allies could not even see it, much less reach it. Dead harracks were heaped in great piles around the impenetrable shields. Whenever they managed to beat down a dwarf, the formation closed up again and the shields locked, leaving their fallen comrade to add to the corpse wall which was proving a great obstacle to their foes.

It was the arrival of the goblins that proved the undoing of the dwarves. They came late to the fight as fresh reinforcements now that the harrack onslaught had been checked. Sifting between their bulky allies, or clambering over them like ghastly gymnasts, they came whooping and hollering into the fight. Dozens of them leapt on top of the dwarvish shield-wall and scrabbled over it like sadistic monkeys. With long wicked daggers and javelin points, they found the tiny gaps in the defences and jabbed down. Underneath the shields, the helmets and armour of the dwarves were a solid second line of defence, but the attack from above succeeded in breaking the tight cohesion of their formation. As they started to shift about in a bid to protect themselves from the blades above, more goblins attacked from all sides, jumping up and seizing shield-rims. Clinging on with all four limbs and careless of the hands and feet they lost, they used their weight to pull the shields out and expose the warriors behind. When the gaps appeared, the harracks hurled their weapons in to batter and stun.

Within minutes of the goblins' arrival, the dwarf formation had disintegrated and they were left to fight as individuals. Then their axes really went to work, splitting helms, cutting off limbs and disembowelling harracks and goblins alike. Yet more of their own number were falling now, perishing to face-crushing hammer-blows or bleeding to death from scores of little knife-wounds.

The Hendarians found themselves in a similar predicament, able to match their enemies man for man but being worn slowly down. Bishop Nurvo went down to a hammer-blow and was thrust unceremoniously from the fight, his attendant priests dragging him free from the melee while the knights fought on. The young King Adhanor was giving a good account of himself, with the towering Earl Onandur on one side warding off blows and a sturdy knight on the other. Count Xavion and Duke Reubun were nowhere to be seen.

Beside the Hendarians, the Aranese were no less beset. Goblin arrows whistled from overhead to bring death and injury from every angle, whilst all about them their enemies were swarming. Yet they employed the skills they had honed at many tournaments, fighting skilfully at close quarters and giving their enemies as few openings as possible. At the Hamid Tournament, their great men fought for the right to be called Jeantar, and at dozens of small tourneys their young warriors were blooded and showed off their prowess. Now they were not fighting for prizes or prestige, they were fighting for their very lives. Caiasan had a bloodied head but was still on his feet and giving as good as he got. Southilar was using his great strength to deal out ferocious sword-blows. He loomed over the harracks like a highland tree above dry stone walls, but nothing they could do seemed to hinder him. Several arrows already jutted out from his armour, having been cheated of any effect, and his Pegasus men defended him well.

By the cavern's far wall, Elrinde and his companions were fighting a very different battle, avoiding the tight-packed bludgeoning going on elsewhere by keeping their enemies at sword's length with agile skill. Every time a club or hammer swung at them, they were no longer there, but had danced away to lash out another lethal thrust from a new position. They seemed able to dodge the javelins flung at them and wriggle aside when charged. Elrinde thwarted every attempt to pen him up against the wall and deny him space by ceaselessly moving, weaving and feinting.

The Alanai were used to the cramped conditions of shipboard fighting and threw themselves into the fight with deadly effect. No rules or disciplines governed their approach, so they scrapped tooth and nail, kicking, wrestling, gouging and stamping. Their pikes were useless after the first charge, but they were deadly with their sabres and their knives, both throwing and slashing. Each of them seemed to have an inexhaustible supply of throwing knives stashed about their person, flinging them like a storm of waves crashing over a ship. Time and again a rush of harracks was reduced to a pile of gurgling bodies, but when they succeeded in getting close, the Alanai proved no less lethal at close quarters, stabbing and ripping.

But the enemy that the harracks most feared was the armist king. Curillian fought like a tornado, combining the speed and skill of Elrinde with the brute power of the big Hendarians. Whenever a weapon came close to him, the Sword of Maristonia shore clean through handles and hafts, and arrows were powerless against his cunning armour. Lancoir was close by his side, guarding his flank, killing with ruthless efficiency. The enemy shied away from them only to run smack into the whirling mace of Lionenn or the greatswords of the Royal Guards. Aleinus, though, had advanced too far and found himself cut off with the young Ciricien warrior Kaspain. They fought back-to-back, desperately trying to fend off the enemy. But a low-swung mattock smashed into the armist's knees and his legs crumpled under him. As he fell, a javelin passed clean through his neck, finding the exposed throat above his mail-coat. Blood bubbled out of his mouth as he slid to the floor, eyes glazing over. Moments later, a sickening thud knocked Kaspain down over him, blood matting his blonde hair.

Roujeark was gasping for breath and almost spent. He didn't see the death of Aleinus, but he was distracted by the cry of anguish that went up from his right, piercing above the battle-storm. He watched a tall Ciricien with the physique of a prize-fighter charge into a press of enemies where his comrade had fallen. He broke a goblin's neck with one punch and smashed the heads of two others together. He cast the bodies aside contemptuously and then lifted a harrack clean off the ground. Roujeark was amazed at the feat of strength, and watched, captivated, as the warrior, whose name was Rhyard, threw the squealing harrack into his gang of subordinates. With hardly a break in stride, the massive man plunged into the gap he had created, but death found him an eyeblink later. A dwarvish axe, taken from its trampled owner, came hurtling out of nowhere and struck Rhyard full in the face. Like a fallen oak, he crashed back in ruin, the axe still buried deep.

Roujeark turned away, sickened by the sight. Whatever Sir Theonar said, he was not cut out for this wholesale slaughter. No amount of magical power could galvanise his heart in the face of such butchery. Others in the cavern might be inured to the horror of battle, but he was not. The sight of Findor losing a leg to a goblin scimitar and falling was too much for him. He dropped back and sank to his knees, tears brimming in his eyes. Through the tears the cavern shimmered, and its ghastly clamour receded to just a dull echo in his ears. His comrades seemed to be falling thick and fast about him, and he lost sight of Lancoir and the king.

Theonar found him in that state. The tall knight knew something was wrong when the booming sound of the wizard-pupil's fireballs ceased, and he extricated himself from his position near Earl Culdon, who fought stoically despite grisly wounds. Theonar himself bore countless small hurts, and his sword was rinsed in blood, but he had great reserves of stamina. When he saw Roujeark whimpering in abject despair, he seized him by the scruff of his scorched and blood-soaked robes and dragged him along.

'Pull yourself together Roujeark, we need you!' he yelled in his ear. With one hand, he pulled him back into the thick of the battle and with the other he cut down any goblin who scampered near. He reached the spot he was aiming for and saw a case of desperate need dead ahead of him. He manhandled Roujeark upright and pointed out the dense press of harracks ahead of them.

'Now, Roujeark, fire!' But Roujeark's knees were buckling and his thoughts were scattered. He could no more summon a fireball than conjure a wolverine from thin air. Theonar saw there was nothing for it. Stooping, he scooped the young armist onto his shoulder and turned his back on the scene. Fearlessly he stood in harm's way and prayed, sword outstretched in supplication.

'Now Roujeark, DO IT! NOW! NOW!'

Held over the knight's shoulder, Roujeark could barely see or hear. He felt consciousness sliding from him when a gust of vitality swept in and through him. Borne on the wings of prayer, it invigorated him with a sharp rush of life, like a cascade of icy water over a groggy man. In a split second, his eyes focused. A few moments later, his arms stretched out rigidly, and twin fireballs shot out. The group of harracks in their path was devastated. One moment they had been mobbing a fallen enemy, the next they lay flung about in charred ruin. Roujeark's eyes widened still further when he saw a dwarf in the midst of the ruckus, beard alight and rippling with flame. Theonar was still murmuring a silent prayer of thanks when he felt Roujeark slide from his shoulder. He was too slow to catch him as he darted forward, heading for the blazing apparition. Lancoir saw him go, plunging recklessly into the flame-licked charnel-house, and went after him, leaving the king's side.

Roujeark reached the dwarf and stopped short, horror and wonder mingling in him. The warrior was still standing, but his beard was half-gone and his face was badly burned. A moment ago, the flames had been writhing all over him, but now they were gone, dispelled as if by magic. It was Hoth, the chieftain of the dwarves. Seeing his brothers dying around him, he had charged, maddened, into a knot of his foes, ploughing deep into them. He had been on the point of being overwhelmed when Roujeark's thunderbolts had struck the harracks near him. What followed was an inferno that consumed his axe-handle like tallow and part-melted the buckle on his belt. But his new armour had saved him, cheating the flames. He had put it on shortly before the fight began, taking Kulothiel at his word. Now, ignoring Roujeark completely, he tottered unsteadily away, leaving the battle. Roujeark gaped open-mouthed after him, astonished.

Yet the battle went on. Virtually everyone had paused when the great explosion rocked the cavern, and many a goblin had fled, but enough harracks loitered nearby to converge on Roujeark in a rush. He did not even heed his danger, so dumbstruck was he by the scene which he had just witnessed. Lancoir arrived just in time to intercept the enemies who came straight for him. They thought to put an end to this accursed wizard once and for all, but instead they found themselves face to face with the death-eyed Captain of the Guard. Lancoir cut down the first harrack and quickly recovered his blade to hack down another. He moved fast, knowing the ring of enemies was all around. He didn't have time to land a killing blow on each of them, so he abandoned his own advice and slashed just enough to drive each one back.

A ring of them closed about him and Roujeark, who was slowly coming back to his senses again. Lancoir buried his sword in a harrack's chest, but there it stuck fast, and when he tugged it would not come. A heavy fist clobbered his head and poleaxed him. Roujeark found himself seized by a harrack and squeezed in a deadly embrace, but he slapped at the hate-filled face with his hands. Grasping the angular temples in both palms, he felt steam rise and the harrack's grunts turn into gasps of pain. The tight-stretched skin seemed to start melting, and then it burst into flame. Roujeark cried out in pain as his own hands were burnt, but he felt the vicelike grip about his waist slacken. He dropped to the floor as the harrack fled howling, burning like a living torch.

Out of the corner of his eye he saw Lancoir struggling to his feet, shaking his head. Bereft of his sword, he looked helpless as a harrack swung at him with a crooked blade. But Lancoir ducked under the swing, which cut home instead into the harrack who had been coming up behind him. Suddenly there appeared in Lancoir's fist the demonbane dagger that was his prize. Forgotten until now, he buried it in his assailant's throat. In a split second the harrack completely disintegrated, falling like a pile of ash to the floor. The very next second Lancoir reversed the lethal weapon into the other harrack, finishing him off in the same way.

Roujeark saw a harrack looming over him with a club, and he swung upwards with the hammer he had found lying on the floor. His hands were throbbing with blistering pain, but he managed to catch the harrack a savage blow which crunched teeth and sent him reeling. Roujeark lurched upright in time to see a goblin arrow embed itself in the back of Lancoir's shoulders. It was foiled by his armour, but another one followed hard on its heels and struck his arm with strength-sapping force. It found a gap in between the lacings of the knight's vambrace and he dropped the dagger with a grunt of pain. Lancoir took a fist-blow to his kidneys from behind and staggered forwards. He stumbled over a harrack who was coming in low to tackle him to the ground. He seized up his dagger again with his good arm and the harrack vanished from underneath him. Heavy boots kicked Lancoir while he was on the floor, and he slashed about him furiously, trying to regain his feet.

Roujeark was sobbing with pain, but he did his best to fight off Lancoir's attackers. They seemed to be alone amongst their enemies. Where were the others? A jarring blow to his elbow made him drop the borrowed hammer. With his hands in agony, and now weaponless, Roujeark felt panic rising. Another blow hit him somewhere on his back, and he fell forward, stunned.

Lancoir killed another harrack, then another, and another, but they kept coming. He saw Roujeark under attack, saw him fall. He went in that direction, trying to reach him. He slew the harrack standing over him with a swing of the dagger that left him at full stretch and off balance. Another harrack appeared fast and seized the hand that held the dagger. From the opposite side, another seized his throat. Pinioned from both sides, Lancoir looked down at Roujeark, and Roujeark looked up at him. The jagged sword seemed to grow out of his middle. The blow, dealt by a hulking brute of a harrack, had enough force to puncture through the armist-mail, jerkin, body and right out the other side. Lancoir hung, impaled, eyes defiant to the last, but his face overtaken by the throes of death. Roujeark's cry of loss seemed to sear across the ghastly frozen tableau. A moment later the sword withdrew, the vicious hands let go, and Lancoir fell heavily on top of Roujeark. The wind was driven from the young armist, cutting off his strangled cry of anguish. Lancoir's dying eyes bored into his, and he watched close-up as death claimed him. With his last tortured breath, the Captain of the Guard uttered one word.

'Lancaro.'

※

XXI
At The Sight Of The Flaming Sword

INALLY The battle lulled. Whether it was the terror of the wizard's fire, or a desire to fall back and regroup, the harracks backed away and departed from the cavern. The goblins went with them, their screeches dying away into the rock with horrid echoes. A pitiful remnant of the Free Peoples were left behind, standing amid a carpet of corpses. It was a horrific scene, the survivors standing like the lonely sentinels of some long-felled forest. Acrid smoke drifted about, stinging eyes which were already raw with weeping. A smell of charred flesh and blood hung in the air. Dreadful wounds were staunched and tended as best as could be contrived, and the weary warriors gulped in air. Elrinde cleaned his sword and Southilar squatted amongst the bodies of his fallen comrades. The Hendarians gathered protectively around their ebullient king, who exhilarated after surviving his first bloodletting, whilst beside them the Ciriciens sat around, exhausted, bloodied and smoke-grimed. Parthir's Alanai scurried about retrieving arrows and thrown knives and Hoth's dwarves, now pitifully few in number, stood like statues, singing a dirge over their fallen kin.

Roujeark saw none of it, though. All he saw, close as a lover, was the dead face of Lancoir. The captain's sweat had coursed little channels through the grime on his skin. He could barely breathe, still less shift the captain's weight off him. Moments passed like hours, and then a new face appeared over Lancoir's shoulder. It was

Theonar, stooping down from on high, full of concern. With him was Andil, fresh from slaying the harracks who had done the deed. Then came Caréysin as well. Together they heaved Lancoir's body aside and liberated the shell-shocked Roujeark. Theonar helped him sit up while the two armists knelt over Lancoir.

'My friend,' said Theonar breathlessly, 'I am so sorry. I couldn't get to you in time. A charge of harracks came between us. I am so sorry...I should have been here...' Andil and Caréysin were incredulous. They could not believe that their indestructible captain had actually fallen. They had seen it happen, as helpless as Theonar to intervene through the enemies in between, but they still didn't believe it. Andil picked up the demonbane dagger and retrieved Lancoir's sword from the harrack it had killed and become stuck in, and after he had cleaned it, he laid it at the captain's side. Caréysin was holding his lifeless hand and murmuring a prayer over him, tears pouring down his cheeks.

That was when Curillian saw them. The tides of the battle had swept them apart, though he still had Antaya and Lionenn with him. He had been stooping over the maimed Findor, but when he had straightened, eyes smarting in the foul air, he had sensed something amiss. Looking around for the cause of it, his eyes fell on the sorry scene of his comrades stooping over a fallen body. All the rest of the battlefield vanished from his sight. Andil. Caréysin. Roujeark. But he could not see who they crowded around. He had watched Aleinus die, Findor he had just come from, and Antaya and Lionenn were with him. His heart went cold as he ran out of names. The sound of his heartbeat became the only thing he could hear, diminished to the barest of background flutters. Time itself seemed to stand still. He could not feel his arms or legs, could not move. The grief-stricken eyes of his surviving comrades looked at him, helpless to make it untrue.

Roujeark had never known pain like it. He was battered and bruised, groggy, parched and exhausted. His hands were horribly burnt. The stricken field filled him with horror and the smell nauseated him. Far worse was the knowledge of what he had done. He had contributed to this slaughter, his own hands had brought forth the flames which had burned friends and foes alike and now wafted about, stinging the nostrils of the survivors. The smell of the flesh he had charred lingered like an unclean spirit refusing to depart. But he had also been the cause of this. He looked down at Lancoir, whose face was now at peace. He looked up at the king. Curillian was frozen with disbelief and horror. He just stared at them. Roujeark's skin crawled under that baleful glance, guilt gnawing at him like rodents in his clothes. Weeping freely, he leaned over Lancoir.

'Lancoir...I...I can't...'

The words would not come. The gratitude he felt was swamped with guilt and shame and fear, and from that tangle nothing articulate would come. He squeezed the brave captain's hand and looked into his sightless staring eyes. How could such a valiant fighter be dead? Wouldn't Prélan save such a one? Yet if his lips and tongue would not cooperate, his fingers knew what to do. He pulled off the ring. He felt its loss like a silent but loyal friend. The plain silver band was scuffed and worn and possessed almost no shine. *Where I come from, rings are given in token of a debt of honour. I give this to you. I will not forget until I have repaid.* The long-ago words of the captain filled his head, making him choke with emotion. Gripping the ring, Roujeark leant forward and kissed the fallen armist's forehead. He left the ring on his breast. *You have paid your debt, Lancoir, my friend. Far more than was owed.*

Then he looked up and Curillian was standing over them, his face a mask of sorrow. Roujeark backed away as the king slumped down beside the body. Slowly the tears came, and then all of a sudden there was a flood. All semblance of dignity was gone from the great monarch as he wept in great sobs that seemed wrenched from his depths. Curillian dug his fingers into his friend's hair and caressed his face. All his armists and Sir Theonar stood about, sharing in the grief of their sovereign. Curillian pulled Lancoir's head into his lap so that tears fell on the captain's battle-grimed features. Then his hands reached out, grasped Lancoir's sword and pressed it into the lifeless fingers. With both hands he held it against Lancoir's breast, holding it tight.

'He saved me,' Roujeark said, feeling desperately that he had to say something. 'He came after me. He fought them off...but there were too many. He saved my life.' Painfully long seconds stretched out as Curillian's eyes bored into his, trying to understand what he was saying. Then the wizard saw a fell light come into the eyes. Curillian lurched, and Roujeark fell back. The king rose, getting unsteadily to his feet, his eyes still fixed on Roujeark. There was open accusation in them now, and furious, blood-chilling anger. Theonar stepped between them and then Curillian was ushered away by his guards. Theonar draped an arm protectively about Roujeark's shoulders and together they watched the other armists depart. But Curillian pushed his companions away and staggered into the centre of the battlefield. Unaware of all else, he sank to his knees, staring into space.

The survivors of the other nations, scarcely forty in all now, gathered about him slowly. All but Elrinde gave him a wide berth. The elf crouched down and looked into his face. He raised the armist king back up again and held him by the shoulders. Curillian's head hung limp, shaking as if refusing to heed what Elrinde was whispering to him in elvish. Then he thrust Elrinde away as well, and the elf, grave-faced, stepped back away from him. Curillian was shaking violently now, as if some great force stirred within him that could scarce be contained. Then the cry came, a great shout torn from the caverns of his soul. It blasted across the battlefield, through the tunnels and reverberated around the caverns beyond, powered by sheer hatred and carrying the promise of vengeance. The harracks heard it and blanched. Kulothiel heard it in his high chamber and closed his eyes in sorrow. On and on it went, until Curillian slumped again, drained by the effort of it. None were able to look upon his face, which quivered and twitched with storms of emotion. He took a step forward, his great sword clenched in his hand.

'Curillian.' A voice called, that of Earl Onandur. He ignored it and took another step.

'Curillian!' another voice called, this time King Adhanor. Again, Curillian took no notice, but carried on forward.

'Curillian, now is not the time,' called Earl Culdon, gasping from his wounds. 'We need to regroup.' Curillian kept going.

Sir Hardos from Southilar's party strode after him, shouting angrily for him to stay. He caught him up and grasped him by the shoulder. In a flash Curillian turned and struck him to the floor with a great blow. Such was his force that he left the big man reeling and dazed on the floor, spitting blood. Fury reigned unassuaged in Curillian's face, and madness was in his eyes. Not even Lancoir, were he still alive to see it, could claim to have seen anything like it. Then Curillian turned and strode from the chamber.

The armists hurried after him, fearful for what he might do, Roujeark included. Andil bore the body of Lancoir over his shoulder, and Theonar went with them. The others were not far behind. Southilar had been enraged by the assault on his lieutenant, and he yelled at his remaining men to apprehend the armist king.

But Curillian was well ahead of them now, picking up his pace until he was running full pelt through the tunnel. He erupted from it like a cannonball and sped down the steps of the great cavern beyond, the one they had fled through after the shield-wall collapsed. The harracks and goblins had withdrawn there, and now waited in an uncertain mob. Should they attack again or slink off with the partial victory they had scored? Then a strange noise cut through their indecision. An echoing cry, quite unlike anything any of them had ever heard, drifted through the high cavern and came to their ears. Moments later they heard the rumour of his coming, and they trembled. A single warrior came charging out of the tunnel, alone and enraged. His sword was bright and his face was a herald of death. They looked around, took comfort from their numbers, and hefted their weapons ready to receive him.

Despite being weak and feeling sick Roujeark stumbled on, driven by a renewed sense of urgency. In the tunnel he pushed past the other armists and so was next to emerge into the cavern they had so lately evacuated. The sight that greeted him took his breath away. Curillian was charging across the floor, heading straight for the whole harrack army, which was still hundreds strong. With the goblin mobs there must have been several thousand foes still in the Mountain, and in a dark, torch-lit mass they waited for the lone warrior. The other armists came alongside, and they too checked in horror and awe. None of them had ever witnessed such reckless courage. This was the Curillian that legends spoke of, the destroyer of armies, the champion of the Silver Empire, Kurundar's nemesis.

Yet he was going to his death. The enemies waiting for him would surround him in seconds and he would be overwhelmed, driven by madness to his death. Not if Roujeark could help it. He went to one knee, ignoring the throbbing pain from his hands, and raised them up. His companions watched, spellbound, as he drew a thunderbolt from his living flesh. A sinewy coil of fire snaked out of his palm and fizzled in his hands as he shaped it into a sorcerous spear. Then, with a strength they didn't know he had, he threw it. With the speed of lightning striking, it hurtled across the cavern, lighting it up and ripping the air asunder. The very floor seemed to ripple under its blistering onset. From behind Curillian's shoulder it sped, zooming past him and smashing home into the harrack ranks. They had been rooted to the spot as it came, filled with fear yet unable to discern what it was. It exploded on their front rank and burst through, flinging bodies into the air and punching through rank after rank. It did not expend its energy until it had torn the harrack army almost in two, incinerating dozens and blasting dozens more to either side.

And Curillian leapt into the carnage, following the lightning with a different kind of flame, the Sword of Maristonia. As Roujeark sagged down, spent, and as the others recovered from their shock to continue the pursuit, Curillian tore into the harracks. Half of them had already turned to run, and those that stayed were cut down left, right and centre. The Sword of Maristonia was like a living thing among them, striking death like a serpent. Fuelled by rage, Curillian cut them down and set them all to flight. And he went after them, chasing them through the corridor where the shield-walls had clashed. Theonar led those that came after. He called over his shoulder as he ran.

'Everyone take a shield. The goblin archers are still out there.' Many took his advice, snatching up the crude shields of the harracks and then carried on running. Still they could not catch Curillian, who charged on as if no weariness could ever come over him. He chased the harracks through the pillared cavern where Roujeark had first sensed their presence, cutting them down as they ran. Goblins to either side took pot shots at him, but none managed to do any damage. Curillian ignored the monstrous drum and its crew and heeded not the pockets of foes which he bypassed. His bloodlust drove him recklessly on, filled with an intense desire to kill every last one of them.

Theonar and the frontrunners crossed the pillared cavern, and they too ignored the harrack drum. Hoth's dwarves, coming behind, smashed it to pieces, stopping its great beats from throbbing out. Andil, burdened with the body of Lancoir, fell way behind, but Parthir came unexpectedly to his aid and helped him on. The goblins were massing again now for another attack, and their arrows were building up ominously in volume. Theonar's advice showed its value as their shields cheated most of the arrows. Unable to do anything else, the long straggling line of the contestants struggled on, desperate to keep pace with each other. There were enough enemies left alive in this place to swamp them yet, Curillian or no Curillian.

At length they came to the grand entrance hall, the very threshold of Oron Amular and the greatest cavern yet. They had not come in this way, and no eyes did they have now for the wondrous architecture and statuary around them. That final cavern before the open world was reached from a great balcony from which broad flights of stairs led down. Curillian was already on the floor, striving towards the great gates where pale daylight showed cold and alien to their sight. Theonar despaired of reaching the berserk king, but before going further he deployed archers on the balcony to fire down and try and cover Curillian. Then he somersaulted down, scorning the steps. Others charged down the steps, whilst the Hendarians formed a rearguard, fighting off the harracks and goblins who came at them from behind now.

Curillian was in grave danger. His vast strength was flagging, and his onslaught had carried him deep into the mass of his enemy. He did not notice the great engines of war that were being set up by harracks who hadn't yet joined any of the fighting. He was slowed by several small wounds and a great weariness which seemed to be stealing over him. All the great exertion of the Tournament was at last catching up with him and swamping his adrenaline. Yet even the end of his strength was still incredibly strong, and he kept fighting doggedly. Whirling around, he struck again and again, the great Sword of Maristonia making light of the harrack armour. No longer pressing forward, he made a ring of slain about him. But the enemy kept coming. Recovering again from their panic at the magic levelled against them, they returned to the assault. Only too late did the Free Peoples realise quite how outnumbered they had been.

Now their great engines, ballistas and catapults cunningly assembled from portable parts were deployed, and great arrows half the height of a man and thick as spear-shafts came hurtling through the cavern. Theonar narrowly evaded one, and another turned a dwarf almost inside out. With them whooshed great chunks of masonry torn from the walls; the Mountain itself was being turned against them. A Ciricien went down, and a Hendarian, then another and another was slain. The pitifully small remnant was being gradually encircled and slain to a man. Unchecked slaughter raged, and still Curillian fought on.

Yet cold sense and realisation were beginning to get through to him, and the awful predicament he had led them into slowly dawned on him. The enemy was all around; death lapped at their feet. His limbs were leaden and his heart was heavy. Feeling old and tired, he looked despairingly towards the arched gateway. Out there, so close, was sunlight and fresh air. So close. They had come so close to escaping...and now they would all die.

As he looked, the light in the gateway seemed to dim. Something was cutting off the light. A great banner. He lifted his eyes, not daring to believe what he saw. Though the cavern was dark otherwise, lit only feebly by a few braziers, he could make out the silver stitching on the great rectangular flag. A sword. The image of his own, sewn in shimmering thread and fringed with fire on a royal blue field. Beneath it marched legionaries of Maristonia in disciplined ranks, and Royal Guards with them. Beyond all hope, his troops had somehow found them. Somewhere behind him he heard armist voices lifted in ragged cheers, and a shrill trumpet blared out defiantly, shaking the ancient walls.

Ready to collapse, he watched a moment longer. Suddenly the flaming sword was cast into shadow by the passing of a shining object, flying in through the gateway. A great falcon, shimmering with silver wings, soared in above the advancing battle-line. It cast radiance on the scene below. The eyes of the Free Peoples were lifted in hope, but the hearts of the goblins and harracks were chilled. The mysterious falcon sped down like an arrow, but as it neared the earth it suddenly morphed into a pegasus, its bright wings now flanking a sleek equine body. It came to land by Curillian, all graceful strength and shining white. With his last strength he slid onto its bare back and slumped there. At last Theonar caught up with Curillian, and he fought off the enemies who menaced the king and the newly come creature.

Yet the strange beast and the Maristonian troops were not the only newcomers. Bringing gusts of sudden cold air, lines of snow-elves rushed into the hall like a snowstorm. Seeming to glide over the cavern walls above the heads of the goblins, they made straight for the war-engines, which had now been turned on the reinforcements and were doing grievous damage. Leaving behind frosted trails of ice, they descended like hail in savage anger on the harrack artillerymen and slew them with cold daggers. The machines themselves they froze solid, never to be fired again.

The Maristonian troops fought their way forward until they met the survivors. Curillian's companions were delighted to see their old comrades among the newcomers, Surumo and those members of the Third Cohort that they had left behind at Tol Ankil, and several of the trackers and scouts as well. Yet they had no time to greet them, for escape was their pressing need. The legionaries closed protectively around them, a great outward-facing square. There were several hundred of them, a couple of cohorts' worth, still fewer than the enemy but enough to hold them at bay. All the remaining contestants reached safety within the square, and Andil wearily passed the body of Lancoir up to lie draped in front of Curillian on the horse. Curillian clung to his dead friend as the newly arrived armist officers shouted orders at their troops. Slowly, pace by pace, they conceded ground and marched back towards the gate. The snow-elves went as suddenly as they had come, leaving the square to bunch through the gateway and spill out into bright daylight.

The sun was hot and riding high. The light was searingly bright in their eyes after so much time spent in dark caverns, and they raised their hands to shelter their faces. Gusts of fresh wind smote their faces, wafting with it the scent of wildflowers. Gravel and loose stones crunching under their boots, the square slowly reformed as it emerged from the great gate and made its way slowly downhill.

From within the Mountain the harracks and goblins hurled themselves against the retreating formation, but they were held at bay. Nor did the soldiery of Maristonia panic. They had trained long and learned well. Slowly, and with great fortitude, they kept up the ordered retreat. When they had all emerged into the daylight, the rearmost side of the square faced the enemy defiantly. Hard on their heels, the harracks and goblins fanned out onto the grassy slopes of the Mountain's toes. The goblins did not like the sunshine, which they usually avoided, and were not eager to renew the combat in its glare. The harracks egged them on, clashing weapons and shouting gruff encouragement. Yet they let the enemy square make it to the far side of the trough and take up a defensive position on the facing slope.

Curillian was only dimly aware of what was going on. Once upon the pegasus, his mind had switched off, his one and only thought being to keep a tight hold on Lancoir's body. Clutching it to him and slumped over the horse, his squinting eyes registered the change from cool gloom to warm summer air, but little else. The horse's measured hoofbeats lulled him as they crossed over the trough, and the sounds of battle died away in his ears. Then weariness and sorrow overcame him. As the winged horse knelt, he slid from its back and lay inert upon the fragrant grass.

His guards stood vigil over him. Roujeark sat nearby, forlorn and forgotten by all but Theonar. The rest of the Free Peoples stood and awaited the next stage. The legionaries of Mariston and the Tournament's contestants were equally weary, for the rescuers had pushed themselves through many forced marches to arrive in the nick of time. Now they watched the enemy gather and steel themselves. The senior officer in the rescuing contingent was a colonel called Estalor. He took charge and had the square formation change to a long line. He had done the impossible, and reached his king in time, but now it all seemed futile. More and more of the enemy were piling out into the open air, and every time he thought there could be no more, another mob emerged. He felt the spirits of his armists sag as the full strength of the enemy became evident. They needed a full legion here, not just the crack cohorts who could be deployed in haste.

Despairing cries went up as new enemies were spied. 'Look, there are more! Coming around the flanks of the Mountain. Hundreds of them...thousands!'

Like a swarm of ants, more and more goblins were coming to the fray. It seemed that some had not even gone inside the Mountain but had taken up positions on its lower spurs. Fresh and unbloodied, they came eager to the last confrontation. Despite the strong sun, and despite the unlooked-for arrival of the legionaries under their accursed banner, they knew they were going to win. One more push, and then they would be free to pillage the Mountain.

Roujeark was weeping now. Hope died in him as death came rushing across the valley towards him. It had all been for nothing. The long-delayed journey, his long years of carefully nurtured hope, the labours of the armists, the gruelling Tournament, the horrible underground battle. Why had Kulothiel bothered giving out his prizes and his missions if this was where it would end, just hours later? Why had *he* not done something? Now Roujeark would be denied again, and all talk of the future was vain. The battle joined, the slaughter resumed, and he let out a bitter, blasphemous curse. The end had come.

XXII

The Bloody Vale

BLOOD Ran down the green slopes in slick streams. The cries of wounded and dying warriors rent the air and weapons clashed in a relentless din. The goblins had reached the armist lines first and they paid dearly for their onslaught. A whole rank was cut down before the second rank sprang up and hauled down the Maristonian shields. Armist by armist, they carved their way into the last stand, aiming for the banner that they hated so much. The Free Peoples fended them off for as long as they could, but their strength was fading, their numbers dwindling.

Yet so absorbed were the goblins in their orgy of killing that they did not see it coming. Theonar was the first to notice. Standing tense and erect above Roujeark, his ears heard the faint sounds above the roar of battle. His face turned, eyes boring into the distance. The harracks felt it next. They felt the tremor in the ground, faint at first but building in strength. They were accustomed to the movements of the earth, but no cause could they find for this.

The trumpet did not sound until the first horse had emerged from behind a spur of the Mountain. Theonar's eyes fixed on it in a split second. It was a great grey stallion, a beautiful creature galloping in full flow. Silver-shoed and caparisoned in ivory barding, it was the tip of a blade-shaped cavalcade. As each new horse thundered into view, another trumpet sang out until the whole vale was full of a brazen music. Louder and louder blew the stirring notes until the heights on all side were ringing. All the while, the ground shook as if the Mountain were flexing buried limbs. The elven cavalry swept across the flat bottom of the trough like a ship in full sail. For cavalry they were, mounted warriors in their war-glory. Dressed in flowing silk and mail so bright it hurt to look at, here were the noblest riders in Kalimar. They wore tall helms and above their heads a thousand pennons rippled in the breeze. A forest of spears glittered in the sun and golden hair streamed out behind beasts and riders alike.

The fighting had faltered at the first trumpet blast, then the goblins had fallen back altogether as each rolling note smote them. Mortals, dwarves and armists watched in awe as the elven charge gathered speed and came hurtling to the attack. Spears were lowered and warhorses snorted. The goblins broke in panic, but their retreat from the armist line only put them straight in the riders' path. The leading horses smashed the goblins over like wattle hurdles and then ploughed straight on through. Steel-shoes smashed foreheads and leaf-bladed spearpoints gored torsos. The momentum of the charge carried it clean through the goblin host with appalling ease. Those not slaughtered in the first moments were knocked over and trampled by the following riders. A storm of hooves crushed and smeared goblins into the ground. No mercy was shown. Gems flashed and blood spurted bright. The onlookers' eyes were drawn irresistibly from left to right as the charge swept by. In its wake it left a flattened horde. Where once hundreds of goblins had been swarming to victory, now a riot of bodies lay in red ruin. The pitifully few survivors were hunted down and put to the sword.

Nor did the harracks escape. They might have fallen behind the faster goblins in the last assault, but they had nowhere to hide. The elves employed slightly different tactics with them, knowing that they were heavy enough to disrupt a charge that tried to simply overrun them, so they rode either side of them instead and lashed out with long blades. Many fell in the first pass, but then the leading riders wheeled about in a fluid display of horsemanship and returned the way they had come. Down swung the swords again, and the harracks were too slow to either flee or dodge. By the end of the third pass none were left alive, and not so much as a single elf had fallen. Imperiously they rode on and clear. Passing under the eyes of the awestruck defenders, they looked like angels of death, proud and terrible.

The first trumpet call had awoken Curillian. Standing shakily, he watched the elven charge smash home and pulverise the enemy. Gasping in disbelief at this second unexpected rescue, his eyes shone with unshed tears. Then he noticed someone standing beside him. This person too was watching the massacre, eyes bright and shining, jaw set firm and cheekbones standing proud and shapely. Rich dark hair tumbled out of a mail coif and over a sleek mailshirt. She was tall and slim, standing like a queen dressed for war. She gleamed in the sun, looking more beautiful than any person had a right to. Curillian studied her from the side for a few moments before she turned her golden eyes on him.

'Carea,' he breathed. She smiled, but there was sadness in the smile. 'Was it you?' he asked unnecessarily. 'The falcon, the pegasus...' His mind struggled to catch up with his flapping tongue. 'The reinforcements...'

'It was all me,' she said. 'Don't look so surprised, Curillian. I told you before. I told you I would prepare the help you needed, and I did. I knew you would run into trouble here, and so I found troops to rescue you. Your 5th legion is still encamped on the marches of the East-fold. Horuistan is a very unworthy general, but the young colonel, Estalor, was willing to come. Defying a threat of court-martial, he led his cohorts over the mountains under my guidance. The rest of your cohort from Tol Ankil joined us also, desperate to rejoin their king. And so we came here on a road known to none but the Cuherai.'

'Estalor…I know the name. And the snow-elves, you brought them too?'

'They needed little persuading. As soon as I told them about the goblins, they were all aflame, and the thought of their evil presence in Oron Amular had them boiling over. They went ahead of us in time of storm, some to summon extra help, some to block the enemy's retreat, and some to clear our path. Your legionaries endured the cold and the speed of their march to fight beside them.'

Suddenly it was all too much, and Curillian collapsed back to the floor. Carea crouched by him, full of concern. He grasped her arm.

'Thank you,' he said feelingly. 'Thank you.'

'My debt to you is paid. Now we have rescued each other from the harracks. But you, Curillian, you look as if you have barely survived…' She saw the grief welling up afresh in the king's face, and she knew its cause, but she was dismayed to see the sudden age and fatigue in her friend's eyes. She squeezed his hands.

'I know of your loss. He is with Prélan.'

'But I want him here still.'

'Mourn him, noble king, but let him go.'

Further words were prevented by the approach of another person. Curillian watched the ranks of men and armists part and draw back in awe as an immensely tall rider with others in attendance strode up the slope to where he sat. Once again Curillian struggled to his feet, only to go to his knees along with everyone else. For it was Lithan, High King of the elves. His tall riding boots came level with the kneeling faces, and when they looked up, they saw his scarlet tunic and gleaming Zimmerill armour, his jewel-crusted sword-belt and flowing cloak of the most gorgeous fabric. A star was on his brow and at his throat.

'Rise, Curillian, rise,' he said as he came up. Curillian stood shakily, finding himself level with the rune-chased fabric of the elven-king's surcoat. He looked up into the ever-young face, where a fell light was shining. This was only the second time he had ever seen Lithan, but whereas the first time he had been graciously serene, now he was angry. Anger too was in the eyes of his companions, all grave elven warriors.

'Your Grace,' Curillian began with an effort, 'thank you. We are all indebted to you and your cavalry.'

'I wish I could say you are welcome, but it is not so. I came because I had to.' Curillian had nothing to say. 'This is a bitter end to a foolish undertaking,' Lithan went on, 'and I grieve that I have been forced to intervene.' The High King swept his gaze over the survivors, none of whom could meet his eye. His eyes lingered long on Theonar, who alone of those present was prepared to return his gaze. The High King's lip curled in distaste. 'Look at this,' he said, seemingly to no one in particular. 'Every race under the sun gathered in a holy place, all lusting for glory and understanding nothing. Rogues and wanderers and stripling kings of men. And goblins – *goblins in Oron Amular*. Kulothiel has brought things to a sorry pass.'

He looked up at the Mountain as he said this, as if casting his eyes towards the Keeper. The assembled chieftains and lords all heard his words, and some bridled, but none could bring themselves to challenge this lofty sovereign. Lithan was older and greater than any of them. Lithan visibly struggled to control himself, gripping his sword hilt and sighing deeply. He looked at the leaders of the contestants.

'You all have my leave to depart. You shall not be molested, so long as you go in peace. First you will help us clear away the stricken from the field, but then you must leave. However you go, by land or by stream, go quickly. The land of Kalimar is not open for you to linger or ever return.' Then he turned to Curillian. 'Come, Curillian, walk with me.'

Curillian turned and walked stiffly with him. With them went Carea and one elf warrior, who seemed to be a close companion of the High King. Roujeark watched them go and noticed how Theonar also followed them with his eyes. He also heard the unhappy mutterings of those around him and felt the hostility of the dismounted elves as they set about their gruesome task.

Lithan led Curillian a way up the slope and then stopped, far beyond earshot of the others. 'Was it worth it?' he asked suddenly. Curillian's tired mind did not at first understand. 'Are you happy with your prize?' the High King asked. Curillian glanced at Carea, whose expression wordlessly conveyed that he should not be surprised that Lithan knew.

'It is...not...not what I expected.' He felt rather than heard Lithan judging what he might have expected. 'Kulothiel has laid a heavy burden on me.'

'On *us*, you mean,' Lithan corrected him. 'I know what prizes were given, and to whom.' Curillian could not guess how Lithan knew, but such things were quite beyond him. So, he listened. 'And what will you do with them?' The High King pressed him harshly. 'Do you have any idea what you are getting involved with? What you're up against?' He sighed again. 'Curillian, forgive my anger, but none of this is as it should have been.'

What do you mean? Curillian wondered, but did not voice the question.

'Though all mortals have short memories,' Lithan said, 'you at least of those here can remember the last war. You remember how close we came to utter ruin. This time, it will be worse. Curillian, I admire you more than any mortal, but I cannot approve of what Kulothiel has done.' At last, Curillian found his tongue.

'He said he was acting under the guidance of the Oracle.' Lithan looked at him long and sadly.

'So he says.' He turned away, looking once more towards the Mountain. 'But to me it seems that he is staking all his hopes on a very thin thread, trading the vestiges of his heritage for an alliance that will never come to be.' He turned back to the armist and spoke very slowly and gravely. 'Curillian, you cannot win this war.'

'Then fight with us, Your Grace...' Lithan cut him off.

'No, the elves of Kalimar will not fight. We have fought enough in this world, and we will not do so again.' Curillian glanced out of the corner of his eye at Carea, and he saw neither agreement nor rebellion in her face. Lithan came close and laid a gloved hand on Curillian's shoulder. 'Lancearon may fight with you, but I cannot. You know not what you ask. You have my blessing, though. I pray that Prélan helps you achieve the impossible, but my heart doubts.' He paused. 'But I am glad to have at least kept you alive to try. And you can thank *her* for that. Farewell.'

Curillian turned and suddenly noticed another elf close at hand. Different to the others, she was clad in pale furs and her eyes were downcast. When she looked up, Curillian found himself staring into familiar ice-blue eyes. It was Aiiyosha, the mysterious snow-elf who had rescued them after they had left Tol Ankil. For a moment her face was fixed in cold composure, but then a smile spread across her face as swift and bright as sunrise in the mountains.

'Aiiyosha came to my aid when I brought your troops across the Mountain,' Carea explained. 'Her folk led them by secret paths, and Aiiyosha herself sent a message ahead to High King Lithan in Paeyeir. For that reason alone, he was able to come in time. It was a long ride from Avarianmar to this remote vale. Thank her well, Curillian, for it is little likely that you will ever see her folk again.'

Curillian thanked the smiling snow-elf chieftain repeatedly, feeling clumsy in his effusion. Understanding not a word of what the strange elf said in reply, he bowed low and then watched her vanish up the hillside. When Curillian turned back, Lithan had gone too, striding down the slope to where his horse waited. He and Carea watched as Elrinde intercepted him with Astacar and Linvion in tow, and they exchanged words. Then Lithan continued to his horse, while the Ithrillian elves came up to them.

'I expect the High King did not have cheerful words for you,' Elrinde observed.

'What did you say to him?'

'I told him what Kulothiel told me, so that he may know the tidings I take back to my lord, his kin.'

'Which is?'

Elrinde shook his head.

'Ugh,' said Curillian disgustedly. 'The secretive ways of elves never change.'

'Do not fall out with us, King Curillian,' Astacar spoke for the first time. 'Not when we are ready to fight with you. Even if Kalimar will not.'

Curillian smiled ruefully at him, and when he looked to Elrinde for confirmation, his old friend nodded grimly.

'When the war comes, our lord Lancearon will send word. Yet it is not us you need to worry about, O King,' Astacar went on, 'but them.' He gestured back down the slope to where the other leaders were gathered.

Then the Ithrillian elves took their leave too, leaving Curillian alone with Carea.

'Are you the next to leave?' he asked her. She looked long at him, but though he could not perceive her thoughts he knew she could read his.

'Yes,' she answered at length.

'Will I ever see you again?' his voice sounded plaintive, even to him. Another long pause.

'I do not know. It depends on many things. My own course is yet unclear to me and I must seek Prélan's will. I urge you to do the same.' She came close and took his face in her hands. She looked deep into his eyes. 'Go home now, *Ruthion Curillian*, go home to your wife and to your son.' An unshed tear glistened in her eye, and he almost broke down. Recovering himself, he backed away and started to trudge down the slope. Carea called after him.

'Curillian, the decisions you take now will reach far. Have a care.' When he turned back, she was gone, but he watched the falcon winging high into the sky until it was lost amid the western peaks.

'You! We have a score to settle.' Southilar confronted him ferociously as soon as he came back. The Jeantar came aggressively forward with the other leaders close at hand. Curillian blinked, struggling to adjust from a very different conversation. 'You did grievous harm to Sir Hardos and honour demands that you make amends.' King Adhanor, Earl Culdon, Theonar, Hoth, Parthir and Colonel Estalor were all there to witness the accusation, and they all waited for Curillian's response.

'A single punch seems small recompense for how you betrayed us in the tunnel,' the armist king said quietly and tonelessly. There was a faraway look in his eyes as he spoke. As if wrenching himself from some heavy dream, the armist king raised cold eyes to the Jeantar. 'Let us leave it at that.' Southilar had been spoiling for a fight, but he did not press the issue, and withdrew in bad grace. In truth, none of them could muster the energy for any more confrontation.

Curillian summoned the last of his wits and addressed them, speaking slowly. Yet the far-away look remained in his eyes.

'My lords, our time here is done. Home beckons each of us. There are hurts to be healed and losses to mourn. But before we go, let us agree on something.'

'What do you have in mind?' Earl Culdon was grievously wounded, but he still spoke lucidly from under a bandaged head.

'Let us meet, a year from now, at midsummer. What happened here should be discussed in the cold light of day, after careful reflection and with due deliberation. None of us now are in any state to decide anything, but Kulothiel's wishes should not be forgotten.'

They all assented, some more willingly than others.

'I nominate Hamid as a location for this council,' said Adhanor formally. 'It is the most central place for all of us, if the Lord Jeantar is willing.' They all looked to Southilar, who was nursing his anger still.

'So be it.'

When the lords dispersed, Roujeark hurried to meet Curillian. Anxiety gnawed at him and he longed for some reassurance that all as well. But Curillian turned his face away.

'Stay away,' he said. Roujeark was thunderstruck.

'Curillian, please…my lord…' But Curillian was walking quickly, and at a nod from him, Colonel Estalor stepped in front of Roujeark. He was a beefy armist and he barred the way. Roujeark looked past him and called out again, but Curillian kept walking. For a moment he was tempted to fight, knowing he could blast this soldier out of the way if he had a mind to, but somehow he could not summon the energy. Estalor, a tough, capable looking armist, had no reason to think him anything other than a scruffy vagabond, and so looked down with confident disdain. He only turned away to follow his king when someone laid a hand on Roujeark's shoulder.

The young wizard turned to see Theonar standing by him. Theonar looked to the king, but then he turned sad eyes down on Roujeark.

'His grief is raw. He…' Even the eloquent Theonar seemed not to know what to say. Instead, he held out something in his hand. Roujeark opened his palm and Theonar pressed Lancoir's ring into it. Roujeark's burned flesh throbbed, but he held the ring tight.

'I took it from his corpse. I thought he would want you to keep it.'

Theonar helped him bandage his hands, expressing with regret that he could do no more. Yet healing would soon be at hand, he foretold. With nothing else to do, they stood in companionable silence as the battlefield was set in order. The dead goblins and harracks were piled in a great heap, and fire was set to their mangled flesh. The fallen men and armists were gathered and tended by their comrades, to be taken away for proper burial. The elves of Kalimar shared in the labour, silent and efficient, but they mounted up as soon as the flames took hold and a noisome smoke billowed out. The High King surveyed the dismal scene, then turned away. His cavalry left as suddenly as they had come, the thunder of their hooves dying away as the crackling of the flames became the predominant sound.

The various companies of contestants prepared to leave as well. Conversing little with each other, they packed up and made ready to leave. Their camp had been destroyed whilst they had been inside the Mountain and all their horses were butchered by the marauding goblins, so they went on foot with little more than what they had on their backs. The High King offered them neither pack-animals nor provisions. Lithan's contempt left a feeling of shame and resentment with them, so they departed in low spirits, their prizes forgotten for the time being. Sudden clouds came up the valley, casting shade over the palls of smoke that fouled the once-bright summer's day.

Roujeark and Theonar watched all this happen, and the tall knight seemed in no hurry to rejoin his Aranese companions. They watched as Curillian greeted Surumo and Piron, who were among the reinforcements brought by Carea. Royal Guards and legionaries mingled, the Maristonians formed up in a column, ready to leave. They began to march past, weary and downcast. Lancoir was borne on a makeshift stretcher, carried by Caréysin, Lionenn and two legionaries. Roujeark watched his fallen friend go but was unable to reach him. His surviving friends drew level. One-legged Findor was being helped along by Antaya and Andil, his wound cauterised and bandaged. Together they broke ranks to come and stand by Roujeark.

'This is a bitter end,' said Findor, 'and I leave more than a leg behind. We all loved him, but we also knew that he would give his life for any of us. As it happened, he gave it for you. And I, for one, do not begrudge you that.'

'Nor do I,' said Antaya, squeezing the wizard's shoulder. 'I wish we did not have to part so. You got us here, and you kept us alive.

You have my thanks, my friendship, and my prayers.'

'I, too, wish to part in friendship from you, Roujeark,' Andil joined in. 'We've come a long way since I taught you how to hold a bow – remember, when the corsairs attacked?' He chucked briefly. 'And now look at you. You have no need of arrows, that's for sure. But if this is the last we see of you, then I'm a dwarf. When you come to Mariston, look for me.'

Roujeark embraced them one by one, blinking away tears as they rejoined the column. He looked for the king, who was further back in the line. As he approached, he looked earnestly for some sign of a change of heart. Curillian had his face set hard and looking resolutely ahead. Estalor marched by his side. Roujeark's heart sank lower when it looked like the king would march straight past without another word. He went by without even a break in his step. Roujeark fought to hold back his tears, trembling and sorely hurt. He watched the king keep going. Then, suddenly, Curillian broke ranks. He kept facing ahead, but he was no longer moving, letting the column pass him by. Then he turned around and looked at Roujeark and Theonar. His face was a mask, frozen in grief and anger. He approached.

'He should be marching home with me,' he said coldly, looking at the Mountain with tears in his own eyes, which the wind blew across his cheeks. Then he turned to look savagely at Roujeark. 'But he's dead and *you* survived. No prize is worth that.' Roujeark quailed under his gaze, and he felt each of the king's next words as a separate hammer blow. 'If you had not come, he would not have fallen. I regret now that I offered you the hand of friendship. You will find no such friendship if ever you come again to my realm. Stay here and do what you must.'

'Curillian!' Theonar barked sharply, surprising the king. 'This is not right. It doesn't have to be this way.' Curillian turned his eyes on the knight.

'It is how it is, sir.'

'We have a mission, Curillian,' Theonar tried again. 'We are called to something greater than any of our lives, greater than yours, greater than mine, greater than Lancoir's. We should let nothing come between us, for we must work together in days to come.'

'Don't use his name to preach to me, sir!' Curillian snapped. 'With you at least I have no quarrel, so let us keep it that way. When the times comes, you will find me ready to do what I must, but ask nothing of me now. Our mission can wait until we meet again. Farewell.'

He turned and walked away. The column had passed, and he followed it. A cold wind blew harsh through the valley. Smoke from the great burning billowed across between them, obscuring the marching armists from view. It stung Roujeark's nostrils and made his eyes smart. Suddenly the smoke was so thick that it completely engulfed him, concealing all else.

'Farewell, my friend,' he heard Theonar say, 'the last recruit of Oron Amular. Farewell, until our next meeting.'

'And what do you do now, Theonar?' he asked. But there was no reply. He looked for him but did not see him. 'Theonar?'

Panicking at the thought of being left alone, he hurried about, trying to get clear of the smoke. He couldn't do so, stumbling blindly across the valley. Only when he ascended the far slope and rose above the smoke did he escape. Suddenly the wind changed, and the battlefield became visible again. The grass was stained red and blackened, and the fire still burned fiercely. But no living soul was there, neither good nor evil. Theonar was nowhere to be seen. He had vanished in the smoke, to follow his own road.

And me? What should I do now? He thought miserably. *Everyone else has left, and I am here all alone.* He turned, looking up at the Mountain. The great gates were open wide, empty and dark. Only a short while ago a battle had spilled out of them, but now all was eerily silent. The cold wind gusted again, smiting him as he stood exposed. He shivered, feeling the cold caress the tears on his face. Of all he had hoped and dreamed for, this was very different.

Yet the Mountain beckoned him. The empty doors radiated power. They drew him upwards. Winter was in his heart, his hands throbbed in pain and his mind was blank, but his feet at least knew what to do. They carried him up the slope, right to the threshold. As he had done on the night of the full moon when the Tournament began, he paused and gazed upwards. Oron Amular rose impossibly high above him. He felt very small. He took one last longing gaze down the valley, but they had all gone. So he went inside, and the Mountain swallowed him.

※

XXIII
The Apprentice & The King

S O. *You have come. Welcome.* Roujeark heard the voice in his
head first, then the words echoed around the chamber. At
first, he couldn't recall how he had come here, but then he
remembered. His feet had wandered through the dark passages of
the Mountain whilst he wallowed in grief and loneliness. He thought
perhaps that he might just find a dark corner and lie down and die,
but instead he had passed through a portal without realising it. Then
suddenly he was transported upwards, so fast it made his head spin.
And now here he was, somewhere in the roof of Oron Amular.

A spectral blue light was shimmering in front of him. Leaving the
smooth path he was on, he crossed over gnarled rock, and as he went
forward a ghostly lake came into view. It lay limpid in the middle of
the cavern, lapping a wave-smoothed shoreline of rock like polished
glass. Strange mists seem to hover above the water to thicken the air
and fill the cavern with fragrant warmth. Reflected patterns danced
around the ceiling above. He was bewitched by the sight. It was like
the time Prélan had spoken to him under the Aravell Bridge but
amplified a thousandfold. When he broke out of his reverie some
time later, he realised that he still had not seen the speaker, whose
words seemed able to penetrate both rock and bone. The mist-filled
air cheated his eyes when they roved about in search of him, so all
they reported was strange reflections and time-carved rock.

The voice spoke again, the words seeming to come from the mist itself.

Come to the pool.

Obediently he walked down towards the pool. He passed by tall menhirs of mottled stone that seemed to guard the perimeter and shivered in their shadow. Both the temperature and the mesmerising effect of the pool seemed to increase as he came closer. He was swaying and felt quite disorientated by the time he stopped at the point where the tiniest movement of water lapped the rock. His eyes were drawn forward until he was leaning over the water. He marvelled to see strange patterns and currents eddying in the deeps, though never a ripple disturbed the surface.

You are hurt. What magic has scarred, let magic heal. Take off your bandages and put your hands in the water.

Roujeark felt unsure about this command, but he was too tired and too dispirited to resist. He sank to his knees and felt that he would faint. If he were not careful, all of him would fall in, not just his hands, so he made a great effort to control his body. Gingerly he removed the bandages that Theonar had applied. The scorched skin underneath was a suppurating mass of flesh and blackened weals of skin. Suddenly it hurt more than at any point previously. Tentatively he leaned down and lowered his hands towards the surface. His whole body tensed, and he winced as if expecting great pain, but when his fingertips brushed the water the sensation was like nothing he had ever experienced. It did not feel like water, somehow thicker and smoother. It was burning hot and searing cold at the same time, rough and smooth, yielding yet crackling with an unearthly energy. Shocked, he jerked his fingers away almost as soon as they had had touched the water. The tips were tingling but unharmed.

He lowered his hands a second time, and this time plunged them in up to the wrists. He cried aloud in shock and gasped as his skin was subjected to extraordinary ministrations. At once it felt soothing, like the hot baths in the palace at Welton, and also so painful that it made him hiss and grit his teeth. The pain built to a vicious crescendo and plumes of steam rose off the surface. It felt as if his skin was being sloughed off like boiled meat from a bone, but just as he was about to withdraw his hands, the pain passed. What replaced it was a delightful, comforting heat that seemed to seep inside him and spread a warm glow right through him. It felt like gentle fingers were smearing warmed oil across his skin, massaging and soothing. He relished the sensation, feeling it drive away the hurts and the cares of the last few days and weeks. Then curiosity overcame him and he reluctantly lifted his hands out again, fearful at what he might see.

What he saw when he inspected his palms made him gasp again and jerk upright to his feet. Gone was the festering, oozing flesh and the burn marks, gone was the livid skin and blackened scabs. What was there instead was brand new flesh, soft as a baby's and completely unmarked. Were these even his old hands? He flexed the fingers and brushed the palms, making sure his eyes weren't deceiving him. For a split second, as the front of his mind marvelled, he was seized by an impulse to strip naked and cast himself in, but just then the voice spoke again, checking him.

Now we can begin again. Come here Rutharth. Follow my voice. The soporific words seemed to lead him on, repeating on the still air in front of him to guide him. He traced a route around the pool and then back over the knotted rocky depression. He rejoined the path that he had left before and followed it beyond the pool's end to where a great luminescence now shone amid the pall of bluish steam. He had not noticed the great light before, raised dais, but by the time he reached the steps that led up to it his eyes could not look directly at it. Covering them with his hand, he ascended the steps hesitantly. Not knowing what he might find, he went with infinite slowness, groping about with his feet before planting them each time. His other hand felt about in front of him too, and it touched a sculpted surface. The dazzling light seemed to be held aloft on a pedestal of some sort, and he stepped around it. The light was so bright that he could see nothing, but at a soft command from the voice, which now sounded very close by, it dimmed instantaneously. Suddenly he was looking at Kulothiel, Keeper of the Mountain.

⅄

The great wizard was a pitifully shrunken man, sitting in a great carven throne that looked designed to accommodate someone much bigger and less bent. His face was haggard, his eyes shrunken and his skin pallid. His hair and beard were thin and white as bone. Painfully thin hands gripped the arms of the throne with white knuckles. He did not look directly at Roujeark, so he seemed to be glancing sidelong, his gaze steady but lopsided. Roujeark felt like a newborn next to him and seemed to have an infant's capacity for rational thought and speech. The old man appeared to tire of his gawping, for annoyance flickered half-heartedly in his features and he sighed deeply, the breath coming slowly and uneven.

'An old man grows tired of being looked at thus.' The voice was real this time, spoken from frail lungs and through cracked lips. No more sonorous intonations that seemed to seep from the rock-walls and reverberate around his head. This was the real Kulothiel, and every syllable seemed an effort. Still Roujeark did not know what to say, but he made a great effort to change his expression.

'You are Kulothiel?'

The Keeper inched his head round a fraction and the deep-set eyes flashed. The countless lines etched in his face quivered with the effort as he spoke as forcefully as he could.

'Newly-arrived apprentices should address me as Lord Keeper.' His indignant outburst tailed off in muttering, from which Roujeark just about caught the word 'impudent'. Yet the effort seemed to have tired the old man out, for he said no more at first.

'I...I'm sorry,' stammered Roujeark. 'It's just...just that you've ch-changed so much since last I saw you.' His mind flashed back to their meeting on a narrow mountain-ledge on the path to Oron Amular. That had been on his first journey to the Mountain, a fruitless effort which led to forty years of waiting. He had almost forgotten the face of the wizard-lord he had met then, but now it came back suddenly, a much younger version of the ancient visage before him now. He would swear that more than forty years had been added to the face since then. He had been old yes, but still hale. He had leaned on a staff, but he had been mobile. This decrepit creature seemed chair-bound, more than nine-tenths dead already. There were livid scars across the hollow cheeks which hadn't been there before, and the cares of the world had redoubled around his eyes.

'Yes,' the old man spoke again, scarce above a whisper. 'I am Kulothiel. Head of the League of Wizardry, Keeper of the Mountain, and the last wizard...until now. You are Roujeark, my final apprentice. I say again: welcome.'

For some reason it was at that moment that the tears came. All his sadness, born of long years of loneliness, and rejection both fresh and forgotten, came bubbling over. He couldn't have felt less like the person he was supposed to be, or more pathetic in front of such an illustrious name. He felt like a snivelling schoolboy in front of an old master, and although he cuffed at his eyes and sniffed, the tears kept coming. Yet Kulothiel showed no impatience or embarrassment. No, there was compassion in his eyes, and his next words were kindly.

'Do not be ashamed of your tears. You have suffered much, and your grief has now caught up with you. The pool has had that effect before. Come, let us speak no more. There will be a time for all that must be said, and a time for lamentation. For now, let us go, I will take you to a place where you can rest.'

Roujeark had never watched anyone rise more slowly or with more discomfort, even with the aid of a stout staff. It was as if the skeleton of Kulothiel had long ago withered, and only fading enchantment was holding skin and bone together.

'Help me, young apprentice.' Roujeark came close and took his frail arm. 'The first service you shall render me is to get me to yonder portal.' With painful slowness they walked in that direction, Kulothiel clutching his arm fiercely the whole way, but explaining as he went. 'I have no energy for magical assistance, and no power to spare if I am to train you properly. It is just as well that the first Keeper had the foresight to install these *celagien*, otherwise this would be quite impossible. The name means 'from far', a network of convenience for the privileged, the lazy and those in dire haste. Or, in my case, for the infirm.' For an old man whose voice seemed ready to pack up at any minute, Kulothiel was proving quite the talker, but Roujeark had no idea what he was talking about until they reached the portal. Then, he understood. It looked just like that which had whisked him from the lower levels to this height just a short while before, and similar to that door he had passed through when summoned to the prize-giving ceremony. The fine-wrought spirals of shimmering steel, the luminescent stone set at the centre, the halo of runes about the frame, it was all the same. Now, as before, a gesture of the hand caused the stone to vanish and the spirals to unwind, allowing admittance to a confined space beyond, a claustrophobic cylinder bathed in a blue glow.

Once they were inside, Kulothiel gestured again and the portal closed behind them.

'Do keep hold, young one,' he beseeched the armist at his side. 'As you have already discovered, they move quite fast.' No sooner had he finished speaking than they set off, the flawless platform beneath their feet dropping away into the space below. They fell like a stone, whizzing through one of the Mountain's secret arteries, and Roujeark's stomach lurched into his mouth. He remembered the sensation from last time, though this was longer and faster than before, and there also seemed to be stretches of lateral movement as well, though so smooth was the motion that he couldn't be sure. Still, he clutched Kulothiel as firmly as the old man was clutching him and didn't let go till the platform hissed to a serene halt. Looking across, he felt sure Kulothiel was markedly less perturbed than himself, but doubtless the old mage had long ago mastered the art of this ride.

'Marvellous things, don't you know,' the Keeper commented, patting Roujeark's arm. 'Some time ago I found myself using them more and more, and now, if it weren't for them, I wouldn't have left the Chamber of the Pool for years.' Then the portal opened again, and they stepped out, after waiting for the metal spirals to retreat far enough.

'What are they?' Roujeark asked, his voice as shaky as his legs.

'Magical shafts. They criss-cross the Mountain, connecting all the important parts. Avatar made them. You are fortunate to get to use them so soon; in the old days, novices had to wait until they had graduated to the Second Circle before they were permitted to use them. There are less elegant means of getting about, but you will discover that for yourself in due course.' As he was speaking, he guided Roujeark up a dimly lit corridor. 'But for now, as I said, you need your rest. This will be your chamber.' Roujeark saw they had halted outside a door, one of many in the corridor. At first glance it looked quite ordinary, but around the edge were traces of gold paint and faded carvings. No lock was there, but a single glowing rune instead. Kulothiel touched a thumb to the rune, it pulsed, and the door gave silently inwards.

'It belonged to a former apprentice of mine and has housed many a Mage-Lord in its time. I hope you find it comfortable – everything you need should be inside. Rest now, and tomorrow we shall speak further.'

With that, the old wizard shuffled off down the corridor. Roujeark lingered outside, watching him dematerialise into the gloom. He fancied he saw him turn and vanish into another chamber further along, but he couldn't be sure. He went into his own chamber. It was black. Totally pitch black. He stumbled about, looking for some means of illumination, but all he managed to do was clatter into a table and smash a vial of some sort. He was too tired to do anything other than discover the bed by touch and cast himself in. His mind went blank as soon as he hit the pillow.

⚔

The journey was long and dispiriting. While they should have been admiring the luscious Kalimari countryside, they trudged on with heads hung low. Instead of the normally benign summer of the region, cast-iron clouds dogged them the whole way, and the ever-present escort of baleful riders was oppressive. If every other party was being treated the same as the footsore Maristonians, then High King Lithan was clearly serious about making sure that every single contestant left his kingdom fully accounted for. Few songs were sung, and conversations were short and whispered from armist to armist. Every now and then a jovial soul like Andil would lift up his voice in a barrack-room chant, but it soon died away under the disapproving stare of the elven riders.

They were steered away from all the wondrous sights that the oldest kingdom in Astrom had to offer, barred from even seeing the beautiful cities and waterfalls. When they came to the great forest of Therenmar, they were guarded even more jealously, as if their guards expected them at any moment to break into the trees and contaminate them. They were not permitted to cut wood for fires, nor to stray from their designated path to hunt, so their meals were hard-tack and their nights chilly. Sheer exhaustion weighed them down. The Tournament seemed to have sucked the life out of the contestants, while Estalor's cohort had been marching hard for weeks, right over the Black Mountains and now all through Kalimar. Findor had to be helped every step of the way, and the king's mood was black.

None of them had travelled with Curillian before, and so could not be expected to know how out of character he was, but his glowering brows and obstinate silence was quite at odds with the easy-going reputation they all held dear. He spoke to no one at all for the first few days, then only to a few, and even then, curt orders were all they got. He did not bother to protest about the elves' lack of kindness, but just trudged on with his soldiers, shoulders weighed down but still more tireless than the youngsters around him. Every night he stood silent vigil over the body of Lancoir, which lay in its shroud upon the makeshift stretcher. Everyone else kept well clear, unnerved by the intensity of the attachment.

Not even when the weather improved did Curillian emerge out of his grim withdrawal. When the late summer sun rode hot overhead, he turned neither right to see shapely tree-clad hills nor left to drink in the broad green vistas of vale and meadow. The great traveller-king had no appetite for anything around him, which was in keeping with the meagre portions he dolorously spooned down at mealtimes.

Yet when at last they reached the border, Curillian sprang into action. Trudging down the Armist Road with the smell of the nearby sea in their nostrils, they were abandoned at the frontier, which was marked by a line of white menhirs. No words were spoken except a grave warning not to return from the leader of their escort. On the other side they were met by a party of riders, armists from the 5th Legion. When Carea brought Estalor and Surumo's cohorts over the mountains, she had at least persuaded the truculent General Horuistan to decamp to the south, for he could expect his sovereign to return that way before long. And the legion's scouts had received word from elvish outriders, so they knew the hour of their king's coming. They had brought spare horses, which Curillian and Estalor mounted. With no delay, Curillian sent the other riders back to the nearest settlement, bidding them return swiftly with supplies and a waggon to bear the dead and wounded. The last spare horse he gave to Caréysin, with whom he held a hasty private conversation. With a smart salute the skilled archer had mounted and galloped away, and only later did the rest learn that he had been sent post-haste to Mariston with special instructions.

All through the long miles of the East-fold the Armist Road was lined with posting stations where fresh horses were kept for royal couriers, who could cover astonishing distances by regularly changing mounts. Caréysin would set the system in motion at Baldan before continuing on himself. While he rode fast with a personal message, the important state tidings would far outstrip him and reach the capital in under a week.

Baldan itself was the nearest town to the Kalimari border, but it was still many miles away. Long before they reached it, they met supplies coming the other way, which the legion's riders had procured for them. Lancoir's body was reverently laid in a large waggon, whilst the other corpses were interred in a nearby army cemetery. Not even pausing to eat, Curillian rode straightaway in the waggon with his fallen friend. With him he took only Findor, Antaya, Andil and Lionenn, although a cohort of the 5th Legion's cavalry rode too as an escort. The rest of Estalor's men were left in Baldan to recuperate and seek healing – they would return to their unit later. The king remembered to send a message to Horuistan via one of his subordinates that Estalor and his men were not to suffer for disobeying orders – they had rescued their king and were all in line to receive royal honours. But with that, Curillian forgot the legion and all other matters. He set off west, absorbed in his grief.

⋀

When Roujeark awoke it was still pitch black. So dark was it that at first, he wasn't sure whether he had really woken, or whether this was actually just another avenue of his dreams. But his fingers clutched the soft sheets and his nose inhaled the faintly musty odour of the chamber. He sat up, put his feet to the floor and rubbed his face. It was neither warm nor cold. No breath of air nor any chink of light. He could see nothing. He began to get uneasy, wondering what he had let himself in for.

'So, you are awake at last?' The voice of Kulothiel startled him, coming from somewhere close by in the chamber.

'Kulothiel?' He cursed inwardly. 'I mean, Lord Keeper.'

'You may call me Master for the time being. You are now an apprentice of the League of Wizardry, so you shall be treated like one.'

'But how did you get in here, why did I not hear you?'

There came something like a faint chuckle. 'My dear boy, you were so fast asleep you wouldn't have heard if a troll had come in. You have been asleep for a day and a half.'

'A day and a half!' exclaimed Roujeark.

'You were very weary, both in body and in spirit. Best you rested before we begin.'

'Begin what?'

'Your training.' That statement hung in the sightless air for a while.

'Why can we not have light?' Roujeark asked.

'You have no need of light for now. Just listen and speak. All apprentices begin their noviciate in darkness, to attune other senses and to refocus their minds. So shall you, but...first I imagine you have some questions...'

So many questions, thought Roujeark, *but where to begin*? His mind went blank, but out blurted the thing most preoccupying his heart.

'Why did Lancoir have to die?' Kulothiel did not answer at first, Roujeark just heard the sound of his breathing, so he carried on. 'He was my friend, and he died.' His voice caught in this throat. 'He died to save me, but the king would rather that I died, and Lancoir lived.' More tears flowed down his cheeks. Soon his gentle sobbing turned into huge wracks of grief that filled the chamber with hoarse, tortured sounds. Above it he was dimly aware of Kulothiel speaking soothingly.

'Yes, let it come. Let it come. Let all the tears out. Hold nothing back within yourself. Let nothing remain to distract you.' Then his words changed to a low, strange chanting that he couldn't make out.

Some time later the storm subsided, and his convulsions calmed down to gentle sobbing again. He became aware of Kulothiel praying, and in the midst of the darkness he felt a warm glow of peace touch him. Slowly, ever so slowly, it spread throughout him, quieting his inner turmoil.

'They just left.' He spoke aloud to the darkness, recalling how Curillian and his guards had all abandoned him that day. He had experienced rejection many times, being turned away from villages and denounced by rural clergy, but never like this. Never had he felt so abandoned. The memory was still raw, but he felt much better for having expressed his distress.

'This world is full of trouble, Roujeark,' Kulothiel said, 'and those with Prélan's calling upon them receive more than their fair share. Yes, mourn, but do not hold on to what is past. It was Lancoir's time to die, but for you also your old life is over. Another lies before you, and that is what you must look to. Yes, Curillian was unjust in his treatment of you, and if he clings to his anger it will hurt him sorely, more so even than the loss of his friend. Even for one who has confronted death many times, losing a friend never gets any easier, and Lancoir was dearer to Curillian than any other comrade. But do not carry the same hurt yourself. Leave it here in the darkness, leave it with Prélan. Unforgiveness will kill you, and thwart your mission before ever you come to it.'

Silence fell as Roujeark considered those words. It hurt, and what Kulothiel was telling him was hard, but he would try and do it. Kulothiel was content to let his young apprentice ruminate in silence for a long time. Then, slowly, other questions came.

'What was it all really about? The Tournament I mean.'

'Were you not there when I spoke to all the contestants?' Kulothiel responded. 'I needed to bring the Free Peoples together. They must learn to unite before it is too late.'

'But couldn't you have done that anyway? Why a tournament?' Kulothiel nodded, as if accepting that further explanation was required.

'The Oracle ordained it.'

'The Oracle?'

'Yes, the Oracle. The mouthpiece of Prélan, the principal means by which He reveals His will to us. It is beyond our control, and what it is we still do not know, but ever and anon it arises from the Pool of High Magic and speaks to us, to me. Sometimes it is silent for centuries, and at other times it speaks often and at great length. Its meaning is rarely clear to the undiscerning, but to those who have been given the gift of interpretation, and who respond with faith and prayer, it provides wisdom and direction from Prélan Most High.'

Kulothiel spoke in reverent tones before lapsing into silence. After a time, he spoken again, enlarging his answer.

'I'm not sure they would have come otherwise. There had to be some compelling reason for the representatives of so many different nations and races to come so far. Something to break through their preoccupations, command attention, rouse them to action and overcome their suspicion of old Kalimar, and of each other.

'In truth, the simplest answer is that Prélan commanded it. All I have done is merely to obey His bidding. Many years ago, the Oracle appeared to me and spoke a revelation from Prélan. It confirmed my fears about the return of evil to the north and warned of coming war. It foretold your coming, the last wizard. Your coming would coincide with the onset of a great struggle, and the world must be ready. Prélan had chosen champions to lead the Free Peoples, but it was my task to find them and to arm them. The Oracle decreed that a tournament in this Mountain would bring them forth and reveal who they were. I had the prizes prepared in advance, but it was the performance of each contestant that showed which reward they merited.

'Understand that I could not simply give the prizes, they had to be earned. The Tournament was the perfect vehicle for revealing each one's true nature. When pushed to the limit, you see who a person really is, and what they are capable of. You of all people should know that, after all that you have been through.

'At first, I was as perplexed as you are now, and the High King thought it was foolishness when I told him of my plans. He still does. But I have given it much thought and have had many years to consider why things had to be as they were. The more I meditate on the will of Prélan, the more I understand it. Some things cannot simply be told to a person. They must be shown. The Free Peoples had to see for themselves that there is no longer a League of Wizardry to protect them. Only here could they see the greater matters which transcend their petty priorities, both the great danger they all face and the common bond they share.

'Some of this I told to Curillian after his victory, enough to guide him. It will fall to you, though, after I am gone, to ensure that this knowledge is imparted to those who need to hear it.'

Roujeark thought about all that he had heard, sitting there in the perfect darkness. So much of it seemed far above him, too lofty for him to attain. The thought that his own destiny had been foretold was staggering to him. With an effort he pushed the thought aside, lest he drown in it, and asked his next question.

'Did you know that Curillian would win?'

'Know? I would not say so,' said the wizard lord, 'but I suspected. Hoped, even. There are few in Astrom like Curillian Harolin. Yet I wondered if perhaps his time had passed, for a new generation is rising and others there are who might have triumphed instead. The winners, if you could call them that, have a hard road ahead of them, the Harolins not least. Their worth has been proved, but it will be tested again and again in the years to come. I can only put my faith in Prélan that He will empower them and work through their weaknesses to bring about deliverance. No, I believe things have transpired as Prélan intended, though my heart tells me that there may be more yet that I do not understand.'

Again Roujeark pondered the words, and a certain phrase seemed to hover in the darkness, sparking in his mind.

'As Prélan intended,' he mused, half to himself. 'Did Prélan intend all this?'

'What do you mean?'

'The Tournament, the prizes, the winners...'

'Yes, even as I have said.'

'And the battle afterwards? Was that too as Prélan intended? How could He wish so many slain?'

Kulothiel made a strange noise, almost like a little laugh, as of one hearing something anticipated and being delighted that it has come.

'A fine question, young armist. And I will answer as best I may. "Intended", I think, is the wrong word. I do not believe that Prélan desired the battle or brought it about. Rather He worked *through* it. Not all that happens in this world is from Prélan, but evil chances, selfish decisions and the misguided desires of created beings can all be made to redound to His glory, abhorrent though they may be in the first seeming. We none of us see the whole story, how every thread and theme fit together, so no one is qualified to judge the true significance of every event. Even in tragedy and loss, there may lie great purpose that we cannot see. If nothing else, bonds of brotherhood have been reforged between erstwhile enemies, and they will be dearly needed in the times to come.'

'I'm not sure I understand,' Roujeark said, frustrated. 'But where did the harracks come from? How did they invade Oron Amular? I thought this Mountain was so strong, that no evil could ever come here.'

'Alas,' said Kulothiel feelingly, 'would that it were so. Verily, though it lies on the edge of tranquil Kalimar, Oron Amular has been beset by enemies for millennia. Goblins have prowled the Black Mountains for time immemorial, and harracks hold sway over their hidden vales. Long have they desired to come here and despoil the Mountain. It stands for everything they hate, and they are goaded on by the Great Enemy.'

'Kurundar?'

'Yes, Kurundar.' Kulothiel's voice was heavy. 'He is the mover of all that is evil in this world. He is not content with Oron Cavardul, his own sinister abode, but wishes to have Oron Amular as well. For millennia the League was always too strong, and our enemies were kept at bay. Yet over time our strength waned, while evil prospered. We spent what little power we had left forty years ago in a futile venture, and ever since then this Mountain has been exposed. No battalions of warrior-wizards to fight our foes, no Mage-Lords to bar our gates. Only one frail old master. Yet even so, the goblins and harracks could never have come here without help. We were betrayed. An old friend, who long ago turned to evil, gave them help, and revealed the ways here.'

⋏

As Curillian trudged home, and as Roujeark learned at the feet of Kulothiel, the goblins climbed the mountain. Slogging through the snows and driving wind, they came to a fist of rock standing proud of the high pass. This was their rendezvous, here on the saddle between Ustanzor and Hundereth, two mighty peaks of the Black Mountains, and *he* was waiting. A dark figure stood atop the fist. He was motionless, but his black robes blew wildly in the wind and snow frittered about. The goblins came as close as they dared, careful not to look at the masked face. The dark figure waited impassively for them to report.

'Master,' the goblin chieftain began, having to shout above the gale. 'We were defeated. They had reinforcements. Immortals came out of nowhere, riding their cursed horses, and we were routed.'

'Why did you not complete your task inside?' Somehow the words cut through the wind, and though softly spoken there was no mistaking the impatient malice behind them. The goblin chieftain cringed.

'The foreign lords fought harder than expected. They had magic on their side.' Keenly interested eyes bored holes in the goblin as he spoke, though they could not be seen through the rune-chased mask.

'Did you get what you went for?' The goblin hesitated a long moment, then shook his head fearfully. He heard the heavy exhalation of displeasure and braced himself for the inevitable blast. The dark figure looked away and was silent a long time, as if deliberating how to dispense death. Instead he spoke again, quiet and menacing.

'So…the old man made one final effort?'

'Him...and another.' The dark figure snapped his gaze down on the cringing figure, his intensity redoubled.

'Another?' Suddenly the goblin felt himself lifted up through the air and held close under the mask. He dangled, held by an invisible force.

'What other?' The goblin didn't know and couldn't speak either. Holding his victim in limbo, the dark figure stared out beyond the pass to where Oron Amular stood wreathed in storm-clouds driven up out of the eastern ocean.

Who are you? Lightning crackled and struck the flanks of the mountain, flaking away great shards of ice. The figure gazed at the Mountain as if trying to penetrate both rock and snow to discover who lay within. *It matters not. I will discover soon enough.* There would be time aplenty to deal with whatever final mischief the Keeper was brewing. His master would know what was to be done. Soon he would take back his tidings of the battle and the unexpected resistance, but with the elf-king and his woodwitch holding vigil in the guarded valleys, he could uncover no more.

Turning his attention back to the goblin, he found that the wretched creature had suffocated whilst he had been lost in thought. The ugly face had turned a fascinating shade of blue, making it still more repulsive. Disgustedly he tossed the corpse aside, where the snowdrifts would soon cover it. He looked down at the others, who cowered under his malice.

'Return to your maggot-holes. You may thank your petty gods that you will get a chance to redeem yourselves for this failure. Await my signal. It will begin soon.' Then he turned and strode north, putting the Mountain to his back.

‹ᛝ›

'Who is this old friend?' asked Roujeark, feeling horribly out of his depth.

'That you shall know in due time. Some questions should not be answered yet.'

'But I have other questions…will you not answer those?' Roujeark heard the pleading tone in his voice and hoped that Kulothiel was looking kindly at him, for it was still pitch dark and he could not see the Mage-Lord's face.

'Ask your questions,' came the answer, neither kind nor harsh.

'You say that the harracks and goblins were led here, that we were betrayed, but did this traitor also open the Mountain for them? Or if not, how did they get inside? I had to use a Seal of the League of Wizardry to open the doors before the Tournament began.'

'The doors were not shut after the contestants entered. The Mountain remained open.'

'But why? Did you not know that enemies were approaching?'

'Yes, I knew.'

Roujeark was startled by the confession.

'Then why…'

Kulothiel cut him off impatiently, voice rising.

'Because an end needed to be made. I do not need to justify my decisions to you…' he snapped. Roujeark heard him sigh deeply before continuing. 'But I will explain, if it helps you find peace. Matters had built to a head and had to be dealt with. The threat had to be ended. When a hostile army that size is on your doorstep, you do not leave it to do as it pleases in a land of peace. Not when the inside of your home is much more dangerous than the outside. I did not know that High King Lithan knew of their coming – that was Carea's work – and so for all I knew, it fell to us to destroy the invaders.'

'But you gave us no warning,' protested Roujeark, thinking of how they had been trapped inside the mountain at unawares. 'Could you not have…' he trailed off, interrupted by another memory. The chill air rushing over him before the battle, the book about the harracks fallen from its place in the library. He saw himself leaning over it on the patterned floor, and sudden realisation dawned on him.

'…You did warn us.' A deep exhalation in the darkness was answer enough. Roujeark had more questions, though.

'But could you not have helped us? I know there were the traps that Sir Theonar showed me,' he went on, other memories flashing back through his mind, 'and I saw you destroy that group that followed us, but why did you not do more? Surely you could have?'

'Why are you so sure of that?' Kulothiel challenged him. 'You have no idea how much of my remaining strength I used to achieve even that much. You have seen awesome things, Roujeark, but I am not all-powerful. All the power of the Pool will not avail when the host is too frail to channel it. My strength and my energy are fading, and I must steward it with great care. Perhaps I could have shut the invaders out, or destroyed more of them, but then I would have had nothing left of myself with which to train you. I had hard choices to make, but make them I did. It grieved me sorely, not to be able to do more, not to save more lives, but I had to prioritise that which is of the utmost importance: you. I had to keep back what I needed to equip you. Do you understand?'

'Am I really worth so much?' Roujeark felt sick and overwhelmed. Struggling with his words, he said, 'given the choice, I would not have purchased my training with so much blood.'

'But the choice was not yours.' Kulothiel's voice was stern, but thick with emotion. 'You might not like it, but this is an investment that I have to make. If I could not train you, no one else could. If we were not here now, with the barest resource spared for your training, then all would be lost. You must look beyond the lives that were lost and think of the countless more that would have been lost had things gone otherwise.'

Roujeark was struggling to take it all in, mind churning with all that he had been told, so much of which he hated or could not understand and so many questions yet unanswered. He felt exhausted, so great was the inner turmoil, but he forced himself to ask one more question. *The question.* The question which had been long buried, but which burned close to his heart. Now at last he could ask it.

'Then tell me this: why now? Why turn me away before? Why have you kept me waiting *forty* years?' All Roujeark's frustration boiled up as he asked the question, but the anger and resentment in his words seemed to melt into the blackness, perturbing the voice which responded not at all.

'The reason is simply this: it was your ill fortune to arrive just when we could not welcome you.'

'What does that mean?

'You will speak respectfully.' The rebuke was softly given, but it shut Roujeark up instantly. He suddenly remembered that he was just a low-born foreigner, and that Kulothiel was a prince of wizards.

'It means just this, Roujeark: you came to us on the eve of war.' *War? What war?* Roujeark had not heard of any wars, but he managed to keep the questions in his head, sensing that Kulothiel would provide the answers anyway. 'A war that few participated in, and about which fewer still will ever hear, but a more grievous conflict there never was. The League of Wizardry marched out to fight its final campaign.' Roujeark suddenly remembered the strange lights he had seen the night Kulothiel turned him away. Now he realised they had been the illuminated staves of wizards issuing from the Mountain. 'We left Oron Amular and went north to confront the evil of Urunmar. Too long its power had grown unchallenged. Too many young wizards had been seduced to its allegiance. So, we fought...' There was a quiver in his voice as he spoke. 'Before it was too late.' As if oppressed by the memories, Kulothiel lapsed into silence, and a great weight came upon the air of the lightless chamber. At long last, the old mage spoke again.

'It *was* too late. The power of Oron Cavardul had outmeasured all our most fearful guesses, and I led our last wizards into a trap. There, amid the frozen wastes of Urunmar, and under the eerie lights of the northern sky, we contested with the forces of darkness. Bolts of magic scorched the freezing air and blasts of sorcery smote the snow to tremble the earth and throw up great pillars of steam. We were outnumbered, but we had the greater knowledge of the *Valiroen*. That much good I accomplished: we arrived before too many of the defectors were able to rise to their full potential. They went north to join the winning side, but instead they were cut down, their youthful promise as dead and frozen as their corpses. I wept as I fought, striking down one old pupil after another, using my strength in the worst possible way. Once I even dared to hope that we might prevail...would Prélan grant us victory on that day and stop the war before it even began? Alas, no. We, too, endured our losses. Friends died on either side of me, fellow workers over many lives of men.

'Reydoeir, Timell, Finarion, and dozens of young warriors. The old masters were slain alongside the flower of our last intake, and our enemies took heart. Orcs, trolls and fell beasts flocked to the battlefield so that we were surrounded. While we kept those hordes at bay, the dark wizards gained the upper hand. Baradon, valiant Baradon, was struck down by his own apprentice, and his eyes watched me as his spirit departed. Such grief I have never known. Our circle shrank as one by one we died. Iorcar slew the chimeras of the underworld, but died in the jaws of the last, burned and rent even as he struck his final deathblow. Elucar warded off one blast of sorcery after another, and might even at that hour have extricated himself, but he stood firm and met his maker on his own terms. Even as he contended at my side with Kurundar, he was cut down from behind by him whom I shall not yet name. Together, we might have overthrown Kurundar, and averted much evil, but I was left alone.

'My ancient foe, my brother, waged war from an outcrop of the volcano, and it burst into life even as he brandished his staff and sword. Fire and smoke filled the sky, cutting off the stars and raining ruin upon the field. Those who had no cloak of protection were smothered or incinerated. Thus, only a handful witnessed that final struggle. We had been at odds for three thousand years, the champions of good and evil, and this was our last confrontation. Neither of us could overmaster the other, and the very ground was riven by our contest. Yet at the last, I yielded. I could not fight him and yet also ward off his minions, both great and small. These wounds I bore on that day, a payment for my retreat, and I barely escaped with my life. I had expended the greater part of my power and sacrificed the lives of every wizard under my care. Every last one. The League failed. I failed.'

There was a long silence before he spoke again.

'And now we teeter on the very brink of doom. So, you see, my young apprentice, why you could not stay?'

Roujeark was weeping. Kulothiel's words had moved him to anguish, and the visions he had cast of death and fire and ice tormented his waking mind.

'Yes…I see. I understand now. And how I wish that I didn't.'

∧

Every lord and dignitary in the East-fold heard the news of the king's return. Few had known of his going, but in his absence the rumours had multiplied and gained credence. They had all been wondering what he had been doing and when he would come back; now they flocked to his column as it trundled along the Armist Road. Yet few of them were allowed near and the king paid little heed. Barons and magistrates of immense dignity and wealth were left by the wayside, and the grim procession continued unabated. Curillian eschewed creature comforts even more than normal and camped in the open country beside the road rather than in the towns and abbeys. That was, when he remembered to rest at all. His companions left him to his introspection, their unease growing with every day that passed.

At last they reached the Delarom Pass, that winding mountain corridor that climbed up out of the East-fold over the Carthaki Mountains. The last peaks of that mighty range, which curled around the Central Lands of the kingdom like a defensive hide, stood like great sentinels on either side of the narrow way. Ruined elven towers disfigured the rocky slopes like shattered teeth, but the modern fortifications were higher up, and stronger. At the height of the pass, where the mountain-bastions were barely more than a quarter mile apart, the armist kings had built a formidable rampart, sealing off the heart of their realm. Five other walls of increasing width guarded the lower slopes as they descended into the rich heartland of Maristonia. Together they made the fastness of Delarom, a statement of strength and a burden of inconvenience to the mercantile traffic that laboured unceasingly over the pass.

The crowds of merchants and peasants and travellers parted to let the royal riding go by unrestricted. Hats were removed and armists knelt, but no heed did the pale-faced king pay. He was greeted at the final and highest rampart by a deputation of officers and a fanfare of trumpets that set the ravines to ringing. Passing under the arch, Curillian walked on foot past the towers and across the pass which old labour had made smooth as a pavement. Through the midst of a parade-ground the flag-marked road ran west and downhill, and in the distance could be seen the fertile fields and forests of central Maristonia.

From the barracks on either side spilled a multitude of soldiers. They approached the cortege and surrounded the funeral-waggon of Lancoir. Curillian did not stop them but wept fresh tears as their honest faces crumpled in grief at the sight of their fallen captain. Helmets were removed, spears were dipped, and hundreds of blades were placed lovingly around the corpse. Lancoir had been Captain of the Guard in the palace of Mariston, but he had been of the legions' own, a soldiers' general. His reputation bestrode the realm, and not a one was willing at first to believe the grim news that he had been slain.

But slain he was, and now he embarked upon the last leg of his long journey home.

⋀

'Is there any hope?' Roujeark asked plaintively of the darkness. They had been many days in the darkness, days of penitence and prayer and self-reflection. And from the darkness, Kulothiel responded without hesitation.

'Hope remains. Hope can never die, for an end to hope means that He in whom we hope has deserted us. That, He will never do. Prélan lives and reigns, and His power will make a way. His light shines in the darkness...'

A single flame appeared in the blackness, slender and frail, but dazzlingly bright after so long in darkness, and waxing stronger.

'...and the darkness cannot overcome it.' And behold, the flame danced between Kulothiel's gnarled hands, growing ever larger and larger until it illuminated the whole chamber, driving the shadows back into the farthest recesses. For the first time Roujeark was able to see the chamber in which he had spent so long. There was a bed raised on a small platform, a well-worn table and chair, and many niche-shelves filled with manuscripts and old artefacts. The privy which hitherto he had found and used by smell alone he now saw was a well-separated side-chamber, and the cold draught that kept it fresh came down from a fissure high above.

'So, you have learnt your first lesson, Roujeark,' Kulothiel told him. 'Learn it well. Never will you hear from me anything so vital. Prélan is the source of all hope, and in Him you will ever replenish your own, no matter how low it ebbs. No matter how dark it gets, no matter how close the storm clouds press, there is nothing that can overcome the light of Prélan. Come,' he said, standing. 'The rest of your lessons await. But first, I will show you the Mountain that is to be your home for a while.'

Roujeark followed Kulothiel and received sustenance to strengthen him on his tour of Oron Amular. It was vast and intricate beyond his wildest imaginings. True, the great mountain had seemed gigantic from the outside, but he had never guessed how much lay contained within. How many miles of tunnels, how many great caverns, how many armouries and smithies and pools and streams and chapels and holy places. There were kitchens, pantries, larders, refectories, dormitories, libraries, workshops and assembly rooms, none of which he had seen during the Tournament. Dimly, slowly, he began to perceive how they fitted around what he had seen: the Tear of Mírianna, the Hall of Tapestried History, the Map Chamber, the Amphitheatre where Curillian had vanquished the last guardian. Even with this vague knowledge he felt keenly his ignorance, for untold districts of the wizards' city lay unexplored and unknown to him.

'There were once thousands of wizards here,' Kulothiel told him. 'Prélan's own army, to match on Astrom below the hosts of angels in Eluvatar above. So many had to be housed and fed and entertained as well as trained. Thus, we acquired here the richest trappings of civilised life that has ever been seen. Not in storied Paeyeir or amongst the marvels of Avamar could such wealth and intricacy be found. Oron Amular was the mystery and wonder of the world, a place of unfathomable learning, of unshakable strength and of unending nobility. The elves of Kalimar barricaded their ancient arts from the outside world, but we, we taught the teachers, healed the healers, equipped the explorers, trained the warriors and schooled the loremasters. Here was the vision of Avatar, Prélan's great design for the succour and betterment of His world. The great plagues? We banished them. The mighty floods? We rolled them back. The suspicions of nations? We dispelled them. Peace we kept, knowledge we spread, virtue and honour of Prélan we upheld. All this we did... for six and a half thousand years.'

Slowly, by masterly told chapters, Roujeark heard the story of Astrom in its long history. Kulothiel took him to the Great Library, high in the uppermost levels, where marvellous books came alive and told their story with sounds and visions that sprang alive from the pages. In the Map Chamber, he watched the tale of nations unfold as the elves spread across Astrom in the dimmest recesses of antiquity. He watched the wars and great endeavours unfold, witnessed the fall of elvendom as great swathes of it forsook the faith of Prélan and beheld the dawn of mortality. From the ashes of the heathen altars mortal nations arose and contended with each other. Maristonia was born and Curillian's ancestors roamed its shores. The shadow of Kurundar darkened the north, and the south rose up in unison against it in the First War. But their victorious union broke apart, and from the ruins of shattered agreements dissension bred new wars and fresh tragedies. Lancearon's Silver Empire tried to forge a new peace and alliance against Kurundar, and Roujeark watched spellbound as it both failed and succeeded. Rapt until the end, he watched as history caught up with his own lifetime, where newly invigorated nations flexed their muscles as the Silver Empire retreated and evil grew once again.

He watched and learned until he felt his mind would burst, but after each spell of rest he came back thirsty for more. Something in him had awoken, a great yearning for knowledge. Kulothiel supplied his appetite from a limitless supply, teaching him theology, medicine, astronomy, rhetoric, mathematics, geography and weaponcraft. What Kulothiel himself could not do in his enfeebled state, he had magical denizens to do for him. Sentinels, like those they had fought during the Tournament, came awake again to drill and train him, and portals of knowledge poured forth in their respective disciplines while Kulothiel slumbered.

The Keeper put him through his paces, sending him on long runs and explorations of the Mountain, some of which had him away for weeks at a time. He learnt that the lowest levels of the Mountain were set aside for training areas, where novice wizards and apprentices were subjected to gruelling regimes of physical challenges. Some of these training areas had provided the backdrop for the Tournament, and Roujeark came across familiar spots. But there were many more they hadn't passed through, vast and labyrinthine. His sense of direction sharpened to a fine point and his muscles grew hard, but no matter how many miles he traversed, there was always more to discover.

Mariston was a changed city, for the king himself had changed. He rode beneath the gates in a mood as grey as the cloak that swathed him; as grey as the walls looming above him, as grey as the leaden skies and as grey as the cold seas buffeting the coast of Mariston Bay. A poor harvest had been followed by the onset of a winter as harsh and early as it was unusual. He had been many months upon the road, and he had not hurried. Now cold winds blew through the streets he loved so much, and crinkled leaves fluttered amongst the plane trees.

Joyful crowds had gathered to welcome him home, for news had gone ahead of his party that royal banners were approaching the city, but their cheers had swiftly tailed off when he did not stop or show any of his customary warmth. He and his escort had ridden on past, neither rushing nor pausing, and passed silently through the city. All who saw them pass knew something was wrong. No trumpets rang out, no armour glittered, no gifts were given, just a grey company winding its way into the heart of the city.

All had heard the rumour of Lancoir's fall, but they saw no body and heard no confirmation. Curillian had left the corpse in the care of a monastery on the slopes below Delarom Pass, reluctantly parting with it in order that his friend might be properly tended. The body had decayed on its long passage through Kalimar on foot, and it had only been crudely preserved on the East-fold leg. Now the monks would do what they could for the fallen knight and make him presentable while arrangements were made for his funeral. The other Knights of Thainen had all been recalled in haste from far-flung postings and missions, and all but a few reached Mariston before Curillian did, convening with the speed of devotion. Their sudden convergence on the capital was a rare event and a sure sign to the masses that something was afoot. Other preparations were set in train by Ophryior, the Lord High Chancellor, who met his sovereign at the gates of the Carimir Palace with Earl Cardanor the regent and a handful of other dignitaries.

The queen had not come to meet him. She had remained tearfully in her chamber, not wanting to believe what she had heard. The official post-riders had come first, bringing news of a distant victory and the king's return, and all had seemed well, but Carmen knew that something was amiss when orders were given for the recall of the Knights of Thainen. Then came Caréysin, and his news was less good. He brought the grievous tidings personally from her husband, and while he tried to remain cool and factual, he could not hide that some terrible change had come over the king. Since then, other rumours had reached her ears: his refusal to meet some of his most senior subjects along the way, uncharacteristic gloom and a seeming reluctance to speed his return.

Now she watched from her high balcony as he rode between the lines of Royal Guards who had formed up in perfect lines either side of the palace road. Her concerns grew when she watched his manner and bearing. His head, which normally gazed about in absolute command of all he saw, was bowed, and there was no spring in his step. When he dismounted, it was with barely a trace of his usual agility. Only a small, ragged party was with him, looking like armists who had endured great privations. They dispersed when Téthan, the king's son, had come hurtling from the gardens to greet his father. Carmen watched the two embrace, and then she held his gaze when he at last looked up at her balcony. Her breath caught in her throat. Even at this distance, the change was noticeable. His shoulders were slumped, his hair was long and unkempt; his whole demeanour was burdened. He had gone forth the greatest monarch in Astrom, evergreen and strong, and come back a weary traveller. He had left a colossus and returned a shadow.

'Why did you take so long?' She had not meant to accuse him like this, but the bitter words burst forth as soon as they were alone. With an effort, she had composed herself to receive him in sight of others down below, but now in their chambers, with all their servants gone, her anger flared. Yet it dissipated almost immediately when she watched him lingering uncertainly by the door. He was grey-faced and wayworn and looked ready to collapse. Where had her husband gone? A stranger stood before her, unassured and weary.

'Curillian?' She walked towards him, full of concern, and he too took a few unsteady steps.

'Curillian, my darling, what has happened?' She was shocked when she looked into his eyes. She knew those eyes, though she had never seen them so sad. Not since his return from exile and the tragic revelations of what had passed under the usurper had she seen a sorrow like to it, but then he had been in the summer of his strength and the grief had not clung to him as it did now. There was a look of defeat in those eyes and an air of utter dejection. Could Lancoir's death alone have wrought so terrible a change?

He spoke not a word, but when she folded him into her arms, wrinkling her nose against the smell, he began to weep. Trembling with shock, it was all she could do to stay strong for him. He had wept before, of course, but never had he seemed so helpless, so spent. She stroked the rough hairs of his beard and caressed the tears on his cheeks, all the while murmuring into his ear.

'Oh, my darling, my darling Curillian. It's all right, you're home now. You're home.'

⋀

Ever and anon Kulothiel would recall him to his one-on-one studies, and there at length the subject turned to the League itself. All until now had apparently been background knowledge and context, but now Kulothiel taught him about the League itself.

'The League has four circles and its members progress from one to the other.' He illustrated his point by indicating a diagram on the floor of the library. Underneath the tables and benches and between the colossal bookshelves, the entire floor was taken up with one great spherical design. There were four circles, one within the other, each coloured slightly differently. Kulothiel explained each circle as they stepped from one to the next.

'The Fourth and Outer Circle is the junior-most. This is where apprentices join the League and commence their training. Only once they have passed their tests and proved themselves do they become initiated as *Amthaen*, warrior-wizards. The warrior-wizards of the Third Circle were the backbone of the League, its foot-soldiers and primary agents. A warrior-wizard is assigned a master to give him more in-depth training, for the requirements of the next circle are much more demanding. Most wizards only ever attained to the third circle; it was only a gifted few who entered the Second Circle to become *Kenapayen*, or Overseers. The *Kenapayen* were powerful wizards with deep and wide-ranging powers. They conducted most of the day-to-day affairs of the Mountain, trained the outer circles and served as ambassadors in the courts of the world, where they spoke with the authority of the League. The final destination and aspiration of every wizard is the First Circle, the heart of the League. A wizard of the First Circle is an *Amulira*, a Master Mage. Rarely were there more than six at any one time, the elder statesmen of the League, its greatest minds and most exceptional workers of magic. From among them was chosen the Keeper, he who ruled the Mountain.'

When he had finished speaking, they were in the centre of the library, standing in the smallest circle of the design.

'You are in the Fourth Circle, my apprentice,' Kulothiel told him. 'Apprentices are able to discern the presence of magic and recognise it in others. We made it our business to identify mortals and elves the world over who showed a magical gifting, knowing that even the smallest spark could be trained into a great prowess. Before coming to the Mountain, they might perform small conjuring tricks or illusions, as you yourself have, but you are exceptional in being able to weaponise your skills without any instruction. You should not be able to do what you have done. Normally it would take an apprentice many months, if not years, of practice and schooling before he could fight with magic, and yet you have done so. In the past, magically gifted elves found it far easier to nurture and govern their talent, and indeed, many of the great among the elves have had wizard-like powers without having ever dabbled with magic, such is their innate ability. But with men and women it took longer, and progress was never quite so smooth. My brother and I were reckoned prodigies for being able to work magic before going to the Pool. You are one of only a few since our day to show such promise.'

Roujeark flushed with pride and felt much better about his early struggles with magic. They had left him feeling confused and afraid at the time, but now he was beginning to see that he had already progressed further and quicker than any observer would have expected. Yet he was also uneasy, not knowing what this meant. He asked the question of Kulothiel.

'Master, why have I been given such power? What does it signify?'

'Because you need it. Your coming was foretold: *the last wizard*. It was revealed to me that you were coming by the same Oracle which later instructed me to hold the Tournament. I was told that I would have no trouble in recognising you when you came, nor did I. When first we met on the mountain-path all those years ago, I knew at once that you were he. There was such an aura about you, though you yourself had no idea. It was with great sadness and trepidation that I sent you back, for the reason I have already told you.' Kulothiel looked away, a distant look in his eyes. 'You have been given ability equal to your need. All magic is a gift from Prélan, and always it should be used to serve Him. It is because He has such great purposes for you that you have been endowed as you have. And, I suspect, there is another reason.'

'What reason is that?' Roujeark prompted him. He waited for his tutor to look him in the eye again.

'You needed a head start, because I may not be able to complete your training.'

'Of course, you also needed a little bit of extra protection on your second journey here,' Kulothiel pontificated later that day. 'The perils confronting you were such that if your magic had not announced itself when it did, you might very well have died before ever you returned to me. Often it is thus, a situation of grave danger or extreme stress brings out the magical gift, which will otherwise lie dormant and undiscovered. With you, it happened to be somewhat more, err, incendiary.'

They had returned to the Chamber of the Pool and sat on chairs by the water's edge. It was only his second visit to the chamber, but Roujeark already felt more relaxed in the odd atmosphere, his brain and lungs adjusting to the potency of the air in the Mountain's upper levels.

'Most wizards naturally have an affinity with one or other of the elements. Some wizards have gifts that manifest themselves in control of water, some can shape the earth and others, much the rarest specimen, can manipulate the air. A fourth kind can, like yourself, master fire. But all have the same origin, given birth by the same Spirit of Prélan. It is time for you to learn the essence of magic. To know what it is you have already done, and how.

'Everything in this world, whether animal, vegetable or mineral, is made up of particles, units of matter so small the mind can scarcely conceive. And for every particle there is a *Valiron*, the magical counterpart of that which is ordinary. A *Valiron* is a spark of the divine, and together in their innumerable millions they make up the unseen fabric of magic which pervades this world. All things contain *Valiroen*, living or inanimate…these chairs, the walls around us, your very body. The vast majority of people in this world go through life have no inkling of the existence of *Valiroen*, still less any ability to control them.' Kulothiel cast out his hand over the water of the Pool, and his fingers seemed to summon a mysterious vapour. 'But for the wizard, for the servant of Prélan, they are the key to all things, an elemental source of power.' The vapour came upon silent command to Kulothiel's fingers, a fine mist that glowed with countless little pricks of light.

Roujeark watched, hypnotised, as Kulothiel gathered the mist like a barely visible net between his fingers. As if he were working a web of silken threads, he compressed it and shaped it into a glittering sphere.

'*Valiroen*, once trained, will obey your commands, and can be shaped into anything, for any purpose. Thus...' He moved his hands up and down, back and forth, and from side to side, and the magical ball mirrored his movements. Then suddenly it changed into a flower, and then a halo, which the old wizard raised above their heads. Setting it spinning, Kulothiel stretched it outwards and it expanded across the whole ceiling like a great net. He dropped his hands, and the whole thing slowly settled back into the Pool with a faint sigh.

'Master, are you saying that I have commanded *Valiroen* before without knowing it?' Kulothiel nodded. 'That when I cast missiles of fire, it was *Valiroen* at work?'

'Yes,' said his tutor. 'That is exactly what happened.'

'I remember seeing strange words form in my head, letters of an unknown language that screeched through my mind too fast for me to catch them.'

'Yes, yes,' said Kulothiel. 'Those were secret words of command, the only tongue which *Valiroen* respond to. It is based on elvish but devised by Avatar, with the guidance of Prélan's Spirit. It is known only to those who are taught here in Oron Amular, a language of creative power and boundless subtlety. An apprentice begins by learning just a few sounds and letters, with which he can affect small results, but he must utter them slowly and deliberately. A more advanced wizard can speak it fluently, while the greatest do not need to speak it at all, they merely think it, faster than any other kind of thought.

'I can only suppose that Prélan Himself spoke those words through you, for it is known intuitively to none; it must be taught. Now, having had experience with it, you must learn to speak it, then think it. I will teach you.'

Roujeark learned slowly, methodically, painfully at times. Kulothiel was patient, gradually teaching him the elusive and otherworldly sounds of *Amuyar*, the language of magic. As the weeks and months went by, he formed the sounds into syllables, then words. Next, he strung the words together into phrases of power and sentences of command. The earliest sounds could nudge a small object, ripple some water or conjure a fleeting spark, but with words he was able to create towering fountains of water, shift great boulders and move fire around in artistic whirls. Unlike before, it hurt him not at all, for he was able to channel it correctly. It no longer burst out of him like a wild arrow, but came and went at command. Soon he was speaking and even thinking nothing but *Amuyar*, and he gained steadily in fluency and confidence. Thus did Kulothiel open a world of wonders to him, and he forgot his loneliness in the amazement of it all.

Then, one day, Kulothiel sent him on a new kind of mission. For the first time, he was to go out of the Mountain. He was to find a tree and bring back a branch of suitable size and shape. He exited the Mountain by a hidden door and found himself on a high promontory. The cold smote him and the wind gusted around his robes. Clinging to the rock, he cringed against the elements. After so long indoors it took some getting used to it, but after a while he began to relish it. The sky was dramatic, half inky black and half bright sunshine. Shielding his eyes against the glare of the afternoon sun, he gazed northwards to where thick storms were brewing over the Black Mountains. He would have to be quick if he wanted to avoid getting caught in that. He scrambled down a steep path and came out on the plateau that separated the lower slopes of the Mountain from its higher flanks. On this plateau, a few hardy trees grew in wind-blasted copses, tough, bent and gnarled. Among these wizened old specimens, he searched for a long time before he found a straight enough branch. Unstrapping a hatchet from his back, he lopped it off and carried it away.

Reclimbing the dizzying steps to the door was challenging in the wind, and his heart was in his mouth the whole time, but he managed to regain the safety of the interior with his branch. It was only moments before the storm struck, with perilous winds whose howling could be heard for a long time as he walked back into the Mountain's passages. He took the branch to one of the Mountain's workshops, where a carpenter's bench and tools lay waiting. He stripped off the unwanted twigs and outer bark and then left it for several weeks to dry, returning every now and then to treat it with oil and ensure it was still straight. When things were ready, he bent over the cold fireplace and swiftly built up some wood and kindling from a nearby basket. Uttering a whispered phrase of *Amuyar*, he conjured fire and set the hearth blazing. Then he set to work. He hardened the stave in the fire and then applied more oil. He was instructed in the shaping of the wood, setting to work with an ancient plane, devotedly smoothing and sculpting the wood. He honed it to perfection and bound a breast-high indent with smooth leather binding for a grip. Into the top he carved a little hollow at Kulothiel's behest.

When it was ready, after many weeks of work, he took it to the Chamber of the Pool, where Kulothiel was waiting for him. He loved the feel of it in his hand as he walked and felt emboldened by the sense of dignity it gave him. His back even straightened as he walked. The old wizard inspected it and seemed content. He took his apprentice to a far recess of the cave where they had not yet been. They passed through what seemed to be a gossamer curtain and Roujeark gasped. They were in an alcove that was filled with glittering light. A thousand precious stones were embedded in the rock walls, catching and scattering the luminescence of the pool in a marvellous radiance. He stood entranced, seeing every kind of gem he had ever heard of, and many more besides.

'These stones have been here as long as the pool,' Kulothiel said, 'and none know whence they came. This is a privileged place, where a wizard comes just once, or twice if he returns with an apprentice. To come here uninvited is forbidden, and a frightful death awaits the one who tries to take one of the stones without leave. They are sacred to Prélan and set aside for His service. Each wizard is given one, to last a lifetime. Now, choose yours.'

Roujeark walked about dazedly, drinking in the marvellous hues and textures. He was dazzled, but eventually his eye settled on one blood-red ruby the size of a large coin. Putting his hand to it, he felt a strange pulsing, as if it were the very heartbeat of the Mountain. Breathless with anticipation and nerves, he prised it loose, and it came willingly enough. It did not quite fill his palm, but it captivated his vision, glowing faintly and filled with wispy patterns. Kulothiel held out his hand, and, with a fierce reluctance, Roujeark gave it to him. Kulothiel weighed it in his palm, caressed it with his fingers, and held it up to his eye. He murmured to himself and eventually grunted affirmation.

'Verily, that is your stone. It is a jewel of pain, of toil, and of sacrifice. It signifies passion and labours which will require your whole heart. It is your stone.' He looked his apprentice in the eye. 'Do you want it?'

Roujeark looked at it in a new light. The ruby seemed to throb in the old wizard's hand, as if promising all the things Kulothiel had foretold. He hesitated. A feeling of great trepidation stole up on him. He reached out his fingers, then checked.

'Yes,' he said at last, and reached out further to take it back, but Kulothiel retained it.

'Good,' he said, turning on his heel and exiting the veiled space. 'Then follow me.'

Kulothiel led him back to the pool. Roujeark looked at him expectantly. He was commanded to strip to the waist, then to kneel. His master held both his staff and his stone above his head.

'Roujeark, do you accept the calling of Prélan upon your life?'

'I do.'

'And do you acknowledge both His authority and His love?'

'I do.'

'And do you swear to serve Him faithfully to the end of your days, wherever the road may lead, giving your utmost for His glory? Do you swear to use the gift of magic He has given you only for His ends, for what is good and true, forsaking all other allegiances?'

'I do.'

'And do you pledge yourself to The League of Wizardry, to obey the word of the Lord Keeper and to uphold the sacred mission and values handed down to us by King Avatar?'

'I do.'

'Then, with the authority given me as Keeper and as your master, I anoint you with the holy water of the Pool of High Magic.' As he spoke, Roujeark sensed something strange happening beside him. The pool, normally so placid, was bubbling and hissing. Obeying Kulothiel's command, a plume of shimmering liquid rose into the air and snaked across to the wizard's waiting hand. Kulothiel wetted his fingertips and then drew a circle upon Roujeark's forehead. It was hot to his touch, and his skin tingled. An aromatic vapour filled his nostrils. But Kulothiel did not let the water go. Instead, he wrapped it around the ruby, and then plunged the gemstone into the hollow atop the staff. There was a flash and a crack, and a temporarily blinded Roujeark feared his masterpiece had broken. But when his sight returned, he saw the staff was well and whole, but with the gemstone soundly lodged into its tip. Upending the staff, Kulothiel pressed the staff stone-first against Roujeark's breast, digging it in above his heart. He endured a moment of pain and then a thrilling pulse of power. Looking down, he saw a mark had been left, a circle bearing a strange rune.

He looked up expectantly at Kulothiel, but the old wizard was not done yet. He pressed the staff against several more parts of his body, each touch accompanied by a brief flash of pain.

'A touch of Prélan for your ear, for your hand, and for your foot, so that you might hear His voice, serve Him in your deeds, and walk faithfully in His ways.' He righted the staff again, and suddenly the faltering old man's voice regained some of its old power. 'Now, arise a wizard, a chosen champion of Prélan.' Roujeark rose to his feet, feeling stronger and bolder than ever before. He pulled his robes back over his shoulders. Slowly, reverently, Kulothiel laid the staff horizontally in his hands. His eyes fixed Roujeark's with unearthly intensity.

'This staff is your companion for life. Your guide, your support, your weapon. Never, ever, let it go.'

Roujeark gripped it fiercely, resolving to do no such thing.

'Now,' Kulothiel spoke again, 'dip it into the pool. Receive its power.'

Roujeark turned, and with infinite care he dipped the staff, stone-first, into the pool. He expected to feel a shock, like when he had put his hands in, but there was no resistance. Leaning over, he lowered the staff as far as the handgrip. At first nothing happened, then a glow lit up the stone. A red light suffused the water around the insertion and the staff started to throb. Roujeark watched the power surge visibly up it, the wood warping and flexing gently. At last an end point came, and the glow faded away. He lifted the staff out and brought it close. It carried a strange fragrance and was hot to his touch, but never a drip did it make, for every last bead of water soaked into it. He looked at the staff, his face aglow in the red ruby's light, and knew that he was a wizard at last.

⅄

After the emotional reunion with his wife, Curillian had slept for a week, barely stirring in all that time. When at last he rose, the queen ordered that he be taken care of. He was washed and shaved, massaged and dressed in soft garments. He was given what seemed to have been his first proper meal in weeks. Slowly he regained some of his former self, and slowly the tale of his adventures came out. Carmen had heard all his tales, but she was shocked by what he had been through this time. She began to understand the burden he had brought back from Oron Amular, a burden not just of grief and weariness and impending war, but of guilt and self-reproach. He no longer prayed like he used to, and he sat stony-faced in church. Gone was his perennial restlessness which used to take him all around the city and the surrounding country in pursuit of distraction and exertion. Now he kept to the palace, going no further abroad than the well-tended gardens.

A full season had passed, and only once did he leave the palace. They bade farewell to Lancoir in a packed city square surrounded by legions of mourners, mostly soldiers of many units but also city-dwellers and nobles and dignitaries from far and wide. Under cold dreary skies the funeral torches had burned fiercely, and the immaculate black procession had borne Lancoir in grave dignity. Curillian had led it with Lancoir's son, Lancaro, and all were able to see their grief. The rest of the royal family had watched from a balcony, black-veiled spectators all in a row. Sadly, they watched the scene unfold below with rigid posture and faces trembling with emotion. Curillian had roused himself to give an oration and a prayer worthy of the occasion, but the effort seemed to take a lot out of him. For many, it would be the last time they ever saw their king in public. With full military honours Lancoir had been buried in the sombre grove outside the city where a few privileged champions were permitted to rest alongside the kings and queens of Maristonia.

Once more the king departed the city, and stirred himself in a brief glimpse of the old Curillian, when the time came for a great council of the nations in Hamid, Aranar. With his knights and councillors he had ridden away, but this absence, although less mysterious, was more protracted. And it was futile. He came home more despondent than ever, laden with fresh worries after fruitless diplomacy.

Carmen had watched the pain of bereavement in Curillian turn from a fierce pain to a dull ache. She watched his faith crumble. She watched his energy and vitality seep away. She watched illnesses come and go and she watched old age set in at last. Always she watched, for she could not get through to him. His manners were impeccable, and kindness still flickered in him, but there was no passion, no intimacy. She wept for the romance of bygone days, recalling with tears what they had once enjoyed. Only Téthan now could make the old king come alive, and even he not for long. Carmen watched as the prince grew into a fine young armist, but with less input from his father than there should have been.

And so, age and sorrow had come upon the queen as well. She knew he must decline at some point, that age would catch up with him, but she was horrified by how suddenly it had happened, stealing up like a thief. She resented that his spirits had been so sapped that they could not enjoy their winter seasons together. She cursed the day that he had ridden off to Oron Amular. He did not speak of that quest anymore, but in all that he had told her, he had never uttered words of regret. With the last shreds of his faith, he believed that he had gone with Prélan's blessing and with a high purpose before him. He just no longer knew what that purpose was and doubted his strength to perform it even if he knew. Carmen prayed that the task would no longer need performing, that the rumours out of the north were worse than reality justified. If only they could live out their days in peace and leave Téthan a legacy of stability. Yet in her unhappy heart, the queen knew that prayer would not be answered.

⋀

'The stone is both the entry point for magic into the staff and its conduit for releasing the magic again. Without the stone, the wood would have just vapourised in the pool, just as would anything else unholy.' Another of Roujeark's endless questions came to his lips.

'But why have a staff at all, if control of the *Valiroen* is achieved by mastery of *Amuyar*?'

'A staff is to a wizard what a spear is to a warrior,' Kulothiel answered. 'The warrior's arm and fist might be animated by great strength and valour, but with the spear it can do vastly more damage. The staff is a means by which you may draw upon deeper magic. That power which lies in the pool is vastly more potent than the *Valiroen* of ordinary matter. Your staff is now charged with enormous power, extending and enhancing that ability which you already have. Some wizards never gain sufficient mastery in *Amuyar* to be independent of their staff, and so it is to them a lifeline. A wizard who is weary and at the end of his wits will find it easier to draw upon power through the staff than through his mind. It is a subtle art which you learn, but practical too. The staff will eventually lose its charge, of course, but the length of time will vary according to the stone and the purpose of the bearer. Young warrior-wizards are given only a little, sufficient for small errands, but as they grow wiser and more trusted, they are given longer doses. I have given you a surfeit, enough to last for many years, decades if used sparingly.'

Roujeark's lessons had taught him that the staff's power was drained by the performance of magic, and the drain would be greater for harder spells and greater feats. An irresponsible wizard could waste its power haphazardly and then be left vulnerable, but a wise custodian could nurse its strength for a long time of service.

'Master, why have you given me so much? I am still so junior, and untried in the field.'

'Roujeark, you are untried in the field because once you go out you will never come back. I have tried to train you as best as I am now able, but you will not undergo the full regime of tests and trials and expeditions. There is no time. *My* time is running out. It is needful that you be accelerated through the process. And Prélan be praised that He has given me so much to work with. Only a little time remains to us, my apprentice. Let us use it wisely.'

Roujeark continued to train both physically and mentally, not letting his body lose its fitness nor his mind its sharp edge. But his formal lessons grew fewer and further between. Kulothiel, increasingly frail and drawn, retired for ever longer periods to his bed. Many times Roujeark thought him dead, only for him to stir once more. Then came the day of his final lesson.

He went to Kulothiel in his chamber, a wondrous repository of many ancient and marvellous things. The Keeper had acquired many keepsakes and souvenirs on his journey through life, and their memories kept him company in the cold dark hours. Now he lay, ashen-faced and barely breathing, upon a bed beneath crimson covers.

'Roujeark,' the old man croaked. 'I have brought you to me for one last lesson. And to bestow upon you some final gifts that...may help you.' He motioned for Roujeark to sit in a chair beside the bed. In another part of the chamber a small fire burned, its light casting moving shadows upon the Keeper's death-postponed face. Every syllable seemed to take a whole minute for the old man to utter.

'Roujeark, you must face Kurundar.'

The young wizard grimaced, fear clutching at his heart. Those words hung upon the air a long while. All this time he had known this to be true, that it was the whole reason for him being here, but he had tried to forget. Tried to pretend that it was not so.

'My brother seized the second pool of magic, the twin of ours, and corrupted it. With it he has afflicted the world for long enough. Now, matters must be settled. A day of reckoning beckons. Your task, lest you forget, is to destroy the Pool of Dark Magic, as it has now become. Take the Star-shard, drop it in the pool, and that is all.'

Roujeark took out the Star-shard from the pouch tied securely within his robes. The arrowhead-shaped hunk of rock glimmered in the firelight as its many crystals caught the light. It looked so little, and yet so much. The rock was like no other, deep and cold and mottled, and yet he could not imagine what it could do. It would not keep him upon the road, nor grant him any extra powers. All he could do was bear it into grave danger.

'What will happen when I drop it in?'

'I do not know.'

Roujeark was shocked. 'What do you mean you don't know? How, then, do you know it will work?'

His master was now weary beyond rebuking him, so he just summoned the strength to answer.

'Because Prélan has said so. The Star-shard came from Him, from the heavenly star of Eluvatar. Back to Him the dark magic will go, for cleansing. How this is to be done precisely, I do not know. I only know what I have been told to pass on to you. What I do know is that Kurundar will guard his prize to the very last. It is long since he ventured abroad, and my foolhardy last venture achieved this much at least: he is no longer as agile as once he was. We have both lived far beyond the span of our years, and he has not weathered it to this point any better than I. While I relinquish my life willingly, my service done, He clings to life unnatural and is sustained only by dark powers. Great emissaries of evil have been welcomed to his dark throne, and they brought with them the life of the undead and power bereft of all joy or light.

'He will be there. He guards the pool jealously. His own minions he suspects, lest an able lieutenant usurp his place as Dark Lord and Tyrant of the World. He will send forth his armies, hurl his full strength against the world of mortals, but he will remain. So, you must go to him. You must confront him. Only by overcoming him can you get to the pool. Prélan preserve you, that you might get that far. And Prélan empower you to win that final combat.'

Roujeark felt his blood run cold. He had not volunteered for this. This had never been part of the bargain. Even when Kulothiel had first told him his mission at the Tournament's end, he had made no mention of such things. One on one combat with the greatest sorcerer who ever lived? It was absurd. Terrifying. His mind shrank from even contemplating it.

'You are afraid, Roujeark, I see it in your eyes. Do not let your heart falter. For mortal man it is impossible, but with Prélan all things are possible. He never ordains what He does not enable, nor demand what He does not supply. You have been called, therefore You have been made able. What you have within yourself you will never know until the time comes. If your heart will only remain steadfast, you will reach your goal at the journey's end.'

The old man lapsed into another long silence, eyes half-closed. Roujeark feared he was dead, and concern for his master temporarily superseded his own dread. But Kulothiel stirred, looking up as if surprised to see Roujeark still there. Then he recovered his wits and smiled feebly.

'Forgive an old man rambling on.' He motioned with his hand towards a stout wooden box beside the bed. 'Everything in the chest is for you. Things I have acquired over the years, which may prove useful to you…'

Roujeark got up from his chair and crouched by the chest. It was locked, but Kulothiel twitched his fingers and the clasps came away. Opening the lid, Roujeark looked inside. He frowned. The box seemed to be empty. Looking harder, he saw that there was a strange garment of some fine silver-black material. It was glossy and lightweight, like no fabric he had ever handled.

'That is a shadow-cloak,' said Kulothiel. 'Three times it will render you invisible, when danger presses too close, but only for a while.

Wear it wisely, for after the third time has worn off it will be useless to you.'

Beneath the cloak lay other items which had been concealed. There was a dagger, a miniature manuscript, a pale coin and a blue crystal vial. Kulothiel explained each one.

'Let the dirk be your weapon, for I know you have none. It cannot compare with your staff, of course, but there may come times when you need something for close-quarters work. And it may come in useful in other ways. The blade is Mountain-forged, and spells of power lie upon it.'

'What spells?' Roujeark asked.

'Spells to make it unbreakable and sharp enough to cut any substance. In the dark it can be made to glow like a torch, and you can be sure it will never be turned against you.'

'How so?' For answer Kulothiel just muttered something, and the glowing runes on the grip seemed to extinguish.

'I have just released it from my service. Take it, it's yours. Now speak these words, and it will be bound to you. Any other hand that touches it shall be burned.' Roujeark gripped the hilt and repeated the phrase spoken by Kulothiel. Beneath his palm the runes flashed into life again, his own magical signature. Laying it reverently to one side, he turned his attention to the next item.

'What can I learn from so small a book?' he asked, handling the tiny codex. It was wallet-sized and fitted snugly in his hand.

'Everything,' Kulothiel answered. 'Almost…Open it.' Roujeark did so, and suddenly the manuscript grew in his hands till he was holding a vast tome. He nearly overbalanced from the weight of it, but he recovered himself and sat down with the volume. Wonderingly he turned page after page, seeing encyclopaedic entries on everything under the sun. There were histories, medical treatises, spells, maps, charts, letters and songs of lore. He shut the cover, thinking he would never be able to carry it with him, but he watched in amazement as it shrank back to its original size. Kulothiel chuckled, or as nearly as he could in his weakened state.

'A gift from a former librarian here. He was a wonderful one for books and tricks,' the old wizard said wistfully. 'Take it with you, and perhaps you will not feel my absence so keenly.'

Roujeark laid the manuscript aside and picked up the coin, turning it in his fingers. It was gold, heavy and traced with strange designs.

'The currency of the mountain?' he guessed, smiling in jest. But Kulothiel was serious.

'Verily. A most rare and precious coin. Few were ever made, and they were reserved for the most trustworthy of hands. For these coins can both pay and yet remain. When you give of it, you will not find yourself with less. Keep it well, for you have needs ahead of you that you do not guess.' Roujeark tucked it away, remembering that something similar had been awarded as Adhanor's prize during the Tournament. He could not imagine what use he would have for it, but perhaps it would prove useful.

Finally, Roujeark inspected the vial, which contained a clear fluid. He wondered what it was. He unstoppered it and sniffed. His nose wrinkled at the strong smell.

'What is it? Poison?'

'Nothing so base,' said Kulothiel. 'It is an elixir of great virtue, the recipe for which is now lost. How I miss its creator. It is designed to be of use in extreme situations: it will bring both warmth in deadly cold and refreshment in the direst heat. It also has a restorative power when all other sustenance fails. But, as with the cloak, use it sparingly. What you see there is all that remains of it; you will be the last to ever taste it.'

Roujeark placed the vial on the cloak alongside the codex and the dirk. Tears came to his eyes when he reflected on his master's generosity. These were gifts beyond price, treasures fit for a prince of mages. He knelt by the bed and clasped Kulothiel's hand. It was so cold.

'Master Kulothiel, I cannot thank you fitly for these gifts, nor indeed for any of your kindnesses.'

'Don't try.' The old man's words were so faint now that Roujeark could barely catch them. 'I'm just sorry I cannot do more.' Kulothiel's colourless lips still quivered, as if trying to frame more words the voice no longer had the power to utter. Roujeark leaned in closer, his tears wetting the coverlet on the bed.

'Master?' he called. Kulothiel squeezed his hand ever so slightly, and his eyes flickered one last time.

'*Prélan ditiios eres.*' Roujeark bowed his head to receive this last benediction, his tears streaming freely now. He felt the faint pressure on his hand relinquish and then disappear altogether. Looking up, he saw that the end had come. The old man had gone. Roujeark wailed at the ceiling and wept hoarsely, clinging onto the Keeper's arm as if to wrench him back. But he was gone. And Roujeark was alone.

XXIV

Storm's Herald

The horsemen flew through the dark city streets in a storm of hooves. They splashed through puddles and rattled over the flagstones, cloaks swirling and nostrils steaming. Folk watched uneasily from upper windows as they passed, wondering what haste drove the small group on such a foul night. Round corners, under arches, through plazas and over bridges, the riders did not relent until they came to the guardpost. There they dismounted and made themselves known. Their mud-spattered cloaks dragged on the floor as they were ushered into shelter. They stood dripping and panting in the candlelit shelter while the officer of the watch was fetched. When he appeared, the officer stifled a yawn and eyed them darkly before listening to his subordinates, who showed him the damp parchment they had been given. After a moment he looked up with a worried expression.

Feet hurried up the empty corridor, echoing loudly in the alcoves of the deserted palace. Moonlight broke through the ragged storm clouds and cast pale luminance across the halls and window-lined passageways as he made his way to the Royal Apartments. The urgent message rang in his ears. *Go to the king. He must hear this straightaway.* Normally the Doorkeeper would have acted with more reserve, and even at this godless hour detained the visitors until the Royal Audience Chamber could be made ready, but not tonight. No, tonight he sent the messenger hot-foot straight to the king's own private residence, there to disturb him without delay. It mattered not if the king were sleeping. Of course, the Royal Guards at the door did not realise that, and they brought him up sharp. But he just thrust out his hand and showed them the token he carried. It was a seal from the Doorkeeper, the armist responsible for the comings and goings of the palace. He had a few such, and they bore the king's own authority. The bearer could pass any guard and go through any door. Anyone who hindered the bearer of a seal could expect to be dismissed, or worse. So he pushed past the astonished guards and burst into the antechamber.

Seated inside was Sir Cardeyn, the senior-most Knight of Thainen. Candlelight shimmered and reflected off his armour. He looked up in surprise but understood the situation at a glance. He was up out of his seat in a heartbeat, moving to intercept the breathless messenger. A Knight of Thainen ranked higher than any seal, save the king's own, and there was no way he would let this runner-boy get through the next set of doors into the inner sanctum.

'Give me the message, boy,' commanded the knight. The runner nervously divulged his message, and then beat a hasty retreat. Frowning, Sir Cardeyn thought for a moment, then knocked upon the inner doors. When there was no answer he slipped inside, bearing a small oil-lamp. On the inside he met a sleepy-looking young woman, one of the queen's handmaidens, coming the other way with a lamp of her own. She looked startled at the intrusion.

'Sir Cardeyn, what is it?'

'Wake Their Majesties please, an urgent message has come.'

In the combined light of their lamps he watched as she crossed the richly furnished room and slipped through another pair of gilt doors. A few moments elapsed before the queen emerged, hair tousled, in a rich velvet dressing-gown. A few moments later the king followed, massaging his face with his hands. Dressed in leggings and a loose shirt, the old king looked pale, thin and drawn. Blinking away his sleep, he looked wearily at his guardian knight. The sight of him made the knight hesitate.

'Well Cardeyn…what is it?' the king said impatiently.

Cardeyn recovered quickly. Clearing his throat, he said, 'Sire, King Adhanor of Hendar sends urgent word from the north; he thinks the war has started.'

For a long while the king just looked at him in silent shock. Once so imperturbable, now the monarch looked unsettled, scared even. So long did he pause that Cardeyn felt the need to prompt him.

'Sire, the messengers of Hendar are in your palace. They request an immediate audience. Will you go to them?' Still Curillian said nothing, but kept staring at the knight. Then he started, as if recovering himself. He half turned away.

'No, I will not.' He started walking towards another door. 'Have the Crown Prince speak to them.' He walked to the door, leaving Sir Cardeyn staring in consternation at his back.

'Sire?' the knight asked, unsure what else to say. The king did not turn.

'Do as I say.' Then he pushed through the doors and was gone. Queen Carmen mustered a slight smile of apology, then withdrew. Sir Cardeyn went at once to the prince's apartments.

⋏

Prince Téthan emerged much fresher than his elderly parents, in fact barely looking as if he had been asleep. He shrugged on a supple robe and smiled benevolently.

'Do foreign embassies often turf us out of our beds?' he asked ruefully. Yet he seemed not to mind, and went willingly enough. A manservant brought him a thick cloak and soft shoes, then they left the chamber. A squad of Royal Guards fell in with them as they left the prince's apartments and walked up the candlelit corridor. They found the emissaries waiting in a smaller audience chamber, still wet and mud-stained from their frantic journey. With them were more guards, for Commander Surumo took no chances, but others were in the room too. Lord High Chancellor Ophryior, who despite his advanced years never seemed to sleep, lurked in the shadows and watched from under heavy-lidded eyes. Standing by a giant candlestick was Commander Surumo, and seated discreetly off to one side was Eremiah, the prince's chaplain and private confessor. Someone had been efficient in waking the right people, and the cleric even sat ready with parchment and quill to take notes.

'My friends, I hope you've been offered refreshments?' the prince addressed the emissaries. They were all grim-faced men, weary but resolute and wearing the livery of the King of Hendar. Such men were rarely seen in Mariston, and never in living memory had they come with such urgency. Despite their evident fatigue, they all bowed, and then their leader responded, courteous but forceful.

'Lord Prince, I come with grim tidings. Ridgun of Belovern am I, personal envoy of His Majesty, Adhanor, son of Idunar. We have come straight from my sovereign and ridden hard for long weeks to deliver this message. When it is told, my companions and I shall gladly accept your hospitality.' His face was worn like a peasant's, but his voice was cultured, and he displayed great poise in his speech after a hard ride. The prince took a seat and accepted a goblet of wine from a newly appeared servant.

'Speak on,' he invited with a wave of his hand. The prince's manners were affable and assured, but he set his jaw firm and clasped his seat's arms in expectance of bad news. Ridgun said his piece.

'Lord Prince, war has come to Hendar again. The north is aflame. Kurundar's hordes are mounting ever larger incursions, bringing war and destruction out of the Haunted Pass. The signs have been mounting. The raids have been growing in intensity and black fumes now clog the northern sky permanently. After months of ominous build-up, Urunmar now looks set to play its hand.'

Crown Prince Téthan took the news calmly, but his clenched forearms betrayed the great effort it cost him. 'When was this?' he asked.

'A week before we set out, so two moons ago now. The war-beacons of the Guard Hills brought the news to Kalator, and a council of war was summoned.'

'There have been raids before,' the prince pointed out.

'This is no raid,' Ridgun said tersely.

'Large-scale raids,' the prince persisted.

'This is different.' The envoy was insistent, eyes set hard. 'Lord Prince, I was bidden to impress the gravity of the situation upon the King of the South and to seek his aid. In his stead, I beg you to hear my words. We are well-versed enough by now in the stratagems of the enemy to know how serious this is. What has been unleashed upon us is neither raid nor feint…but the beginning of the end.'

His last words hung on the air, and the candles guttered. The armists in the room exchanged worried glances, but Téthan stared straight ahead. Gazing fixedly at a carving on the wall, he thought for a few heartbeats. Then he sprang out of his chair. Striding closer to the envoy, he inclined his head.

'Thank you for bringing us this news, Ridgun of Belovern. I know how long the road is, and your heart must be heavy. Lay aside your cares for a while now. Eat, drink, rest. Rooms shall be made available for you and your men.' The prince nodded to Ophryior, who silently conveyed instructions to a waiting servant. The armists made to leave, led by their prince, but Ridgun stood his ground.

'Lord Prince, we have come for Maristonia's aid in time of great peril. What answer does she give?' Téthan turned and looked back at the man, whose resolute face showed the anguish of his cares.

'You shall have your answer...in due time. No pronouncement will I make in haste, until I have consulted with my father and his advisors. But Hendar can rest assured, Ridgun – Maristonia will do what must be done.'

A

Curillian stumbled across his night-dark apartments, banging into furniture and knocking things askew. His mind whirled. His breath came in short, ragged gasps. He felt sick and unsteady on his feet. He tottered over to his nightstand, seeking a remedy. His questing fingers knocked over bottles and scattered parchments aside until they found the marble bust of his grandfather Arimaya. Feeling up the shoulders, he found what was hanging there. For months he had gotten out of the habit of wearing it, but now he had need of it. the fine metal links of the chain were cool under his fingertips, and he traced down to the charm suspended at the end. He pulled up the stone and held it before his eyes. Bending over it, he scrutinised it, fixing all his attention on the strange colours and wispy patterns. It shone faintly, and a roving blue light seemed to flit across the veins and whirlpools in the depths. It was a blue gem, not so brilliant as a sapphire, but altogether more captivating. It was like a small corner of some storm-tossed sky had been captured in a glass prison, the shapes inside as elusive and indescribable as roiling clouds. It was long and slender, shaped like an elven menhir, bulbous at the top and tapering down to a slender point.

As he lost himself in the shifting forms within, his breathing calmed and his mind cleared. More and more now it seemed to grow in power the more he needed it. Maybe that was why it had seemed dull and lifeless when first he received it, and why he had forgotten about it in some drawer for so long.

Now it gave him strength. Taking it from the bust, he put it around his own neck, letting it fall within his gaping nightshirt. It also reminded him to pray. In the wake of Lancoir's passing he had let lapse the habit of a lifetime, but now he started to turn his fears into prayers again. *Can I do this? Will You give me what it takes, one last time?* Prélan did not answer so that he could hear Him, but the king did feel the peace of God enter into his troubled heart. *I cannot do this*, he prayed on, *but You can. Make a way, where there is no way. If You will spare me, I will do what I have vowed; but if not, let not our hope stumble with me. Raise up another, someone who can do what must be done. Make a way...*

A cool night breeze flowed in and wafted around his bare legs. Slowly he turned and followed the direction of the air to come out onto his balcony. Pushing the thin curtains aside, he walked out, the tiles cold against his bare feet. He made it to the rail and leaned heavily upon it. He felt so old. Where had his strength gone? Each passing season seemed to have taken a decade's toll, and now every day was wearisome and every night disturbed. He pushed this latest intrusion to the back of his mind. Whatever Hendar had to say, he had no energy to deal with it. Let it wait. Let Téthan deal with it. The boy was on the cusp of manhood, yet already he handled matters of state so well.

The cool night air was less refreshing than the king had hoped. It turned cold and clutched at his sparse frame where the muscles had wasted away. His skin broke out in goosebumps, and he shivered. Yet he did not want to go back in, back to the nightmares. Instead he looked out over his city. The view from this most privileged vantage-point was breath-taking: all Mariston lay spread before him in its concentric zones, awash with lamps and murmuring with its soft night-time noises. But then a cloud swept over the moon, and the city was doused in a deeper shade. Curillian looked up and saw that the rainclouds were scudding by, torn and shredded by the wind. But this wind came not from the south, whence it usually came, bearing the salty tang of Mariston Bay, but from the north. It was cold, and harsh, filled with the icy spite of the mountains. It bore with it a new storm. A bigger storm. Vast, menacing cloudbanks filled the northern sky and they rolled down upon the plains like siege-engines. Curillian shivered again. He could not face the onset, but neither could he turn away. He just clutched the charm and kept staring into the raging tempest, where thunder boomed and sheet lightning flashed. The storm was coming.

A

He shouldn't have looked, shouldn't have read. Now he spun away and fled the library, wondering what madness had possessed him to open that book. Knowing your enemy was supposed to empower you, but by the time he had dropped the manuscript he had terrified himself half witless. Reading about Kurundar, the Arch-Mage and sorcerer, about his fearsome history and devastating powers, had been a mistake. How could he face such a foe? The thought appalled him, sliding like a hill in ruin and crushing his quavering hopes. Now he came away in a blind panic, snivelling and struggling to breathe. The Star-shard lay abandoned on the dreadful pages, and his staff was cast aside. *Roujeark.* He heard his name called faintly, as if echoing in his mind. But no one was here to call him. He stumbled on, knowing not where he went, just aware that he had to get away. He found himself in a narrow tunnel and, with arms outstretched to feel the rock, he tottered along. A sharp wind gusted down from an opening somewhere ahead to smite him, trying to drive him back. *Roujeark.*

'No,' he called aloud, denying whomever was trying to reach him. He drove onward, striving with the wind. He was alone. His mentor was dead. He had no friends, no support, no hope. So he thrust his responsibilities away also, resolving to have nothing. Perhaps he should find some high precipice and cast himself off? The last wizard of Oron Amular? He sneered despairingly at the notion. What could the last wizard do except end himself upon the empty Mountain?

The tunnel ended in a high balcony, and he came to a pulpit-sized projection on the mountainside. The wind was awesome in this high, lonely place, and the air was so thin that his breath came in thin gasps. Below him the icy flanks of the Mountain fell away into mist-shrouded obscurity, but out there the view was terrific, looking out right over Kalimar and to the sea beyond. An immense storm was brewing in the north, where lightning lit the horizon and illuminated swollen storm clouds in nightmarish colours. His hands gripped the thin rock wall of the balcony, which came only up to his waist. Looking down, he gulped. Would he feel the impact, or would he freeze to death before the rocks broke his body?

'Roujeark!' That was a voice, a living sound. Lurching back from the edge, he turned around and saw a dark shape filling the tunnel. The person came towards him, calling his name again.

'Roujeark?'

Sir Theonar joined him on the balcony, straightening up as he escaped the confines of the tunnel. The tall man filled the rest of the remaining space. He placed a hand on Roujeark's shoulder and looked down at him.

'Roujeark? What are you doing here?' The young wizard backed away, as much as was possible, until he felt the rock wall behind him. His stomach reeled when he thought how easily he could topple backwards. With an effort, he opened his eyes against the wind's ferocity and focused on the blurry shape before him. Slowly his friend the knight came into focus.

'What are you doing here?' he yelled, just as the wind suddenly dropped, so it came out in a shrill cry.

'Paying my respects,' the man said simply. 'Now come inside, Roujeark, this is no place to be with a storm rising. A lightning strike could bring an avalanche down on our heads or a sudden gust might pluck us both to oblivion.' Roujeark glanced up at the dizzying heights of the Mountain above, which were lost in frigid, ferocious clouds. Theonar ducked to re-enter the tunnel, but Roujeark cried again, still needlessly loud.

'No, I will not. Why should I? What's the point?' Theonar straightened again, keeping his eyes on the armist's.

'We still have a job to do, my friend.' Freezing cold tears were driven across Roujeark's face as he shook his head.

'No. I can't. It's not possible, what he asked of me.' Compassion was in Theonar's eyes as he regarded him.

'No one ever said it would be easy. But you're not alone, Roujeark. We're in this struggle together.'

'But I can't,' sobbed Roujeark. 'I can't do it. Such evil is beyond me.' Theonar took him by both shoulders and looked deep into his eyes. Distant flashes made the handsome face flicker and almost glow with a strange intensity.

'Roujeark, listen to me. Prélan does not command what He does not enable. He does not call where He does not make a way. He does not send what He does not equip. His strength within you is more than you will ever need.' His next words he had to shout, as the wind rose again. 'You only have to let Him in. Lean on Him, and there will be nothing you cannot do.'

No sooner had he said it than Theonar was distracted, his eyes flicking urgently upwards. A great whooshing rumble descended on them from on high. Theonar shoved Roujeark back into the tunnel and dove in after him. Moments later, a mass of snow crashed upon the balcony. It was snapped off and swept clean away by a great cascade tumbling down the mountainside. The noise in the tunnel was deafening, even though Theonar's bulk was covering him and stifling his ears. As the rumbling faded, Theonar extricated himself and crawled on past Roujeark. Sitting with his back to the tunnel, he looked over at his friend. Roujeark was pale and wide-eyed, but when his heart stopped pounding, he managed a smile.

'That was not your path, my friend,' Theonar said. 'Your way takes you out of the doors of this Mountain and into the world. When the time comes, you'll know where to be.' Roujeark nodded. Though he felt shaken, he had drawn away from the brink. Glancing around his mind, he found that his fears had, for the moment, fled.

'What about you?' he asked. 'Don't you have to go back to Aranar?' Theonar smiled enigmatically.

'Yes, I will go back to Aranar in time, but I have business also in the south and in the north. Many tasks beckon me.' He got up to crouching. 'Prélan go with you, friend Roujeark…oh, and you'll be needing this…' he passed Roujeark's staff to him. The ruby-stone shone warmly as Roujeark passed his hands over it. '…and this.' Theonar pressed something hard into his hand, and then he was gone, slipping back up the tunnel.

Shakily Roujeark got to his feet, leaning heavily on his staff. He went as close as he dared to the tunnel-mouth, where now a void yawned. Looking out, he saw the same view again but through a fine shower of snow. He opened his palm and saw the Star-shard nestled there. Closing his fist protectively over the prize, he looked up again. In the north the storm was still raging, seeming to fill his vision. But in his heart, there was peace. Now he felt he could face it.

✳

The adventure will continue…

Subscribe at www.worldofastrom.com to get updates on the sequel.

Character List

Characters listed in alphabetical order, with a syllabic guide to pronunciation and short description for each entry.

ACIL, SIR (Ah-sill) – Man, Hawk Clan Knight from Aranar

ADHANOR (Ad-an-or) – Man, newly-succeeded King of Hendar

AIIYOSHA (Eye-yo-sha) – Elf, chieftain of the Cuherai, the snow-elves of the Black Mountains

ALEINUS (Ah-lee-nus) – Armist, member of Curillian's Royal Guards

ANDIL (An-dil) – Armist, Royal Guardsman; native to the Phirmar

ANRHUS (An-rous) – Man, Culdon's scout

ANTAYA (An-tie-ah) – Armist, member of Curillian's Royal Guards

ANTHAB (An-thab) – Man, free-rider of Aranar

ANTRUPHAN (An-truh-fan) – Armist, architect to King Curillian

ARAMIST (Ara-mist) – Armist, younger brother of Curillian, died young

ARDIR (Ar-deer) – Angelic messenger of Prélan, usually taking elven form

ARIMAYA (Ah-rih-my-ah) – Armist, late king of Maristonia; grandfather of Curillian

ARVAYA (Ar-vaya) – Elf, late king of Kalimar; great-grandfather of Lithan

ARTON/CARDANOR (Car-da-nor) – Armist, duke of Arton who acted as regent in Curillian's absence

ASTACAR (As-ta-kar) – Elf of Ithrill, companion of Elrinde

ATELLIA (A-tell-ee-ah) – Armist, servant-girl working as a masseuse in the duke of Welton's palace; a favourite of Lancoir's

ATHRICK (Ath-rick) – Man of Hendar, squire to Adhanor

AVALAR (A-va-lar) – Elf, late king of Kalimar; grandfather of Lithan

AVAR (Ah-var) – Elf, long-dead prince of the Avatar; a relation of Lithan

AVARONE (Ava-rone) – Elf, former High King of Kalimar and eldest son of Avatar

AVATAR (Ah-vah-tar) – Eldest elf and first High King of Kalimar

BARADON (Bara-don) – Man, erstwhile Master-Mage of Oron Amular

BENEK THUNDER-EYE (Ben-ek) – Man of Aranar, member of Raspald's band

CAIASAN (Kya-san) – Man, scribe and healer of the Pegasus Clan

CARDEYN (Kar-dane) – armist, Knight of Thainen

CAREA (Sah-ree-ah) – Elf, princess of the wood-elves

CARÉYSIN (Car-ay-sin) – Armist, army tracker and expert archer

CARION (Cah-ree-on) – Elf, noble wood-elf, father of Dácariel

CARMEN (Car-men) – Armist, queen of Maristonia and wife of Curillian

CELKENORÉ (Kel-ken-or-ray) – Man, former Jeantar of Aranar, of the Unicorn Clan

COMMANGEN (Coh-man-gen) – Armist, clerk in the Royal Library

CUHERL (Soo-hurl) – Elf, father of Aiiyosha

CULDON (Kul-don) – Man, Earl of Centaur, a fiefdom of Ciricen

CURILLIAN (Su-rill-ee-an) – Armist, king of Maristonia and husband of Carmen

CYRON (Ky-ron) – Armist, member of Curillian's Royal Guards

DÁCARIEL (Dah-sah-ree-ell) – Elf, queen of Tol Ankil, niece of Carea and mother of the triplets Sin-Solar, Sin-Tolor & Sin-Serin

DAULASTIR (Daw-luh-stee-ah) – Armist, Lord High Chancellor under King Mirkan. He murdered his master and usurped the throne of the young Curillian, before later being overthrown by the prince when he returned from exile

DEÀREG, SIR (Day-ah-regg) – Man, Falcon Clan Knight from Aranar

DENCARIL (Den-kar-ill) – Man of Hendar, Duke of Nalator and uncle of Adhanor

DUBARNIK (Do-bar-nick) – Armist, conjuror and father of Roujeark

EDRIST (Ed-wrist) – Armist, member of Curillian's Royal Guards

ELRINDE (El-rind) – Elf, a statesman representing King Lancearon of Ithrill

ELUCAR (El-oo-kar) – Elf, erstwhile Master-Mage of Oron Amular

EQUERRIN (Eh-queh-rin) – Man of Hendar, physician to Adhanor

ESTALOR (es-tah-lore) – Armist, cohort commander in the 5th Legion

FINARION (Fin-ah-ree-on) – Elf, erstwhile Master-Mage of Oron Amular

FINDOR (Fin-dor) – Armist, member of Curillian's Royal Guards

FIRWAN (fir-wan) – Armist, former King of Maristonia and ancestor of Curillian

GAEON (Guy-on) – Armist, tutor to Prince Téthan

GANNODIN (Gan-no-din) – Armist, general of the elite 1st Legion, garrisoned in Mariston

GARTHAN (Gar-than) – Man, master-of-arms to Earl Culdon

GERENDAYN (geh-ren-dane) – Wood-elf, antiquary and gatherer of news

HARDOS, SIR (Har-dos) – Man, Pegasus Clan Knight and close ally of Southilar

HAROTH (Hah-roth) – Armist, member of Curillian's Royal Guards

HORUISTAN (hor-uh-stan) – Armist, general of the 15th legion

HOTH (Hoth) – Dwarf-lord from the subterranean realm of Carthak

IDUNAR (Ee-doo-nar) – Man, late King of Hendar, father of Adhanor

ILLYIR (Ill-year) – Armist, duke of Welton; cousin to Curillian

IORCAR (yor-kar) – Dwarf, erstwhile Master-Mage of Oron Amular

JEANNOR (Jean-or) – Man, free-rider of Aranar. The first syllable is pronounced as in the French *Jean*, not the English Jean.

KASPAIN (Kas-pain) – Man, household warrior of Earl Culdon

KULOTHIEL (Koo-low-thee-ell) – Man, Head of the League of Wizardry and Keeper of Oron Amular

KURUNDAR (Kuh-run-dar) – Man, sorcerer from Urunmar, brother to Kulothiel

LANCEARON (Larn-sa-ron) – High-elf, king of Ithrill and former Silver Emperor

LANCOIR (Larn-swa) – Armist, Captain of the Royal Guards

LINDAL, SIR (Lin-dal) – Man, Unicorn Clan Knight from Aranar

LINVION (Lin-vee-on) – Elf-woman of Ithrill, diplomat and companion of Elrinde

LIONENN (Lee-oh-nen) – Armist, army tracker and expert archer

LIOTOR (Leo-tor) – Man, former King of Ciricen, father of Thónarion

LITHAN (Lee-than) – Elf, king of Kalimar

LOSATHEN THE LUCKLESS, SIR (Loss-ah-then) – Man of Aranar, a knight errant

LUCASK LIGHTFOOT (Loo-cas-k) – Man of Aranar, member of Raspald's band

MANRION (Man-ree-on) – Armist, member of Curillian's Royal Guards

MARINTOR (Ma-rin-tor) – Elf, king of the eponymous sea-elf kindred, ancestor of Aiiyosha

MELNOVA (Mel-no-va) – Armist, celebrated poet of Maristonia

MÍRIANNA (Mih-ree-ah-nah) – Elf, second oldest elf and first High Queen of Kalimar

MIRKAN (Mur-kan) – Armist, prior king of Maristonia; father and predecessor of Curillian

NADIHOAN (Nad-ee-ho-an) – Alias of Curillian during exile

NARHEYN (Nar-hayn) – Man, household warrior of Earl Culdon

NIMARION (Nim-ah-ree-on) – Elf of Kalimar

NORSCINDE (Nor-sind) – Armist, member of Curillian's Royal Guards

NURVO (Nur-vo) – Man of Hendar, Bishop of Losantum

ONANDUR (Oh-nan-durh) – Man, Earl of Oloyir in Hendar and Captain of Adhanor's bodyguards

OPHRYIOR (Off-ree-or) – Armist, Lord High Chancellor of Maristonia; Curillian's chief minister

OTAKEN (O-tah-ken) – Armist, general in the Maristonian army

PARTHIR (Par-thear) – Man of Raduthon, a barbarian principality in the south

PERETHOR (Peh-reh-thor) – Elf, resident of Faudunum

PIRON (Peer-on) – Armist, junior officer of the third cohort of The Royal Guards; second-in-command to Surumo

PRÉLAN (Pray-larn) – God, deity of the elves and all believing folk. Prélan is one and the same as the Triune God of Christianity. He reveals Himself differently to the inhabitants of Astrom than He has to us on Earth.

RANE (Rain) – Man of Aranar, knight of the Pegasus Clan

RASPALD THE KIN-SLAYER (Ras-pald) – Man of Aranar, bandit chieftain

REUBUN (Roo-bun) – Man of Hendar, Duke of Lalator and favourite of Adhanor

REYDOEIR (Ray-doe-ear) – Elf, erstwhile Master-Mage of Oron Amular

RHYARD (Ry-ard) – Man, household warrior of Earl Culdon

RIDGUN (rid-gun) – man, emissary of Hendar to Maristonia

ROMANTHONY, SIR (Row-man-tho-nee) – Man, Eagle Clan Knight from Aranar

ROTHGER (Roth-guh) – Man, a Hendarian sheriff and pathfinder

ROUJEARK (Roo-jark) – Armist, a gifted young magician; son of Dubarnik. The second syllable, 'jeark' is pronounced similarly to the South African forename 'Jacques', with an accented first vowel; not like the flat-vowelled English 'Jack' or 'Jake'.

RUFIN (Roo-fin) – Man, household warrior of Earl Culdon

RUMORIL (Roo-mor-ill) – Man of Hendar, Duke of Malator and uncle of Adhanor

RUTHARTH (Roo-tharth) – Correct pronunciation of the elvish form of Roujeark's name

RUTHION (RUE-THEE-ON) – Alias of Curillian during his service to the Silver Empire

SAMPA THE SMOOTH (Sam-pah) – Man of Aranar, member of Raspald's band

SCEANT (Skee-ant) – Man of Aranar, member of Raspald's band

SIN-SERIN (Sin-seh-rin) – Elf, princess of Tol Ankil, sister of the brothers Sin-Solar and Sin-Tolor

SIN-SOLAR (Sin-so-lar) – Elf, prince of Tol Ankil

SIN-TOLOR (Sin-toe-lore) – Elf, prince of Tol Ankil and brother of Sin-Solar

SOUTHILAR (Soo-thi-lar) – Man, Jeantar and lord of Aranar, of the Pegasus Clan

SURUMO (Suh-roo-mo) – Armist, commanding officer of the third cohort of The Royal Guards

TEKKA (Tech-ah) – Pony, erstwhile mount and companion of Roujeark in his youth

TÉTHAN (Tay-than) – Armist, prince of Maristonia; son and heir of Curillian

THEAMACE (Theam-ace) – Horse, favourite mount of Curillian

THEONAR, SIR (Theo-nar) – Man, Pegasus Clan Knight and rival of Southilar

THERENDIR (Theh-ren-deer) – Elf, king of the wood-elves, father of Carea

THÓNARION (Tho-nah-ree-on) – Man, King of Ciricen and liege-lord of Earl Culdon

TIMELL (Tim-ell) – Man, erstwhile Master-Mage of Oron Amular

TORLAS (Tor-las) – Elf, prince and swordsmith who forged the Sword of Maristonia for King Armista

UTARION (You-tah-ree-on) – Armist, member of Curillian's Royal Guards

VAMPANA (Vam-par-nah) – Woman of Aranar, member of Raspald's band

XAVION (Zay-vee-on) – Man of Hendar, Earl of Koros and favourite of Adhanor

The Races of Astrom

A short guide to introduce the main races of Astrom that we meet in *Oron Amular*. More information on the people and places of Astrom can be found in the online glossary at **www.worldofastrom.com**.

Armists

A hardy mountain race originally from the foothills of the Carthaki Mountains. They awoke at the dawn of the Second Chapter, the second of the Free Peoples, and shortly before the coming of the dwarves. Fostered and taught by the elves, they moved into the lowlands and slowly spread across Maristonia, which in the passing of time became their own kingdom. They are a species apart, sharing some features with their elven and mortal neighbours but being quite unlike them in others. As a rule, they are short and stockily-built, are adaptable and persevere well in difficult tasks. They have a reputation for valour and stubbornness.

Dwarves

Like the armists, the dwarves are children of the mountains and they awoke in the Carthaki Mountains at around the same time as the armists. But whereas the armists were befriended and tutored by the elves, becoming like them in their worldview and habits, the dwarves were long isolated in a remote part of Astrom. They had a different temperament, being more secretive, more industrious, and preferring to live underground in excavated halls and caverns. With time they also built an overground civilisation and dwelt side by side with the elven kingdom of Alanmar. In this time of peace, they sent forth colonists and delved halls in many of the far-flung mountains of

Astrom, from which came many different breeds of their race, some noble and some less so. After the ruinous Carthaki Wars they shut themselves underground and forsook the outside world. For long centuries they were not heard from at all, but later they did venture forth to participate in the great events of the world. The dwarves are short, rarely exceeding five feet, but incredibly strong. They are excellent craftsmen and ingenious artisans, working wonders in stone, wood, metal and minerals of all kinds. They are fearless tunnelers, hardy mountaineers and formidable warriors. They do not share the elven view of Prélan but have their own conception of the divine and their own law-codes to govern their affairs.

Elves

The elves are the eldest children of Prélan, exalted and excellent among the Free Peoples. They were the first to awake in Astrom, having come to the world in star-capsules. They were known as *Avarian*, the People of the Stars, but they called themselves *Genesi*, the First. There are three main kindreds, the Avatar, the Firnai and the Marintors.

The *Avatar* are the eldest of all, named after their first king, Avatar. Also known as the High-elves, the Avatar are the most senior of the elven kindreds, and also the most populous and powerful. They are great scholars, warriors and craftsmen, preferring to live in cities or in the open country.

Firnai is the elvish name for the Wood-elves, named after their first king, Firnar. The wood-elves are the most secretive of the three main kindreds of the elves, rarely coming out of their woodland fastnesses to interact with the outside world. They are as varied as the trees they love, some loving oaks, some building high homes in giant beeches and some loving riverside willows and alders. They are wonderful weavers, passionate storytellers and great lovers of animals. Some of them even have the gift of shape-shifting into the forms of beasts. Most Firnai dwell deep within Kalimar, but one colony live in the forest of Tol Ankil, on the borders of Maristonia.

Marintors are Sea-elves, dwelling by the coasts and enamoured of all the sea. Dwelling in caves, grottoes and white-walled havens, they are the mariners, explorers and traders of the elves. Their realm once embraced all the coasts of Astrom, but whilst in latter days they may have relinquished much of it to armists and Mortals, they also have innumerable havens and colonies on the far-flung islands and continents of the planet. The Marintors are great singers and lovers of music, but they are also the most worldly of the elves, and the readiest to have dealings with Mortals.

The *Cuherai* (Snow-elves), who dwell amid the high snows and ice-fields, and the *Irynthai* (Deep-elves), whose mansions and workshops are underground, are amongst the many lesser kindreds of the elves, but the rest do not feature in this tale.

Harracks

A mysterious race who inhabit subterranean halls and caverns in the land of Stonad. Lying in the southern Black Mountains, this mountainous domain lies between Kalimar proper and the wood-elven realm of Tol Ankil. The harracks are little known to their neighbours except as a source of trouble and few among either armists or elves know the secrets of their origins. In fact, they are an ancient race of dwarves, descended from an outcast chieftain of

Carthak who journeyed north in exile with a few followers. These were ignoble individuals who founded a nation which bore their own traits of harshness, injustice and ferocious insularity. Through long millennia of isolation the harracks degenerated into a fallen race of coarse, unlovely warriors and craftsmen, barely recognisable to their old dwarvish kin but not dis-similar from the Black Dwarves of the Goragath Mountains, another evil scion of old Carthak. The harracks are short, stocky and incredibly tough, strong and with thick skin that is difficult to harm. They are ruthless with outsiders and extremely secretive about their ways. However, they do have redeeming features, being quite capable of great feats of engineering, excavation and construction. They are frightful to look upon, for not only were they unlovely to begin with, but they have also added to their horrifying demeanour by affecting brutal customs like head-binding and eschewing all but the most rustic garments and decorations.

Mortals

The elves are the only immortal race among the Free Peoples, and though the armists and dwarves are also mortal, the name Mortals is reserved for those elves who forfeited their immortality for rebellion against Prélan. Though by the time of Oron Amular they may resemble human beings, they are in fact the descendants of elves who fell from grace. In the second half of the Second Chapter, large swathes of the population of Elvendom fell away from the true faith and embraced manifold heresies and false religions. In a cataclysmic event known as the Great Betrayal, those who forsook Prélan were cursed with mortality, losing their deathlessness and many of the virtues of mind and body that went with it. The faithful elves remained in Kalimar and Ithrill, but the Mortals were to be found across much of the rest of Ciroken, in Aranar, Hendar and Ciricen.

In all these countries there arose mortal nations and kingdoms which lived uneasily alongside their immortal neighbours. They were still related by blood, but utterly estranged in mindset and values. Mortals were subject to sickness and deformity, as well as ageing, but they made up for their limited years with a great zest for life that expressed itself in invention, literature, art and zealous politics. As such, their realms were characterised by rapid change and frequent upheavals. Had they refrained from fighting each other and amongst themselves, mortal civilisation might have rivalled that of the elves, in accomplishment, if not in longevity. Opinion is divided among the loremasters of Astrom as to whether mortality was in fact a curse, denying Mortals the long bliss of the elves, or a blessing in disguise, speeding their way back to Prélan.

Follow Michael J Harvey
on social media:

Facebook.com/worldofastrom

X: @worldofastrom

Instagram: @worldofastrom

Website: worldofastrom.com

Sign up for more World of Astrom content
by scanning the code below

Scan to continue the adventure